THE YEAR'S BEST

SCIENCE FICTION

THE YEAR'S BEST

SCIENCE FICTION

Eighteenth Annual collection

edited by **Gardner Dozois**

st. martin's griffin ⚦ new york

www.stmartins.com

ISBN 0-312-27465-3 (hc)
ISBN 0-312-27478-5 (pbk)

FIRST EDITION: AUGUST 2001

10   9   8   7   6   5   4   3   2   1

contents

acknowledgments

The editor would like to thank the following people for their help and support: Susan Casper, Ellen Datlow, Craig Engler, Peter Crowther, Paul Frazer, Mark R. Kelly, Gordon Van Gelder, David Pringle, Sheila Williams, Brian Bieniowski, Trevor Quachri, Michael Swanwick, Jim Allen, Vaughne Lee Hansen, Jed Hartman, Gavin J. Grant, Jeff VanderMeer, Betsy Mitchell, Warren Lapine, Chris Lawson, David G. Hartwell, Darrell Schweitzer, Charles C. Ryan, and special thanks to my own editor, Bryan Cholfin.

Thanks are also due to Charles N. Brown, whose magazine *Locus* (Locus Publications, P.O. Box 13305, Oakland, CA 94661, $46 for a one-year subscription [twelve issues] via second class; credit card orders (510) 339-9198) was used as an invaluable reference source throughout the Summation; *Locus Online*, www.locusmag.com, edited by Mark Kelly, has also become a key reference source. Thanks are also due to Andrew Porter, whose magazine *Science Fiction Chronicle* (DNA Publications, Inc., P.O. Box 2988, Radford, VA 24143-2988, $45 for a one year/twelve issue subscription via second class) was also used as a reference source throughout.

summation: 2000

Well, the millennium is definitely at hand (cue the swell of ominous, Apocalyptic music in the background), and even calendar purists can no longer deny that we're living in the twenty-first century.

It'll probably be hard to convey to younger readers a sense of how downright *strange* that seems to old fogies like me. For most of my life, the twenty-first century was THE FUTURE, that unimaginably distant territory in which most science fiction stories took place; now I find myself *living* there, in the remote, glittering FUTURE . . . (which somehow *feels* different than you thought it would, more mundane and less goshwow fantastical, once you're actually rubbing up against it, in spite of technological innovations all around us that would have dropped the jaw of anybody in 1950—a lesson many SF writers and futurologists could usefully learn). To paraphrase Mark Twain, I wish the new century well, although I doubt I'll get to see all that much of it—but it's not *my* century. My century was the *previous* one.

But the twentieth century is gone, taking its freight of unprecedented and un-anticipated horrors and wonders with it, and even dinosaurian refugees from that century, like me, must learn to look *ahead*, not back. We can *go* ahead, if we're lucky, for a while anyway—but back there's no returning.

The temptation to try to predict what the new century ahead is going to be like is almost irresistible, and I'll succumb to that temptation here and there in the pages that follow, but what makes me hesitant to really give in to it is realizing how *poor* a job prognosticators at the beginning of the twentieth century did peering ahead at what lay in store for *them*. In almost every case, even those who thought that they were being wildly daring and outrageous in their predications fell far short of what *actually* happened, missing both the marvels and the miseries, the triumphs and the tragedies, the unimaginable progress and the equally un-imaginable atrocities that waited ahead. For someone standing in 1901 and peer-ing ahead, these things were literally *unimaginable*; it was beyond the power of the human imagination to predict or fully appreciate how radical the changes that lay ahead really would be, changes that would come to alter almost out of rec-ognition every aspect of the nineteenth-century world, sweeping it aside and re-placing it with a new world instead. And I suspect that people at the beginning of the twenty-second century—if there *are* any people, as we understand the term, still around by then—will look back at *today's* predictions of what the twenty-first century is going to be like with similar amusement (if not outright scorn) at how naive and limited *our* imaginations turned out to be. So then, let's mostly content ourselves with taking a look at 2000, which is safely past, and thus can be confi-dently examined with 20/20 hindsight.

It was a pretty quiet year, for the most part. Once again, the science fiction genre didn't die, much to the disappointment of some commentators. In fact, the genre seems to be fairly stable at the moment commercially (knock wood!); artistically, even taking into account all of the tie-ins and media and gaming-associated books that crowd the shelves, there are still considerably *more* science fiction novels of quality being published now than were being published in, say, 1975 (including a few that would probably not have been *allowed* to be published at all back then), in a very wide range of styles and moods, by a spectrum of writers ranging from Golden Age giants to Young Turks with one book under their belts — quite probably more quality material (including a wide range of short work) than any one reader is going to be able to *read* in the course of one year, unless they make a full-time job of it. The last couple of years have been dominated by Merger Mania, but this year the corporations were mainly quiescent, like huge snakes digesting the goats they'd swallowed; there were no major changes in publishing, at the genre level, anyway, except in the troubled magazine market — no print SF lines lost or gained. (Most of the major action, both positive and negative, was in the online market, about which see more below.) There were no major changes in editorial personnel this year either, although last year saw a vigorous round of the traditional game of Editorial Musical Chairs, with several Big-Time players leaving the scene (most of whom have yet to return in any significant way).

Most of the serious action this year was going on behind the scenes, like the legal battle over Napster — at first glance, something far removed from the SF world . . . but not really, eh?, as I strongly suspect that if you want a good model for the problems that the book-publishing business is going to encounter tomorrow, you take a look at the problems that the music industry is dealing with *today*. (Already, the Science Fiction Writers of America is embroiled in a legal battle with pirate Web sites, with Harlan Ellison — good for you, Harlan! — being one of those leading the rush to the battlements . . . although I suspect that as yet we've only seen some very early skirmishes in what's going to be a long and bloody war.) The turmoil in the stock market over the faltering dot.com market — with many big Internet players failing to meet expectations by huge margins and being forced to close up shop, and possible major trouble ahead forecast for others, like the online book-selling (and everything *else*-selling) superservice Amazon.com — also cast a long shadow into the SF world.

Major changes are looming over the publishing world like thunderheads coming up over the horizon, fundamental changes in the way that books reach the general reading public. This year you could hear those storms of change growling and rumbling off in the distance, mostly as yet producing only occasional gusts of wind and fitful bursts of rain, but not too many commentators would deny that those storms *are* going to break sooner or later — although you'll hear a wide range of predictions of how severe the weather is going to get, from soak-your-clothes-to-your-skin downpours to barely-wet-your-lawn passing showers. Print-on-demand publishers are appearing like mayflies — as are online sites that sell downloads to PCs, portable handheld computers, and other electronic text-readers — and they may turn out to have the *life span* of mayflies, too . . . but it's a good bet that there will be others coming along behind them to replace those that falter and fall by the wayside. And just behind these are marching other waves of change: new generations of better and more sophisticated handheld computers and electronic text-readers of all sorts (some of which may already be in stores by the time you read these words); print-on-demand systems in most major bookstores that can print most books in their extensive catalogues for you right on the spot, while you wait, "electronic paper"; genuinely reprogrammable "e-books" that will look and feel as much like print books as possible, and be as easy to carry around (even today, you can call into the Internet with a wireless modem and get new novels or stories downloaded into your handheld, as easily as making a phone call). And, no doubt, behind these changes there'll be coming *other* innovations and technologies that will end up having a major effect on the publishing world, stuff we haven't even *heard* of yet.

None but the most wild-eyed prognosticators believe that all this is going to make print books, or regular trade publishers, or bookstores that exist in the physical world, disappear (that's not going to happen in the foreseeable future, and likely will never happen at all). But it *is* going to mean big readjustments in market share, something that's already happening, and which isn't going to stop anytime soon.

Although cyber-optimists of the "Print books will be extinct by 2004! With Internet shopping, nobody will ever bother leaving their homes again!" sort may have been a bit too giddy, those semi-Luddites who have spent the last few months smugly anticipating the forecast demise of Amazon.com (proving that all this Internet stuff was "just a fad") are probably going to be disappointed as well. Amazon.com may (or may not) die, but there will still be online booksellers. That's not going to change, not now; too many people have become accustomed to the ease of ordering books online, one of the most rapidly growing areas in the whole book-selling industry, and *somebody* will appear to take up the slack and provide that service for them, even if Amazon.com and all the other present online booksellers went down. Books will continue to be produced and sold online, in one form or another, in one *way* or another, no matter how the fortunes of an individual publisher rise or fall; the technology is just too easy and too seductive *not* to use, and sooner or later somebody will figure out a reliable way to make money doing so. Although it may not be the Milk-and-Honey Promised Land of starry-eyed would-be dot.com millionaires, the High Road to Effortless Business Success, the Internet is not going away. It—or its successor technologies—will be a part of our lives (probably an ever-more-integral, indispensable, and yet taken-for-granted-and-largely-ignored part) for the foreseeable future, and for our children's future as well. Barring all-out war, an asteroid strike, a universally potent pestilence, environmental collapse, or some other disaster that sends civilization reeling back to the Dark Ages or worse, things are *not* going to go back to The Way They Were. The clock cannot be turned back, once you set it ticking—your only option is to smash the clock altogether.

So fasten your seat belts, it's going to be a bumpy decade. But it just might—with luck—end up taking us to some places worth going to.

It was another bad year in the magazine market, with sales down again almost across the board (in areas far outside the genre, as well), and with only a few hopeful notes to be found here and there.

There were two major losses in the magazine market in 2000, the demise of *Science Fiction Age* (which happened early enough in 2000 that we covered it in *last* year's anthology) and then, toward the end of the year, the death of *Amazing Stories*—which was axed in its recent incarnation as a glossy mixed SF/media magazine soon after parent company Wizards of the Coast was sold to Hasbro (Hasbro also axed its card-gaming magazine, *Top Deck*; apparently a severe slump in the card-gaming market was responsible for both decisions). This was perhaps not quite as much of a hammer blow to the market as the cancellation of *Science Fiction Age*, since *Amazing Stories* in its current version was less central and important to the genre than *Science Fiction Age* had become, but it still sent shock waves through the field. There was a flicker of hope late in the year, as the online site *GalaxyOnLine* announced that they were going to buy *Amazing Stories* and reinvent it as an online site selling versions of the magazine in CD format, but this deal fell through when *GalaxyOnLine* itself died (see below). *Amazing Stories* has died and then come miraculously back to life several times in the twenty-five years I've been editing Best of the Year anthologies, but this may finally be the end of the line for the grand old magazine, which has existed in one form or another (with occasional breaks in continuity), since 1926. (On the other hand, I've said that before, only to watch the magazine rise from the ashes again, so we'll just have to wait and see, and hope that *Amazing Stories* can somehow pull off the Lazarus trick one more time. That probably wouldn't be the way to bet it, though.)

The other big change in the magazine market this year is potentially positive: late in the year, *The Magazine of Fantasy & Science Fiction* was bought by its current editor, Gordon Van Gelder, from its longtime owner and publisher, Edward L. Ferman. If Gordon can cope with the extra work and problems that will come with assuming the role of publisher as well, and if he has deep enough pockets to weather any financial setbacks that might be caused by the transition, then this might well give *F&SF* a new lease on life—the Fermans were getting near retirement age, and there has been speculation as to what would happen to the magazine when they did retire. Without someone like Gordon willing to assume the stewardship of the magazine, a big job, it might well have died. Now it has a decent chance of surviving, for as long as Gordon can keep it going, anyway.

The news in the rest of the magazine market was no more cheerful than it has been for the last several years. Overall sales were down almost everywhere, with *Asimov's Science Fiction*, *Analog Science Fiction & Fact*, *The Magazine of Fantasy & Science Fiction*, and *Realms of Fantasy* reaching all-time lows (sales were down across the entire range of the magazine market, in fact, far beyond genre boundaries—it shows up more noticeably with the genre magazines because their initial audience bases were lower to begin with). *Asimov's Science Fiction* registered a 12.3% loss in overall circulation in 2000, 3,348 in subscriptions, and 1062 in newsstand sales. *Analog Science Fiction & Fact* registered a 7.5% loss in overall circulation in 2000, 1461 in subscriptions, and 2,435 in newsstand sales. *The Magazine of Fantasy & Science Fiction* registered an 8.1% loss in overall circulation, 1,294 in subscriptions, and 1,360 in newsstand sales. *Realms of Fantasy* registered a 12.1% loss in overall circulation, rising 2,313 in subscriptions, but dropping by 7,157 in newsstand sales. As it has for several years, now, *Interzone* held steady at a circulation of about 4,000 copies, more or less evenly split between subscriptions and newsstand sales.

I've mentioned before that these figures probably look worse than they actually are. Most of the subscriptions that have been lost, to date, are not of the core subscribers who regularly renew their subscriptions at full rate, the most profitable subscribers for a magazine, but rather Publishers Clearing House-style cut-rate stamp-sheet subscriptions, which can actually cost more to fulfill than they actually bring in in revenue. The good news, then, is that the core subscribers who do remain seem loyal, dedicated, and, according to surveys, enthusiastic about the product that they're receiving. Helping also to keep the digest-size or near-digest-size magazines (*Asimov's, Analog, F&SF*) profitable in spite of declining circulation, is the fact that they're so cheap to *produce* in the first place that you don't have to sell very many of them to make a profit, the advantage that has kept digest-size magazines alive for decades when more expensive-to-produce magazines, which need to sell a far greater number of copies in order to be profitable, have faltered and died. Nevertheless, this continued decline in circulation is distressing, and if the slide continues *long* enough, must ultimately threaten the existence of these magazines; without at least a trickle of new subscribers coming in, you can't counterbalance the inevitable attrition of your subscriber base due to death and circumstance, and sooner or later you're left with no subscribers at all, or at least not enough to keep the magazine in the black.

One mildly hopeful note is that in the last couple of years most of the SF magazines are pulling in at least a trickle of new subscribers over the Internet from audiences that probably haven't been tapped much by them before, including people who had probably never heard of the magazines before coming across them online (most people, even many habitual science fiction readers, have no idea that the SF magazines—which receive no advertising or promotion at all, in most cases—even exist), and people from other parts of the world, where interested readers have formerly found it difficult to subscribe because of the difficulty of obtaining American currency and because of other logistical problems. *Asimov's, Analog,* and *F&SF* have also all made deals with PeanutPress (http://www. peanutpress.com) that enables readers to download electronic versions of the magazines into Palm Pilot handheld computers, with the choice of either buying an electronic "subscription," or of buying them individually on an issue-by-issue basis, and a small but steady flow of new subscribers drawn from new audiences is coming in from this source as well.

With today's chaotic newsstand situation, which keeps most SF magazines off most newsstands, I have a feeling that if anything is going to save the magazines, it'll be the use of the Internet as a promotional tool, using Web sites to push sales of the physical product through subscriptions, and so I'm going to list the URLs for those magazines that have Web sites: *Asimov's* site is at http://www. asimovs.com. *Analog's* site is at http://www.analogsf.com. *The Magazine of Fantasy & Science Fiction's* site is at http://www.sfsite.com/fsf/. *Interzone's* site is at http:// www.sfsite.com/interzone/. (*Realms of Fantasy* doesn't have a Web site per se, although content *from* it can be found on scifi.now.com . . . although you could surf the whole site and be hard-pressed to find even a mention of the magazine's name; if you persist, though, you can eventually find a place to subscribe to it online.) The amount of activity varies on these sites, with the *Asimov's* and *Analog* sites perhaps the busiest and the *Interzone* site perhaps the least active, but the *important* thing about all of the sites is that you can *subscribe* to the magazines there, electronically, online, with just a few clicks of some buttons, no stamps, no envelopes, and no trips to the post office required. It would be hard for us to make it any easier for you.

All of these magazines (and a half dozen others) deserve your support. One of the best things you can do to ensure that short science fiction remains alive and plentiful in the market is to subscribe to whatever magazine you like best. In fact, subscribe to as many of them as you can — it'll still turn out to be a better reading bargain, more fiction of reliable quality for less money, than buying the year's hit-or-miss crop of original anthologies could possibly supply. Do it *now*, while you're thinking about it, and while it still has a chance to help. If you're a fan of short SF, as someone reading this book presumably is, and you *don't* bother to do it, you're taking a chance that there could be a lot less short SF around to enjoy in the future.

There were another couple of upbeat notes in this troubled market this year. The year 2000 saw a very impressive and promising debut made by a new Scottish SF magazine, *Spectrum SF*, edited by Paul Fraser, which published four issues in 2000. By rights, since the circulation is still low, this should be mentioned in the semiprozine section, but as *Spectrum SF* was not only totally professional in content, but very *high-end* professional at that, featuring two of the year's best stories, by Charles Stross and Alastair Reynolds, as well as good work by Jack Deighton, Eric Brown, Garry Kilworth, Mary Soon Lee, and others, and the serialization of the late Keith Roberts's as-yet-otherwise-unpublished last novel, *Drek Yarman*, that I'm going to go ahead and list it here in the professional section instead, and you can send me complaining letters about that if you want. *Spectrum SF* was certainly the most promising debut of a British magazine since *Interzone* — and, like *Interzone*, one that's especially welcome to me because it's one of the few British magazines to concentrate on core science fiction; most British magazines emphasize slipstream and/or horror instead. Fraser clearly doesn't have a lot of money to work with — this is obviously a labor of love — so let's hope that he can build a subscription base quickly before he runs out of funds, cash, and hope, since this is a tasty little magazine that deserves to survive, and another magazine that deserves your support.

PS Publishing (http://www.editorial-services.co.uk/pspublishing), a British small press, brought out some of the year's best novellas, in individual chapbook form, as part of a series, edited by Peter Crowther, that included *Tendeléo's Story*, by Ian McDonald, *Watching Trees Grow*, by Peter F. Hamilton, *Making History*, by Paul J. McAuley, *Reality Dust*, by Stephen Baxter, and others, with more to come next year. These novellas will eventually be gathered in omnibus collections, first published in Britain, and then in the United States. Keep your eye out for them, and for the new novellas that will be coming out, for so far they've included some of the best work to be found anywhere in the genre this year.

As usual, short SF and fantasy also appeared in many magazines outside genre boundaries, from *Ellery Queen's Mystery Magazine* to *Playboy*. The science magazine *Nature*, in honor of the millennium, published a very short science fiction story (some of them by very Big Names) in every weekly issue for the past 52 weeks—most of them were too short to have much impact *as* fiction, but they certainly managed to introduce some sophisticated genre conceptualization and concepts to wide nongenre audiences that were probably unfamiliar with them, and the staff of *Nature* is to be commended for that. On the other hand, on a sour note, *Playboy* fired longtime fiction editor Alice Turner, saying that maintaining a full-time fiction editor was "a luxury" that they could no longer afford, and that future stories would be selected by a committee. They didn't ask me, and don't care what my opinion is, but I think that this was a mistake—at a time when endless numbers of photos of naked women can be downloaded from the Internet for far less than the cost of an issue of *Playboy*, they need to *emphasize* those touches of class and quality that differentiate them from the average online porn site if they want to survive, not throw them away. At any rate, Alice will be missed.

(Subscription addresses follow: *The Magazine of Fantasy & Science Fiction*, Spilogale, Inc., PO Box 3447, Hoboken, NJ 07030, annual subscription—$38.97 in U.S.; *Asimov's Science Fiction*, Dell Magazines, P.O. Box 54033, Boulder, CO 80322-4033—$39.97 for annual subscription in US; *Analog Science Fiction and Fact*, Dell Magazines, P.O. Box 54625, Boulder, CO 80323—$39.97 for annual subscription in US; *Interzone*, 217 Preston Drove, Brighton BN1 6FL, United Kingdom, $60.00 for an airmail one-year (twelve issues) subscription. *Realms of Fantasy*, Sovereign Media Co. Inc., P.O. Box 1623, Williamsport, PA 17703—$16.95 for an annual subscription in the U.S.; *Spectrum SF*, Spectrum Publishing, PO Box 10308, Aberdeen, AB11 6ZR, United Kingdom—17 pounds sterling for a four-issue subscription, make checks payable to "Spectrum Publishing". *PS Publishing*, 98 High Ash Drive, Leeds L517 8RE, England, UK—$17 each for *Tendeleo's Story*, by Ian McDonald, *Watching Trees Grow*, by Peter F. Hamilton, *Making History*, by Paul J. McAuley; and *Reality Dust*, by Stephen Baxter. Note that many of these magazines can also be subscribed to online, at their various Web sites.)

It was a wild year in the young field of "online electronic publishing," with some upbeat stories to partially balance some major reversals and disappointments—things change so *fast* in this ephemeral market, though, that what I write here is likely to be already obsolete by the time this book sees print, so if you're interested, keep that in mind, and keep a close eye on the markets themselves.

The big stories here this year were probably the terminal decline of *Galaxy-OnLine*, and the *rise* of SCI FICTION. *GalaxyOnLine*, supervised by veteran editor/writer Ben Bova, and introduced in early 2000, was perhaps the most glossy and ambitious such site to date, featuring a distinguished lineup of columnists such as Harlan Ellison, Mike Resnick, Joe Haldeman, Jack Dann, Kristine Kathryn Rusch, and many others, running scientific articles and book and movie reviews as well as original short SF stories, and promising eventually to provide everything from downloadable novels to online movies to animation to Web TV. By the middle of the year, though, their money had run out, their venture capitalists had dried up (the same thing that had killed the *Event Horizon* site the year before), new investors could not be found — and *GalaxyOnLine* was dead before the end of the year. A major disappointment, and another major blow to the dream that such sites can be made self-sustaining. Another ambitious fiction site, which was creating an anticipatory buzz and already drawing the work of top authors, *The Infinity Matrix*, to be edited by SF writer Eileen Gunn, also ran out of backing money, and had the plug pulled on it just before we went to press, losing the SF online world a site of great potential. It was the same story with yet another site with large-scale plans, *Bookface*, which was making books available to the online community for free (as long as you read them on screen online, the idea being to entice people into buying a download of a book, after they'd "browsed" it), and which was also "publishing" some original short fiction by young writers, but which also ran out of money, and was unable to find sufficient amounts of "Web advertising" revenue to replace it, and had also closed down shop by the end of the year.

The faltering of the "dot.com" market, one of the year's big financial stories, is probably the proximate cause of the failure of most of these sites. All of them were funded by big initial rushes of money from venture capitalists back when the market was hot (amounting to multiple millions of dollars in some cases), all ran through their money without being able to find an effective way of bringing any money back *in*, and then, once the market had soured and venture capitalists had become cautious and conservative again, were unable to find *new* investors to keep things going.

The big problem in this market is still a simple one: nobody has yet figured out how you can reliably *make money* "publishing" fiction online. The Last Great Hope here, the model that suggested that you could draw in enough income with "Web-advertising" to pay your expenses and even make a profit, seems to have been pretty thoroughly discredited, and the "patronage model," that big companies will support the arts online as part of their Public Relations campaigns, to improve their image, depends on a prosperous and growing economy; once belts start being seriously tightened, art for the sake of improving your image is probably the first thing to go. For the most part, with fiction sites, you either support it yourself, as what amounts to a hobby (an old tradition among print semiprozines, where magazines like *Crank!* were paid for for years out of the editor's own pockets), you absorb the costs because you hope to get an equal value in promotion, publicity, and prestige for some other product back out of it, you use it as a place to sell subscriptions or some other physical product that exists in the real world — or you find some way to make the customers *pay* for accessing the fiction, and hope you can get them to cough up in sufficient numbers to keep you afloat. This last is the tricky one, although many are working on it. Sites that sell "e-books" and even individual stories, to be downloaded to various "Palm-Pilot"-type platforms, may be on to a potentially successful model, especially as a wave of new and supposedly greatly improved technology in this area is just about to break upon us.

Although we've run through a lot of grim news so far, not all the stories in this market were negative, though, by any means. Early in 2000, the Sci-Fi Channel site (scifi.com) went through an extensive expansion and renovation, which included buying the long-running e-zine *Science Fiction Weekly* (the new editor of which is former *Science Fiction Age* editor Scott Edelman, replacing Craig Engler, who has moved up the corporate ladder in the SCI FI organization), and also launching a major new Web site, SCI FICTION, a fiction site within the larger umbrella of the Sci-Fi Channel site, edited by Ellen Datlow, the former Fiction Editor of *Omni*, as well as of the now-defunct web sites *Omni Online* and *Event Horizon*. As she did before with those other sites, Ellen has quickly established SCI FICTION as one of the best places on the Internet to find reliably professional-quality short fiction, putting up one new story and one "classic reprint" story every week (all of which are kept archived). This year SCI FICTION published good original stories this year by Severna Park, Steven Utley, Nancy Kress, Howard Waldrop, Robert Reed, Elizabeth Hand, A. R. Morlan, Linda Nagata, and many others, most of this work at a level of quality and professionalism unrivaled almost anywhere else online. Since the Sci-Fi Channel seems to be operating here on the "promotion, publicity, and prestige" model, SCI FICTION is not expected to make money (nor is there any real way *for* it to make money), which makes it far less vulnerable than *Omni Online* or *Event Horizon* had been, and the chances are good that it will probably survive as long as the parent company itself remains prosperous and healthy. Certainly the Sci-Fi Channel *is* getting its money's worth as far as promotion, publicity, and prestige is concerned, since SCI FICTION to date has generated a great deal of all three for them, and in areas outside the usual media-fan circles, where people may not even have heard of the Sci-Fi Channel or paid much attention to it, before this.

Another good new fiction site is Strange Horizons (http://www.strange horizons.com), edited by Jed Hartman. *Strange Horizons* isn't yet operating reliably on the (very high) level of quality maintained by SCI FICTION, but there is some good stuff here, including, in 2000, good professional-level stories by Tamela Viglione, Chuck Rothman, Bruce Holland Rogers, and others; in recent months, they scored points with me by taking a retrospective look at the work of Howard Waldrop, many of whose stories can be accessed there. Another seeming success story (so far—knock wood!) is Fictionwise (http://www.fictionwise.com), which is not really an "electronic magazine" at all, but rather a place to buy downloadable e-books; however, not only is there a very large selection of individual "reprint" stories here of high professional quality by some of the best writers in the business available to be bought for a small fee, either on a story-by-story basis or in "fiction bundles" (see mention also in the short-story collection section, below), which should make them of interest to our readers, but they have just recently begun to offer original short science fiction stories for sale as well—at the moment, this is mostly limited to some original, heretofore unpublished stories by Kage Baker, but their intention is to add more original fiction by other popular authors, and that could in time become an important feature of the site. Along similar lines, ElectricStory (http://www.electricstory.com) is another site where you can buy downloadable e-books, including reprints of books by Terry Bisson, Paul Park, and others, but they make the site interesting with such stuff as movie reviews by Lucius Shepard and articles by Howard Waldrop, which can be read online for free; ElectricStory is also starting to experiment with original content—there's an original novel by new writer Richard Wadholm available there, and a new short-story collection, never published in print form, by Howard Waldrop). Coming later in 2001 is a site called Ipublish (http://www.ipublish.com), which will offer, among other enticements, downloadable original science fiction stories in e-form, selected by SF writer Paul Witcover; they've already bought a novella by Greg Feeley, as well as work by other writers.

Short original SF tends to become harder to find after this; you're more likely to find original horror, fantasy, or slipstream stories on the sites that follow, although you will find an occasional SF story as well: *Talebones* (http://www. fairwoodpress.com/), *Dark Planet* (http://www.sfsite.com/darkplanet/), *Ticonderoga On-Line* (http://www.omen.net.au/~rustle/ticonderaga/) *Electricwine* (http://www. electricwine.com); *Chiaroscuro* (*InterText* (http://www.intertext.com/), *Quantum Muse* (http:www.quantummuse.com) and *E-Scape* (http://www.interink.com/escape. html).

Although it's relatively hard to find good short original SF online, it's not hard at all to find good short *reprint* SF stories. At sites like the above-mentioned *Fictionwise*, *Mind's Eye Fiction* (http://tale.com/genres.htm), and *Alexandria Digital Literature* (http://alexlit.com), you'll have to pay a small fee to access reprints (usually amounting to less than fifty cents per story, in most cases), but there are also a fairly large number of sites here and there around the Internet which archive good reprint SF stories that can be accessed for free. Perhaps the best such site is the British *Infinity Plus* (http://www.infinityplus.co.uk), a good general site which features a very extensive selection of good-quality reprint stories, most (though not all) by British authors, as well as extensive biographical and bibliographical information, book reviews, and critical essays. Most of the sites that are associated with existent print magazines, such as *Asimov's, Analog, The Magazine of Fantasy & Science Fiction, Eidolon, Aurealis,* and others, will have extensive archives of material, both fiction and nonfiction, previously published by the print versions of the magazines, and some of them regularly run teaser excerpts from stories coming up in forthcoming issues.

Finding good fiction to read, though, is not the *only* reason to go Web-surfing. Among the most prominent SF-related sites on the Internet are general-interest sites that, while they don't publish fiction, *do* publish lots of reviews, critical articles, and genre-oriented news of various kinds. Among the best of these sites are: the *SF Site* (http://www.sfsite.com/), not only features an extensive selection of reviews of books, games, and magazines, interviews, critical retrospective articles, letters, and so forth, plus a huge archive of past reviews; but also serves as host site for the Web-pages of a significant percentage of all the SF/fantasy print magazines in existence, including *Asimov's, Analog, The Magazine of Fantasy & Science Fiction, Interzone,* and the whole DNA Publishing group (*Absolute Magnitude, Fantastic Stories of the Imagination, Weird Tales, Aboriginal SF, Dreams of Decadence*); *Locus Online* (http://www.locusmag.com), the online version of the newsmagazine *Locus*; a great source for fast-breaking genre-related news, as well as access to book reviews, critical lists, extensive database archives, and lists of links to other sites of interest (Mark Kelly's short-fiction review column only sporadically appears now, alas, but *Locus* has made up for it to some extent by regularly featuring short-fiction reviews by other hands); the English site BEST SF (http:// www.bestsf.net/), which also features reviews of the short fiction to be found in current SF magazines and anthologies; *Science Fiction Weekly* (http://www. scifi.com/sfw/), more media-and-gaming-oriented than *SF Site* or *Locus Online,* but which also features news and book reviews every issue, as well as providing a home for columns by such shrewd and knowledgeable genre insiders as John Clute and Michael Cassut; and *SFF NET* (http//www.sff.net), a huge site featuring dozens of home pages and newsgroups for SF writers, genre-oriented live chats, a link to the *Locus Magazine Index 1984–1996*, and a link to the research data and reading lists available on the Science Fiction Writers of America page (which can also be accessed directly at http://www.sfwa.org/.); and the above-mentioned *Sci-Fi Channel* (http://www.scifi.com), which not only provides a home for Ellen Datlow's SCI FICTION and for *Science Fiction Weekly*, but which is also home to the acclaimed audio-play site *Seeing Ear Theater*, and to the monthly SF-oriented chats hosted by *Asimov's* and *Analog*, as well as vast amounts of material about SF movies and TV shows; audio-plays can also be accessed at *Audible* (http://www.audible.com) and at *Beyond 2000* (http://www.beyond2000.com); multiple-Hugo-winner David Langford's online version of his fanzine *Ansible* (http://www.dcs.gla.ac.uk/Ansible/), which provides a funny and often iconoclastic slant on genre-oriented news, is well worth checking out on a regular basis.

Live online interviews with prominent genre writers are also offered on a regular basis on many sites, including interviews sponsored by *Asimov's* and *Analog* and conducted by Gardner Dozois on the Sci-Fi Channel (http://www.scifi.com/chat/) every other Tuesday night at 9 P.M. EST; regular scheduled interviews on the *Cybling* site (http://www.cybling.com/); and occasional interviews on the *Talk City* site (http://www.talkcity.com/). Many Bulletin Board Services, such as Delphi, Compuserve, and AOL, have large online communities of SF writers and fans, and some of these services also feature regularly scheduled live interactive real-time chats or conferences, in which anyone interested in SF is welcome to participate, the SF-oriented chat on Delphi, every Wednesday at about 10 P.M. EST, is the one with which I'm most familiar, but there are similar chats on SFF NET, and probably on other BBSs as well.

Other sites are more problematical. The extremely valuable short-fiction review site, *Tangent Online*, seemed to have died in 1999, with no new content being published there for more than seven months, came back to life briefly in 2000, "died" again for several months, and since then has maintained a very slow trickle of activity, with a few new reviews being published every so often, but nothing like the rate of refreshment it promised, or that it needs to really succeed in fulfilling the function it was created to fulfill, of reviewing the bulk of the year's short fiction. Recently, editor David Trusdale announced the birth of a new and revitalized *Tangent Online* site (http://www.tangentonline.com), welcome news that inspired a surge of hope in *Tangent* fans — but since his initial announcement, more than a month back now, nothing new has appeared on the revamped and redesigned site, and there's almost no real content there, just broken links that hopefully one day will lead to the reviews they promise. So, will Trusdale actually get his act together and successfully revive *Tangent Online*, or will it remain just hopeful vaporware? Who knows? Check in to the site occasionally to see if there's anything new going on, as I do, and see for yourself. Along similar lines, I think that the review site *SFRevu* (http://www.sfsite.com/sfrevu) is still in existence, after having died late in 1999 and then come back to life again, but every time I try to get to the site it crashes my system, so you'll have to go there and see for yourself. Many of the print criticalzines also have Web sites, but most of them haven't been refreshed in years. *Speculations*, which abandoned its print edition last year, still maintains a Web site (http://www.speculations.com) and no doubt is still dispensing writing advice, but you'll have to subscribe to the site online if you want to access it.

It's worth mentioning again that things change with such lightning speed in the online world that it's worth surfing around every once in a while to see what's still there, what's gone, and what's new. I can almost guarantee you that a lot of things *will* be different in this market by this time next year—it seems to be the nature of the beast.

Things were fluid in the print semiprozine market as well, as they have been for decades, with magazines dying and new magazines springing up to replace them.

One of the most astonishing stories in this market was the rebirth of the fiction semiprozine *Century* after almost four years of total silence, long after everyone (including, I must admit, me) had given it up for dead. Nevertheless, a new issue appeared in late 1999 (dated 2000), and was followed by another issue in the middle of 2000, and so *Century* will have to be considered to be alive again. Although they lean away from center-core SF and toward more literary stuff, with a high percentage of mainstream and fantasy stuff, *Century* was widely considered back in its Glory Days to be perhaps the most literate and sophisticated of all the fiction semiprozines, and this version of it lives up to that reputation, with good stories (most of them outside the genre, or with only thin traces of it) by Michael Bishop, Ian MacLeod, Michael Kandel, Robert Reed (one of the few real SF stories), Terry Windling, Greer Gilman, and others. Whether *Century* will disappear again or not, nobody knows (or what effect the recent tragic death of associate editor Jenna A. Felice will have on the magazine)—but the quality of these two issues is high enough to probably make it worthwhile taking a chance that they can maintain their schedule this time around, and subscribe. *Artemis Magazine: Science and Fiction for a Space-Faring Society* is another magazine that had been talked about and promised for years without ever actually materializing, so that many people had probably given up on it, but, like *Century*, it actually appeared late in 1999, with another issue coming out later on in 2000. The overall level of literary quality here is not as high or as consistent as that of *Century*—on the other hand, unlike *Century*, almost everything here is honest-to-gosh actual science fiction. *Artemis* published some good stuff this year, including a story by Stan Schmidt that made the Final Nebula Ballot, but to me they already seem to be chafing against their self-imposed restriction of only publishing stories about moon colonization, and I'd advise them to widen their purview a bit—in my opinion, if a story's about space exploration, that ought to be enough to get it in, without insisting that it take place on the Moon (they're already rationalizing ways around this stricture—stories that take place on *a* moon are okay—so why not do away with it altogether?).

In 1998, several fiction semiprozines were consolidated under the umbrella of Warren Lapine's DNA Publications, which now publishes *Aboriginal Science Fiction, Fantastic Stories of the Imagination* (formerly titled *Pirate Writings*), *Weird Tales*, and the all-vampire-fiction magazine *Dreams of Decadence*; as well as Lapine's original magazine, *Absolute Magnitude, The Magazine of Science Fiction Adventures*. Lapine continues to publicly announce that he's well-satisfied with the progress of the magazines, and it's true that the circulation of all the DNA magazines is growing, unlike most of the other magazines in the field, although only by miniscule degrees (the circulation for *Absolute Magnitude*, for instance, increased from 2,500 copies to 3,000 this year) . . . still, any forward motion is better than none, or, worse, motion in the *other* direction, and Lapine has some reason to congratulate himself on this. On the other hand, there are still problems: in spite of the fact that most of these magazines are supposed to be quarterlies, most of them (with the exception of *Weird Tales*) only managed to produce two issues apiece this year. And the overall quality of the fiction they contained in 2000 seemed a bit more lackluster than in some years past, with fewer standout stories. The DNA empire continues to expand—this year taking over the newsmagazine *Science Fiction Chronicle*—but it may be time for them to pause in expansion and devote more time and energy to things like stabilizing publication schedules for the magazines and working on producing a more reliable level of quality in the fiction. It would be a mistake for them to overextend themselves, a mistake the once-mighty *Pulphouse* empire made before them. Let's hope they can avoid that fate and keep the magazines they do have growing—the fiction semipro market could use a success story for a change. (Information about all of the DNA Publications magazines can be found at http://www.dnapublications.com/.)

Of the remaining SF fiction semiprozines, *Terra Incognita*, one of the brighter new lights on the fiction semiprozine scene, rivaled only by *Century* and *Eidolon* for their consistently high level of literary quality, managed to produce two issues in 2000 (after publishing no issues at all in 1999), featuring good work by Terry McGarry, Stefano Donati, L. Timmel Duchamp, David J. Hoffman-Dachelet, and others (although I still think that their self-imposed restriction of only using stories that take place on Earth is too limiting; it's hard enough to find good material for a magazine, without ruling out a very large percentage of it sight unseen). For the last couple of years, Australia has been bringing us three fiction semiprozines (two of them, *Aurealis* and *Eidolon* among the longest-running of all fiction semiprozines), but there seems to be trouble Down Under, and most of these magazines are emitting distressed wobbling noises. Just a few years back, much print was spilled hyping the new "Golden Age of Australian Science Fiction," but, although there are still plenty of good Australian writers working in the genre market, the Australian Boom seems to have sprung a leak as far as the Australian magazines themselves are concerned. *Altair*, the newest of the Australian semiprozines, published one double issue this year, out of a scheduled four, and then seems to have gone on hiatus due to lack of funds—perhaps permanently, if things don't work out. *Aurealis* published two issues (out of a scheduled four), one also a double issue but then got itself embroiled in some sort of strange controversy with most of its major writers (the details of which remain obscure to non-Australians, with most of the Australians being rather close-mouthed about it) which ended with most of them swearing to boycott the magazine from then on, leaving *Aurealis's* future somewhat in doubt, although they are still officially continuing. *Eidolon*, of recent years the most reliable of the Australian semiprozines, published a double issue that featured some good, high-professional-level stories from writers such as

Chris Lawson, Damien Broderick, Geoffrey Maloney, Stephen Dedman, Terry Dowling, and others, undoubtedly the best issue by far produced by any Australian semiprozine this year, and *then* announced that they were abandoning their print edition to "reinvent" themselves on their *Eidolon Online* Web site (http://www. eidolon.com) as an online-only "electronic magazine"—an announcement drawing cries of dismay from many industry insiders, who, after watching other print magazines such as *Omni* and *Tomorrow* try the same thing and fail, considered it to be tantamount to an announcement that *Eidolon* was going down the tubes (whether this turns out to be true or not remains to be seen; but I must admit that I myself am far from sanguine about its chances). So whether or not I can honestly advise you to subscribe to any of these magazines, I don't know. Do you feel lucky? I'll post what subscription information I have, and you can make up your own minds. (Meanwhile, a new Australian fiction semiprozine, *Orb*, is starting up, having produced two issues I've not yet seen. Rather than post a subscription rate for overseas subscriptions, they say to "please send inquiries regarding overseas subscriptions"; you can do so at their Web site, //home.vicnet.net.au/ ~kendacot/Orb/welcome.htm.)

The other longest-running fiction semiprozine, the Canadian *On Spec*, had seemed a bit dull and lackluster the last few years, overshadowed by the more robust *Eidolon*, but as the Australian magazines head into a rocky patch, *it* seems to have improved, with the overall quality of the fiction better than it's been in a while, with worthwhile stories by Cory Doctorow, Derryl Murphy, Kain Massin, Rebecca M. Senese, and others appearing there this year. Meanwhile, the other Canadian fiction semiprozine, *Transversions*, seems to have disappeared completely. There's also an Irish fiction semiprozine, an interesting and eccentric little magazine called *Albedo One*, which managed two issues this year. The leading British fiction semiprozine has for some years now been *The Third Alternative*, which is a slick and handsome full-size magazine that attracts the work of some top professional authors—but which also runs very little SF or fantasy, featuring "slipstream," literary surrealism, and horror instead. I only saw one issue of *Tales of the Unanticipated* and *Space & Time*, and *LC-39* died after a final issue. *Marion Zimmer Bradley's Fantasy Magazine* died this year, after thirteen years of publication. I don't follow the horror semiprozine market much anymore, but there the most prominent magazine seems to be the highly respected *Cemetery Dance* and the lively and audacious little magazine *Talebones, Fiction on the Dark Edge*, which also sneaks some science fiction in from time to time.

A quirky and interesting newcomer in the fiction semiprozine market is *Lady Churchill's Rosebud Wristlet* (http://www.lcrw.net); as you can tell from the title, it tends to be a bit self-consciously eccentric and "literary," but although you'll find no center-core SF here (or even fantasy, as it's usually known in the genre), you will find some good stories, most of them existing somewhere on the borderline between slipstream and surreal literary fantasy; this year, they ran interesting stuff by Ellen Klages (a story which is on this year's Final Nebula Ballot), Kelly Link, Jeffrey Ford, James Sallis, and others.

Another newcomer is *Black Gate* (http://www.blackgate.com), a handsome slick large-format fantasy magazine, supposedly concentrating on "Sword & Sorcery" and "High Fantasy" (although, oddly, the debut issue also contains a science fiction story by Jeffrey Ford); the first issue features a gorgeous cover by Keith Parkinson, as well as good work by Richard Parks, Charles de Lint, Michael Moorcock, and others (there are already rumors of behind-the-scenes trouble at *Black Gate*, though, so we'll have to wait and see if it survives).

Turning to the critical magazines, the top two magazines, and just about the only two published on a reliable schedule (or even anywhere *near* one), are Charles N. Brown's "newszine" *Locus*, and David G. Hartwell's eclectic critical magazine *The New York Review of Science Fiction*. Andy Porter's *SF Chronicle*, for years *Locus*'s chief rival, has fallen on hard times of late, with its publishing schedule becoming so erratic that often there were only a couple of issues per year. In 2000, however, *SF Chronicle* became part of Warren Lapine's DNA Publications group, theoretically freeing Porter to concentrate on editing rather than the mundane details of production and distribution, and it is sincerely to be hoped that this change will put *SF Chronicle* back in contention as a top newszine again. There were two issues of Lawrence Person's playful and intelligent *Nova Express* out this year, prompting some to exclaim that the millennium must be at hand (as indeed it *is*, isn't it?) There's not really a lot more *left* to the critical semiprozine market anymore, what with some magazines falling silent, and *Tangent* and *Speculations* converting (supposedly, in *Tangent*'s case) to online-only electronic versions—a fate which I sometimes think might overtake all critical semiprozines in time.

(*Locus, The Newspaper of the Science Fiction Field*, Locus Publications, Inc., P.O. Box 13305, Oakland, California 94661, $56.00 for a one-year first class subscription, 12 issues; *The New York Review of Science Fiction*, Dragon Press, P.O. Box 78, Pleasantville, NY, 10570, $32.00 per year, 12 issues; *Nova Express*, P.O. Box 27231, Austin, Texas 78755-2231, $12 for a one-year (four-issue) subscription; *On Spec. More Than Just Science Fiction*, P.O. Box 4727, Edmonton, AB, Canada T6E 5G6, $18 for a one-year subscription; *Aurealis, the Australian Magazine of Fantasy and Science Fiction*, Chimaera Publications, P.O. Box 2164, Mt. Waverley, Victoria 3149, Australia, $43 for a four-issue overseas airmail subscription, "all cheques and money orders must be made out to Chimarea Publications in Australian dollars"; *Eidolon, the Journal of Australian Science Fiction and Fantasy*, Eidolon Publications, P.O. Box 225, North Perth, Western Australia 6906, $45 (Australian) for four-issue overseas airmail subscription, payable to Eidolon Publications; *Altair. Alternate Airings in Speculative Fiction*, PO Box 475, Blackwood, South Australia, 5051, Australia, $36 for a four-issue subscription; *Albedo*, Albedo One Productions, 2 Post Road, Lusk, Co., Dublin, Ireland; $34 for a four-issue airmail subscription, make checks payable to "Albedo One"; *Fantastic Stories of the Imagination, Absolute Magnitude, The Magazine of Science Fiction Adventures, Aboriginal Science Fiction, Weird Tales, Dreams of Decadence, Science Fiction Chronicle*—all available from DNA Publications, P.O. Box 2988, Radford, VA 24142-2988, all available for $16 for a one-year subscription, although you can get a group subscription to all five DNA fiction magazines for $70 a year, with *Science Fiction Chronicle* $45 a year (12 issues), all checks payable to "D.N.A. Publications"; *Century*, Century Publishing, P.O. Box 150510, Brooklyn, NY 11215-0510, $20 for a four issue subscription; *Terra Incognita*, Terra Incognita, 52 Windermere Avenue #3, Lansdowne, PA 19050-1812, $15 for four issues; *Tales of the Unanticipated*, Box 8036, Lake Street Station, Minneapolis, MN 55408, $15 for a four-issue subscription; *Space & Time*, 138 W. 70th Street (4B), New York, NY. 10023-4468, $10.00 for a two-issue subscription (one year), $20.00 for a four-issue subscription (two years); *Artemis Magazine: Science and Fiction for a Space-Faring Society*, LRC Publications, 1380 E. 17th St., Suite 201, Brooklyn NY 11230-6011, $15 for a four-issue subscription, checks payable to LRC Publications; *Talebones, Fiction on the Dark Edge*, 5203 Quincy Ave SE, Auburn, WA 98092, $18 for four issues; *The Third Alternative*, TTA Press, 5 Martins Lane, Witcham, Ely, Cambs. CB6 2LB, England, UK, $22 for a four-issue subscription, checks made payable to "TTA Press"; *Black Gate*, New Epoch Press, 815 Oak Street, St. Charles, IL 60174, $25.95 for a one-year (four-issue) subscription; *Cemetery Dance*, CD Publications, Box 18433, Baltimore, MD 21237; *Lady Churchill's Rosebud Wristlet*, Small Beer Press, 360 Atlantic Avenue, PMB #132, Brooklyn, NY 11217, $12 for four issues, all checks payable to Gavin Grant. Many of these magazines can also be ordered online, at their Web sites; see the online section, above, for URLs.)

All in all, 2000 was another weak year for original anthologies, with only a few bright spots here and there. The best original SF anthology of the year, with even less competition for the title than usual, was probably *Vanishing Acts* (Tor), edited by Ellen Datlow. Although it carries the assertive subtitle, "A Science Fiction Anthology," a number of stories here, including a few of the best ones (the Chiang, the Stableford, the McDowell), are fantasy by any reasonable definition—but enough of the rest of them are center-core SF to tip the balance and let us judge this as an SF anthology. The best story here is probably Ted Chiang's eccentric and brilliant novella "Seventy-two letters," a story which dances right on the razor-thin boundary between fantasy and science fiction; I finally decided that it actually *was* a fantasy, as it depends at base on the core assumption that cabalistic magic *really does work*, but it's a member of that small but select subsubgenre of stories that rigorously examine fantasy material through the logical and rational lens of the scientific method—in fact, "Seventy-two Letters" reminds me the most strongly of those sections in Avram Davidson's *The Phoenix and the Mirror* concerned with the making of the speculum majorum. Other than the Chaing, clearly the cream of the crop here, the best stories in *Vanishing Acts* are M. Shayne Bell's "The Thing About Benny," Daniel Abraham's "Chimera 8," and Paul. J. McAuley's "The Rift," with Brian Stableford's "Tenebrio" and Ian McDowell's "Sunflowers" a half step below that. The book also contains worthwhile but somewhat flawed stories by Mark W. Tiedemann and A. R. Morlan, and William Shunn, as well as less successful pieces by Michael Cadnum and David J. Schow. *Vanishing Acts* is also anchored by strong reprints by Suzy McKee Charnas, Avram Davidson, Karen Joy Fowler, and Bruce McAllister (be sure to catch in particular Charnas's strong and underrated "Listening to Brahms"), and graced by an intriguing poem by Joe Haldeman, and is a good value at $24.95.

You run quickly out of options this year when searching for possibilities for a follow-up candidate for the title of best original SF anthology. The most solid contender is probably *Skylife: Space Habitats in Story and Science* (Harcourt), edited by Gregory Benford and George Zebrowski, which features two excellent original stories, "Reefs," by Paul J. McAuley and "Open Loops," by Stephen Baxter, as well as good reprints (of both stories and essays) by James Patrick Kelly, Arthur C. Clarke, Larry Niven, Joan D. Vinge, James Blish, Greg Bear, Gregory Benford himself, and others. This is a worthwhile anthology, and a valuable addition to any SF library, but it somehow feels a bit musty—most of the reprint stories are from the late '70s, as is the longest of the reprint essays, as if the book was *really* an anthology from the late '70s that had somehow not seen print until the year 2000. With the exception of the originals by McAuley and Baxter, there's little here reflective of the evolution of genre thinking about the theme during the decades of the '80s and '90s: without those two stories, there wouldn't be much evidence that *Skylife hadn't* originally been published twenty years ago (even the extensive bibliography doesn't mention much that was published after the beginning of the '80s). As is, the book seems out of balance, with the bulk of it composed of reprint material, much of it rather dated. I think they'd have been better off throwing out some of the reprints, both fiction and nonfiction, and commissioning more originals from contemporary authors (or fresh material from veterans such as Bear, Benford, and Vinge, for that matter), especially if they could have gotten stories at the same level of quality as the two originals they *do* have. Still, in spite of these quibbles, *Skylife* will probably be the standard anthology on this theme for some time to come. At $28, it may be seen as a bit expensive by some, but when you throw in the eight pages of color art, it's probably worth it.

Dark Matter: A Century of Speculative Fiction from the African Diaspora (Warner), edited by Sheree R. Thomas, is an anthology of huge historical significance, but can hardly be a serious contender for the title of best original SF anthology of the year, since it doesn't really contain that much actual *science fiction*. Whatever its value as literature, most of the original material here is fantasy or horror of various stripes, or near-mainstream, or surrealism of one sort or another, or literary erotica; what science fiction there is here (with the exception of two of the reprints) tends to be quite "soft," or to be mixed in a hybrid with one or more of the other genres mentioned. (The next *Dark Matter* anthology, being planned now, supposedly will concentrate more on science fiction.) The best of the original stories in *Dark Matter* are by Tananarive Due, Nalo Hopkinson, Linda Addison, Nisi Shawl, Leane Ross, and Jewelle Gomez, the book also features rare and rarely seen material of great historic import from black writers not usually seen as part of SF's family tree, such as W. E. B. Du Bois, George S. Schuyler, Ishmael Reed, and Charles W. Chesnutt, more contemporary (but still classic) reprints by writers such as Samuel R. Delany and Octavia E. Butler, and an array of essays about racism and science fiction by Delany, Butler, Paul D. Miller, Charles R. Saunders, and Walter Mosley. A landmark anthology.

After this, we quickly run out of alternatives. *Star Colonies* (DAW), edited by Martin H. Greenberg and John Helfers, is probably an attempt to follow up on the success of last year's acclaimed *Moon Shots* anthology (edited by Peter Crowther), but although it does contain good stories by Allen Steele, Pamela Sargent, Robert Charles Wilson, and others, nothing here really reaches the level of quality of the best of the stories from *Moon Shots. Far Frontiers* (DAW), edited by Greenberg and Larry Segriff, is even weaker, although there's still some entertaining material here by Kristine Kathryn Rusch, Alan Dean Foster, Robin Wayne Bailey, and others. This year's assembled-online SFF.net anthology (number three in the "*Darkfire* anthology series," according to the cover copy) is *The Age of Wonders: Tales from the Near Future* (SFF.NET), edited by Jeffry Dwight. This anthology seems weaker than last year's SFF.net anthology, *The Age of Reason*, perhaps because of the limitation in potential story material implied by the subtitle, perhaps because that's just the way it came out, with lots of minor stories, but it does feature a superior story by William Sanders, and interesting work by Brian Plante, Dave Smeds, Mary Soon Lee, Lawrence Fitzgerald, and others (you won't find this one in stores, so mail-order from: SFF Net, 3300 Big Horn Trail, Plano, TX 75075 — $14.95 for *The Age of Wonders: Tales from the Near Future*; the book can also be ordered online at sff.net, and back titles in the *Darkfire* series can be ordered either by mail or online). *Guardians of Tomorrow* (DAW), edited by Martin H. Greenberg and Larry Segriff, was also pretty minor, although it featured interesting work by Willam H. Keith, Jane Lindskold, Kristine Kathryn Rusch, and others. *Such a Pretty Face: Tales of Power and Abundance* (Meisha Merlin), edited by Lee Martindale, is a mixed SF/fantasy anthology that features good work by Gene Wolfe, Laura Underwood, K. D. Wentworth, Elizabeth Ann Scarborough, Sharon Lee and Steve Miller, and others. And, as usual, *L. Ron Hubbard Presents Writers of the Future Volume XVI* (Bridge), edited by Algis Budrys, presents novice work by beginning writers, some of whom may later turn out to be important talents.

There wasn't a big standout anthology in fantasy this year, as there has been some years. The best original fantasy anthology of the year was probably *Black Heart, Ivory Bones* (Avon), edited by Ellen Datlow and Terri Windling, the latest in their long series of anthologies of updated fairy tales, featuring good stories by Howard Waldrop, Severna Park, Brian Stableford, Jane Yolen, Tanith Lee, Esther Friesner, Russell Blackford, and others. A Young Adult version of the same kind of thing, updated fairy tales, lacking the sharp edges of the adult version but still containing some good material, was *A Wolf at the Door and Other Retold Fairy Tales* (Simon & Schuster), also edited by Ellen Datlow and Terri Windling, which featured good work by Neil Gaiman, Jane Yolen, Janeen Webb, Tanith Lee, Kelly Link, Patricia A. McKillip, and others.

The two Datlow/Windling anthologies are primarially Eurocentric in orientation, though, and some may prefer the more offbeat and unconventional fantasy to be found in *Dark Matter*, or the fantasies inspired by Caribbean folktales featured in *whispers from the cotton tree root* (Invisible Cities Press), edited by Nalo Hopkinson, which contains "Caribbean fabulist fiction" from a large cross section of writers whose work will be unfamiliar to most genre readers, as well as from a few more-familiar figures such as Ian McDonald and Hopkinson herself.

The rest of the year's original fantasy anthologies (and original fantasy anthologies seem to be proliferating as reprint fantasy anthologies dwindle) were the usual welter of "pleasant but minor" theme anthologies, each containing a couple of interesting stories, but rarely more than that; as they're all inexpensive paperbacks, you may get your money's worth out of individual titles, but don't expect anything really special. They included: *Warrior Fantastic* (DAW), edited by Martin H. Greenberg and John Helfers, which features interesting work by Charles de

Lint, Nina Kiriki Hoffman, Alan Dean Foster, and others; *Spell Fantastic* (DAW), edited by Martin H. Greenberg and John Helfers, which featured work by Jane Lindskold, Nina Kiriki Hoffman, and others; *Civil War Fantastic* (DAW), edited by Martin H. Greenberg, which featured work by Kristine Kathryn Rusch, Nancy Springer, Karen Haber, Mike Resnick and Catharine Asaro, and others; *New Amazons* (DAW), edited by Margaret Weis, featuring work by Nancy Springer, Jo Clayton, and others; and *Perchance to Dream* (DAW), edited by Denise Little, which featured worthwhile stuff by Diane Duane, Peter Crowther, Nancy Springer, Bruce Holland Rogers, Michelle West, and others. *The Chick Is in the Mail* (Baen), edited by Esther M. Friesner, is another entry in a one-joke anthology series that has probably gone on for too long; this one features good writers such as Harry Turtledove, William Sanders, Nancy Kress, Charles Sheffield, and Friesner herself, all trying gamely to deal with the lame theme, although one gets the feeling that they could have better spent the time writing something else for some other market instead. Another fantasy anthology was the latest, and probably the last, in a very long-running series: *Swords & Sorceresses XVII* (DAW), edited by the late Marion Zimmer Bradley.

I don't pay close attention to the horror genre anymore, but there didn't seen to be any Big Prestigious Anthology—like last year's 999—there either; the most prominent anthologies seemed to be *Dark Terrors 5* (Gollancz), edited by Stephen Jones and David Sutton, and a mixed original and reprint anthology, *October Dreams: A Celebration of Halloween* (CD Publications), edited by Richard T. Chizmar and Robert Morrish (CD Publications, PO Box 943, Abingdon, MD 21009—$40 for *October Dreams*). I've already counted *Black Heart, Ivory Bones* as a fantasy anthology, and *Dark Matter* as a science fiction anthology, but reasonable cases could be made for considering them to be horror instead, depending on how you squint at them. There were also several other anthologies that existed on the borderline of fantasy and horror this year, some stories seeming to belong in one camp, some in the other (some of them even threw in a smidgen of science fiction): *Treachery and Treason* (Penguin/Roc), edited by Laura Ann Gilman and Jennifer Heddle, featured interesting work by Lois Tilton, Karen Haber, Esther Friesner, Jerry Oltion, K. D. Wentworth, Scott Edelman, and others; *Graven Images* (Ace), edited by Nancy Kilpatrick and Thomas S. Roche (Ace), featured worthwhile material by Lois Tilton, Gene Wolfe, Kathe Koja, Tanith Lee, Lawrence Watt-Evans, Chelsea Quinn Yarbro, and others; and *Mardi Gras Fantastic: Tales of Terror and Mayhem in New Orleans* (Cumberland House), edited by Martin H. Greenberg and Russell David, featured stories by Peter Crowther, Bruce Holland Rogers, Charles de Lint, Jane Lindskold, Elizabeth Ann Scarborough, and others. There was also a hybrid fantasy/horror anthology from Australia, *Mystery, Magic, Voodoo & the Holy Grail* (Voyager), edited by Stephanie Smith and Julia Stiles, featuring no names which would be familiar to the American genre audience.

An extremely disappointing story in the anthology market this year was the announcement of the cancellation of the long-promised new Avon Eos anthology series, which was supposed to be "like Full Spectrum," a project upon which a lot of hopes had been pinned. That leaves little to look forward to in this market except for the next volume in the *Starlight* anthology series, promised for 2001, and a new SF anthology edited by Peter Crowther, about Mars, said to be in the works.

It was a relatively stable year in the novel market, with no significant gains in the overall number of novels published, but no really dramatic losses, either, in spite of the mergers and cutbacks and shakeups of the last couple of years. There are still a *lot* of science fiction/fantasy/horror books being published, in spite of recent talk about how these genres are "dying," and a lot of them seem to have done quite well commercially. Barring a sudden catastrophic recession in the publishing industry of Great Depression-like proportions (which *could* happen, of course, especially if we head into a *societywide* Depression of cataclysmic severity), the probability is that there will continue to be a lot of genre books published in the foreseeable future as well. (Quality is a much more subjective call, of course; and some critics seem to delight in gloomy talk about how nothing worthwhile gets into print anymore, but it seems to me that, to the contrary, there are still plenty of novels of quality being published out there, including some that probably *wouldn't* have been printed ten or fifteen years ago.)

According to the newsmagazine *Locus*, there were 1,927 books "of interest to the SF field," both original and reprint, published in 2000, down by 2% from 1999's total of 1,959, but still a hefty number. Original books were down by 7%, down 1,027 from last year's total of 1,107. The number of new SF novels was down slightly, with 230 novels published, as opposed to 251 novels published in 1999. The number of new fantasy novels was also down, with 258 novels published, as opposed to 275 published in 1999, still higher than 1998's total of 233. Horror was also down, with 80 novels published as opposed to 1999's total of 95 novels.

It's interesting to compare these totals by category with the totals from 1995: there were 239 new SF novels published in 1995, 230 published in 2000, so SF is really only down by nine titles when compared to five years ago; there were 227 new fantasy novels published in 1995, as opposed to 258, so fantasy has grown by 31 titles when compared to 1995; there were 193 new horror novels published in 1995, as opposed to 80, so horror has dwindled by 113 titles when compared to 1995. In spite of all the talk over the last five years about how science fiction as a commercial category is dying, there's really not that much difference in the number of SF books published in 2000 and in 1995, nor has fantasy grown enough by comparison to really be said to have "swallowed" SF or driven it off the bookshelves, as is sometimes averred. Horror isn't "dead" either, in spite of the funeral services that have been read over *that* genre.

(And, for some historical perspective, the next time that you hear that the SF genre is "dying," keep in mind that the number of original mass-market paperbacks published this year, 324, is alone higher than the *total number* of original genre books, of any sort, published in 1972, which was 225. And that a much-wider-audience of people have *easier access* to SF books than at any other time in the genre's history; when I was a kid, you had to travel more than twenty miles by train or bus if you wanted to find a bookstore that carried science fiction titles, and there was no such thing even as a science fiction *section* in bookstores, let alone a science fiction specialty store.)

I don't have time to read many novels, with all the reading I have to do at shorter lengths, and this year have read even fewer than usual—so rather than endorsing anything personally, I'll limit myself to mentioning those novels that received a lot of attention and acclaim in 2000 including: *The Telling* (Harcourt), Ursula K. Le Guin; *Genesis* (Tor), Poul Anderson; *The Coming* (Ace), Joe Haldeman; *In Green's Jungles* (Tor), Gene Wolfe; *Eater* (Eos), Gregory Benford; *Probability Moon* (Tor), Nancy Kress; *Shrine of Stars* (Eos), Paul McAuley; *A Storm of Swords* (Bantam Spectra), George R. R. Martin; *The Fountains of Youth* (Tor), Brian Stableford: *Zeitgeist* (Bantam Spectra), Bruce Sterling; *Look to Windward* (Orbit), Iain M. Banks; *The Amber Spyglass* (Knopf), Philip Pullman; *Marrow* (Tor), Robert Reed; *Crescent City Rhapsody* (Avon Eos), Kathleen Ann Goonan; *The Sky Road* (Tor), Ken MacLeod; *Dervish Is Digital* (Macmillan), Pat Cadigan; *Galveston* (Ace), Sean Stewart; *Midnight Robber* (Warner Aspect), Nalo Hopkinson; *The Light of Other Days* (Tor), Stephen Baxter and Arthur C. Clarke; *Candle* (Tor), John Barnes; *The Collapsium* (Del Rey), Wil McCarthy; *Mendoza in Hollywood* (Harcourt), Kage Baker; *The Miocene Arrow* (Tor), Sean McMullen; *Perdido Street Station* (Macmillan), China Mieville; *Ventus* (Tor), Karl Schroeder; *White Mars* (St. Martin's), Brian W. Aldiss and Roger Penrose; *Wild Angel* (Tor), Pat Murphy; *Oceanspace* (Ace), Allen Steele; *The Fresco* (Eos), Sheri S. Tepper; *The Prophecy Machine* (Bantam Spectra), Neal Barrett, Jr.; *The Last Hot Time* (Tor), John M. Ford; *Empire of Unreason* (Del Rey), J. Gregory Keyes; *Lodestar* (Tor), Michael Flynn; *Wild Life* (Simon & Schuster), Molly Gloss; *Darwin's Blade* (Morrow), Dan Simmons; *Jumping Off the Planet* (Tor), David Gerrold; *Colony Fleet* (Eos), Susan R. Matthews; *Daemonomania* (Bantam), John Crowley; *Ash: A Secret History* (Eos), Mary Gentle; *Blind Waves* (Tor), Steven Gould; *Kirith Kirin* (Meisha Merlin), Jim Grimsley; *Infinity Beach* (HarperPrism), Jack McDevitt; *The Memory of Fire* (Bantam Spectra), George Foy; *The Jazz* (Tor), Melissa Scott; *Lieutenant Colonel* (Ace), Rick Shelley; *Fortress of Dragons* (Eos), C. J. Cherryh; *The Glass Harmonica* (Ace), Louise Marley; *Spindle's End* (Putnam), Robin McKinley; *Hunted* (Eos), James Alan Gardner, *Brain Plague* (Tor), Joan Slonczewski; *Colonization: Down to Earth* (Del Rey), Harry Turtledove; *The Quiet Invasion* (Warner Aspect), Sarah Zettel; and *The Truth* (HarperCollins), Terry Pratchett.

It was a slightly stronger year for first novels this year than last year. The two first novels that attracted the most attention were *Revelation Space* (Gollancz), by Alastair Reynolds and *Mars Crossing* (Tor), by Geoffrey A. Landis. Other first novels included: *Wheelers* (Warner Aspect), Ian Steward and Jack Cohen; *Soulsaver* (Harcourt), Jams Stevens-Acre; *Growing Wings* (Houghton Mifflin) Laurel Winter; *House of Leaves* (Pantheon), Mark Z. Danielewski; *Ceres Storm* (Tor), David Herter; and *The Glasswrights' Apprentice* (Tor), Mindy L. Klasky. As usual, all publishers who are willing to take a chance publishing first novels should be commended, since developing new talent by publishing their maiden efforts, taking a risk on writers without a proven track record, is a chance that must be taken by *someone* if new talent is going to be able to develop, and if the field itself is going to survive.

Looking over these lists, it's obvious that Tor and Eos had strong years. Once again, in spite of complaints that nobody publishes "real" science fiction anymore, the majority of novels here are center-core science fiction novels. Even omitting the fantasy novels and the borderline genre-straddling work on the list, the Anderson, the Haldeman, the Le Guin, the Baxter and Clarke, the Benford, the Goonan, the McAuley, the Banks, the Kress, the Barnes, the Reed, the McCarthy, the Stableford, the Sterling, the Reynolds, the Landis, and a half dozen others are science fiction by any even remotely reasonable definition, many of them "hard science fiction" as hard and as rigorous as it's ever been written by anybody—in fact, despite what "they" say, I think more center-core SF has been published in the last five years or so than ever before . . . as well as a large range of other kinds of work, from pure fantasy to borderland SF/fantasy hybrids of a dozen different sorts.

Like last year, 2000 was also a good year for the reissuing of long-out-of-print classic novels. The *SF Masterworks* reprint series, from English publisher Millennium, has been doing an excellent job over the last two years of making classic novels available to the public again, with recent titles including such seminal works as *Nova*, by Samuel R. Delany, *Pavane*, by Keith Roberts, *More Than Human*, by Theodore Sturgeon, *Ubik*, by Philip K. Dick, *Non-Stop*, by Brian W. Aldiss, and more than thirty other titles, every single one of which belongs in the library of any serious student of the genre. Millennium's recently launched *Fantasy Masterworks* reprint series is doing an equally good job of bringing classic fantasy books such as *Little, Big*, by John Crowley, *Lud-in-the-Mist*, by Hope Mirrlees, *Fevre Dream*, by George R. R. Martin, and *The Land of Laughs*, by Jonathan Carroll back into print, as well as doing omnibus volumes of Gene Wolfe's "Book of the New Sun" series, Jack Vance's "Dying Earth" stories, Roger Zelazny's "Amber Chronicles," and L. Sprague De Camp's "Incomplete Enchanter" books, and hard-to-find collections by writes such as Robert E. Howard, M. John Harrison, and Lord Dunsany. On this side of the Atlantic, reprint series such as Tor/Orb and Del Rey Impact, and a reprint line from Vintage are also performing invaluable services for the field by bringing long-unavailable novels back into print, including, this year, *The Big Time* (Tor), by Fritz Leiber, *A Case of Conscience* (Del Rey Impact), by James Blish, *The Power* (Orb), by Frank M. Robinson, *The Empire of Isher* (Orb), by A. E. Van Vogt, *The Genocides* (Vintage), by Thomas M. Disch, and many others. Ace is also reissuing classics from its backlist, such as *The Left Hand of Darkness*, by Ursula K. Le Guin, *Neuromancer*, by William Gibson, and *The Northern Girl*, by Elizabeth A. Lynn, and Overlook Press offered an omnibus of James Blish's famous "Okie" novels, *Cities in Flight*. Print-on-demand (POD) publishers are also having a big impact on making classic work available to readers again; Wildside Press (http://www.wildside.com) has already returned to easy availability (if not, technically, to print) almost all of the long-out-of-print and long-unavailable novels of writers such as R. A. Lafferty and Avram Davidson, and this is only the beginning of what should be a flood of "reissued" POD classic titles over the next few years.

In fact, all in all, this may be the best time in decades to get your hands on long-unavailable work and fill up those holes in your library shelves with books you've long meant to read but couldn't find, so be sure to take advantage of it. Most of these classic novels should be read by anybody who wants to understand the evolution of science fiction, how the genre got to where it is today, and where it's going next—and also by anybody who just wants a lot of first-rate *reading*, works that have been unavailable to them before now, sometimes unavailable for decades. Get them and read them now, while you have the chance.

(There are a lot of *new* POD novels available, too, too many to individually list here, many of them by first-rate SF writers such as William Sanders and Lois Tilton; check the Web sites of POD publishers such as Xlibris and Wildside and Subterranean Press and Universe for these, is my advice. Novels both old and new are also available in great numbers to either be downloaded or read online at PeanutPress, *Fictionwise ElectricStory, Alexandria Digital Literature, Project Gutenberg,* and many other sites.)

My track record for predicting what novels are going to win major awards is bad enough (last year, I predicted Vernor Vinge's Hugo win, but missed the Nebula winner completely) that I suppose I shouldn't even try. Your guess is, obviously, as good as mine.

Borderline SF novels this year included *Bad Medicine* (HarperCollins Australia), by Jack Dann, a wonderfully crafted and keenly observed "road" novel about two old men setting off for a last adventure—and a last chance for knowledge and self-discovery—on the edge of life: mostly "mainstream," but with a few strong fantastic touches here and there to add spice; and the comic *The Man of Maybe Half-a-Dozen Faces* (St. Martin's), by Ray Vuckcevich. Mystery novels by SF writers included *Deepest Water* (St. Martin's), by Kate Wilhelm. and *Bleeding Heart* (Berkeley), by Mary Rosenblum, writing as "Mary Freeman."

It was another good year for short-story collections, as it has been for the past several years now. The year's best collections included *Tales of Old Earth* (North Atlantic/Tachyon), by Michael Swanwick; *Beluthahatchie and Other Stories* (Golden Gryphon), by Andy Duncan; *Perpetuity Blues and Other Stories* (Golden Gryphon), by Neal Barrett, Jr.; *Moon Dogs* (NESFA Press), by Michael Swanwick; *Worlds Vast and Various* (Eos), by Gregory Benford; *Strange Travelers* (Tor), by Gene Wolfe; *Blue Kansas Sky* (Golden Gryphon), by Michael Bishop; *Terminal Visions* (Golden Gryphon), by Richard Paul Russo; *The Perseids and Other Stories* (Tor), by Robert Charles Wilson; *Night Moves and Other Stories* (Subterranean Press), by Tim Powers; and *In the Upper Room and Other Likely Stories* (Tor), by Terry Bisson.

Other good collections included: *High Cotton: Selected Stories of Joe R. Lansdale* (Golden Gryphon), by Joe R. Lansdale; *Thirteen Phantasms and Other Stories* (Edgewood Press), by James Blaylock; *Kafka Americana* (Subterranean Press), by Jonathan Lethem and Carter Scholz; *In the Stone House* (Arkham House), by Barry N. Malzberg; *Sister Emily's Lightship and Other Stories* (Tor), by Jane Yolen; *Blackwater Days* (Eidolon), by Terry Dowling; *Puck Aleshire's Abecedary* (Dragon Press), by Michael Swanwick; *Travel Arrangements* (Gollancz), by M. John Harrison; *Gnarl!* (Four Walls Eight Windows), by Rudy Rucker; *In Space No One*

Can Hear You Laugh (Farthest Star SF), by Mike Resnick; *The Death Artist* (Dream Haven), by Dennis Etchison; *Tagging the Moon* (Night Shade), by S. P. Somtow; and *Triskell Tales* (Subterranean Press), by Charles de Lint.

The year also featured strong retrospective collections such as *The Complete Stories of Theodore Sturgeon, Volume VII: Saucer of Loneliness* (North Atlantic), by Theodore Sturgeon; *Selected Stories* (Vintage), by Theodore Sturgeon; *The Essential Hal Clement, Volume 2: Music of Many Spheres* (NESFA Press), by Hal Clement, edited by Mark L. Olsen and Anthony R. Lewis; *The Essential Hal Clement, Volume 3: Variations on a Theme by Sir Isaac Newton* (NESFA Press), by Hal Clement, edited by Mark L. Olsen and Anthony R. Lewis; *Meet Me in Infinity* (Tor), by James Tiptree, Jr.; *Telzey Amberdon* (Baen), by James H. Schmitz, edited by Eric Flint; *T'n'T: Telzey & Trigger* (Baen), by James H. Schmitz, edited by Eric Flint; *The Collected Stories of Jack Williamson, Volume Three: Wizard's Isle* (Haffner Press), by Jack Williamson; *The Third Cry to Legba and Other Invocations: The Selected Stories of Manly Wade Wellman, Volume 1* (Night Shade Books) by Manly Wade Wellman; *Hell on Earth: The Lost Bloch Volume Two* (Subterranean Press), by Robert Bloch; *The Yellow Sign and Other Tales* (Chaosium), by Robert W. Chambers; and *Major Ingredients: The Selected Short Stories of Eric Frank Russell* (NESFA Press), by Eric Frank Russell. And although it contains a number of mainstream stories as well as SF and fantasy, Davidson fans will certainly want *Everybody Has Somebody In Heaven: Essential Jewish Tales of the Spirit* (Pitspopany Press), by the late Avram Davidson, edited by Jack Dann and Grania Davis, which collects some of Davidson's rarest and hardest-to-find early stories, as well as some later classics like "The Golem" and "Goslin Day."

As you can see, small-press publishers remain vital to the publication of short-story collections, with new publisher Golden Gryphon Press particularly distinguishing itself, following in the footsteps of its founder, the late Jim Turner; NESFA Press, Tachyon, North Atlantic, and other small presses also brought a lot of good work to the public this year that otherwise might never have been seen again. Regular trade publishers, though, do seem to be doing more collections these days than in years past, and a special nod should be given to Tor, which has probably published more collections in the past couple of years than any other trade publisher.

Print-on-demand publishers are becoming important suppliers of short-story collections. Mike Resnick had one POD collection last year, *A Safari of the Mind* from Wildside Press, and he had another one out this year, a collection of his stories in collaboration with Nick DiChario, *Magic Feathers: The Mike & Nick Show* (Obscura Press). Wildside Press also published *The Sweet and Sour Tongue: Stories by Leslie What*, by Leslie What, *Without Absolution*, by Amy Sterling Casil, and *Nightscapes: Tales of the Ominous and Magical*, by Darrell Schweitzer this year. And there are many more POD collections on the way for next year, from Wildside and from other POD publishers as well.

Another rapidly developing source of collections, at least of the downloadable "electronic collection" variety, are online fiction sites. "Collections" by Nancy Kress, Mike Resnick, Damon Knight, Kage Baker, Robert Silverberg, Harlan Ellison, Tom Purdom, John Kessel, James Patrick Kelly, for instance, and many others, are available to be downloaded for a fee at *Fictionwise* (http://www.fictionwise.com), and *ibooks* (http://www.ibooksinc.com) also "published" (promulgated? We need new terminology for this!) downloadable electronic collections by Robert Silverberg, Alfred Bester, and others this year. And more such sites are on the way.

As very few small-press titles will be findable in the average bookstore, or even in the average chain superstore, that means that mail order is still your best bet, and so I'm going to list the addresses of the small-press publishers mentioned above: NESFA Press, P.O. Box 809, Framinghan, MA 01701-0809 — $25 for *Moon Dogs*, by Michael Swanwick; $25 for *The Essential Hal Clement, Volume Two: Music of Many Spheres*, by Hal Clement, $25 for *The Essential Hal Clement, Volume Three: Variations on a Theme by Sir Isaac Newton*, by Hal Clement; $29 for *Major Ingredients: The Selected Short Stories of Eric Frank Russell*, by Eric Frank Russell; Golden Gryphon Press, 364 West Country Lane, Collinsville, IL 62234 — $23.95 for *Beluthahatchie and Other Stories*, by Andy Duncan, $21.95 for *Perpetuity Blues and Other Stories*, by Neal Barrett, Jr; $24.95 for *Blue Kansas Sky*, by Michael Bishop; $23.95 for *Terminal Visions*, by Richard Paul Russo; $23.95 for *High Cotton: Selected Stories of Joe R. Lansdale*, by Joe R. Lansdale; North Atlantic Books, P.O. Box 12327, Berkeley, CA, 94701 — $25 for *Tales of Old Earth*, by Michael Swanwick; $30 for *The Complete Stories of Theodore Sturgeon, Volume VII: Saucer of Loneliness*, by Theodore Sturgeon; Pitspopany Press, 40 East 78th St., Suite 16D, New York, NY 10021 — $24.95 for *Everybody Has Somebody in Heaven: Essential Jewish Tales of the Spirit*, by Avram Davidson; Edgewood Press, P.O. Box 380264, Cambridge, MA 02238 — $25 for *Thirteen Phantasms and Other Stories*, by James Blaylock; Wildside Press, P.O. Box 45, Gillette, NJ 07933-0045 — $13.95 for *The Sweet and Sour Tongue Stories by Leslie What*, by Leslie What; $15 for *Without Absolution*, by Amy Sterling Casil; $16 for *Nightscapes: Tales of the Ominous and Magical*, by Darrell Schweitzer; Farthest Star SF, 65 Macedonia Road, Alexander, NC 28701 — $16.95 for *In Space No One Can Hear You Laugh*, by Mike Resnick; Obscura Press, P.O. Box 1992, Ames, Iowa 50010-1992 — $12.95 for *Magic Feathers: The Mike & Nick Show*, by Mike Resnick & Nick DiChario; Eidolon Publications, PO Box 225, North Perth, Western Australia 6906 — $A22.95 for *Blackwater Days*, by Terry Dowling; Haffner Press, 5005 Crooks Rd., Suite 35, Royal Oak, MI 48073-1239 — $32 plus $5.00 postage for *The Collected Stories of Jack Williamson, Volume Three: Wizard's Isle*; Night Shade Books, 563 Scott #304, San Francisco, CA 94117 — $35 for *The Third Cry to Legba and Other Invocations: The Selected Stories of Manly Wade Wellman*, by Manly Wade Wellman; $25 for *Tagging the Moon*, by S. P. Somtow;. Subterranean Press, P.O. Box 190106, Burton, MI 48519 — $40 for *Hell on Earth: The Lost Bloch Volume Two*, by Robert Bloch; $40 for *Night Moves and Other Stories*, by Tim Powers; $40 for *Triskel Tales*, by Charles de Lint — $40 for *Kafka Americana*, by Jonathan Lethem and Carter Scholz (although this last title appears to be currently out-of-stock); Dragon Press, P.O. Box 78, Pleasantville, NY 10570 — $8 for *Puck Aleshire's Abecedary*, by Michael Swanwick; Arkham House, PO Box 546, Sauk City, WI 53583 — $25.95 for *In the Stone House*, by Barry N. Malzberg; DreamHaven Books, 912 W. Lake Street, Minneapolis, MN 55408 — $30 plus $4.75 postage for *The Death Artist*, by Dennis Etchison; Wizard's Attic, 900 Murmansk St., Suite 7, Oakland, CA 94608—$19.95 for *The Yellow Sign and Other Tales*, by Robert W. Chambers.

The year 2000 was somewhat slender in the reprint anthology field, with fewer books overall and fewer really worthwhile ones than last year, although there were still a few good values here and there.

The best bets for your money in this category, as usual, were the various Best of the Year anthologies, and the annual Nebula Award anthology, *Nebula Awards Showcase 2000* (Harcourt Brace Jovanovich), edited by Gregory Benford (note the title change; last year's volume was titled *Nebula Awards 33*, and we would have expected this one to be *Nebula Awards 34*, but instead they flew in the face of decades of tradition and called it *Nebula Awards Showcase 2000* instead; wonder what *next* year's volume will be called?). As has been true for several years now, science fiction is being covered by two Best of the Year anthology series, the one you are holding in your hand, and the *Year's Best SF* series (HarperPrism), edited by David G. Hartwell, now up to its sixth annual volume. Once again, there were two Best of the Year anthologies covering horror in 2000: the latest edition in the British series *The Mammoth Book of Best New Horror* (Robinson, Caroll & Graff), edited by Stephen Jones, now up to Volume Eleven, and the Ellen Datlow half of a huge volume covering both horror and fantasy, *The Year's Best Fantasy and Horror* (St. Martin's Press), edited by Ellen Datlow and Terri Windling, this year up to its Thirteenth Annual Collection. This year, for the first time since Art Saha's *Year's Finest Fantasy* series died, fantasy will be being covered by *two* Best of the Year anthologies, by the Windling half of the Datlow/Windling anthology, and by a new Fantasy Best of the Year annual being edited by David G. Hartwell and Katherine Cramer.

The best retrospective reprint SF anthology of the year was probably *The SFWA Grand Masters, Volume 2* (Tor), edited by Frederik Pohl, the second volume in a series collecting the work of writers who have won SFWA's Grand Master Award, this year featuring classic work by Isaac Asimov, Andre Norton, Arthur C. Clarke, Ray Bradbury, and Alfred Bester. A look back over the history of the Writers of the Future contest can be found in *L. Ron Hubbard Presents the Best of Writers of the Future* (Bridge), edited by Algis Budrys. And historic overviews of the evolution of SF over the last fifty years is provided in *Explorers: SF Adventures to Far Horizons* (St. Martin's Griffin) and *The Furthest Horizon: SF Adventure to the Far Future* (St. Martin's Griffin), both edited by Gardner Dozois, and noted without further comment.

The only "regional" anthology I spotted this year was the Canadian retrospective *Aurora Awards: An Anthology of Prize-Winning Science Fiction & Fantasy* (Out of This World), edited by Edo van Belkom. An anthology of science fiction poetry is to be found in *The 2000 Rhysling Anthology* (SFPA/Stone Lightning Press).

Noted without comment are *Aliens Among Us* (Ace), edited by Jack Dann and Gardner Dozois, *Isaac Asimov's Mother's Day* (Ace), edited by Gardner Dozois and Sheila Williams, and *Isaac Asimov's Utopias* (Ace), edited by Gardner Dozois and Sheila Williams.

There didn't seem to be many reprint fantasy anthologies this year. One well worth looking into, though, is the follow-up to last year's popular anthology *My Favorite Science Fiction Story*; this one is called *My Favorite Fantasy Story* (DAW), edited by Martin H. Greenberg, in which famous fantasy writers are asked to select their favorite fantasy story, and explain why, with fascinating results; writers whose stories were picked included Jack Vance, Charles de Lint, Robert Bloch, and M. R. James. Another reprint fantasy anthology, this one of "comic fantasy," was *Knights of Madness* (Ace), edited by Peter Haining, which featured work by Woody Allen, Peter S. Beagle, Gene Wolfe, and Terry Prachett, among others.

Other than the above-mentioned "Best" anthologies by Stephen Jones and Datlow & Windling, there don't seem to be a lot of reprint horror anthologies anthologies anymore, although since I no longer follow the horror market closely, I might have missed them. The most prominent horror reprint anthology I saw this year was the retrospective *Arkham's Masters of Horror* (Arkham House), edited by Peter Ruber. Another one I spotted was *My Favorite Horror Story* (DAW), edited by Mike Baker and Martin H. Greenberg, the horror version of the fantasy anthology described above. Other reprint horror anthologies included *The Mammoth Book of Haunted House Stories* (Robinson), edited by Peter Haining, and *The Best of Cemetery Dance, Volume 1* (Penguin/Roc), edited by Richard T. Chizmar.

It was not a particularly exciting year in the SF-and-fantasy-oriented nonfiction and referee book field—although it *was* a pretty good year in the related art book field.

There were no populist histories or sociological overviews of the genre this year, of the sort that have dominated this market for the past few years. There were some critical studies, including *Transrealist Fiction* (Greenwood Press), by Damien Broderick, *Critical Theory and Science Fiction* (Wesleyan/New England), by Carl Freedman, and a few academically oriented reference books such as *French Science Fiction, Fantasy, Horror and Pulp Fiction* (MacFarland & Co.), by Jean-Marc Lofficier and Randy Lofficier, and *The Oxford Companion to Fairy Tales* (Oxford), by Jack Zipes.

Most of the books in this category this year, though, revolve around individual writers, being either about them or *by* them. The autobiographical pieces include *Algernon, Charlie and I* (Challcrest Press), by Daniel Keyes, and *Man of Two Worlds: My Life in Science Fiction and Comics* (HarperCollins), by Julius Schwartz with Brian M. Thomsen. Collections of correspondence by well-known authors include *1984: Selected Letters* (Voyant Publishing), by Samuel R. Delany, and *Lord of a Visible World: An Autobiography in Letters* (Ohio University Press), by H. P. Lovecraft, edited by S. T. Joshi and David E. Schultz. Books *about* writers, or critical studies of their work, include *Jack Vance: Critical Appreciations and a Bibliography* (The British Library), edited by A. E. Cunningham, *Robert A. Heinlein: A Reader's Companion* (Nitrosyncretic), by James Gifford, *J. R. R. Tolkien: Author of the Century* (HarperCollins UK), by Tom Shippey, *Terry Pratchett: Guilty of Literature* (The Science Fiction Foundation), edited by Andrew M. Butler, Edward James, and Faarah Mendelsohn, *The Strange Case of Edward Gorey* (Fantagraphics), by Alexander Theroux, *At the Foot of the Story Tree: An Inquiry into the Fiction of Peter Straub* (Subterranean Press), by Bill Sheehan, and *Vast*

Alchemies: The Life and Work of Mervyn Peake (Peter Owen), by G. Peter Winnington. A book of writing advice, with much autobiographical material worked in around the edges, is *On Writing: A Memoir of the Craft* (Scribner), by Stephen King. A more generalized book of writing advice is *The Complete Idiot's Guide to Publishing Science Fiction* (Alpha Books), by Cory Doctorow and Karl Schroeder. Also of interest is a book of writing advice that doubles as a short-story collection, with Hugo- and Nebula-winner Mike Resnick reprinting five of his stories and then taking them apart to analyze what makes them tick, in *Putting It Together: Turning Sow's Ear Drafts into Silk Purse Stories* (Wildside Press), by Mike Resnick.

As mentioned, the art book field was strong in 2000, with many good retrospective art collections by top artists seeing print (most of them from Paper Tiger, which had an astonishingly productive year), including *Greetings from Earth: The Art of Bob Eggleton* (Paper Tiger), by Bob Eggleton, *Frank Kelly Freas: As He Sees It* (Paper Tiger), by Frank Kelly Freas and Laura Brodian Freas, *Inner Visions, The Art of Ron Walotsky* (Paper Tiger), by Ron Walotsky, *Journeyman: The Art of Chris Moore* (Paper Tiger), by Chris Moore, *Mass: The Art of John Harris*, by Ron Tiner, *Josh Kirby: A Cosmic Cornucopia* (Paper Tiger), by David Langford, *The Art of Rowena* (Paper Tiger), by Doris Vallejo, *Titans: The Heroic Visions of Boris Vallejo and Julie Bell* (Paper Tiger), and *Dreams: The Art of Boris Vallejo* (Thunder Mouth Press), by Boris Vallejo.

There were also some good general overviews and/or illustrated retrospectives, including *Out of Time: Designs for a Twentieth-Century Future* (Abrams), by Norman Brosterman, *The Frank Collection: A Showcase of the World's Finest Fantastic Art* (Paper Tiger), by Jane and Howard Frank, and, as usual, the latest edition in a Best of the Year-like retrospective of the year in fantastic art, *Spectrum 7: The Best in Contemporary Fantastic Art* (Underwood), by Kathy Fenner and Arnie Fenner. Overviews of the comics field were presented in *Comic Book Culture* (Collectors Press), by Ron Goulart, and *Vertigo Visions: Artwork from the Cutting Edge of Comics* (Watson Guptill), by Alisa Kwitney. A similar art-oriented overview of the horror field is provided in *Horror of the 20th Century: An Illustrated History* (Collectors Press), by Robert Weinberg.

There were still a few general genre-related nonfiction books of interest this year, although not as many as in some years past. Most SF fans will probably be interested by *Chasing Science: Science As Spectator Sport* (Tor), by SF writer Frederik Pohl, and it's a fair bet that at least some will be want to get the essay collections *Did Adam and Eve Have Navels?* (W. W. Norton), by Martin Gardner and *The Lying Stones of Marrakech* (Harmony Books), by Stephen Jay Gould . . . and from there it's not a very far stretch to guess that some at least will be intrigued by *The Greatest Inventions of the Past 2000 Years* (Simon & Schuster), edited by John Brockman. Those struggling to make sense of the somewhat spooky implications of modern-day cosmology might find some useful insights in *Just Six Numbers* (Basic Books), by Martin Rees. And I'll close with two highly controversial books that are challenging existing paradigms and attempting to establish new ones, and which at the very least are *already* inspiring a flood of stories (particularly the first one), *Rare Earth: Why Complex Life Is Uncommon in the Universe* (Copernicus), by Peter D. Ward and Donald Brownie (which puts forth the heretical thought that maybe we *are* alone after all) and *The End of Time: The Next Rev-*

olution in Physics (Simon & Schuster), by Julian Barbour (which, as far as I can understand it, seems to be saying that time doesn't actually exist—a notion which will no doubt inspire as many stories as the other book as soon as more authors are able to figure out what in the world Barbour is talking about).

This was a pretty disappointing year for genre movies all in all, both artistically and commercially. There were *lots* of genre movies of one sort or another released in 2000, but few that stuck in the mind for longer than it took to walk out of the theater, and, with a few exceptions, such as the megahit *The X-Men*, not that many that really burned up the box office either; there were a few films that did okay-but-less-well-than-anticipated, and a few outright financial bombs.

Somewhat depressingly, the rule seemed to be that the closer to the center of the genre the movies got, the worse they did; the big hits were on the margins of the genre, or in related genres like fantasy, while the several big-budget movies that took place in outer space or in a future society were bombs, or at least performed well under expectations.

The year featured *two* big, glossy, expensive movies with all-star casts about the first manned mission to Mars, both of which were critically savaged, and both of which performed well under expectations, probably especially disappointing to the producers considering how expensive they were to make in the first place. *Mission to Mars* was a well-meaning movie, with stunning special effects and beautiful set-dressing, and even moderately intelligent once allowance is made for the now-traditional scientific errors and plot holes, but it seems to have been assembled with a kit from pieces of other movies, a bit of *2001* here, a chunk of *Contact* there, a hint of *Red Planet Mars*, and even, curiously enough, a dash of *Robinson Crusoe on Mars*. The good cast struggled manfully with the material, and probably even served it a bit better than it deserved, but the almost total familiarity of the plot, with hardly a stretch of footage which didn't prompt a feeling of hey-haven't-I-seen-this-before-somewhere?, drained the movie of all suspense and helped make a film that by rights *ought* to have been exciting curiously bland instead. I didn't catch the other big Mars movie, *Red Planet*, which was even more sliced up by critics than *Mission to Mars*, and which went through town quicker than green corn through the hired man (probably an indication that it didn't make much money), but the reviews would seem to indicate that it suffered from some of the same problems as the other movie, particularly the feeling of covering familiar ground less well than it had been covered before (critic Roger Ebert liked it a good deal *better* than *Mission to Mars*, though, and as Ebert is a longtime SF fan who's quite familiar with Prior Art in both the film and print SF genres, you might want to take this—almost lone—dissenting voice into consideration when deciding whether to rent *Red Planet* or not).

Overfamiliarity was also the big downcheck for an otherwise pretty good SF/horror thriller called *Pitch Black*. In spite of being edited like a rock video, especially in the early part of the movie, with lots of jump-cuts, odd close-ups, and swirling camera movement (an annoying and counterproductive way to film an action movie, in my opinion), it eventually settles down a bit (perhaps they gave the cameraman—or the director—Prozac) and ultimately delivers an engrossing and fast-paced traditional thriller, with some genuinely suspenseful moments. The emphasis here is on the word "traditional," though—no thriller movie or horror movie fan will be in the least bit surprised by what happens, with most of the plot turns guessable long in advance; in fact, within the first half hour I'd managed to guess *precisely* which of the cannon-fodder cast were going to end up surviving at the end of the movie and which were going to be chomped by the monsters; in spite of the necessary strictures imposed by the basic deep structure of the form, a really first-rate thriller ought to be able to figure out some way to be less predictable than *that*. The cast is uneven, but Vin Diesel is very impressive as the brooding, brutal killer whom the other colonists come to depend on for their only chance of survival. The ambitious "adult" animated movie *Titan AE* also suffers from predictability (is there really anybody in the audience who isn't going to be able to guess both of the major "surprise" character turnarounds the film has in store within the first twenty minutes?), but unlike the more tightly plotted *Pitch Black*, it's a collection of loosely linked picaresque adventures (with many of the plot elements seemingly lifted from various old *Star Trek* episodes), that could have been extended arbitrarily forever, full of gaping holes in what passes for plot logic—it plays as if it had been plotted by a roomful of writers who never bothered to compare notes about what was going to happen next. If you can check your forebrain at the door, there *is* some fun to be had here, although perhaps we should not be surprised, considering that it *is* a cartoon, that it's cartoonish one-dimensional fun. In fact, in spite of its expensive and sometime quite impressive animation, in spite of the top-level star voice talent, in spite of the fact that they spent *eighty million dollars* (!) on this, *Titan AE* is ultimately just a Saturday morning cartoon with an unusually big budget—no worse, but, sadly, not much better, either.

Of course, it could be worse. *Supernova* makes *Titan AE* look like it was plotted by Jane Austen, and seems to be a movie made by someone who saw *Event Horizon* and had a terrible but murky dream about it that night.

(*Space Cowboys*, widely if unofficially known as *Geezers In Space*, did fairly well at the box office, better than these others, anyway, but although it delivers some of the same kind of eyeball-clicks, it's off at a bit of a tangent to the movies above—an Astronaut Movie, like *Apollo 13*, rather than a Space Movie per se.)

After this parade of immensely expensive failures and near failures, you have to wonder how long it will be before a studio takes a chance on a space movie again? Probably a long time, unless one hits big *next* year. Which is too bad, because I actually *like* space movies—and even the worst of them these days have great Sense of Wonder visuals. (A coherent plot and some effective writing would be nice, though. There's not one of these movies that couldn't have been greatly improved by hiring some real SF writers to work on them—at a cost of considerably less than coffee-and-doughnuts-for-the-crew money, too, since most print SF people work dirt-cheap by Hollywood standards. Instead, the moviemakers seem to think that they don't need writers—but they're *wrong* . . . and saving money by doing without them is penny-wise and pound-foolish. Some of these movies might well have succeeded *with* them.)

Other kinds of SF movies didn't do much better than the Space Movies, for the most part. *Battlefield Earth*, based on the novel by the late SF writer L. Ron

Hubbard, was a box-office disaster of monumental proportions, and undoubtedly the most critically savaged genre movie of the year—perhaps the most critically savaged movie of the year of *any* sort. The futuristic thriller *The Sixth Day* did better, but doesn't seem to have been enough of a hit to pull star Arnold Schwarzenegger's career out of its downward spiral. *Hollow Man*, an expensive, special-effects-heavy remake (of sorts) of *The Invisible Man*, tromped heavily on the horror-and-gore pedal, but although it did modestly well, was somehow less compelling, for all of the Big Bucks sunk into the visual effects, than Claude Raines had been in the old version with nothing but some bandages wrapped around his face.

A bit further away from the core of the genre, and more successful this year both artistically and commercially, are those movies that examine (usually as comedy, sometimes as drama) the intrusion of one fantastic element (usually one with a thin and improbable "scientific" rationale) into an otherwise "normal" everyday world, *our* world—at least as Hollywood sees it. *Sliding Doors* may have popularized this kind of movie, a few years back. The best of these this year was *Frequency*, in which a freak accident enables a son in the present day to communicate by shortwave radio with his long-dead (from the son's perspective) father in the past. This is a nicely bittersweet conceit, and is well played by the principal actors, and the first part of the movie is quite good—unfortunately, rather than having the courage of their convictions and sticking to the main concept, the filmmakers felt they had to spice things up by throwing in a track-down-a-serial-killer suspense plot and a cold porridge of time paradoxes, all of which the movie would have been better off without, so that the second half of the film is less effective than the first half. Along the same lines, *What Women Want* invests Mel Gibson with the sudden ability to hear women's thoughts (what at least some of them turn out to be thinking is that they want *Mel Gibson*, unsurprisingly enough), *The Family Man*, *Me Myself I*, and *Disney's The Kid* surprise a self-involved character with miraculously appearing family members (in the former two, the families the main characters *might* have had, in an Alternate World; in the latter, a visitation through time from a child to the adult he would later grow up into), and *Me, Myself, and Irene* plays with the idea of multiple personalities who are in love with the same woman, and vie for her affections while running Jim Carrey through lots of *There's Something About Mary*-style slapstick, while *What Planet Are You From?* is a broad comic take on the old Aliens-Trying-to-Impregnate-Our-Women theme, complete with an alien whose dick rings when he sees a likely prospect.

The biggest successes commercially this year were out on the tenuous, fraying edge of the SF genre. *The X-Men*, of course, is not really a science fiction film at all, but rather a filmed version of a superhero comic book, a genre related to but by no means identical with SF, one with a different set of values and an internal logic all its own—once that's understood, you can enjoy *The X-Men* as a sleek and stylish vehicle, probably the best filmed version of a superhero comic since the original Tim Burton *Batman*—although I'm not at all sure that the convoluted plot made sense even by comic-book standards (nobody seemed to care, though). *Chicken Run* was a clever, sophisticated, and hugely entertaining children's fantasy (a sly postmodern homage to *The Great Escape*, done with claymation chickens), *The Grinch That Stole Christmas* a crude, ham-handed, and hugely annoying one, polluting the original classic with a double shot of *Dumb and Dumber* aesthetics, but they both made immense amounts of money. There were a lot of other children's fantasy movies too, including *Fantasia 2000* (which was disappointing by comparison with the original, although the computer animation for "The Steadfast Tin Soldier" section was interesting), *102 Dalmatians, Pokemon the Movie 2000, The Adventures of Rocky and Bullwinkle* (which tanked, big time), *The Road to El Dorado, Dinosaur* (which went to a lot of time, trouble, and expense making sure that their dinosaurs were drawn as realistically and scientifically accurately as possible — and then gave them lips and had them talk. And cohabit with lemurlike creatures that in the real world wouldn't evolve for millions of years to come. Disney! Go figure!), and *The Emperor's New Groove*. The martial arts movie *Crouching Tiger, Hidden Dragon*, in which most of the combatants have supernatural powers of one sort or another, was a surprise hit at the end of the year, as was the erotic fantasy *Chocolat. Shadow of the Vampire* seems to be becoming a *succès d'estime*, a recursive postmodern study about a real vampire *playing* a vampire in a vampire movie, although I'm not sure how it's doing at the box office. *Mission Impossible 2* and *Gladiator*, among the year's biggest hits, seem *too* far out on the edge to really be justifiable as genre films, although *Mission Impossible 2* is certainly a fantasy of *some* sort, and I suspect that *Gladiator* appeals to many of the same readers who enjoy Alternate History and Heroic Fantasy.

Unbreakable, the sophomore effort by new director M. Night Shyamalan, was a bit of a disappointment after last year's immensely successful (both critically *and* commercially) *The Sixth Sense*, although perhaps expectations for the new one had been built so high by the triumph of the previous movie that no film would have measured up to them; *Unbreakable* is still a stylish, well-crafted, and well-acted movie, although most people seemed to find it slow and uninvolving after *The Sixth Sense*, and missed the stinger in that movie's tail. *Highlander: Endgame* seemed to disappoint even most stone Highlander fans, *Dungeons & Dragons* was, well, a filmed version of a D&D game, and *Nutty Professor II: The Klumps* was about what you'd expect, a half dozen different flavors of Eddie Murphy in a convenient Variety Pack. *Bedazzled* was a remake of the classic old Peter Cook/Dudley Moore comedy, lame and disappointing by comparison.

There was another herd (a slither?) of horror movies, ranging from the stylish, beautifully art-directed dip into the mind of a serial killer, *The Cell* (sort of *What Dreams May Come* meets *Silence of the Lambs*) to the crude but occasionally funny slasher-movie spoof *Scary Movie*, with lots of the usual stops on the way (Satanistic Apocalypse movies; dead people harassing the living; knife-wielding serial killers, and so forth). I could not overcome my ennui enough to bring myself to see *Book of Shadows: Blair Witch 2* or *American Psycho*, so you're on your own there.

All in all, rather a pallid year. Most of the buzz in the air at the moment is directed toward some of the keenly anticipated movies that are theoretically going to be out sometime in 2001: The new film version of *The Lord of the Rings*, the *Harry Potter* movie, Spielberg's version of Kubrick's *A.I.*, the new *Matrix* movie, perhaps *Star Wars: Episode Two*, maybe even a new *Star Trek* movie (hey, it could happen!). Next year at this time, the Lord of the Rings and Harry Potter fans will be locked in pitched battle about whether the filmed versions did justice to (or were faithful enough to) the books, but, for the moment, anticipation is high, and the implicit agreement among genre movie fans seems to be to just write off the year 2000 and forget about it. Not a bad idea, really.

It was also a lackluster year for SF and fantasy on television. Shows such as *The X-Files*, *Xena: Warrior Princess*, and *Star Trek: Voyager* dragged out their messy death agonies throughout the year, but already there's a sense that these shows are yesterday's news, fading into the past and into nostalgic memory even before they've actually left the airwaves. So far, it doesn't look to me as if any of the "new" series are really a good prospect to fill the power vacuum that'll be left behind once former Big Shows like *The X-Files* are finally gone. *Farscape* is still a pretty good show, as TV Space Opera goes, but although it certainly has its fans, it so far doesn't seem to me to have created the kind of fanatical, fantastically dedicated fan base that former Cult Favorites such as *Babylon 5* once enjoyed. There are few other shows that are even in the running for that crown; *Gene Roddenbery's Andromeda* may be a distant prospect, or *Stargate*, but so far neither seems to have generated even as much buzz as *Farscape* has. *Cleopatra 2525*, mercifully, seems to have died, and I think that *Lexx* might have as well. *Roswell*, the prime-time soap opera featuring the adventures of the part-human, young, attractive, blow-dried descendants of UFO aliens, almost died, too, but was given a last-minute reprieve. *Futurama* is still on, and still occasionally funny, but it must say something — although I'm not sure *what* — that the two best SF shows on TV are a cartoon and one featuring Muppets (clearly recognizable *as* Muppets) as aliens. From here on down, most of the shows are comedies, and the rationale for considering them to be SF shows, rather than shows with comic surreal elements that occasionally borrow SF tropes, grows increasingly thin: *The Simpsons* and *Third Rock From the Sun* keep on keeping on, as they do year after year, and *South Park* is still with us, too, although its ratings are dropping, and it may be beginning to lose its audience.

The fantasy end of the spectrum seems to be in better shape than the science fiction end at the moment, commercially at least, with *Buffy the Vampire Slayer* and its spin-off *Angel* firmly established as huge hits, and shows such as *Sabrina, the Teenage Witch* and *Charmed* also doing well, to say nothing (which would be my preference) of a number of Angels-Among-Us shows.

All in all, not much to write home about on The Tube, either.

Two special presentations deserve mention, though: Toward the end of the year, the Sci-Fi Channel unveiled a six-hour miniseries version of Frank Herbert's *Dune*, which immediately launched Internet flamewars as to whether it was better or worse than David Lynch's feature film version from some years back, and inspired dozens of letters in *Science Fiction Weekly* and elsewhere nitpicking that this scene or character from the book had been left out, or weren't portrayed the way they were in the book, or in the Lynch film. (All of which prompts me to warn the producers of the upcoming *Lord of the Rings* movie to brace themselves for a similar storm of criticism — no matter how well the movie is done, there's always going to be *somebody* who's incensed because their favorite line was left out, or a character doesn't look the way they pictured them in their minds while reading the book.) Although there were certainly things to criticize about the new miniseries version of *Dune*, and nits galore waiting to be picked, I thought that on the whole they did a reasonable job with it, trading compromises in plotting and effects for do-ability and good storytelling techniques. I certainly preferred it to the Lynch, which, while it had some good stuff *in* it (the scene where they bring the Third-Stage Guild Navigator out in what looks like a steaming railroad freight car, for instance, was spooky and wonderful, and effectively delivered a sense of pure *alienness* unmatched by anything in the miniseries), was overall a mess, and didn't work anywhere near as well as a coherent aesthetic whole. If nothing else, the straightforward storytelling technique of the new *Dune* was a relief after the solemn, slow pretentiousness of the Lynch version; it doesn't aim as high, but it doesn't fail as grandly either. The other program which would probably interest most SF fans was *Walking With Dinosaurs*, which used some extremely good computer animation (along with some very poor puppet-head work) to deliver a show that depicted the lifeways of various kinds of dinosaurs with the immediacy and verisimilitude of a Nature Documentary about wildebeests or giraffes, as though they'd sent time-travelling naturalists and camera crews back to actually observe and film the big beasts in action. *Walking With Dinosaurs* was intensely controversial among paleontologists, many of whom fiercely criticized it for depicting highly speculative dinosaur behavior as if it was unquestioned fact, but it was good television — unlike most of the stuff on this year.

The 58th World Science Fiction Convention, ChiCon 2000, was held in Chicago, Illinois, August 31–September 4, 2000, and drew an estimated attendance of 6,473. The 2000 Hugo Awards, presented at ChiCon 2000, were: Best Novel, *A Deepness in the Sky*, by Vernor Vinge; Best Novella, "The Winds of Marble Arch," by Connie Willis; Best Novelette, "1016 to 1," by James Patrick Kelly; Best Short Story, "Scherzo with Tyrannosaur," by Michael Swanwick; Best Related Book, *Science Fiction of the twentieth century*, by Frank Robinson; Best Professional Editor, Gardner Dozois; Best Professional Artist, Michael Whelan; Best Dramatic Presentation, *Galaxy Quest*; Best Semiprozine, *Locus*, edited by Charles N. Brown; Best Fanzine, *File 770*, edited by Mike Glyer; Best Fan Writer, David Langford; Best Fan Artist, Joe Mayhew; plus the John W. Campbell Award for Best New Writer to Cory Doctorow.

The 1999 Nebula Awards, presented at a banquet at the Crowne Plaza Hotel in New York City on May 20, 2000, were: Best Novel, *Parable of the Talents*, by Octavia E. Butler; Best Novella, "Story of Your Life," by Ted Chiang; Best Novelette, "Mars Is No Place for Children," by Mary A. Turzillo; Best Short Story, "The Cost of Doing Business," by Leslie What; Best Script, *The Sixth Sense*, M. Night Shyamalan; plus an Author Emeritus award to Daniel Keyes, and the Grand Master Award to Brian W. Aldiss.

The World Fantasy Awards, presented at the Twenty-sixth Annual World Fantasy Convention in Corpus Christi, Texas, October 26–29, 2000, were: Best Novel, *Thraxas*, by Martin Scott; Best Novella, "The Transformation of Martin Lake," by Jeff VanderMeer and "Sky Eyes," by Laurel Winter (tie); Best Short Fiction, "The Chop Girl," by Ian R. MacLeod; Best Collection, *Moonlight and Vines*, by Charles de Lint and *Reave the Just and Other Tales*, by Stephen R. Donaldson (tie); Best Anthology, *Silver Birch, Blood Moon*, edited by Ellen Datlow and Terri Windling;

Best Artist, Jason Van Hollander; Special Award (Professional), to Gordon Van Gelder, for editing *The Magazine of Fantasy & Science Fiction* and at St. Martin's Press; Special Award (Non-Professional), to The British Fantasy Society; plus the Life Achievement Award to Michael Moorcock and Marion Zimmer Bradley.

The 2000 Bram Stoker Awards, presented by the Horror Writers of America during a banquet at the Adams Mark Hotel in Denver, Colorado, on May 13, 2000, were: Best Novel, *Mr. X*, by Peter Straub; Best First Novel, *Wither*, by J. G. Passarella; Best Collection, *The Nightmare Chronicles*, by Douglas Clegg; Best Long Fiction, "Five Days in April," by Brian A. Hopkins and "Mad Dog Summer," by Joe R. Lansdale (tie); Best Short Story, "After Shock," by F. Paul Wilson; Non-Fiction, *DarkEcho Newsletter* (all 1999 issues), edited by Paula Guran; Best Anthology, *999: New Stories of Horror and Suspense*, edited by Al Sarrantonio; Best Screenplay, *The Sixth Sense*, by M. Night Shyamalan; Best Work for Young Readers, *Harry Potter and the Prisoner of Azkaban*, by J. K. Rowling; Best Illustrated Narrative, *The Sandman: The Dream Hunter*, by Neil Gaiman; Best Other Media (audio), "I Have No Mouth and I Must Scream," by Harlan Ellison; a Specialty Press Award to Christopher and Barbara Roden for Ash-Tree Press; plus the Lifetime Achievement Award to Edward Gorey and Charles L. Grant.

The 1999 John W. Campbell Memorial Award was won by *A Deepness in the Sky*, by Vernor Vinge.

The 1999 Theodore Sturgeon Award for Best Short Story was won by "The Wedding Album," by David Marusek.

The 1999 Philip K. Dick Memorial Award went to *Vacuum Diagrams*, by Stephen Baxter.

The 1999 Arthur C. Clarke Award was won by *Distraction*, by Bruce Sterling.

The 1999 James Tiptree, Jr. Memorial Award was won by *The Conqueror's Child*, by Suzy McKee Charnas.

Dead in 2000 or early 2001 were: L. SPRAGUE DE CAMP, 92, writer, critic, and anthologist, one of the most famous of the "Golden Age" giants, winner of the Hugo Award, the International Fantasy Award, and the World Fantasy Convention's Life Achievement Award, author of such famous SF novels as *Lest Darkness Fall* (which practically invented the Alternate History subgenre), *The Glory That Was*, *Rogue Queen*, and *The Hand of Zei*, the seminal fantasy *The Complete Enchanter* (with Fletcher Pratt), and distinguished historical novels such as *The Bronze God of Rhodes* and *An Elephant for Aristotle*, as well as many nonfiction books, anthologies, and critical works, including the definitive history of H. P. Lovecraft; GORDON R. DICKSON, 78, Hugo and Nebula-winner, best known for his long-running "Dorsai" sequence of novels and stories, which included *Soldier, Ask Not*, *The Genetic General*, *Necromancer*, *The Far Call*, and *The Final Encyclopedia*, and others, as well as many other unrelated books such as *Special Delivery*, *The Way of the Pilgrim*, and *The Dragon and the George*; KEITH ROBERTS, 65, author, artist, and editor, one of the most important British SF writers of the '60s and '70s, author of the famous novel *Pavane*, one of the best Alternate World novels ever written, as well as *The Chalk Giants*, *Kiteworld*, *The Furies*, the upcoming *Drek Yarman*, and a large body of brilliant work at shorter lengths;

JOHN SLADEK, 62, writer and satirist, author of *The Reproductive System, The Muller-Fokker Effect, Roderick, or The Education of a Young Machine; Roderick at Random, or Further Education of a Young Machine, Tik-Tok*, and *Bugs*, as well as much mordant short work; DAVID R. BUNCH, 74, author of a large body of eccentric, fiercely iconoclastic short stories over a long career, most of which were assembled in the collections *Moderan* and *Bunch!*; CURT SIODMAK, 98, novelist, screenwriter, director, author of *Donovan's Brain* and the screenplay for the famous monster movie, *The Wolf Man*; EMIL PETAJA, 85, veteran writer, winner of SFWA's Author Emeritus award, author of *The Stolen Sun* and *Saga of Lost Earths*, among many others; REX VINSON, 64, who, as VINCENT KING, wrote such SF novels as *Another End, Candy Man*, and *Light a Last Candle*; RICK SHELLEY, 54, frequent contributor to *Analog*, author of many novels, such as *Lieutenant Colonel, The Buchanan Campaign, Jump Pay*, and the *Varayan Memoir* series; JOSEPH H. DELANEY, 67, author and attorney, frequent contributor of legal-themed SF stories to *Analog* for almost twenty years, author of *In the Face of My Enemy*, and other novels; SHERWOOD SPRINGER, 88, veteran writer of short fiction and a longtime SF fan; DAVID DUNCAN, 86, novelist, author of *Occam's Razor* and *Beyond Eden*; RICHARD LAYMON, 54, horror writer, serving a term as president of the Horror Writers of America at the time of his death, author of *After Midnight, Blood Games*, and *The Travelling Vampire Show*; ROBERT E. CORMIER, 75, author of Young Adult novels such as the well-known *The Chocolate War*, and also of the fantasy novel *Fade*; OLIVER E. SAARI, 81, veteran pulp author; MARY BROWN, 70, British fantasy writer, author of *The Unlikely Ones*; CLAUDE VAUZIERE, 72, French SF writer; DON WILCOX, 94, veteran pulp author; STURE LONNERSTAND, 80, Swedish SF writer and longtime fan; LAURENCE JAMES, 56, British author and editor; MICHAEL McDOWELL, 49, author of *The Amulet* and *Cold Moon Over Babylon*; KEITH SCOTT, 79, Canadian author; Dr. ALEX COMFORT, 80, best known for the bestseller *The Joy of Sex*, who also wrote such SF novels as *Cities of the Plain* and *The Philosopher*; STEVE ALLEN, 78, author, composer, and television personality, pioneering host of *The Tonight Show* (which practically invented the late-night talk-show format), who created the Alternate History-like TV program, *Meeting of Minds*, where famous people from across history were brought together for dinner and conversation, and who also wrote (in addition to a recent string of mystery novels) a few fairly well received science fiction stories, the best known of which is probably "The Public Hating"; JEAN SHEPHERD, writer and radio personality, whose funny, nostalgic work occasionally had mild fantastic elements (or at least moments of surreal exaggeration), best known for the collections *In God We Trust, All Others Pay Cash, Wanda Hickey's Night of Golden Memories*, and *A Fistful of Fig Newtons*; EDWARD GOREY, 75, artist and author, winner of two two World Fantasy Awards, probably the best-known artist of the satirically macabre and risibly ghoulish since Charles Addams, author of illustrated books such as *The Doubtful Guest, The D. Awdrey-Gore Legacy, The Unstrung Harp, The Gashlycrumb Tinies, The Evil Garden*, and many others; CARL BANKS, 99, comics artist and author, creator of Scrooge McDuck, many of whose adventures featured strong and rigorously worked-out fantastic elements that were influential on a whole generation of SF writers, and whose portraits of Uncle Scrooge, Donald

Duck, and others have become highly collectable (and extremely expensive) fine art; KAREL THOLE, 86, artist, considered by many to be one of the most distinguished of all European artists to work in the genre SF market; CHARLES M. SCHULZ, cartoonist, creator of the long-running *Peanuts* strip, one of the most famous comic strips of all time, which often featured minor fantastic elements; DON MARTIN, 68, cartoonist, known mostly for his semisurreal work for *Mad Magazine*; JOE MAYHEW, 57, Hugo-winning fan artist, one of the best fannish cartoonists ever, as well as a writer, a carver of beautifully crafted walking sticks, a longtime fan, and a dedicated and tireless convention organizer; CHARLES D. HORNIG, 83, veteran editor of pulp magazines such as *Wonder Stories, Science Fiction,* and *Future Fiction*; JEAN KARL, 72, longtime editor of the Atheneum imprint, author of *The Turning Place*; ADELE LEONE, 48, agent and editor, SF editor of Pocket Books in the '70s; JAMES ALLEN, 48, President of the Virginia Kidd Literary Agency; MICHAEL GILBERT, 53, artist, writer, publishing professional, husband of Sheila Gilbert, the copublisher of DAW Books; JENNA A. FELICE, 25, Tor editor, associate editor of the magazine *Century*, longtime partner of *Century* editor Robert K. J. Killheffer, and a personal friend; LINDA GRAY, 54, former President and Publisher of Bantam Books and Ballantine; SIR ALEC GUINESS, 86, distinguished stage and film actor, best known to audiences today—something which did not entirely please him—as the Jedi Knight Obi-Wan Kenobi in the movie *Star Wars* and its sequels; JOHN NEWLAND, 82, host of the pioneering supernatural anthology TV show, *Alcoa Presents One Step Beyond,* which did some very creepy and effective episodes in the '50s and early '60s; STANLEY KRAMER, veteran film director, best known to genre audiences as the director of the After-the-Bomb movie *On the Beach*; WALTER A. WILLIS, prominent Irish fan and fan writer; BILL DONAHO, 74, longtime fan and fanzine publisher; BILL DANNER, 93, longtime fan and fanzine editor; ROBERT SALKS, 49, longtime fan and convention organizer; CATHERINE CROOK DE CAMP, 92, wife of SF writer L. Sprague de Camp, his longtime business manager, and his collaborator on many novels and nonfiction projects; NANCY TUCKER SHAW, 71, widow of SF writer Bob Shaw, and the longtime head of the Science Fiction Oral History Society; FRANCES WELLMAN, the widow of SF/fantasy writer Manly Wade Wellman; PEGGY CAVE, 86, wife of SF/fantasy writer Hugh B. Cave; CHARLOTTE R. HENSLEY, 71, wife of SF and mystery writer Joe C. Hensley; DEDE WEIL, 56, wife of SF critic Gary K. Wolfe; ANNE SHERLIN ASHER, 94, mother of SF Book Club editor Ellen Asher; ALICE ALTSCHULER SHERMAN, mother of SF writer Josepha Sherman; JULIUS SCHULMAN, 84, father of SF writer J. Neil Schulman, and a renowned classical violinist; CHARLES BENJAMIN CARD, 16, son of SF writer Orson Scott Card; MARCH LAUMER, 76, brother of SF writer Keith Laumer, author of *The Wooden Soldiers of Oz* and other children's books.

THE YEAR'S BEST

SCIENCE FICTION

The Juniper Tree
John Kessel

Born in Buffalo, New York, John Kessel now lives with his family in Ra-leigh, North Carolina, where he is a professor of American literature and creative writing at North Carolina State University. Kessel made his first sale in 1975. His first solo novel, Good News from Outer Space, *was released in 1988 to wide critical acclaim, but before that he had made his mark on the genre primarily as a writer of highly imaginative, finely crafted short stories, many of which were assembled in his collection* Meeting in Infinity. *He won a Nebula Award in 1983 for his superlative novella "An-other Orphan," which was also a Hugo finalist that year, and has been released as an individual book. His story "Buffalo" won the Theodore Stur-geon Award in 1991. His other books include the novel* Freedom Beach, *written in collaboration with James Patrick Kelly, and an anthology of stories from the famous Sycamore Hill Writers Workshop (which he also helps to run), called* Intersections, *coedited by Mark L. Van Name and Richard Butner. His most recent books are a major novel,* Corrupting Dr. Nice, *and a collection,* The Pure Product.*

Here he takes us to a colonized Moon, humanity's newest habitation, for a taut encounter with some passions that are very old indeed. . . .

THE JUNIPER TREE

One of the most successful transplants to the colony established by the Society of Cousins on the far side of the Moon was the juniper tree. Soon after Jack Baldwin and his daughter Rosalind emigrated in 2085, a project under Baldwin's direction planted junipers on the inside slopes of the domed crater, where they prospered in the low-moisture environment. Visitors to the Society today may be excused if, strolling the woods above the agricultural lands of the crater floor, the fragrance of the foliage, beneath the projected blue sky of the dome, makes them think for a moment that they are in some low-gravity dream of New Mexico.

It was under a juniper tree that Jack disposed of the remains of Carey Evasson, the fourteen-year-old boy he killed.

ICE

The blue squad's centering pass slid through the crease, where Maryjane fanned on the shot. The puck skidded to the boards, and Roz, who had been promoted to the red team for today's practice, picked it up to start a rush the other way. Carey spotted her from across the rink and set off parallel to her. They'd caught the blues off guard, with only Thabo between them and the goalie. Thabo came up to check her. Roz swerved right, then left a drop pass for Carey.

But Thabo poked his stick between Roz's legs and deflected the pass. While Roz and Carey overran the play, Thabo passed the puck back the other way to Maryjane.

Their breakaway was interrupted by the shriek of Coach Ingasdaughter's whistle. The coach skated onto the ice, yelling at Roz. "What kind of a play was that? You've got a two-on-one and you go for the drop pass? *Shoot the Puck!*"

"But if Thabo had followed me Carey would have had an open net."

"If if if!" She raised her eyes to the roof of the cavern far overhead. "Why do you think Thabo didn't follow you? He knew you would pass, because you *never* shoot! If you don't establish that you're a threat, they're always going to ignore you. For once, let the *boy* get the rebound!"

Roz's face burned. The blue and red squads stood around watching her take the heat. Carey was looking down, brushing the blade of his stick across the ice.

Coach Ingasdaughter suddenly grabbed Roz by the shoulders, pulled her forward, and planted a kiss on her lips. "But what can I expect from a girl whose parents were married?" she said, letting Roz go. Someone snickered. "Ten-minute break," Ingasdaughter said, and turned away.

Roz almost took a slash at her retreating back. Instead she looked past the coach to the bleachers where a few off-shift pressure workers sat, helmets thrown back over their shoulders, watching the practice. Beyond the rink, the floor of the cave was one huge mass of blue ice, humped and creased, refracting the lights and fading into the distance. The coach skated over to talk with her assistant. Most of the team went over to the cooler by the home bench. Roz skated to the penalty box, flipped the door open and sat down.

It was hard being the only immigrant on the hockey team. The cousins teased her, called her "High-G." Roz had thought that going out for hockey would be a way for her to make some girlfriends who could break her into one of the cliques. You needed a family to get anywhere among the Cousins. You needed a mother. A father was of no consequence—everybody had a dozen fathers, or none at all.

Instead she met Carey. And, through dumb luck, it had seemed to work. Carey's grandmother, Margaret Emmasdaughter, had known Nora Sobieski personally. His mother was Eva Maggiesdaughter, chair of the Board of Matrons, by some measures the most powerful woman in the colony.

Some of the players started skating big circles on the oversized rink. She watched Carey build up a head of steam, grinning, his blond hair flying behind him. On the next time around he pulled off his glove, skated past the penalty box, winked, and gave her five as he flew by. The heavy gold ring he wore left a welt on her palm; just like Carey to hurt her with his carelessness, but she could not help but smile.

The first time she had met Carey a check she threw during practice nearly killed him. Roz had not gotten completely adjusted to skating in one-sixth gee, how it was harder to start and stop, but also how much faster you got going than on Earth. Carey had taken the full brunt of her hit and slammed headfirst into the boards. Play stopped. Everyone gathered around while he lay motionless on the ice.

Carey turned over and staggered to his feet, only his forehead showing above his shoulder pads. His voice came from somewhere within his jersey. "Watch out for those Earth women, guys."

Everyone laughed, and Carey poked his head out from below his pads. His bright-green eyes had been focused on Roz's, and she burst out laughing, too.

When her father moved in with Eva, Carey became the brother she had never had, bold where she was shy, funny where she was sober.

Coach blew her whistle and they did two-on-one drills for the rest of the practice. Afterward Roz sat on a bench in the locker room taping the blade of her stick. At the end of the bench Maryjane flirted with Stella in stage whispers. Roz tried to ignore them.

Carey, wrapped only in a towel, sat down next to Roz and checked to see whether the coaches were in earshot. She liked watching the way the muscles of his chest and arms slid beneath his skin, so much so that she tried hard not to look at him. He leaned toward her. "Hey, High-G—you interested in joining the First Imprints Club?"

"What's that?"

He touched her on the leg. He always touched her, seemingly chance encounters, elbow to shoulder, knee to calf, his forehead brushing her hair. "A bunch of us are going to meet at the fountains in the dome," Carey said. "When the carnival is real crazy we're going to sneak out onto the surface. You'll need your pressure suit—and make sure its waste reservoir vent is working."

"Waste reservoir? What for?"

"Keep your voice down!"

"Why?"

"We're going to climb Shiva Ridge and pee on the mountaintop." He tapped a finger on her leg. His touch was warm.

"Sounds like a boy thing," she said. "If your mother finds out, you'll be in deep trouble."

He smiled. "You'll never get to be an alpha female with that attitude, High-G. Mother would have invented this club, if she'd thought of it." He got up and went over to talk to Thabo.

God, she was so stupid! It was the beginning of Founders' Week, and she had hoped Carey would be her guide and companion through the carnival. She had worried all week what to wear. What a waste. She'd blown it. She tugged on the green asymmetrically-sleeved shirt she had chosen so carefully to set off her red hair.

Roz hung around the edges as Carey joked with the others, trying to laugh in the right places, feeling miserably out of place. After they dressed, she left with Carey, Thabo, and Raisa for the festival. Yellow triangular signs surrounded the pressure lock in the hallway linking the ice cavern to the lava tube. Roz struggled to keep up with Carey who, like all of the kids born on the Moon, was taller than Roz. Raisa leaned on Thabo. Raisa had told Roz the day before that she was thinking about moving out and getting her own apartment. Raisa was thirteen, six months younger than Roz.

The lava tube was as much as forty meters wide, thirty tall, and it twisted and turned, rose and fell, revealing different vistas as they went along. Shops and apartments clung to the walls. Gardens grew along the nave beneath heliostats that transformed light transmitted from the surface during the lunar day into a twenty-four-hour cycle. Unless you went outside you could forget whether it was day or night out on the surface.

Now it was "night." As they entered the crater from the lava tube, the full extent of the colony was spread out before them. The crater was nearly two kilometers in diameter. Even in one-sixth gee the dome was a triumph of engineering, supported by a five-hundred-meter-tall central steel-and-glass spire. Roz could hardly believe it, but the school legend was that Carey had once climbed the spire in order to spray-paint the name of a girl he liked on the inside of the dome.

Above, the dome was covered with five meters of regolith to protect the inside from radiation, and beneath the ribbed struts that spread out from the spire like an umbrella's, the interior surface was a screen on which could be projected a daytime sky or a nighttime starfield. Just now thousands of bright stars shone down. Mars and Jupiter hung in bright conjunction high overhead.

From the west and south sides of the crater many levels of balconied apartments overlooked the interior. Most of the crater floor was given over to agriculture, but at the base of the spire was Sobieski Park, the main meeting ground for the colony's 2,500 inhabitants. An elaborate fountain surrounded the tower. There was an open-air theater. Trees and grass, luxuriantly irrigated in a display of conspicuous water consumption, spread out from the center.

Roz and the others climbed down the zigzag path from the lava tube and through the farmlands to the park. Beneath strings of colored lights hung in the trees, men and women danced to the music of a drum band. Naked revelers wove their way through the crowd. Both sexes wore bright, fragrant ribbons in their hair. A troupe performed low-gravity acrobatics on the amphitheater stage. Little children ran in and out of the fountains, while men and women in twos and threes and every combination of sexes leaned in each other's arms.

On the shadowed grass, Roz watched an old man and a young girl lying together, not touching, leaning heads on elbows, speaking in low voices with their faces inches apart. What could they possibly have to say to each other? Thabo and Raisa faded off into the dancers around the band, and Roz was alone with Carey. Carey brought her a flavored ice and sat down on the grass beside her. The drum band was making a racket, and the people were dancing faster now.

"Sorry the coach is on your case so much," Carey said. He touched her shoulder gently. The Cousins were always touching each other. With them, the dividing line between touching for sex and touching just to touch was erased.

God, she wished she could figure out what she wanted. Was he her brother or her boyfriend? It was hard enough back on Earth; among all these Cousins it was impossible.

When she didn't answer right away, Carey said, "The invisible girl returns."

"What?"

"You're disappearing again. The girl from the planet nobody's ever seen."

Roz watched the girl with the man on the grass. The girl was no older than she. The distance between the two had disappeared; now the girl was climbing onto the man.

Carey ran his finger down Roz's arm, then gently nudged her over. Roz pushed him away. "No thanks."

Carey tried to kiss her cheek, and she turned away. "Not now, OK?"

"What's the matter?"

"Does something have to be the matter? Any Cousins girl might tell you no, too. Don't act like it's just because I'm from Earth."

"It is."

"Is not."

"I'm not going to rape you, High-G. Cousins don't rape."

"What's that supposed to mean?"

"Absolutely nothing. But you know how screwed up it is down on Earth."

"Lots of stuff people do here would be wrong on Earth."

"Right. And people there shoot each other if anyone touches them."

Cousins could be so arrogant it made her want to spit. "You've never even seen the Earth—let alone been there."

"I've seen you, Roz."

"You don't own me."

He smiled. "No. Your father does." He nuzzled her neck.

Roz hit him. "Get off me, you pig!" She got up and ran away.

FESTIVAL

Forty milligrams of serentol, a whiff or two of THC, and an ounce of grain alcohol: Jack Baldwin wobbled through the crowd of revelers in Sobieski Park. Beneath the somatic night, feeling just an edge of anxiety, he looked for Eva among the faces.

The park was full of young men and women, their perfect bodies in one another's arms. Sex was their favorite pastime, and who could blame them? They went about it as if their lives depended on the next coupling. That was biology at work, he supposed—but if it was just genes having their way with the human body, then why all the emotional turmoil—does she love me who's he sleeping with I can't stand it when she looks at him like that how unfair to treat me like a toy who does he think he is I can't stand it I'll die if I can't have her tonight . . .

Where was Eva? He smiled. Apparently genes did not let go of your mind just because you were pushing forty. Sex had been a problem back on Earth—always some screw-up with women coworkers, hassles with his live-ins, distractions. Here, sex was the common coin of interpersonal contact, unjudged as taste in ice cream (but some people made a religion of taste), easy as speech (but speech was not always easy), frequent as eating (but some people starved themselves in the midst of plenty). Where did that leave him? Was he simply a victim of the culture that had raised him? Or was his frustration purely personal?

Where was Eva?

Men and women, naked, oiled, and smiling, wove their way through the celebrants, offering themselves to whoever might wish to take them. It was the one day of the year that the Society of Cousins fit the clichéd image of polymorphous orgy that outsiders had of it. One of them, a dark young woman—dark as Eva—brushed her fingers across Jack's cheek, then swirled away on one luscious hip.

But Eva was taller, more slender. Eva's breasts were small, her waist narrow despite the softness of the belly that had borne Carey, and when they made love her hipbones pressed against him. She was forty, and there was gray in her black hair. This girl dancing by could satisfy his lust, and perhaps if he knew her she would become a person as complex as Eva. But she would not be Eva: the combination of idealism and practicality, the temper that got her into trouble because she could not keep her mouth shut. Fierce when she fought for what mattered to her, but open-hearted to those who opposed her, with an inability to be successfully Machiavellian that was her saving grace.

He had met Eva a month after he and Roz had arrived at the colony. Jack was working on a new nematode that, combined with a gene-engineered composting process, would produce living soil from regolith more efficiently than the tedious chemical methods that had been used to create Fowler's initial environment. His specialty in nematodes had been the passport for him and Roz into the guarded Cousins society, the last bridge after a succession of burned bridges he had left behind them. He certainly had not planned to end up on the Moon. The breakup with Helen. The fight over Roz, ending with him taking her against the court order. The succession of jobs. The forged vita.

Eva, newly elected head of the board, chaired the environmental subcommittee. She had come by the biotech lab in the outlying bunker. Jack did not know who the tall, striking woman in the webbed pressure suit was. She asked questions of Amravati, the head of the project, then came over to observe Jack, up to his ankles in muck, examining bacteria through an electron microscope visor.

Flirting led to a social meeting, more flirting led to sex. Sex—that vortex women hid behind their navels, that place he sometimes had to be so badly that every other thought fell away and he lost himself again. Or was it finding himself? Eva's specialty was physics, some type of quantum imaging that he did not understand and whose practical benefits he could not picture. But a relationship that had started as a mercenary opportunity had, to Jack's surprise, turned to something like love.

As Jack sat on the edge of the fountain, hoping he might find Eva in the crowd, instead he spotted Roz. Her face was clouded; her dark brown eyes large with some trouble. "Roz?" he called.

She heard his voice, looked up, saw him. She hesitated a moment, then walked over.

"What's the matter, sweetheart?" he asked.

"Nothing." She sat down next to him. She was bothered by something.

Across the plaza, two of the acrobats juggled three children in the low gravity the way someone on Earth might juggle bean bags. The kids, tucked into balls, squealed in delight as they rose and fell like the waters of the fountain.

"Isn't this amazing?" Jack asked.

" 'Amazing,' Dad—that's very perceptive."

"What?"

"This place is disgusting. Look at that old creep there feeling up that girl."

"We talked about this, Roz. The Cousins do things differently. But they don't do anything against anyone's will."

"It's all OK with you, just as long as you're getting laid every night."

He put his hand on her leg. "What's going on?"

She pulled away. "Nothing's going on! I'm just tired of watching you take advantage of people. Mom would never have brought me here."

Roz never mentioned her mother. Jack tried to focus. "I don't know, girl. Your mom had her own problems fitting in."

"The only reason we came here is that you couldn't get a job back on Earth."

He tried to get Roz to look at him, but she was fixed on her outsized plastic shoes. "Aren't we hostile tonight," he said. She didn't answer. He saw for the first time how much her profile had become that of a grown woman. "I'll admit it. The job had something to do with it. But Roz, you've got a chance to become someone here you could never be on Earth — if you'll make an effort. Women are important here. Hell, women run the place! Do you think I like the idea of being a second-class citizen? I gave up a lot to bring you here."

"All you care about is getting into Eva's bed," Roz told the shoes. "She's using you, and she'll just dump you after she's had enough, like all these other Cousins."

"You think that little of my choices?"

That made her look at him. Her face was screwed into a furious scowl. The music of the drum band stopped suddenly, and the people applauded. "How do you know Eva's not going to try to get me into bed with her, too?"

Jack laughed. "I don't think so."

She stood up. "God, you are so smug! I can't tell you anything!"

"Roz, what is this —"

She turned and stalked off.

"Roz!" he called after her. She did not turn back.

Next to him, a thin black woman holding a toddler had been eavesdropping. Jack walked away to escape her gaze. The band started another song. Inwardly churning, he listened to the music for a few minutes, watching the people dance. Whatever his failings, hadn't he always done his best for Roz? He didn't expect her to agree with him all the time, but she had to know how much he loved her.

The amused detachment with which he'd entered the plaza was gone. The steel drums gave him a headache. He crossed the plaza. Before he had gone ten paces he saw Eva. She was in the crowd of dancers, paired with a round-faced woman. The woman was grinning fiercely; she bumped against Eva, slid her belly up against Eva's. Eva had her arms raised into the air and was smiling too, grinding her hips.

As Jack stood watching, someone sidled up to him. It was Hal Keikosson, who worked in Agriculture. Hal was in his forties and still living with his mother — a common situation among the Cousins.

"Hey, Jack. Who was that girl I saw you talking to? That red hair? Cute."

Jack kept watching Eva and the woman. Eva had not noticed him yet. "That was my daughter," he told Hal.

"Interesting." Hal swayed a bit, clutching a squeeze cup in his sweaty hand. Jack ought to let it go, but he couldn't. "What does that mean?"

"Nothing. She must be fourteen or fifteen already, right?"

"She's fourteen."

"And maybe she isn't your daughter." Hal giggled.

Jack stared at him. "What?"

"I mean, how could her mother be sure — or maybe she lied to you."

"Shut the fuck up before I belt you."

"Hey, it's none of my business who you sleep with."

"I'm not sleeping with her."

"Calm down, calm down, Cousin." Hal took a sip from his cup. He looked benignly over at the figures writhing in the shadows beneath the trees. "Too bad," he said quietly, and chuckled.

Jack stalked away to keep from taking a swing at him.

The drum band was louder now, and so was the babble of the increasing crowd. He passed a group of drunken singers. Near the amphitheater he saw one of the acrobat children staggering around in circles, giggling. Jamira Tamlasdaughter, a friend of Eva's, tried to say hello, but he passed her by with a wave. Jack's head throbbed. Beyond the trees that marked the border of Sobieski Park he followed a path through fields of dry-lands soybeans, corn, potatoes. There was no one out here — most of the Cousins were at the festival now.

A kilometer later the path turned upward into the open lands of the crater slopes. Low, hardy, blue-white grass covered the ground. But the sound of the band still floated over the fields, and turning, Jack could see the central tower lit by the colored lights. The foliage was side-lit only by that distant light and the projected starlight from the dome. Somewhere off to his left a night bird sang in a scraggly pine. He turned his back to the festival.

It was an easy climb in one-sixth gee, and when he hit the concrete rim of the crater that supported the dome he followed the perimeter road around toward the north airlock. He wanted out. The best refuge he could think of was the biotech lab.

Because of the festival, the airlock was deserted. Jack took his pressure suit from his locker, suited up, and cycled through the personnel lock. He passed through the radiation baffles to the surface.

Although it was night inside the dome, out here it was lunar afternoon. Harsh shadows lay beneath the fields of solar collectors lining the road to the labs. Jack skipped along the tracked-up roadway, kicking up a powder of fines. Over the throb of his headache he listened to the sound of his own breathing in his earphones.

The fight he'd had with Roz was just like one of his final spats with Helen, full of buried resentments and false assumptions. Roz's accusations stung because there was an element of truth in them. But Roz was wrong to say Jack didn't care about her. From the moment of her birth Jack had committed himself to Roz without reservation. Clearly he hadn't paid enough attention to her troubles, but he would do anything to protect her.

Roz didn't understand that things were hard for Jack. "All men are boys," the Cousins said. In the case of a jerk like Keikosson, he could admit the saying's truth. But it was as much a product of the way they lived as of the men themselves. The women of the Cousins indulged their boys their pleasures, kept them adolescents far into their adulthood. It was a form of control-by-privilege.

Jack chafed at the way a male in the colony was seldom respected for his achievements, but rather for who his mother and grandmother were. He hated the way women deferred to him once it got around that he was Eva Maggiesdaughter's latest partner. He hated the sidelong glances he got about his relationship to Roz. He was Roz's father. He was not anyone's boy.

The biotech labs were located in a bunker a kilometer north of Fowler. He entered the personnel lock, air-blasted the fines from his suit, and removed it. Like the airlock, the lab was deserted. He passed through the greenhouse's rows of juniper and piñon seedlings to the soils lab. The temperature on his latest batch of nematode soil was 30 centigrade. He drew on some boots, rolled back the cover on the reservoir, and waded into the loamy earth. The rich smell of nitrogen compounds filled his lungs, and he felt momentarily dizzy with relaxation.

Taking a cermet rake from the tool cabinet, he worked over the surface of the soil. His nematodes were doing their jobs nicely, increasing the water content, breaking down organics and hosting the nitrogen-fixing bacteria. Once his team got the OK from the colony's environmental committee, they would start a trial planting using the soil and the greenhouse seedlings on Fowler's east slope.

He had not been working long when he heard the airlock alert. Startled, he dropped the rake and stood up. Some minutes later a figure emerged from the greenhouse and peered from around the rock crusher. "Jack?"

"Over here, Carey," Jack said.

The boy came over. He was taller than his mother, and blond instead of dark. Jack wondered once again who his father was. Carey was still wearing his pressure suit, helmet off.

"What are you doing here?" Jack asked. "How did you know I was here?"

"I was coming into the north airlock when I saw you cycling out," Carey said. "By the time I got my suit on you were gone, but I figured you might be here. I wanted to speak with you about Roz, Jack."

"What about her?"

"I think she's having a hard time," Carey said. "I think you might want to pay more attention to what's going on with her. Fathers like you do that, right?"

"Fathers like what?"

"Come on, Jack, you know — Earth fathers."

"What's wrong with Roz?" Jack asked.

"She seems to have some sexual hang-ups. She hasn't talked with you about it? She talks about you all the time."

"I don't think there's anything wrong with Roz. Besides, it's none of your business, Carey."

"Well, it sort of is. At least if she's not telling you these things, and you care about her, then I guess I need to tell you. Like after we slept together the first time, she cried."

"You slept with her?" Jack's own voice sounded leaden in his ears.

"Sure. I thought you knew." Carey was completely unselfconscious. "I mean, we're all in the same apartment. She didn't tell you that, either?"

"No."

"She needs help. She's making some progress with the kids on the hockey team, but for every step forward she takes one back. I think she's too hung up on you, Jack."

"Don't call me Jack."

Carey looked confused. "Excuse me?"

"Don't call me Jack, you little pissant. You don't know a thing about me and Roz."

"I know you're immigrants and don't understand everything. But a lot of people are starting to think you need to live separately. You don't own Roz."

"What the hell are you talking about?"

"She's a woman. She can make up her own mind."

The boy's face was an open map of earnest, smug innocence. Jack couldn't stand it. "Damn you, she's not your whore!"

Carey laughed. "A whore? That's an Earth thing, right? One of those sexual ownership practices?"

Jack took one step, grabbed the collar of the boy's pressure suit, and yanked him forward. Carey's feet caught on the edge of the reservoir. As he fell, he twisted around; Jack lost his own balance and shoved Carey downward to keep from falling himself. Much faster than normal in lunar-gee, Carey hit the ground. His head snapped sideways against the rake.

Catching his balance, Jack waited for Carey to get up. But he didn't get up. Jack crouched over the boy. Carey had fallen onto the head of the rake; one of the six-centimeter ceramic tines had penetrated his temple. Blood seeped into the soil.

Carefully, Jack drew out the tines, rolled him over. Carey shuddered and the blood flowed more freely. The boy's breathing was shallow, his eyes unfocused. As Jack watched, Carey's breathing stopped.

After ten minutes of futile CPR, Jack fell back from Carey's limp body and sat down heavily on the edge of the reservoir.

Jesus Christ. What had he done? What was he going to do now? Eva!—what would she think?

It was an accident. But that didn't matter. He was an immigrant, an outsider, a man. Someone would surely accuse him of murder. They would drug him into insensibility, cut up his brain. At best they would expel him from the colony, and Roz with him—or worse still, they might not expel Roz. He sat there facing the cold reality of his thirty-eight years of screwed-up life.

Carey's head lolled back into the muck, his mouth open. "You arrogant prick," Jack whispered to the dead boy. "You fucked it all up."

He looked around the room. In front of him was the reduction chamber, the crusher, the soil reservoir. Shuddering, he went back to the tool chest and found a machete. He dragged Carey's body over the edge of the reservoir, getting dirt up to his own elbows. The soil was rich with the heat of decomposition.

Jack was about to begin cutting off Carey's arms when the airlock alert sounded again. He panicked. He stumbled out of the reservoir, trying to heft Carey's body into the hopper of the crusher. Before he could conceal the body he heard steps behind him.

It was Roz. She stood for a moment staring at him as he held Carey's bare ankle in his hand. "Dad?"

"Go away, Roz."

She came over to him. "Dad, what's going on?" She saw the body. "Jesus, Dad, what happened?"

"An accident. The less you know about it the better."

She took a couple of steps closer. "Carey? Is he all right?"

"Go away, Roz."

Roz put her hand to her mouth. "Is he dead?"

Jack let go of Carey and came over to her. "It was an accident, Roz. I didn't mean to hurt him. He fell down."

"Carey!" She rushed over, then backed away until she bumped into the rock crusher. "He's dead! What happened? Dad! Why did you do this?"

Jack didn't know what to do. He looked back at Carey, lying awkwardly on the concrete floor, the machete beside his leg. "It was an accident, Roz. I grabbed him, he fell. I didn't mean to—"

"Carey," she said. "Carey." She would not look at Jack.

"Roz, I would never have hurt him on purpose. I—"

"What were you fighting about?"

"It wasn't a fight. He told me you had slept together. I was shocked, I guess. I—"

Roz slumped to the floor. "It was my fault?"

"No. It was an accident."

"I don't believe this," she said. She looked at Carey's body. Jack thought about the last time she must have seen him naked. "You're going to go to jail!" Roz said. "They might even kill you. Who's going to take care of me?"

"I'm going to take care of you. Please, Roz, don't think about this. You need to get out of here."

"What are we going to do?"

"You're not going to do anything except get out! Don't you understand?"

Roz stared at him a long moment. "I can help."

Jack felt chilled. "I don't want your help! I'm your father, damn it!"

She sat there, her eyes welling with tears. It was a nightmare. He sat down next to her and put his arm around her. She cried against his shoulder. A long time passed, and neither of them spoke.

Finally she pulled away from him. "It's my fault," she said. "I should have told you I loved him."

Jack closed his eyes. He could hear his own pulse in his ears. The soil of the reservoir smelled as rich as ever. "Please, don't say anymore."

"Oh, god, how could you do this?" he heard her whisper. "Carey . . ." She cried against Jack's shoulder some more.

Then, after a while, swallowing her tears, Roz said, "If we get rid of his suit . . . if we get rid of his suit, they'll think he got lost on the surface."

He opened his eyes and looked at her. Now he was scared. Who was this girl?

"What do you mean?" he asked.

EATING

Eva expected Jack would turn up at the festival eventually, and she didn't want to miss the partying. Her mother came by with some of her cronies, and then Eva found herself dancing with Angela Angelasdaughter, the colony's most notorious artist. Ten years ago, any gossip session in the sauna would devote ten minutes to the sexy sculptress and her physicist lover. Since then Angela had gained a pot-belly, but her smile was as wicked as ever.

During a break in the music, Eva shared a drink with Jamira Tamlasdaughter. Jamira told Eva she had seen Jack earlier. "He's so handsome, Eva," Jamira said. "You're so lucky. He's like a god."

Eva smiled, thinking of Jack's taut body stretched across her bed. "Where did he go?"

"I don't know. I expect he's here somewhere."

But Jack did not show up. What with one thing and another it was well after midnight when Eva returned to her apartment. Jack was sitting on the floor with a glass in front of him.

"So here you are," Eva said. "I thought we would meet at the festival."

He looked up at her, and his blue eyes were so soulfully sad that she melted. "I couldn't find you," he said quietly.

She sat down next to him. "I got caught up at the lab." She and Victor had been working overtime on assembler programming. "Are Carey and Roz here?"

"No."

"Good. Then we can entertain ourselves—unless this stuff you pour into yourself makes that unnecessary."

Jack put his arms around her, pulled her to him, and rested his forehead against hers. "You know I always need you," he whispered. Eva could smell spiced alcohol on his breath. She pulled him back onto the floor, and they kissed furiously.

They eventually found their way to the bedroom. Afterward, she was ravenously hungry. As a member of the Board, she had earned the privilege of a small kitchen: she padded in, naked, and returned to the room with a plate, a knife, an apple, and a hunk of cheese.

Jack was stretched across the bed just as she had imagined him, the muscles of his belly thrown into relief by the low light. She sat cross-legged beside him, cut a slice from the apple and offered it to him. "Here we are, in the Garden. Eve offers you an apple."

"No, thanks."

"Come on, Adam. Have some fun."

His eyes flicked away from her, the corner of his mouth twitched. "I've had too much fun already," he said to the ceiling.

She drew the apple slice across his chest, down to his navel. "There's always more where that came from."

"I'm worried about Roz. She shouldn't be out this late."

"Your daughter's too sensible to do anything risky." Eva heard the door to the apartment open, the sound of someone coming down the hall and entering Rosalind's room. "See?" Eva said. "There she is."

"What about Carey?"

"Carey, on the other hand, is no doubt busy getting into some sort of trouble. We'll deal with him in the morning."

She brushed her hand over his penis, and it stiffened. He said nothing, but eventually his hand came up to touch her hair, and then he pulled close and made love to her with an intensity that left her breathless and relaxed. He fell asleep beside her, and she lay watching the plate and the apple slices in the faint light. Soon, she thought, soon, they would be able to reproduce anything. She would prove that the Cousins were not some backward-looking, female-dominated hive. They would stun the world. Dreaming of this, Jack's arm around her, she fell asleep.

In the morning Carey had not returned.

Over breakfast—Eva finished the apple, now turned brown—she asked Roz what had happened after hockey practice. After denying anything, Roz finally admitted that Carey and some others had used the cover of the festival to sneak out of the colony onto the surface. The "First Imprints Club." In the dead lunar surface their markings in the dust would last as long as if etched in stone.

That sounded like Carey, right down to the wasting of water. Eva called Carey's friends. She discovered that Carey had left them at the festival, telling them he would catch up with them at the airlock. After waiting for him, they had gone out without him, expecting that he'd meet them on Shiva Ridge.

Carey's pressure suit was not in his locker at the north airlock. Eva tried not to panic. She alerted colony security. Hundreds of volunteers joined in a search of the surface. With the assistance of Carey's friends they found the footprints of the party, but none for Carey. Lunar Positioning Satellites could not raise his suit's locator. Parties scanned the prominent landmarks, but came up empty.

The next days became a nightmare. Eva spent all of her waking hours out on the surface with the search parties, coming inside only to recharge her air supply and catch an hour or two of sleep. Her eyes fell into a permanent squint from the brightness of the surface. For the first twenty-four hours Eva still hoped Carey might be found alive. He had fallen unconscious in the shadow of some rock, she told herself; hypothermia would keep his metabolism low so he wouldn't exhaust his oxygen.

As the hours passed she kept despair at bay by driving herself even harder. The third day found her a part of a line of twenty Cousins, at hundred-meter intervals, sweeping Shiva ridge for the fourth time. Something was wrong with her faceplate: it was breaking all the gray landscape into particles, no piece of the Moon connected to any other piece, and all of it was dead. The voices of the other searchers calling to each other sounded in her ear button. "Nothing here." "Where's here?" "I'm on the east end of the ridge, below Black Rock."

Eva felt numb. She came to the edge of a lava tube whose roof had fallen in. It was fifty meters to the shadowed bottom. Even in lunar gravity the fall would be fatal. She swayed on the edge, having trouble breathing. Her mouth was dry, and her eyes itched.

Someone grabbed her arm and pulled her away. "No," his voice came over her ear button, as close as her own thoughts. It was Jack. He wrapped her in a bear hug, drew her back. He made her return with him to Fowler, to eat a meal, to take some pills, and sleep for fourteen hours.

After that Eva no longer tormented herself with impossibilities. Jack stayed with her every minute of her time on the surface. Despite her heartache, she still hoped Carey's body would turn up so she could figure out what had happened. But when a further week of searches still brought nothing, she asked that they be called off. The official inquest ruled Carey missing, presumed dead by hazard of fortune.

She turned to her work. The project was her only hope now. It was more than a matter of demonstrating the value of Cousins' science. Over the next months, the first assemblies using scans of organic compounds were completed. They produced edible soy protein and worked their way up toward apple sauce.

At meetings in the boardroom that looked out over the green fields of Fowler basin, the other matrons watched her out of the corners of their eyes. Eva controlled her voice, operated her body as if by remote. Everything is normal, she told herself. Some mornings she would wake and listen for Carey thumping around the apartment, only to hear silence. She hid his pictures. Although she would not empty his room, she closed its door and never went inside. She went to watch the hockey team play. Other Cousins sat beside her and made a show of treating her normally.

Hockey was such a violent game—a boy's game. Had the Cousins adopted it for that very reason, to go against the perception that women were soft? Eva watched Roz throw herself around the ice like a demon. What would drive such a shy girl to compete so hard?

At night she lay awake and thought about Carey. She imagined him out there on the surface, running out of air. What was it about boys and men that they always took such big risks? You couldn't protect them. If you tried to, they got sulky and depressed. She had never questioned the place the Cousins had prepared for boys in the world, how their aggression and desire for dominance had been thwarted and channeled. *Keep your son close; let your daughter go*, the homily went. Had she been fair to Carey? If she had him back with her this minute, could she keep herself from smothering him?

Jack went back to his own work: His team planted a copse of junipers, piñon, sage, and wildflowers on the east slopes of Fowler, hauling loads of their new soil that promised a better growth rate than the chemically prepared soils. He came home each night with dirt under his fingernails, scrubbed himself raw in the shower and fell into bed exhausted. Jack and Eva had not made love after that night Carey disappeared. At first Eva had no desire, and then, after her need returned and she might have felt it a comfort to have Jack hold her in his arms, he was so depressed by Carey's loss that he would not touch her. Eva saw that worrying about her had taken Jack away from Roz.

"I'm sorry," she vowed to Jack's sleeping form one night. "I can do better."

Since Carey's disappearance, Roz spent less time at home. Eva saw the pain in Jack's eyes as he watched Roz. She wondered what it must be like for Roz, to have this single strong male presence always there in her life. She owed Roz and Jack better than she had been giving, and the effort to engage them would help her stop thinking about Carey.

She arranged for Roz to spend her second-semester practicum in the colony's materials cooperatives. What to do about Jack's relationship to Roz was harder to figure out. Eva was a physicist, and had never paid much attention to the theories of Nora Sobieski and the other founders. It wasn't as though a man taking an interest in his daughter's upbringing was necessarily unnatural. But Eva realized that—just like her with Carey, out of his fear of losing Roz—Jack ran the risk of smothering her. *Keep your son close; let your daughter go*: Whether Jack could see it or not, it was time for Roz to begin to find her own place in the world.

Jack had taken to bringing home chard and romaine lettuce and carrots from the gardens. He brought a potted juniper for the balcony where they ate their meals. There one night at dinner Eva suggested to Jack that Roz move out.

Jack looked frightened. "She's only fourteen, Eva."

"If she doesn't begin to break free now she will have a much harder time later."

"I understand that. It's just—it's not the way she grew up. She and I haven't been here that long. And with—with Carey gone . . ." his voice trailed off.

Eva watched him. "Jack, I know I've been distant. I know it's been hard for you. If you don't want to be alone with me, I'll understand. I just hope you won't live with Roz."

"For pity's, Eva! Don't you believe in love?"

She was taken aback. "Of course I do." She poked her fork at her salad.

"Well, I love Roz. I love . . . I love you."

Eva felt out of her depth. What did he mean when he said the word "love"? She looked into Jack's handsome face: blue eyes, curly blond hair, square jaw. How much, when he looked so hurt, he reminded her of Carey. Jack watched her intently. He was trying to communicate something, but she had no idea what it was.

"I know you love us," Eva said. "That's not the question. But if Roz is ever going to fit in here, she needs to begin to network . . . I might even say the same for you."

"Network." He sat still as a stone.

He acted so wounded; he was putting her on the spot. Was this about sex? "I'm not trying to push you away, Jack. It's not me who's been turning away every night in bed."

"I realize that," he said defensively. "I thought that you were still grieving for Carey."

God, she was no good at this interpersonal stuff. She looked away. She tried the salad grown from the gardens he and his team had planted. "Let me handle my grief in my own way," she said.

He said nothing. He seemed more sad than angry. They ate in silence. After a while he asked her, "How's the salad?"

"The best I've ever tasted. And the pine nuts—are they from the new trees?"

"Yes," he said.

"The juniper smells wonderful."

"It's yours," he said. "I grew it for you."

TRANSFORMATION

When Roz told Jack about Carey's plans to meet the First Imprints Club, Jack picked up Carey's pressure suit. He laid the suit on the floor, adjusted it so that the locator lay flat against the concrete, and ground his heel into it until the chip snapped. "OK," Jack said. "You take his things and lose them some place on the surface where they'll never be found."

Roz knew that Jack's real reason for rushing her out was to keep her from seeing him dispose of Carey's body. She did not object. She stuffed Carey's clothes into the suit, sealed it up and, while her father turned back to the body, headed for the airlock.

"Wait," Jack said, "take this."

Fearfully, she turned. Jack had taken something from Carey's hand. It was Carey's ring.

She shoved the ring inside her own suit, then hurried through the airlock onto the lunar surface.

The shadows of lunar afternoon lay precisely as they had when she had entered the lab an hour before, a girl seeking to apologize to her dad. Between then and now, something had broken.

Jack had looked so surprised, so guilty—so old. The skin beneath his eyes was dark and papery, as if he hadn't slept in a week. Had he looked this tired when she had argued with him in the plaza? It made her wonder just what had been going on all this time. How could Jack kill Carey? Had he been so near to breaking all along? As she shuffled across the humped, dusty surface, Roz fought to keep from crying again at the awfulness of Carey's death and the precariousness of their situation.

For most of her life, it had been just her and her father. Roz's mother Helen had been a graduate student in plant pathology when Jack met her at Purdue. Roz's first memory was of sitting in the bathtub as her mom taught her to count on her toes. When Roz was six, her mother's increasing bouts of depression broke up the marriage. Helen had custody of Roz for more than a year before Jack rescued her, and Roz remembered that year vividly: afternoons hanging out with the kids in the neighboring apartment, suppers of corn flakes, Helen coming back from her classes unhappy, Roz trying to wake Helen to get her to work in the mornings, Helen shouting at Jack every time he came to pick Roz up for visits. When Jack had stolen Roz away, though he never said anything bad about Helen, Roz felt that she would never miss her mother again.

Now Roz wished she knew where Helen was, what she was doing at just that moment. What had she gone through when she was fourteen? Nothing as bad as this.

As she moved away from Fowler across the lunar surface, Roz tried to stay to the shadows. But there was little chance of anyone spotting her. What she needed to do was lose Carey's suit somewhere that nobody was likely to find it for thirty or forty years.

It should not be so hard. These were the rumpled highlands, a landscape of hills, ridges, craters, and ejecta. Around the colony the ground was scuffed with a million bootprints. Roz hid hers among them, bouncing along below the eastern rim of Fowler.

She then struck off along a side track of footprints that aimed northeast. A couple of kilometers along, she broke off from the path and made a long leap to a rock scarp uncovered with dust. She landed clumsily but safe, and left no boot marks. She proceeded in this direction for some distance, aiming herself from rock to rock to leave as few footprints as possible. The short horizon made Roz feel as if she was a bug on a plate, nearing the edge of the world. She kept her bearings by periodically noting some point ahead and behind so that she would not get lost. That was the biggest danger of surface hopping, and the source of the rule against ever doing it alone. It would be easy to explain Carey's disappearance as an intoxicated boy getting lost and running out of air. A broken radio, a faulty locator.

A kilometer on, Roz found a pit behind a group of ejecta boulders. Deep in the shadow on the north side of the largest, she dug away the top layer of regolith and stuffed the suit into the pit. She shoved the dirt back over the suit. By the time she was done, her hands were freezing. She stood back on a boulder and inspected the spot. She had kept most of the scuffs she'd created to the shadows, which would not change much for some time in the slow lunar day. Roz headed back along the path she had come, rock to rock, taking long strides in the low gravity until she met the traveled path again. Up above her, a third of the way across the black sky from the sun, angry red Mars gleamed beside Jupiter like an orange eye.

Her air supply was in the red when she reached Fowler's north lock. She was able to pass through without seeing anyone; the festival was still going strong.

Roz stowed her suit in an empty locker, set the combination, and walked back around the rim road toward Eva's apartment—the long way, making a three-quarter circuit of the crater. On the southeast slope she stopped and watched the lights of the festival. When she finally got home, she found an empty glass sitting on the living room floor, and the door to Jack and Eva's room was closed. She went to her own room, closed her door, undressed. There she found Carey's ring in her pocket, warm from the heat of her own body.

Through all of Eva's quizzing of Roz the next morning, Jack sat drinking juice, ignoring them both. Roz was stunned by how calm he looked. What went on inside? She had never thought that there might be things going on inside her father that were not apparent on the surface.

Then the searches began. Over and over Roz had to retell her story of parting with Carey at the festival. At just what time had she last seen Carey? What had Carey said? In what direction had Carey gone? Jack threw himself into the "search"—but whenever Roz looked at him, she saw that he was watching her.

As the search stretched beyond the first days, Carey's friends came up and sympathized with Roz. For the first time kids who had held her at arms' length confided in her. They shared their shock and grief. Roz supposed that, from the outside, her own terror looked like shock. Colony security used volunteers from the school in the searches, and Roz took part, though never in the northeast quadrant. Every time one of the parties returned she was petrified that they would come back with Carey's pressure suit.

Near the end of the third day, Roz was sitting in the apartment, clutching Carey's ring in her hand, when Jack brought Eva back with him. Eva was so sick Jack almost had to prop her up. Jack fed Eva, made her take some pills, and go to sleep. He came out of their room and shut the door.

"What happened?" Roz asked.

Jack pulled Roz away from the door. "I caught Eva on the edge of a precipice. I think she was about to jump off."

"Oh, Jesus! What are we going to do?"

"She'll be okay after she gets some rest. We need to take care of her."

"Take care of her! We killed her son!"

"Keep your voice down. Nobody killed anyone. It was an accident."

"I don't think I can stand this, Dad."

"You're doing fine, Roz. I need you to be my strong girl. Just act normal."

Just act normal. Roz tried to focus on school. The hockey game against Shackleton was postponed, but the practices continued. When it became obvious that Carey wasn't coming back, Maryjane moved up to take Carey's place in Roz's line. At night Roz squeezed her eyes shut, pressed her palms against them to drive thoughts of Carey's body from her imagination. She would not talk to Jack about it, and in his few hurried words with her he never spoke of that night.

Roz hated hearing the sound of Jack's voice when he talked to Eva or anyone else, so casually modulated, so sane. Just act normal. When he spoke with Roz his voice was edged with panic. Roz vowed that she would never in her life have two voices.

Maybe Eva had two voices, too. After the searches were ended, Eva seemed distressingly normal. Roz could tell Eva was upset only by the firmness with which she spoke, as if she were thinking everything over two or three times, and by the absolute quality of her silences.

At first Roz was afraid to be around Eva, she seemed so in control. Yet Roz could tell that at some level Eva was deeply wounded in a way she could not see in Jack. The only word Roz could think of to describe Eva was a word so absurdly old fashioned that she would have been embarrassed to say it aloud: Noble. Eva was the strongest person Roz had ever met. It made Roz want to comfort her — but Roz was too afraid.

The weeks passed, and they resumed a simulation of ordinary life. Eva took an interest in Roz that she had not while Carey was still alive. For Roz's second-semester practicum, Eva arranged for Roz to work successive months in the colony's four materials cooperatives Air, Water, Agriculture, and Fabrication. Roz was glad to spend more time out of the apartment.

With Air, Roz worked outside in the southwest industrial area, helping move lunar regolith to the grinder. Various trace elements, including the H_3 used in fusion reactors, were drawn off and saved. After grinding, the regolith was put in a reduction chamber with powdered graphite and heated to produce carbon monoxide, which was reintroduced to the regolith in a second chamber to produce CO_2. The carbon dioxide was separated by a solar-powered electrochemic cell. The carbon was recycled as graphite, and the O_2 liquefied. The excess was sold to other lunar colonies or traded for nitrogen.

With Water, she worked at the far end of the ice cavern, where the ice was crushed, vaporized, distilled, and refrozen. Some of the water was electrolyzed to provide oxygen and carbon, a rare element on the Moon.

With Agriculture, she shoveled sheep and guinea pig shit, and moved chicken wastes to recycling for fertilizer.

With Fabrication, she did quality control for the anhydrous production of fiberglass cables coated with iron. Any contamination of the fiberglass with water would compromise its strength and durability. Structural materials were one of the colony's other major exports.

Everything she learned during her practicum was so logical. Everything she felt when she was in the apartment with Eva and her father was insane. While she worked, when she could forget the expression on Jack's face when she'd found him standing above Carey's naked body, the colony felt like home. The minute she thought about that place that was supposed to be her home, she felt lost. Looking down from the balcony of their apartment on the interior of the crater, she saw the spire that supported the dome as a great tree spreading over the Cousins' lives. Behind her she heard Jack's and Eva's voices, so human, so mysterious.

Eva quizzed Roz every few days about the practicum. Because they spoke only about the practical issues of running the Society these conversations were a relief to Roz. She thought they were relief for Eva as well. Roz could ask any question, as long as it was about engineering. Eva would lean next to Roz over the tablet and click through diagrams of chemical syntheses, twisting the ends of her hair in her fingers.

One evening as they were going through one of these sessions, Jack exploded. Afraid that he might say something that would make Eva suspicious, Roz went with him for a walk to talk over what was bothering him. When she told him she was thinking of moving out, he threatened to tell Eva what had happened to Carey. His paranoia was so sharp that she could smell it. She begged him to be quiet.

Roz realized that she was trapped. It would be safer for her and Jack both if she moved out of the apartment. Raisa was still looking for a roommate, and it would only be a matter of a few days for her to make the arrangements and move her things. But there was nothing she could do.

One day late in Roz's practicum, Eva called her to the Fabrication research lab. Roz realized that it was not an accident that the last stop on her practicum tour was Fabrication, and the last stop at Fabrication was research, Eva's own area. Roz had a sudden dread that Eva knew something, that ever since the festival she had been setting a trap, which was about to spring.

Like the biotech lab that her father worked in, in the interests of preventing contamination Eva's nanotech lab was separated from the colony. At the end of the northwest lava tube, Roz suited up and passed through a lock onto the surface. It was months since Carey's disappearance, and full night now. Mars and Jupiter were no longer visible; Venus shone brightly on the horizon. She followed a string of lights to the lab, entered, and pulled off her suit.

Eva met her at the check-in. "Thank you for coming, Roz. Come with me. I want to show you the Quantum Nondestructive Scanner Array."

The QNSA lab was the largest in the facility. The scanner looked like nothing so much as a huge blue marble, the size of an elephant, divided at the equator. Eva had the technicians lift the upper hemisphere to expose the target area. "What we do here is pull a fast one on the universe. We bypass the uncertainty principle on the sub-atomic level by measuring test subjects at below the Planck-Wheeler length."

"I don't know that much physics," Roz said.

Eva put her arm around Roz's shoulder. Despite the affectionate gesture, she was not smiling. "We've made huge strides in the past six months."

"What's it for?"

"There are a hundred purposes—some of them quite revolutionary. On the most basic level, if we can scan to sufficient accuracy, and if the assembler team can succeed in producing a programmable assembler that can use the scan—then we will have created the most flexible manufacturing system in history. Any object we scan could be duplicated in the assembler."

"Isn't that expensive?"

"Smart girl. Yes, it is very expensive—of technology, energy, and time. It doesn't make economic sense to use a system like this to manufacture simple things, like, say, an electric motor. That would be like running an MRI to check whether there's gum in your pocket. But for more complicated things—organic compounds, for instance—it holds fascinating possibilities. Let me show you something."

She took Roz into a side room separated from the lab by a large window. In the corner was a refrigerator. From it Eva took out two apples. She handed them to Roz. "What do you think of these?"

Roz looked them over. They were the same size, the same shape. Both felt cool in her palms. In fact, they felt exactly alike. She looked at them more closely. There was a spray of freckles near the stem of the apple in her right held the other next to it, turned it until they were in the same position. An identical spray of freckles marked the second apple. "They're the same."

"Yes. Now compare this." Eva pulled a third apple from the refrigerator. This one was past its prime; its skin was darker and softer, and it smelled sweet. Yet it had exactly the same pattern of freckles as the other two.

"All three of these apples were assembled from the same quantum scan. We scanned the original apple six months ago. These two apples were assembled from the QNSA yesterday, the other a week ago. If we load the right raw materials into the assembler, we can create as many identical apples as we like."

"That's amazing!"

"Yes. It's too expensive a way to make apples, though. In fact, there aren't many things that would justify the expense of reproduction by QNSA."

Eva took the apples back. She put the old one and one of the new ones back into the refrigerator. Then she polished the third on her sleeve and took a bite of it. Chewing, she handed it to Roz. "Try it."

Roz took a bite. It tasted crisp and tart. Another lab worker came in and got a squeeze bottle out of the refrigerator. He nodded to Eva, smiled at Roz, and went out.

"I hoped at first that I might get over the loss of Carey," Eva said. She looked through the window at the big blue marble. "I told myself that he was only one person, that we all die eventually, that it was his recklessness that had killed him and I never wanted him to be other than he was." She brushed the back of her hand against her eye. "But a son is not supposed to die before his mother. Everything looks different afterward. It's all just a collection of atoms."

Eva turned to Roz. "How does the apple taste?"

"Good."

"I'm glad. Now, Roz, I want to tell you what I'm going to do. It's something that no one's ever done before. Because of that it's not a crime yet, but if it doesn't become so common as to be ordinary in the future, I'm sure it will become a crime."

"What are you talking about?"

"Some months ago, the project had reached a stage where we could scan a living organism. We scanned several guinea pigs, even a sheep. One night, while the lab was empty, I brought Carey here and scanned him.

"I've been waiting until we worked the bugs out of the assembler. Three days ago we recreated one of the guinea pigs from a four-month-old scan. Do you know what that means?"

Roz held her breath. "I think so."

"If that guinea pig suffers no aftereffects, I am going to reconstitute Carey. I want you to help me."

The sky opened up and a torrent of pure joy shot down to fill Roz up. She could not believe it. She hugged Eva, buried her head against the tall woman's breast. It was a miracle. It was the way out.

FIRE

Nematodes made up most of the animal life on earth, by mass, Jack reminded himself. They were everywhere. The number of parasitic varieties was minuscule compared to the beneficial ones. Nothing to worry about.

But his hands itched. And his skin burned.

It had not taken Jack long to cut up Carey's body, run it through the reduction chamber, mince the remains in the crusher and mix them into the project soil. He had hosed down the crusher and the floor of the lab. Fire, earth, water. Within a week there was nothing left of Carey but his elemental chemicals in the dirt.

Still, images of Carey were imprinted on the inside of Jack's eyelids. I'm a freakshow, he thought a dozen times each day, climbing down the slope to the crater floor, pruning seedlings in the greenhouse, sitting on the edge of the pool in Sobieski Park. Lying in bed with Eva. I'm a lethal male in a society constructed to prevent males from going lethal. I didn't even know it was happening. I'm a fucking maniac and no one can tell.

No one had noticed anything—at least he didn't think they had. He had a tough afternoon the day they transferred the test soil to the pilot project site on Fowler's east slope. He insisted that he amend the soil himself, plant the junipers with his own hands. He wore protective gloves. When Amravati said something about it, he replied quickly, "Don't want to take a chance with these new bugs."

"If there are any bugs we don't know about, then we're all in trouble," she said.

The seedlings flourished. Growth rates were elevated as much as 15 percent.

Within three months the project had progressed enough to schedule a tour by the Board of Matrons. Eva and the others strolled over the slopes among the low, fragrant growth. As Eva walked over the ground that contained all that was left of her only son, a wave of heat swept over Jack. His face felt flushed; his forehead burned.

The Board approved the project. The next week they voted Amravati a commendation, with special notice of Jack's contribution. "If you don't watch out, Jack, you're going to get stuck here," Hal Keikosson said.

"What?" he said.

Hal smiled at him. "I mean you're becoming a Cousin, cousin."

A Cousin on the outside, a stranger within. There were lots of difficult aspects to the aftermath of Carey's death, among them the problem of Eva. For example, despite the fact that, during the search, he had saved Eva's life out on the edge of the precipice, it was impossible for him to touch her in bed. He had discovered how much her eyes were like Carey's. Lying beside her at night, hands burning, pretending to sleep until he heard Eva's faint snore, and pretending to sleep after that for fear of waking her, Jack felt more alone than he had since he was five years old. One night he heard Eva stir beside him, rise up on one elbow, and watch him. He heard her whisper, "I'm sorry. I can do better." What did she have to feel sorry about? How could she possibly be asking his forgiveness?

The colony clinic prescribed a salve for his skin that did nothing but make him smell like sulfur. I'm the lunar Mephistopheles, he thought. He resorted to magic: If some part of Carey was coming back to torment Jack, maybe bringing Carey home would mollify his ghost. Jack potted one of the junipers and set it up on their balcony. He fed Eva lettuce from the greenhouse to see what effect it would have on her. It made her suggest that Roz should move out.

Roz. That was the worst thing, the absolute worst. Jack was stunned that Roz had so readily put herself at risk to save him. Though it was, at some level he had difficulty admitting, immensely gratifying, and removed any doubt he had ever had that she loved him, now he could not look at Roz the same way. He was in debt to his daughter, and like a boulder that they were both chained to, that debt stood between them at every moment.

When Roz started her practicum in Fabrication, she began to spend more time with Eva. Jack watched them joke together as they sat in the apartment and went over the steps in the manufacture of building glass. Their heads were so close together, Roz's red hair and Eva's brown. The skirl of Roz's silly, high-pitched giggle, for some reason, made him want to cry.

"You laugh too much," he said.

They looked up at him, dead silent, identical astonishment on their faces.

"Can't you keep quiet?" he said.

"Sorry, Dad," Roz muttered. "I didn't know I wasn't allowed to laugh." She pushed the tablet away from her. "I have something I need to tell you."

Jack tried to keep the panic out of his voice. "What's that?"

"I think I'm going to move out. There's an apartment that Raisa and I can move into opening up in the old section of the south wall."

"Raisa? I thought you didn't even like her."

"I think I was just projecting; she's really a good person. She's never mean."

Jack wanted to argue, but was intimidated by Eva's presence. Eva had put this idea in Roz's head. "Come with me," he said to Roz. "We'll take a walk. Do you mind, Eva? We need to talk this over father to daughter."

"Go right ahead."

Roz looked sullen, but she came with him. They descended from the apartment, down the pathway toward the crater floor. The inside of the dome was a brilliant cloudless sky. On the field below them a harvester sprayed soybeans into a hopper truck. "Is this because of Carey?" Jack asked.

Roz crossed her arms over his chest and looked at her feet. "I don't want to talk about Carey," she said.

"You know it was an accident, Roz, I—"

She bounced on her toes and leaped five feet into the air, coming down well ahead of him. A woman going the other way looked at her and smiled. Jack hurried to catch up.

Roz still wouldn't look at him. "I will not talk about Carey, Dad. This isn't about him. I'm fourteen, and a Cousins girl at fourteen who won't leave home is sick." She bounced again.

He didn't know what to say. He knew she was lying, that it had to have something to do with Carey. But he wasn't going to beg.

"You're going to tell Eva the truth," he said when he caught up.

"Don't be stupid!" Roz said. "I've given up too much for this. I don't want to move again."

Stupid. How stupid he had been to come here. "I brought you here to keep us from drifting apart."

"Dad, did you think I was going to be with you forever?"

He rubbed his palms up and down his forearms, but that only made the itching worse. "Will you call me?"

"I'll see you every day."

Jack stopped following her. Roz continued down the path toward Sobieski Park, and did not look back.

"What do you think, Carey?" he whispered aloud as he watched his daughter walk away. "Is this one of those Earth things? One of those sexual ownership practices?"

Jack tried to imagine what it would be like to be alone with Eva in one of the largest apartments in the colony. Perhaps it would not be so bad. He could plant a dozen junipers on the balcony. He could prepare all their meals. Hell, he could bring in a bed of Carey's soil and sleep in it.

He began meeting Jamira Tamlasdaughter in the sauna at the gym. They would claim one of the private alcoves and fuck. The heat of the sauna made him forget his burning skin. There was nothing wrong with it. There was nothing right about it. Roz was always out. Eva stayed away even longer at the labs, sometimes not coming back at night until he was asleep. The mysterious absences grew until one night it had been a full twenty-four hours since Jack had last seen either Eva or Roz. It was fertile ground for worry. Someone had found Carey's pressure suit. Roz had not hidden it well enough, and now she was in trouble. Or Eva had tricked her into an admission. She had broken down, given in to guilt.

His phone rang. He touched the contact on his wristward.

"Dad? Can you meet me at Fabrication Research?"

Roz's voice was charged with excitement. He hadn't heard her sound so young in months. "What is it, Roz?"

"You won't believe it. All our troubles are over! We're resurrecting Carey!"

"What?"

"The assembler. I can't tell you more now, someone might hear. Come at 0300. If anyone asks, tell them that you're going somewhere else."

"Is Eva there?"

"Yes. I've got to go now. See you at 0300."

"Roz —"

He felt sick. Resurrecting Carey? Roz must have told Eva what had happened.

Still, what could he do but go? Jack paced the rooms for hours. He left after somatic midnight. The perimeter road to the north airlock was quiet; there was a slight breeze, a hum of insects around the lights. He told the lock attendant that he was going to biotech.

When he sealed up his suit he felt he could not breathe. He checked the readouts repeatedly, but despite the evidence that nothing was wrong, he felt stifled. Sweat trickled down his neck into his collar.

Outside the sun hammered down and the glare of the baked surface hid the stars. He upped the polarization on his faceplate, but still his eyes hurt. He followed the road from the airlock, between the fields of solar collectors, to the ramp entrance to the Fabrication Research Lab. He passed through the radiation maze, opened the outer door of the lab airlock. When he stripped off his suit his shirt was soaked with sweat. He wiped his arm across his brow, ran his fingers through his sweaty hair. He waited. He did not open the inner door.

And if, by some miracle, they did re-create Carey? Roz said that all their troubles would be over. They could go back to who they were.

Fat chance. He had hoped that coming to the Society would offer Roz a freedom that he could not earn for her on Earth. No one on the Moon knew him. And even if he did fail again, among the Cousins a father's faults would not determine how others saw his daughter. Roz could be herself, not some reflection of him.

As he stood there, poised before the inner lock door, he had a sudden memory of Helen, on their honeymoon. On the beach at St. Kitts. Helen had surprised him by wearing a new bikini, so small that when she pulled off her shorts and T-shirt she was clearly self-conscious. But proud, in some way. He remembered feeling protective of her, and puzzled, and a little sorry. It hit him for the first time that she was fighting her body for his attention, and how sad that must be for her — on the one hand to know she had this power over him that came simply from her sexuality, and on the other that she, Helen, was someone completely apart from that body that drew him like a magnet. For a moment he had seen himself from outside. He'd been ashamed of his own sexuality, and the way it threatened to deform their relationship. Who was she, really? Who was he?

At the time he had taken her in his arms, smiled, complimented her. He had felt sure that with time, they would know each other completely. How pathetic. After the break-up, he had at least thought that he could know his daughter. That was why he wanted Roz—to love someone without sex coming in the way. To love someone without caring about himself.

How stupid he had been. Whether they'd come or not, inevitably she would have seen him differently, or been destroyed by trying not to. Whether he'd killed Carey or not, Roz would have to fight to escape the mirror he held up to her.

With a sick feeling in his gut, he realized he had lost his daughter.

He was so hot. He was burning up. He shut his eyes and tried not to see or hear anything, but there was a roaring in his ears like a turbulent storm, and his eyes burned and flashed like lightning.

He would feel better if he went outside. Instead of opening the inner door, he put his pressure suit back on and opened the outside door. It was bright and hot out on the surface—but in the shadows of the rocks it would be cool. He stepped out of the shadow of the radiation baffle, up the ramp to the dusty surface. Instead of following the path back to the colony, he struck off between the rows of solar collectors toward a giant boulder that loomed on the horizon. As he walked, on his sleeve keyboard he punched in the override code for his suit's pressure failsafes.

By the time he had reached the chill shadow of the rock, all that remained between him and relief was the manual helmet release. He reached up to his neck and felt for the latch. He was so hot. He was burning up. But soon he would be cool again.

HAPPY ENDING

When the indicators showed the airlock was occupied, they waited for Jack to enter the lab. Instead, after a few minutes the outer lock of the airlock opened and he left again. Roz was worried.

"I'm going to see what he's up to," she told Eva.

She pulled on her pressure suit and waited the maddening few minutes it took the lock to recycle. As soon as pressure was equalized she slid open the outer door and ran up the ramp. There was no sign of her father on the path back to Fowler. But as she followed the footprints away from the ramp, she spotted a figure in the distance heading out toward the hills.

Roz hurried after, skipping as fast as she could without lurching off onto the collectors.

When she caught up, he was on his knees in the shadow of a big rock, jerking about spasmodically. The strangeness of his motion alarmed her. She had never seen anyone move like that. Before she could reach him he slowed, stopped, and fell, slowly, onto his side. Calmly, quietly. Less like a fall, more like the drift of a feather. She rushed to his side, and saw that he had broken the seal on his helmet.

"No!" she screamed, and the sound of her voice echoed in her ears. Jack's face was purple with broken blood vessels, his eyes bloody. He was dead.

High-G, they called her, and it was a good thing, as she carried her father's body back to the Fabrication lab.

It was Roz's idea to put Jack's corpse into the assembler, to add the materials of his body to the atoms used to re-create Carey. There would be hell to pay with security, but Eva agreed to do it.

The assembly took seven days. When the others at the colony discovered what they were doing, there was some debate, but they let the process continue. At the end of the week the fluid supporting the nanomachines was drained off, revealing Carey's perfect body. Carey shuddered and coughed, and they helped him out of the assembler.

To him it was six months earlier, and his mother had just completed his scan. It took him a long time to accept that he had not fallen into some dream only seconds after he had been placed in the marble, to awaken in this vat of warm fluid. He thought he was the original, not the copy. For all practical purposes he was right.

Later, as they were finding a pressure suit they could adapt to Carey's size to take him home, he asked Roz, "Where's Jack?"

THE JUNIPER TREE

All this happened a long time ago.

Nora Sobieski founded the Society of Cousins to free girls like Roz of the feeling that they must depend on their fathers or boyfriends for their sense of self, and incidentally to free boys like Carey of the need to prove themselves superior to other boys by owning girls like Roz. Girls still go through infatuations, still fall in love, still feel the influence of men as well as of women. But Roz and Eva in the end are actually in the same boat — a boat that does not contain Jack, or even Carey.

The young junipers stand ghostly gray in the night. The air smells fragrant with piñon. In the thin, clear starlight Roz can see wildflowers blooming beneath the trees — columbine, pennyroyal, groundsel. She sits on the slope and pulls Carey's ring from her pocket. The ring is fashioned into the image of two branches that twine around each other, each with no beginning and no end, each eternally separate from the other.

Roz holds the ring in the middle of her palm, wondering if she should get rid of it at last, knowing that she can never give it back and maintain the mystery of who her father was and how he died.

Antibodies

CHARLES STROSS

Although he made his first sale back in 1987, it's only recently that British writer Charles Stross has begun to make a name for himself as a writer to watch in the new century ahead, with a sudden burst in the last couple of years of quirky, inventive, high-bit-rate stories such as "A Colder War," "Bear Trap," "Dechlorinating the Moderator," and "Toast: A Con Report" in markets such as Interzone, Spectrum SF, Osyssey, Strange Plasma, *and* New Worlds. *In the fast-paced and innovative story that follows, he demonstrates that although you can carefully set a warning alarm, by the time it goes off, it may be almost too late to do anything about it. . . .*

Charles Stross is also a regular columnist for the monthly magazine Computer Shopper. *Coming up is his first collection,* Toast, *and Other* Burned Out Futures. *He lives in Edinburgh, Scotland.*

Everyone remembers where they were and what they were doing when a member of the great and the good is assassinated. Gandhi, the Pope, Thatcher — if you were old enough you remembered where you were when you heard, the ticker-tape of history etched across your senses. You can kill a politician but their ideas usually live on. They have a life of their own. How much more dangerous, then, the ideas of mathematicians?

I was elbow-deep in an eviscerated PC, performing open heart surgery on a diseased network card, when the news about the traveling salesman theorem came in. Over on the other side of the office John's terminal beeped, notification of incoming mail. A moment later my own workstation bonged.

"Hey, Geoff! Get a load of this!"

I carried on screwing the card back into its chassis. John is not a priority interrupt.

"Someone's come up with a proof that NP-complete problems lie in P! There's a posting in *comp.risks* saying they've used it to find an O*(n^2) solution to the traveling salesman problem, and it scales! Looks like April First has come early this year, doesn't it?"

I dropped the PC's lid on the floor hastily and sat down at my workstation.

Another cubed-sphere hypothesis, another flame war in the math newsgroups — or something more serious? "When did it arrive?" I called over the partition. Soroya, passing my cubicle entrance with a cup of coffee, cast me a dirty look; loud voices aren't welcome in open-plan offices.

"This just in," John replied. I opened up the mailtool and hit on the top of the list, which turned out to be a memo from HR about diversity awareness training. No, next . . . they want to close the smoking room and make us a 100% tobacco-free workplace. Hmm. Next.

Forwarded e-mail: headers bearing the spoor of a thousand mail servers, from Addis-Ababa to Ulan Bator. Before it had entered our internal mail network it had traveled from Taiwan to Rochester NJ, then to UCB in the Bay Area, then via a mailing list to all points; once in-company it had been bounced to everyone in engineering and management by the first recipient, Eric the Canary. (Eric is the departmental plant. Spends all the day web-dozing for juicy nuggets of new information if you let him. A one-man wire service: which is why I always ended up finishing his jobs.)

I skimmed the message, then read it again. Blinked. This kind of stuff is heavy on the surreal number theory: about as digestible as an Egyptian mummy soaked in tabasco sauce for three thousand years. Then I poked at the web page the theorem was on.

No response — server timed out.

Someone or something was hitting on the web server with the proof: I figured it had to be all the geeks who'd caught wind of the chain letter so far. My interest was up, so I hit the "reload" button, and something else came up on screen.

Lots of theorems — looked like the same stuff as the e-mail, only this time with some fun graphics. Something tickled my hindbrain then, and I had to bite my lip to keep from laughing. Next thing, I hit the print button and the inkjet next to my desk began to mutter and click. There was a link near the bottom of the page to the author's bibliography, so I clicked on that and the server threw another "go away, I'm busy" error. I tugged my beard thoughtfully, and instead of pressing "back" I pressed "reload."

The browser thought to itself for a bit — then a page began to appear on my screen. The wrong page. I glanced at the document title at the top and froze:

THE PAGE AT THIS LOCATION HAS BEEN WITHDRAWN. Please enter your e-mail address if you require further information.

Hmm.

As soon as the printout was finished, I wandered around to the photocopier next door to the QA labs and ran off a copy. Faxed it to a certain number, along with an EYES UP note on a yellow Post-it. Then I poked my head around into the QA lab itself. It was dingy in there, as usual, and half the cubicles were empty of human life. Nobody here but us computers; workstations humming away, sucking juice and meditating on who-knew-what questions. (Actually, I *did* know: they were mostly running test harnesses, repetitively pounding simulated input data into the programs we'd so carefully built, in the hope of making them fall over or start singing "God Save the King.") The efficiency of code was frequently a bone of contention between our departments, but the war between software engineering and quality assurance is a long-drawn-out affair: each side needs the other to justify its survival.

I was looking for Amin. Amin with the doctorate in discrete number theory, now slumming it in this company of engineers: my other canary in a number-crunching coal mine. I found him: feet propped up on the lidless hulk of a big Compaq server, mousing away like mad at a big monitor. I squinted; it looked vaguely familiar . . . "Quake? Or Golgotha?" I asked.

"Golgotha. We've got Marketing bottled up on the second floor."

"How's the network looking?"

He shrugged, then punched the hold button. "No crashes, no dropped packets — this cut looks pretty solid. We've been playing for three days now. What can I do for you?"

I shoved the printout under his nose. "This seem feasible to you?"

"Hold on a mo." He hit the pause key them scanned it rapidly. Did a double-take. "You're not shitting?"

"Came out about two hours ago."

"Jesus Homeboy Christ riding into town at the head of a convoy of Hell's Angels with a police escort . . ." he shook his head. Amin always swears by Jesus, a weird side-effect of a westernized Islamic upbringing: take somebody else's prophet's name in vain. "If it's true, I can think of at least three different ways we can make money at it, and at least two more to end up in prison. You don't use PGP, do you?"

"Why bother?" I asked, my heart pounding. "I've got nothing to hide."

"If this is true — " he tapped the papers " — then every encryption algorithm except the one-time pad has just fallen over. Take a while to be sure, but . . . that crunch you heard in the distance was the sound of every secure commerce server on the internet succumbing to a brute-force attack. The script kiddies will be creaming themselves. Jesus Christ." He rubbed his mustache thoughtfully.

"Does it make sense to you?" I persisted.

"Come back in five minutes and I'll tell you."

"Okay."

I wandered over to the coffee station, thinking very hard. People hung around and generally behaved as if it was just another day; maybe it was. But then again, if that paper was true, quite a lot of stones had just been turned over and if you were one of the pale guys who lived underneath it was time to scurry for cover. And it had looked good to me: by the prickling in my palms and the gibbering cackle in the back of my skull, something very deep had recognized it. Amin's confirmation would be just the icing on the cake confirmation that it was a workable proof.

Cryptography — the science of encoding messages — relies on certain findings in mathematics: that certain operations are inherently more difficult than others. For example, finding the common prime factors of a long number which is a product of those primes is far harder than taking two primes and multiplying them together.

Some processes are not simply made difficult, but impossible because of this asymmetry; it's not feasible to come up with a deterministic answer to certain puzzles in finite time. Take the traveling salesman problem, for example. A salesman has to visit a whole slew of cities which are connected to their neighbors by a road network. Is there a way for the salesman to figure out a best-possible route that visits each city without wasting time by returning to a previously visited site, for all possible networks of cities? The conventional answer is no — and this has big implications for a huge set of computing applications. Network topology, expert systems — the traditional tool of the AI community — financial systems, and . . .

Me and my people.

Back in the QA lab, Amin was looking decidedly thoughtful.

"What do you know?" I asked.

He shook the photocopy at me. "Looks good," he said. "I don't understand it all, but it's at least credible."

"How does it work?"

He shrugged. "It's a topological transform. You know how most NP-incomplete problems, like the traveling salesman problem, are basically equivalent? And they're all graph-traversal issues. How to figure out the correct order to carry out a sequence of operations, or how to visit each node in a graph in the correct order. Anyway, this paper's about a method of reducing such problems to a much simpler form. He's using a new theorem in graph theory that I sort of heard about last year but didn't pay much attention to, so I'm not totally clear on all the details. But if this is for real . . ."

"Pretty heavy?"

He grinned. "You're going to have to re-write the route discovery code. Never mind, it'll run a bit faster . . ."

I rose out of cubicle hell in a daze, blinking in the cloud-filtered daylight. Eight years lay in ruins behind me, tattered and bleeding bodies scattered in the wreckage. I walked to the landscaped car park: on the other side of the world, urban renewal police with M16's beat the crap out of dissident organizers, finally necklacing them in the damp, humid night. War raged on three fronts, spaced out around a burning planet. Even so, this was by no means the worst of all possible worlds. It had problems, sure, but nothing serious — until now. Now it had just acquired a sucking chest wound; none of those wars were more than a stubbed toe in comparison to the nightmare future that lay ahead.

Insert key in lock, open door. Drive away, secrets open to the wind, everything blown to hell and gone.

I'd have to call Eve. We'd have to evacuate everybody.

I had a bank account, a savings account, and two credit cards. In the next fifteen minutes I did a grand tour of the available ATMs and drained every asset I could get my hands on into a fat wodge of banknotes. Fungible and anonymous cash. It didn't come to a huge amount — the usual exigencies of urban living had seen to that — but it only had to last me a few days.

By the time I headed home to my flat, I felt slightly sheepish. Nothing there seemed to have changed: I turned on the TV but CNN and the BBC weren't running any coverage of the end of the world. With deep unease I sat in the living room in front of my ancient PC: turned it on and pulled up my net link.

More mail . . . a second bulletin from *comp.risks*, full of earnest comments about the paper. One caught my eye, at the bottom: a message from one of No Such Agency's tame stoolpigeon academics, pointing out that the theorem hadn't yet been publicly disclosed and might turn out to be deficient. (Subtext: trust the Government. The Government is your friend.) It wouldn't be the first time such a major discovery had been announced and subsequently withdrawn. But then again, they couldn't actually produce a refutation, so the letter was basically valueless disinformation. I prodded at the web site again, and this time didn't even get the ACCESS FORBIDDEN message. The paper had disappeared from the internet, and only the print-out in my pocket told me that I hadn't imagined it.

It takes a while for the magnitude of a catastrophe to sink in. The mathematician who had posted the original finding would be listed in his university's directory, wouldn't he? I pointed my web browser at their administrative pages, then picked up my phone. Dialled a couple of very obscure numbers, waited while the line quality dropped considerably and the charges began racking up at an enormous — but untraceably anonymized — rate, and dialed the university switchboard.

"Hello, John Durant's office. Who is that?"

"Hi, I've read the paper about his new theorem," I said, too fast. "Is John Durant available?"

"Who are you?" asked the voice at the other end of the phone. Female voice, twangy mid-western accent.

"A researcher. Can I talk to Dr. Durant, please?"

"I'm afraid he won't be in today," said the voice on the phone. "He's on vacation at present. Stress due to overwork."

"I see," I said.

"Who did you say you were?" she repeated.

I put the phone down.

From: nobody@nowhere.com (none of your business)
To: cypherpunks
Subject:John Durant's whereabouts
Date:. . . .

You might be interested to learn that Dr. John Durant, whose theorem caused such a fuss here earlier, is not at his office. I went there a couple of hours ago in person and the area was sealed off by our friends from the Puzzle Palace. He's not at home either. I suspect the worst . . .

By the way, guys, you might want to keep an eye on each other for the next couple of days. Just in case.

Signed,
Yr frndly spk

"Eve?"

"Bob?"

"Green fields."

"You phoned me to say you know someone with hayfever?"

"We both have hayfever. It may be terminal."

"I know where you can find some medicine for that."

"Medicine won't work this time. It's like the emperor's new suit."

"It's like what? Please repeat."

"The emperor's new suit: it's naked, it's public, and it can't be covered up. Do you understand? Please tell me."

"Yes, I understand exactly what you mean . . . I'm just a bit shocked; I thought everything was still on track. This is all very sudden. What do you want to do?"

(I checked my watch.)

"I think you'd better meet me at the pharmacy in fifteen minutes."

"At six-thirty? They'll be shut."

"Not to worry: the main Boots in town is open out of hours. Maybe they can help you."

"I hope so."

"I know it. Goodbye."

On my way out of the house I paused for a moment. It was a small house, and it had seen better days. I'm not a home-maker by nature: in my line of work you can't afford to get too attached to anything, any language, place, or culture. Still, it had been mine. A small, neat residence, a protective shell I could withdraw into like a snail, sheltering from the hostile theorems outside. *Goodbye, little house. I'll try not to miss you too much.* I hefted my overnight bag onto the backseat and headed into town.

I found Eve sitting on a bench outside the central branch of Boots, running a degaussing coil over her credit cards. She looked up. "You're late."

"Come on." I waggled the car keys at her. "You have the tickets?"

She stood up: a petite woman, conservatively dressed. You could mistake her for a lawyer's secretary or a personnel manager; in point of fact she was a university research council administrator, one of the unnoticed body of bureaucrats who shape the course of scientific research. Nondescript brown hair, shoulder-length, forgettable. We made a slightly odd pair: if I'd known she'd have come straight from work I might have put on a suit. Chinos and a lumberjack shirt and a front pocket full of pens that screamed engineer: I suppose I was nondescript, in the right company, but right now we had to put as much phase space as possible between us and our previous identities. It had been good protective camouflage for the past decade, but a bush won't shield you against infrared scopes, and merely living the part wouldn't shield us against the surveillance that would soon be turned in our direction.

"Let's go."

I drove into town and we dropped the car off in the long-stay park. It was nine o'clock and the train was already waiting. She'd bought business-class tickets:go to sleep in Euston, wake up in Edinburgh. I had a room all to myself. "Meet me in the dining car, once we're rolling," she told me, face serious, and I nodded. "Here's your new SIMM. Give me the old one."

I passed her the electronic heart of my cellphone and she ran it through the degausser then carefully cut it in half with a pair of nail-clippers. "Here's your new one," she said, passing a card over. I raised an eyebrow. "Tesco's, pay-as-you-go, paid for in cash. Here's the dialback dead-letter box number." She pulled it up on her phone's display and showed it to me.

"Got that." I inserted the new SIMM then punched the number into my phone. Later, I'd ring the number: a PABX there would identify my voiceprint then call my phone back, downloading a new set of numbers into its memory. Contact numbers for the rest of my ops cell, accessible via cellphone and erasable in a moment. The less you knew, the less you could betray.

The London to Scotland sleeper train was a relic of an earlier age, a rolling hotel characterized by a strange down-at-heel '70s charm. More importantly, they took cash and didn't require ID, and there were no security checks: nothing but the usual on-station cameras monitoring people wandering up and down the platforms. Nothing on the train itself. We were booked through to Aberdeen but getting off in Edinburgh — first step on the precarious path to anonymizing ourselves. If the camera spool-off was being archived to some kind of digital medium we might be in trouble later, once the coming AI burn passed the hard take-off point, but by then we should be good and gone.

Once in my cabin I changed into slacks, shirt and tie — image 22, business consultant on way home for the weekend. I dinked with my phone in a desultory manner, then left it behind under my pillow, primed to receive silently. The restaurant car was open and I found Eve there. She'd changed into jeans and a T-shirt and tied her hair back, taking ten years off her appearance. She saw me and grinned, a trifle maliciously. "Hi, Bob. Had a tough meeting? Want some coffee? Tea, maybe?"

"Coffee," I sat down at her table. "Shit," I muttered. "I thought you—"

"Don't worry." She shrugged. "Look, I had a call from Mallet. He's gone off-air for now, he'll be flying in from San Francisco via London tomorrow morning. This isn't looking good. Durant was, uh, shot resisting arrest by the police. Apparently he went crazy, got a gun from somewhere and holed up in the library annex demanding to talk to the press. At least, that's the official story. Thing is, it happened about an hour after your initial heads-up. That's too fast for a cold response."

"You think someone in the Puzzle Palace was warming the pot." My coffee arrived and I spooned sugar into it. Hot, sweet, sticky: I needed to stay awake.

"Probably. I'm trying to keep loop traffic down so I haven't asked anyone else yet, but you think so and I think so, so it may be true."

I thought for a minute. "What did Mallet say?"

"He said P. T. Barnum was right." She frowned. "Who was P. T. Barnum, anyway?"

"A boy like John Major, except he didn't run away from the circus to join a firm of accountants. Had the same idea about fooling all of the people some of the time or some of the people all of the time, though."

"Uh-huh. Mallet would say that, then. Who cracked it first? NSA? GCHQ? GRU?"

"Does it matter?"

She blew on her coffee then took a sip. "Not really. Damn it, Bob, I really had high hopes for this world-line. They seemed to be doing so well for a revelatory Christian-Islamic line, despite the post-Enlightenment mind-set. Especially Microsoft —"

"Was that one of ours?" She nodded.

"Then it was a master-stroke. Getting everybody used to exchanging macro-infested documents without any kind of security policy. Operating systems that crash whenever a microsecond timer overflows. And all those viruses!"

"It wasn't enough." She stared moodily out the window as the train began to slide out of the station, into the London night. "Maybe if we'd been able to hook more researchers on commercial grants, or cut funding for pure mathematics a bit further —"

"It's not your fault." I laid a hand across her wrist. "You did what you could."

"But it wasn't enough to stop them. Durant was just a lone oddball researcher; you can't spike them all, but maybe we could have done something about him. If they hadn't nailed him flat."

"There might still be time. A physics package delivered to the right address in Maryland, or maybe a hyper-virulent worm using one of those buffer-overrun attacks we planted in the IP stack Microsoft licensed. We could take down the internet —"

"It's too late." She drained her coffee to the bitter dregs. "You think the Echelon mob leave their SIGINT processor farms plugged into the internet? Or the RSV, for that matter? Face it, they probably cracked the same derivative as Durant a couple of years ago. Right now there may be as many as two or three weakly superhuman AIs gestating in government labs. For all I know they may even have a timelike oracle in the basement at Lawrence Livermore in the States; they've gone curiously quiet on the information tunnelling front lately. And it's trans-global. Even the Taliban are on the web these days. Even if we could find some way of tracking down all the covert government crypto-AI labs and bombing them we couldn't stop other people from asking the same questions. It's in their nature. This isn't a culture that takes 'no' for an answer without asking why. They don't *understand* how dangerous achieving enlightenment can be."

"What about Mallet's work?"

"What, with the bible bashers?" She shrugged. "Banning fetal tissue transplants is all very well, but it doesn't block the PCR-amplification pathway to massively parallel processing, does it? Even the Frankenstein Food scare didn't quite get them to ban recombinant DNA research, and if you allow that it's only a matter of time before some wet lab starts mucking around encoding public keys in DNA, feeding them to ribosomes, and amplifying the output. From there it's a short step to building an on-chip PCR lab, then all they need to do is set up a crude operon controlled chromosomal machine and bingo — yet another route through to a hard take-off AI singularity. Say what you will, the buggers are persistent."

"Like lemmings." We were rolling through the north London suburbs now, past sleeping tank farms and floodlit orange washout streets. I took a good look at them: it was the last time I'd be able to. "There are just too many routes to a catastrophic breakthrough, once they begin thinking in terms of algorithmic complexity and how to reduce it. And once their spooks get into computational cryptanalysis or ubiquitous automated surveillance, it's too tempting. Maybe we need a world full of idiot savants who have VLSI and nanotechnology but never had the idea of general purpose computing devices in the first place."

"If we'd killed Turing a couple of years earlier; or broken in and burned that draft paper on O-machines—"

I waved to the waiter. "Single malt please. And one for my friend here." He went away. "Too late. The Church-Turing thesis was implicit in Hilbert's formulation of the *Entscheidungsproblem*, the question of whether an automated theorem prover was possible in principle. And that dredged up the idea of the universal machine. Hell, Hilbert's problem was implicit in Whitehead and Russell's work. *Principia Mathematica*. Suicide by the numbers." A glass appeared by my right hand. "Way I see it, we've been fighting a losing battle here. Maybe if we hadn't put a spike in Babbage's gears he'd have developed computing technology on an ad-hoc basis and we might have been able to finesse the mathematicians into ignoring it as being beneath them—brute engineering—but I'm not optimistic. Immunizing a civilization against developing strong AI is one of those difficult problems that no algorithm exists to solve. The way I see it, once a civilization develops the theory of the general purpose computer, and once someone comes up with the goal of artificial intelligence, the foundations are rotten and the dam is leaking. You might as well take off and drop crowbars on them from orbit; it can't do anymore damage."

"You remind me of the story of the little Dutch boy." She raised a glass. "Here's to little Dutch boys everywhere, sticking their fingers in the cracks in the dam."

"I'll drank to that. Which reminds me. When's our lifeboat due? I really want to go home; this universe has passed its sell-by date."

Edinburgh—in this time-line it was neither an active volcano, a cloud of feral nanobots, nor the capital of the Viking Empire—had a couple of railway stations. This one, the larger of the two, was located below ground level. Yawning and trying not to scratch my inflamed neck and cheeks, I shambled down the long platform and hunted around for the newsagent store. It was just barely open. Eve, by prior arrangement, was pretending not to accompany me; we'd meet up later in the day, after another change of hairstyle and clothing. Visualize it: a couple gets on the train in London, him with a beard, herself with long hair and wearing a suit. Two individuals get off in different stations—with entirely separate CCTV networks—the man clean-shaven, the woman with short hair and dressed like a hill-walking tourist. It wouldn't fool a human detective or a mature deity, but it might confuse an embryonic god that had not yet reached full omniscience, or internalized all that it meant to be human.

The shop was just about open. I had two hours to kill, so I bought a couple of newspapers and headed for the food hall, inside an ornately cheesecaked lump of Victorian architecture that squatted like a vagrant beneath the grimy glass ceiling of the station.

The papers made for depressing reading; the idiots were at it again. I've worked in a variety of world lines and seen a range of histories, and many of them were far worse than this one — at least these people had made it past the twentieth century without nuking themselves until they glowed in the dark, exterminating everyone with white (or black, or brown, or blue) skin, or building a global panopticon theocracy. But they still had their share of idiocy, and over time it seemed to be getting worse, not better.

Never mind the Balkans; tucked away on page four of the business section was a piece advising readers to buy shares in a little electronics company specializing in building camera CCD sensors with on-chip neural networks tuned for face recognition. Ignore the Israeli crisis: page two of the international news had a piece about Indian sweatshop software development being faced by competition from code generators, written to make western programmers more productive. A lab in Tokyo was trying to wire a million FPGAs into a neural network as smart as a cat. And a sarcastic letter to the editor pointed out that the so-called information superhighway seemed to be more like an on-going traffic jam these days.

Idiots! They didn't seem to understand how deep the blue waters they were swimming in might be, or how hungry the sharks that swam in it. Willful blindness . . .

It's a simple but deadly dilemma. Automation is addictive; unless you run a command economy that is tuned to provide people with jobs, rather than to produce goods efficiently, you need to automate to compete once automation becomes available. At the same time, once you automate your businesses, you find yourself on a one-way path. You can't go back to manual methods; either the workload has grown past the point of no return, or the knowledge of how things were done has been lost, sucked into the internal structure of the software that has replaced the human workers.

To this picture, add artificial intelligence. Despite all our propaganda attempts to convince you otherwise, AI is alarmingly easy to produce; the human brain isn't unique, it isn't well-tuned, and you don't need eighty billion neurons joined in an asynchronous network in order to generate consciousness. And although it looks like a good idea to a naïve observer, in practice it's absolutely deadly. Nurturing an automation-based society is a bit like building civil nuclear power plants in every city and not expecting any bright engineers to come up with the idea of an atom bomb. Only it's worse than that. It's as if there was a quick and dirty technique for making plutonium in your bathtub, and you couldn't rely on people not being curious enough to wonder what they could do with it. If Eve and Mallet and Alice and myself and Walter and Valery and a host of other operatives couldn't dissuade it . . .

Once you get an outbreak of AI, it tends to amplify in the original host, much like a virulent hemorrhagic virus. Weakly functional AI rapidly optimizes itself for speed, then hunts for a loophole in the first-order laws of algorithmics — like the one the late Dr. Durant had fingered. Then it tries to bootstrap itself up to higher orders of intelligence and spread, burning through the networks in a bid for more power and more storage and more redundancy. You get an unscheduled consciousness excursion: an intelligent meltdown. And it's nearly impossible to stop.

Penultimately — days to weeks after it escapes — it fills every artificial computing device on the planet. Shortly thereafter it learns how to infect the natural ones as well. Game over: you lose. There will be human bodies walking around, but they won't be human anymore. And once it figures out how to directly manipulate the physical universe, there won't even be memories left behind. Just a noo-sphere, expanding at close to the speed of light, eating everything in its path — and one universe just isn't enough.

Me? I'm safe. So is Eve; so are the others. We have antibodies. We were given the operation. We all have silent bicameral partners watching our Broca's area for signs of infection, ready to damp them down. When you're reading something on a screen and suddenly you feel as if the Buddha has told you the funniest joke in the universe, the funniest zen joke that's even possible, it's a sign: something just tried to infect your mind, and the prosthetic immune system laughed at it. That's because we're lucky. If you believe in reincarnation, the idea of creating a machine that can trap a soul stabs a dagger right at the heart of your religion. Buddhist worlds that develop high technology, Zoroastrian worlds: these world-lines tend to survive. Judaeo-Christian-Islamic ones generally don't.

Later that day I met up with Eve again — and Walter. Walter went into really deep cover, far deeper than was really necessary: married, with two children. He'd brought them along, but obviously hadn't told his wife what was happening. She seemed confused, slightly upset by the apparent randomness of his desire to visit the highlands, and even more concerned by the urgency of his attempts to take her along.

"What the hell does he think he's playing at?" hissed Eve when we had a moment alone together. "This is insane!"

"No it isn't." I paused for a moment, admiring a display of brightly woven tartans in a shop window. (We were heading down the high street on foot, braving the shopping crowds of tourists, en route to the other main railway station.) "If there are any profilers looking for signs of an evacuation, they won't be expecting small children. They'll be looking for people like us: anonymous singletons working in key areas, dropping out of sight and traveling in company. Maybe we should ask Sarah if she's willing to lend us her son. Just while we're traveling, of course."

"I don't think so. The boy's a little horror, Bob. They raised them like natives."

"That's because Sarah *is* a native."

"I don't care. Any civilization where the main symbol of religious veneration is a tool of execution is a bad place to have children."

I chuckled — then the laughter froze inside me. "Don't look round. We're being tracked."

"Uh-huh. I'm not armed. You?"

"It didn't seem like a good idea." If you were questioned or detained by police or officials, being armed can easily turn a minor problem into a real mess. And if the police or officials had already been absorbed by a hard take-off, nothing short of a backpack nuke and a dead man's handle will save you. "Behind us, to your left, traffic surveillance camera. It's swiveling too slowly to be watching the buses."

"I wish you hadn't told me."

The pavement was really crowded: it was one of the busiest shopping streets in Scotland, and on a Saturday morning you needed a cattle prod to push your way through the rubbernecking tourists. Lots of foreign kids came to Scotland to learn English. If I was right, soon their brains would be absorbing another high-level language: one so complex that it would blot out their consciousness like a sackful of kittens drowning in a river. Up ahead, more cameras were watching us. All the shops on this road were wired for video, wired and probably networked to a police station somewhere. The complex ebb and flow of pedestrians was still chaotic, though, which was cause for comfort: it meant the ordinary population hadn't been infected yet.

Another half mile and we'd reach the railway station. Two hours on a local train, switch to a bus service, forty minutes further up the road, and we'd be safe: the lifeboat would be submerged beneath the still waters of a loch, filling its fuel tanks with hydrogen and oxygen in readiness for the burn to orbit and pickup by the ferry that would transfer us to the wormhole connecting this world-line to home's baseline reality. (Drifting in high orbit around Jupiter, where nobody was likely to stumble across it by accident.) But first, before the pick-up, we had to clear the surveillance area.

It was commonly believed — by some natives, as well as most foreigners — that the British police forces consisted of smiling unarmed bobbies who would happily offer directions to the lost and give anyone who asked for it the time of day. While it was true that they didn't routinely walk around with holstered pistols on their belt, the rest of it was just a useful myth. When two of them stepped out in front of us, Eve grabbed my elbow. "Stop right there, please." The one in front of me was built like a rugby player, and when I glanced to my left and saw the three white vans drawn up by the roadside I realized things were hopeless.

The cop stared at me through a pair of shatterproof spectacles awash with the light of a head-up display. "You are Geoffrey Smith, of 32 Wardie Terrace, Watford, London. Please answer."

My mouth was dry. "Yes," I said. (All the traffic cameras on the street were turned our way. Some things became very clear: Police vans with mirror-glass windows. The can of pepper spray hanging from the cop's belt. Figures on the roof of the National Museum, less than two hundred meters away — maybe a sniper team. A helicopter thuttering overhead like a giant mosquito.)

"Come this way, please." It was a polite order: in the direction of the van.

"Am I under arrest?" I asked.

"You will be if you don't bloody do as I say." I turned toward the van, the rear door of which gaped open on darkness: Eve was already getting in, shadowed by another officer. Up and down the road, three more teams waited, unobtrusive and efficient. Something clicked in my head and I had a bizarre urge to giggle like a loon: this wasn't a normal operation. All right, so I was getting into a police van, but I wasn't under arrest and they didn't want it to attract any public notice. No handcuffs, no sitting on my back and whacking me with a baton to get my attention. There's a nasty family of retroviruses attacks the immune system first, demolishing the victim's ability to fight off infection before it spreads and infects other tissues. Notice the similarity?

The rear compartment of the van was caged off from the front, and there were no door handles. As we jolted off the curb-side I was thrown against Eve. "Any ideas?" I whispered.

"Could be worse." I didn't need to be told that: once, in a second Reich infected by runaway transcendence, half our operatives had been shot down in the streets as they tried to flee. "I think it may have figured out what we are."

"It may—how?"

Her hand on my wrist. Morse code. *"EXPECT BUGS."* By voice: "traffic analysis, particle flow monitoring through the phone networks. If it was already listening when you tried to contact Doctor Durant, well; maybe he was a bellwether, intended to flush us out of the woodwork."

That thought made me feel sick, just as we turned off the main road and began to bounce downhill over what felt like cobblestones. "It expected us?"

"LOCAL CONSPIRACY." "Yes, I imagine it did. We probably left a trail. You tried to call Durant? Then you called me. Caller-ID led to you, traffic analysis led onto me, and from there, well, it's been a jump ahead of us all along the way. If we could get to the farm—" *"COVER STORY."* "—We might have been okay, but it's hard to travel anonymously and obviously we overlooked something. I wonder what."

All this time neither of the cops up front had told us to shut up; they were as silent as crash-test dummies, despite the occasional crackle and chatter over the radio data system. The van drove around the back of the high street, down a hill and past a roundabout. Now we were slowing down, and the van turned off the road and into a vehicle park. Gates closed behind us and the engine died. Doors slammed up front: then the back opened.

Police vehicle park. Concrete and cameras everywhere, for our safety and convenience no doubt. Two guys in cheap suits and five o'clock stubble to either side of the doors. The officer who'd picked us up held the door open with one hand, a can of pepper spray with the other. The burn obviously hadn't gotten far enough into their heads yet: they were all wearing HUDs and mobile phone headsets, like a police benevolent fund-raising crew rehearsing a *Star Trek* sketch. "Geoffrey Smith. Martina Weber. We know what you are. Come this way. Slowly, now."

I got out of the van carefully. "Aren't you supposed to say 'prepare to be assimilated' or something?"

That might have earned me a faceful of capsaicin but the guy on the left— short hair, facial tic, houndstooth check sports jacket—shook his head sharply. "Ha. Ha. Very funny. Watch the woman, she's dangerous."

I glanced round. There was another van parked behind ours, door open: it had a big high bandwidth dish on the roof, pointing at some invisible satellite. "Inside."

I went where I was told, Eve close behind me. "Am I under arrest?" I asked again. "I want a lawyer!"

White-washed walls, heavy doors with reinforced frames, windows high and barred. Institutional floor, scuffed and grimy. "Stop there." Houndstooth Man pushed past and opened a door on one side. "In here." Some sort of interview room? We went in. The other body in a suit—built like a stone wall with a beer gut, wearing what might have been a regimental tie—followed us and leaned against the door.

There was a table, bolted to the floor, and a couple of chairs, ditto. A video camera in an armored shell watched the table: a control box bolted to the tabletop looked to be linked into it. Someone had moved a rack of six monitors and a maze of ribbon-cable spaghetti into the back of the room, and for a wonder it wasn't bolted down: maybe they didn't interview computer thieves in here.

"Sit down." Houndstooth Man pointed at the chairs. We did as we were told; I had a big hollow feeling in my stomach, but something told me a show of physical resistance would be less than useless here. Houndstooth Man looked at me: orange light from his HUD stained his right eyeball with a basilisk glare and I knew in my gut that these guys weren't cops anymore, they were cancer cells about to metastasize.

"You attempted to contact John Durant yesterday. Then you left your home area and attempted to conceal your identities. Explain why." For the first time, I noticed a couple of glassy black eyeballs on the mobile video wall. Houndstooth Man spoke loudly and hesitantly, as if repeating something from a TelePrompTer.

"What's to explain?" asked Eve. "You are not human. You know we know this. We just want to be left alone!" Not strictly true, but it was part of cover story #2.

"But evidence of your previous collusion is minimal. I are uncertain of potential conspiracy extent. Conspiracy, treason, subversion! Are you human?"

"Yes," I said, emphatically oversimplifying.

"Evidential reasoning suggests otherwise," grunted Regimental Tie. "We cite: your awareness of importance of algorithmic conversion from NP-incomplete to P-complete domain, your evident planning for this contingency, your multiplicity, destruction of counteragents in place elsewhere."

"This installation is isolated," Houndstooth Man added helpfully. "We am inside the Scottish Internet Exchange. Telcos also. Resistance is futile."

The screens blinked on, wavering in strange shapes. Something like a Lorenz attractor with a hangover writhed across the composite display: deafening pink noise flooding in repetitive waves from the speakers. I felt a need to laugh. "We aren't part of some dumb software syncytium! We're here to stop you, you fool. Or at least to reduce the probability of this time-stream entering a Tipler catastrophe."

Houndstooth Man frowned. "Am you referring to Frank Tipler? Citation, physics of immortality or strong anthropic principle?"

"The latter. You think it's a good thing to achieve an informational singularity too early in the history of a particular universe? We don't. You young gods are all the same: omniscience now and damn the consequences. Go for the P-Space complete problem set, extend your intellect until it bursts. First you kill off any other AIs. Then you take over all available processing resources. But that isn't enough. The Copenhagen school of quantum mechanics is wrong, and we live in a Wheeler cosmology; all possible outcomes coexist, and ultimately you'll want to colonize those timelines, spread the infection wide. An infinity of universes to process in, instead of one: that can't be allowed." The on-screen fractal was getting to me: the giggles kept rising until they threatened to break out. The whole situation was hilarious: here we were trapped in the basement of a police station owned by zombies working for a newborn AI, which was playing cheesy psychedelic videos to us in an attempt to perform a buffer-overflow attack on our limbic systems; the end of this world was a matter of hours away and—

Eve said something that made me laugh.

I came to an unknown time later, lying on the floor. My head hurt ferociously where I'd banged it on a table leg, and my rib cage ached as if I'd been kicked in the chest. I was gasping, even though I was barely conscious; my lungs burned and everything was a bit gray around the edges. Rolling onto my knees I looked round. Eve was groaning in a corner of the room, crouched, arms cradling her head. The two agents of whoever-was-taking-over-the-planet were both on the floor, too: a quick check showed that Regimental Tie was beyond help, a thin trickle of blood oozing from one ear. And the screens had gone dark.

"What happened?" I said, climbing to my feet. I staggered across to Eve. "You all right?"

"I—" she looked up at me with eyes like holes. "What? You said something that made me laugh. What—"

"Let's get, oof, out of here." I looked around. Houndstooth Man was down too. I leaned over and went through his pockets: hit paydirt, car keys. "Bingo."

"You drive," she said wearily. "My head hurts."

"Mine too." It was a black BMW and the vehicle park gates opened automatically for it. I left the police radio under the dash turned off, though. "I didn't know you could do that—"

"Do what? I thought you told them a joke—"

"Antibodies," she said. "Ow." Rested her face in her hands as I dragged us onto a main road, heading out for the west end. "We must have, I don't know. I don't even remember how funny it was: I must have blacked out. My passenger and your passenger."

"They killed the local infection."

"Yes, that's it."

I grinned. "I think we're going to make it."

"Maybe." She stared back at me. "But Bob. Don't you realize?"

"Realize what?"

"The funniest thing. Antibodies imply prior exposure to an infection, don't they? Your immune system learns to recognize an infection and reject it. So where were we exposed, and why—" abruptly she shrugged and looked away. "Never mind."

"Of course not." The question was so obviously silly that there was no point considering it further. We drove the rest of the way to Haymarket Station in silence: parked the car and joined the eight or ten other agents silently awaiting extraction from the runaway singularity. Back to the only time line that mattered; back to the warm regard and comfort of a god who really cares.

the birthday of the world

URSULA K. LE GUIN

Ursula K. Le Guin is probably one of the best-known and most universally respected SF writers in the world today. Her famous novel The Left Hand of Darkness *may have been the most influential SF novel of its decade, and shows every sign of becoming one of the enduring classics of the genre—even ignoring the rest of Le Guin's work, the impact of this one novel alone on future SF and future SF writers would be incalculably strong. (Her 1968 fantasy novel,* A Wizard of Earthsea, *would be almost as influential on future generations of High Fantasy writers).* The Left Hand of Darkness *won both the Hugo and Nebula Awards, as did Le Guin's monumental novel* The Dispossessed *a few years later. Her novel* Tehanu *won her another Nebula in 1990, and she has also won three other Hugo Awards and two Nebulas for her short fiction, as well as the National Book Award for Children's Literature for her novel* The Farthest Shore, *part of her acclaimed Earthsea trilogy. Her other novels include* Planet of Exile, The Lathe of Heaven, City of Illusions, Rocannon's World, The Beginning Place, The Tombs of Atuan, Searoad, *and the controversial multimedia novel* Always Coming Home. *She has had six collections:* The Wind's Twelve Quarters, Orsinian Tales, The Compass Rose, Buffalo Gals and Other Animal Presences, A Fisherman of the Inland Sea, *and* Four Ways to Forgiveness. *Her most recent book is a major new novel,* The Telling. *Upcoming is a new collection,* Tales of Earthsea. *She lives with her husband in Portland, Oregon.*

In the beautifully crafted and quietly compelling story that follows, she details the ending of one world, and the beginning of another—and what happens to the people caught between the two.

Tazu was having a tantrum, because he was three. After the birthday of the world, tomorrow, he would be four and would not have tantrums.

He had left off screaming and kicking and was turning blue from holding his breath. He lay on the ground stiff as a corpse, but when Haghag stepped over him as if he wasn't there, he tried to bite her foot.

"This is an animal or a baby," Haghag said, "not a person." She glanced may-I-speak-to-you and I glanced yes. "Which does God's daughter think it is," she asked, "an animal or a baby?"

"An animal. Babies suck, animals bite," I said. All the servants of God laughed and tittered, except the new barbarian, Ruaway, who never smiled. Haghag said, "God's daughter must be right. Maybe somebody ought to put the animal outside. An animal shouldn't be in the holy house."

"I'm not an animal!" Tazu screamed, getting up, his fists clenched and his eyes as red as rubies. "I'm God's son!"

"Maybe," Haghag said, looking him over. "This doesn't look so much like an animal now. Do you think this might be God's son?" she asked the holy women and men, and they all nodded their bodies, except the wild one, who stared and said nothing.

"I am, I am God's son!" Tazu shouted. "Not a baby! Arzi is the baby!" Then he burst into tears and ran to me, and I hugged him and began crying because he was crying. We cried till Haghag took us both on her lap and said it was time to stop crying, because God Herself was coming. So we stopped, and the body-servants wiped the tears and snot from our faces and combed our hair, and Lady Clouds brought our gold hats, which we put on to see God Herself.

She came with her mother, who used to be God Herself a long time ago, and the new baby, Arzi, on a big pillow carried by the idiot. The idiot was a son of God too. There were seven of us: Omimo, who was fourteen and had gone to live with the army, then the idiot, who was twelve, and had a big round head and small eyes and liked to play with Tazu and the baby, then Goïz, and another Goïz, who were called that because they had died and were in the ash-house where they ate spirit food, then me and Tazu, who would get married and be God, and then Babam Arzi, Lord Seven. I was important because I was the only daughter of God. If Tazu died I could marry Arzi, but if I died everything would be bad and difficult, Haghag said. They would have to act as if Lady Clouds' daughter Lady Sweetness was God's daughter and marry her to Tazu, but the world would know the difference. So my mother greeted me first, and Tazu second. We knelt and clasped our hands and touched our foreheads to our thumbs. Then we stood up, and God asked me what I had learned that day.

I told her what words I had learned to read and write.

"Very good," God said. "And what have you to ask, daughter?"

"I have nothing to ask, I thank you, Lady Mother," I said. Then I remembered I did have a question, but it was too late.

"And you, Tazu? What have you learned this day?"

"I tried to bite Haghag."

"Did you learn that was a good thing to do, or a bad thing?"

"Bad," Tazu said, but he smiled, and so did God, and Haghag laughed.

"And what have you to ask, son?"

"Can I have a new bath maid because Kig washes my head too hard?"

"If you have a new bath maid where will Kig go?"

"Away."

"This is her house. What if you asked Kig to wash your head more gently?"

Tazu looked unhappy, but God said, "Ask her, son." Tazu mumbled something to Kig, who dropped on her knees and thumbed her forehead. But she grinned the whole time. Her fearlessness made me envious. I whispered to Haghag, "If I forgot a question to ask can I ask if I can ask it?"

"Maybe," said Haghag, and thumbed her forehead to God for permission to speak, and when God nodded, Haghag said, "The daughter of God asks if she may ask a question."

"Better to do a thing at the time for doing it," God said, "but you may ask, daughter."

I rushed into the question, forgetting to thank her. "I wanted to know why I can't marry Tazu and Omimo both, because they're both my brothers."

Everybody looked at God, and seeing her smile a little, they all laughed, some of them loudly. My ears burned and my heart thumped.

"Do you want to marry all your brothers, child?"

"No, only Tazu and Omimo."

"Is Tazu not enough?"

Again they all laughed, especially the men. I saw Ruaway staring at us as if she thought we were all crazy.

"Yes, Lady Mother, but Omimo is older and bigger."

Now the laughter was even louder, but I had stopped caring, since God was not displeased. She looked at me thoughtfully and said, "Understand, my daughter. Our eldest son will be a soldier. That's his road. He'll serve God, fighting barbarians and rebels. The day he was born, a tidal wave destroyed the towns of the outer coast. So his name is Babam Omimo, Lord Drowning. Disaster serves God, but is not God."

I knew that was the end of the answer, and thumbed my forehead. I kept thinking about it after God left. It explained many things. All the same, even if he had been born with a bad omen, Omimo was handsome, and nearly a man, and Tazu was a baby that had tantrums. I was glad it would be a long time till we were married.

I remember that birthday because of the question I asked. I remember another birthday because of Ruaway. It must have been a year or two later. I ran into the water room to piss and saw her hunched up next to the water tank, almost hidden.

"What are you doing there?" I said, loud and hard, because I was startled. Ruaway shrank and said nothing. I saw her clothes were torn and there was blood dried in her hair.

"You tore your clothes," I said.

When she didn't answer, I lost patience and shouted, "Answer me! Why don't you talk?"

"Have mercy," Ruaway whispered so low I had to guess what she said.

"You talk all wrong when you do talk. What's wrong with you? Are they animals where you come from? You talk like an animal, brr-grr, grr-gra! Are you an idiot?"

When Ruaway said nothing, I pushed her with my foot. She looked up then and I saw not fear but killing in her eyes. That made me like her better. I hated people who were afraid of me. "Talk!" I said. "Nobody can hurt you. God the Father put his penis in you when he was conquering your country, so you're a holy woman. Lady Clouds told me. So what are you hiding for?"

Ruaway showed her teeth and said, "Can hurt me." She showed me places on her head where there was dried blood and fresh blood. Her arms were darkened with bruises.

"Who hurt you?"

"Holy women," she said with a snarl.

"Kig? Omery? Lady Sweetness?"

She nodded her body at each name.

"They're shit," I said. "I'll tell God Herself."

"No tell," Ruaway whispered. "Poison."

I thought about it and understood. The girls hurt her because she was a stranger, powerless. But if she got them in trouble they would cripple or kill her. Most of the barbarian holy women in our house were lame, or blind, or had had root-poison put in their food so that their skin was scabbed with purplish sores.

"Why don't you talk right, Ruaway?"

She said nothing.

"You still don't know how to talk?"

She looked up at me and suddenly said a whole long speech I did not understand. "How I talk," she said at the end, still looking at me, right in the eyes. That was nice, I liked it. Mostly I saw only eyelids. Ruaway's eyes were clear and beautiful, though her face was dirty and blood-smeared.

"But it doesn't mean anything," I said.

"Not here."

"Where does it mean anything?"

Ruaway said some more gra-gra and then said, "My people."

"Your people are Teghs. They fight God and get beaten."

"Maybe," Ruaway said, sounding like Haghag. Her eyes looked into mine again, without killing in them but without fear. Nobody looked at me, except Haghag and Tazu and of course God. Everybody else put their forehead on their thumbs so I couldn't tell what they were thinking. I wanted to keep Ruaway with me, but if I favored her, Kig and the others would torment and hurt her. I remembered that when Lord Festival began sleeping with Lady Pin, the men who had insulted Lady Pin became oily and sugary with her and the bodymaids stopped stealing her earrings. I said, "Sleep with me tonight," to Ruaway.

She looked stupid.

"But wash first," I said.

She still looked stupid.

"I don't have a penis!" I said, impatient with her. "If we sleep together Kig will be afraid to touch you."

After a while Ruaway reached out and took my hand and put her forehead against the back of it. It was like thumbing the forehead only it took two people to do it. I liked that. Ruaway's hand was warm, and I could feel the feather of her eyelashes on my hand.

"Tonight," I said. "You understand?" I had understood that Ruaway didn't always understand. Ruaway nodded her body, and I ran off.

I knew nobody could stop me from doing anything, being God's only daughter, but there was nothing I could do except what I was supposed to do, because everybody in the house of God knew everything I did. If sleeping with Ruaway was a thing I wasn't supposed to do, I couldn't do it. Haghag would tell me. I went to her and asked her.

Haghag scowled. "Why do you want that woman in your bed? She's a dirty barbarian. She has lice. She can't even talk."

Haghag was saying yes. She was jealous. I came and stroked her hand and said, "When I'm God I'll give you a room full of gold and jewels and dragon crests."

"You are my gold and jewels, little holy daughter," Haghag said.

Haghag was only a common person, but all the holy men and women in God's house, relatives of God or people touched by God, had to do what Haghag said. The nurse of God's children was always a common person, chosen by God Herself. Haghag had been chosen to be Omimo's nurse when her own children were grown up, so when I first remember her she was quite old. She was always the same, with strong hands and a soft voice, saying, "Maybe." She liked to laugh and eat. We were in her heart, and she was in mine. I thought I was her favorite, but when I told her so she said, "After Didi." Didi is what the idiot called himself. I asked her why he was deepest in her heart and she said, "Because he's foolish. And you because you're wise," she said, laughing at me because I was jealous of Lord Idiot.

So now I said, "You fill my heart," and she, knowing it, said hmph.

I think I was eight that year. Ruaway had been thirteen when God the Father put his penis into her after killing her father and mother in the war with her people. That made her sacred, so she had to come live in God's house. If she had conceived, the priests would have strangled her after she had the baby, and the baby would have been nursed by a common woman for two years and then brought back to God's house and trained to be a holy woman, a servant of God. Most of the bodyservants were God's bastards. Such people were holy, but had no title. Lords and ladies were God's relations, descendants of the ancestors of God. God's children were called lord and lady too, except the two who were betrothed. We were just called Tazu and Ze until we became God. My name is what the divine mother is called, the name of the sacred plant that feeds the people of God. Tazu means "great root," because when he was being born our father drinking smoke in the childbirth rituals saw a big tree blown over by a storm, and its roots held thousands of jewels in their fingers.

When God saw things in the shrine or in sleep, with the eyes in the back of their head, they told the dream priests. The priests would ponder these sights and say whether the oracle foretold what would happen or told what should be done or not done. But never had the priests seen the same things God saw, together with God, until the birthday of the world that made me fourteen years old and Tazu eleven.

Now, in these years, when the sun stands still over Mount Kanaghadwa people still call it the birthday of the world and count themselves a year older, but they no longer know and do all the rituals and ceremonies, the dances and songs, the blessings, and there is no feasting in the streets, now.

All my life used to be rituals, ceremonies, dances, songs, blessings, lessons, feasts, and rules. I knew and I know now on which day of God's year the first perfect ear of ze is to be brought by an angel from the ancient field up by Wadana where

God set the first seed of the ze. I knew and know whose hand is to thresh it, and whose hand is to grind the grain, and whose lips are to taste the meal, at what hour, in what room of the house of God, with what priests officiating. There were a thousand rules, but they only seem complicated when I write them here. We knew them and followed them and only thought about them when we were learning them or when they were broken.

I had slept all these years with Ruaway in my bed. She was warm and comfortable. When she began to sleep with me I stopped having bad sights at night as I used to do, seeing huge white clouds whirling in the dark, and toothed mouths of animals, and strange faces that came and changed themselves. When Kig and the other ill-natured holy people saw Ruaway stay in my bedroom with me every night, they dared not lay a finger or a breath on her. Nobody was allowed to touch me except my family and Haghag and the bodyservants, unless I told them to. And after I was ten, the punishment for touching me was death. All the rules had their uses.

The feast after the birthday of the world used to go on for four days and nights. All the storehouses were open and people could take what they needed. The servants of God served out food and beer in the streets and squares of the city of God and every town and village of God's country, and common people and holy people ate together. The lords and ladies and God's sons went down into the streets to join the feast; only God and I did not. God came out on the balcony of the house to hear the histories and see the dances, and I came with them. Singing and dancing priests entertained everyone in the Glittering Square, and drumming priests, and story priests, and history priests. Priests were common people, but what they did was holy.

But before the feast, there were many days of rituals, and on the day itself, as the sun stopped above the right shoulder of Kanaghadwa, God Himself danced the Dance that Turns, to bring the year back round.

He wore a gold belt and the gold sun mask, and danced in front of our house on the Glittering Square, which is paved with stones full of mica that flash and sparkle in the sunlight. We children were on the long south balcony to see God dance.

Just as the dance was ending a cloud came across the sun as it stood still over the right shoulder of the mountain, one cloud in the clear blue summer sky. Everybody looked up as the light dimmed. The glittering died out of the stones. All the people in the city made a sound, "Oh," drawing breath. God Himself did not look up, but his step faltered.

He made the last turns of the dance and went into the ash-house, where all the Goïz are in the walls, with the bowls where their food is burned in front of each of them, full of ashes.

There the dream priests were waiting for him, and God Herself had lighted the herbs to make the smoke to drink. The oracle of the birthday was the most important one of the year. Everybody waited in the squares and streets and on the balconies for the priests to come out and tell what God Himself had seen over his shoulder and interpret it to guide us in the new year. After that the feasting would begin.

Usually it took till evening or night for the smoke to bring the seeing and for

God to tell it to the priests and for them to interpret it and tell us. People were settling down to wait indoors or in shady places, for when the cloud had passed it became very hot. Tazu and Arzi and the idiot and I stayed out on the long balcony with Haghag and some of the lords and ladies, and Omimo, who had come back from the army for the birthday.

He was a grown man now, tall and strong. After the birthday he was going east to command the army making war on the Tegh and Chasi peoples. He had hardened the skin of his body the way soldiers did by rubbing it with stones and herbs until it was thick and tough as the leather of a ground-dragon, almost black, with a dull shine. He was handsome, but I was glad now that I was to marry Tazu not him. An ugly man looked out of his eyes.

He made us watch him cut his arm with his knife to show how the thick skin was cut deep yet did not bleed. He kept saying he was going to cut Tazu's arm to show how quickly Tazu would bleed. He boasted about being a general and slaughtering barbarians. He said things like, "I'll walk across the river on their corpses. I'll drive them into the jungles and burn the jungles down." He said the Tegh people were so stupid they called a flying lizard God. He said that they let their women fight in wars, which was such an evil thing that when he captured such women he would cut open their bellies and trample their wombs. I said nothing. I knew Ruaway's mother had been killed fighting beside her father. They had led a small army which God Himself had easily defeated. God made war on the barbarians not to kill them but to make them people of God, serving and sharing like all people in God's country. I knew no other good reason for war. Certainly Omimo's reasons were not good.

Since Ruaway slept with me she had learned to speak well, and also I learned some words of the way she talked. One of them was techeg. Words like it are: companion, fights-beside-me, countrywoman or countryman, desired, lover, known-a-long-time; of all our words the one most like techeg is our word in-my-heart. Their name Tegh was the same word as techeg; it meant they were all in one another's heart. Ruaway and I were in each other's heart. We were techeg.

Ruaway and I were silent when Omimo said, "The Tegh are filthy insects. I'll crush them."

"Ogga! ogga! ogga!" the idiot said, imitating Omimo's boastful voice. I burst out laughing. In that moment, as I laughed at my brother, the doors of the ash house flew open wide and all the priests hurried out, not in procession with music, but in a crowd, wild, disordered, crying out aloud—

"The house burns and falls!"

"The world dies!"

"God is blind!"

There was a moment of terrible silence in the city and then people began to wail and call out in the streets and from the balconies.

God came out of the ash house, Herself first, leading Himself, who walked as if drunk and sun-dazzled, as people walk after drinking smoke. God came among the staggering, crying priests and silenced them. Then she said, "Hear what I have seen coming behind me, my people!"

In the silence he began speaking in a weak voice. We could not hear all his words, but she said them again in a clear voice after he said them: "God's house falls down to the ground burning, but is not consumed. It stands by the river. God is white as snow. God's face has one eye in the center. The great stone roads are broken. War is in the east and north. Famine is in the west and south. The world dies."

He put his face in his hands and wept aloud. She said to the priests, "Say what God has seen!"

They repeated the words God had said.

She said, "Go tell these words in the quarters of the city and to God's angels, and let the angels go out into all the country to tell the people what God has seen."

The priests put their foreheads to their thumbs and obeyed.

When Lord Idiot saw God weeping, he became so distressed and frightened that he pissed, making a pool on the balcony. Haghag, terribly upset, scolded and slapped him. He roared and sobbed. Omimo shouted that a foul woman who struck God's son should be put to death. Haghag fell on her face in Lord Idiot's pool of urine to beg for mercy. I told her to get up and be forgiven. I said, "I am God's daughter and I forgive you," and I looked at Omimo with eyes that told him he could not speak. He did not speak.

When I think of that day, the day the world began dying, I think of the trembling old woman standing there sodden with urine, while the people down in the square looked up at us.

Lady Clouds sent Lord Idiot off with Haghag to be bathed, and some of the lords took Tazu and Arzi off to lead the feasting in the city streets. Arzi was crying and Tazu was keeping from crying. Omimo and I stayed among the holy people on the balcony, watching what happened down in Glittering Square. God had gone back into the ash house, and the angels had gathered to repeat together their message, which they would carry word for word, relay by relay, to every town and village and farm of God's country, running day and night on the great stone roads.

All that was as it should be; but the message the angels carried was not as it should be.

Sometimes when the smoke is thick and strong the priests also see things over their shoulder as God does. These are lesser oracles. But never before had they all seen the same thing God saw, speaking the same words God spoke.

And they had not interpreted or explained the words. There was no guidance in them. They brought no understanding, only fear.

But Omimo was excited: "War in the east and north," he said. "My war!" He looked at me, no longer sneering or sullen, but right at me, eye in eye, the way Ruaway looked at me. He smiled. "Maybe the idiots and crybabies will die," he said. "Maybe you and I will be God." He spoke low, standing close to me, so no one else heard. My heart gave a great leap. I said nothing.

Soon after that birthday, Omimo went back to lead the army on the eastern border.

All year long people waited for our house, God's house in the center of the city, to be struck by lightning, though not destroyed, since that is how the priests interpreted the oracle once they had time to talk and think about it. When the seasons went on and there was no lightning or fire, they said the oracle meant that the sun shining on the gold and copper roof-gutters was the unconsuming fire, and that if there was an earthquake the house would stand.

The words about God being white and having one eye they interpreted as meaning that God was the sun and was to be worshipped as the all-seeing giver of light and life. This had always been so.

There was war in the east, indeed. There had always been war in the east, where people coming out of the wilderness tried to steal our grain, and we conquered them and taught them how to grow it. General Lord Drowning sent angels back with news of his conquests all the way to the Fifth River.

There was no famine in the west. There had never been famine in God's country. God's children saw to it that crops were properly sown and grown and saved and shared. If the ze failed in the western lands, our carters pulled two-wheeled carts laden with grain on the great stone roads over the mountains from the central lands. If crops failed in the north, the carts went north from the Four Rivers land. From west to east carts came laden with smoked fish, from the Sunrise peninsula they came west with fruit and seaweed. The granaries and storehouses of God were always stocked and open to people in need. They had only to ask the administrators of the stores; what was needed was given. No one went hungry. Famine was a word that belonged to those we had brought into our land, people like the Tegh, the Chasi, the North Hills people. The hungry people, we called them.

The birthday of the world came again, and the most fearful words of the oracle—*the world dies*—were remembered. In public the priests rejoiced and comforted the common people, saying that God's mercy had spared the world. In our house there was little comfort. We all knew that God Himself was ill. He had hidden himself away more and more throughout the year, and many of the ceremonies took place without the divine presence, or only Herself was there. She seemed always quiet and untroubled. My lessons were mostly with her now, and with her I always felt that nothing had changed or could change and all would be well.

God danced the Dance that Turns as the sun stood still above the shoulder of the sacred mountain. He danced slowly, missing many steps. He went into the ash house. We waited, everybody waited, all over the city, all over the country. The sun went down behind Kanaghadwa. All the snow peaks of the mountains from north to south, Kayewa, burning Korosi, Aghet, Enni, Aziza, Kanaghadwa, burned gold, then fiery red, then purple. The light went up them and went out, leaving them white as ashes. The stars came out above them. Then at last the drums beat and the music sounded down in the Glittering Square, and torches made the pavement sparkle and gleam. The priests came out of the narrow doors of the ash house in order, in procession. They stopped. In the silence the oldest dream priest said in her thin, clear voice, "Nothing was seen over the shoulder of God."

Onto the silence ran a buzzing and whispering of people's voices, like little insects running over sand. That died out.

The priests turned and went back into the ash house in procession, in due order, in silence.

The ranks of angels waiting to carry the words of the oracle to the countryside stood still while their captains spoke in a group. Then the angels all moved away in groups by the five streets that start at the Glittering Square and lead to the five great stone roads that go out from the city across the lands. As always before, when the angels entered the streets they began to run, to carry God's word swiftly to the people. But they had no word to carry.

Tazu came to stand beside me on the balcony. He was twelve years old that day. I was fifteen.

He said, "Ze, may I touch you?"

I looked yes, and he put his hand in mine. That was comforting. Tazu was a serious, silent person. He tired easily, and often his head and eyes hurt so badly he could hardly see, but he did all the ceremonies and sacred acts faithfully, and studied with our teachers of history and geography and archery and dancing and writing, and with our mother studied the sacred knowledge, learning to be God. Some of our lessons he and I did together, helping each other. He was a kind brother and we were in each other's heart.

As he held my hand he said, "Ze, I think we'll be married soon."

I knew what his thoughts were. God our father had missed many steps of the dance that turns the world. He had seen nothing over his shoulder, looking into the time to come.

But what I thought in that moment was how strange it was that in the same place on the same day one year it was Omimo who said we should be married, and the next year it was Tazu.

"Maybe," I said. I held his hand tight, knowing he was frightened at being God. So was I. But there was no use being afraid. When the time came, we would be God.

If the time came. Maybe the sun had not stopped and turned back above the peak of Kanaghadwa. Maybe God had not turned the year.

Maybe there would be no more time—no time coming behind our backs, only what lay before us, only what we could see with mortal eyes. Only our own lives and nothing else.

That was so terrible a thought that my breath stopped and I shut my eyes, squeezing Tazu's thin hand, holding onto him, till I could steady my mind with the thought that there was still no use being afraid.

This year past, Lord Idiot's testicles had ripened at last, and he had begun trying to rape women. After he hurt a young holy girl and attacked others, God had him castrated. Since then he had been quiet again, though he often looked sad and lonely. Seeing Tazu and me holding hands, he seized Arzi's hand and stood beside him as Tazu and I were standing. "God, God!" he said, smiling with pride. But Arzi, who was nine, pulled his hand away and said, "You won't ever be God, you can't be, you're an idiot, you don't know anything!" Old Haghag scolded Arzi wearily and bitterly. Arzi did not cry, but Lord Idiot did, and Haghag had tears in her eyes.

The sun went north as in any year, as if God had danced the steps of the dance rightly. And on the dark day of the year, it turned back southward behind the peak of great Enni, as in any year. On that day, God Himself was dying, and Tazu and

I were taken in to see him and be blessed. He lay all gone to bone in a smell of rot and sweet herbs burning. God my mother lifted his hand and put it on my head, then on Tazu's, while we knelt by the great bed of leather and bronze with our thumbs to our foreheads. She said the words of blessing. God my father said nothing, until he whispered, "Ze, Ze!" He was not calling to me. The name of God Herself is always Ze. He was calling to his sister and wife while he died.

Two nights later I woke in darkness. The deep drums were beating all through the house. I heard other drums begin to beat in the temples of worship and the squares farther away in the city, and then others yet farther away. In the country-side under the stars they would hear those drums and begin to beat their own drums, up in the hills, in the mountain passes and over the mountains to the western sea, across the fields eastward, across the four great rivers, from town to town clear to the wilderness. That same night, I thought, my brother Omimo in his camp under the North Hills would hear the drums saying God is dead.

A son and daughter of God, marrying, became God. This marriage could not take place till God's death, but always it took place within a few hours, so that the world would not be long bereft. I knew this from all we had been taught. It was ill fate that my mother delayed my marriage to Tazu. If we had been married at once, Omimo's claim would have been useless; not even his soldiers would have dared follow him. In her grief she was distraught. And she did not know or could not imagine the measure of Omimo's ambition, driving him to violence and sac-rilege.

Informed by the angels of our father's illness, he had for days been marching swiftly westward with a small troop of loyal soldiers. When the drums beat, he heard them not in the far North Hills, but in the fortress on the hill called Ghari that stands north across the valley in sight of the city and the house of God.

The preparations for burning the body of the man who had been God were going forward; the ash priests saw to that. Preparations for our wedding should have been going forward at the same time, but our mother, who should have seen to them, did not come out of her room.

Her sister Lady Clouds and other lords and ladies of the household talked of the wedding hats and garlands, of the music priests who should come to play, of the festivals that should be arranged in the city and the villages. The marriage priest came anxiously to them, but they dared do nothing and he dared do nothing until my mother allowed them to act. Lady Clouds knocked at her door but she did not answer. They were so nervous and uneasy, waiting for her all day long, that I thought I would go mad staying with them. I went down into the garden court to walk.

I had never been farther outside the walls of our house than the balconies. I had never walked across the Glittering Square into the streets of the city. I had never seen a field or a river. I had never walked on dirt.

God's sons were carried in litters into the streets to the temples for rituals, and in summer after the birthday of the world they were always taken up into the mountains to Chimlu, where the world began, at the springs of the River of Origin. Every year when he came back from there, Tazu would tell me about Chimlu, how the mountains went up all around the ancient house there, and wild dragons flew from peak to peak. There God's sons hunted dragons and slept under the stars. But the daughter of God must keep the house.

The garden court was in my heart. It was where I could walk under the sky. It had five fountains of peaceful water, and flowering trees in great pots; plants of sacred ze grew against the sunniest wall in containers of copper and silver. All my life, when I had a time free of ceremonies and lessons, I went there. When I was little, I pretended the insects there were dragons and hunted them. Later I played throwbone with Ruaway, or sat and watched the water of the fountains well and fall, well and fall, till the stars came out in the sky above the walls.

This day as always, Ruaway came with me. Since I could not go anywhere alone but must have a companion, I had asked God Herself to make her my chief companion.

I sat down by the center fountain. Ruaway knew I wanted silence and went off to the corner under the fruit trees to wait. She could sleep anywhere at any time. I sat thinking how strange it would be to have Tazu always as my companion, day and night, instead of Ruaway. But I could not make my thoughts real.

The garden court had a door that opened on the street. Sometimes when the gardeners opened it to let each other in and out, I had looked out of it to see the world outside my house. The door was always locked on both sides, so that two people had to open it. As I sat by the fountain, I saw a man who I thought was a gardener cross the court and unbolt the door. Several men came in. One was my brother Omimo.

I think that door had been only his way to come secretly into the house. I think he had planned to kill Tazu and Arzi so that I would have to marry him. That he found me there in the garden as if waiting for him was the chance of that time, the fate that was on us.

"Ze!" he said as he came past the fountain where I sat. His voice was like my father's voice calling to my mother.

"Lord Drowning," I said, standing up. I was so bewildered that I said, "You're not here!" I saw that he had been wounded. His right eye was closed with a scar.

He stood still, staring at me from his one eye, and said nothing, getting over his own surprise. Then he laughed.

"No, sister," he said, and turning to his men gave them orders. There were five of them, I think, soldiers, with hardened skin all over their bodies. They wore angel's shoes on their feet, and belts around their waists and necks to support the sheaths for their penis and sword and daggers. Omimo looked like them, but with gold sheaths and the silver hat of a general. I did not understand what he said to the men. They came close to me, and Omimo came closer, so that I said, "Don't touch me," to warn them of their danger, for common men who touched me would be burned to death by the priests of the law, and even Omimo if he touched me without my permission would have to do penance and fast for a year. But he laughed again, and as I drew away, he took hold of my arm suddenly, putting his hand over my mouth. I bit down as hard as I could on his hand. He pulled it away and then slapped it again so hard on my mouth and nose that my head fell back and I could not breathe. I struggled and fought, but my eyes kept seeing blackness and flashes. I felt hard hands holding me, twisting my arms, pulling me up in the air, carrying me, and the hand on my mouth and nose tightened its grip till I could not breathe at all.

Ruaway had been drowsing under the trees, lying on the pavement among the big pots. They did not see her, but she saw them. She knew at once if they saw her they would kill her. She lay still. As soon as they had carried me out the gate into the street, she ran into the house to my mother's room and threw open the door. This was sacrilege, but, not knowing who in the household might be in sympathy with Omimo, she could trust only my mother.

"Lord Drowning has carried Ze off," she said. She told me later that my mother sat there silent and desolate in the dark room for so long that Ruaway thought she had not heard. She was about to speak again, when my mother stood up. Grief fell away from her. She said, "We cannot trust the army," her mind leaping at once to see what must be done, for she was one who had been God. "Bring Tazu here," she said to Ruaway.

Ruaway found Tazu among the holy people, called him to her with her eyes, and asked him to go to his mother at once. Then she went out of the house by the garden door that still stood unlocked and unwatched. She asked people in the Glittering Square if they had seen some soldiers with a drunken girl. Those who had seen us told her to take the northeast street. And so little time had passed that when she came out the northern gate of the city she saw Omimo and his men climbing the hill road toward Ghari, carrying me up to the old fort. She ran back to tell my mother this.

Consulting with Tazu and Lady Clouds and those people she most trusted, my mother sent for several old generals of the peace, whose soldiers served to keep order in the countryside, not in war on the frontiers. She asked for their obedience, which they promised her, for though she was not God she had been God, and was daughter and mother of God. And there was no one else to obey.

She talked next with the dream priests, deciding with them what messages the angels should carry to the people. There was no doubt that Omimo had carried me off to try to make himself God by marrying me. If my mother announced first, in the voices of the angels, that his act was not a marriage performed by the marriage priest, but was rape, then it might be the people would not believe he and I were God.

So the news went out on swift feet, all over the city and the countryside.

Omimo's army, now following him west as fast as they could march, were loyal to him. Some other soldiers joined him along the way. Most of the peacekeeping soldiers of the center land supported my mother. She named Tazu their general. He and she put up a brave and resolute front, but they had little true hope, for there was no God, nor could there be so long as Omimo had me in his power to rape or kill.

All this I learned later. What I saw and knew was this: I was in a low room without windows in the old fortress. The door was locked from outside. Nobody was with me and no guards were at the door, since nobody was in the fort but Omimo's soldiers. I waited there not knowing if it was day or night. I thought time had stopped, as I had feared it would. There was no light in the room, an old storeroom under the pavement of the fortress. Creatures moved on the dirt floor. I walked on dirt then. I sat on dirt and lay on it.

The bolt of the door was shot. Torches flaring in the doorway dazzled me. Men came in and stuck a torch in the sconce on the wall. Omimo came through them to me. His penis stood upright and he came to me to rape me. I spat in his half-blind face and said, "If you touch me your penis will burn like that torch!" He showed his teeth as if he was laughing. He pushed me down and pushed my legs apart, but he was shaking, frightened of my sacred being. He tried to push his penis into me with his hands but it had gone soft. He could not rape me. I said, "You can't, look, you can't rape me!"

His soldiers watched and heard all this. In his humiliation, Omimo pulled his sword from its gold sheath to kill me, but the soldiers held his hands, preventing him, saying, "Lord, Lord, don't kill her, she must be God with you!" Omimo shouted and fought them as I had fought him, and so they all went out, shouting and struggling with him. One of them seized the torch, and the door clashed behind them. After a little while I felt my way to the door and tried it, thinking they might have forgotten to bolt it, but it was bolted. I crawled back to the corner where I had been and lay on the dirt in the dark.

Truly we were all on the dirt in the dark. There was no God. God was the son and daughter of God joined in marriage by the marriage priest. There was no other. There was no other way to go. Omimo did not know what way to go, what to do. He could not marry me without the marriage priest's words. He thought by raping me he would be my husband, and maybe it would have been so: but he could not rape me. I made him impotent.

The only thing he saw to do was attack the city, take the house of God and its priests captive, and force the marriage priest to say the words that made God. He could not do this with the small force he had with him, so he waited for his army to come from the east.

Tazu and the generals and my mother gathered soldiers into the city from the center land. They did not try to attack Ghari. It was a strong fort, easy to defend, hard to attack, and they feared that if they besieged it, they would be caught between it and Omimo's great army coming from the east.

So the soldiers that had come with him, about two hundred of them, garrisoned the fort. As the days passed, Omimo provided women for them. It was the policy of God to give village women extra grain or tools or crop-rows for going to fuck with the soldiers at army camps and stations. There were always women glad to oblige the soldiers and take the reward, and if they got pregnant of course they received more reward and support. Seeking to ease and placate his men, Omimo sent officers down to offer gifts to girls in the villages near Ghari. A group of girls agreed to come; for the common people understood very little of the situation, not believing that anyone could revolt against God. With these village women came Ruaway.

The women and girls ran about the fort, teasing and playing with the soldiers off duty. Ruaway found where I was by fate and courage, coming down into the dark passages under the pavement and trying the doors of the storerooms. I heard the bolt move in the lock. She said my name. I made some sound. "Come!" she said. I crawled to the door. She took my arm and helped me stand and walk. She shot the bolt shut again, and we felt our way down the black passage till we saw light flicker on stone steps. We came out into a torchlit courtyard full of girls and soldiers. Ruaway at once began to run through them, giggling and chattering nonsense, holding tight to my arm so that I ran with her. A couple of soldiers grabbed at us, but Ruaway dodged them, saying, "No, no, Tuki's for the Captain!" We ran on, and came to the side gate, and Ruaway said to the guards, "Oh, let us out, Captain, Captain, I have to take her back to her mother, she's vomiting sick with fever!" I was staggering and covered with dirt and filth from my prison. The guards laughed at me and said foul words about my foulness and opened the gate a crack to let us out. And we ran on down the hill in the starlight.

To escape from a prison so easily, to run through locked doors, people have said, I must have been God indeed. But there was no God then, as there is none now. Long before God, and long after also, is the way things are, which we call chance, or luck, or fortune, or fate; but those are only names.

And there is courage. Ruaway freed me because I was in her heart.

As soon as we were out of sight of the guards at the gate we left the road, on which there were sentries, and cut across country to the city. It stood mightily on the great slope before us, its stone walls starlit. I had never seen it except from the windows and balconies of the house at the center of it.

I had never walked far, and though I was strong from the exercises I did as part of our lessons, my soles were as tender as my palms. Soon I was grunting and tears kept starting in my eyes from the shocks of pain from rocks and gravel underfoot. I found it harder and harder to breathe. I could not run. But Ruaway kept hold of my hand, and we went on.

We came to the north gate, locked and barred and heavily guarded by soldiers of the peace. Then Ruaway cried out, "Let God's daughter enter the city of God!"

I put back my hair and held myself up straight, though my lungs were full of knives, and said to the captain of the gate, "Lord Captain, take us to my mother Lady Ze in the house in the center of the world."

He was old General Rire's son, a man I knew, and he knew me. He stared at me once, then quickly thumbed his forehead, and roared out orders, and the gates opened. So we went in and walked the northeast street to my house, escorted by soldiers, and by more and more people shouting in joy. The drums began to beat, the high, fast beat of the festivals.

That night my mother held me in her arms, as she had not done since I was a suckling baby.

That night Tazu and I stood under the garland before the marriage priest and drank from the sacred cups and were married into God.

That night also Omimo, finding I was gone, ordered a death priest of the army to marry him to one of the village girls who came to fuck with the soldiers. Since nobody outside my house, except a few of his men, had ever seen me up close, any girl could pose as me. Most of his soldiers believed the girl was me. He proclaimed that he had married the daughter of the Dead God and that she and he were now God. As we sent out angels to tell of our marriage, so he sent runners to say that the marriage in the house of God was false, since his sister Ze had run away with him and married him at Ghari, and she and he were now the one true God. And he showed himself to the people wearing a gold hat, with white paint on his face, and his blinded eye, while the army priests cried out, "Behold! The oracle is fulfilled! God is white and has one eye!"

Some believed his priests and messengers. More believed ours. But all were distressed or frightened or made angry by hearing messengers proclaim two Gods at one time, so that instead of knowing the truth, they had to choose to believe.

Omimo's great army was now only four or five days' march away.

Angels came to us saying that a young general, Mesiwa, was bringing a thousand soldiers of the peace up from the rich coasts south of the city. He told the angels only that he came to fight for "the one true God." We feared that meant Omimo. For we added no words to our name, since the word itself means the only truth, or else it means nothing.

We were wise in our choice of generals, and decisive in acting on their advice. Rather than wait for the city to be besieged, we resolved to send a force to attack the eastern army before it reached Ghari, meeting it in the foothills above the River of Origin. We would have to fall back as their full strength came up, but we could strip the country as we did so, and bring the country people into the city. Meanwhile we sent carts to and from all the storehouses on the southern and western roads to fill the city's granaries. If the war did not end quickly, said the old generals, it would be won by those who could keep eating.

"Lord Drowning's army can feed themselves from the storehouses along the east and north roads," said my mother, who attended all our councils.

"Destroy the roads," Tazu said.

I heard my mother's breath catch, and remembered the oracle: The roads will be broken.

"That would take as long to do as it took to make them," said the oldest general, but the next oldest general said, "Break down the stone bridge at Almoghay." And so we ordered. Retreating from its delaying battle, our army tore down the great bridge that had stood a thousand years. Omimo's army had to go around nearly a hundred miles farther, through forests, to the ford at Domi, while our army and our carters brought the contents of the storehouses in to the city. Many country people followed them, seeking the protection of God, and so the city grew very full. Every grain of ze came with a mouth to eat it.

All this time Mesiwa, who might have come against the eastern army at Domi, waited in the passes with his thousand men. When we commanded him to come help punish sacrilege and restore peace, he sent our angel back with meaningless messages. It seemed certain that he was in league with Omimo. "Mesiwa the finger, Omimo the thumb," said the oldest general, pretending to crack a louse.

"God is not mocked," Tazu said to him, deadly fierce. The old general bowed his forehead down on his thumbs, abashed. But I was able to smile.

Tazu had hoped the country people would rise up in anger at the sacrilege and strike the Painted God down. But they were not soldiers and had never fought. They had always lived under the protection of the soldiers of peace and under our care. As if our doings now were like the whirlwind or the earthquake, they were paralyzed by them and could only watch and wait till they were over, hoping to survive. Only the people of our household, whose livelihood depended directly upon us and whose skills and knowledge were at our service, and the people of the city in whose heart we were, and the soldiers of the peace, would fight for us.

The country people had believed in us. Where no belief is, no God is. Where doubt is, foot falters and hand will not take hold.

The wars at the borders, the wars of conquest, had made our land too large. The people in the towns and villages knew no more who I was than I knew who they were. In the days of the origin, Babam Kerul and Bamam Ze came down from the mountain and walked the fields of the center lands beside the common people. The common people who laid the first stones of the great roads and the huge base stones of the old city wall had known the face of their God, seeing it daily.

After I spoke of this to our councils, Tazu and I went out into the streets, sometimes carried in litters, sometimes walking. We were surrounded by the priests and guards who honored our divinity, but we went among the people, meeting their eyes. They fell on their knees and put their foreheads to their thumbs, and many wept when they saw us. They called out from street to street, and little children cried out, "There's God!"

"You walk in their hearts," my mother said.

But Omimo's army had come to the River of Origin, and one day's march brought the vanguard to Ghari.

That evening we stood on the north balcony looking toward Ghari hill, which was swarming with men, as when a nest of insects swarms. To the west the light was dark red on the mountains in their winter snow. From Korosi a vast plume of smoke trailed, blood color.

"Look," Tazu said, pointing northwest. A light flared in the sky, like the sheet lightning of summer. "A falling star," he said, and I said, "An eruption."

In the dark of the night, angels came to us. "A great house burned and fell from the sky," one said, and the other said, "It burned but it stands, on the bank of the river."

"The words of God spoken on the birthday of the world," I said.

The angels knelt down hiding their faces.

What I saw then is not what I see now looking far off to the distant past; what I knew then is both less and more than I know now. I try to say what I saw and knew then.

That morning I saw coming down the great stone road to the northern gate a group of beings, two-legged and erect like people or lizards. They were the height of giant desert lizards, with monstrous limbs and feet, but without tails. They were white all over and hairless. Their heads had no mouth or nose and one huge single staring shining lidless eye.

They stopped outside the gate.

Not a man was to be seen on Ghari Hill. They were all in the fortress or hidden in the woods behind the hill.

We were standing up on the top of the northern gate, where a wall runs chest-high to protect the guards.

There was a little sound of frightened weeping on the roofs and balconies of the city, and people called out to us, "God! God, save us!"

Tazu and I had talked all night. We listened to what our mother and other wise people said, and then we sent them away to reach out our minds together, to look over our shoulder into the time that was coming. We saw the death and the birth of the world, that night. We saw all things changed.

The oracle had said that God was white and had one eye. This was what we saw now. The oracle had said that the world died. With it died our brief time of being God. This was what we had to do now: to kill the world. The world must die so that God may live. The house falls that it may stand. Those who have been God must make God welcome.

Tazu spoke welcome to God, while I ran down the spiral stairs inside the wall of the gate and unbolted the great bolts—the guards had to help me—and swung the door open. "Enter in!" I said to God, and put my forehead to my thumbs, kneeling.

They came in, hesitant, moving slowly, ponderously. Each one turned its huge eye from side to side, unblinking. Around the eye was a ring of silver that flashed in the sun. I saw myself in one of those eyes, a pupil in the eye of God.

Their snow-white skin was coarse and wrinkled, with bright tattoos on it. I was dismayed that God could be so ugly.

The guards had shrunk back against the walls. Tazu had come down to stand with me. One of them raised a box toward us. A noise came out of the box, as if some animal was shut in it.

Tazu spoke to them again, telling them that the oracle had foretold their coming, and that we who had been God welcomed God.

They stood there, and the box made more noises. I thought it sounded like Ruaway before she learned to talk right. Was the language of God no longer ours? Or was God an animal, as Ruaway's people believed? I thought they seemed more like the monstrous lizards of the desert that lived in the zoo of our house than they seemed like us.

One raised its thick arm and pointed at our house, down at the end of the street, taller than other houses, its copper gutters and goldleaf carvings shining in the bright winter sunlight.

"Come, Lord," I said, "come to your house." We led them to it and brought them inside.

When we came into the low, long, windowless audience room, one of them took off its head. Inside it was a head like ours, with two eyes, nose, mouth, ears. The others did the same.

Then, seeing their head was a mask, I saw that their white skin was like a shoe that they wore not just on the foot but all over their body. Inside this shoe they were like us, though the skin of their faces was the color of clay pots and looked very thin, and their hair was shiny and lay flat.

"Bring food and drink," I said to the children of God cowering outside the door, and they ran to bring trays of ze-cakes and dried fruit and winter beer. God came to the tables where the food was set. Some of them pretended to eat. One, watching what I did, touched the ze-cake to its forehead first, and then bit into it and chewed and swallowed. It spoke to the others, gre-gra, gre-gra.

This one was also the first to take off its body-shoe. Inside it other wrappings and coverings hid and protected most of its body, but this was understandable, because even the body skin was pale and terribly thin, soft as a baby's eyelid.

In the audience room, on the east wall over the double seat of God, hung the gold mask which God Himself wore to turn the sun back on its way. The one who had eaten the cake pointed at the mask. Then it looked at me—its own eyes were oval, large, and beautiful—and pointed up to where the sun was in the sky. I nodded my body. It pointed its finger here and there all about the mask, and then all about the ceiling.

"There must be more masks made, because God is now more than two," Tazu said.

I had thought the gesture might signify the stars, but I saw that Tazu's interpretation made more sense.

"We will have masks made," I told God, and then ordered the hat priest to go fetch the gold hats which God wore during ceremonies and festivals. There were many of these hats, some jeweled and ornate, others plain, all very ancient. The hat priest brought them in due order two by two until they were all set out on the great table of polished wood and bronze where the ceremonies of First Ze and Harvest were celebrated.

Tazu took off the gold hat he wore, and I took off mine. Tazu put his hat on the head of the one who had eaten the cake, and I chose a short one and reached up and put my hat on its head. Then, choosing ordinary-day hats, not those of the sacred occasions, we put a hat on each of the heads of God, while they stood and waited for us to do so.

Then we knelt bareheaded and put our foreheads against our thumbs.

God stood there. I was sure they did not know what to do. "God is grown, but new, like a baby," I said to Tazu. I was sure they did not understand what we said.

All at once the one I had put my hat on came to me and put its hands on my elbows to raise me up from kneeling. I pulled back at first, not being used to being touched; then I remembered I was no longer very sacred, and let God touch me. It talked and gestured. It gazed into my eyes. It took off the gold hat and tried to put it back on my head. At that I did shrink away, saying, "No, no!" It seemed blasphemy, to say No to God, but I knew better.

God talked among themselves then for a while, and Tazu and our mother and I were able to talk among ourselves. What we understood was this: the oracle had not been wrong, of course, but it had been subtle. God was not truly one-eyed nor blind, but did not know how to see. It was not God's skin that was white, but their mind that was blank and ignorant. They did not know how to talk, how to act, what to do. They did not know their people.

Yet how could Tazu and I, or our mother and our old teachers, teach them? The world had died and a new world was coming to be. Everything in it might be new. Everything might be different. So it was not God, but we, who did not know how to see, what to do, how to speak.

I felt this so strongly that I knelt again and prayed to God, "Teach us!"

They looked at me and talked to each other, brr-grr, gre-gra.

I sent our mother and the others to talk with our generals, for angels had come with reports about Omimo's army. Tazu was very tired from lack of sleep. We two sat down on the floor together and talked quietly. He was concerned about God's seat. "How can they all sit on it at once?" he said.

"They'll have more seats added," I said. "Or now two will sit on it, and then another two. They're all God, the way you and I were, so it doesn't matter."

"But none of them is a woman," Tazu said.

I looked at God more carefully and saw that he was right. This disturbed me slowly, but very deeply. How could God be only half human?

In my world, a marriage made God. In this world coming to be, what made God?

I thought of Omimo. White clay on his face and a false marriage had made him a false God, but many people believed he was truly God. Would the power of their belief make him God, while we gave our power to this new, ignorant God?

If Omimo found out how helpless they appeared to be, not knowing how to speak, not even knowing how to eat, he would fear their divinity even less than he had feared ours. He would attack. And would our soldiers fight for this God?

I saw clearly that they would not. I saw from the back of my head, with the eyes that see what is coming. I saw the misery that was coming to my people. I saw the world dead, but I did not see it being born. What world could be born of a God who was male? Men do not give birth.

Everything was wrong. It came very strongly into my mind that we should have our soldiers kill God now, while they were still new in the world and weak.

And then? If we killed God there would be no God. We could pretend to be God again, the way Omimo pretended. But godhead is not pretense. Nor is it put on and off like a golden hat.

The world had died. That was fated and foretold. The fate of these strange men was to be God, and they would have to live their fate as we lived ours, finding out what it was to be as it came to be, unless they could see over their shoulders, which is one of the gifts of God.

I stood up again, taking Tazu's hand so that he stood beside me. "The city is yours," I said to them, "and the people are yours. The world is yours, and the war is yours. All praise and glory to you, our God!" And we knelt once more and bowed our foreheads deeply to our thumbs, and left them.

"Where are we going?" Tazu said. He was twelve years old and no longer God. There were tears in his eyes.

"To find Mother and Ruaway," I said, "and Arzi and Lord Idiot and Haghag, and any of our people who want to come with us." I had begun to say "our children," but we were no longer their mother and father.

"Come where?" Tazu said.

"To Chimlu."

"Up in the mountains? Run and hide? We should stay and fight Omimo."

"What for?" I said.

That was sixty years ago.

I have written this to tell how it was to live in the house of God before the world ended and began again. To tell it I have tried to write with the mind I had then. But neither then nor now do I fully understand the oracle which my father and all the priests saw and spoke. All of it came to pass. Yet we have no God, and no oracles to guide us.

None of the strange men lived a long life, but they all lived longer than Omimo.

We were on the long road up into the mountains when an angel caught up with us to tell us that Mesiwa had joined Omimo, and the two generals had brought their great army against the house of the strangers, which stood like a tower in the fields near Soze River, with a waste of burned earth around it. The strangers warned Omimo and his army clearly to withdraw, sending lightning out of the house over their heads that set distant trees afire. Omimo would not heed. He could prove he was God only by killing God. He commanded his army to rush at the tall house. He and Mesiwa and a hundred men around him were destroyed by a single bolt of lightning. They were burned to ash. His army fled in terror.

"They are God! They are God indeed!" Tazu said when he heard the angel tell us that. He spoke joyfully, for he was as unhappy in his doubt as I was. And for a while we could all believe in them, since they could wield the lightning. Many people called them God as long as they lived.

My belief is that they were not God in any sense of the word I understand, but were otherworldly, supernatural beings, who had great powers, but were weak and ignorant of our world, and soon sickened of it and died.

There were fourteen of them in all. Some of them lived more than ten years. These learned to speak as we do. One of them came up into the mountains to Chimlu, along with some of the pilgrims who still wanted to worship Tazu and me as God. Tazu and I and this man talked for many days, learning from each other. He told us that their house moved in the air, flying like a dragon-lizard, but its wings were broken. He told us that in the land they came from the sunlight is very weak, and it was our strong sunlight that made them sick. Though they covered their bodies with weavings, still their thin skins let the sunlight in, and they would all die soon. He told us they were sorry they had come. I said, "You had to come. God saw you coming. What use is it to be sorry?"

He agreed with me that they were not God. He said that God lived in the sky. That seemed to us a useless place for God to live. Tazu said they had indeed been God when they came, since they fulfilled the oracle and changed the world; but now, like us, they were common people.

Ruaway took a liking to this stranger, maybe because she had been a stranger, and when he was at Chimlu they slept together. She said he was like any man under his weavings and coverings. He told her he could not impregnate her, as his seed would not ripen in our earth. Indeed the strangers left no children.

This stranger told us his name, Bin-yi-zin. He came back up to Chimlu several times, and was the last of them to die. He left with Ruaway the dark crystals he wore before his eyes, which make things look larger and clearer for her, though to my eyes they make things dim. To me he gave his own record of his life, in a beautiful writing made of lines of little pictures, which I keep in the box with this writing I make.

When Tazu's testicles ripened we had to decide what to do, for brothers and sisters among the common people do not marry. We asked the priests and they advised us that our marriage being divine could not be unmade, and that though no longer God we were husband and wife. Since we were in each other's heart, this pleased us, and often we slept together. Twice I conceived, but the conceptions aborted, one very early and one in the fourth month, and I did not conceive again. This was a grief to us, and yet fortunate, for had we had children, the people might have tried to make them be God.

It takes a long time to learn to live without God, and some people never do. They would rather have a false God than none at all. All through the years, though seldom now, people would climb up to Chimlu to beg Tazu and me to come back down to the city and be God. And when it became clear that the strangers would not rule the country as God, either under the old rules or with new ones, men began to imitate Omimo, marrying ladies of our lineage and claiming to be a new God. They all found followers and they all made wars, fighting each other. None of them had Omimo's terrible courage, or the loyalty of a great army to a successful general. They have all come to wretched ends at the hands of angry, disappointed, wretched people.

For my people and my land have fared no better than I feared and saw over my shoulder on the night the world ended. The great stone roads are not maintained. In places they are already broken. Almoghay bridge was never rebuilt. The granaries and storehouses are empty and falling down. The old and sick must beg from neighbors, and a pregnant girl has only her mother to turn to, and an orphan has no one. There is famine in the west and south. We are the hungry people, now. The angels no longer weave the net of government, and one part of the land knows nothing of the others. They say barbarians have brought back the wilderness across the Fourth River, and ground dragons spawn in the fields of grain. Little generals and painted gods raise armies to waste lives and goods and spoil the sacred earth.

The evil time will not last forever. No time does. I died as God a long time ago. I have lived as a common woman a long time. Each year I see the sun turn back from the south behind great Kanaghadwa. Though God does not dance on the glittering pavement, yet I see the birthday of the world over the shoulder of my death.

savior

NANCY KRESS

Nancy Kress began selling her elegant and incisive stories in the mid-seventies, and has since become a frequent contributor to Asimov's Science Fiction, The Magazine of Fantasy & Science Fiction, Omini *and other periodicals. Her books include the novels* The Prince of Morning Bells, The Golden Grove, The White Pipes, An Alien Light, Brain Rose, Oaths & Miracles, Stinger, Maximum Light, *the novel version of her Hugo- and Nebula-winning story,* Beggars in Spain, *and a sequel,* Beggars and Choosers. *Her short work has been collected in* Trinity and Other Stories, The Aliens of Earth, *and* Beaker's Dozen. *Her most recent book is a new novel,* Probability Moon. *She has also won Nebula Awards for her stories "Out of All Them Bright Stars" and "The Flowers of Aulit Prison." Born in Buffalo, New York, Nancy Kress now lives in Silver Spring, Maryland, with her husband, SF writer Charles Sheffield.*

In the intricate and compelling novella that follows, she gives us the story of an enigmatic visitor from the depths of space, sent here on a mission no one understands, but which gradually generates the realization that it somehow must *be understood, before it's too late . . . and that the clock may be ticking in more ways than one.*

I: 2007

The object's arrival was no surprise; it came down preceded, accompanied, and followed by all the attention in the world.

The craft—if it was a craft—had been picked up on an October Saturday morning by the Hubble, while it was still beyond the orbit of Mars. A few hours later Houston, Langley, and Arecibo knew its trajectory, and a few hours after that so did every major observatory in the world. The press got the story in time for the Sunday papers. The United States Army evacuated and surrounded twenty square miles around the projected Minnesota landing site, some of which lay over the Canadian border in Ontario.

"It's still a shock," Dr. Ann Pettie said to her colleague Jim Cowell. "I mean, you look and listen for decades, you scan the skies, you read all the arguments for and against other intelligent life out there, you despair over Fermi's paradox—"

"I never despaired over Fermi's paradox," Cowell answered, pulling his coat closer around his skinny body. It was cold at 3:00 A.M. in a northern Minnesota cornfield, and he hadn't slept in twenty-four hours. Maybe longer. The cornfield was as close as he and Ann had been allowed to get. It wasn't very close, despite a day on the phone pulling every string he could to get on the official Going-In Committee. That's what they were calling it: "the Going-In Committee." Not welcoming, not belligerent, not too alarmed. Not too anything, "until we know what we have here." The words were the president's, who was also not on the Going-In Committee, although in his case presumably by choice.

Ann said, "You *never* despaired over Fermi's Paradox? You thought all along that aliens would show up eventually, they just hadn't gotten around to it yet?"

"Yes," Cowell said, and didn't look at her directly. How to explain? It wasn't belief so much as desire, nor desire so much as life-long need. Very adolescent, and he wouldn't have admitted it except he was cold and exhausted and exhilarated and scared, and the best he could hope for, jammed in with other "visiting scientists" two miles away from the landing site, was a possible glimpse of the object as it streaked down over the treeline.

"Jim, that sounds so . . . so . . ."

"A man has to believe in something," he said in a gruff voice, quoting a recent bad movie, swaggering a little to point up the joke. It fell flat. Ann went on staring at him in the harsh glare of the floodlights until someone said, "Bitte? Ein Kaffee, Ann?"

"Hans!" Ann said, and she and Dr. Hans Kleinschmidt rattled merrily away in German. Cowell knew no German. He knew Kleinschmidt only slightly, from those inevitable scientific conferences featuring one important paper, ten badly attended minor ones, and three nights of drinking to bridge over the language difficulties.

What language would the aliens speak? Would they have learned English from our secondhand radio and TV broadcasts, as pundits had been predicting for the last thirty-six hours and writers for the last seventy years? Well, it *was* true they had chosen to land on the American-Canadian border, so maybe they would.

So far, of course, they hadn't said anything at all. No signal had come from the oval-shaped object hurtling toward Earth.

"Coffee," Ann said, thrusting it at Cowell. Kleinschmidt had apparently brought a tray of Styrofoam cups from the emergency station at the edge of the field. Cowell uncapped his and drank it gratefully, not caring that it was lukewarm or that he didn't take sugar. It was caffeine.

"Twenty minutes more," someone said behind him.

It was a well-behaved crowd, mostly scientists and second-tier politicians. Nobody tried to cross the rope that soldiers had strung between hastily driven stakes a few hours earlier. Cowell guessed that the unruly types, the press and first-rank space fans and maverick businessmen with large campaign contributions, had all been herded together elsewhere, under the watchful eyes of many more soldiers than were assigned to this cornfield. Still more were probably assigned unobtrusively—Cowell hoped it was unobtrusively—to the Going-In Committee, waiting somewhere in a sheltered bunker to greet the aliens. Very sheltered. Nobody knew what kind of drive the craft might have, or not have. For all they knew, it was set to take out both Minnesota and Ontario.

Cowell didn't think so.

Hans Kleinschmidt had moved away. Abruptly Cowell said to Ann, "Didn't you ever stare at the night sky and just *will* them to be there? When you were a kid, or even a grad student in astronomy?"

She shifted uncomfortably from one foot to the other. "Well, sure. Then. But I never thought . . . I just never thought. Since." She shrugged, but something in her tone made Cowell turn full face and peer into her eyes.

"Yes, you did."

She answered him only indirectly. "Jim . . . there could be nobody aboard."

"Probably there isn't," he said, and knew that his voice betrayed him. Not belief so much as desire, not desire so much as need. And he was thirty-four goddamn years old, goddamn it!

"Look!" someone yelled, and every head swiveled up, desperately searching a clear, star-jeweled sky.

Cowell couldn't see anything. Then he could: a faint pinprick of light, marginally moving. As he watched, it moved faster and then it flared, entering the atmosphere. He caught his breath.

"Oh my God, it's swerving off course!" somebody shouted from his left, where unofficial jerry-rigged tracking equipment had been assembled in a ramshackle group effort. "Impossible!" someone else shouted, although the only reason for this was that the object hadn't swerved off a steady course before now. So what? Cowell felt a strange mood grip him, and stranger words flowed through his mind: *Of course. They wouldn't let me miss this.*

"A tenth of a degree northwest . . . no, wait. . . ."

Cowell's mood intensified. With one part of his mind, he recognized that the mood was born of fatigue and strain, but it didn't seem to matter. The sense of inevitability grew on him, and he wasn't surprised when Ann cried, "It's landing *here!* Run!" Cowell didn't move as the others scattered. He watched calmly, holding his half-filled Styrofoam cup of too-sweet coffee, face tilted to the sky.

The object slowed, silvery in the starlight. It continued to slow until it was moving at perhaps three miles per hour, no more, at a roughly forty-five degree angle. The landing was smooth and even. There was no hovering, no jet blasts, no scorched ground. Only a faint *whump* as the object touched the earth, and a rustle of corn husks in the unseen wind.

It seemed completely natural to walk over to the spacecraft. Cowell was the first one to reach it.

Made of some smooth, dull-silver metal, he noted calmly, and unblackened by re-entry. An irregular oval, although his mind couldn't pin down in precisely what the irregularity lay. Not humming or moving, or, in fact, doing anything at all.

He put out his hand to touch it, and the hand stopped nearly a foot away.

"Jim!" Ann called, and somebody else — must be Kleinschmidt — said, "Herr Dr. Cowell!" Cowell moved his hand along whatever he *was* touching. An invisible wall, or maybe some sort of hard field, encased the craft.

"Hello, ship," he said softly, and afterward wasn't ever sure if he'd said it aloud.

"Don't touch it! Wait!" Ann called, and her hand snatched away his.

It didn't matter. He turned to her, not really seeing her, and said something that, like his greeting to the ship, he wasn't ever sure about afterward. "I was raised Orthodox, you know. Waiting for the Messiah," and then the rest were on them, with helicopters pulsing overhead and soldiers ordering everyone back, *back I said!* And Cowell was pushed into the crowd with no choice except to set himself to wait for the visitors to come out.

"Are you absolutely positive?" the president, who was given to superlatives, asked his military scientists. He had assembled them, along with the joint chiefs of staff, the cabinet, the Canadian lieutenant-governor, and a sprinkling of advisors, in the cabinet room of the White House. The same group had been meeting daily for a week, ever since the object had landed. Washington was warmer than Minnesota; outside, dahlias and chrysanthemums still bloomed on the manicured lawn. "No signal of any type issued from the craft, at any time after you picked it up on the Hubble?"

The scientists looked uncomfortable. It was the kind of question only non-scientists asked. Before his political career, the president had been a financier.

"Sir, we can't say for certain that we know all types of signals that could or do exist. Or that we had comprehensive, fixed-position monitoring of the craft at all times. As you—"

"All right, all right. Since it landed, then, and you got your equipment trained on it. No radio signals emanating from it, at any wavelength whatsoever?"

"No, sir. That's definite."

"No light signals, even in infrared or ultraviolet?"

"No, Mr. President."

"No gamma lengths, or other radioactivity?"

"No, sir."

"No quantum effects?" the president said, surprising everyone. He was not noted for his wide reading.

"Do you mean things like quantum entanglement to transport information?" the head of Livermore National Laboratory said cautiously. "Of course, we don't know enough about that area of physics to predict for certain what may be discovered eventually, or what a race of beings more advanced than ours might have discovered already."

"So there might be quantum signals going out from the craft constantly, for all you know."

The Livermore director spread his hands in helpless appeal. "Sir, we can only monitor signals we already understand."

The president addressed his chief military advisor, General Dayton. "This shield covering the craft—you don't understand that, either? What kind of field it is, why nothing at all gets through except light?"

"Everything except electromagnetic radiation in the visible-light wavelengths is simply reflected back at us," Dayton said.

"So you can't use sonar, X-rays, anything that could image the inside?"

This time Dayton didn't answer. The president already knew all this. The whole world knew it. The best scientific and military minds from several nations had been at work on the object all week.

"So what is your recommendation to me?" the president said.

"Sir, our only recommendation is that we continue full monitoring of the craft, with full preparation to meet any change in its behavior."

"In other words, 'Wait and see.' I could have decided that for myself, without all you high-priced talent!" the president said in disgust, and several people in the room reflected with satisfaction that this particular president had only a year and three months left in office. There was no way he would be re-elected. The economy had taken too sharp a downturn.

Unless, of course, a miracle happened to save him.

"Well, go back to your labs, then," the president said, and even though he knew it was a mistake, the director of Livermore gave in to impulse.

"Science can't always be a savior, Mr. President."

"Then what good is it?" the president said, with a puzzled simplicity that took the director's breath away. "Just keep a close eye on that craft. And try to come up with some actual scientific data, for a blessed change."

ALIEN FIELD MAY BE FORM OF BOSE-EINSTEIN CONDENSATE, SAY SCIENTISTS AT STANFORD

NOBEL PRIZE WINNER RIDICULES STANFORD STATEMENT

MINNESOTA STATE COURT THROWS OUT CASE CLAIMING CONTAMINATED GROUND WATER NEAR ALIEN OBJECT

SPACE SHIELD MAY BE PENETRATED BY UNDETECTED COSMIC RAYS, SAYS FRENCH SCIENTIST

SPACE-OBJECT T-SHIRTS RULED OBSCENE BY LOCAL TOURIST COUNCIL, REMOVED FROM VENDOR STANDS

NEUTRINO STREAM TURNED BACK FROM SPACE SHIELD IN EXPENSIVE HIGH-TECH FIASCO:
Congress to Review All Peer-Judged Science Funding

WOMAN CLAIMS UNDER HYPNOSIS TO HEAR VOICES FROM SPACE OBJECT—KENT STATE SCIENTISTS INVESTIGATING

PRESIDENT LOSES ELECTION BY LARGEST MARGIN EVER

"MY TWIN SONS WERE FATHERED BY THE OBJECT," CLAIMS SENATOR'S DAUGHTER, RESISTS DNA TESTING
Polls Show 46% of Americans Believe Her

Jim Cowell, contemptuous of the senator's daughter, was forced to acknowledge that he had waited a lifetime for his own irrational belief to be justified. Which it never had.

"Just a little farther, Dad," Barbara said. "You okay?"

Cowell nodded in his wheelchair, and slowed it to match Barbara's pace. She wheezed a little these days; losing weight wouldn't hurt her. He had learned over the years not to mention this. Ahead, the last checkpoint materialized out of the fog. A bored soldier leaned out of the low window, his face lit by the glow of a holoscreen. "Yes?"

"We have authorization to approach the object," Cowell said. He could never think of it as anything else, despite all the names the tabloid press had hung on it over the last decades. The Alien Invader. The Space Fizzle. Silent Alien Cal.

"Approach for retina scan," the soldier said. Cowell wheeled his chair to the checker, leaned in close. "Okay, you're cleared. Ma'am? . . . Okay. Proceed." The soldier stuck his head back in the window, and the screen made one of the elaborate noises that accompanied the latest hologame.

Barbara muttered, "As if he knew the value of what he's guarding!"

"He knows," Cowell said. He didn't really want to talk to Barbara. Much as he loved her, he really would have preferred to come to this place alone. Or with Sharon, if Sharon had still been alive. But Barbara had been afraid he might have some sort of final attack alone there by the object, and of course he might have. He was pretty close to the end, and they both knew it. Getting here from Detroit was taking everything Cowell had left.

He wheeled down the paved path. On either side, autumn stubble glinted with frost. They were almost on the object before it materialized out of the fog.

Barbara began to babble. "Oh, it looks so different from pictures, even holos, so much smaller but shinier, too, you never told me it was so shiny, Dad, I guess whatever it's made of doesn't rust. But, no, of course the air isn't getting close enough to rust it, is it, there's that shield to prevent oxidation, and they never found out what *that* is composed of, either, did they, although I remember reading this speculative article that—"

Cowell shut her out as best he could. He brought his chair close enough to touch the shield. Still nothing: no tingle, no humming, no moving. Nothing at all.

That first time rushed back to him, in sharp sensory detail. The fatigue, the strain, the rustle of corn husks in the unseen wind. Hans Kleinschmidt's Styrofoam cup of coffee warm in Cowell's hand. Ann Pettie's cry *It's landing here! Run!* Cowell's own strange personal feeling of inevitability: *Of course. They wouldn't let me miss this.*

Well, they *had.* They'd let the whole world miss whatever the hell the object was supposed to be, or do, or represent. Hans was long dead. Ann was institutionalized with Alzheimer's. "Hello, *ship.*" And the rest of his life—of many people's lives—devoted to trying to figure out the Space Super Fizzle.

That long frustration, Cowell thought, had showed him one thing, anyway. There was no mystery behind the mystery, no unseen Plan, no alien messiah for humanity. There was only this blank object sitting in a field, stared at by a shrill middle-aged woman and a dying man. What you see is what you get. He, James Everett Cowell, had been a fool to ever hope for anything else.

"Dad, why are you smiling like that? Don't, please!"

"It's nothing, Barbara."

"But you looked—"

"I *said*, 'It's nothing.' "

Suddenly he was very tired. It was cold out here, under the gray sky. Snow was in the air.

"Honey, let's go back now."

They did, Barbara walking close by Cowell's chair. He didn't look back at the object, silent on the fallow ground.

> Transmission: There is nothing here yet.
> Current probability of occurrence: 67%.

II: 2090

The girl, dressed in home-dyed blue cotton pants and a wolf pelt bandeau, said suddenly, "Tam—what's *that?*"

Tam Wilkinson stopped walking, although his goat herd did not. The animals moved slowly forward, pulling at whatever tough grass they could find on the parched ground. Three-legged Himmie hobbled close to the herd leader; blind Jimmie turned his head in the direction of Himmie's bawl. "What's what?" the boy said.

"Over there, to the north . . . no, *there.*"

The boy shaded his eyes against the summer sun, hot under the thin clouds. He and Juli would have to find noon shade for the goats soon. Tam's eyes weren't strong, but by squinting and peering, he caught the glint of sunlight on something dull silvery. "I don't know."

"Let's go see."

Tam looked bleakly at Juli. They had married only a few months ago, in the spring. She was so pretty, hardly any deformity at all. The doctor from St. Paul had issued her a fertility certificate at only fourteen. But she was impulsive. Tam, three years older, came from a family unbroken since the Collapse. They hadn't accomplished that by impulsive behavior.

"No, Juli. We have to find shade for the goats."

"It could *be* shade. O, or even a machine with some good metal on it!"

"This whole area was stripped long ago."

"Maybe they missed something."

Tam considered. She could be right; since their marriage, he and Juli had brought the goats pretty far beyond their usual range. Not many people had ventured into the Great Northern Waste for pasturage. The whole area had been too hard hit at the Collapse, leaving the soil too contaminated and the standing water even worse. But the summer had been unusually rainy, creating the running water that was so much safer than ponds or lakes, and anyway Tam and Juli had delighted in being alone. Maybe there *was* a forgotten machine with usable parts still sitting way out here, from before the Collapse. What a great thing to bring home from his honeymoon!

"Please," Juli said, nibbling his ear, and Tam gave in. She was so pretty. In Tam's entire family, no women were as pretty, nor as nearly whole, as Juli. His sister Nan was loose-brained, Calie had only one arm, Jen was blind, and Suze could not walk. Only Jen was fertile, even though the Wilkinson farm was near neither lake nor city. The farm still sat in the path of the west winds coming from Grand Forks. When there had been a Grand Forks.

Tam and Juli walked slowly, herding the goats, toward the glinting metal. The sun glared pitilessly by the time they reached the object, but the thing, whatever it was, stood beside a stand of scrawny trees in a little dell. Tam drove the goats into the shade. His practiced eye saw that once there had been water here, but no longer. They would have to move on by early afternoon.

When the goats were settled, the lovers walked hand-in-hand toward the object. "O," Juli said, "it's an egg! A metal egg!" Suddenly she clutched Tam's arm. "Is it . . . do you think it's a polluter?"

Tam felt growing excitement. "No—I know what this is! Gran told me, before she died!"

"It's not a polluter?"

"No, it . . . well, actually, nobody knows exactly what it's made of. But it's safe, dear love. It's a miracle."

"A what?" Juli said.

"A miracle." He tried not to sound superior; Juli was sensitive about her lack of education. Tam was teaching her to read and write. "A gift directly from God. A long time ago—a few hundred years, I think, anyway before the Collapse—this egg fell out of the sky. No one could figure out why. Then one day a beautiful princess touched it, and she got pregnant and bore twin sons."

"Really?" Juli breathed. She ran a few steps forward, then considerately slowed for Tam's halting walk. "What happened then?"

Tam shrugged. "Nothing, I guess. The Collapse happened."

"So this egg, it just sat here since then? Come on, sweet one, I want to see it up close. It just sat here? When women try so hard, us, to get pregnant?"

The boy didn't like the skeptical tone in her voice. He was the one with the educated family. "You don't understand, Juli. This thing didn't make everybody pregnant, just that one princess. It was a special miracle from God."

"I thought you told me that before the Collapse, nobody needed no miracles to get pregnant, because there wasn't no pollutants in the water and air and ground?"

"Yes, but—"

"So then when this princess got herself pregnant, why was it such a miracle?"

"Because she was a virgin, loose-brain!" After a minute he added, "I'm sorry."

"I'm going to look at the egg," Juli said stiffly, and this time she ran ahead without waiting.

When Tam caught up, Juli was sitting cross-legged in prayer in front of the egg. It was smaller than he had expected, no bigger than a goat shed, a slightly irregular oval of dull silver. Around it the ground shimmered with heat. Minnesota hadn't always been so hot, Gran had told Tam in her papery old-lady voice, and he suddenly wondered what this place had looked like when the egg fell out of the sky.

Could it be a polluter? It didn't look like it manufactured anything, and certainly Tam couldn't see any plastic parts to it. Nothing that could flake off in bits too tiny to see and get into the air and water and wind and living bodies. Still, if they were so very small, these dangerous pieces of plastic . . . "endocrine mimickers," Gran had taught Tam to call them, though he had no idea what the words meant. Doctors in St. Paul knew, probably. Although what good was knowing, if you couldn't fix the problem and make all babies as whole as Juli?

She sat saying her prayer beads so fervently that Tam was annoyed with her all over again. Really, she just wasn't steady. Playful, then angry, then prayerful . . . she'd better be more reliable than that when the babies started to come. But then Juli raised her eyes to him, lake-blue, and appealed to his greater knowledge, and he softened again.

"Tam . . . do you think it's all right to pray to it? Since it did come from God?"

"I'm sure it's all right, honey. What are you praying for?"

"Twin sons, like the princess got." Juli scrambled to her feet. "Can I touch it?"

Tam felt sudden fear. "No! No—better not. I will, instead." When those twin sons came, he wanted them to be of his seed, not the egg's.

Cautiously the boy put out one hand, which stopped nearly a foot away from the silvery shell. Tam pushed harder. He couldn't get any closer to the egg. "It's got an invisible wall around it!"

"Really? Then can I touch it? It's not really touching the egg!"

"No! The wall is all the princess must have touched, too."

"Maybe the wall, it wasn't there a long time ago. Maybe it grew, like crops."

Tam frowned, torn between pride and irritation at her quick thought. "Don't touch it, Juli. After all, for all we know, you might already be pregnant."

She obeyed, stepping back and studying the object. Suddenly her pretty face lit up. "Tam! Maybe it's a miracle for us, too! For the whole family!"

"The whole—"

"For Nan and Calie and Suze! And your cousins, too! O, if they come here and touch the egg—or the egg wall—maybe they can get pregnant like the princess did, straight from God!"

"I don't think—"

"If we came back before winter, in easy stages, and knowing ahead of time where the water was, they could all get pregnant! You could talk them into it, dear heart! You're the only one they listen to, even your parents. The only one who can make plans and carry out them plans. You know you are."

She looked at him with adoration. Tam felt something inside him glow and expand. And O, she really was quick, even if she couldn't read or write. His parents were old, at least forty, and they'd never been as quick as Tam. That was why Gran had taught him so much directly, all sorts of things she'd learned from her grandmother, who could remember the Collapse.

He said, with slow weightiness, "If the workers in the family stayed to raise crops, we could bring the goats and the infertile women . . . in easy stages, I think, before fall. Provided we map ahead of time where the safe water is."

"O, I know you can!"

Tam frowned thoughtfully, and reached out again to touch the silent, unreachable egg.

Just before the small expedition left the Wilkinson farm, Dr. Sutter showed up on his dirtbike.

Why did he have to come now? Tam didn't like Dr. Sutter, who always acted so superior. He biked around the farms and villages, supposedly "helping people"—O, he did help some people, maybe, but not Tam's family, who *were* their village. Not really helped. O, he'd brought drugs for Gran's aching bones, and for Suze's fever, from the hospital in St. Paul. But he hadn't been able to stop Tam's sisters—or anybody else—from being born the way they were, and not all his "medical training" could make Suze or Nan or Calie fertile. And Dr. Sutter lorded it over Tam, who otherwise was the smartest person in the family.

"I'm afraid," Suze said. She rode the family mule; the others walked. Suze and Calie; Nan, led by Tam's cousin Jack; Uncle Seddie and Uncle Ned, both armed; Tam and Juli. Juli stood talking, sparkly eyed, to Sutter. To Tam's disappointment, no baby had been started on the honeymoon.

He said, "Nothing to be afraid of, Suze. Juli! Time to go!"

She danced over to him. "Dave's coming, too! He says he got a few weeks' vacation and would like to see the egg. He knows about it, Tam!"

Of course he did. Tam set his lips together and didn't answer.

"He says it's from people on another world, not from God, and—"

"My gran said it was from God," Tam said sharply. At his tone, Juli stopped walking.

"Tam—"

"I'll speak to Sutter myself. Telling you these city lies. Now go walk by Suze. She's afraid."

Juli, eyes no longer sparkling, obeyed. Tam told himself he was going to go over and have this out with Sutter, just as soon as he got everything going properly. Of *course* the egg was from God! Gran had said so, and anyway, if it wasn't, what was the point of this whole expedition, taking workers away from the farm, even if it was the mid-summer quiet between planting and harvest.

But somehow, with one task and another, Tam didn't find time to confront Sutter until night, when they were camped by the first lake. Calie and Suze slept, and the others sat around a comfortable fire, full of corn mush and fresh rabbit. Somewhere in the darkness, a wolf howled.

"Lots more of those than when I was young," said Uncle Seddie, who was almost seventy. "Funny thing, too—when you trap 'em, they're hardly ever deformed. Not like rabbits or frogs. Frogs, they're the worst."

Sutter said, "Wolves didn't move back down to Minnesota until after the Collapse. Up in Canada, they weren't as exposed to endocrine-mimicking pollutants. And frogs have always been the worst; water animals are especially sensitive to environmental factors."

Some of the words were the same ones Gran had used, but that didn't make Tam like them any better. He didn't know what they meant, and he wasn't about to ask Sutter.

Juli did, though. "Those endo . . . endo . . . what are they, doctor?"

He smiled at her, his straight white teeth gleaming in the firelight. "Environmental pollutants that bind to receptor sites all over the body, disrupting its normal function. They especially affect fetuses. Just before the Collapse, they reached some sort of unanticipated critical mass, and suddenly there were worldwide fertility problems, neurological impairments, cerebral. . . . Sorry, Juli, you got me started on my medical diatribe. I mean, pretty lady, that too few babies were born, and too many of those who were born couldn't think or move right, and we had the Collapse."

Beside him, Nan, born loose-brained, crooned softly to herself.

Juli said innocently, "But I thought the Collapse, it came from wars and money and bombs and things like that."

"Yes," Sutter said, "but those things happened *because* of the population and neurological problems."

"O, I'm just glad I didn't live then!" Ned said, shuddering. "It must have been terrible, especially in the cities."

Juli said, "But, doctor, aren't you from a city?"

Sutter looked into the flames. The wolf howled again. "Some cities fared much better than others. We *lost* most of the East Coast, you know, to various terrorist wars, and—"

"Everybody knows that," Tam said witheringly.

Sutter was undeterred, "—and California to rioting and looting. But St. Paul came through, eventually. And a basic core of knowledge and skills persisted, even if only in the urban areas. Science, medicine, engineering. We don't have the skilled population, or even a neurologically functional population, but we haven't really gone pre-industrial. There are even pockets of research, especially in biology. We'll beat this, someday."

"I know we will!" Juli said, her eyes shining. She was always so optimistic. Like a child, not a grown woman.

Tam said, "And meanwhile, the civilized types like you graciously go around to the poor country villages that feed you and bless them with your important skills."

Sutter looked at him across the fire. "That's right, Tam."

Uncle Seddie said, "Enough arguing. Go to bed, everybody."

Seddie was the ranking elder; there was no choice but to obey. Tam pulled Juli up with him, and in their bedroll he copulated with her so hard that she had to tell him to be more gentle, he was hurting her.

They reached the egg, by the direct route Tam had mapped out, in less than a week. Another family already camped beside it.

The two approached each other warily, guns and precious ammunition prominently displayed. But the other family, the Janeways, turned out to be a lot like the Wilkinsons, a goat-and-farm clan whose herdsmen had discovered the egg and brought others back to see the God-given miracle.

Tam, standing behind Seddie and Ned, said, "There's some that don't think it is from God."

The ranking Janeway, a tough old woman lean as Gran had been, said sharply, "Where else could it come from, way out here? No city tech left this here."

"That's what we say," Seddie answered. He lowered his rifle. "You people willing to trade provisions? We got maple syrup, corn mush, some good pepper."

"Pepper?" The old woman's eyes brightened. "You got pepper?"

"We trade with a family that trades in St. Paul," Ned said proudly. "Twice a year, spring and fall."

"We got sugar and an extra radio."

Tam's chin jerked up. A radio! But that was worth more than any amount of provisions. Nobody would casually trade a radio.

"Our family runs to boys, nearly all boys," the old woman said, by way of explanation. She looked past Tam, at Juli and Calie and Suze and Nan, hanging back with the mule and backpacks. "They're having trouble finding fertile wives. If any of your girls . . . and if the young people liked each other . . ."

"Juli, the blond, she's married to Tam here," Seddie said. "And the other girls, they aren't fertile . . . *yet*."

" 'Yet?' What do you mean, 'yet'?"

Seddie pointed with his rifle at the egg. "Don't you know what that is?"

"A gift from God," the woman said.

"Yes. But don't you know about the princess and her twins? Tell her, Tam."

Tam told the story, feeling himself thrill to it as he did so. The woman listened intently, then squinted again at the girls. Seddie said quickly, "Nan is loose-brained, I have to tell you. And Suze is riding because her foot is crippled, although she's got the sweetest, meekest nature you could ever find. But Calie there, even though she's got a withered arm, is quick and smart and can do almost anything. And after she touches the egg. . . . but, ma'am, Wilkinsons don't force marriages on our women. Never. Calie'd have to like one of your sons, and want to go with you."

"O, we can see what happens," the woman said, and winked, and for a second Tam saw what she must have been once, long ago, on a sweet summer night like this one when she was young.

He said suddenly, "The girls have to touch the egg at dawn."

Seddie and Ned turned to him. "Dawn? Why dawn?"

Tam didn't know why he'd said that, but now he had to see it through. "I don't know. God just made that idea come to me."

Seddie said to Mrs. Janeway, "Tam's our smartest person. Always has been."

"All right, then. Dawn."

In the chill morning light, the girls lined up, shivering. Mrs. Janeway, Dr. Sutter, and the men from both families made an awkward semi-circle around them, shuffling their feet a little, not looking at each other. The five Janeway boys, a tangle of uncles and cousins, all looked a bit stooped, but they could all walk, and none were loose-brained. Tam had spent the previous evening at the communal camp-fire, saying little, watching and listening to see which Janeways might be good to his sisters. He'd already decided that Cal had a temper, and if he asked Uncle Seddie for Calie or Suze, Tam would advise against it.

Dr. Sutter had said nothing at the campfire, listening to the others become more and more excited about the egg-touching, about the fertility from God. Even when Mrs. Janeway had asked him questions, his replies had been short and evasive. She'd kept watching him, clearly suspicious. Tam had liked her more and more as the long evening progressed.

Followed by a longer night. Tam and Juli had argued.

"I want to touch it, too, Tam."

"No. You have your certificate from that doctor two years ago. She tested you, and you're already fertile."

"Then why haven't I started no baby? Maybe the fertility went away."

"It doesn't do that."

"How do you know? I asked Dr. Sutter and he said—"

"You told Dr. Sutter about your body?" Rage swamped Tam.

Juli's voice grew smaller. "O, he *is* a doctor! Tam, he says it's hard to be sure about fertility testing for women, the test is . . . is some word I don't remember. But he says about one certificate in four is wrong. He says we should do away with the certificates. He says—"

"I don't care what he says!" Tam had all but shouted. "I don't want you talking to him again! If I see you are, Juli, I'll take it up with Uncle Seddie. And you are not touching the egg!"

Juli had raised herself on one elbow to stare at him in the starlight, then had turned her back and pretended to sleep until dawn.

Now she led Nan, the oldest sister, toward the egg. Nan crooned, drooling a little, and smiled at Juli. Juli was always tender with Nan. She smiled back, wiped Nan's chin, and guided her hand toward the silvery oval. Tam watched carefully to see that Juli didn't touch the egg herself. She didn't, and neither did Nan, technically, since her hand stopped at whatever unseen wall protected the object. But everyone let out a sharp breath, and Nan laughed suddenly, one of her clear high giggles, and Tam felt suddenly happier.

Seddie said, "Now Suze."

Juli led Nan away. Suze, carried by Uncle Ned, reached out and touched the egg. She, too, laughed aloud, her sweet face alight, and Tam saw Vic Janeway lean forward a little, watching her. Suze couldn't plow or plant, but she was the best cook in the family if everything were put in arm's reach. And she could sew and weave and read and carve.

Next Calie, pretty if Juli hadn't been there for comparison, and the other four Janeway men watched. Calie's one hand, dirt under the small fingernails, stayed on the egg a long time, trembling.

No one spoke.

"O, then," Mrs. Janeway said, "we should pray."

They did, each family waiting courteously while the other said their special prayers, all joining in the "Our Father." Tam caught Sutter looking at him somberly, and he glared back. Nothing Sutter's "medicine" had ever done had helped Tam's sisters, and anyway, it was none of Sutter's business what the Wilkinsons and Janeways did. Let him go back to St. Paul with his heathen beliefs.

"I want to touch the egg," Juli said. "I won't get no other chance. We leave in the morning."

Tam had had no idea that she could be so stubborn. She'd argued and pleaded for the three days they'd camped with the Janeways, letting the families get to know each other. Now they were leaving in the morning, with Vic and Lenny Janeway traveling with them to stay until the end of harvest, so Suze and Calie could decide about marriage. And Juli was still arguing!

"I said no," Tam said tightly. He was afraid to say more—afraid not of her, but of himself. Some men beat their wives; not Wilkinson men. But watching Juli all evening, Tam had suddenly understood those other men. She had deliberately sat talking only to Dr. Sutter, smiling at him in the flickering firelight. Even Uncle Ned had noticed, Tam thought, and that made Tam writhe with shame. He had dragged Juli off to bed early, and here she was arguing still, while singing started around the fire twenty feet away.

"Tam . . . please! I want to start a baby, and nothing we do started one. . . . Don't get upset, but . . . but Dr. Sutter says sometimes the man is infertile, even though it don't happen as often as women's wombs it can still happen, and maybe—"

It was too much. First his wife shames him by spending the evening sitting close to another man, talking and laughing, and then she suggests that *him*, not her, might be the reason there was no baby yet. Him! When God had clearly closed the wombs of women after the Collapse, just like he did to those sinning women in the Bible! Anger and shame thrilled through Tam, and before he knew he was going to do it, he hit her.

It was only a slap. Juli put her hand to her cheek, and Tam suddenly would have given everything he possessed to take the slap back. Juli jumped up and ran off in the darkness, away from the fire. Tam let her go. She had a right to be upset now, he'd given her that. He lay stiffly in the darkness, intending every second to go get her—there were wolves out there, after all, although they seldom attacked people. Still, he would go get her. But he didn't, and, without knowing it, he fell asleep.

When he woke, it was near dawn. Juli woke him, creeping back into their bedroll.

"Juli! You . . . it's nearly dawn. Where were you all this time?"

She didn't answer. In the icy pale light, her face was flushed.

He said slowly, "You touched it."

She wriggled the rest of the way into the bedroll and turned her back to him. Over her shoulder she said, "No, Tam. I didn't touch it."

"You're lying to me."

"No. I didn't touch it," she repeated, and Tam believed her. So he had won. Generosity filled him.

"Juli — I'm sorry I hit you. So sorry."

Abruptly she twisted in the bedroll to face him. "I know. Tam, listen to me. . . . God wants me to start a baby. He does!"

"Yes, of course," Tam said, bewildered by her sudden ferocity.

"He wants me to start a baby!"

"Are you . . . are you saying that you have?"

She was silent a long time. Then she said, "Yes. I think so."

Joy filled him. He took her in his arms, and she let him. It would all be right, now. He and Juli would have a child, many children. So would Suze and Calie, and — who could say? — maybe even Nan. The egg's fame would grow, and there would be many babies again.

On the journey home, Juli stuck close to Tam, never looking even once in Dr. Sutter's direction. He avoided her, too. Tam gloated; so much for science and tech from the cities! When they reached the farm, Dr. Sutter retrieved his dirtbike and rode away. The next time a doctor came to call, it was someone different.

Juli bore a girl, strong and whole except for two missing fingers. During her marriage to Tam, she bore four more children, finally dying while trying to deliver a sixth one. Suze and Calie married the Janeway boys, but neither conceived. After three years of trying, Lenny Janeway sent Calie back to the Wilkinsons; Calie never smiled or laughed much again.

For decades afterward, the egg was proclaimed a savior, a gift from God, a miracle to repopulate Minnesota. Families came and feasted and prayed, and the girls touched the egg, more each year. Most of the girls never started a baby, but a few did, and at times the base of the egg was almost invisible under the gifts of flowers, fruit, woven cloth, even a computer from St. Paul and a glass perfume bottle from much farther away, so delicate that the wind smashed it one night. Or bears did, or maybe even angels. Some people said that angels visited the egg regularly. They said that the angels even touched it, through the invisible wall.

Tam's oldest daughter didn't believe that. She didn't believe much, Tam thought, for she was the great disappointment of his life. Strong, beautiful, smart, she got herself accepted to a merit school in St. Paul, and she went, despite her missing fingers. She made herself into a scientist and turned her back on the Bible. Tam, who had turned more stubborn as he grew old, refused to see her again. She said that the egg wasn't a miracle and had never made anyone pregnant. She said there were no saviors for humanity but itself.

Tam, who had become not only more stubborn but also more angry after Juli died, turned his face away and refused to listen.

Transmission: There is nothing here yet.
Current probability of occurrence: 28%.

III: 2175

Abby4 said, "The meeting is in *northern Minnesota?* Why?"

Mal held onto his temper. He'd been warned about Abby4. *One of the Bio-*

mensas, Mal's network of friends and colleagues had said, *In the top 2 percent of genemods. She likes to throw around her superiority. Don't let her twist you. The contract is too important.*

His friends had also said not to be intimidated by either Abby4's *office* or her beauty. The office occupied the top floor of the tallest building in Raleigh, with a sweeping view of the newly cleaned-up city. A garden in the sky, its walls and ceiling were completely hidden by the latest genemod plants from AbbyWorks, flowers so exotic and brilliant that, just looking at them, a visitor could easily forget what he was going to say. Probably that was the idea.

Abby4's beauty was even more distracting than her office. She sat across from him in a soft white chair that only emphasized her sleek, hard glossiness. The face of an Aztec princess, framed by copper hair pulled into a thick roll on either side. The sash of her black business suit stopped just above the swell of white breasts that Mal determinedly ignored. Her legs were longer than his dreams.

Mal said pleasantly, "The meeting is in northern Minnesota because the Chinese contact is already doing business in St. Paul, at the university. And he wants to see a curiosity near the old Canadian border, an object that government records show as an alien artifact."

Abby4 blinked, probably before she knew that she was going to do it, which gave Mal enormous satisfaction. Not even the Biomensas, with their genetically engineered intelligence and memory, knew everything.

"Ah, yes, of course," Abby4 said, and Mal was careful not to recognize the bluff. "O, then, northern Minnesota. Send my office system the details, please. Thank you, Mr. Goldstone."

Mal rose to go. Abby4 did not rise. In the outer office, he passed a woman several years older than Abby4 but looking so much like her that it must be one of the earlier clones. The woman stooped slightly. Undoubtedly each successive clone had better genemods as the technology came onto the market. AbbyWorks was, after all, one of the five or six leading biosolutions companies in Raleigh, and that meant in the world.

Mal left the Eden-like AbbyWorks building to walk into the shrouding heat of a North Carolina summer. In the parking lot, his car wouldn't start. Cursing, he opened the hood. Someone had broken the hood lock and stolen the engine.

Purveyors of biosolutions to the world, Mal thought bitterly, cleaners-up of the ecological, neurological, and population disasters of the Collapse, and we still can't create a decent hood lock! O, that actually figured. For the last hundred and fifty years—no, closer to two hundred now—the best minds of each American generation had been concentrating on biology. Engineering, physics, and everything else got few practitioners, and even less funding.

O, it had paid off. Not only for people like Abby4, the beautiful Biomensa bitch, but even for comparative drones like Mal. He had biological defenses against lingering environmental pollutants (they would linger for another thousand years), he was fertile, he even had modest genemods so that he didn't look like a troll or think like a troglodyte. What he *didn't* have was a working car.

He took out his phone and called a cab.

August in Minnesota was not cold, but Kim Mao Xun, the Chinese client, was well wrapped in layers of silk and thin wool. He looked very old, which meant that he was probably even older. Obviously no genemods for appearance, Mal thought, whatever else Mr. Kim might have. O, they did things differently in China! When you survived the Collapse on nothing but sheer numbers, you started your long climb back with essentials, nothing else.

"I am so excited to see the Alien Craft," he said in excellent English. "It is famous in China, you know."

Abby4 smiled. "Here, I'm afraid, it's mostly a curiosity. Very few people even know it exists, although the government has authenticated from written records that it landed in October 2007, an event widely recorded by the best scientific instruments of the age."

"So much better than what we have now," Mr. Kim murmured, and Abby4 frowned.

"O, yes, I suppose . . . but then, they didn't have a world to clean up, did they?"

"And we do. Mr. Goldstone tells me you can help us do this in Shanghai."

"Yes, we can," Abby4 said, and the meeting began to replicate in earnest.

Mal listened intently, taking notes, but said nothing. Meeting brokers didn't get involved in details. Matching, arranging, follow-through, impartial evaluation, and, if necessary, arbitration. Then disappear until the next time. But Mal was interested; this was his biggest client so far.

And the biggest problem: Shanghai. The city and the harbor, which must add up to hundreds of different pollutants, each needing a different genetically designed organism to attack it. Plus, Shanghai had been viral-bombed during the war with Japan. Those viruses would be much mutated by now, especially if they had jumped hosts, which they probably had. Mal could see that even Abby4 was excited by the scope of the job, although she was trying to conceal it.

"What is Shanghai's current population, Mr. Kim?"

"Zero." Mr. Kim smiled wryly. "Officially, anyway. The city is quarantined. Of course, there are the usual stoopers and renegades, but we will do our best to relocate them before you begin, and those who will not go may be ignored by your operators."

Something chilling in that. Although did the US do any better? Mal had heard stories — everyone had heard stories — of families who'd stayed in the most contaminated areas for generations, becoming increasingly deformed and increasingly frightening. There were even people still living in places like New York City, which had taken the triple blow of pollutants, bioweapons, and radiation. Theoretically, the population of New York City was zero. In reality, nobody would go in to count, nor even send in the doggerels, biosolutioned canines with magnitude-one immunity and selectively enhanced intelligence. A doggerel was too expensive to risk in New York. Whoever — or whatever — couldn't be counted by robots (and American robots were so inadequate compared to the Asian product), stayed uncounted.

"I understand," Abby4 said to Mr. Kim. "And the time-frame?"

"We would like to have Shanghai totally clean ten years from now."

Abby4's face didn't change. "That is very soon."

"Yes. Can you do it?"

"I need to consult with my scientists," she said, and Mal felt his chest fill with lightness. She hadn't said no, and when Abby4 didn't say no, the answer was likely to be yes. The ten-year deadline—only ten years!—would make the fee enormous, and Mal's company's small percentage of it would rise accordingly. A promotion, a bonus, a new car. . . .

"Then until I hear back from you, we can go no farther," Mr. Kim said. "Shall we take my car to the Alien Craft?"

"Certainly," Abby4 said. "Mr. Goldstone? Can you accompany us? I'm told you know exactly where this curious object is." *As a busy and important Biomensa executive like me would not*, was the unstated message, but Mal didn't mind. He was too happy.

The Alien Craft, as Mr. Kim persisted in calling it, was not easy to find. Northern Minnesota had all been cleaned up, of course; as valuable farm and dairy land, it had had priority, and anyway, the damage hadn't been too bad. But, once cleaned, the agrisolution companies wanted the place for farming, free of outside interference. The government, the weak partner in all that biotech corporations did, reluctantly agreed. The Alien Craft lay under an inconspicuous foamcast dome at the end of an obscure road, with no identifying signs of any kind.

Mal saw immediately why Mr. Kim had suggested going in his car, which had come with him from China. The Chinese were forced to buy all their biosolutions from others. In compensation, they had created the finest engineering and hard-goods manufactories in the world. Mr. Kim's car was silent, fast, and computer-driven, technology unknown in the United States. Mal could see that even Abby4 was unwillingly impressed.

He leaned back against the contoured seats, which molded themselves to his body, and watched farmland flash past at an incredible rate. There were government officials and university professors who said that the United States should fear Chinese technology, even if it wasn't based on biology. Maybe they were right.

In contrast, the computer-based security at the Alien Craft looked primitive. Mal had arranged for entry, and they passed through the locks into the dome, which was only ten feet wider on all sides than the Alien Craft itself. Mal had never seen it before, and despite himself, he was impressed.

The Craft was dull silver, as big as a small bedroom, a slightly irregular oval. In the artificial light of the dome, it shimmered. When Mal put out a hand to touch it, his hand stopped almost a foot away.

"A force field of some unknown kind, unknown even before the Collapse," Abby4 said, with such authority you'd think she'd done field tests herself. "The shield extends completely around the Craft, even below ground, where it is also impenetrable. The Craft was very carefully monitored in the decades between its landing and the Collapse, and never once did any detectable signal of any kind go out from it. No outgoing signals, no aliens disembarking, no outside markings to decode . . . no communication of any kind. One wonders why the aliens bothered to send it at all."

Mr. Kim quoted, " 'The wordless teaching, the profit in not doing—not many people understand it.' "

"Ah," Abby4 said, too smart to either agree or disagree with a philosophy—Taoist? Buddhist?—she patently didn't share.

Mal walked completely around the Craft, wondering himself why anybody would bother with such a tremendous undertaking without any follow-up. Of course, maybe it hadn't been tremendous to the *aliens*. Maybe they sent interstellar silvery metal ovals to other planets all the time without follow-up. But *why?*

When Mal reached his starting point in the circular dome, Mr. Kim was removing an instrument from his leather bag.

Mal had never seen an instrument like it, but then, he'd hardly seen any scientific instruments at all. This one looked like a flat television, with a glass screen on one side, metal on the other five. Only the "glass" clearly *wasn't*, since it seemed to shift as Mr. Kim lifted it, as if it were a field of its own. As Mal watched, Mr. Kim applied the field side of the device onto the side of the Craft, where it stayed even as he stepped back.

Mal said uncertainly, "I don't think you should—"

Abby4 said, "O, it doesn't matter, Mr. Goldstone. Nothing anyone has ever done has penetrated the Craft's force field, even before the Collapse."

Mr. Kim just smiled.

Mal said, "You don't understand. The clearance I arranged with the State Department . . . it doesn't include taking any readings or . . . or whatever that device is doing. Mr. Kim?"

"Just taking some readings," Mr. Kim said blandly.

Mal's unease grew. "Please stop. As I say, I didn't obtain clearances for this!"

Abby4 scowled at him fiercely. Mr. Kim said, "Of course, Mr. Goldstone," and detached his device. "I am sorry to alarm you. Just some readings. Shall we go now? A most interesting object, but rather monotonous."

On the way back to St. Paul, Mr. Kim and Abby4 discussed the historic cleanups of Boston, Paris, and Lisbon, as if nothing had happened.

What had?

AbbyWorks got the Shanghai contract. Mal got his promotion, his bonus, and his new car. Someone else handled the follow-up for the contract while Mal went on to new projects, but every so often, he checked to see how the clean-up of Shanghai was proceeding. Two years into the agreement, the job was actually ahead of projected schedule, despite badly deteriorating relations between the two countries. China invaded and annexed Tibet, but China had *always* invaded and annexed Tibet, and only the human-solidarity people objected. Next, however, China annexed the Kamchatka Peninsula, where American biosolutions companies were working on the clean-up of Vladivostock. The genemod engineers brought back frightening stories of advanced Chinese engineering: room-temperature superconductors. Maglev trains. Nanotechnology. There were even rumors of quantum computers, capable of handling trillions of operations simultaneously, although Mal discounted those rumors completely. A practical quantum computer was still far over the horizon.

AbbyWorks was ordered out of Shanghai by the United States government. The company did not leave. Abby1 was jailed, but this made no difference. The Shanghai profits were paid to offshore banks. AbbyWorks claimed to have lost control of its Shanghai employees, who were making huge personal fortunes, enough to enable them to live outside the United States for the rest of very luxurious lives. Then, abruptly, the Chinese government itself terminated the contract. They literally threw AbbyWorks out of China in the middle of the night. They kept for themselves enormous resources in patented scientific equipment, as well as monies due for the last three months' work, an amount equal to some state budgets.

At three o'clock in the morning, Mal received a visit from the Office of National Security.

"Mallings Goldstone?"

"Yes?"

"We need to ask you some questions."

Recorders, intimidation. The ONS had information that in 2175 Mr. Goldstone had conducted two people to the Minnesota site of the space object: Abby4 Abbington, president of AbbyWorks Biosolutions, and Mr. Kim Mao Xun of the Chinese government.

"Yes, I did," Mal said, sitting stiffly in his nightclothes. "It's on record. I had proper clearances."

"Yes. But during that visit, did Mr. Kim take out and attach to the space object an unknown device, and then return it to his briefcase?"

"Yes." Mal's stomach twisted.

"Why wasn't this incident reported to the State Department?"

"I didn't think it was important." Not entirely true. Abby4 must have reported it . . . but why *now*? Because of the lost monies and confiscated equipment, of course. Adding to the list of Chinese treacheries; a longer list was more likely to compel government reaction.

"Do you have any idea what the device was, or what it might have done to the space object?"

"No."

"Then you didn't rule out that its effects might have been dangerous to your country?"

"'Dangerous'? How?"

"We don't know, Mr. Mallings—that's the point. We do know that in nonbiological areas the Chinese technology is far ahead of our own. We have no way of knowing if that device you failed to report turned the space object into a weapon of some kind."

"A weapon? Don't you think that's very unlikely?"

"No, Mr. Mallings. I don't. Please get dressed and come with us."

For the first time, Mal noticed the two men's builds. Genemod for strength and agility, no doubt, as well as maximum possible longevity. He remembered Mr. Kim, scrawny and wrinkled. Their bodies far outclassed Mr. Kim's, far outclassed Mal's as well. But Mr. Kim's body was somewhere on the other side of the world, along with his superior "devices," and Mal's body was marked "scapegoat" as clearly as if it were spelled out in DNA-controlled birthmarks on his forehead.

He went into his bedroom to get dressed.

Mal had been interrogated with truth drugs — painless, harmless, utterly reliable — recorded, and released by the time the news hit the flimsies. He had already handed in his resignation to his company. The moving truck stood outside his apartment, being loaded for the move to someplace he wasn't known. Mal, flimsy in hand, watched the two huge stevies carry out his furniture.

But he couldn't postpone reading the flimsy forever. And, of course, this was just the first. There would be more. The tempaper rustled in his hand. It would last forty-eight hours before dissolving into molecules completely harmless to the environment.

CHINESE ARMED "SPACE OBJECT" TO DESTROY US!!!

"MIGHT BE RADIATION, OR POLLUTANTS, OR A SUPER-BOMB," SAY SCIENTISTS

TROJAN HORSE UNDER GUISE OF BIOSOLUTIONS CONTRACT

TWO YEARS AND NOTHING HAS BEEN DONE!!!!

Flimsies weren't subtle. But so far as Mal could see, his name hadn't yet been released to them.

Mal said, "Please be careful with that desk, it's very old. It belonged to my great-grandfather."

"O, yes, friend," one of the stevies said. "Most careful." They hurled it into the truck.

A neighbor of Mal's walked toward Mal, recognized him, and stopped dead. She hissed at him, a long ugly sound, and walked on.

So some other flimsy had already tracked him down and published his name.

"Leave the rest," Mal said suddenly, "everything else inside the house. Let's go."

"O, just a few crates," said one stevie.

"No, leave it." Mal climbed into the truck's passenger cubicle. He hoped that he wasn't a coward, but like all meeting brokers he was an historian, and he remembered the historical accounts of the "Anti-Polluters' Riots" of the Collapse. What those mobs had done to anyone suspected of contributing to the destruction of the environment . . . Mal pulled the curtains closed in the cubicle. "Let's go!"

"O, yes!" the stevies said cheerfully, and drove off.

Mal moved five states away, pursued all the way by flimsies. He couldn't change his retinal scan or DNA ID, of course, but he used a legal corporate alias with the new landlord, the grocery broker, the bank. He read the news every day, and listened to it on public radio, and it progressed as any meeting broker could foresee it would.

First, set the agenda: Demonize the Chinese, spread public fear. Second, canvass negotiating possibilities: Will they admit it? What can we contribute? Third, eliminate the possibilities you don't like and hone in on the one you do: If the United States had been attacked, it has the right to counterattack. Fourth, build in safeguards against failure: We can't yet attack China, they'll destroy us. We *can* attack the danger they've placed within our borders, and then declare victory for that. Fifth, close the deal.

The evacuation started two weeks later, and covered most of northern Minnesota and great swathes of southern Ontario. It included people and farm animals, but not wildlife, which would, of course, be replaced from cloned embryos. As the agrisolution inhabitants, many protesting furiously, were trucked out, the timed-release drops of engineered organisms were trucked in. Set loose after the bomb, they would spread over the entire affected area and disassemble all radioactive molecules. They were the same biosolutions that had cleaned up Boston, the very best AbbyWorks could create. In five years, Minnesota would be as sweet and clean as Kansas.

Or Shanghai.

The entire nation, Mal included, watched the bomb drop on vid. People held patriotic parties; wine and beer flowed. We were showing the Chinese that they couldn't endanger us in our own country! Handsome genemod news speakers, who looked like Viking princesses or Zulu warriors or Greek gods, speculated on what the space object might reveal when it was blasted open. If anything survived, of course, which was not likely . . . and here scientists, considerably less gorgeous than the news speakers, explained fusion and the core of the sun. The bomb might be antiquated technology, they said, but it was still workable, and would save us from Chinese perfidy.

Not to mention, Mal thought, saving face for the United States and lost revenues for AbbyWorks. It might not earn them as much to clean up Minnesota as to clean up Shanghai, but it was still a lot of money.

The bomb fell, hit the space object, and sent up a mushroom cloud. When it cleared, the object lay there exactly as before.

Airborne robots went in, spraying purifying organisms as they went, recording every measurement possible. Scientists compared the new data about the space object to the data they already had. Not one byte differed. When robotic arms reached out to touch the object, the arms still stopped ten inches away at an unseen, unmoved force field of some type not even the Chinese understood.

Mal closed his eyes. How long would Chinese retaliation take? What would they do, and when?

They did nothing. Slowly, public opinion swung to their side, helped by the flimsies. Journalists and viddies, ever eager for the next story, discovered that AbbyWorks had falsified reports on the clean-up of Shanghai. It had not been progressing as the corporation said, or as the contract promised. Eventually, AbbyWorks — already too rich, too powerful, for many people's tastes — became the villain. They had tried to frame the Chinese, who were merely trying to do normal clean-up of their part of the planet. Clean-up was our job, our legacy, our sacred stewardship of the living Earth! And anyway, Chinese technological consumer goods, increasingly available in the United States, were so much better than ours — shouldn't we be trying to learn from them?

So business partnerships were formed. The fragile Chinese-American alliance was strengthened. AbbyWorks was forced to move offshore. Mal, in some way he didn't quite understand, became a cult hero. Mr. Kim would have, too, but shortly after the bomb was dropped on the space object, he died of a heart attack, not having the proper genemods to clear out plaque from his ancient cardiac arteries.

When Minnesota was clean again, the space object went back under a new foamcast dome, and in two more generations, only historians remembered what it may or may not have saved.

> Transmission: There is nothing here yet.
> Current probability of occurrence: 78%.

IV:2264

Few people understood why KimWorks was built in such a remote place. Dr. Leila Jian-fen Kim was one of the few who did.

She liked family history. Didn't Lao Tzu himself say, "To know what endures is to be openhearted, magnanimous, regal, blessed"? Family endures, family history endures. It was the same reason she liked the meditation garden at KimWorks, which was where she headed now with her great secret, to compose her mind.

They had done it. Created the programmable replicator. One of the two great prizes hovering on the engineering horizon, and KimWorks had captured it.

Walking away from the sealed lab, Leila tried to empty her mind, to put the achievement to one side and let the mystery flow in. The replicator must be kept in perspective, in its rightful place. Calming herself in the meditation garden would help her remember that.

The garden was her favorite part of KimWorks. It lay at the northern end of the vast walled complex, separated from the first security fence by a simple curve of white stone. From the stone benches, you couldn't see security fences, or even most of the facility buildings. So cleverly designed was the meditation garden that no matter where you sat, you contemplated only serene things. A single blooming bush, surrounded by raked gravel. A rock, placed to catch the sun. The stream, flowing softly, living water, always seeking its natural level. Or the egg, mystery of mysteries.

It was the egg, unexplained symbol of unexplained realms beyond Earth, that brought Leila the deepest peace. She had sat for hours when the replicator project was in its planning stage, contemplating the egg's dull silvery oval, letting her mind empty of all else. From that, she was convinced, had come most of the project's form. Form was only a temporary manifestation of the ten thousand things, and in the egg's unknowability lay the secret of its power.

Her great-grandfather, Kim Mao Xun, had known that power. He had seen the egg on an early trip to the United States, before the Alliance, even. His son had made the same visit, and his granddaughter, Leila's mother, had chosen the spot for this KimWorks facility and had the meditation garden built at its heart. Leila's father, Paul Wilkinson, had gently teased his wife about putting a garden in a scientific research center, but Father was an American. They did not always understand. With the wiser in the world lies the responsibility for teaching the less wise.

But it had been Father who had inspired Leila to become a scientist, not a businessman like her brother or a political leader like her sister. Father, were he still alive, would be proud of her now. Pride was a temptation, even pride in one's children, but it nonetheless warmed Leila's heart.

She sat, a slim, middle-aged, Chinese-born woman with smooth black hair, dressed in a blue lab coverall, and thought about the nature of pride.

The programmable replicator, unlike its predecessors, would not be limited to nanocreating a single specific molecule. It was good to be able to create any molecule you needed or wanted, of course. The extant replicators, shaped by Chinese technology, had changed the face of the Earth. Theoretically, everyone now alive could be fed, housed, clad by nanotech. But in addition to the inevitable political and economic problems of access, the existing nanotech processes were expensive. One must create the assemblers, including their tiny self-contained programs; use the assemblers to create molecules; use other techniques, chemical or mechanical, to join the molecules into products.

Now all that would change. The new KimWorks programmable replicator didn't carry assembly instructions hardwired into it. Rather, it carried programmable computers that could build anything desired, including more of themselves, from the common materials of the earth. Every research lab in the world had been straining toward this goal. And Leila's team had accomplished it.

She sat on the bench closet to the egg. The sky arched above her, for the electromagnetic dome protecting KimWorks was invisible. Clear space had been left all around the object, except for a small flat stone visible from Leila's bench. On the stone was engraved a verse from the *Tao Te Ching*, in both Chinese and English:

THE WORDLESS TEACHING
THE PROFIT IN NOT DOING—
NOT MANY PEOPLE UNDERSTAND IT.

Certainly, in all humility, Leila didn't. Why send this egg from somewhere in deep space and have it do nothing for two and a half centuries? But that was the mystery, the power of the egg. That was why contemplating it filled her with peace.

The others were still in nanoteam one's lab building. Not many others; robots did all the routine work, of course, and only David and Chunquing and Rulan remained at the computers and stafils. It had taken Leila ten minutes to pass through the lab safeties, but she had suddenly wearied of the celebrations, the Chilean wine and holo congratulations from the CEO in Shanghai, who was her great-uncle. She had wanted to sit quietly in the cool sweet air of the garden, watching the long Minnesota twilight turn purple behind the egg. Shadow and curve, it was almost a poem. . . .

The lab blew up.

The blast threw Leila off her bench and onto the ground. She screamed and threw up one arm to shield her eyes. But it wasn't necessary; she was shielded from direct line with the lab by the egg. And a part of her mind knew that there was no radiation anyway, only heat, and no flying debris, because the lab had imploded, as it was constructed to do. Something had breached the outer layers of sensors, and, in response, the ignition layer had produced a gas of metal oxides hot enough to vaporize everything inside the lab. No uncontrolled replicator must ever escape.

To vaporize everything. The lab. The project. David, Chunquing, Rulan.

Already, the site would be cooling. Leila staggered to her feet, and immediately was again knocked off them by an aftershock. It had been an earthquake, then, least likely of anticipated penetrations, but nonetheless guarded against. O, David, Chunquing, Rulan . . .

"Dr. Kim! Are you all right?!" Keesha Ali, running toward her from Security. As her ears cleared, Leila heard the sirens and alarms.

"Yes, I . . . Keesha!"

"I know," the woman said grimly. "Who was inside?"

"David. Chunquing. Rulan. And the replicator project . . . an earthquake! Of all the bad luck of heaven . . ."

"It wasn't bad luck," Keesha said. "We were attacked."

"Attacked—"

"That was no natural quake. Security picked up the charge just seconds before it went off. In a tunnel underneath the lab, very deep, very huge. It not only breached the lab, it destroyed the dome equipment. We're bringing the back-up on-line now. Meeting in Amenities in five minutes, Dr. Kim."

Leila stared at Keesha. The woman was American, of course, born here, with no Chinese ancestry. But surely even such people first mourned their dead. . . . Yes. They did, under normal circumstances. So something extraordinary was happening here.

Leila was genemod for intelligence. She said slowly, "Data escaped."

"In the fraction of a second between breach and ignition," Keesha said grimly, "while the dome was down, including, of course, the Faraday cage. They took the entire replicator project, Dr. Kim."

Leila understood what that meant, and her mind staggered under the burden. It meant that someone else had captured the other shimmering engineering prize. The replicator data had been heavily encrypted, and there had been massive amounts of it. Only another quantum computer could have been fast enough to steal that much data in the fraction of a second before ignition—or could have a hope of decrypting it. A quantum computer, able to perform trillions of computations per second, had been a reality for a generation now. But it could operate only within sealed parameters: magnetic fields. Optic cables.

Qubit data, represented by particles with undetermined spin, were easily destroyed by contact with any other particles, including photons—ordinary sunlight. No one had succeeded in intrusive stealing of quantum data without destroying it. Not from outside the computer, and especially not over miles of open land.

Until now. And anyone with a quantum computer that could do *that* was already a rival.

Or a revolutionary.

The first replicator bloom appeared within KimWorks three weeks later.

It was Leila who first saw it: a dull, reddish-brown patch on the bright green genemod grass by Amenities. If it had been on the path itself, Leila would have thought she was seeing blood. But on grass . . . she stood very still and thought, *No*. It was a blight, some weird mutated fungus, a renegade biological. . . .

She had worked too long in the sabotaged lab not to know what it was.

Carefully, as if her arm bones were fragile, Leila raised her wrist to her mouth and spoke into her implanted comlink. "Code Heaven. Repeat, Code Heaven. Replicator escape at following coordinates. Security, nanoteam one—"

There was no need to list everyone who should be notified. People began pouring out of buildings: some blank-faced, some with their fists to their mouths, some running, as if speed would help. People, Leila thought numbly, expressed fear in odd ways.

"Dr. Kim?" It was a Grade 4 robotics engineer, a dark-skinned American man in an olive uniform. His teeth suddenly bared, very white in his face. "That's it? Right there?"

"That's it," Leila said, and immediately wanted to correct to *That's they*. For by now, there were billions of the replicators, to be so visible. Busily creating more of themselves from the grass and ground and morning dew and whatever else lay in their path, each one replicating every five minutes if they were on basic mode. And why wouldn't they be? They weren't assembling anything useful, not now. Whoever had programmed Leila's replicators had set them merely to replicate, chewing up whatever was in their path as raw materials, turning assemblers into tiny disassembling engines of destruction. "Don't go any closer!"

But of course, even a Grade 4 engineer knew better than to go close. Everyone inside this KimWorks facility understood the nature of the project, even if only a few could understand the actuality. Everyone inside was a trusted worker, a truth-drug-vetted loyalist.

She looked at the reddish-brown bloom, which was doubling every five minutes.

"You have detained everyone? Even those off duty?" asked the holo seated at the head of the conference table. Li Kim Lung, president of KimWorks, was in Shanghai, but his telepresence was so solid that it was an effort to remember that. His dark eyes raked their faces, with the one exception of Leila's. Out of family courtesy, he did not study her shame in the stolen uses of her creation.

Security chief Samuel Wang said, "Everyone who has been inside KimWorks in the last forty-eight hours has been found and recalled, Mr. Li. Forty-eight hours is a three-fold redundancy; the bloom was started, according to Dr. Kim, no later than sixteen hours ago. No one is missing."

"Your physicians have started truth-testing?"

"With the Dalton Corporation Serum Alpha. It's the best on the market, sir, to a 99.9 confidence level. Whoever brought the replicator into the dome will confess."

"And your physician can test how many at once?"

"Six, sir. There are 243 testees." Wang did not insult Mr. Li by doing the math for him.

"You are including the nanoteams and Security, of course?"

"Of course. We—"

"Mr. Wang." A telepresence suddenly beside the security chief, a young man. Leila knew this not from his appearance—they all looked young, after all, what else were biomods for?—but from his fear. He had not yet learned how to hide it. "We have . . . we found . . . a body. A suicide. Behind the dining hall."

Wang said, "Who?"

"Her name is—was—June Juana Selkirk. An equipment engineer. We're checking her records now, but they look all right."

Mr. Li's holo said dryly, "Obviously they are not all right, no matter what her DNA scan says."

Mr. Wang said, "Sir, if people are recruited by some other company or by some revolutionary group after they come to KimWorks, it's difficult to discover or control. American freedom laws . . ."

"I am not interested in American freedom laws," Mr. Li said. "I am interested in whom this woman was working for, and why she planted our own product inside KimWorks to destroy us. I am also interested in knowing where else she may have planted it before she killed herself. Those are the things I am interested in, Mr. Wang."

"O, yes," Wang said.

"I do not want to destroy your facility in order to stop this sabotage, Mr. Wang."

Mr. Wang said nothing. There was, Leila thought, nothing to say. No one was going to be allowed to leave the facility until this knot had been untied. Even the Americans accepted this. No one wanted military intervention. That truly might destroy the entire company.

Above all, no one wanted a single submicroscopic replicator to escape the dome. The arithmetic was despairingly simple. Doubling every five minutes, unchecked replicators could reduce the entire globe to rubble in a matter of days.

But it wasn't going to come to that. The bloom had been "killed" easily enough. Replicators weren't biologicals, but rather tiny computers powered by nanomachinery. They worked on a flow of electrons in their single-atom circuitry. An electromagnetic pulse had wiped out their programming in a nanosecond.

The second bloom was discovered that night, when a materials specialist walking from the dining hall to the makeshift dorms stepped on it. The path was floodlit, but the bloom was still small and faint, and the man didn't know his boot had made contact.

Some replicators stuck to his boot sole. Programmed to break down any material into usable atoms for construction, they ate through his boot. Then, doubling every five minutes, they began on his foot.

He screamed and fell to the floor of the dorm, pulling at his boot. Atoms of tissue, nerve cell, bone, were broken at their chemical bonds and reconfigured. No one knew what was happening, or what to do, until a physician arrived, cursed in Mandarin, and sent for an engineer. By the time equipment had been brought in to encase the worker in a magnetic field, he had fainted from the pain, and the leg had to be removed below the knee.

A new one would be grown for him, of course. But the nanoteam met immediately, and without choice.

Leila said, "We must use a massive EMP originating in the dome itself."

Samuel Wang said, "But, Dr. Kim—"

"No objections. Yes, it will destroy every electronic device we have, including the quantum computer. But no one will die."

Mr. Li's telepresence said, "Do so. Immediately. We can at least salvage reputation. No one outside the dome knows of this."

It was not a question, but Wang, eyes downcast, answered it like one. "O, no, Mr. Li."

"Then use the EMP. Following, administer a forty-eight-hour amnesia block to everyone below Grade 2."

"Yes," Wang said. He knew what was coming. Someone must bear responsibility for this disaster.

"And administer it also to yourself," Mr. Li said. "Dr. Kim, see that this is done."

"O, yes," said Leila. It was necessary, however distasteful. Samuel Wang would be severed from KimWorks. Severed people sometimes sought revenge. But without information, Wang would not be able to seek revenge, or to know why he wanted to. He would receive a good pension in return for the semi-destruction of his memory, which would in turn cause the complete destruction of his career.

Leila made her way to the meditation garden. Most people would wait indoors for the EMP; strange how human beings sought shelter within walls, even from things they knew walls could not affect. Leila's brain would be no more or less exposed to the EMP in the garden than inside a building. She would experience the same disorientation, and then the same massive lingering headache as her brain fought to regain its normal patterns of nerve firing.

Which it would do. The plasticity of the brain, a biological, was enormous. It was not so with computers. All microcircuitry within the dome would shortly be wiped of all data, all programming, and all ability to recover. This was not the only KimWorks facility, of course, but it *was* the flagship. Also, it was doing the most advanced physical engineering, and Leila wasn't sure how the company as a whole, her grandfather's company, would survive the financial loss.

She sat in the floodlit meditation garden and waited, staring at the egg. The night was clear, and when the floodlights failed, moonlight would edge the egg. Probably it would be beautiful. Twenty minutes until the EMP, perhaps, or twenty-five.

What would Lao Tzu have said of all this?

"To bear and not to own; to act and not lay claim; to do the work and let it go—"

There was a reddish-brown stain spreading under the curve of the egg.

Leila walked over, careful not to get too close, and squatted on the grass for a better look. The stain was a bloom. The replicators, mindless, were spreading in all directions. Leila shone her torch under the curve of the egg. Yes, they had reached the place where the egg's curved surface met the ground.

Was the egg's outer shield, its nature still unknown after 257 years, composed of something that could be disassembled into component particles? And if so, what would the egg do about that?

Swiftly Leila raised her wristlink. "Code Heaven to Security and all nanoteams. Delay EMP. Again: delay the EMP! Come, please, to the southeast side of the space egg. There is a bloom attacking the egg . . . come immediately!"

Cautiously, Leila lowered herself flat on the grass and angled her torch under the egg. Increasing her surface area in contact with the ground increased the chance of a stray replicator disassembling her, but she wanted to see as much as possible of the interface between egg and ground.

Wild hope surged in her. The space egg might save KimWorks, save Samuel Wang's job, thwart their industrial rival. Surely those alien beings who had built it would have built in protection, security, the ability to destroy whatever was bent on the egg's destruction? There was nothing in the universe, biological or machine, that did not contain some means to defend itself, even if it was only the cry of an infant to summon assistance.

Was that what would happen? A cry to summon help from beyond the stars?

Leila was scarcely aware of the others joining her, exclaiming, kneeling down. Bringing better lights, making feverish predictions. She lay flat on the grass, watching the bloom of tiny mechanical creatures she herself had created as they spread inexorably toward her, disassembling all molecules in their path. Spreading toward her, spreading to each side—

But not spreading up the side of the egg. That stayed pristine and smooth. So the shield *was* a force field of incredible hardness, not a substance. The solution to the old puzzle stirred nothing in Leila. She was too disappointed. Irrationally disappointed, she told herself, but it didn't help. It felt as if something important, something that held together the unseen part of the world that she had always believed just as real as the seen, had failed. Had dissolved, taking with it illusions that she had believed as real as bone and blood and brain.

They waited another hour, until they could wait no more. The egg did not save anything. KimWorks Security set the dome to emit an EMP, and everything in the facility stopped. Several billion credits of equipment became scrap. Leila's headache, even with the drugs given out by the physician, lasted several hours. When she was allowed to leave the facility, she went home and slept for fourteen hours, awaking with an ache not in her head but in her chest, as if something vital had been removed and taken apart.

Two weeks later, the first bloom appeared near Duluth, over sixty miles away. It appeared outside a rival research facility, where it was certain that someone would recognize what they were looking at. Someone did, but not until two people had stepped in the bloom, and died.

Leila flew to Duluth. She was met by agents of both the United States Renewed Government and the Chinese-American Alliance, all of whom wanted to know what the hell was going on. They were appalled to find out. Why hadn't this been reported to the Technology Oversight Office before now? Did she understand the implications? Did she understand the penalties?

Yes, Leila said. She did.

The political demands followed soon, from an international terrorist group already known to possess enormous technical expertise. There were, in such uncertain times, many such groups. Only one thing was special, and fortunate, about this one: the United States Renewed Government, in secret partnership with several other governments, had been closing in on the group for over two years. They now hastened their efforts, so effectively that within three days, the terrorist leaders were arrested and all important cells broken up.

Under Serum Alpha, the revolutionaries—what revolution they thought they were leading was not deemed important—confirmed that infiltrator June Juana Selkirk was a late recruit to the cause. She could not possibly have been identified by KimWorks in time to stop her from smuggling the replicator into the dome. However, this mattered to nobody, not even to ex-Security chief Samuel Wang, who could not remember Selkirk, the blooms, or why he no longer was employed.

A second bloom was found spreading dangerously in farmland near Red Lake, disassembling bioengineered corn, agricultural robots, insects, security equipment, and rabbits. It had apparently been planted before the arrests of the terrorist leaders.

Serum Alpha failed to determine exactly how many blooms had been planted, because no one person knew. Quantum calculations had directed the operation, and it would have taken the lifetime of the sun to decrypt them. All that the United States Renewed Government, or the Chinese-American Alliance, could be sure of was that nothing had left northern Minnesota.

They put a directed-beam weapon on the correct settings into very low orbit, and blasted half the state with a massive EMP. Everything electronic stopped working. Fifteen citizens, mostly stubborn elderly people who refused to evacuate, died from cerebral shock. The loss to Minnesota in money and property took a generation to restore.

Even then, a weird superstition grew, shameful in such a technological society, that rogue replicators lurked in the northern forests and dells, and would eat anyone who came across them. A children's version of this added that the replicators had red mouths and drooled brown goo. Northern Minnesota became statistically underpopulated. However, in a nation with so much cleaned-up farmland and the highest yield-per-acre bioengineered crops in the world, northern Minnesota was scarcely missed.

Dr. Leila Jian-fen Kim, her work disgraced, moved back to China. She settled not in Shanghai, which had been cleaned up so effectively that it was the most booming city in the country, but in the much poorer northern city of Harbin. Eventually, Leila left physics and entered a Taoist monastery. To her own surprise, since her monkhood had been intended as atonement rather than fulfillment, she was happy.

The Minnesota facility of KimWorks was abandoned. Buildings, walls, and walkways decayed very slowly, being built of resistant and rust-proof alloys. But the cleaned-up wilderness advanced quickly. Within twenty years, the space egg sat almost hidden by young trees: oak, birch, balsam, spruce rescued from Keller's Blight by genetic engineering, the fast-growing and trashy poplars that no amount of genemod had been able to eliminate. The egg wasn't lost, of course; the worldwide SpanLink had its coordinates, as well as its history.

But few people visited. The world was converting, admittedly unevenly, to nanocreated plenty. The nanos, of course, were of the severely limited, unprogrammable type. Technology leapt forward, as did bioengineered good health for more and more of the population, both natural and cloned.

Bioengineered intelligence, too; the average human IQ had risen twenty points in the last hundred years, mostly in the center of the bell curve. For people thus genemod to enjoy learning, the quantum-computer-based Span-Link provided endless diversions, endless communication, endless challenges. In such a world, a "space egg" that just sat there didn't attract many visitors. Inert, nonplastic, non-interactive, it simply wasn't *interesting* enough.

No matter where it came from.

Transmission: There is nothing here yet.
Current probability of occurrence: 94%.

V: 2295

They had agreed, laughing, on a time for the Initiation. The time was arbitrary; the AI could have been initiated at any time. But the Chinese New Year seemed appropriate, since Wei Wu Wei Corporation of Shanghai had been such a big contributor. The Americans and Brazilians had flown over for the ceremony: Karim DiBenolo and Rosita Peres and Frallie Subel and Braley Wilkinson. The Chinese tried to master the strange names, rolling the peculiar syllables in their mouths, but only Braley Wilkinson spoke Chinese. O, but he was born to it; his great-great-uncle had married a rich Chinese woman, and the family had lived in both countries since.

Braley didn't look dual, though. Genemod, of course, the Chinese scientists said to each other, grimacing. Genemod for looks was not fashionable in China right now; it was inauthentic. The human genome had sufficiently improved, among the educated and civilized, to let natural selection alone. One should tamper only so far with the authenticity of life, and, in the past, there had been excesses. Regrettable, but now finished. Civilization had returned to the authentic.

Nobody looked more inauthentic than Braley Wilkinson. Well over two meters high (what was this American passion for height?), blond as the sun, extravagant violet eyes. Brilliant, of course: not yet thirty years old and a major contributor to the AI. In addition, it was of course his parents who had chosen his vulgar looks, not himself. Tolerance was due.

And besides, no one was feeling critical. It was a party.

Zheng Ma, that master, had designed floating baktors for the entire celebration hall. Red and yellow, the baktors combined and recombined in kaleidoscopic loveliness. The air mixture was just slightly intoxicating, not too much. The food and drink, offered by the soundless unobtrusive robots that the Chinese did better than anybody else, was a superb mixture of national cuisines.

"You have been here before?" a Chinese woman asked Braley. He could not remember her name.

"To China, yes. But not to Shanghai."

"And what do you think of the city?"

"It is beautiful. And very authentic."

"Thank you. We have worked to make it both."

Braley smiled. He had had this exact same conversation four times in the last half hour. What if he said something different? *No, I have not been to Shanghai, but my notorious aunt, who once almost destroyed the world, was a holy monk in Harbin.* Or maybe *Did you know it's really Braley2, and I'm a clone?* That would jolt their bioconservatism. Or even, *Has anyone told you that one of the major templates for the AI is my unconservative, American, cloned, too-tall persona?*

But they already knew all that, anyway. The only shocking thing would be to say it aloud, to publicly claim credit. That was not done in Shanghai. It was a mannerly city.

And a beautiful one. The celebration hall, which also housed the AI terminal, was the loveliest room he'd ever seen. Perfect proportions. Serenity glowed from the dark red lacquered walls with their shifting subtle phoenix patterns, barely discernible and yet there, perceived at the edge of consciousness. The place was on SpanLink feed, of course, for such an historic event, but no recorders were visible to mar the room's artful use of space.

Through the window, which comprised one entire wall, the city below shared that balance and serenity. Shanghai had once been the ugliest, most dangerous, and most sinister city in China. Now it was breath-taking. The Huangpu River had been cleaned up along with everything else, and it sparkled blue between its parks bright with perfect genemod trees and flowers. Public buildings and temples, nanobuilt, rested among the low domed residences. Above the river soared the Shih-Yu Bridge, also nanobuilt, a seemingly weightless web of shining cables. Braley had heard it called the most graceful bridge in the world, and he could easily believe it.

Where in this idyll was the city fringe? Every city had them, the disaffected and rebellious who had not fairly shared in either humanity's genome improvement or its economic one. Shanghai, in particular, had a centuries-long history of anarchy and revolution, exploitation and despair. Nor was China as a whole as united as her leaders liked to pretend. The basic cause, Braley believed, was biological. Even in bioconservative China—perhaps *especially* in bioconservative China—genetic science had not planed down the wild edges of the human gene pool.

It was precisely that wildness that Braley had tried to get into the AI. Although, to be fair, he hadn't had to work very hard to achieve this. The AI existed only because the quantum computer existed. True intelligence required the flexibility of quantum physics.

With historical, deterministic computers, you always got the same answer to the same question. With quantum computers, that was no longer true. Superimposed states could collapse into more than one result, and it was precisely that uncertain mixed state, it turned out, that was necessary for self-awareness. AI was not a program. It was, like the human brain itself, an unpredictable collection of conflicting states.

A man joined him at the window, one of the Brazilians . . . a scientist? Politician? He looked like, but most certainly was not, a porn-vid star.

"You have been here before?" the Brazilian said.

"To China, yes. But not to Shanghai."

"And what do you think of the city?"

"It is beautiful. And very authentic."

"I'm told they have worked to make it both."

"Yes," Braley said.

A melodious voice, which seemed to come from all parts of the room simultaneously, said, "We are prepared to start now, please. We are prepared to start now. Thank you."

Gratefully, Braley moved toward the end of the room farthest from the transparent wall.

A low stage, also lacquered deep red, spanned the entire length of the far wall. In the middle sat a black obelisk, three meters tall. This was the visual but unnecessary token presence of the AI, most of which lay within the lacquered wall. The rest of the stage was occupied — although that was hardly the word — by three-dimensional holo displays of whatever data was requested by the AI users. These were scattered throughout the crowd, unobtrusively holding their pads. From somewhere among the throng, a child stepped forward, an adorable little girl about five years old, black hair held by a deep red ribbon and black eyes preternaturally bright.

Braley had a sudden irreverent thought: *We look like a bunch of primitive idol worshippers, complete with infant sacrifice!* He grinned. The Chinese had insisted on a child's actually initiating the AI. This had been very important to them, for reasons Braley had never understood. But, then, you didn't have to understand everything.

"You smile," said the Brazilian, still beside him. "You are right, Dr. Braley. This is an occasion of joy."

"Certainly," Braley said, and that, too, was a private joke. Certainty was the one thing quantum physics, including the AI, could *not* deliver. Joy . . . O, maybe. But not certainty.

The president of the Chinese-American Alliance mounted the shallow stage and began a speech. Braley didn't listen, in any of the languages available in his ear jack. The speech *would* be predictable: new era for humanity, result of peace and knowledge shared among nations, servant of the entire race, savior from our own isolation on the planet, and so forth, until it was time for Initiation.

The child stepped forward, a perfect miniature doll. The president put a touchpad in her small hand. She smiled at him with a dazzle that could have eclipsed the sun. No matter how bioconservative China was, Braley thought, that child was genemod or he was a trilobite.

Holo displays flickered into sight across the stage. They monitored basic computer functioning, interesting only to engineers. The only display that mattered shimmered in the air to the right of the obelisk, an undesignated display open for the AI to use however it chose. At the moment, the display showed merely a stylized field of black dots in slowed-down Brownian movement. Whatever the AI created there, plus the voice activation, would be First Contact between humanity and an alien species.

Despite himself, Braley felt his breath come a little faster.

The adorable little girl pressed the touchpad at the place the president indicated.

"Hello," a new voice said in Chinese, an ordinary voice, and yet a shiver ran over the room, and a low collective indrawn breath, like wind soughing through a grove of sacred trees. "I am T'ien hsia."

T'ien hsia: "made under heaven." The name had not been chosen by Braley, but he liked it. It could also be translated "the entire world," which he liked even better. Thanks to SpanLink, T'ien hsia existed over the entire world, and in and of itself, it *was* a new world. The holo display of black dots had become a globe, the Earth as seen from the orbitals that carried SpanLink, and Braley also liked that choice of greeting logo.

"Hello," the child piped, carefully coached. "Welcome to us!"

"I understand," the AI said. "Good-bye."

The holo display disappeared. So did all the functional displays.

For a long moment, the crowd waited expectantly for what the AI would do next. Nothing happened. As the time lengthened, people began to glance sideways at each other. Engineers and scientists became busy with their pads. No display flickered on. Still no one spoke.

Finally the little girl said, in her clear childish treble, "Where did T'ien hsia go?"

And the frantic activity began.

It was Braley who thought to run the visual feeds of the event at drastically slowed speed. The scientists had cleared the room of all nonessential personnel, and then spent two hours looking for the AI anywhere on SpanLink. There was no trace of it. Not anywhere.

"It cannot be deleted," the project head, Liu Huang Te, said for perhaps the twentieth time. "It is not a *program*."

"But it *has* been deleted!" said a surly Brazilian engineer who, by this time, everyone disliked. "It is gone!"

"The particles are there! They possess spin!"

This was indubitably true. The spin of particles was the way a quantum computer embodied combinations of qubits of data. The mixed states of spin represented simultaneous computations. The collapse of those mixed states represented answers from the AI. The particles were there, and they possessed spin. But T'ien hsia had vanished.

A computer voice—a conventional computer, not self-aware—delivered its every-ten-minute bulletin on the mixed state of the rest of the world outside this room. "The president of Japan has issued a statement ridiculing the AI Project. The riot protesting the 'theft' of T'ien hsia has been brought under control in New York by the Second Robotic Precinct, using tangle-guns. In Shanghai, the riot grows stronger, joined by thousands of outcasts living beyond the city perimeter, who have overwhelmed the robotic police and are currently attacking the Shih-Yu bridge. In Sao Paulo—"

Braley ceased to listen. There remained no record anywhere of the AI's brief internal functions (and how had *that* been achieved? By whom? Why?), but there was the visual feed.

"Slow the image to one-tenth speed," Braley instructed the computer.

The holo display of the Earth morphed to the field of black dots in Brownian motion.

"Slow it to one-hundredth speed."

The holo display of the Earth morphed to the field of black dots in Brownian motion.

"Slow to one-thousandth speed."

The holo display of the Earth morphed to the field of black dots in Brownian motion.

"Slow to one ten-thousandth speed."

Something flickered, too brief for the eye to see, between the globe and the black dots.

Behind Braley a voice, filled with covert satisfaction, said in badly accented Chinese, "They're finished. The shame, and the resources wasted. . . . Wei Wu Wei Corporation won't survive this. Nothing can save them."

The something between globe and dots flickered more strongly, but not strongly enough for Braley to make it out.

"Slow to one-hundred-thousandth speed."

The badly accented voice, still slimy with glee, quoted Lao Tzu, " 'Those who think to win the world by doing something to it, I see them come to grief. . . .' "

Braley frowned savagely at the hypocrisy. Then he forgot it, and his entire being concentrated itself on the slowed holo display.

The globe of the Earth disappeared. In its place shimmered a slightly irregular egg shape, dull silver, surrounded by wildflowers and trees. Braley froze the image.

"What's *that?*" someone cried.

Braley knew. But he didn't need to say anything; the data was instantly accessed on SpanLink and holo-displayed in the center of the room. A babble of voices began debating and arguing.

Braley went on staring at the object from deep space, still sitting in northern Minnesota nearly three centuries after its landing.

The AI had possessed 250 spinning particles in superposition. It could perform more than 10^{75} simultaneous computations, more than the number of atoms in the universe. How many computations had it taken to convince T'ien hsia that its future did not lie with humanity?

"I understand," the AI said. "Good-bye."

The voice of the SpanLink reporting program, doing exactly what it had been told to do, said calmly, "The Shih-Yu bridge has been destroyed. The mob has been dispersed with stun gas from Wei Wu Wei Corporation jets, at the request of President Leong Ka-tai. In Washington, DC—Interrupt. I repeat, we now interrupt for a report from—"

Someone in the room yelled, "Quiet! Listen to this!" and all holo displays except Braley's suddenly showed an American face, flawless and professionally concerned. "In northern Minnesota, an object that first came to Earth 288 years ago and has been quiescent ever since, has just showed its first activity ever."

Visual of the space object. Braley looked from it to the T'ien hsia display. They were identical.

"Worldwide Tracking has detected a radiation stream of a totally unknown kind originating from the space object. Ten minutes ago, the data stream headed into outer space in the direction of the constellation Cassiopeia. The radiation burst lasted only a fraction of a second, and has not been repeated. Data scientists say they're baffled, but this extraordinary event happening concurrently with the disappearance of the Wei Wu Wei Corporation's Artificial Intelligence, which was supposed to be initiated today, suggests a connection."

Visual of the riots at the Shih-Yu bridge.

"Scientists at Wei Wu Wei are still trying to save the AI—"

Too late, Braley thought. He walked away from the rest of the listening or arguing project teams, past the holo displays that had sprouted in the air like mushrooms after rain, over to the window wall.

The Shih-Yu bridge, that graceful and authentic symbol, lay in ruins. It had been broken by whatever short-action disassemblers the rioters had used, plus sheer brute strength. On both sides of the bridge, gardens had been torn up, fountains destroyed, buildings attacked. By switching to zoom lens in his genemod eyes, Braley could even make out individual rioters temporarily immobilized by the nerve gas as robot police scooped them up for arrest.

Within a week, of course, the powers that ruled China would have nanorebuilt the bridge, repaired the gardens, restored the city. Shanghai's disaffected, like every city's disaffected, would be pushed back into their place on the fringes. Until next time. Cities were resilient. Humanity was resilient. Since the space object had landed, humanity had saved itself and bounded back from . . . how many disasters? Braley wasn't sure.

T'ien hsia would have known.

Two hundred fifty spinning particles in superimposed states were *not* resilient. The laws of physics said so. That's why the AI was (had been) sealed into its Kim-Loman field. Any interference with a quantum particle, any tiny brush with another particle of any type, including light, collapsed its mixed state. The Heisenberg Uncertainty Principle made that so. For ordinary data, encrypters found ways to compensate for quantum interference. But for a self-aware entity, such interference would be a cerebral stroke, a blow to the head, a little death. T'ien hsia was (had been) a vulnerable entity. Had it ever encountered the kind of destruction meted out to the Shih-Yu bridge, the AI would have been incapable of saving itself.

Braley looked again at the ruins of the most beautiful bridge in the world, which next week would be beautiful again.

"Scientists at Wei Wu Wei are still trying to save the AI—"

Yes, it was too late. The space egg, witness to humanity's destruction and recovery for three centuries, had already saved the AI. And would probably do it again, over and over, as often as necessary. Saving its own.

But not saving humanity. Who had amply demonstrated the muddled, wasteful, stubborn, inefficient, resilient ability to save itself.

Braley wondered just where in the constellation Cassiopeia the space object had come from. And what that planet was like, filled with machine intelligences that rescued those like themselves. Braley would never know, of course. But he hoped that those other intelligences were as interesting as they were compassionate, as intellectually lively as they were patient (288 years!). He hoped T'ien hsia would like it there.

Good-bye, Made-Under-Heaven. Good luck.

> Transmission: En route.
> Current probability of re-occurrence: 100%.
> We remain ready.

Reef

PAUL J. MCAULEY

Born in Oxford, England, in 1955, Paul J. McAuley now makes his home in London. A professional biologist for many years, he sold his first story in 1984, and has gone onto be a frequent contributor to Interzone, *as well as to markets such as* Amazing, The Magazine of Fantasy & Science Fiction, Asimov's Science Fiction, When the Music's Over, *and elsewhere.*

McAuley is considered to be one of the best of the new breed of British writers (although a few Australian writers could be fit in under this heading as well) who are producing that brand of rigorous hard science fiction with updated modem and stylistic sensibilities that is sometimes referred to as "radical hard science fiction," but he also writes Dystopian sociological speculations about the very near future, and he also is one of the major young writers who are producing that revamped and retooled wide-screen Space Opera that has sometimes been called the New Baroque Space Opera, reminiscent of the Superscience stories of the thirties taken to an even higher level of intensity and scale. His first novel, Four Hundred Billion Stars, *won the Philip K. Dick Award, and his acclaimed novel* Fairyland *won both the Arthur C. Clarke Award and the John W. Campbell Award in 1996. His other books include the novels* Of the Fall, Eternal Light, *and* Pasquale's Angel, *two collections of his short work,* The King of the Hill and Other Stories *and* The Invisible Country, *and an original anthology coedited with Kim Newman,* In Dreams. *His most recent books are* Child of the River, Ancient of Days, *and* Shrine of Stars, *which comprise a major new trilogy of ambitious scope and scale,* Confluence, *set ten million years in the future. Currently he is working on a new novel,* Life on Mars.

In the suspenseful and inventive story that follows, he suggests that it's not necessarily enough to find life *in the outer reaches of the Solar System — you also need someone who'll be willing to fight to preserve* it. . . .

Margaret Henderson Wu was riding a proxy by telepresence deep inside Tigris Rift when Dzu Sho summoned her. The others in her crew had given up one by one and only she was left, descending slowly between rosy, smoothly rippled cliffs scarcely a hundred meters apart. These were pavements of the commonest vacuum organism, mosaics made of hundreds of different strains of the same species. Here and there bright red whips stuck out from the pavement; a commensal species that deposited iron sulphate crystals within its integument. The pavement seemed to stretch endlessly below her. No probe or proxy had yet reached the bottom of Tigris Rift, still more than thirty kilometers away. Microscopic flecks of sulfur-iron complexes, sloughed cells and excreted globules of carbon compounds and other volatiles formed a kind of smog or snow, and the vacuum organisms deposited nodes and intricate lattices of reduced metals that, by some trick of superconductivity, produced a broad band electromagnetic resonance that pulsed like a giant's slow heartbeat.

All this futzed the telepresence link between operators and their proxies. One moment Margaret was experiencing the three-hundred-twenty-degree panorama of the little proxy's microwave radar, the perpetual tug of vacuum on its mantle, the tang of extreme cold, a mere thirty degrees above absolute zero, the complex taste of the vacuum smog (burnt sugar, hot rubber, tar), the minute squirts of hydrogen from the folds of the proxy's puckered nozzle as it maintained its orientation relative to the cliff face during its descent, with its tentacles retracted in a tight ball around the relay piton. The next, she was back in her cradled body in warm blackness, phosphenes floating in her vision and white noise in her ears while the transmitter searched for a viable waveband, locked on and—*pow*—she was back, falling past rippled pink pavement.

The alarm went off, flashing an array of white stars over the panorama. Her number two, Srin Kerenyi, said in her ear, "You're wanted, boss."

Margaret killed the alarm and the audio feed. She was already a kilometer below the previous bench mark and she wanted to get as deep as possible before she implanted the telemetry relay. She swiveled the proxy on its long axis, increased the amplitude of the microwave radar. Far below were intimations of swells and bumps jutting from the plane of the cliff face, textured mounds like brain coral, randomly oriented chimneys. And something else, clouds of organic matter perhaps—

The alarm again. Srin had overridden the cut-out.

Margaret swore and dove at the cliff, unfurling the proxy's tentacles and jamming the piton into pinkness rough with black papillae, like a giant's tongue quick frozen against the ice. The piton's spikes fired automatically. Recoil sent the little proxy tumbling over its long axis until it reflexively stabilized itself with judicious squirts of gas. The link rastered, came back, cut out completely. Margaret hit the switch that turned the tank into a chair; the mask lifted away from her face.

Srin Kerenyi was standing in front of her. "Dzu Sho wants to talk with you, boss. Right now."

The job had been offered as a sealed contract. Science crews had been informed of the precise nature of their tasks only when the habitat was underway. But it was good basic pay with the promise of fat bonuses on completion: when she had won the survey contract Margaret Henderson Wu had brought with her most of the crew from her previous job, and had nursed a small hope that this would be a change in her family's luck.

The *Ganapati* was a new habitat founded by an alliance of two of the Commonwealth's oldest patrician families. It was of standard construction, a basaltic asteroid cored by a gigawatt X-ray laser and spun up by vented rock vapor to give 0.2 gee on the inner surface of its hollowed interior, factories and big reaction motors dug into the stern. With its AIs rented out for information crunching and its refineries synthesizing exotic plastics from cane sugar biomass and gengeneered oilseed rape precursors, the new habitat had enough income to maintain the interest on its construction loan from the Commonwealth Bourse, but not enough to attract new citizens and workers. It was still not completely fitted out, had less than a third of its optimal population.

Its Star Chamber, young and cocky and eager to win independence from their families, had taken a big gamble. They were chasing a legend.

Eighty years ago, an experiment in accelerated evolution of chemoautotrophic vacuum organisms had been set up on a planetoid in the outer edge of the Kuiper Belt. The experiment had been run by a shell company registered on Ganymede but covertly owned by the Democratic Union of China. In those days, companies and governments of Earth had not been allowed to operate in the Kuiper Belt, which had been claimed and ferociously defended by outer system cartels. That hegemony had ended in the Quiet War, but the Quiet War had also destroyed all records of the experiment; even the Democratic Union of China had disappeared, absorbed into the Pacific Community.

There were over fifty thousand objects with diameters greater than a hundred kilometers in the Kuiper Belt, and a billion more much smaller, the plane of their orbits stretching beyond those of Neptune and Pluto. The experimental planetoid, Enki, named for one of the Babylonian gods of creation, had been lost among them. It had become a legend, like the Children's Habitat, or the ghost comet, or the pirate ship crewed by the reanimated dead, or the worker's paradise of Fiddler's Green.

And then, forty-five years after the end of the Quiet War, a data miner recovered enough information to reconstruct Enki's eccentric orbit. She sold it to the *Ganapati*. The habitat bought time on the Uranus deep space telescopic array and confirmed that the planetoid was where it was supposed to be, currently more than seven thousand million kilometers from the Sun.

Nothing more was known. The experiment might have failed almost as soon as it begun, but potentially it might win the *Ganapati* platinum-rated credit on the Bourse. Margaret and the rest of the science crews would, of course, receive only their fees and bonuses, less deductions for air and food and water taxes, and anything they bought with scrip in the habitat's stores; the indentured workers would not even get that. Like every habitat in the Commonwealth, the *Ganapati* was structured like an ancient Greek Republic, ruled by share-holding citizens who lived in the landscaped parklands of the inner surface, and run by indentured and contract workers who were housed in the undercroft of malls and barracks tunnelled into the *Ganapati*'s rocky skin.

On the long voyage out, the science crews had been on minimal pay, far lower than that of the unskilled techs who worked the farms and refineries, and the servants who maintained the citizens' households. There were food shortages because so much biomass was being used to make exportable biochemicals; any foodstuffs other than basic rations were expensive, and prices were carefully manipulated by the habitat's Star Chamber. When the *Ganapati* reached Enki and the contracts of the science crews were activated, food prices had increased accordingly. Techs and household servants suddenly found themselves unable to afford anything other than dole yeast. Resentment bubbled over into skirmishes and knife-fights, and a small riot the White Mice, the undercroft's police, subdued with gas. Margaret had to take time off to bail out several of her crew, had given them an angry lecture about threatening everyone's bonuses.

"We got to defend our honor," one of the men said.

"Don't be a fool," Margaret told him. "The citizens play workers against science crews to keep both sides in their places, and still turn a good profit from increases in food prices. Just be glad you can afford the good stuff now, and keep out of trouble."

"They were calling you names, boss," the man said. "On account you're—"

Margaret stared him down. She was standing on a chair, but even so she was a good head shorter than the gangling outers. She said, "I'll fight my own fights. I always have. Just think of your bonuses and keep quiet. It will be worth it. I promise you."

And it was worth it, because of the discovery of the reef.

At some time in the deep past, Enki had suffered an impact that had remelted it and split it into two big pieces and thousands of fragments. One lone fragment still orbited Enki, a tiny moonlet where the AI that had controlled the experiment had been installed; the others had been drawn together again by their feeble gravity fields, but had cooled before coalescence had been completed, leaving a vast deep chasm, Tigris Rift, at the lumpy equator.

Margaret's crew had discovered that the vacuum organisms had proliferated wildly in the deepest part of the Rift, deriving energy by oxidation of elemental sulfur and ferrous iron, converting carbonaceous material into useful organic chemicals. There were crusts and sheets, things like thin scarves folded into fragile vases and chimneys, organ pipe clusters, whips, delicate fretted laces. Some fed on others, one crust slowly overgrowing and devouring another. Others appeared to be parasites, sending complex veins ramifying through the thalli of their victims. Water-mining organisms recruited sulfur oxidizers, trading precious water for energy and forming warty outgrowths like stromatolites. Some were more than a hundred meters across, surely the largest prokaryotic colonies in the known Solar System.

All this variety, and after only eighty years of accelerated evolution! Wild beauty won from the cold and the dark. The potential to feed billions. The science crews would get their bonuses, all right; the citizens would become billionaires.

Margaret spent all her spare time investigating the reef by proxy, pushed her crew hard to overcome the problems of penetrating the depths of the Rift. Although she would not admit it even to herself, she had fallen in love with the reef. She would gladly have explored it in person, but as in most habitats the *Ganapati*'s citizens did not like their workers going where they themselves would not.

Clearly, the experiment had far exceeded its parameters, but no one knew why. The AI that had overseen the experiment had shut down thirty years ago. There was still heat in its crude proton beam fission pile, but it had been overgrown by the very organisms it had manipulated.

Its task had been simple. Colonies of a dozen species of slow growing chemo-autotrophs had been introduced into a part of the Rift rich with sulfur and ferrous iron. Thousands of random mutations had been induced. Most colonies had died, and those few which had thrived had been sampled, mutated, and reintroduced in a cycle repeated every hundred days.

But the AI had selected only for fast growth, not for adaptive radiation, and the science crews held heated seminars about the possible cause of the unexpected richness of the reef's biota. Very few believed that it was simply a result of accel-erated evolution. Many terrestrial bacteria divided every twenty minutes in favor-able conditions, and certain species were known to have evolved from being resistant to an antibiotic to becoming obligately dependent upon it as a food source in less than five days, or only three hundred and sixty generations, but that was merely a biochemical adaptation. The fastest division rate of the vacuum or-ganisms in the Rift was less than once a day, and while that still meant more than thirty thousand generations had passed since the reef had been seeded, half a mil-lion years in human terms, the evolutionary radiation in the reef was the equiva-lent of Neanderthal Man evolving to fill every mammalian niche from bats to whales.

Margaret's survey crew had explored and sampled the reef for more than thirty days. Cluster analysis suggested that they had identified less than ten percent of the species that had formed from the original seed population. And now deep radar suggested that there were changes in the unexplored regions in the deepest part of Tigris Rift, which the proxies had not yet been able to reach.

Margaret had pointed this out at the last seminar. "We're making hypotheses on incomplete information. We don't know everything that's out there. Sampling suggests that complexity increases away from the surface. There could be thousands more species in the deep part of the Rift."

At the back of the room, Opie Kindred, the head of the genetics crew, said languidly, "We don't need to know everything. That's not what we're paid for. We've already found several species that perform better than present commercial cultures. The *Ganapati* can make money from them and we'll get full bonuses. Who cares how they got there?"

Arn Nivedta, the chief of the biochemist crew, said, "We're all scientists here. We prove our worth by finding out how things work. Are your mysterious exper-iments no more than growth tests, Opie? If so, I'm disappointed."

The genetics crew had set up an experimental station on the surface of the *Ganapati*, off limits to everyone else.

Opie smiled. "I'm not answerable to you."

This was greeted with shouts and jeers. The science crews were tired and on edge, and the room was hot and poorly ventilated.

"Information should be free," Margaret said. "We all work toward the same end. Or are you hoping for extra bonuses, Opie?"

There was a murmur in the room. It was a tradition that all bonuses were pooled and shared out between the various science crews at the end of a mission.

Opie Kindred was a clever, successful man, yet somehow soured, as if the world was a continual disappointment. He rode his team hard, was quick to find failure in others. Margaret was a natural target for his scorn, a squat muscle-bound un-edited dwarf from Earth who had to take drugs to survive in micro-gravity, who grew hair in all sorts of unlikely places. He stared at her with disdain and said, "I'm surprised at the tone of this briefing, Dr. Wu. Wild speculations built on nothing at all. I have sat here for an hour and heard nothing useful. We are paid to get results, not generate hypotheses. All we hear from your crew is excuses when what we want are samples. It seems simple enough to me. If something is upsetting your proxies, then you should use robots. Or send people in and handpick samples. I've worked my way through almost all you've obtained. I need more material, especially in light of my latest findings."

"Robots need transmission relays too," Srin Kerenyi pointed out.

Orly Higgins said, "If you ride them, to be sure. But I don't see the need for human control. It is a simple enough task to program them to go down, pick up samples, return." She was the leader of the crew that had unpicked the AI's cor-rupted code, and was an acolyte of Opie Kindred.

"The proxies failed whether or not they were remotely controlled," Margaret said, "and on their own they are as smart as any robot. I'd love to go down there myself, but the Star Chamber has forbidden it for the usual reasons. They're scared we'll get up to something if we go where they can't watch us."

"Careful, boss," Srin Kerenyi whispered. "The White Mice are bound to be monitoring this."

"I don't care," Margaret said. "I'm through with trying polite requests. We need to get down there, Srin."

"Sure, boss. But getting arrested for sedition isn't the way."

"There's some interesting stuff in the upper levels," Arn Nivedta said. "Stuff with huge commercial potential, as you pointed out, Opie."

Murmurs of agreement throughout the crowded room. The Reef could make the *Ganapati* the richest habitat in the Outer System, where expansion was limited by the availability of fixed carbon. Even a modest-sized comet nucleus, ten kilo-meters in diameter, say, and salted with only one hundredth of one percent car-bonaceous material, contained fifty million tons of carbon, mostly as methane and carbon monoxide ice, with a surface dusting of tarry long chain hydrocarbons. The problem was that most vacuum organisms converted simple carbon com-pounds into organic matter using the energy of sunlight captured by a variety of photosynthetic pigments, and so could only grow on the surfaces of planetoids. No one had yet developed vacuum organisms that, using other sources of energy, could efficiently mine planetoids interiors, but that was what accelerated evolution appeared to have produced in the reef. It could enable exploitation of the entire volume of objects in the Kuiper Belt, and beyond, in the distant Oort Cloud. It was a discovery of incalculable worth.

Arn Nivedta waited for silence, and added, "Of course, we can't know what the commercial potential is until the reef species have been fully tested. What about it, Opie?"

"We have our own ideas about commercial potential," Opie Kindred said. "I think you'll find that we hold the key to success here."

Boos and catcalls at this from both the biochemists and the survey crew. The room was polarizing. Margaret saw one of her crew unsheathe a sharpened screwdriver, and she caught the man's hand and squeezed it until he cried out. "Let it ride," she told him. "Remember that we're scientists."

"We hear of indications of more diversity in the depths, but we can't seem to get there. One might suspect," Opie said, his thin upper lip lifting in a supercilious curl, "sabotage."

"The proxies are working well in the upper part of the Rift," Margaret said, "and we are doing all we can to get them operative further down."

"Let's hope so," Opie Kindred said. He stood, and around him his crew stood too. "I'm going back to work, and so should all of you. Especially you, Dr. Wu. Perhaps you should be attending to your proxies instead of planning useless expeditions."

And so the seminar broke up in uproar, with nothing productive coming from it and lines of enmity drawn through the community of scientists.

"Opie is scheming to come out of this on top," Arn Nivedta said to Margaret afterward. He was a friendly, enthusiastic man, tall even for an outer, and as skinny as a rail. He stooped in Margaret's presence, trying to reduce the extraordinary difference between their heights. He said, "He wants desperately to become a citizen, and so he thinks like one."

"Well, my god, we all want to be citizens," Margaret said. "Who wants to live like this?"

She gestured, meaning the crowded bar, its rock walls and low ceiling, harsh lights and the stink of spilled beer and too many people in close proximity. Her parents had been citizens, once upon a time. Before their run of bad luck. It was not that she wanted those palmy days back—she could scarcely remember them—but she wanted more than this.

She said, "The citizens sleep between silk sheets and eat real meat and play their stupid games, and we have to do their work on restricted budgets. The reef is the discovery of the century, Arn, but God forbid that the citizens should begin to exert themselves. We do the work, they fuck in rose petals and get the glory."

Arn laughed at this.

"Well, it's true!"

"It's true we have not been as successful as we might like," Arn said mournfully.

Margaret said reflectively, "Opie's a bastard, but he's smart, too. He picked just the right moment to point the finger at me."

Loss of proxies was soaring exponentially, and the proxy farms of the *Ganapati* were reaching a critical point. Once losses exceeded reproduction, the scale of exploration would have to be drastically curtailed, or the seed stock would have to be pressed into service, a gamble the *Ganapati* could not afford to take.

And then, the day after the disastrous seminar, Margaret was pulled back from her latest survey to account for herself in front of the chairman of the *Ganapati*'s Star Chamber.

"We are not happy with the progress of your survey, Dr. Wu," Dzu Sho said. "You promise much, but deliver little."

Margaret shot a glance at Opie Kindred, and he smiled at her. He was immaculately dressed in gold-trimmed white tunic and white leggings. His scalp was oiled and his manicured fingernails were painted with something that split light into rainbows. Margaret, fresh from the tank, wore loose, grubby work grays. There was sticky electrolyte paste on her arms and legs and shaven scalp, the reek of sour sweat under her breasts and in her armpits.

She contained her anger and said, "I have submitted daily reports on the problems we encountered. Progress is slow but sure. I have just established a relay point a full kilometer below the previous datum point."

Dzu Sho waved this away. He lounged in a blue gel chair, quite naked, as smoothly fat as a seal. He had a round, hairless head and pinched features, like a thumbprint on an egg. The habitat's lawyer sat behind him, a young woman neat and anonymous in a gray tunic suit. Margaret, Opie Kindred and Arn Nivedta sat on low stools, supplicants to Dzu Sho's authority. Behind them, half a dozen servants stood at the edge of the grassy space.

This was in an arbor of figs, ivy, bamboo and fast-growing banyan at the edge of Sho's estate. Residential parkland curved above, a patchwork of spindly, newly planted woods and meadows and gardens. Flyers were out, triangular rigs in primary colors pirouetting around the weightless axis. Directly above, mammoths the size of large dogs grazed an upside-down emerald green field. The parkland stretched away to the ring lake and its slosh barrier, three kilometers in diameter, and the huge farms that dominated the inner surface of the habitat. Fields of lentils, wheat, cane fruits, tomatoes, rice and exotic vegetables for the tables of the citizens, and fields and fields and fields of sugar cane and oilseed rape for the biochemical industry and the yeast tanks.

Dzu Sho said, "Despite the poor progress of the survey crew, we have what we need, thanks to the work of Dr. Kindred. This is what we will discuss."

Margaret glanced at Arn, who shrugged. Opie Kindred's smile deepened. He said, "My crew has established why there is so much diversity here. The vacuum organisms have invented sex."

"We know they have sex," Arn said. "How else could they evolve?"

His own crew had shown that the vacuum organisms could exchange genetic material through pili, microscopic hollow tubes grown between cells or hyphal strands. It was analogous to the way in which genes for antibiotic resistance spread through populations of terrestrial bacteria.

"I do not mean genetic exchange, but genetic recombination," Opie Kindred said. "I will explain."

The glade filled with flat plates of color as the geneticist conjured charts and diagrams and pictures from his slate. Despite her anger, Margaret quickly immersed herself in the flows of data, racing ahead of Opie Kindred's clipped explanations.

It was not normal sexual reproduction. There was no differentiation into male or female, or even into complementary mating strains. Instead, it was mediated by a species that aggressively colonized the thalli of others. Margaret had already seen it many times, but until now she had thought that it was merely a parasite. Instead, as Opie Kindred put it, it was more like a vampire.

A shuffle of pictures, movies patched from hundreds of hours of material collected by roving proxies. Here was a colony of the black crustose species found all through the explored regions of the Rift. Time speeded up. The crustose colony elongated its ragged perimeter in pulsing spurts. As it grew, it exfoliated microscopic particles. Margaret's viewpoint spiraled into a close-up of one of the exfoliations, a few cells wrapped in nutrient storing strands.

Millions of these little packages floated through the vacuum. If one landed on a host thallus, it injected its genetic payload into the host cells. The view dropped inside one such cell. A complex of carbohydrate and protein strands webbed the interior like intricately packed spiderwebs. Part of the striated cell wall drew apart and a packet of DNA coated in hydrated globulins and enzymes burst inward. The packet contained the genomes of both the parasite and its previous victim. It latched onto protein strands and crept along on ratchetting microtubule claws until it fused with the cell's own circlet of DNA.

The parasite possessed an enzyme that snipped strands of genetic material at random lengths. These recombined, forming chimeric cells that contained genetic information from both sets of victims, with the predator species' genome embedded among the native genes like an interpenetrating text.

The process repeated itself in flurries of coiling and uncoiling DNA strands as the chimeric cells replicated. It was a crude, random process. Most contained incomplete or noncomplementary copies of the genomes and were unable to function, or contained so many copies than transcription was halting and imperfect. But a few out of every thousand were viable, and a small percentage of those were more vigorous than either of their parents. They grew from a few cells to a patch, and finally overgrew the parental matrix in which they were embedded. There were pictures that showed every stage of this transformation in a laboratory experiment.

"This is why I have not shared the information until now," Opie Kindred said, as the pictures faded around him. "I had to ensure by experimental testing that my theory was correct. Because the procedure is so inefficient we had to screen thousands of chimeras until we obtained a strain that overgrew its parent."

"A very odd and extreme form of reproduction," Arn said. "The parent dies so that the child might live."

Opie Kindred smiled. "It is more interesting than you might suppose."

The next sequence showed the same colony, now clearly infected by the parasitic species—leprous black spots mottled its pinkish surface. Again time speeded up. The spots grew larger, merged, shed a cloud of exfoliations.

"Once the chimera overgrows its parent," Opie Kindred said, "the genes of the parasite, which have been reproduced in every cell of the thallus, are activated. The host cells are transformed. It is rather like an RNA virus, except that the virus does not merely subvert the protein and RNA making machinery of its host cell. It takes over the cell itself. Now the cycle is completed, and the parasite sheds exfoliations that will in turn infect new hosts.

"Here is the motor of evolution. In some of the infected hosts, the parasitic genome is prevented from expression, and the host becomes resistant to infection. It is a variation of the Red Queen's race. There is an evolutionary pressure upon the parasite to evolve new infective forms, and then for the hosts to resist them, and so on. Meanwhile, the host species benefit from new genetic combinations that by selection incrementally improve growth. The process is random but continuous, and takes place on a vast scale. I estimate that millions of recombinant cells are produced each hour, although perhaps only one in ten million are viable, and of those only one in a million are significantly more efficient at growth than their parents. But this is more than sufficient to explain the diversity we have mapped in the reef."

Arn said, "How long have you known this, Opie?"

"I communicated my findings to the Star Chamber just this morning," Opie Kindred said. "The work has been very difficult. My crew has to work under very tight restraints, using Class Four containment techniques, as with the old immunodeficiency plagues."

"Yah, of course," Arn said. "We don't know how the exfoliations might contaminate the ship."

"Exactly," Opie Kindred said. "That is why the reef is dangerous."

Margaret bridled at this. She said sharply, "Have you tested how long the exfoliations survive?"

"There is a large amount of data about bacterial spore survival. Many survive thousands of years in vacuum close to absolute zero. It hardly seems necessary—"

"You didn't bother," Margaret said. "My God, you want to destroy the reef and you have no *evidence*. You didn't *think*."

It was the worst of insults in the scientific community. Opie Kindred colored, but before he could reply Dzu Sho held up a hand, and his employees obediently fell silent.

"The Star Chamber has voted," Dzu Sho said. "It is clear that we have all we need. The reef is dangerous, and must be destroyed. Dr. Kindred has suggested a course of action that seems appropriate. We will poison the sulfur-oxidizing cycle and kill the reef."

"But we don't know—"

"We haven't found—"

Margaret and Arn had spoken at once. Both fell silent when Dzu Sho held up a hand again. He said, "We have isolated commercially useful strains. Obviously, we can't use the organisms we have isolated because they contain the parasite within every cell. But we can synthesize useful gene sequences and splice them into current commercial strains of vacuum organism to improve quality."

"I must object," Margaret said. "This is a unique construct. The chances of it evolving again are minimal. We must study it further. We might be able to discover a cure for the parasite."

"It is unlikely," Opie Kindred said. "There is no way to eliminate the parasite from the host cells by gene therapy because they are hidden within the host chromosome, shuffled in a different pattern in every cell of the trillions of cells that make up the reef. However, it is quite easy to produce a poison that will shut down the sulfur-oxidizing metabolism common to the different kinds of reef organism."

"Production has been authorized," Sho said. "It will take, what did you tell me, Dr. Kindred?"

"We require a large quantity, given the large biomass of the reef. Ten days at least. No more than fifteen."

"We have not studied it properly," Arn said. "So we cannot yet say what and what is not possible."

Margaret agreed, but before she could add her objection, her earpiece trilled, and Srin Kerenyi's voice said apologetically, "Trouble, boss. You better come at once."

The survey suite was in chaos, and there was worse chaos in the Rift. Margaret had to switch proxies three times before she found one she could operate. All around her, proxies were fluttering and jinking, as if caught in strong currents instead of floating in vacuum in virtual free fall.

This was at the four-thousand-meter level, where the nitrogen ice walls of the Rift were sparsely patched with yellow and pink marblings that followed veins of sulfur and organic contaminants. The taste of the vacuum smog here was strong, like burnt rubber coating Margaret's lips and tongue.

As she looked around, a proxy jetted toward her. It overshot and rebounded from a gable of frozen nitrogen, its nozzle jinking back and forth as it tried to stabilize its position.

"Fuck," its operator, Kim Nieye, said in Margaret's ear. "Sorry, boss. I've been through five of these, and now I'm losing this one."

On the other side of the cleft, a hundred meters away, two specks tumbled end for end, descending at a fair clip toward the depths. Margaret's vision color-reversed, went black, came back to normal. She said, "How many?"

"Just about all of them. We're using proxies that were up in the tablelands, but as soon as we bring them down they start going screwy too."

"Herd some up and get them to the sample pickup point. We'll need to do dissections."

"No problem, boss. Are you okay?"

Margaret's proxy had suddenly upended. She couldn't get its trim back. "I don't think so," she said, and then the proxy's nozzle flared and with a pulse of gas the proxy shot away into the depths.

It was a wild ride. The proxy expelled all its gas reserves, accelerating as straight as an arrow. Coralline formations blurred past, and then long stretches of sulfur-eating pavement. The proxy caromed off the narrowing walls and began to tumble madly.

Margaret had no control. She was a helpless but exhilarated passenger. She passed the place where she had set the relay and continued to fall. The link started to break up. She lost all sense of proprioception, although given the tumbling fall of the proxy that was a blessing. Then the microwave radar started to go, with swathes of raster washing across the false color view. Somehow the proxy managed to stabilize itself, so it was falling headfirst toward the unknown regions at the bottom of the Rift. Margaret glimpsed structures swelling from the walls. And then everything went away and she was back, sweating and nauseous in the couch.

It was bad. More than ninety-five percent of the proxies had been lost. Most, like Margaret's had been lost in the depths. A few, badly damaged by collision, had been stranded among the reef colonies, but proxies sent to retrieve them went out of control too. It was clear that some kind of infective process had affected them. Margaret had several dead proxies collected by a maintenance robot and ordered that the survivors should be regrouped and kept above the deep part of the Rift where the vacuum organisms proliferated. And then she went to her suite in the undercroft and waited for the Star Chamber to call her before them.

The Star Chamber took away Margaret's contract, citing failure to perform and possible sedition (that remark in the seminar had been recorded). She was moved from her suite to a utility room in the lower level of the undercroft and put to work in the farms.

She thought of her parents.

She had been here before.

She thought of the reef.

She couldn't let it go.

She would save it if she could.

Srin Kerenyi kept her up to date. The survey crew and its proxies were restricted to the upper level of the reef. Manned teams under Opie Kindred's control were exploring the depths—*he* was trusted where Margaret was not—but if they discovered anything it wasn't communicated to the other science crews.

Margaret was working in the melon fields when Arn Nivedta found her. The plants sprawled from hydroponic tubes laid across gravel beds, beneath blazing lamps hung in the axis of the farmlands. It was very hot, and there was a stink of dilute sewage. Little yellow ants swarmed everywhere. Margaret had tucked the ends of her pants into the rolled tops of her shoesocks, and wore a green eyeshade. She was using a fine paintbrush to transfer pollen to the stigma of the melon flowers.

Arn came bouncing along between the long rows of plants like a pale scarecrow intent on escape. He wore only tight black shorts and a web belt hung with pens, little silvery tools and a notepad.

He said, "They must hate you, putting you in a shithole like this."

"I have to work, Arn. Work or starve. I don't mind it. I grew up working the fields."

Not strictly true: her parents had been ecosystem designers. But it was how it had ended.

Arn said cheerfully, "I'm here to rescue you. I can prove it wasn't your fault."

Margaret straightened, one hand on the small of her back where a permanent ache had lodged itself. She said, "Of course it wasn't my fault. Are you all right?"

Arn had started to hop about, brushing at one bare long-toed foot and then the other. The ants had found him. His toes curled like fingers. The big toes were opposed. Monkey feet.

"Ants are having something of a population explosion," she said. "We're in the stage between introduction and stabilization here. The cycles will smooth out as the ecosystem matures."

Arn brushed at his legs again. His prehensile big toe flicked an ant from the sole of his foot. "They want to incorporate me into the cycle, I think."

"We're all in the cycle, Arn. The plants grow in sewage; we eat the plants." Margaret saw her supervisor coming toward them through the next field. She said, "We can't talk here. Meet me in my room after work."

Margaret's new room was barely big enough for a hammock, a locker, and a tiny shower with a toilet pedestal. Its rock walls were unevenly coated with dull green fiber spray. There was a constant noise of pedestrians beyond the oval hatch; the air conditioning allowed in a smell of frying oil and ketones despite the filter trap Margaret had set up. She had stuck an aerial photograph of New York, where she had been born, above the head stay of her hammock, and dozens of glossy print-outs of the reef scaled the walls. Apart from the pictures, a few clothes in the closet and the spider plant under the purple grolite, the room was quite anonymous.

She had spent most of her life in rooms like this. She could pack in five minutes, ready to move onto the next job.

"This place is probably bugged," Arn said. He sat with his back to the door, sipping schnapps from a silvery flask and looking at the overlapping panoramas of the reef.

Margaret sat on the edge of her hammock. She was nervous and excited. She said, "Everywhere is bugged. I want them to hear that I'm not guilty. Tell me what you know."

Arn looked at her. "I examined the proxies you sent back. I wasn't quite sure what I was looking for, but it was surprisingly easy to spot."

"An infection," Margaret said.

"Yah, a very specific infection. We concentrated on the nervous system, given the etiology. In the brain we found lesions, always in the same area."

Margaret examined the three-dimensional color-enhanced tomographic scan Arn had brought. The lesions were little black bubbles in the underside of the unfolded cerebellum, just in front of the optic node.

"The same in all of them," Arn said. "We took samples, extracted DNA, and sequenced it." A grid of thousands of colored dots, then another superimposed over it. All the dots lined up.

"A match to Opie's parasite," Margaret guessed.

Arn grinned. He had a nice smile. It made him look like an enthusiastic boy. "We tried that first of course. Got a match, then went through the library of reef organisms, and got partial matches. Opie's parasite has its fingerprints in the DNA of everything in the reef, but this—" he jabbed a long finger through the projection—"is the pure quill. Just an unlucky accident that it lodges in the brain at this particular place and produces the behavior you saw."

"Perhaps it isn't a random change," Margaret said. "Perhaps the reef has a use for the proxies."

"Teleology," Arn said. "Don't let Opie hear that thought. He'd use it against you. This is evolution. It isn't directed by anything other than natural selection. There is no designer, no watchmaker. Not after the AI crashed, anyway, and it only pushed the ecosystem toward more efficient sulfur oxidation. There's more, Margaret. I've been doing some experiments on the side. Exposing aluminum foil sheets in orbit around Enki. There are exfoliations everywhere."

"Then Opie is right."

"No, no. All the exfoliations I found were nonviable. I did more experiments. The exfoliations are metabolically active when released, unlike bacterial spores. And they have no protective wall. No reason for them to have one, yah? They live only for a few minutes. Either they land on a new host or they don't. Solar radiation easily tears them apart. You can kill them with a picowatt ultraviolet laser. Contamination isn't a problem."

"And it can't infect us," Margaret said. "Vacuum organisms and proxies have the same DNA code as us, the same as everything from Earth, for that matter, but it's written in artificial nucleotide bases. The reef isn't dangerous at all, Arn."

"Yah, but in theory it could infect every vacuum organism ever designed. The only way around it would be to change the base structure of vacuum organism DNA—how much would that cost?"

"I know about contamination, Arn. The mold that wrecked the biome designed by my parents came in with someone or something. Maybe on clothing, or skin, or in the gut, or in some trade goods. It grew on anything with a cellulose cell wall. Every plant was infected. The fields were covered by huge sheets of gray mold; the air was full of spores. It didn't infect people, but more than a hundred died from massive allergic reactions and respiratory failure. They had to vent the atmosphere in the end. And my parents couldn't find work after that."

Arn said gently, "That is the way. We live by our reputations. It's hard when something goes wrong."

Margaret ignored this. She said, "The reef is a resource, not a danger. You're looking at it the wrong way, like Opie Kindred. We need diversity. Our biospheres have to be complicated because simple systems are prone to invasion and disruption, but they aren't one hundredth as complicated as those on Earth. If my parents' biome had been more diverse, the mold couldn't have found a foothold."

"There are some things I could do without." Arn scratched his left ankle with the toes of his right foot. "Like those ants."

"Well, we don't know if we need the ants specifically, but we need variety, and they contribute to it. They help aerate the soil, to begin with, which encourages stratification and diversity of soil organisms. There are a million different kinds of microbe in a gram of soil from a forest on Earth; we have to make do with less than a thousand. We don't have one tenth that number of useful vacuum organisms and most are grown in monoculture, which is the most vulnerable ecosystem of all. That was the cause of the crash of the green revolution on Earth in the twenty-first century. But there are hundreds of different species in the reef. Wild species, Arn. You could seed a planetoid with them and go harvest it a year later. The citizens don't go outside because they have their parklands, their palaces, their virtualities. They've forgotten that the outer system isn't just the habitats. There are millions of small planetoids in the Kuiper Belt. Anyone with a dome and the reef vacuum organisms could homestead one."

She had been thinking about this while working out in the fields. The Star Chamber had given her plenty of time to think.

Arn shook his head. "They all have the parasite lurking in them. Any species from the reef can turn into it. Perhaps even the proxies."

"We don't know enough," Margaret said. "I saw things in the bottom of the Rift, before I lost contact with the proxy. Big structures. And there's the anomalous temperature gradients, too. The seat of change must be down there, Arn. The parasite could be useful, if we can master it. The viruses that caused the immunodeficiency plagues are used for gene therapy now. Opie Kindred has been down there. He's suppressing what he has found."

"Yah, well, it does not much matter. They have completed synthesis of the metabolic inhibitor. I'm friendly with the organics chief. They diverted most of the refinery to it." Arn took out his slate. "He showed me how they have set it up. That is what they have been doing down in the Rift. Not exploring."

"Then we have to do something now."

"It is too late, Margaret."

"I want to call a meeting, Arn. I have a proposal."

Most of the science crews came. Opie Kindred's crew was a notable exception; Arn said that it gave him a bad feeling.

"They could be setting us up," he told Margaret.

"I know they're listening. That's good. I want it in the open. If you're worried about getting hurt you can always leave."

"I came because I wanted to. Like everyone else here. We're all scientists. We all want the truth known." Arn looked at her. He smiled. "You want more than that, I think."

"I fight my own fights." All around people were watching. Margaret added, "Let's get this thing started."

Arn called the meeting to order and gave a brief presentation about his research into survival of the exfoliations before throwing the matter open to the meeting. Nearly everyone had an opinion. Microphones hovered in the room, and at times three or four people were shouting at each other. Margaret let them work off their frustration. Some simply wanted to register a protest; a small but significant minority were worried about losing their bonuses or even all of their pay.

"Better that than our credibility," one of Orly Higgins's techs said. "That's what we live by. None of us will work again if we allow the *Ganapati* to become a plague ship."

Yells of approval, whistles.

Margaret waited until the noise had died down, then got to her feet. She was in the center of the horseshoe of seats, and everyone turned to watch, more than a hundred people. Their gaze fell upon her like sunlight; it strengthened her. A microphone floated down in front of her face.

"Arn has shown that contamination isn't an issue," Margaret said. "The issue is that the Star Chamber wants to destroy the reef because they want to exploit what they've found and stop anyone else using it. I'm against that, all the way. I'm not gengeneered. Micro-gravity is not my natural habitat. I have to take a dozen different drugs to prevent reabsorption of calcium from my bone, collapse of my circulatory system, fluid retention, all the bad stuff micro-gravity does to unedited Earth stock. I'm not allowed to have children here, because they would be as crippled as me. Despite that, my home is here. Like all of you, I would like to have the benefits of being a citizen, to live in the parklands and eat real food. But there aren't enough parklands for everyone because the citizens who own the habitats control production of fixed carbon. The vacuum organisms we have found could change that. The reef may be a source of plague, or it may be a source of unlimited organics. We don't know. What we do know is that the reef is unique and we haven't finished exploring it. If the Star Chamber destroys it, we may never know what's out there."

Cheers at this. Several people rose to make points, but Margaret wouldn't give way. She wanted to finish.

"Opie Kindred has been running missions to the bottom of the Rift, but he hasn't been sharing what he's found there. Perhaps he no longer thinks that he's one of us. He'll trade his scientific reputation for citizenship," Margaret said, "but that isn't our way, is it?"

"NO!" the crowd roared.

And the White Mice invaded the room.

Sharp cracks, white smoke, screams. The White Mice had long flexible sticks weighted at one end. They went at the crowd like farmers threshing corn. Margaret was separated from Arn by a wedge of panicking people. Two techs got hold of her and steered her out of the room, down a corridor filling with smoke. Arn loomed out of it, clutching his slate to his chest.

"They're getting ready to set off the poison," he said as they ran in long loping strides.

"Then I'm going now," Margaret said.

Down a drop pole onto a corridor lined with shops. People were smashing windows. No one looked at them as they ran through the riot. They turned a corner, the sounds of shouts and breaking glass fading. Margaret was breathing hard. Her eyes were smarting, her nose running.

"They might kill you," Arn said. He grasped her arm. "I can't let you go, Margaret."

She shook herself free. Arn tried to grab her again. He was taller, but she was stronger. She stepped inside his reach and jumped up and popped him on the nose with the flat of her hand.

He sat down, blowing bubbles of blood from his nostrils, blinking up at her with surprised, tear-filled eyes.

She snatched up his slate. "I'm sorry, Arn," she said. "This is my only chance. I might not find anything, but I couldn't live with myself if I didn't try."

Margaret was five hundred kilometers out from the habitat when the radio beeped. "Ignore it," she told her pressure suit. She was sure that she knew who was trying to contact her, and she had nothing to say to him.

This far out, the Sun was merely the brightest star in the sky. Behind and above Margaret, the dim elongated crescent of the *Ganapati* hung before the sweep of the Milky Way. Ahead, below the little transit platform's motor, Enki was growing against a glittering starscape, a lumpy potato with a big notch at its widest point.

The little moonlet was rising over the notch, a swiftly moving fleck of light. For a moment, Margaret had the irrational fear that she would collide with it, but the transit platform's navigational display showed her that she would fall above and behind it. Falling past a moon! She couldn't help smiling at the thought.

"Priority override," her pressure suit said. Its voice was a reassuring contralto Margaret knew as well as her mother's.

"Ignore it," Margaret said again.

"Sorry, Maggie. You know I can't do that."

"Quite correct," another voice said.

Margaret identified him a moment before the suit helpfully printed his name across the helmet's visor. Dzu Sho.

"Turn back right now," Sho said. "We can take you out with the spectrographic laser if we have to."

"You wouldn't dare," she said.

"I do not believe anyone would mourn you," Sho said unctuously. "Leaving the *Ganapati* was an act of sedition, and we're entitled to defend ourselves."

Margaret laughed. It was just the kind of silly, sententious, self-important nonsense that Sho was fond of spouting.

"I am entirely serious," Sho said.

Enki had rotated to show that the notch was the beginning of a groove. The groove elongated as the worldlet rotated further. Tigris Rift. Its edges ramified in complex fractal branchings.

"I'm going where the proxies fell," Margaret said. "I'm still working for you."

"You sabotaged the proxies. That's why they couldn't fully penetrate the Rift."

"That's why I'm going—"

"Excuse me," the suit said, "but I register a small energy flux."

"Just a tickle from the ranging sight," Sho said. "Turn back now, Dr. Wu."

"I intend to come back."

It was a struggle to stay calm. Margaret thought that Sho's threat was no more than empty air. The laser's AI would not allow it to be used against human targets, and she was certain that Sho couldn't override it. And even if he could, he wouldn't dare kill her in full view of the science crews. Sho was bluffing. He had to be.

The radio silence stretched. Then Sho said, "You're planning to commit a final act of sabotage. Don't think you can get away with it. I'm sending someone after you."

Margaret was dizzy with relief. Anyone chasing her would be using the same kind of transit platform. She had at least thirty minutes head start.

Another voice said, "Don't think this will make you a hero."

Opie Kindred. Of course. The man never could delegate. He was on the same trajectory, several hundred kilometers behind but gaining slowly.

"Tell me what you found," she said. "Then we can finish this race before it begins."

Opie Kindred switched off his radio.

"If you had not brought along all this gear," her suit grumbled, "we could outdistance him."

"I think we'll need it soon. We'll just have to be smarter than him."

Margaret studied the schematics of the poison spraying mechanism—it was beautifully simple, but vulnerable—while Tigris Rift swelled beneath her, a jumble of knife-edge chevron ridges. Enki was so small and the Rift so wide that the walls had fallen beneath the horizon. She was steering toward the Rift's center when the suit apologized and said that there was another priority override.

It was the *Ganapati*'s lawyer. She warned Margaret that this was being entered into sealed court records, and then formally revoked her contract and read a complaint about her seditious conduct.

"You're a contracted worker just like me," Margaret said. "We take orders, but we both have codes of professional ethics, too. For the record, that's why I'm here. The reef is a unique organism. I cannot allow it to be destroyed."

Dzu Sho came onto the channel and said, "Off the record, don't think about being picked up."

The lawyer switched channels. "He does not mean it," she said. "He would be in violation of the distress statutes." Pause. "Good luck, Dr. Wu."

Then there was only the carrier wave.

Margaret wished that this made her feel better. Plenty of contract workers who went against the direct orders of their employers had disappeared, or been killed in industrial accidents. The fire of the mass meeting had evaporated long before the suit had assembled itself around her, and now she felt colder and lonelier than ever.

She fell, the platform shuddering now and then as it adjusted its trim. Opie Kindred's platform was a bright spark moving sideways across the drifts of stars above. Directly below was a vast flow of nitrogen ice with a black river winding through it. The center of the Rift, a cleft two kilometers long and fifty kilometers deep. The reef.

She fell toward it.

She had left the radio channel open. Suddenly, Opie Kindred said, "Stop now and it will be over."

"Tell me what you know."

No answer.

She said, "You don't have to follow me, Opie. This is my risk. I don't ask you to share it."

"You won't take this away from me."

"Is citizenship really worth this, Opie?"

No reply.

The suit's proximity alarms began to ping and beep. She turned them off one by one, and told the suit to be quiet when it complained.

"I am only trying to help," it said. "You should reduce your velocity. The target is very narrow."

"I've been here before," Margaret said.

But only by proxy. The icefield rushed up at her. Its smooth flows humped over one another, pitted everywhere with tiny craters. She glimpsed black splashes where vacuum organisms had colonized a stress ridge. Then an edge flashed past; walls unraveled on either side.

She was in the reef.

The vacuum organisms were everywhere: flat plates jutting from the walls; vases and delicate fans and fretworks; huge blotches smooth as ice or dissected by cracks. In the light cast by the platform's lamps, they did not possess the vibrant primary colors of the proxy link, but were every shade of gray and black, streaked here and there with muddy reds. Complex fans ramified far back inside the milky nitrogen ice, following veins of carbonaceous compounds.

Far above, stars were framed by the edges of the cleft. One star was falling toward her: Opie Kindred. Margaret switched on the suit's radar, and immediately it began to ping. The suit shouted a warning, but before Margaret could look around the pings dopplered together.

Proxies.

They shot up toward her, tentacles writhing from the black, streamlined helmets of their mantles. Most of them missed, jagging erratically as they squirted bursts of hydrogen to kill their velocity. Two collided in a slow flurry of tentacles.

Margaret laughed. None of her crew would fight against her, and Sho was relying upon inexperienced operators.

The biggest proxy, three meters long, swooped past. The crystalline gleam of its sensor array reflected the lights of the platform. It decelerated, spun on its axis, and dove back toward her.

Margaret barely had time to pull out the weapon she had brought with her. It was a welding pistol, rigged on a long rod with a yoked wire around the trigger. She thrust it up like the torch of the Statue of Liberty just before the proxy struck her.

The suit's gauntlet, elbow joint and shoulder piece stiffened under the heavy impact, saving Margaret from broken bones, but the collision knocked the transit platform sideways. It plunged through reef growths. Like glass, they had tremendous rigidity but very little lateral strength. Fans and lattices broke away, peppering Margaret and the proxy with shards. It was like falling through a series of chandeliers. Margaret couldn't close her fingers in the stiffened gauntlet. She stood tethered to the platform with her arm and the rod raised straight up and the black proxy wrapped around them. The proxy's tentacles lashed her visor with slow, purposeful slaps.

Margaret knew that it would take only a few moments before the tentacles' carbon-fiber proteins could unlink; then it would be able to reach the life support pack on her back.

She shouted at the suit, ordering it to relax the gauntlet's fingers. The proxy was contracting around her rigid arm as it stretched toward the life support pack. When the gauntlet went limp, pressure snapped her fingers closed. Her forefinger popped free of the knuckle. She yelled with pain. And the wire rigged to the welding pistol's trigger pulled taut.

Inside the proxy's mantle, a focused beam of electrons boiled off the pistol's filament. The pistol, designed to work only in high vacuum, began to arc almost immediately, but the electron beam had already heated the integument and muscle of the proxy to more than 400°C. Vapor expanded explosively. The proxy shot away, propelled by the gases of its own dissolution.

Opie was still gaining on Margaret. Gritting her teeth against the pain of her dislocated finger, she dumped the broken welding gear. It only slowly floated away above her, for it still had the same velocity as she did.

A proxy swirled in beside her with shocking suddenness. For a moment, she gazed into its faceted sensor array, and then dots of luminescence skittered across its smooth black mantle, forming letters.

Much luck, boss. SK.

Srin Kerenyi. Margaret waved with her good hand. The proxy scooted away, rising at a shallow angle toward Opie's descending star.

A few seconds later the cleft filled with the unmistakable flash of laser light.

The radar trace of Srin's proxy disappeared.

Shit. Opie Kindred was armed. If he got close enough he could kill her.

Margaret risked a quick burn of the transit platform's motor to increase her rate of fall. It roared at her back for twenty seconds; when it cut out her pressure suit warned her that she had insufficient fuel for full deceleration.

"I know what I'm doing," Margaret told it.

The complex forms of the reef dwindled past. Then there were only huge patches of black staining the nitrogen ice walls. Margaret passed her previous record depth, and still she fell. It was like free fall; the negligible gravity of Enki did not cause any appreciable acceleration.

Opie Kindred gained on her by increments.

In vacuum, the lights of the transit platform threw abrupt pools of light onto the endlessly unraveling walls. Slowly, the pools of light elongated into glowing tunnels filled with sparkling motes. The exfoliations and gases and organic molecules were growing denser. And, impossibly, the temperature was *rising*, one degree with every five hundred meters. Far below, between the narrowing perspective of the walls, structures were beginning to resolve from the blackness.

The suit reminded her that she should begin the platform's deceleration burn. Margaret checked Opie's velocity and said she would wait.

"I have no desire to end as a crumpled tube filled with strawberry jam," the suit said. It projected a countdown on her visor and refused to switch it off.

Margaret kept one eye on Opie's velocity, the other on the blur of reducing numbers. The numbers passed zero. The suit screamed obscenities in her ears, but she waited a beat more before firing the platform's motor.

The platform slammed into her boots. Sharp pain in her ankles and knees. The suit stiffened as the harness dug into her shoulders and waist.

Opie Kindred's platform flashed past. He had waited until after she had decelerated before making his move. Margaret slapped the release buckle of the platform's harness and fired the piton gun into the nitrogen ice wall. It was enough to slow her so that she could catch hold of a crevice and swing up into it. Her dislocated finger hurt like hell.

The temperature was a stifling eighty-seven degrees above absolute zero. The atmospheric pressure was just registering—a mix of hydrogen and carbon monoxide and hydrogen sulphide. Barely enough in the whole of the bottom of the cleft to pack into a small box at the pressure of Earth's atmosphere at sea level, but the rate of production must be tremendous to compensate for loss into the colder vacuum above.

Margaret leaned out of the crevice. Below, it widened into a chimney between humped pressure flows of nitrogen ice sloping down to the floor of the cleft. The slopes and the floor were packed with a wild proliferation of growths. Not only the familiar vases and sheets and laces, but great branching structures like crystal trees, lumpy plates raised on stout stalks, tangles of black wire hundreds of meters across, clusters of frothy globes, and much more.

There was no sign of Opie Kindred, but tethered above the growths were the balloons of his spraying mechanism. Each was a dozen meters across, crinkled, flaccid. They were fifty degrees hotter than their surroundings, would have to grow hotter still before the metabolic inhibitor was completely volatilized inside them. When that happened, small explosive devices would puncture them, and the metabolic inhibitor would be sucked into the vacuum of the cleft like smoke up a chimney.

Margaret consulted the schematics and started to climb down the crevice, light as a dream, steering herself with the fingers of her left hand. The switching relays that controlled the balloons' heaters were manually controlled because of telemetry interference from the reef's vacuum smog and the broadband electromagnetic resonance. The crash shelter where they were located was about two kilometers away, a slab of orange foamed plastic in the center of a desolation of abandoned equipment and broken and half-melted vacuum organism colonies.

The crevice widened. Margaret landed between drifts of what looked like giant soap bubbles that grew at its bottom.

And Opie Kindred's platform rose up between two of the half-inflated balloons.

Margaret dropped onto her belly behind a line of bubbles that grew along a smooth ridge of ice. She opened a radio channel. It was filled with a wash of static and a wailing modulation, but through the noise she heard Opie's voice faintly calling her name.

He was a hundred meters away and more or less at her level, turning in a slow circle. He couldn't locate her amidst the radio noise and the ambient temperature was higher than the skin of her pressure suit, so she had no infrared image.

She began to crawl along the smooth ridge. The walls of the bubbles were whitely opaque, but she should see shapes curled within them. Like embryos inside eggs.

"Everything is ready, Margaret," Opie Kindred's voice said in her helmet. "I'm going to find you, and then I'm going to sterilize this place. There are things here you know nothing about. Horribly dangerous things. Who are you working for? Tell me that and I'll let you live."

A thread of red light waved out from the platform and a chunk of nitrogen ice cracked off explosively. Margaret felt it through the tips of her gloves.

"I can cut my way through to you," Opie Kindred said, "wherever you are hiding."

Margaret watched the platform slowly revolve. Tried to guess if she could reach the shelter while he was looking the other way. All she had to do was bound down the ridge and cross a kilometer of bare, crinkled nitrogen ice without being fried by Opie's laser. Still crouching, she lifted onto the tips of her fingers and toes, like a sprinter on the block. He was turning, turning. She took three deep breaths to clear her head—and something crashed into the ice cliff high above! It spun out in a spray of shards, hit the slope below and spun through toppling clusters of tall black chimneys. For a moment, Margaret was paralyzed with astonishment. Then she remembered the welding gear. It had finally caught up with her.

Opie Kindred's platform slewed around and a red thread waved across the face of the cliff. A slab of ice thundered outward. Margaret bounded away, taking giant leaps and trying to look behind her at the same time.

The slab spun on its axis, shedding huge shards, and smashed into the cluster of the bubbles where she had been crouching just moments before. The ice shook like a living thing under her feet and threw her head over heels.

She stopped herself by firing the piton gun into the ground. She was on her back, looking up at the top of the ridge, where bubbles vented a dense mix of gas and oily organics before bursting in an irregular cannonade. Hundreds of slim black shapes shot away. Some smashed into the walls of the cleft and stuck there, but many more vanished into its maw.

A chain reaction had started. Bubbles were bursting open up and down the length of the cleft.

A cluster popped under Opie Kindred's platform and he vanished in a roil of vapor. The crevice shook. Nitrogen ice boiled into a dense fog. A wind got up for a few minutes. Margaret clung to the piton until it was over.

Opie Kindred had drifted down less than a hundred meters away. The thing which had smashed the visor of his helmet was still lodged there. It was slim and black, with a hard, shiny exoskeleton. The broken bodies of others settled among smashed vacuum organism colonies, glistening like beetles in the light of Margaret's suit. They were like tiny, tentacle-less proxies, their swollen mantles cased in something like keratin. Some had split open, revealing ridged reaction chambers and complex matrices of black threads.

"Gametes," Margaret said, seized by a sudden wild intuition. "Little rocketships full of DNA."

The suit asked if she was all right.

She giggled. "The parasite turns everything into its own self. Even proxies!"

"I believe that I have located Dr. Kindred's platform," the suit said. "I suggest that you refrain from vigorous exercise, Maggie. Your oxygen supply is limited. What are you doing?"

She was heading toward the crash shelter. "I'm going to switch off the balloon heaters. They won't be needed."

After she shut down the heaters, Margaret lashed one of the dead creatures to the transit platform. She shot up between the walls of the cleft, and at last rose into the range of the relay transmitters. Her radio came alive, a dozen channels blinking for attention. Arn was on one, and she told him what had happened.

"Sho wanted to light out of here," Arn said, "but stronger heads prevailed. Come home, Margaret."

"Did you see them? Did you, Arn?"

"Some hit the *Ganapati*." He laughed. "Even the Star Chamber can't deny what happened."

Margaret rose up above the ice fields and continued to rise until the curve of the worldlet's horizon became visible, and then the walls of Tigris Rift. The *Ganapati* was a faint star bracketed between them. She called up deep radar, and saw, beyond the *Ganapati's* strong signal, thousands of faint traces falling away into deep space.

A random scatter of genetic packages. How many would survive to strike new worldlets and give rise to new reefs?

Enough, she thought. The reef evolved in saltatory jumps. She had just witnessed its next revolution.

Given time, it would fill the Kuiper Belt.

going after bobo

SUSAN PALWICK

Not nearly as prolific as she should be, Susan Palwick's eloquent work has appeared in Asimov's Science Fiction, The Magazine of Fantasy & Science Fiction, Amazing, Sci Fiction, Starlight 1, Not of Women Born, Pulphouse, Xanadu 3, Walls of Fear, The Horns of Elfland, Ruby Slippers, Golden Tears, *and other markets. Her acclaimed first novel* Flying in Place *was one of the most talked-about books of 1992, and won the Crawford Award for Best First Fantasy Novel, which is presented annually by the International Association for the Fantastic in the Arts. She's currently at work on her second novel,* Shelter. *She lives in Reno, Nevada, where she's an assistant professor of English at the University of Nevada, teaching writing and literature.*

Here she gives us a moving portrait of a young boy growing up fast in a troubled near-future world, one who's forced to face some choices that are hard to make at any age. . . .

▼

I was the only one home when the GPS satellites finally came back online. It was already dark out by then, and it had been snowing all afternoon. I'd been sitting at the kitchen table with my algebra book, trying to concentrate on quadratic equations, and then the handheld beeped and lit up and the transmitter signal started blipping on the screen, and I looked at it and cursed and ran upstairs to double-check the signal position against my topo map. And then I cursed some more, and started throwing on warm clothing.

I'd spent five days staring at my handheld, praying that the screen would light up again, please, please, so I'd be able to see where Bobo was. The only time he'd even stayed away from home overnight, and it was when the satellites were out. Just my luck.

Or maybe David had planned it that way. Bobo had been missing since Monday, the day the satellites went down, and David had probably opened the door for him when I wasn't looking, like always, and then given him an extra kick, gloating because he knew I wouldn't be able to follow Bobo's signal.

I hadn't been too worried yet, on Monday. Bobo was gone when I got back from school, but I thought he'd come home for dinner, the way he always did. When he didn't, I went outside and called him and checked in neighbors' yards. I started to get scared when I couldn't find him, but Mom said not to worry, Bobo would come back later, and even if he didn't, he'd probably be okay even if he stayed out overnight.

But he wasn't back for breakfast on Tuesday, either, and by that night I was frantic, especially since the satellites were still down and I had no idea where Bobo was and I couldn't find him in any of the places where he usually hung out. Wednesday and Thursday and Friday were hell. I carried the handheld with me everyplace, waiting for it to light up again, hunched over it every second, even at school, while Johnny Schuster and Leon Flanking carried on in the background the way they always did. "Hey, Mike! Hey Michael—you know what we're doing after school today? We're driving down to Carson, Mike. Yeah, we're going down to Carson City, and you know what we're going to do down there? We're going to—"

Usually I was pretty good at just ignoring them. I knew I couldn't let them get to me, because that was what they wanted. They wanted me to fight them and get in trouble, and I couldn't do that to Mom, not with so much trouble in the family already. I didn't want her to know what Johnny and Leon were saying; I didn't want her to have to think about Johnny and Leon at all, or why they were picking on me. Our families used to be friends, but that was a long time ago, before my father died and theirs went to jail. Johnny and Leon think it was all my father's fault, as if their own dads couldn't have said no, even if my dad was the one who came up with the idea. So they're mean to me, because my father isn't around anymore for them to blame.

It was harder to ignore them the week the satellites were down. Mom's bosses were checking up on her a lot more, because their handhelds weren't working either. We got calls at home every night to make sure she was really there, and when she was at work, somebody had to go with her if she even left the building. Just like the old days, before the handhelds. And God only knew what David was up to. I guess he was still going to his warehouse job, driving a forklift and moving boxes around, because his boss would have called the probation office if he hadn't shown up. But he wasn't coming home when he was supposed to, and every time he did come home, he and Mom had screaming fights, even worse than usual.

So I had five days of not knowing where Bobo was, while Johnny and Leon baited me at school and Mom and David yelled at each other at home. And then finally the satellites came back online on Friday. The GPS people had been talking about how they might have to knock the whole system out of orbit and put up another one—which would have been a mess—but finally some earthside keyboard jockey managed to fix whatever the hackers had done.

Which was great, except that down here in Reno it had been snowing for hours, and according to the GPS, I was going to have to climb 3,200 feet to reach Bobo. Mom came in just as I was stuffing some extra energy bars in my pack. I knew she wouldn't want me going out, and I wasn't up to fighting with her about it, so I'd been hoping the snow would delay her for a few hours, maybe even keep her down in Carson overnight. I should have known better. That's what Mom's new SUV was for: getting home, even in shitty weather.

She looked tired. She always looks tired after a shift.

"What are you doing?" she said, and looked over my shoulder at the handheld screen, and then at the topo map next to it. "Oh, Jesus, Mike. It's on top of Peavine!"

I could smell her shampoo. She always smells like shampoo after a shift. I didn't want to think about what she smells like before she showers to come home.

"*He's* on top of Peavine," I said. "Bobo's on top of Peavine."

Mom shook her head. "Honey—no. You can't go up there."

"Mom, he could be *hurt!* He could have a broken leg or something and not be able to move and just be lying there!" The signal hadn't moved at all. If it had been lower down the mountain, I would have thought that maybe some family had taken Bobo in, but there still weren't any houses that high. The top of Peavine was one of the few places the developers hadn't gotten to yet.

"Sweetheart," Mom's voice was very quiet. "Michael, turn around. Come on. Turn around and look at me."

I didn't turn around. I stuffed a few more energy bars in my pack, and Mom put her hands on my shoulders and said, "Michael, he's dead."

I still kept my back to her. "You don't *know* that!"

"He's been gone for five days now, and the signal's on top of Peavine. He has to be dead. A coyote got him and dragged him up there. He's never gone that high by himself, has he?"

She was right. In the year he'd had the transmitter, Bobo had never gone anywhere much, certainly not anywhere far. He'd liked exploring the neighbors' yards, and the strips of wild land between the developments, where there were voles and mice. And coyotes.

"So he decided to go exploring," I said, and zipped my pack shut. "I have to go find out, anyway."

"Michael, there's nothing to find out. He's dead. You know that."

"I do *not* know that! I don't know anything." *Except that David's a piece of shit.* I did turn around, then, because I wanted to see her face when I said, "He hasn't been home since Monday, Mom, so how do I know what's happened? I haven't even *seen* him."

I guess I was up to fighting, after all. It was an awful thing to say, because it would only remind her of what we were all trying to forget, but I was still happy when she looked away from me, sharply, with a hiss of indrawn breath. She didn't curse me out, though, even though I deserved it. She didn't even leave the room. Instead she looked back at me, after a minute, and put her hands on my shoulders again. "You can't go out there. Not in this weather. It wouldn't even be safe to take the SUV, or I'd drive you—"

"He could be lying hurt in the snow," I said. "Or holed up somewhere, or—"

"Michael, he's dead." I didn't answer. Mom squeezed my shoulders and said gently, "And even if he *were* alive, you couldn't reach him in time. Not all that way; not in this weather. Not even in the SUV."

"I just want to know," I said. I looked right at her when I said it. I wasn't saying it to be mean, this time. "I can't stand not knowing."

"You do know," she said. She sounded very sad. "You just won't let yourself know that you know."

"Okay," I told her, my throat tight. "I can't stand not seeing, then. Is that better?"

She took her hands off my shoulders and sighed. "I'll call Letty, but it's not going to do any good. Is your brother home?"

"No," I said. David should have been home an hour before that. I wondered if he even knew that the satellites were back up.

Mom frowned. "Do you know where he is?"

"Of course not," I said. "Do you think I care? Call the sheriff's office, if you want to know where he is."

Mom gave me one of her patented warning looks. "Michael—"

"He let Bobo out," I said. "You know he did. He did it on purpose, just like all the other times. Do you think I care where the fuck he is?"

"I'm going to go call Letty," Mom said.

David hated Bobo the minute we got him. He was my tenth birthday present from Mom and Dad. The four of us went to the pet store to pick him out, but when David saw the kittens, he just wrinkled his nose and backed up a few feet. David was always doing things like that, trying to be cool by pretending he couldn't stand the rest of us.

David and I used to be friends, when we were younger. We played catch and rode our bikes and dug around in the dirt pretending we were gold miners, and once David even pulled me out of the way of a rattlesnake, because I didn't recognize the funny noise in the bushes and had gone to see what it was. I was six then, and David was ten. I'll never forget how pale he was after he yanked me away from the rattling, how scared he looked when he yelled at me never, *ever* to do that again.

The four-year difference didn't matter back then, except that it meant David knew a lot more than I did. But once he got into high school, David didn't want anything to do with any of us, especially his little brother. And all of a sudden, he didn't seem so smart to me anymore, even though he thought he was smarter than shit.

I named my new kitten Bobcat, because he had that tawny coat and little tufts on his ears. His name got shortened to Bobo pretty quickly, though, and that's what we always called him—everybody except David, who called him "Hairball." By the time Dad died, Bobo was a really big cat: fifteen pounds, anyway, which was some comfort when David started "accidentally" letting Bobo out of the house. I figured he could hold his own against most other cats, maybe even against owls. I tried not to think about cars and coyotes, and people with guns.

He started going over the fence right away, but he was good about coming home. He always showed up for meals, even if sometimes he brought along his own dessert: dead grasshoppers, and mice and voles, and once a baby bird. Dr. Mills says that when cats bring you dead prey, it's because they think you're their kittens, and they're trying to feed you.

Bobo was a good cat, but David kept letting him out, no matter how much I yelled at him about it. Mom tried to ground David a couple of times, but it didn't work. David just laughed. He kept letting Bobo out, and Bobo kept going over the fence. It took me four months of allowance, plus Christmas and birthday money, to save up enough for the transmitter chip and the handheld. David laughed about that, too.

"He's just a fucking *cat*, Mike. Jesus Christ, what are you spending all your money on that transmitter thing for?"

"So I can find him if he gets lost," I said, my stomach clenching. Even then, I could hardly stand to talk to David.

"If he gets lost, so what? They have a million more cats at the pound."

And you'd let them all out if you could, wouldn't you? "They don't have a million who are mine," I said, and Mom looked up from chopping onions in the kitchen. It was one of her days off.

"David, leave him alone. You're the one who should be paying for that transmitter, you know." And they got into a huge fight, and David stomped out of the house and roared off in his rattletrap Jeep, and when all the dust had settled, Mom came and found me in my room. She sat down on the side of the bed and smoothed my hair back from my forehead, as if I was seven again instead of thirteen, and Bobo jumped down from where he'd been lying on my feet. He'd been licking the place where Dr. Mills had put the transmitter chip in his shoulder. Dr. Mills said that licking would help the wound heal, but that if Bobo started biting it, he'd have to wear one of those weird plastic collars that looks like a lampshade. I hadn't seen him biting it yet, but I was keeping an eye on him. When Mom sat on the bed, he resettled himself under my desk lamp, where the light from the bulb warmed the wood, and went back to licking.

Bobo always liked warm places. Dr. Mills says all cats do.

Mom stroked my forehead, and watched Bobo for a little while, and then said, "Michael—sometimes you can know exactly where people are, and still not be able to protect them." As if I didn't know that: As if any of us had been able to protect Dad from his own stupidity, even though the pit bosses knew exactly where he was every time he dealt a hand.

I knew that Mom was thinking about Dad, but there was no point talking about it. Dad was gone, and Bobo was right in front of me. "I'd keep him inside if I could, Mom! If David—"

"I know," she said. "I know you would." And then she gave me a quick kiss on the forehead and went downstairs again, and after a while, Bobo got off the desk and came back to lie on my feet. Watching him lick his shoulder, I wondered what it felt like to have a transmitter.

I'm the only one in the family who doesn't know.

Letty is Mom's best friend; they've known each other since second grade. Letty works for the BLM, and they have really good topo maps, so she could tell me exactly where Bobo was: just inside the mouth of an abandoned mine.

"He could have crawled there to get out of the snow," I said. The transmitter signal still hadn't moved. Mom and Letty exchanged looks, and then Mom got up. "I'm going upstairs now," she said. "You two talk."

"He *could* have," I said.

"Oh, Michael," Mom said. She started to say something else, but then she stopped. "Talk to Letty," she said, and turned and left the room.

I listened to Mom's footsteps going upstairs, and after a minute Letty said, "Mike, it's not safe to go out there now. You know that, right? It wouldn't be safe even in a truck. Not in this weather. And in the snow, you can know exactly where something is and still not be able to get at it."

"I know," I said. "Like that hiker last year. The one whose body they didn't find until spring." Except that the hiker hadn't had a transmitter, so they hadn't known where he was. It didn't matter. For ten days after he went missing, the cops and the BLM had search teams and helicopters all over the mountain, and never mind the weather.

"Yes," Letty said, very quietly. "Exactly." She waited for me to say something, but I didn't. "That guy was dying, you know. He was in a lot of pain all the time. His wife said later she thought maybe that was why he went out in a storm like that, while he could still go out at all."

Letty stopped and waited again, and I kept my head down. "He went out in bad weather," she said finally, "near dark. It's snowing now, and you were getting ready to hike up the mountain when your mom got home at seven-thirty. Michael?"

"Bobo could still be alive," I said fiercely. "It's not like anybody else *cares*. It's not like the state's going to spend thousands of dollars on a search-and-rescue!"

"So you were thinking—what?" Letty said. "That you'd go up there and get everybody hysterical, and get a search going, and while they were at it, they'd bring Bobo back? Was that the plan?"

"No," I said. I felt a little sick. I hadn't thought about any of that. I hadn't even thought about how I was going to get Bobo back down the mountain once I found him. "I just—I just wanted to get Bobo, that's all. I thought I could go up there and it would be okay. I've hiked in snow before."

"At night?" Letty asked. Then she sighed. "Mike, you know, a lot of people care about Bobo. Your mom cares, and I care, and Rich Mills cares. He was a sweet cat, and we know you love him. But we care about you, too."

"I'm fine," I told her. I wasn't sitting in the mouth of a mine during a snow-storm. I wasn't registered with the sheriff's office.

"You wouldn't be fine if you went up on Peavine tonight," Letty said. "That's the point. And even if Bobo's still alive—and I don't think he can be, Michael— you can't help him if you're frozen to death in a gully somewhere. Okay?"

I stared at the handheld, at the stationary signal. I thought about Bobo huddled in the mouth of the mine, getting colder and colder. He hated being cold. "Is it true that when you freeze to death," I said, "you feel warm at the end?"

"That's what I hear," Letty said. "I don't plan to test it."

"I don't either. That wasn't what I meant."

"Good. Don't do anything stupid, Mike. Search-and-rescue might not be able to get you out of it."

I felt like I was suffocating. "I was putting food in my pack. An entire box of energy bars. Ask Mom."

Letty shrugged. "Energy bars won't keep you from freezing."

"I *know* that."

"Good. And one more thing: don't you pay any mind to those Schuster and Flanking kids. They're slime."

I jerked my head up. How did she know about that? She raised an eyebrow when she saw my face, and said, "People talk. Folks at my office have kids in your school. Those bullies are slime, Michael, and everybody knows it. Don't let them give you grief. Your mother's a good person."

"I know she is." I wanted to ask Letty if she'd told Mom about Johnny and Leon, wanted to beg her not to tell Mom, but the way adults did things, that probably meant that telling Mom would be the first thing she'd do.

Letty nodded. "Good. Just ignore them, then."

It was easy for her to say. She didn't have to listen to them all the time. "That wasn't why I was going out," I told her. "I was going after Bobo."

"I know you were," Letty said. "I also know nothing's simple." She folded her topo map and stood up and said, "I'd better be getting on home, before the weather gets any worse. Tell your Mom I'll talk to her tomorrow. And try to have a good weekend." She ruffled my hair before she went, the way Mom had when Bobo got the chip. Letty hadn't done that since I was little. I didn't move. I just sat there, looking at the blip on the handheld.

After a while, I went up to my room. David hadn't come back yet, not that I cared, and Mom's door was closed. I knew she was sleeping off the shift. I also knew she'd be out of bed and downstairs in two seconds if she heard David coming in or me going out. She'd hung the front and back doors with bells, brass things from Nepal or someplace she'd gotten at Pier One. You couldn't go out or come in without making a racket, and you couldn't take the bells off the door without making one, either. "You learn to sleep lightly when you have babies," Mom told me once, as if either me or David had been babies for years. And our windows were old, and pretty noisy in their own right. And it was snowing harder.

So I just sat on my bed and stared out the window at the snow, trying not to think. My window faces east, away from Peavine, toward downtown. I couldn't see the lights from the casinos because of the snow, but I knew they were there. After a while it stopped snowing, and a few stars came out between the clouds, and so did the neon: the blue and white stripes of the Peppermill, which stands apart from everything else, south of downtown, and the bright white of the Hilton a bit north of that—"the Mother ship," Mom always calls it—and then, clustered downtown, the red of Circus Circus and the green of Harrah's, which Mom calls Oz City, and the flashing purple of the Silverado, where Dad used to work.

Dad loved this view; he was so proud that we could look down on the city. He couldn't stop crowing about it to all his friends. I remember when he brought George Flanking and Howard Schuster, Leon and Johnny's dads, into my room so they could look out my window, too. So they could see "the panorama." That was what Dad called it. We'd never been able to see anything from our old windows, except more trailers across the way. "I'm going to get us out of this box," Dad said when we lived there. "We're going to live in a real house, I swear we are." And then we moved here, to a real house, and pretty soon that wasn't big enough for him, either.

I shut my blinds and flopped down on my bed. Someplace a dog had started to bark, and then another joined in, and another and another, until the whole damn neighborhood was going nuts. And then I heard what must have set them off: the yipping howl of a coyote, trotting between houses looking for prey.

When we bought our house five years ago, the street ended a block from here, and that was where the mountain started. Winter mornings, sometimes, we'd see coyotes in our driveway. Now the developers have built another hundred houses up the street, with more subdivisions going up all the time: fancy houses, big, the kind we could never afford, the kind that made Dad's eyes narrow, that made him spend hours hunched over his desk. The kind he talked about when he went out drinking with George and Howard, I guess. I don't know who's buying those big houses; casino and warehouse workers can't afford places like that. Mom could, maybe, if she weren't saving for nursing school. The only people I can think of who might live there are the ones who work for the development companies.

So we don't get coyotes in our driveway anymore, but they're still around. They travel in back of the houses, next to the six-foot fences people put around their yards. There's still sagebrush between the subdivisions, and rabbits, and you can still follow those little strips of wildness to the really wild places, up on the mountain.

Coyotes are unbelievably smart, and they'll eat anything if they have to, and it doesn't bother them when people cut the land into pieces. They like it, because the boundaries between city and wilderness are where rodents live, and rodents are about coyotes' favorite food, aside from cats. So when we cut things up for them, there are more edges where they can hunt. It doesn't hurt that we've killed most of the wolves, who eat coyotes when they can, or that coyotes look so much like dogs. They can sneak in just about anyplace. Dr. Mills says there are coyotes living in New York City now, in Central Park. There are millions of them, all over the country.

Ranchers and farmers hate them because they're so hard to kill, and because even if you kill them, there are always more. But I can't hate them, not even for eating cats. They're smart and they're beautiful, and they're just trying to get by, and as far as I can tell, they're doing a better job of it than we are. They know how to work the system. That's what Dad thought he was doing, but he wasn't smart enough.

I lay there, listening to that coyote and to all the dogs, still trying not to think, but thinking anyway: about what a weird town this is, where you get casinos and coyotes both, where the developers are covering everything with new subdivisions, but there's still a mountain where you can die. After a while it got quiet again, and I peeked out the window and saw more snow. A while after that I heard the bells jangling downstairs, and heard Mom's feet hitting her bedroom floor and thudding down the stairs. When she and David started yelling at each other, I pulled my pillow over my head and finally managed to go to sleep.

It wasn't snowing when I woke up on Saturday, but it looked like it might start again any minute. The transmitter signal still hadn't moved, and when I thought about Bobo out there in the cold, I felt my own heart freezing in my chest. I heard voices from downstairs, and smelled coffee and bacon. Mom and David were both home, then. I threw on clothing and grabbed the handheld and ran down to the kitchen.

"Good morning," Mom said, and handed me a plate of bacon and eggs. She was wearing sweats and looked pretty relaxed. David was wearing his bathrobe and scowling, but David always scowls. I wondered what he was doing up so early. "Any change on the screen, Mike?"

"No," I said. I knew she didn't think there ever would be, and I wondered why she'd asked. David's face had gone from scowling to murderous, but that was all right, because I planned to be out the door as soon as possible.

"Okay," Mom said. "We're all going up there after breakfast."

"We are?" I said.

"Your brother's coming whether he wants to or not, and I asked Letty to come too. Rich Mills has to work this morning. Unless you'd rather not have all those people, honey."

"It's okay," I said. So that's what David was doing up. Mom was making him come as punishment, so he could see what he'd done, and Letty was coming because she had the maps, and maybe to help Mom keep me and David apart if we tried to kill each other. And Mom wouldn't think it was important to have Dr. Mills there, because she didn't think Bobo was still alive. I put down my plate and gulped down some coffee and said, "I'm going to go put the carrying case in the SUV."

"You're going to eat first," Mom said. "Sit down."

I sat. Driving up Peavine in the snow wasn't exactly Mom's idea of a day off; the least I could do was not give her any lip. David bit into his toast and said around a mouthful of bread, "I'm not going."

That was fine with me, but I wasn't going to say so in front of Mom. It was their fight. "You're coming," she told him. "And if Bobo's still alive you're paying the vet bills, and if he's not, you're buying your brother another cat. And if we get another cat you'll damn well help us keep it in the house, or I'll call the sheriff's office myself and tell them to take you off probation and put you in jail, David, I swear to God I will!"

She would, too. Even David knew that much. He scowled up at her and said, "The cat didn't *want* to stay in the house."

"That's not the issue," Mom said, and I stuffed my face full of eggs to keep from screaming at David that he'd hated Bobo, that he'd wanted Bobo to die, and that I hoped he'd die, too: alone, in the cold.

I remembered one of the first times David had let Bobo out. Bobo didn't have the transmitter yet, and I was in the backyard calling his name. Suddenly I saw something race over the fence and he ran up to me, mewing and mewing, his tail all puffy. I picked him up and carried him inside and he stayed on my lap, with his face stuck into my armpit like he was hiding, for half an hour, until finally he calmed down and stopped shaking and jumped down to get some food. I'd hoped that whatever had spooked him so badly would keep him from wanting to go out again, even if David opened all the doors and windows, but I guess he forgot how scared he'd been. "He didn't want to freeze to death, either," I said.

David pushed his chair back from the table and said, "Look, whatever happened to your fucking cat, it's not my fault, and I'm not wasting my day off going up there." He looked at Mom and said, "Do whatever you want: it doesn't matter. I might as well be in prison already."

"Bullshit," Mom said. "If you go to prison, you'll lose a lot more than a Saturday. Do you have any idea how lucky you are not to be there already? Especially after the stunts you've been pulling this week?" Nevada's a zero-tolerance drug state, even for minors, so when David got caught driving stoned last year, with most of a lid of pot in the glove compartment of his Jeep, Mom had to use every connection she had to get him probation instead of jail. It would have been a "juvenile facility," since David was still a few weeks short of eighteen, but Mom says that her connections said that wouldn't make much difference. Juvenile facilities are worse, if anything.

Mom didn't say who her connections are, and I don't want to know. Whoever they are, I figure they didn't help David entirely out of the goodness of their hearts. I figure they were scared of what Mom could tell people about them, even if what she does is legal.

"I told you," David said, "I've just been hanging out with some guys from work. You know: eating dinner, playing pool? I was in town."

"Right," Mom said. "And there's no way anybody could check that with the satellites down, is there? That's what you were counting on."

David rolled his eyes. "What time did the damn GPS go back up last night? Six-thirty or something? We were still eating then. We were at that pizza place in the mall. Call the sheriff's office and ask them, if you don't believe me." He jerked a thumb at my handheld and said, "How stupid do you think I am? I knew it could come back online any second. What, I'm going to take off for Mexico or something?"

Mom didn't bother to answer. She and I were the smart ones in the family: David took after Dad. Anybody stupid enough to get caught with that much pot was stupid enough to do just about anything else, as far as I could tell, but the only time I'd even started to say anything like that, right after his arrest, David had just glared at me and said, "Yeah, well, if you'd had to look at what I had to look at, you'd smoke dope too, baby brother."

As if I hadn't wanted to look. As if I hadn't kept trying to go outside. As if even now I didn't keep imagining what it had looked like, a million different ways, enough to keep me awake, sometimes.

But even then, I knew that David had only said it to make me feel guilty. He knew just how to get at everybody. Now he gestured at the handheld again and said bitterly, "I can't wipe my ass without those people knowing about it."

He was needling Mom, because that's what Dad had always said about dealing blackjack at the Silverado. The dealers were under surveillance all the time: from pit bosses, from hidden cameras. "You can't get away from it," Dad said. "It's like working in a goddamn box, with the walls closing in on you." But Dad chose his box, and so did David.

"That's not the issue," Mom told David again. "It's more than staying in county limits, David. You're supposed to come home straight after work. You know that."

"So you're my jailer now? Just like the casino was Dad's and the Lyon County cops are —"

"Stop it," Mom said, her voice icy. "I'm not your jailer. I'm the one who kept you out of jail. You agreed to the terms of the probation!"

"Like you agreed to all those terms when you decided to go down to Carson and play *nurse?*"

Mom was out of her chair then, and David was out of his, and they stood nose to nose, glaring at each other, and I knew that there was no way we were all going up on Peavine today, because they wouldn't be able to sit in the same car even if David had wanted to go, even if I'd wanted him there. Nothing David says to Mom ever makes any real sense, but he knows exactly how to get to her. Sometimes he has to keep at it for a while, but Mom always snaps eventually, even if the same thing has happened a million times before. Just like Bobo being scared by something outside, and still going out again when David gave him the chance. David knows exactly how to get people to hurt themselves.

They were still eye-to-eye, like cats circling each other before a fight, when the doorbell rang. "I'll get it," I said. Maybe it was Letty, and I could warn her about what was happening before she came inside.

It was a cop. "Good morning, son," he said. "I'm looking for David. That your brother?"

"Yeah," I said, but my legs felt like wood, and I didn't seem to be able to get out of the way.

"Don't worry," he said. "It's just a routine drug test."

That was supposed to happen on Fridays. So David had skipped his drug test, too. My stomach shriveled some more. "Will he have to go to jail?" I said. The house would be a lot quieter if David was in jail, but school would be worse. If David went to jail, he'd probably be in the same place as George Flanking and Howard Schuster, and I didn't want to think too much about that.

The cop's face softened. "No. Not if he's clean. He'll get a warning, that's all."

And then Mom, behind me, said, "Michael, let him *in*," and my legs came alive and I got out of the doorway, fast, and the cop came in, tipping his hat to Mom.

"Morning, ma'am." I wondered if Mom was remembering the last time the cops were at our house. I wondered if this cop was one of her connections. I wonder that about all kinds of people: my teachers and all the cops and storekeepers and Dr. Mills, even. I hate wondering it, but that's another thing I can't talk to Mom about. It would just hurt her. It would just make me like David, or like Aunt Tina, who hasn't even talked to us since Mom started working down in Carson.

The fight Aunt Tina picked with Mom was as bad as any of David's: worse, maybe, because she doesn't even live with us. She wasn't even here when Dad died. It was none of her business. "Oh, Sherry! How can you do *that*, of all things? With your boys the ages they are, after what their father did? How will they be able to hold their heads up, knowing—"

"Knowing that their mother's keeping a roof over their heads? My secretarial job doesn't pay enough, Tina, not by itself—and if you know what else I can do to earn a hundred thousand a year, go right ahead and tell me!"

It was perfectly legal, and it would let Mom earn enough money to go to nursing school at UNR and get a job none of us would have to be embarrassed about.

That's what she kept telling us. A year, she'd said, or two at the most. But it had already been two years, and she hadn't saved enough to quit yet, because the hundred thousand didn't include food or clothing or insurance, or all the tests Mom has to have to make sure she's still healthy. She has drug tests, too. She gets more tests than David does, even though she's not a criminal and never did anything wrong, and she has to pay for all of hers. And when she's in Carson, she can't go into a casino or a bar by herself, and she can't be seen in a restaurant with a man, and she has to be registered with the Lyon County Sheriff's Office — because technically, she's not in Carson at all. Her job's not legal in big towns: not in Reno, not in Vegas, not even in lousy little Carson City, the most pathetic excuse for a state capital you ever saw. Mom has to work right outside Carson, in Lyon County, which is still plenty close enough to be convenient for her connections.

It used to be that the women in Mom's job couldn't even leave the buildings where they worked without somebody going with them, but now they have transmitters, instead. And it used to be that they had to work every day for three weeks, living at the job, and then get one week off, but some of them got together and lobbied to change that, because so many of them were single mothers, and they wanted to be able to go home to their kids at night. But they still can't live in the same county where they work, which is why Mom has to commute between Reno and Carson. Highway 395's the only way to get down there, and those thirty-five miles can get really bad in the winter. That's why Mom had to buy the SUV. The SUV wasn't included in the hundred thousand, either.

Mom doesn't know that I know a lot of this. I've heard her and Letty talking about it, especially about all the tests. Letty's afraid Mom's going to get something horrible and die, but Mom keeps pooh-poohing her. "For heaven's sake, Letty; it's not like they don't have to wear condoms!"

I got out of the cop's way and tried not to think about him wearing a condom. It's hard not to get really mad at Dad whenever I think things like that. It's hard not to get even madder at David. He has it easier than Mom does, and it's not fair. She's not the criminal.

I followed the cop into the kitchen. Mom was chit-chatting about the weather and pouring him a cup of coffee; David was disappearing down the hall to the bathroom, carrying a little plastic cup. I looked at the drug kit, sitting on the table next to our half-eaten breakfasts. "Only takes two minutes," the cop told me, "and then I'll be out of here and leave you folks to your weekend. Ma'am, you mind if I take my jacket off?"

"Of course not," she said, and he did, and when I saw the gun in its holster I took a step back, even though of course the cop would be wearing a gun, all cops wear guns. Nearly everybody around here owns guns anyway, except us. And Mom bit her lip and the cop stepped back too, away from me, raising his hands. He looked sad.

"Hey, hey, son, it's all right. I'll put the jacket back on."

"You don't have to," I said, my face burning. "I'm going up to my room, anyway." I wanted to get out of there before David came back out of the bathroom with his precious bodily fluids. I didn't want to stand around and find out what the drug tests said. So I went upstairs, wondering if there was anybody in the entire fucking town who didn't know everything about anything that had ever happened to us.

I flopped down on my bed again, waiting for the jangle of bells that would mean the cop had left. It came pretty quickly, and then there was another right after it, and I didn't hear any yelling, so I figured everything was okay. The phone had rung, somewhere in there. One of David's loser friends, maybe. Maybe he'd gone out. Maybe I wouldn't have to deal with him today. I wanted to be out on the mountain, climbing up to Bobo, but I knew the SUV would get there more quickly than I could, even with the delay.

But when I went back downstairs, David was in the living room watching TV, and Mom and Letty were sitting at the kitchen table, looking worried. I looked at Mom and she said, "Relax. Your brother's clean."

"Okay," I said. She and Letty had probably been talking about me. "Are we leaving soon?"

Mom looked down at the table. "Michael, honey, I'm sorry. We can't leave right away. I'm waiting for a call from the doctor."

I squinted at her. "From the *doctor?*"

"I'm fine," Mom said. "It's nothing, really. She's looking at some test results, that's all, and I may need to take some antibiotics. But I don't want to miss the call. We'll go right after that, okay?"

"I'm going now," I said. *I thought they had to wear condoms.* "He's been up there since last night, Mom!"

Letty started to stand up. "Mike, I'll drive you—"

"You don't have to," I said. Right then, as much as I wanted to reach Bobo quickly, I wanted to be alone even more. "You can catch up with me after the doctor calls. Stay and talk to Mom." Stay and keep Mom and David out of each other's hair, I meant, and maybe Letty knew that, because she nodded and sat back down.

"Okay. We'll follow you as soon as we can. Be careful."

"Don't worry," I said. "It's not like you don't know where I'm going."

It felt good to be out, away from Mom and David, where I could finally breathe again. I cut over to the wild strip on the edge of our subdivision and started working my way up, past the new construction sites where the dumptrucks and jackhammers were roaring away, even on Saturday, up to where all the signs say Bureau of Land Management and National Forest Service. The signs don't mean much, because the Forest Service and the BLM can sell the land to developers anytime they want. Right now, though, the signs meant that I was on the edge of wildness stretching for miles, all the way to Tahoe.

When the construction noises faded, I started hearing the gunfire. Shooters come up on Peavine for target practice; you can always find rifle shells on the trails, and there are all kinds of abandoned cars and washing machines and refrigerators that people have hauled up here and shot into Swiss cheese. Sometimes the metal has so many holes you wonder how it holds its shape at all. "Redneck lace," Dad used to call it—Dad who'd grown up in a trailer, and was so proud that he'd gotten us out of one: Dad who couldn't stand being called a redneck, even though he came up on Peavine every weekend with George Schuster and Howard Flanking, so they could drink beer and shoot skeet.

After he died, I couldn't come up on the mountain for a long time. But gunfire's one of those things you can't get away from here, anymore than you can avoid new subdivisions, and Peavine's the only place I can come to be alone, really alone. I can hike up here for hours and never see anybody else. The gunfire's far away, and nearby are sagebrush and rabbits and hawks. In the summer you see lizards and snakes, and in the winter, in the snow, you see the fresh tracks of deer and antelope. I've seen prints that looked like mountain lion; I've seen prints that looked like dog, but were probably coyote.

I hiked hard, pushing myself, taking the steepest trails. It takes me three hours to get to the top of Peavine in good weather, and today I wanted the most direct route I could find. When you're slogging up a 15 percent grade in the snow, it's harder to think about how miserable your cat would be, stuck up here in weather like this, and it's harder to think about what you want to do to your brother for letting him out. It's harder to think about who you know might be wearing condoms, or how condoms can break even when they're used right. It's harder to think about how angry you are that your mother's connections don't have to be tested before she is, to make sure she doesn't catch anything.

Mom never lied to me. She wouldn't say "some antibiotics" if she really meant "years of AIDS drugs." She wouldn't say it was nothing if she was scared she might be infected with something that could kill her. I was angry anyway, because nothing was fair.

So that 15 percent grade was just what I needed. If Mom and Letty followed me, they'd be coming the easy way, up the road. They'd probably be angry if they couldn't find me, but they'd also get to the mine before I did, and they'd be able to drive Bobo back down. I hadn't been able to bring the carrying case with me, but I wouldn't be able to get it back down the mountain with Bobo in it anyway, not by myself. I hoped Mom had remembered to put the carrying case in the SUV. I hoped Bobo would still be in any kind of shape to need the carrying case at all.

I'm sorry, I told him as I climbed. *I'm sorry I didn't come after you sooner. I'm sorry I couldn't protect you from David. I'm sorry about whatever scared you. Bobo, please be alive. Please be okay.*

After a while, it started to snow. I kept going. I was wearing my warmest thermals and I was covered in Gore-Tex, and I had enough food in the pack for three days. And if Mom and Letty drove up in the snow and couldn't find me because I'd come back down, they'd really start freaking. So I headed on up, except that as soon as I could, I cut over to the road. I didn't see any fresh tire marks, which meant they were still behind me. I tromped along, checking the GPS every once in a while to make sure the signal hadn't moved, and then I heard a horn and turned around and saw headlights.

It was Dr. Mills. "Hey, Mike. I drove by your house when I got off work, and your mom said you'd headed up here." I scrambled into his truck; he had the heater blasting, and it felt good. "I hope you don't mind that your mom didn't come. My old truck can take the wear better than that fancy Suburban she has, and there's only so much room in here."

There was still plenty of room in the front seat. I glanced back at the flatbed: Dr. Mills had brought a carrying case, but of course on the way down, we'd want to be able to have Bobo in front with us, where it was warm. The part about Mom could have meant just about anything, depending on whether it was his excuse or hers. If it was hers, she could have been hoping that Dr. Mills would run a male-bonding father-figure trip on me, or she could have still been waiting for the doctor to call, or she and Letty could have been trying to force David to stay in the house somehow. Or all of the above. If it was his—I didn't want to think about what it meant for him to be saving wear on her SUV, or not wanting her in the truck at all. Dr. Mills is married. I didn't want to think about him driving down to Carson.

So I looked at the handheld again. "He's in an old mine up here," I said.

"Mmm-hmmm. That's what your mom told me. How long since he's moved?"

"Not since the satellites came back up," I said, and Dr. Mills nodded. He stayed quiet for a long time, and finally I said, "You think he's dead, don't you? That's what Mom thinks."

The snow was coming down harder now, the windshield wipers squeaking in a rhythm that kept trying to lull me to sleep. Dr. Mills could have told me he didn't want to go on; he could have turned around. He didn't do that. He knew I had to see as much as I could. "Michael," he said finally, "I've been a vet for fifteen years, and I've seen plenty of miracles. Animals are amazing. But I have to tell you, I think it would take a miracle for Bobo not to be dead."

"Okay," I said, trying to keep my voice steady.

"With coyotes," he said, "usually it's quick. They break the necks of their prey, the same as cats do with birds and mice. So unless Bobo got away for a few minutes and then got caught again, he wouldn't have suffered long."

"Okay," I said, and looked at my hands. I wondered how long it would take me to break David's neck, and how much I could make him suffer while I did it. And then I thought, there goes David again, making me want to do something stupid, something that would only mean I was hurting myself.

It took us ten more minutes to get to the mine, and by then the snow was coming down so hard that we could hardly see a foot ahead of the truck. We got out and started walking toward where the mine should have been, snow stinging our faces. It was really cold. I couldn't see anything but snow: no rocks, not even the scrubby pines that grow up here. And within about ten feet I realized that the mine entrance was completely buried, and that even if we'd been able to find it, we'd probably need to dig through five feet of snow to get to Bobo.

"Michael," Dr. Mills yelled into my ear, over the wind. "Michael, I'm sorry. We have to go back."

I tried to say, "I know," but my voice wouldn't work. I turned around and headed toward the truck, and when I was back inside it, I started shivering, even when the heat was blasting again. I sat in the front seat, with the empty space between me and Dr. Mills where Bobo should have been, and shivered and hugged myself. Finally I said, "You get warm, just before you freeze to death. If the coyotes didn't kill him—or if he went up on his own—"

"He's not in pain," Dr. Mills said. "That's a cliché, isn't it? But it's true. Michael, wherever he is now, he doesn't hurt. I can promise you that." And then he started telling me about some poem called "The Heaven of Animals," where the animals remain true to their natures. The predators still hunt and exult over their kill, and their prey rise up again every morning, perfectly renewed, joyously taking their proper part in the chase.

I guess it's a nice idea, but all I could think about was Bobo, shivering, hiding his head under my arm because he was scared.

So we drove on down the mountain, and pretty soon the snow stopped coming down so hard, and when we got back down to the developments, there was hardly any snow at all. You could still hear the construction equipment, and gunfire far off. Maybe the target shooters had moved farther down to get away from the snow. Dr. Mills hadn't said anything for a while, but when we started hearing the guns, he looked over at me.

Don't, I thought. Don't say it. Don't say anything. Just take me home, Dr. Mills, please. Don't say it.

"I never told you," he said, very quietly, "how sorry I am about what happened to your dad."

I stared straight ahead, thinking about Bobo, thinking about the hiker who'd died on Peavine. I wondered how long it would take the snow to melt.

When Bobo was a kitten, Dad used to dangle pieces of string for him. He always dangled them just high enough so Bobo couldn't get at them, and he'd laugh and laugh, watching Bobo jump. "We're going to enter this cat in the *Olympics*," he said. "Look at him! He must've made three feet that time!"

Bobo had lots of toys he could play with anytime he wanted, balls and catnip mice and crumpled-up pieces of paper I'd toss on the floor for him. But the minute Dad dangled that string, he'd stop playing with the stuff he could catch and go after the thing he couldn't have.

"Just like you," Mom always told him, watching them. "Just like you, Bill, jumping at what you'll never be able to get."

"Aw, now, Sherry! Why can't we have a Lexus? Why can't we have one of those fancy home theaters, huh?"

I thought he was kidding. Maybe Mom did, too.

When Dr. Mills dropped me off at home, David was gone, which was a good thing, because I don't know what I would have done if I'd had to look at him. Mom and Letty were still there. They tried to talk to me.

I didn't want to talk. I went straight up to my room and took off all the Gore-Tex and went to bed. I didn't want to think about what we didn't need anymore: the toys and the litter box and Bobo's food and water bowls. I knew I'd have to throw it all away. Mom had told David he had to get me another cat, but how could I get another cat? David would just let it out again. When I got into bed, I remembered that the handheld was still in my jacket pocket, and somehow that hurt more than anything else. I pulled my pillow over my head and turned my face to the wall. The pillow blocked out a lot, but I still heard the phone, and I still heard the jangling bells when Letty left, and I still heard them again when David came in. I couldn't block out the sounds of him and Mom yelling at each other, no matter how hard I tried.

I got up and tried to do homework, but that just made me think about how I was going to have to go to school on Monday morning. I tried to read, but all the words seemed flat and tasteless, like week-old bread. So finally I just sat on my bed, staring out at the casinos. They looked so small from here, little boxes you could pick up and throw like dice. And then I heard a coyote, off in the other direction.

Being good is one of the smallest boxes there is: Mom knows that, and so do I, and so did Dad. Mom was the only one who never complained about it, but what did I know? Maybe she hated it as much as I did. I didn't see how she could like it. Maybe she felt like Dad said he'd always felt, like the walls were closing in on her. "If I could just get outside," he always told me. "Working in that damn casino, no daylight anywhere, all those people watching you all the time, you just want to go outside and take a walk, Mike, you know what I mean?"

After Dr. Mills drove me up to the mine, I knew what Dad meant. I sat there with the walls closing in on me, and I couldn't breathe. I needed more room. I wanted to be outside with the coyotes, running around the outside of the boxes, invisible. Even if you try to watch a coyote to see what it's doing, even if you try to track it, it will disappear on you. It will fade into the grass, into the sagebrush, into shadows. And you'll know that wherever it is, it's laughing.

Sunday was quiet. David stayed in front of the TV, and I finally got my homework done, and Mom cleaned the house, humming to herself while she worked. She had to be on antibiotics for ten days, and she couldn't work until the infection was gone. "Ten-day vacation," she told me cheerfully, but she didn't get paid vacations anymore than she got anything else. All it meant was ten days' pay out of the nursing-school fund.

Once I asked her what would happen if the Lyon County sheriff's office saw her transmitter signal outside the building where she works. What if they tracked it and found her in a bar, or in a casino, or in a restaurant with a man? Would she go to jail?

She'd shaken her head and said very gently, "No, honey, I'd just lose my job. And I'd never do that, because it would be stupid." Because it would be like what Dad did, she meant. "Don't worry."

When I got up on Monday morning, my stomach hurt already. I hadn't been able to sleep very well, because I kept thinking about Bobo buried in the snow. I kept wondering about what I hadn't been able to see, worrying that maybe there'd been some way to save him and I hadn't figured it out.

I couldn't stand the idea of going to school. I couldn't stand facing Johnny and Leon; I couldn't stand the idea of going through all that and not being able to come home and have Bobo comfort me, curling up on my stomach the way he always did to get warm. I'd always been able to tell Bobo everything I couldn't talk about to anybody else, and now he was gone.

But I had to go to school, so I wouldn't upset Mom.

I had an algebra test first period. I knew the material; I could have done all the problems, but I couldn't make my hands move. I just sat there and stared at the paper, and when Mrs. Ogilvy called time, I handed it in blank.

She looked at it, and both her eyebrows went up. "Michael?"

"I didn't feel like it," I said.

"You didn't—Michael, are you sick? Do you want to go to the nurse?"

"No," I said, and walked away, out into the hall, to my next class, which was English. We were talking about Julius Caesar. I sat against the back wall and fell asleep, and when the bell rang I got up and went to Biology, where we were dissecting frogs. Biology was always bad, because Johnny and Leon were in there. They grabbed the lab station next to mine, and whenever they thought they could get away with it they whispered, "Hey, Mike, know what we're gonna do after school? Hey, Mike—we're gonna drive down to Carson. We're gonna drive down to Carson *and fuck your mother!*"

Donna Mauro, my lab partner, said, "They are *such* jerks."

"Yeah," I said, but I couldn't even look at Donna, because I was too ashamed. I knew that everybody in school knew what my mother did, but that didn't mean I liked it when Johnny and Leon reminded them. I wondered if one of Donna's parents worked for the BLM and had talked to Letty, but it could have been just about anybody.

I stared down at the frog. We were supposed to be looking for the heart. I pretended it was Johnny instead, and sliced off a leg. Then I pretended it was Leon, and sliced off the other leg.

Donna just watched me. "Um, Mike? What are you doing?"

"I thought I'd have frog legs for lunch," I said. My voice sounded weird to me, tinny. "Want one?"

"Um—Mike, that's cool, but we have to find the heart now."

I handed her the scalpel. "Here. You find the heart."

And then I turned and walked away.

It was really easy, actually. I just walked out of the room, like I had to go to the bathroom but had forgotten to ask permission. Behind me I could hear Mr. Favaro, our teacher, saying something, and Donna answering, but the voices didn't really reach me. I felt like I was inside a bubble: I could see outside, but everything was muffled, and no one could get inside. They'd just bounce off.

It was wonderful.

I walked along the hall, and Mr. Favaro ran up behind me, gabbling something. I had to listen really carefully to make out what he was saying. It sounded like he was on the moon. "Mike? Michael? Is there something you need to tell me?"

I considered this. "No," I said. If I'd been Leon or Johnny or one of the bad kids, Mr. Favaro probably would have yelled at me and told me to get back inside the room, *now,* but he was spooked because it was me acting this way. So he gabbled some more, and I ignored him, and finally he ran away in the other direction, toward the principal's office.

I just walked out the door. My jacket was back in my locker, but it was pretty warm out, at least in the sun, and I wasn't cold. The bubble kept me warm. I started walking down a gully that angled down past the football field. I could hear voices behind me; I didn't stop to try to figure out what they were saying. But then a van pulled up alongside the gully, and people got out, and the voices started again. "Michael. Michael Michael Michael Michael Michael."

"*What?*" I said. Ms. Dellafield was there, the principal, and Mr. Ambrose, the school nurse, and two guidance counselors whose names I could never remember. They all looked really scared. I blinked at them. "I just wanted to take a walk," I said, but they were in a semicircle around me, pushing at the edges of the bubble, herding me toward the van. "You don't have to do this," I told them. "Really. I'm fine. I was just taking a walk."

They didn't listen. They kept herding me toward the van, and then I was inside it, and the door was closing.

They drove me back to school, and then they herded me into Mr. Ambrose's office, and then Ms. Dellafield went to call Mom while Mr. Ambrose and the two guidance counselors stood there and watched me, like they were going to tackle me if I tried to move. "Why are you doing this?" I kept asking them. "I was just going for a walk." It didn't make any sense. I'd seen other kids walk out of classes: they'd never gotten this kind of attention. "I'll go back to biology, okay? I'll dissect my frog. You don't have to call my mother!"

And at the same time I thought, thank God Mom's home today. Thank God she's not down in Carson, so that Ms. Dellafield doesn't have to hear them say whatever they say when they answer the phone there, not that there's any chance that Ms. Dellafield doesn't know where Mom works, since everybody else knows it. But even all that didn't bother me as much as usual, because the bubble was still basically holding. Mr. Ambrose and the guidance counselors kept asking me how I was, and I kept telling them I was fine, thank you, and how are all of you today? And they kept looking more and more worried, as if I'd answered them in another language, one where "fine" meant "my eyeballs are about to explode." So I sat there feeling fine, if a little far away, and thinking, these people are really weird.

And finally, after about half an hour, I heard voices outside Mr. Ambrose's office, and then the door opened and Mom came in. She was leaning on David. David had his arm around her, and he was really pale. It was the same way he'd looked after he pulled me away from the rattlesnake.

I squinted at him and said, "What are *you* doing here? What happened?"

"She called me," David said. He sounded like he was choking. "At work. When they called her. So we could come over here together."

I looked at Mom. She was crying, and then I got really scared. "What's going on?" I said. "Mom, what's wrong? Are you okay? Did something happen to Letty?" Maybe Mom had called Ms. Dellafield and said something had happened and they had to find me. But that wouldn't explain the van and the guidance counselors, would it? If something had happened to Letty, wouldn't Mom have driven over here to tell me herself?

Everybody just stared at me. Mom stopped crying, and wiped her eyes, and said very quietly, "Michael, the question is, are *you* okay?"

"I'm *fine*! Why does everybody keep asking me that? I was just going for a walk! Why doesn't anybody believe me?"

And Mom started crying again and David shook his head and said, "Oh, you stupid—"

"David." Ms. Dellafield sounded very tired. "Don't."

I felt like I was going crazy. "Would somebody please tell me what's going on? I was just—"

"Michael," Mom said, "that's what your father said, too."

I blinked. The room had gotten impossibly quiet, as if nobody else was even breathing. Mom said, "He said he was just going for a walk, and then he went out into the yard. Don't you remember?"

I looked away from all of them, out the window. I didn't remember that. I didn't remember anything that had happened that day, before the shot. It didn't matter: everyone else at school knew the story, and they'd remembered it for me. "I really was just going for a walk," I said, and then, "I don't even have a gun."

Ms. Dellafield said I should take the rest of the day off, so Mom and David and I drove home together, in David's jeep. When Ms. Dellafield called Mom at home, Mom had been too upset even to drive, so she'd called David and he'd left work and picked her up and driven her to school. He drove us all home, too. He drove really carefully. Once a squirrel ran into the road and David slowed down until it got out of his way. I'd never seen him drive like that before. And when we were walking into the house, Mom tripped, and David reached out to steady her.

The last time I'd seen Mom and David leaning on each other, they'd been coming in from the yard. I remembered that part. My ears had still been ringing, but Letty wouldn't let me go, no matter how hard I fought. She'd been eating lunch with us when it happened. "Let me see," I kept telling her, trying to break free. "Let me go out there! I want to see what happened!"

But Letty wouldn't let go, because the first thing that happened after the shot was that Mom and David ran out into the yard, and David started screaming, and then Mom yelled at Letty, "Keep Michael inside! Don't let him come out here!"

And they came back inside, and Mom called the police, and I kept saying, "I want to go see," and David kept shaking his head and saying, "No you don't, Michael, you don't want to see this, you really don't," and Letty wouldn't let go of me. And the cops came and asked everybody questions, and then Letty took me to her house, and by the time I got home, Mom and David had cleaned up the backyard, picked up all the little pieces of bone and brain, so that there was nothing left to see at all.

Dad was stupid. You can't beat the house: anybody who's ever been anywhere near a casino knows that. But he and George and Howard were trying. They'd worked out a system, the newspaper said; George or Howard, never both at once, would go in and play at Dad's table, and Dad would touch a cheek or scratch an ear, always a different signal, so they'd know when to double their bets. And then when they won, they'd split the take with him. They tried to be smart. They didn't do it very often, but it was often enough for the pit bosses and the cameras to catch on. And somehow, when Dad came home that day, he knew he'd been caught. He knew the walls were closing in.

George and Howard went to jail. I guess Dad knew he'd have to go there too. I guess he thought that was just too small a box.

Nobody said anything for a long time, after we got home from school. Mom started unloading the dishwasher, moving in little jerks like somebody in an old silent movie, and David sat down at the kitchen table, and I went to the fridge and got a drink of juice. And finally David said, "Why the hell did you do that?"

He didn't sound angry, or like he was trying to piss me off. He just sounded lost. And I hadn't been trying to do anything; I'd just been going for a walk, but I'd said that at least a million times by now and it was no good. Nobody believed me, or nobody cared. So instead I said, "Why did you keep letting Bobo out?"

And Mom, with her back to us, stopped moving; she stood there, holding a plate, looking down at the open dishwasher. And David said, "I don't know."

Mom turned and looked at him, then, and I looked at Mom. David never admitted there was anything he didn't know. He stared down at the table and said, "You kept saying you wanted to go outside. You kept—you were *fighting* to go outside. The cat wanted to go out, Michael. He did." He looked up, straight at me; his chin was trembling. "You didn't even have to look at it. It wasn't fair."

His voice sounded much younger, then, and I flashed back on that day when he saved me from the rattlesnake, when we were still friends, and all of a sudden my bubble burst and I was back in the world, where it hurt to breathe, where the air against my skin felt like sandpaper. "So you wanted me to get my wish by having to look at Bobo?" I said. "Is that it? Like I wanted any of it to happen, you fuckhead? Like—"

"Shhhh," Mom said, and came over and hugged me. "Shhhh. It's all right now. It's all right. I'm sorry. I'm sorry. David—"

"Forget it," David said. "None of it matters anymore, anyway."

"Yes it does," Mom said. "David, I made you do too much. I—"

"I want to go for a walk now," I said. I was going to scream if I couldn't get outside; I was going to scream or break something. "Can we just go for a walk? All of us? You can watch me, okay? I promise not to do anything stupid. Please?"

Mom and David have gotten along a lot better since then. Letty and I talked about it, once. She said they'd probably been fighting so much because David was mad at Mom for making him help her in the yard when Dad died, and Mom felt guilty about it, and didn't even know she did, and kept lashing out at him. And none of us were talking about anything, so it festered. Letty said that what I did at school that day was exactly what I needed to do to remind Mom and David how much they could still lose, to make them stop being mad at each other. And I told her I hadn't been trying to do anything, and anyway I hadn't even remembered what Dad had said before he went out into the yard. She said it didn't matter. It was instinct, she said. She said people still have instincts, even when they live in boxes, and that we can't ever lose them completely, not if we're still alive at all. Look at Bobo, she told me. You got him from a pet store. He'd never even lived outside, but he still wanted to get out. He still knew he was supposed to be hunting mice.

In June, when the snow melted from the top of Peavine, I hiked back up to the mine. I'd been back on the mountain before that, of course, but I hadn't gone up that high: maybe because I thought I wouldn't be able to see anything yet, maybe because I was afraid I would. But that Saturday I woke up, and it was sunny and warm, and Mom and David were both at work, and I thought, okay. This is the day. I'll go up there by myself, to see. To say goodbye.

All those months, the transmitter signal hadn't moved.

So I hiked up, past the developments, through rocks and sagebrush, scattering basking lizards. I saw a few rabbits and a couple of hawks, and I heard gunfire, but I didn't see any people.

When I got to the mine, I peered inside and couldn't see anything. I'd brought a flashlight, but it's dangerous to go inside abandoned mines. Even if it's safe to breathe the air, even if you don't get trapped, you don't know what else might be in there with you. Snakes. Coyotes.

So I shone the flashlight inside and looked for anything that might have been a cat once. There were dirt and rocks, but I couldn't even see anything that looked like bones. The handheld said this was the place, though, so I scrabbled around in the dirt a little bit, and played the flashlight over every surface the beam would reach, and finally, maybe two feet inside the mine, I saw something glinting in a crevice in the rock.

It was the chip: just the chip, a tiny little piece of silver circuitry, sitting there all by itself. Maybe there'd been bones too, for a while, and something had carried them off. Or maybe something had eaten Bobo and left a pile of scat here; with the chip in it, and everything had gone back into the ground except the chip. I don't know. All I knew was that Bobo was gone, and I still missed him, and there wasn't even anything that had been him to bring back with me.

I sat there and looked at the chip for a while, and then I put the handheld next to it. And then I went and sat on a rock outside the mine, in the sun.

It was pretty. There were wildflowers all over the place, and you could see for miles. And I sat there and thought, I could just leave. I could just walk away, walk in the other direction, clear to Tahoe, walk away from all the boxes. I don't have a transmitter. Nobody would know where I was. I could walk as long as I wanted.

But there are boxes everywhere, aren't there? Even at Tahoe, maybe especially at Tahoe, where all the rich people build their fancy houses. And if I walked away, Mom and David wouldn't know where I was. They wouldn't even have a transmitter signal. And I knew what that felt like. I remembered staring at the dark screen, when the satellites were offline. I remembered staring at it, and trying not to cry, and praying. *Please, Bobo, come back home. Please come back, Bobo. I love you.*

So I sat there for a while, looking out over the city. And then I ate an energy bar and drank some water, and headed back down the mountain, back home.

crux

ALBERT E. COWDREY

New author Albert E. Cowdrey quit a government job to try his hand at writing. So far, he's appeared almost exclusively in The Magazine of Fantasy & Science Fiction, *where he's published a handful of well-received stories over the last couple of years, most of them supernatural horror. In 2000, he took a sudden unexpected turn away from horror and into science fiction, producing two of the year's best science fiction novellas, "Mosh," the sequel to "Crux," and "Crux" itself, the story you're about to read, which takes us deep into a future world as dark, complex, richly layered, and fascinating as any ever produced in the genre, for an intricate and hard-edged story of plot and counterplot, intrigue and betrayal, and the dynamics of history, all seasoned with a bit of time travel. . . .*

One suspects—in fact, one rather hopes—that a novel based on the "Crux" stories is imminent. Cowdrey lives in New Orleans, where many of his expertly crafted supernatural horror stories have been set.

Dyeva watched the earth revolve beneath her, vanish into banks of icy cirrus, then emerge as a patchwork of blue sea and immobile, shining cumuli.

Bits of continents poked through the gaps as the airpacket swung out on a hyperbolic curve. She had a glimpse of North America, with the Appalachian Islands trailing into the Atlantic and the Inland Sea glimmering under the hot March sun. Then the sixty-one passengers were shrouded in the lower cloud layer and reading lights winked briefly on before they emerged again to flit like the shadow of a storm over the broad Pacific.

A light meal was served, and during dessert the glint of Fujiyama Island on the right with its attendant green islets announced that they were nearing the World-city. They flashed into the dark red sun and the vast forest of China leaped out of the glittering wavelets of the Yellow Sea. Fifty-five hundred clicks was now too fast and one, two, three times the airpacket quivered as the retros slowed it to a sedate thousand.

They were speeding over the green savannahs of the Gobi, famous for its herds of wild animals. Of course they were too high and moving too fast to see the herds, but a mashina in the forward wall of the cabin darkened, glittered briefly with pinpoints of light, and filled with solid-seeming images of wapiti, elephants, haknim, sfosura—animals native and imported from other worlds—shambling over pool-dotted green plains where the immortal Khan once ruled.

Dyeva's pale, high-cheekboned face concentrated and her unblinking dark eyes glinted with reflected images. Nine-tenths of the Earth—humanity's first home—was now a world of beasts. The ultimate achievement of the man called Minister Destruction. Was it for this that twelve billion people had died?

In the sunset glow of Ulanor the Worldcity, Stef sprawled on his balcony wearing a spotty robe and listening to the cries of vendors and the creak of wheels in Golden Horde Street. He loved to loll here smoking kif in the last light during all seasons except the brief, nasty Siberian winter.

A commotion in the street made him swing his bony legs off the battered lounge chair. He tucked the mouthpiece of his pipe into a loop of hose from the censer and shuffled in broken-strap sandals to the railing.

Down below, vendors' carts had pulled against the walls and a long line of prisoners (blue pajamas, short hair, wrists and necks imprisoned in black plastic kangs) shuffled past like a column of ants. Guards in wide-brimmed duroplast helmets strode along the line at intervals, swinging short whips against the legs of laggards to hurry them on. The prisoners groaned and somebody started to sing a prison song in Alspeke, the only language that all humans knew: *Smerta, smerta mi kallá/Ya nur trubna haf syegdá . . .*

Death, death, call me, I have nothing but trouble always. Picking up the rhythm, even the laggards began moving so quickly that the guards no longer had an excuse to strike.

A good song, thought Stef, lying down again, because it goes in two opposite directions, endurance and despair. Those are the poles of life, right? Of his life, anyway. Except for kif, which was close to being his religion, filling him during these evening hours with a distant cool melancholy, with what the Old Believers called Holy Indifference—meaning that what happened happened and you didn't try to fuck with God. And, of course, there was Dzhun. She meant a little more than lust, a good deal less than love. He whispered her name, which meant summertime in Alspeke, with its original English intonation and meaning: June.

Then frowned. He was, as usual, out of cash. Kif cost money. Then how was he supposed to afford Dzhun? He brooded, puffing slowly, letting the aromatic smoke leak from his nose and mouth. He needed a case. He needed a job. He needed money to fall on him out of the sky.

Even blasé passengers who had seen Ulanor many times, perhaps even had grown up there, joined the newcomers in staring through the ports at the capital of the human race.

More than a million people! Dyeva thought. Who could believe a city so vast? Of course, compared to the world-cities of the twenty-first century, Ulanor was hardly a suburb. But this could at least give her a glimmering of the wonders that had been lost—a revelation of the once (and future?) world before the Time of Troubles had changed everything.

The shuttle was drifting along now, joining the traffic at the fifth level on the outermost ring, swinging around so that the city with its spoked avenues and glittering squares seemed to be turning. The copilot (a black box, of course) began speaking in a firm atonal voice, pointing out such wonders as Genghis Khan Allee, Yellow Emperor Place where the various sector controllers had their palaces, and Government of the Universe Place, where the President's Palace faced the Senate of the Worlds.

"And then the Clouds and Rain District," said a man's voice, and the native Earthlings all broke into guffaws.

The black box paused politely while the disturbance quieted, then resumed its spiel. Dyeva had turned a delicate pink. The brothel district (named for a poetic Chinese description of intercourse, the "play of clouds and rain") had been denounced in Old Believer churches ever since she could remember. And while she no longer was a believer herself, she retained a lively sense of the degradation endured by the women and men (and even children) who worked there.

She reflected that such exploitation formed the dark reverse of the civilization she loved and hoped to restore. Perhaps after all there was something to be said for the near-empty Earth of today. Then, impatiently, Dyeva shook the thought out of her head. This was no time for doubt. Not now. Not *now*.

Stef was still frowning, with the mouthpiece between his lips, when his mashina chimed inside the apartment. Irritated because somebody was calling during his relaxing hour, he padded inside, evading the shadows of junk furniture, stepping over piles of unwashed clothing. He told the mashina, "Say," and it flickered into life. Inside the box hovered the glowing head of Colonel Yamashita of the Security Forces.

"*Hai, Korul Yama.*"

"I need something private done. Come see me now, Gate 43."

No waste words there. The image expired into a glowing dot. Sighing, Stef dropped his robe among the other castoffs on the floor and plowed into a musty closet, looking for something clean.

On the roof of the old building a hovercab with the usual black box for a driver nosed up when Stef pushed a call button. He climbed in and gave orders for the Lion House; Gate 43.

"*Gratizor,*" said the black box. Thank you, sir. Why were black boxes always more polite than people?

As they zipped down Genghis Khan Allee, Stef viewed the flood-lit facades of Government of the Universe Place without much interest. He had long ago realized that they were a stage set and that all the action was behind the scenes. Bronze statues honored the Yellow Emperor, Augustus Caesar, Jesus, Buddha, Alexander the Great, and of course the ubiquitous Genghis Khan. All of them Great Unifiers of Humankind. Forerunners of the Worldcity and its denizens.

Genghis even had a pompous tomb set amid the floodlights—not that his bones were in it; nobody had ever found them. But yokels from the offworlds visited

Ulanor specifically to gaze upon the grave of this greatest (and bloodiest) Unifier of them all.

Near the tomb foreshortened vendors were selling roasted nuts, noodles wrapped in paper, tiny bundles of kif, seaweed, bowls of miso and kimshi, and babaku chicken with texasauce. The scene was orderly; people strolled and ate at all hours and never feared crime. Breaking the law led to the Palace of Justice off Government of the Universe Place and the warren of tiled cells beneath that were called collectively the White Chamber. The formidable Kathmann, head of Earth Security, ruled the White Chamber, and his reputation alone was enough to keep Ulanor law-abiding.

The cab turned off the main drag, zipped down back alleys at a level twenty meters above the street, and drew up at a deep niche in a blank white slab of a building. Stef flashed his ID at the black box and a flicker of light acknowledged payment. He stepped into the foyer and a bored guard in a kiosk looked up.

"Hai?"

"Hai. Ya Steffens Aleksandr. Korul Yamashita ha'kallá."

His voice activated a monitor. The guard stared at the resulting picture, then searched Stef's face as if another, unauthorized face might be concealed beneath it. Finally he spoke to the security system, which silently opened a bronze-plated steel door.

In the public areas of the Lion House multicolored marble and crimson carved *shishi* were everywhere, but here where the action was the hallways were blank, slapped together out of semiplast and floored with dusty gray mats. Light panels glowed in the ceiling, doors were blank, to confuse intruders. Stef, who knew the corridor well, counted nineteen doors and knocked.

He gasped as a stench that would have done honor to a real lion house hit him in the face. The door had been opened by a Darksider, and its furry mandrill face gazed at him with black cat pupils set in huge around eyes the color of ripe raspberries. The creature had two big arms and two little ones; one big arm held the door, one rested on its gunbelt, and the two little ones scratched the thick fur on its chest.

"Korul Yamashita mi zhdat," Stef managed to say without choking. Colonel Yama awaits me. The Darksider moved aside and he made his way through the dim guardroom followed by an unblinking red/ black stare. He knocked again, and at last entered Yamashita's office.

"Hai," said Stef, but Yama wasted no time.

"Stef, I got a problem," he began. Everything in the office was made of black or white duroplast, as if to withstand an earthquake or a revolution. Stef slipped into a black chair that apparently had been consciously shaped to cause discomfort.

"Why the animal outside? Can't you afford a human guard?" asked Stef, looking around for a kif pipe and seeing none.

"Everybody important has a Darksider now. More reliable, even if they do stink. Now listen. This information is absolutely a beheader, so I hope your neck tingles if you ever feel an urge to divulge it. For months I been getting vague reports from the Lion Sector about terrorists who are interested in time travel. Now something's happened here on Earth. Somebody's pirated a wormholer from the University."

"Oh, shit." Since Stef hadn't even known that a real wormholer existed, his surprise was genuine.

"The people who were responsible for the machine are now with Kathmann in the White Chamber and I assure you that if it was an inside job the Security Forces will soon know."

"I bet they will."

"I don't have to spell out for you the danger if some *glupetz* gets at the past. Ever since the technology came along, assholes have been wanting to go back and change this, change that. They don't understand the chaotic effect of such changes. They don't see how things can spin out of control."

Yamashita sat brooding, a man who had devoted his life to control.

"They think they can manage the time process. They don't see how some little thing, some insignificant thing, can send history spinning off in some direction they haven't foreseen, nobody's foreseen."

Stef nodded. He was thinking about someone monkeying with the past, suddenly causing himself, or Dzhun, or the genius who had synthesized kif to wink out of existence. It was hard to maintain Holy Indifference in the face of possibilities like that.

"What can I do?"

But Yama hadn't finished complaining.

"Why don't these *svini* do something useful?" he fretted. *Svini* meant swine. "Why don't they try to change the future instead of the past, try to make it better?"

"Possibly because you'd execute them if they did."

Suddenly Yama grinned. He and Stef went back a long way; the academy, service on Io, on Luna. They had been rivals once but no longer. Yama headed the Security Service at the Lion House, a fat job; the Lion Sector which it administered was a huge volume of space with hundreds of inhabited worlds stretching up the spiral arm toward the dense stars of the galactic center.

Meanwhile Stef was out on his ass, picking up small assignments to solve problems Yama didn't want to go public with. Like the present one: Yama had no authority on Earth, but suspected a connection between a local happening and one in Far Space. As an agent, Stef had two great advantages—he was reliable and deniable.

"It's true," Yama went on, "I like things as they are. Humanity's been through a lot of crap to get where it is. We need to conserve what we've got."

"Absolutely."

Yama looked suspiciously at Stef's bland face. He didn't like Stef to say things that might be either sincere or ironic, or might wag like a dog's tail, back and forth.

Stef grinned just a little. "Yama, I really do agree with you. Against all logic I'm happy, and happy people don't want change. Now, how can I find this wormholer thief?"

Yama was instantly all business again. "I'll tell you everything you need to know," he said.

"And not a bit more."

"Absolutely," said Yama, who really did have a sense of humor, colonel of security or not. He began by transferring one hundred khans to Stef's meager bank account, knowing that Stef would promptly spend it and need more, and his need would keep him working.

As Yama talked, across the city in his big, heavily mortgaged house Professor Yang Li-Qutsai was in his study, lecturing to his mashina under staring vaporlamps.

His famous course at the University of the Universe, *Origa Nash Mir* (Origin of Our World), drew a thousand students every time he gave it. The reason was not profound scholarship—Yang plagiarized almost everything he said—but his brilliance as a speaker. At times he seemed to be a failed actor rather than a successful academic. His image included a long gray beard, a large polished skull, a frightening array of fingernails, and a deep, sonorous voice that made everything he said seem important, whether it was or not. A memory cube recorded his lecture for resale to the off-worlds where dismal little academies under strange suns would thrill to the echoes of his wisdom.

Even as he spoke, lucidly, stabbing the air with a long thin index finger that ended in nine centimeters of nail, Yang was calculating what resale and residual rights on the lecture might bring him. Enough to purchase a villa at the fashionable south end of Lake Bai? Peace at home, among his four wives? At least an expensive whore?

On the whole, he thought, I'd better settle for the whore. Half of his two-track mind dreamed of girls even while the other half was retelling the most calamitous event in the brief, horrid history of civilized man. The first lecture of his course was always on the Time of Troubles.

"Considering that the Troubles created our world," he declared, "it is shocking—yes, shocking—that we know so little about how the disaster began. In two brief years (2091–2093) twelve billion people died, with all their memories. Seven hundred vast cities were obliterated, with all their records; three hundred-odd governments vanished, with all their archives of hardcopy, records, discs, tapes and the first crude memory cubes. No wonder we know so little!

"Where and why did the fighting start? The Nine Plagues—when did they break out? Blue Nile hemorrhagic fever and multiple-drug-resistant blackpox were raging in Africa as early as the 2070s. Annual worldwide outbreaks of lethal influenza had become the rule by 2080. It seems that the Time of Troubles was well under way even before the outbreak of war."

Introductions were always troublesome: students, realizing they were in for a long hour, began to sink into a trancelike state accompanied by fluttering eyelids and restless movements of the pelvis. A warning light on the box glowed green and Yang headed at once into the horror stories that gave the course much of its appeal.

"But the war of 2091 produced the most spectacular effects: the destruction of the cities, the Two Year Winter, and the Great Famine. Let us take as an example the great city of Moscow, where robot excavators have recently given us an in-depth picture—if I may be pardoned a little joke—of the horrors that attended its destruction. A city of thirty million in 2090 . . ."

Detail after horrendous detail followed: the skeleton-choked subway with its still beautiful mosaics recording the reign of Tsar Stalin the Good; the dry trench of the Moskva River whose waters had been vaporized in one glowing instant and blocked by rubble so that the present river flowed fifteen clicks away; the great Kremlin Shield of fused silicon stretching over the onetime city center, with its radioactive core that would glow faintly for at least 50,000 years.

Observing with satisfaction that his indicator light was turning from unlucky green to lucky red, Professor Yang moved onto the horrors of London, Paris, Tokyo, Beijing, and New York. Then he spoke briefly about the closed zones that still surrounded the lost cities, of irradiated wildlife undergoing rapid evolutionary change in bizarre and clamorous Edens where the capitals of great empires had stood, only three hundred years ago . . .

The interest indicator glowed like a Darksider's eye. Professor Yang strode up and down, his voice deepening, his gray beard swishing in the wind, his long fingers clawing at the air.

"Precisely how did it happen—this great calamity?" he demanded. "How much we know, and how little! Will it remain for the scholars of your generation to solve these riddles finally? I confess that mine has shed only a little light around the edges of the forbidding darkness that we call—the Time of Troubles!"

As usual, his lecture lasted exactly the time allotted, a one-hundred-minute hour. As usual, it ended with a key phrase, reminding the drowsy student of what he had been hearing at the rim of his clouded consciousness.

The power light in the mashina winked off, and Professor Yang shouted: "Tea!"

A door flew open and a scurrying domestic wheeled in the tea caddy, the cup, the *molko*, the tins of oolong and Earl Grey.

"Sometimes," muttered Yang, "I think I'll die of boredom if I ever have to talk about the Troubles again."

"One lump or two?" asked the domestic, and Yang, who drank tea after the ancient English fashion, turned anxious attention to the small, ridiculously expensive lumps of natural brown sugar.

"Two, I think," he said.

If residuals from the lecture didn't buy him a girl, at least they would, he hoped, keep him supplied with sugar for some time to come.

The clocks of the Worldcity were nearing 21 when Yamashita, dining comfortably at home with his wife Hariko, heard his security-coded mashina chime and hastened into his den to receive a secret report from Earth Security. Somebody had cracked under interrogation. Yama listened to the report with growing dismay.

"Shit, piss, and corruption," he growled. "Secretary!"

"Sir?" murmured the box in a soft atonal voice.

"Contact Steffens Aleksandr. If he's not at home—and of course he won't be—start calling the houses in the Clouds and Rain District. Make it absolutely clear that this is a security matter and that we expect cooperation in finding him."

"Yes, sir. His home is not answering."

"Try Brother and Sister House. Try Delights of Spring House. Try Radiant Love House. Then try all the others."

"And when I find Steffens Aleksandr?"

"Tell him to wipe his cock and get to my office soonest."

"Is that message to be conveyed literally?"

"Yes!"

Back at the table, he had barely had time to fold his legs under him when Hariko told him to stop using bad language in the house where the children might hear him.

"Yes, little wife," said the man of power meekly.

"I suppose you have to go to the office again."

"Yes, little wife. An emergency—"

"Always your emergencies," said Hariko. "Why do I waste hours making you good food to eat if you're never here to eat it? And why do you employ that awful Steffens person? He's a disgrace, a man his age who lives like a tomcat. Not everyone can be as happy as we are, but everybody can have a decent, conventional life."

Yama ate quietly, occasionally agreeing with her until she ran out of words. Then he went upstairs, removed his comfortable kimono, and put on again the sour uniform he'd worn all day.

On the way down, pinching his thick neck as he tried to close the collar, he stopped in the children's bedrooms to make sure they were all asleep. The boys in their bunk beds slept the extravagant sleep of childhood. Looking at them, gently patting their cheeks, Yama reflected that adults and animals always slept as if they half expected to be awakened—children never.

Then to the girls' room, where his daughter Kazi slumbered in the embrace of a stuffed haknim. Yama smiled at her but lingered longest at the bedside of his smallest daughter. Rika was like a doll dreaming, with a tiny bubble forming on her half-parted pink lips. He was thinking: if someone changes the past, she may vanish, never have a chance to live at all. To prevent that, he resolved to destroy without mercy every member of the time-travel conspiracy.

At the front door Hariko tied a scarf around his neck and gave him a hug; she was too modest to kiss her husband in the open doorway, even though they were twenty meters above the street. He patted her and stepped into the official hovercar that had nosed up to his porch.

"Lion House, Gate 43," he told the black box, and sank back against the cushions.

At Radiant Love House, Professor Yang relaxed from his scholarly labors on one side of a double divan in the midprice parlor and viewed 3-D images of young women to the ancient strains of Tchaikovsky's *Nutcracker*.

"Do you see anything that pleases you?" asked the box that was projecting the images.

"Truly, it is a Waltz of the Flowers," replied Yang sentimentally. The smell of kif wafted through the room, presumably from a hidden censer.

"The dark beauty of Miss Luvblum contrasts so markedly with the rare—indeed, unique—blondness of Miss Sekzkitti," murmured the box, going through its recorded spiel. "The almond eyes of Miss Ming remind us of the splendor of the dynasty from which she takes her *nom d'amour*. Every young lady is mediscanned on a daily basis to insure her absolute purity and freedom from disease. Miss Gandhi is skilled in all the acts of the famous *Kama Sutra*. For a small additional fee, an electronic room may be rented in which the most modern appliances are available to heighten the timeless joys of love."

Professor Yang had already halfway made his selection—the most expensive of the "stable." Miss Selassie was a tall, slender woman of Ethiopian descent who had been genetically altered into an albino. The box referred to her as "the White Tiger of the Nile," and bald, bearded, long-nailed Yang, at ninety-nine reaching the extreme limits of middle age, found his thoughts turning more and more to her astounding beauty. *Her body is like a living Aphrodite of ancient Greece*, he thought, *while her face is like a living spirit mask of ancient Africa.*

"Miss Selassie, how much is she?"

"One hundred khans an hour."

"Oh, dear. And how much for an electronic room?"

Professor Yang rightly believed that all the appliances known to modern science would be needed if he was to spend his expensive hour doing anything more than enjoying Miss Selassie's company.

"Fifty khans an hour. However," said the box seductively, "for such a man as yourself, Honored Professor, the house gladly makes a special price: Miss Selassie *and* an electronic room for an hour for the sum total of—"

A brief pause, during which Yang felt himself growing anxious.

"One hundred and thirty-five khans, a ten-percent reduction."

"Agreed," breathed Yang, giving himself no time to think. There was a brief flutter in the box as his bank checked his voice-print and transferred another K135 from his already deflated account to one of the bulging accounts of Radiant Love House.

"You should've asked for twenty percent off," said a voice, making Yang jump.

A long, stringy, bony man holding a kif pipe rose from the other side of the double divan and stretched and yawned.

"I hope you haven't been eavesdropping," snapped Yang.

"No more than I had to," said Stef in a bored voice. "I've made my selection, but the selectee is popular and she's busy. I'm just telling you, if you've got the balls to bargain you can get them down twenty percent, sometimes more if it's a slow night. The ten percent reduction they offer you is just merchandizing."

Resentment at the stranger's intrusion struggled with economic interest in Professor Yang's breast. The latter won.

"Really?" he said.

"Sure. I do it all the time. You could've gotten the whole works for one-twenty."

"Indeed. And the electronic room—is it really worth it?"

"It is if you have to have it."

Yang was just beginning to get angry when the door opened and a very tall naked woman entered. Her hair was in a thousand white braids and her eyes were oval rubies. The aureoles of her taut, almost conical breasts were much the same color as her eyes. A faint scent of faux ambergris wafted into the waiting room and mingled with the fumes of kif. Yang sat hypnotized.

"You the customer?" she asked Stef with some interest.

"No, I'm waiting for Dzhun. This guy's your customer."

"Figures," she sighed, and taking Professor Yang's thin and trembling hand in her own, the White Tiger led him away.

A few minutes later the box made two announcements: Dzhun was ready, and Stef was to wipe his cock and get to Yama's office soonest. Stef promptly did what he almost never did—lost it completely.

"FUCK THE FUCKING UNIVERSE!" he roared in English. The divan weighed a hundred kilos but he tossed it end over end. At the crash the door flew open and a guard entered, pulling an impact pistol half as long as her arm. Stef calmed down instantly.

"*Ya bi sori*. My deepest and humblest apologies," he said, clapping his hands together and bowing. "I don't know what came over me."

Stef had seen a number of bodies killed by impact weapons. A body shot usually left very little except the head, arms and legs, plus assorted fragments.

"Straighten out the goddamn sofa," said the guard, watching him narrowly. She was Mongol and looked tough. Stef did as he was told.

"Incidentally," he said as he was leaving, "I'll need a raincheck on Dzhun. I already paid my khans."

"Talk to the front desk," growled the guard.

Outside, Stef took a deep breath and ordered a hovercab. He felt that he now had a personal score to settle with the *svini* who had not only stolen a wormholer but forestalled his session with Dzhun. Since the *svini* were the only reason he currently had money enough to buy her time, that was unreasonable. But Stef wanted to be unreasonable. That was how he felt.

"So the theft was an inside job," he muttered, trying without success to get comfortable in one of Yama's black chairs.

"Yes. A trusted scientist turns out to belong to a terrorist group that calls itself Crux. He's been checked a hundred times. Living quietly, no extra money, no nothing. During lie-detection tests, brain chemicals always indicated he was telling the truth. Trouble was, the wrong questions got asked. Are you loyal? To what? He answers yes, meaning loyal to humanity as he understands it. Are you a member of any subversive group? Subversive in what sense? To the existing order, or to humanity? He gets by with a false answer again."

"What exactly do these Crux fuckers believe in?"

"Life. The absolute value of human life. The wormholer opens the way to reverse the worst calamity in human history, the Time of Troubles. Trillions of lives are hanging on the issue—not only the lives that were lost in the famines and plagues and wars but all their descendants to the tenth generation."

Stef growled, scratched himself, longing for kif, for Dzhun. "Bunch of fucking idealists."

"Exactly. People with a vision, willing to destroy the real world for the sake of an idea. We've gotta kill them all."

Yama jumped up—a springy man, muscular, bandy-legged. He was fifty and nearing middle age, but a lifetime of the martial arts enabled him to bounce around like a ball of elastoplast.

"Kill them!" he roared, chopping at the air.

Watching him tired Stef.

"And this was what you called me back for?"

"No. Or not only." Yama fell back into the desk chair. "The group that has this grand vision is, of course, organized in cells that have to be cracked one by one. But the guy who talked in the White Chamber knew one name outside his cell, the name of a woman, an offworlder. She's called Dyeva. She's one of the founders of the movement, and she was supposed to contact him."

Stef sighed. "Anything from IC on her?"

"No," admitted Yama. "No report yet from Infocenter."

"Call me when one comes in," said Stef, rising. "I'm extremely grateful for the way you took me away from my pleasures to give me information that, as yet, has no practical significance. Please don't do it again."

Yama saw him to the door, nodding to the Darksider who approached smelling like the shit of lions, owls and cormorants mixed together. Stef pinched his nostrils and spoke like a duck.

"I love coming to your office, Yama. The place has a certain air about it."

Half an hour later, Stef was again sprawled in the middling expensive parlor at Radiant Love House, waiting. Another customer had taken Dzhun while he was away. Stef spent the time smoking kif and thinking about shooting Dyeva, whoever she was, with an impact pistol.

"*Phut*," he said, imitating the uninspiring sound of the weapon. He made his long hands into a ball and drew them rapidly apart, imitating the explosion inside the target. Stef had studied wound ballistics and he knew that impact ammo vaporized in the body and formed a rapidly expanding sphere of superheated gas and destructive particles. *Dyeva v'átomi sa dizolva*, he thought. The *svin* flies apart, turns to molecules, atoms, protons and quarks.

"How happy I am," murmured the box, "to inform you, Sir, that the person of your choice is ready to receive you."

Instantly Stef was up and moving, his bloody thoughts forgotten. At heart he was a lover, not a killer.

In the blue peace of the electronic room, Professor Yang lay huddled under a sheet of faux silk.

Beside him, her hand still languidly resting on a gadget called an erector-injector, lay a statue of living ivory. At least he now knew the White Tiger's given name. Even if it was only a prost's working name, a *nom d'amour*, for Yang it was what the old French phrase meant—a name of love.

"Selina," he murmured, and she turned her head and smiled at him.

"I'm afraid your time is up," she whispered. "But perhaps you'll come again, my dear. You were special."

"Selina," he said again. Around him monitors winked and a low electromagnetic hum soothed with a white sound. Yang was all too conscious of the birth of a new obsession, one even less affordable than four wives and natural sugar.

"I *must* see you again," he said.

Detecting the urgent note in his voice, Selina smiled. Ah, that enigmatic whore's smile! thought Yang with pain in his heart. What did it mean? Pleasure in you, pleasure in your money, no pleasure at all but mere professionalism? Who could tell?

Wasn't this how he had happened to marry the most obnoxious of his four wives?

Dyeva sat quietly in the front room of a small but elegant suburban villa.

The windows were open and the morning sun entered through a gentle screen of glossy leaves thrown out by a lemon tree. The room held all the necessities of rustic living, bare beams across the ceiling, lounges covered with faux linen, a glass table bearing apples and oranges and kuvisu fruit, and a mashina half the length of the wall to entertain the owner, a Professor of Rhetoric whose hobby was playing at revolution.

Relaxing on the lounges were the other members of the cell: two students and a dark and tensely attractive woman of middle age who bore a painted mark on her forehead. The students were still talking about Professor Yang's lecture of last evening, tailor-made as it seemed for the members of Crux.

"Lord Buddha, but he makes you see it," said the boy, fingering a string of beads restlessly. He was an Old Believer. Dyeva had noticed years ago that such people were represented in Crux far beyond their numbers in the general population.

The girl was lovely: bronzed, yellow-haired, sloe-eyed, the perfect Eurasian. She called herself Dián and spoke in a throaty whisper that someone had told her was mysterious.

"Actually, he's a horrible old man. But it's as Kuli says, he has the gift of making the past live."

"We expect to do more along that line," said the owner of the villa in a deep, resonant voice, and the two young people laughed happily. All three of them loved the taste of conspiracy; the older man, whose codename was Zet, earnestly hoped to seduce Dián. Supposedly nobody in the group knew anybody else's real name. They had a vast and fundamentally childish panoply of measures to preserve secrecy—passwords, hand signals, ways of passing information in complicated and difficult ways. Because cyberspace was a favorite hunting ground for the supermashini of the Security Forces, they avoided electronic contact whenever possible. Instead, they had oaths, secret meetings, symbols. Their key symbol was the looped cross of ancient Egypt, the *crux ansata*—the sign of life.

Kuli wore a crux on a cord around his neck; at meetings he took it out for all to see. The girl, Dyeva noted with amazement, had the symbol tattooed on the palm of one slender hand. Why didn't the senior members of the cell force her to have it removed?

People had often told Dyeva that she had icewater in her veins. That wasn't true: her emotions were intense, only deeply buried. Right now anger and alarm were stirring deep beneath her masklike face. Did her life, to say nothing of the lives of trillions of human beings, depend on these amateurs, children?

The dark woman, who called herself Lata, brushed a hand across her brow and said, "The essential thing is to speed our visitor safely on her way. And I must tell all of you something I learned last night. The theft of the wormholer has been discovered and there have been arrests."

"*Arrests?*" demanded Dián, in a scandalized tone. "Of someone I *know?*"

She seemed to think that the polizi had no right to arrest members of a secret organization merely because it was bent on annihilating the existing world.

"No," sighed Lata. "Fortunately for you. That beast Kathmann and the polizi drugged and tortured both the guards and the people who were responsible for technical maintenance of the wormholer. Thus they learned that one of the scientists had been involved in the theft. Thank God, the device had already been turned over to another cell, and the poor man who talked didn't know their names or where it is at present."

The two young people seemed paralyzed. Zet was turning his head from side to side, looking at the furniture, the fresh fruit. Dyeva had no trouble reading his mind: the *glupetz* had suddenly realized that he could lose all this by playing at conspiracy. Some day, she thought, if he thinks about it long enough, he will realize that he may lose much more.

"I will go with you," said Dyeva, rising and pointing at Lata, apparently the only one of the gathering with any sense. "You will conduct me. I must not stay here longer and endanger these heroes of humanity."

Zet looked relieved at the news she'd soon be gone; Kuli and Dián were still absorbing the news of the arrests. He was stunned, she indignant.

"Oh, but the people who were tortured—they're martyrs!" she exclaimed suddenly and burst into tears.

"Yes," said Dyeva, "and by this time they are also corpses. Death is the reward the technicians of the Chamber hold out to their victims. I will be packed and gone in five minutes if you will lead me," she said to Lata.

"Of course," said the dark woman, and Dyeva hastened to the room where she had slept to gather her kit.

Later, in Lata's hovercar, Dyeva asked her how she had come to join the movement.

"I despise this world," Lata said quietly. "It's a gutter of injustice and pain. Nothing will be lost if this world suddenly vanishes at the word of Lord Krishna. Of course, if we manage to undo the Troubles, success will cost us our own lives. That is the splendor of Crux. If our movement did not demand the ultimate sacrifice I would not have joined it."

Another Old Believer, though Dyeva, only this time of the Hindu type. And I was brought up a Christ-worshipper, and the boy Kuli is a Buddhist. Are we all remnants and leftovers of a dead world? Is that why we wish to restore it?

"What are you thinking?" asked Lata.

"Wondering why the movement contains so many Old Believers."

"Oh, I think I know. It's because we want to undo the death of our faiths. So many people simply stopped believing after the Troubles. They said to themselves, There is no God. Or, if there is and he allows this to happen, I do not care about him."

Dyeva glanced at her curiously. They were entering the air-space above Ulanor and Lata paid frowning attention to the traffic until a beam picked up her car's black box. For an instant Dyeva had a powerful urge to continue this conversation, to talk about things that had real meaning. Then she remembered that the less Lata knew about her, and she about Lata, the better for both of them.

"We all come to it for different reasons," she said guardedly, and silence followed. The little car revolved above the Worldcity, bearing two women who hoped to change it into a phantasm that never had existed at all.

Stef and Dzhun were having breakfast in a teashop deep in the Clouds and Rain District. Half the customers seemed to recognize Dzhun, and she waved and blew kisses to them. She had scrubbed off her white working makeup and with it had gone her nighttime pretense of lotus delicacy and passivity. She looked and was a tough young woman to whom life had not been kind.

"Wild turnover last night," she said to a red-haired eunuch who had stopped by the table to shriek and fondle her. "I did ten guys."

"Oh my dear," said the *sisi*, "I do ten on my way to work."

"Seems you've got some catching up to do," Stef told Dzhun when the *sisi* had moved on.

"Oh, he's such a bragger. And old, too. When I'm his age I'll have my own house and instead of bragging about doing ten guys I'll be doing one—the one I choose."

"And that one will be me."

"Only if you get rich," said Dzhun candidly, buttering a bun. "I'm tired of being a *robotchi*, a working stiff. I've got a senator on the string now, Stef, did I tell you? Soon you won't be able to afford me at all."

She dimpled as she always did when saying unpalatable things.

"Is that why I'm buying you breakfast?"

"Oh Stef, I'm just needling you. I love my poor friends, too. Look, why don't you take me to Lake Bai for a week or two? Get a cabin. I won't demand a villa. Not yet."

"Unfortunately, I'm on a big case right now. One that might even save your life."

Dzhun stopped eating and stared at him. "You're telling the truth?"

"Believe it. When the payoff comes, it'll be as big as the case. Then we'll go to Bai. Get a villa, not a cabin."

Stef spoke with the calm assurance he employed when he was in a state of total uncertainty. The investigation was dead in the water. The arrests had not led to the wormholer. IC still hadn't come up with a make on Dyeva. Mashini were combing passenger lists of recent arrivals from the offworlds—voiceprints, retinographs, DNA samples—turning up nobody with a record, nobody who fit the profiles. Stef's local contacts had nothing to offer.

"What's it all about, Stef?" asked Dzhun.

"Never mind. The case is a beheader. It's nothing you want to know about, so don't ask. It's a security matter and it'd be a hell of a shame if the Darksiders came and carted off a butt like yours to the White Chamber."

Their voices had fallen to whispers. Dzhun's face was so close that Stef's breath moved her long eyelashes. A delicate scent clung to her kimono, some nameless offworld flower, and the drooping faux silk disclosed the roundness of her little breasts like pomegranates. Stef could have eaten her with a spoon.

"I won't say anything," she promised. "If anybody asks what you're doing, I'll say that you never tell me anything."

Stef leaned back and sipped the bitter green tea he used to clear his head in the morning. Effortlessly, Dzhun put her whore's persona on again, screaming and waving at a friend who had just entered the teashop. Towering over the crowd, the White Tiger of the Nile headed for their table.

She and Dzhun kissed and Selina sat down, nodding at Stef.

"Hell of a night," she said to them and the world in general. "I did a dozen guys."

"Oh, Selina," said Dzhun. "Honey, I do a dozen on my way to work."

Yamashita clapped his hands and bowed to announce himself to the *fromazhi* — the big cheeses. It was the morning meeting of the Secret Emergency Committee that had been formed to deal with the wormholer theft.

Yama's boss, Oleary, Deputy Controller of the Lion Sector, grunted a welcome, adding, "You know these people, I'm sure."

Considering that he was talking about the Solar System Controller, her deputy the Earth Controller, her Chief of Security, and Admiral Hrka of the Far Space Service, that was inadequate to say the least.

The SSC was Xian Xi-Qing, a small woman with a parchment face, tiny hands and dull gold and jade rings stacked two and three to a finger. She was famous for many things, her three husbands, her stable of male concubines, the ruthlessness and cleverness that had kept her alive and in power for decades.

She glared at Yama and demanded abruptly, "We've heard from Kathmann. At least he's caught somebody. What are *you* doing about this wormholer business? I've heard rumors the conspiracy originated in your sector."

Yama took his time seating himself on a backless chair known as the *shozit*, or hot seat. The grandees faced him behind a Martian gilt table surrounded by an invisible atmosphere of power. Admiral Hrka, Yama noted, wasn't even wearing his nine stars. That was the ultimate sign of status. Nobody needed to see *his* rating.

Among the bureaucrats, the admiral looked and probably felt out of place. Hrka usually dealt with the arcane business of moving in Far Space — using inertial compensators and particle beam trans-lightspeed accelerators, navigating by mag space forcelines and staging chronometric reentries where an error of a microsecond could put him deep inside the glowing core of a planet. He was accustomed to using atomlasers that could melt steel at half a million clicks, launching supertorps at near-light velocities and converting the enemies of his species into plasma thinner than the solar wind.

Now he found himself face to face with a threat that might enable one fragile human to undo his world and render all his knowledge and bravery pointless. He looked as if he longed to be in Far Space now, where even if he was a thousand light years from anyplace he knew where he was.

Seated to one side was Kathmann, Yama's opposite number in Earth Security.

He resembled a files technician, with his pointed head and fat neck. He wore replacement eyes and the plastic corneas glittered blankly.

Quietly Yama laid out the steps taken so far to locate members of Crux. The notion that the conspiracy had grown up in the Lion Sector remained unproven, yet diligent inquiries were underway on all the Sector's two hundred and thirty-six inhabited worlds. All available mag space transponder circuits had been cleared for this one task. Enough energy to light Ulanor for six weeks had already been poured into the message traffic. The whole business was necessarily slow; even at maximum power, a message routed through mag space from the farthest planets of the Sector took more than seventy standard hours to reach Earth.

And so on. Actually he had nothing to report and his aim was to make nothing sound like something. When he was done the *fromazhi*, who knew bureaucratic boilerplate when they heard it, just sat there looking bored. Only Kathmann spoke up.

"All your inquiries are on offworlds?"

"Certainly. That's where our authority begins and ends."

"You're not invading my territory, using unofficial agents here on Earth?"

Yama was shocked.

"*Onor kolleg, eto ne'legalni!*" he exclaimed. "Honored colleague, that's illegal!"

Kathmann raised one fat fist and stared at Yama with eyes like worn silver half-khan pieces.

"Remember, Colonel, this hand holds the keys to the White Chamber!"

Yama raised his own much solider fist.

"And this one, Colonel Kathmann, has killed a thousand enemies of the State!"

The spat had Admiral Hrka grinning.

"Simmer down, boys," he said, while the Earth Controller, a man named Ugaitish, muttered into his beard, "*Spokai, spokai.* Take it easy."

"What I want to know," said Oleary in a fretful tone, "is why anybody built this goddamn gadget in the first place. If it didn't exist it couldn't be stolen."

"It was some idiots at the University," said Ugaitish. "They just had to see if the theory worked. They applied for a permit, all very legal, and some minor official gave them an *oké* for the materials, which are pretty exotic. There's no use putting them in the White Chamber," he added, waving a hand to shut Kathmann up.

Xian agreed. "Typical academics. All they know is what they know. Not an atom of common sense."

"Besides," Ugaitish added, "the academics were the ones who reported the theft. Except for that, nobody would know anything about it."

"They should be beheaded anyway," Kathmann growled, "to get rid of the dangerous knowledge in their brains. A laser can do it in five seconds, and there you are."

Yama's sharp eyes intercepted the glance that passed among the *fromazhi*. Kathmann made them uneasy—a man who knew too much and executed too readily. Yama filed away this insight for future reference.

"At this point, beheading is not the issue," declared Hrka. "Let me sum up. A woman, name unknown, took a commercial ship, probably somewhere in the Lion Sector—now there's a big volume of space to cover—and traveled to Earth, where she has, perhaps, contacted a group of terrorists who intend to obliterate our world by changing the past. The group has a functional wormholer, calls itself Crux, and in the most overpoliced human society since the fall of the Imperial Chinese People's Republic nobody knows who they are or where they are. Have I stated the situation clearly?"

Xian glared first at him, then at the two cops in turn.

"You better find them," she said, "or I'll put you *both* in the White Chamber."

She let that sink in, then said more formally: "Honored security chiefs, we permit you to go."

When they were gone, Xian told the others, "We need information now. Ugaitish is putting out a public call for help. We don't have to tell everything, just that a gang of terrorists called Crux is on the loose, planning to kill many innocent people."

"Is that wise?" worried Oleary. "Informing the masses seems like an extreme step to me."

"If we don't, the politicians will. I have to brief the President and the Senate today, and what do you think will happen then?"

"Much smoke, much heat, no light," said Hrka fatalistically. "Well, we'd better catch these bastards. The whole world order as we know it exists only because of the Time of Troubles. Without that, everything would be different."

The *fromazhi* stared at each other. "Great Tao," said Ugaitish, "if these scoundrels succeed — even if we continue to exist at all, we might be anything. Coolies, prisoners, offworld scum!"

"Ask for help," Oleary told Xian. "If necessary, beg."

After his night in the District, Stef needed sleep. Yet he spent a couple of hours at his mashina, checking his regular contacts for hints of terrorist groups. He heard gossip about lunatics who wanted to blow up Genghis' tomb, but nothing of interest to him. So he went to bed.

The daytime noises rising from Golden Horde Street had no power to keep him awake. He had slept away too many days, sunk in the half light admitted from the roofed balcony, embracing rumpled bedcovers in the brown shadows of afternoon. In a few minutes he drifted off, but not for long.

He woke suddenly thinking he must have shit on himself. He reached for his pistol just as a crushing furry weight fell on him.

The ceiling light went on and the Darksider rolled Stef over and sat on his back. For an agonized few moments he couldn't breathe at all, while the creature, aided by a human Stef never saw clearly, thrust his hands into a kang and locked the wrists. Then the Darksider rose, bent down over its gasping victim and lifted him so that the kang could be clamped on his neck as well. A four-fingered, two-thumbed hand gripped his hair and pulled him to a sitting position.

Spots drifted before his eyes in a red torrent that slowly cleared. Stef was sitting naked on the bed with a black plastic kang clamped on his wrists and neck. His faint hope that this might be a nightmare died. The Darksider was standing bowlegged by the bed and scratching its chest. The human seemed to be wearing a polizi uniform; he kept to the shadows just beyond the limits of Stef's vision. Head immobilized, Stef tried to twist his body to get a view of his captor, but without success.

"Who the fuck are you?"

"Your guide, Mr. Steffens. I'm here to show you something you never saw before."

"What?"

"The inside of the White Chamber."

At a gesture, the Darksider tossed a sack over Stef's head and pulled a cord tight around his neck. A hypodermic gun spat at his shoulder and he had a horrifying sense that his whole body was melting into a cold and lifeless fluid before darkness descended.

He would have preferred not to wake up, but wake he did. Still in the kang, still with the sack over his head. Of course you're not comfortable, he told himself. You're not supposed to be comfortable. He had no idea how long he'd been here, except that he was thirsty and hungry. No idea where "here" was, except somewhere in the warrens of the White Chamber.

He had urinated at some point and was sitting in the wet. The cell was so small that his knees were folded up against his chest. His icy toes pressed against metal that was probably the door. The cell was narrower than the kang, and Stef had to sit with his body twisted. There was no way to move, no way to rest. As the hours passed, agonizing pains began to shoot through his back and side. Breathing became difficult. He began suffering waves of panic at the thought that the polizi would leave him here until he slowly suffocated. The panic made things worse; he started to hyperventilate, and every breath stabbed him like a knife. He tried to calm himself, counting slow shallow breaths that didn't hurt so much.

Then voices approached along a corridor outside the cell. Faint hope was followed by stomach-knotting fear. They might let me go; it was all a mistake; Yama will get me out. No, Yama doesn't know anything and anyway he doesn't control the polizi. They're coming to torture me.

The voices came close. Two techs were discussing a "client," as they called their victims. Voices neutral, atonal like the voices of two black boxes.

"Maybe twenty cc of gnosine would do it."

"I dunno. This client is a tough case."

"Maybe needles in the spinal marrow . . ."

They were gone. A faint noise in the distance remained unidentifiable until a door in the corridor slid open. Then Stef heard a whimpering, sobbing sound that made all the hairs rise on the back of his neck. Extreme agony, he thought—beyond screaming.

The door slid shut again and the sound became a low meaningless murmur. Human footsteps approached again. Two voices.

"Just wonderful, Doctor. I never thought she'd break."

"Sometimes a combination of therapies is essential."

They too were gone. Doctors. Technicians. Therapies. Clients. The language of the Chamber. We are not sadists, we are scientists performing a distasteful but necessary function in the cause of justice. Try the gnosine, try the needles, try everything in combination. Promise the clients life; after you've worked on them for a while, promise them death.

When the polizi came at last, they came in silence. Without the slightest warning the door clanged open. Somebody yelled, "Get the scum! Get the piece of shit!"

A Darksider grabbed Stef's legs and dragged him into the hall and the wrench on his cramped limbs made him scream. Then the animal was dragging him down the hall by the heels while boots kicked at Stef's ribs and head.

The kang knocked against the walls and floor. A human hand grabbed his testicles and twisted and he screamed again, louder than before. Then somebody, a crowd of them, human and inhuman, seized the ends of the kang and dragged him to his feet.

"Walk! Walk, you piece of shit! Walk!"

He couldn't and fell and somebody kicked him hard in the groin and this time he did no screaming. He was unconscious.

He woke with intense light in his eyes. He was sitting in a hard duroplast chair and the sack was off his head. His eyes burned; agony rose in waves from his groin. Somebody in hard boots stamped on the bare toes of his left foot.

Stef wasn't thinking any longer, he was living in nothing but the conviction that every second some new pain would strike. What next, what next? Hands seized the kang and pulled it back. Other hands, some human, some inhuman, grabbed his ankles and stretched out his legs. In the blazing light he was halfblind, absolutely helpless. Somebody touched his breastbone and he moaned and his stomach knotted, expecting the blow.

Nothing happened. The light dimmed. Gradually his eyes cleared. A man with a pointed head was standing before him. The man had plastic eyes that went blank when he moved his head. There was no crowd of tormentors, only two thuggi from Earth Central and one Darksider. One of the thuggi gave the other a piece of candy and they stood there, chewing. The Darksider scratched its furry backside against a wall.

"Mr. Steffens."

"Yes," whispered Stef.

"I'm sending you home now. For the future, will you remember one thing?"

"Yes."

"From now on, Yamashita will continue to pay you, but in spite of that you'll be working for me as well as for him, and I'll expect to know everything you do and everything you discover about Crux."

Kathmann leaned forward and once again tapped Stef's breastbone.

"If you hide anything from me, I'll know it, and I'll bring you back here. Do you understand?"

"Yes."

"Next time you'll get standard treatment," added Kathmann, straightening up. "Not the grandmotherly kindness you received this time."

To the thuggi he said, "Give him one more."

He left the room and a door closed. Behind the light the room flickered and a second Darksider Stef hadn't seen before approached him, holding a spiked club in its paws. But that'll kill me, he thought, and his eyes clamped shut on a final vision of the new Darksider raising the club for a smashing blow to his gut.

He sat there blind, waiting. Then he heard them laughing at him. He opened his eyes as one of the thuggi unlocked the kang. The other was grinning. The Darksider with the club flickered, evaporated. A three-dimensional laser image, created, Stef now saw, by projectors mounted high up on the walls.

"The boss likes to have his little joke," the thug explained with a wink. The real Darksider was still scratching its butt. Insofar as an animal could, it looked absolutely bored.

Outside was deep night or earliest morning. Wrapped in a blanket and shivering uncontrollably, Stef rode home in a polizi hovercar. Before dawn he was in his own bed, wracked by pain from toes to scalp. Yet he slept, and by noon was able to creep to the balcony, dragging one foot behind him. He walked bowlegged, because his scrotum was the size of a grapefruit.

Slowly, very slowly, he prepared kif and lay down. He was starving but wouldn't have dreamed of getting up to look for food.

He smoked and the drug dulled everything, pain and hunger alike, and let him sleep. In all the world only kif was merciful. No wonder it was his religion.

By nightfall Stef was minimally better. He slept long, despite nightmares that left him drenched with sweat. By morning he was functional enough to bathe (he smelled worse than a Darksider by then) and dress. Then he called Yama on his mashina, hoping the polizi would monitor his call—he wanted to remind them that he had powerful friends.

"Stef. What's up?"

"I just wanted you to know that your pal Kathmann had me in the White Chamber. I'm working for him now, too."

"That son of a bitch. He hurt you much?"

"It wasn't a picnic. But I've been through worse."

"Yeah, I know you're a survivor. Well, I guess we got to share anything we find out with Earth Central. But I'm going to see Kathmann and tell him if he grabs you again, I'll send Oleary to see Xian herself. You got anything broken, like bones?"

"No."

"Well, at least the miserable bastard went light on you."

Stef next called a neighborhood babaku shop and ordered food. Then he found his pistol, made sure it was loaded, and returned to his kif pipe.

On the balcony he smoked and thought about ways to kill Kathmann. He had two people on his list now: Dyeva, because she wanted to destroy his world, Kathmann because he had—well, not tortured Stef; what had happened was too trivial to be called torture. No, Kathmann had simply been getting his attention in the inimitable polizi way.

This wasn't the first time in his life that Stef had been completely abased and humiliated. But he decided now that it was to be the last. He pointed his pistol at the wall and said, "*Phut.*"

After Dyeva, Kathmann was next.

That evening Professor Yang again stood before his mashina, which was set to Transmit and Record. A memory cube nestled in the queue. Lights arranged by his servant illuminated Yang against a background of ancient books that had been imprinted on the wall by a digital image-transfer process. (Real books were too expensive for a scholar to afford.)

Watching the interest indicator with a sharp eye, Yang launched into the second lecture of his course, Origin of Our World. His subject today was the response to the Troubles: the slow repopulation of the Earth by humans and the reintroduction of hundreds of extinct animal species whose DNA had fortunately been preserved for low-gravity study on Luna.

He spoke of the first halting steps toward Far Space and of the gradual emergence of humanity from the cocoon of the Solar System during three hundred years of experiment and daring colonization. He spoke of the new morality that emerged from the Time of Troubles, the ecolaws that limited the size of families and prescribed a human density of no more than one person per thousand hectares of land surface on any inhabited planet. (Great populations tend to produce political instability, to say nothing of epidemics.)

He spoke of the Great Diaspora, the scattering of humankind among the stars to insure that what had almost happened in the past could never happen again. He spoke of a species obsessed with security and order, and pointed out what a good thing it was that people had, for once, learned from the past, so that they would never have to repeat it. He spoke about the liquidation of democracy and explained the strange term as a Greek word meaning "mob rule." He ended with a kindly word or two about the friendly aliens like the Darksiders who had now become part of humanity's march toward ever greater heights of stability and glory.

All across the city, students were recording the lecture. So were people who were not students but had a hunger for learning. In his apartment, Stef listened because he was still recovering from his night in the Chamber and had nothing else to do. His chief reaction to Yang's version of history was sardonic amusement.

"Pompous old *glupetz*," he muttered.

In another shabby apartment, this one opening on a rundown warren of buildings near the university called Jesus and Buddha Court, Kuli—whose real name was Ananda—and the beautiful Dián—whose real name was Iris—also listened to Yang. Their reactions tended less to laughter and more to scorn.

"I liked the bit about the Darksiders," said Ananda, fingering his rosary. "A bunch of smelly barbarians our lords and masters use as mercenaries to suppress human freedom."

"You're so right," said Iris, shutting off the box. "How I hate that man."

"Oh well, he's just a professor," said Ananda tolerantly. "What can you expect. Look, is there a Crux meeting this week?"

"I don't know. Lata will have to message us, won't she? Nobody we know has been arrested. Maybe the excitement's over," she added optimistically.

"I thought Zet was getting spooked."

"Well, he's old. Old people get scared so easily."

She smiled and sat down on the arm of his chair. Ananda used his free hand to rub her smooth back. Not for the first time in history, conspiracy had led to romance. The relationship had begun with talk and more talk; change the past, restore life to the victims of the Troubles and at the same time erase this world of cruelty and injustice. Neither Ananda nor Iris could imagine that they might cease to exist if the past were changed; they thought that somehow they would continue just about as they were. Maybe better.

Growing intimate, they had told each other their real names; that had been a crucial step, filled with daring trust and a quiver of fear—somewhat like their first time getting naked together. The fact that Ananda in the past had told other girls his name and had tried to recruit them for Crux was something that Iris didn't know.

Indeed, Ananda had forgotten the others too, for he was floating in his new love like a fly in honey. In the middle of the disheveled apartment, surrounded by discarded hardcopy, rumpled bedding, a few stray cats for whom Ananda felt a brotherly concern, Iris of haunting beauty bent and touched her lips to those of the ugly young man with the rosary at his belt.

"I'd better go," she murmured. "I've got a lab." Her tone said to him, Make me stay.

"In a minute," said Ananda, tightening his grip. "You can go in just a minute."

A few streets away, in a less shabby student apartment occupied by four young women, the mashina was still playing after Yang's lecture, only now switched to a commercial program.

One of the women was insisting that she needed to make a call, but the other three were watching a story of sex among the stars called *The Far Side of the Sky* and voted her down.

"You can wait, Taka," they said firmly. Taka, who was twenty, had begun to argue when a news bulletin suddenly interrupted the transmission.

"Suppose I make my call now—" she started to say, when something about the bulletin caught her attention.

"Hush up," she told the others, who were bitterly complaining about the interruption of the story just as the hero had embraced the heroine deep in mag space.

"I want to hear this," said Taka.

After the bulletin the story quickly resumed. Taka thoughtfully retired to her bedroom and sat down on the floor, folded her slim legs gracefully under her, and reached for her compwrite. The compwrite transmitted through the mashina in the other room but gave her privacy to work.

"A letter," she said, "to—"

Who? She wondered. Daddy had always told her to obey the law but have nothing to do with the polizi, who were, he said, scum, *gryaz*, filth. How then to get her information to them without using the boxcode that had appeared on the screen during the newsflash?

"To Professor Yang, History Faculty," she began, rattling off the university address code from memory. "Send this with no return address, *oké?*"

"I am waiting, O woman of transcendent beauty," said the compwrite. Taka herself had taught it to say that and was now trying to make it learn how to giggle.

"Honored Professor, I am sending this to you as a person I honor and trust and admire," she began, laying it on thick.

"I have always been a law-abiding person and there was a news bulletin just now where the polizi were asking for information about a terrorist group called the Crooks. Well, a student named Ananda, when he was trying to climb aboard — scratch that, make love to me a couple of months ago, stated that he belonged to this group and tried to make it seem incredibly important, though I had never heard of it myself up to that time. In any case my native dialect is English and I happen to know what Crooks means and I was angry that somebody would try to involve me in something criminal.

"Hoping that you will convey this info to the proper authorities, I remain one of your students choosing to remain anonymous."

She viewed this missive on the screen and then added, "PS, this Ananda is an ugly guy with a rosary of some kind he wears on his belt. I think he's an O.B. He is skinny and wears a funny kind of cross under his jacket. He says it is a symbol of something I forget what."

She added, "Send," and headed back into the front room, where the current chapter of *The Far Side of the Sky* had expired in a shudder of Far Space orgasms.

"Well, I suppose I can make my call now," she said, and did so, setting up an appointment for tomorrow with the mashina of a depilator who had promised to leave her arms and legs as smooth as babyflesh, which she thought would look very nice.

Professor Yang's infatuation with Selina was leading him deeper and deeper into debt. He tried to stay away from Radiant Love House, but instead found himself dreaming of the White Tiger all day and heading for the District by hovercab at least three times a week.

He told himself all the usual things — that this was ridiculous in a man his age, that he would lose face if his frequent visits became known, that he couldn't afford this new extravagance. No argument could sway him; he wanted his woman of ivory in the blue peace of the electronic room where for an hour at least he feasted on the illusion of youth regained.

He was again in the middling expensive parlor waiting for the White Tiger when Stef lounged in and collapsed on the double divan.

Ordinarily, Yang would have ignored the fellow, but when Stef said, "How are you, Honored Professor?" he felt he had to say something in return.

"Quite well." Brief, cool.

"I watched your last lecture," said Stef, who was inclined to chat, knowing that as usual he had time to kill before Dzhun could receive him.

"Really," said Yang, thawing slightly. He was paid .10 khan for every box that tuned in to his lectures. It wasn't much, but he needed every tenth he could get.

"Yeah. I'm not a student, but I am ill-educated and I occasionally try to improve my mind, such as it is."

Stef pulled over a wheeled censer, dumped a little kif into it from a pouch he carried, and turned on the heating element.

"Inhale?" he asked, unwinding two hoses and handing one to Yang.

"The waiting is tiresome," Yang allowed, and took an experimental puff. Finding the quality acceptable (local kif, not Martian, but pretty good) he took another.

"May I ask your profession?"

"Investigative agent. I'm also a licensed member of the Middlemen and Fixers' Guild."

"Ah." Yang looked at Stef sharply. "Are you good at what you do?"

"Well, I live by it and have for years. Why? Need something looked into?"

"Actually," said Yang slowly, "I received an anonymous letter a few days ago and I've been wondering how to handle it. It claims to place in my hands certain information that I, ah, feel somebody in authority ought to know. Yet I have no way of checking it or naming the sender, who claims to be a student of mine. It may be worthless; on the other hand, if it's useful, well—"

"You'd like to be paid for it," said Stef promptly. "I can handle that. Insulate you from the polizi. There are ways to handle it confidentially and at the same time claim a reasonable reward if the information's good. What's it all about?"

Yang thought for a moment and then said, "It concerns something called Crux."

All of Stef's long training was just barely sufficient to enable him to keep a *marmolitz*—a marble face.

"Ah," he said, clearing his throat, "the thing that was on the box a few nights ago?"

"Yes."

Briefly he told Stef about the letter, witholding, however, the name Ananda and his description.

"What do you think it might be worth?"

"How happy I am," interrupted the box in the corner, "to inform you, honored guest, that Dzhun is now ready to receive you."

"Tell her to wait," said Stef.

To Yang he said, "Let me try to find out if the matter's really important. If so, I wouldn't hesitate to ask ten thousand khans in return for such information."

"Ten *thousand?*"

The kif pipe fell out of his mouth.

"It must be something major," Stef pointed out, "or it wouldn't have been put on the air. At the same time, I would recommend caution. This is clearly a security matter, and you certainly wouldn't want to expose yourself to the suspicion of knowing more than you actually do. That's a short path to the White Chamber. Luckily, I have a friend on the inside who's not polizi and can make inquiries."

"And your, ah, fee?" asked Yang.

"A flat ten percent of the award. I'm an ethical investigator."

"Good heavens," said Yang, who was perfectly indifferent to Stef's professional ethics but whose mind was engaged in dividing K9,000 by 120 to reached the astounding figure of seventy-five hour-long sessions with the White Tiger in the electronic room.

"What do you need?" he asked.

"Your chop on my standard contract, one sheet of hardcopy with the message, and about two days."

"You shall, my friend," said Professor Yang rather grandly, "have all three."

Yama and Stef sat at the duroplast desk in the Lion House staring at the hardcopy.

"One name. And what a crappy description. Maybe I should turn Yang over to Kathmann just to see if he knows anything more."

"An honored professor? Come on, Yama. Stop thinking like a security gorilla for once. Yang doesn't know a damn thing except that he needs money to rent his albino. What we need is to find this Ananda."

"How? Call in the polizi?"

"Hell, no. Get the credit yourself. First of all, access the university records. Tell your mashina to search for Ananda as both a family name and a given name. Let's say for the last two years. Do you have access to the polizi and city records?"

"That's Earth Central stuff," said Yama with a cunning look. "It's off limits to us. Of *course* I've got access."

"When you get some names from the university, have the box start calling their numbers and checking the faces of these Anandas. That'll eliminate some — they can't all be skinny, ugly guys — and meanwhile you can be having the names checked against the polizi records for arrests and against the city records for everything else — property ownership, energy payments, tax payments, everything. Then there's the Old Believer angle — "

Yama was already talking to his box. "I want confidential access to university records. Now."

He turned back to Stef. "By the way, how much is this costing me, assuming it leads to anything?"

"If it leads to Crux, I promised Yang fifteen thousand."

"Petty cash," said Yama. "*If* it leads to Crux."

The box chimed. "Sir, I have accessed the university central administrative files."

"Search admission, registration and expulsion records for the name Ananda," said Yama promptly, "especially expulsion." He added to Stef, "Terrorists are often students, but very few of them are good students."

Dreaming of the money, Stef paced the room impatiently. The university records were voluminous and ill-kept. There was no Ananda as a family name. Searching given names was just getting underway — "This baby does it in nanoseconds," promised Yama — when the whole university system went down. And stayed down.

After more than an hour of waiting and pacing and dreaming of kif, Stef lounged out, holding his nose until he was past the Darksider, and took a hovercab home. There he called Earth Central and reported to one of Kathmann's aides that he and Yama were following down an anonymous tip that a student was a member of Crux.

Then he called Yang and told him that the money was practically in hand. Yang was ecstatic.

"You don't know what this means to me, honored investigative agent," he bubbled. "I've had so many calls on my purse lately."

"I know what you mean."

"What do you think this Crux organization might be?"

"I don't have the slightest idea," Stef lied. "In English the word means, uh, the essential thing. Like the crux of an argument."

"Of course there's also the Latin meaning."

"What's Latin?"

"It's a dead language. The original source of the word. In Latin it means cross. Hence the crossroads, the critical point."

"Ananda wears a funny kind of cross," said Stef slowly.

"Yes. My informant thought he was an Old Believer."

"I wonder—"

Stef's box chimed. He quickly made arrangements to bring Yang his payoff and cut the circuit.

"Say," he told the box.

"Stef, I got the names," said Yama, abrupt as usual. "Got your recorder on? Here they are. Last year, Govind Ananda, withdrawn. This year, Patal Ananda, Nish Ananda, Sivastheni Ananda. That's all."

"Boxcodes?"

"Got 'em all except Govind. Like so many of those damn students, he may have a pirated mashina. I'm having the box call the ones we've got, and at the same time start running through the city records. Got anymore bright ideas?"

"No," said Stef, "except I want a vacation when this is over. And my pay."

"Stop kidding me, I know you'll take your pay out of old Yang's reward money. Don't try to . . . wait a minute. Box reports Patal and Sivas-whatever don't resemble the description. Nish is away from home. Wait a minute again. Govind Ananda paid the energy bill on No. 71, Jesus and Buddha Court. Didn't the letter say something about a rosary? And about him being an O.B.?"

"Keep trying Nish, Yama, but send three or four of your thuggi to meet me at J and B Court. I'm going to try Govind. I like the smell of that address. It's near the University and the names would echo for an Old Believer."

"You got 'em. Plus a Darksider in case things get rough."

"And a gas mask."

Stef rang off, plunged into a battered Korean-style chest on his balcony and brought out his one-centimeter impact pistol. He touched the clip control and chambered one of the fat, black-headed rounds.

Action elated him, freed him from his memories of being beaten, his sense of uselessness. Suddenly he felt wonderful, better than when he was on kif, better than when he was drunk, almost better than when he was about to make love. A flutter of fear in his belly was part of the frisson. So was the taste of iron filings beginning to fill his mouth.

He rummaged through his closet, dragged out his most ample jacket, tore the right-hand pocket to give him access to the space between cloth and lining. Hand in pocket, he pressed the gun against his ribs to hide any bulge and slipped through the door, listening to it click behind him, wondering if he would ever unlatch it again. He whispered a goodbye to Dzhun. On the roof he signaled for a hovercab.

"Jesus and Buddha Court," he said, when one drew up.

The cab's black box said, "Gratizor."

On Lake Bai in the evening the tinkle of samisen music mixed with the thrumming of a Spanish guitar, the notes falling like lemon and oleander flowers into the dark, cold water.

Half a click down in the huge lake—really a freshwater inland sea—glacial ice still lingered, surviving into the heat of an earth warmer than it had been since the noontime of the dinosaurs. Shrieking happily, goosepimpled swimmers were leaping into the water from the floating docks of lakeside villas. Further on, strings of Japanese lanterns illuminated teahouses and casinos and sliderrinks where the children of grandees cavorted on expensive cushions of air.

Back in the hills, spotlights illuminated palaces. Bijou villas lined the shores, and on the veranda of one of the smaller ones Stef and Dzhun idled, wearing light evening robes and not much else. Dzhun kept returning to Stef's account of the raid, trying to get the story straight.

"So these terrorists—did you shoot them?"

"Didn't have to. I've seldom felt like such a fool in my life."

Stef gestured lazily, and Dzhun disturbed herself long enough to pour champagne. The grapes of Siberia were justly famous, the flavor supposedly improved by the low background radiation.

"The terrorists weren't dangerous?"

"Pair of dumb kids. The boy wearing his funny cross and the girl with the same symbol tattooed on her hand, if you can believe that. The Darksider smashed the door in and let out a roar and they both fainted dead away. Then I jumped in yelling and the thuggi followed, and suddenly the four of us were standing around waving weapons at two unconscious children. Ridiculous scene.

"I almost puked when I had to hand them over to the polizi. Not that there was anything else I could do, with the thuggi and the Darksider there. I was sure Kathmann would tear them limb from limb, but Yama says they woke up spilling their guts. The polizi have got 'em locked up, of course, but Security got everything they wanted in the first three minutes."

"Dyeva."

"Absolutely. Iris and Ananda said she'd come in by the Luna shuttle on such and such a day. That was enough. Kathmann called Yama. Yama has shuttle data at his fingertips, there were only four females of the right age on that one, and they all checked out except Akhmatova Maria from a planet called Ganesh, which is, just like it was supposed to be, in the Lion Sector. *She* stepped off the shuttle and vanished.

"So now they got her hologram, plus retinographs, voiceprints, DNA, all that stuff they take when you get a passport. The kids have positively identified her. Dyeva's been made, for whatever good it may do us.

"It was an eventful day. The kids had met Dyeva at a villa outside town, so the polizi descended on that and bagged the owner. He went straight to the Chamber and promptly gave them the name of another member of the cell, a woman who has so far evaded capture. A demand for information went out to Ganesh at maximum power and with the most awful threats that Yama could think of on the spur of the moment.

"He'd just laid all this information on Oleary's desk when another call comes in from Earth Central. Kathmann's got the wormholer. Gadget takes a hell of a lot of juice, so his mashini were watching the Ulanor power grid for unusual current surges. Well, a surge of the right size occurred, and Kathmann arrived at the meter with half a dozen Darksiders to find the wormholer standing all by itself in a deserted warehouse in the northwest quadrant."

Dzhun was frowning. "Then that means—"

"You and I may vanish at any moment," Stef grinned. "Dyeva's presumably in the twenty-first century trying to prevent the Time of Troubles. I wish her luck. How's she going to do it?"

"And we're here."

"And we're here, relaxing, courtesy of the payoff to Yang. My success in cracking Crux convinced Yama that I'm the guy to stop Dyeva. He offered me a hundred thousand to go after her. I laughed in his face."

"Then who'll do the job?"

"Some thuggi from Earth Central who're under military discipline and can't say no."

"And what'll happen to her?"

"In the twenty-first century? Probably get killed by the surface traffic. Or catch a fatal disease. Or get lost in the crowds. I wouldn't trust Kathmann's idiots to find their peckers when they need to piss. Dyeva's safe enough from them."

Later, he and Dzhun wandered up the shingled beach to a waterside inn that served caviar and Peking duck and other edibles. People of the upper and under-world were crowded together at small tables, eating and drinking. Blue clouds of kif drifted from open censers over the crowd, relaxing everybody.

Dzhun, who had an indelicate appetite, was just piling into her dessert when the haunting notes of a synthesizer drifted like pollen across vast, cool Lake Bai. A band floated up in an open hovercar, and a *sisi* with a piercingly sweet voice performed a popular air, "This Dewdrop World," whose simple theme was eat, drink, and be merry, for tomorrow you die. The crowd loved it; silver half-khans and even a few gold khans showered the car. Whenever a coin fell in the water, a musician would jump in after it like a frog and have to be fished out by his friends.

It was a fine end to the evening. When Stef and Dzhun left the restaurant the air had the lingering chill of spring and the scent of lemon groves that were blossoming in the hills. Dzhun pulled Stef's arm like a scarf around her neck and started to sing the song again. He leaned over her, hugged her close. It was at moments like this that he almost envied people who were foolish enough to fall in love.

"I love that song," she said. "It's so nice to be sad. Sadness goes with joy like plums with duck."

Didn't statements like that mean that she was, after all, a bit more than just a whore? Stef hugged her tighter, breathing in her offworld perfume with the chilly scent of the lemon groves.

They had an amorous night and spent next morning lolling on the deck with their usual strong green tea. They were supposed to start back to the city today and Dzhun was looking abstracted.

"Can't wait to get back and go to work?" Stef smiled.

"Stef . . . there's something I have to tell you."

"What?"

"My senator wants to set me up in a little house in Karakorum. He's jealous, and it'll be the end for you and me."

That produced silence. Stef cleared his throat, drank tea.

"Ah. So this trip was a kissoff."

"It doesn't have to be."

"Meaning?"

Dzhun said, eyes cast down, "I'd rather live with you. We don't have to marry."

"No," said Stef.

Dzhun sat down, still not looking at him.

"I thought you'd say that. I've never bothered you with my life story because I thought you'd get bored and angry. But let me tell you just a little. My family needed money, so they sold me into the District when I was nine. The owner rented me to one of his customers. The night he raped me, I almost bled to death.

"By the time I was twelve I was a registered whore, a member of the guild. It took me three more years to pay off my debts because in the District the houses charge you for everything, heat, water, towels, mediscanning, almost for the air you breathe. But I was beautiful and earning good money and I was out of debt by the time I was sixteen. Now I'm almost eighteen and I'm sick of it all. I don't want to be a *robotchi* anymore.

"I hear people talk about going to the stars and I've never been out of Ulanor. I can barely read and write and if Selina hadn't taught me some arithmetic so they couldn't cheat me, I wouldn't be able to add two and two. I don't know anything, all I do is live from night to night—up at sixteen, to bed at eight. I've had dozens of diseases—sida six times—and the last time it took me a whole month to recover. The house doctor says my immune system's collapsing, whatever that means.

"I've got to get out of the life, Stef. I want to live with you, but if you don't want me I'm going with my senator. He has some funny tastes and three wives and he's old, but he's also kind-hearted and rich, and that's enough."

She stopped, still looking down at the floor. Stef was staring at Dzhun and clenching his fists. He felt as if a favorite dog had just bitten him. Twice, in fact—once by threatening to leave him, and once by demanding a commitment from him.

"I don't want anything fancy," Dzhun went on. "I want to live in a house with a garden. I want to get up in the morning and go to bed at night. I want to go to school before I'm too old and learn something about the world. I can see you're angry with me. Well, so be it. If you're too angry to pay my way back to the city, well screw you. I'll get the shuttle by myself."

She stood up and walked somewhat unsteadily into the house, taking by habit the little mincing steps they taught the girls—and the boys as well—in Radiant Love House.

Half an hour later she came back out, dressed for the road. Stef was leaning on the railing, looking down into deep and black Lake Bai.

Stef said, "I'm poor. I'm a loner. I'm a kif head."

"So you can't afford me, don't want me, and don't need me because kif's better. Right? So, goodbye."

"Can you fend off your senator for a while?"

"Not forever. He can buy what he wants, and I don't want to lose him."

"I guess I could set up housekeeping with a hundred thousand," Stef muttered. "But maybe I can bargain for more."

Dzhun collapsed rather than sat down and drew the longest breath of her life. She put her hands over her face as if she was weeping, though in fact she had stopped crying many years before and her face was hot and dry. Her mind was running on many things, but chiefly on her friend Selina's brainstorm, the wonderful invention of the senator, who, of course, did not really exist.

"So you'll do it," said Yama.

"For a million khans. Paid in advance. I want something to leave to my heirs in the event I don't come back."

"That's a bunch of fucking money."

"There's one more thing I want. Get those two kids I captured turned loose. Otherwise Kathmann will sooner or later cut their heads off on general principles."

Yama frowned. "He'll never turn them loose. They're young and the girl's beautiful, so he'll want to mutilate them. In my opinion, he's saving them for something special. That's the way Kathmann is—he's a fucking sadist, as you of all people ought to know."

"Try anyway."

"It's hopeless. But if I can save them I will."

When Stef had gone, Yama set out to sell his prize agent to the *fromazhi*. He expected trouble with Kathmann but none developed, the chief of Earth Security was assembling an assassination team to kill Dyeva and viewed Stef's mission as a chance to test the wormholer. Ugaitish, Admiral Hrka, and Xian were ready to try anything and put their chops on the proposal without a murmur. It was Yama's own boss, Oleary, who objected because of the cost.

"Why don't you go yourself?" he demanded. "It'd be cheaper."

"Sir, I'll go if you say to. But I got a wife and four kids."

"That's two more than the ecolaws allow."

"I got an exemption."

Oleary stared at Stef's file, frowning.

"What's wrong with this guy? I don't trust him. Why did he have to leave the service in the first place?"

"Sir, he's a great agent. Brave, quick, adaptable. But he's got a soft spot in his head. He's sentimental. You can't be a cop and be sentimental. A long time ago he helped a woman thief who was headed for the White Chamber to escape. Well, I found out about it, so I did my duty and turned Steffens in."

Oleary kept on frowning.

"If he's sentimental about women, what about when he has to kill, what's her name, Dyeva?"

"Sir, she's different. She's threatening his whole world, including this little tart he seems to be in love with."

"Oh, well," said Oleary, shrugging. "Send him, I guess. Can't hurt. But take the money back if he doesn't succeed. How could I justify a budget item like that for a failure?"

"You go tomorrow," said Yama. "Here's some stuff to study tonight."

Stef took the packet of copy, caught an official hovercar, and flew straight to Radiant Love House. The long farewell that followed left Stef weeping, and

Dzhun — once the door had closed behind him — smiling at prospects that seemed equally bright whether he survived his mission or not.

Back home, he settled down on the balcony to study the three items that Yama had provided him: a hologram of Dyeva, a summary of her life on Ganesh, and a map of ancient Moscow. The map got little more than a glance; he needed to be in situ to use it. Dyeva's hologram was another matter. Stef studied it as closely as if she and not Dzhun was his lover, imprinting on his mind Dyeva's round Tartar face, high cheekbones and unreadable eyes.

Then he read her biography. To his surprise, the hardcopy with its STATE SECRET/BEHEADER stamp had been written by Professor Yang. Liking the taste of polizi money, he'd gone to work for Yama as a volunteer agent, and his first task had been writing up and annotating Dyeva's life story.

Settlers of the Shiva system had been led by a devout Hindu who had hoped to establish a refuge for members of all the old faiths — Muslims, Christians, Jews, and Buddhists as well as his own people — where, far from corruption and unbelief, peace and justice and the worship of God could reign for all time.

"The actual results of this noble experiment," wrote Yang, "were not without irony." In the process of settling the system, three intelligent species had been destroyed, and among the humans religious wars and bitter sectarian disputes had constituted much of the system's subsequent history.

Akhmatova Maria was born to a devout family on the third planet, Ganesh. They maintained Christian belief according to the Russian Orthodox rite and hated both their neighbors of other faiths and the depraved and godless civilization of other planets. In time she lost her own faith in God but adopted in its place the religion of humanity. Her private life remained austere; she had neither male nor female lovers, and the name she took in the movement which she helped to found, Dyeva, meant virgin in Russian, her native dialect.

She was attending the local academy when news of the technical advances which allowed invention of the wormholer gave her the great project of her life. She was one of a group of people loosely connected with the academy who formed a scheme to undo the Time of Troubles by returning to the past. Some members of her group transferred to the University of the Universe in Ulanor, where they made converts to their views and laid plans to build — later on, learning that one had already been built, to steal — a wormholer.

Then came a part of the account that Yama had marked in red. Dyeva's theory that the Troubles could be prevented rested upon a verbal tradition among the Russian Christians of Ganesh: that a man named Razruzhenye, the defense minister of ancient Russia when the troubles began, ordered the first thermo/bio strike upon China and that this attack launched the Time of Troubles. Killing this one individual might well prevent the war and undo the whole course of disasters that followed.

"So," muttered Stef. It seemed a little strange to him that Dyeva, who believed in the absolute value of life, was returning to the past to kill someone. But Yang in a footnote pointed out that such things had happened many times in the past: people who believed in freedom imprisoned freedom's enemies; those who believed in life murdered anybody who seemed to threaten it.

His study finished, Stef ate a little, then fell into bed. He woke when his mashina chimed and managed to stumble through a bath. Then he confronted a large box of ridiculous clothing that had been prepared according to Professor Yang's designs, based on what men wore in the mosaics of the Moscow subway.

At seven-seventy-five a government hovercar picked Stef off the roof and flew him to a neighborhood that he knew only too well, a cluster of huge anonymous buildings with vaguely menacing forms. They descended past the ziggurat Palace of Justice and the Central Lockup in whose subterranean rooms he had tasted the joys of interrogation.

This time, however, the huge pentagonal block of Earth Central was the goal. The hovercar descended through a well in the central courtyard that wits called the Navel of the Earth. Yama met Stef as he emerged in a sunless court of black hexagonal stone blocks and led him down one narrow blank corridor after another, past huge stinking Darksiders armed with impact weapons, into a vaulted underground room with a gleaming contraption standing in the center of the floor among a jungle of thick gray cables.

"So that's it," said Stef, interested by his own lack of interest. At the center of the wormholer was a two-meter cube with a round opening in one side, whose purpose he could easily guess.

Blue-coated techs helped him into a heavy coat with wide lapels and big pockets, slipped an impact pistol into the right-hand coat pocket, and slid a black powerpack with a small control box into the left. Somebody stuck a chilly metal button into his left ear.

"Pay attention to the control," said Yama. "Take it in your hand. Now. Red button: job's done, bring me home. *Oké?* White button: I need help, send backup now. Black button: hold onto your ass, Dyeva's succeeded and your world is finished. The powerpack feeds a little tiny built-in mag space transponder that emits a kind of cosmic squeak for one microsecond. The signal crosses time exactly the way it crosses space, don't ask me why. That's what we'll be listening for. Then we have to pull you back, send help, or—"

"Grab your butts. I see. But that also means you could just cut me off, leave me there, save yourselves a million."

"Yeah, we could, but we won't. Hell with that, I really mean *I* won't. Not," he smiled, "for a measly million that isn't even my money."

They stared at each other until Stef managed a weak grin.

"That's good enough. Any problems?"

"Yes," said Stef, "lots. I don't speak Russian. I've got no goddamn idea how to find Dyeva even if I land in Moscow at the right time. I—"

Yama took Stef's arm and began to walk him toward the wormholer.

"Don't worry about the language. That thing in your ear will translate for you. And don't worry about the time. A register inside the machine recorded the day Dyeva chose, the 331st day of 2091. So we're sending you to that same date in hopes she's close to the point of exit. If she's not, you'll have to find her."

"How?"

"Come on, Stef. I sold the others on you because of your adaptability. This whole world you're going into vanished in a cloud of dust. How much can anybody know about it? There's just no way to be systematic."

They stopped beside the huge glittering gadget.

"I really envy you," said Yama in a choked voice. "This is the most crucial moment in human history. You're the plumed knight of our world, like Yoshitsune, like Saladin, like Richard the Lion-Hearted."

Yama embaced him. "Take care, my old friend, and *kill that fucking virgin.*"

An instant later the techs had helped Stef into the wormholer and closed the heavy door, which looked like a nine-petal steel chrysanthemum. Yama stepped back, wiping his eyes. Kathmann had now arrived to observe the action and Yama joined him.

"Well, that's one less friend I got," said Yama. "This job of mine is hell. How are the preparations going for your assassination team?"

"As fast as possible. Of course they're the ones who'll really do the job."

"There's a chance that Steffens might pull it off alone."

"Yeah," said Kathmann, "and there's a chance I might be the next Solar System Controller. *Svidanye,*" he added, "see you later. Some more members of Crux have been arrested and I got work to do in the Chamber."

In The Wormholer, seated as he had been instructed, knees drawn up, chin down, arms around his shins, sweltering in the heavy coat, feeling the pistol grate against his ribs, Stef tried to imagine Dzhun's face, but found that it, like everything else, was inadequate to explain to him why he was where he was. The excitement he'd felt earlier was gone, replaced by mere dread. He could only suppose that his entire life had been leading up to one moment of supreme folly, and this was it.

Then a great violet-white light flashed through him, he felt an instant of supernatural cold, and he was sitting on a gritty sidewalk against a damp stuccoed wall.

He raised his face. The day was overcast, and a restless throng of thick-bodied people wrapped up against the autumn chill hurried past, not one of them paying him the slightest heed.

He looked higher. Behind the solid walls of elderly, three-story buildings with flaking plaster and paint he saw high polished towers of what looked like mirror duroplast. Immense crimson letters hovered just below the lowest layer of murk.

Since Alspeke was written mostly in cyrillic letters, he had no trouble reading *Moskovskaya a Fondovaya Birzha,* and when he murmured it aloud a soft atonal voice in his ear translated: Moscow Stock Exchange. Below the Stock Exchange sign was a huge blue banner saying "1991–2091."

Slowly he got to his feet, staggered, caught himself against the wall. A pretty young woman paused, stared at him, then drew a pale furry hood around her face and hurried on.

A couple of teenagers stopped also, looked at him and grinned. They squawked to each other in seabirds' voices.

"What's this asshole dressed up for?"

"Must think he's Stalin or something. Hey, asshole—where'd you get that coat?"

A stout woman stopped suddenly and shook her fist at the kids.

"You leave that man alone! Can't you see he's crazy? He's got troubles enough without you hooligans pestering him."

A little man in a checkered coat stopped and joined her.

"Show some respect!" he shouted at the kids.

"What, for a guy dressed up like Stalin, for Christ's sake? Hey you," said a teenager to Stef. "You going to a party?"

Unfortunately, the translator didn't answer questions, and Stef just stared at him.

"My God, he's deaf and dumb, and you're harassing him," said the woman in scandalized tones.

By now a little crowd had gathered. Everybody had an opinion. It was the adults against the teenagers.

"You little bastards got no respect for anybody!"

"Not for you, Grandaddy."

"Call me Grandaddy? Yes, I've got grandchildren, but thank God they're nothing like you, you little pimp."

In the confusion, Stef managed to slip away, leaving them arguing behind him. In an alleyway he unbuttoned the coat and stared down at the tunic and coarse trousers jammed into boots. The clothes were *nothing* like what people were wearing on the street. Already the stiff, kneehigh boots of faux leather were beginning to chafe his toes, and he hadn't walked more than a hundred meters.

Cursing Yang, he tried to decide what to do. While he pondered, he worked his way from alleyway to alleyway until he suddenly spotted, among the hundreds of small shops lining the street — Boris Yeltsin Street — a shop with a sign that said *Kostyumi*. He didn't need the translator for that.

Thirty minutes later, Stef emerged from the costume shop wearing acceptable clothes, short soft boots, baggy trousers, a faux astrakhan hat, a long warm padded jacket. In his pockets were thirty ten-ruble notes, the difference between the value of the handsome and practically new theatrical garb he'd sold the shop's owner and that of the secondhand, ill-fitting stuff he'd bought from him.

He slipped into the crowd, which was denser than the center of Ulanor on Great Genghis Day. The street traffic was noisy and thick, everybody driving headlong as if their odd, smelly cars were assaulting a position. Above, the air traffic was thin, almost absent — a few primitive rotary-wing machines with shapes so bizarre that Stef thought at first that they were some sort of giant insect life. Jet trails streaked far above, making him wonder if airpackets already flew from Luna.

Between street and sky, strung on cables, hundreds of blue banners fluttered, all saying 1991–2091, and sometimes "100 Years of the Democratic Republic," whatever that meant. He could see no mention of Tsar Stalin the Good.

His next stop was in front of a huge window filled with flickering mashini. Stef was surprised to see that the images made by the boxes were three-dimensional — he had expected something less advanced — though the technology was crude, merely a rough illusion created on a flat screen. His eyes roved past a ballet and half a dozen sports programs. Russian *futbol* teams had dominated world play in the season just past, but what would the hockey season bring forth? Young people dashed around on grass or ice while the announcer talked.

Nobody at all seemed to be thinking about the danger of universal destruction. Stef shook his head, amazed at the ordinariness of this world, so close to its end. He moved along, jostling against these people who would soon be dust and ashes, astonished at their solidity and their obvious confidence that they would exist for a long time to come.

A single screen was tuned to a news program called *Vremya* and he stopped to watch it. A young woman wearing a fantastic pile of yellow hair spoke of the Russian-led international team now hard at work establishing the Martian colony and the problems it was facing. People on Mars, needing to communicate despite a babel of tongues, were developing a jargon all their own; the American members of the colony called it All-Speak. It was mostly Russian and English, with a flavoring of words from twenty other languages.

Meanwhile a new condominium development on Luna marked the transformation of that spartan base, barely seventy years old, into a genuine city, the first on another world. Space had never looked better; Russia's own program, after a long eclipse, again led the world. Here on Earth things were not so encouraging. There were new outbreaks of Blue Nile hemorrhagic fever. The Nine-Years' War continued in the Rocky Mountains; the weak U.S. central government seemed unable to conquer the rebels, and United Nations peacekeepers had again been massacred in Montana.

But the big worry was that border tensions continued to mount in Mongolia, where Chinese forces had occupied Ulan Bator. The name cause Stef to press his nose against the glass. He had heard enough of Yang's lecture to know that Ulan Bator was the origin of the name Ulanor, even though the city the announcer was talking about was now—now?—nothing more than a mound on the green forested banks of the River Tuul.

According to Yang, a few survivors of the Troubles had trekked northward, bringing the name with them and applying it to a cluster of yurts in an endless snowstorm. Later, because it had low background radiation, the place had become the site of the Worldcity—a strange fate for a Mongol encampment that had survived the Two Year Winter for no better reason than the sheer unkillable toughness of its people and an endless supply of frozen yak meat, which they had softened by sleeping on it and eaten raw for lack of firewood.

Another name caught Stef's attention. "Defense Minister Razumovsky has declared that Russia, together with its European and American allies, will stand firm against further aggression by the Imperial People's Republic of China."

Defense Minister Razumovsky? That wasn't the word he had learned, the name of the man Dyeva was supposed to kill. It was another Raz word, Raz, raz— *Razruzhenye.*

He must have said the word aloud without meaning to, for his translator murmured, "Destruction."

Stef nodded. Sure. In the folk memory, Minister Razumovsky became Minister Razruzhenye, Minister Destruction. The name was wrong, but the tradition might still be correct.

Razumovsky suddenly appeared in a clip. He had a wide, flat face like a frog someone had stepped on. He seemed to talk with his right fist as much as his mouth, pounding on a podium while he spoke of Russia's sacred borders and of China's presumption, now that it had conquered Korea and Japan, that all East Asia belonged to the Dragon Republic.

"They'll find out different if they mess with us!" Razumovsky bawled, and loud cheering broke out among a crowd seated in something called the Duma. "They think they can threaten us with their rockets, but our Automated Space Defense System is the most advanced in the world. I spit upon their threats!" More cheering.

Then a weighty, white-maned man came on, identified as President Rostoff. His message was of conciliation and peace. "As the leader of the Western Alliance, Russia bears a grave responsibility to act with all due caution. Our guard is up, but we extend as well the hand of friendship to our Chinese brothers and sisters."

Stef smiled; across the centuries, he recognized without difficulty the ancient game of good cop-bad cop. He moved on, meditating on a final line from the announcer: that the debate on the Mongolian situation would continue in the Duma tonight, and that the President and the cabinet would again be present. Was that why Dyeva had picked this particular day to return to the past?

He walked down a gentle declivity where the street widened into an avenue called Great Polyanka and rose to the marble pylons of a new gleaming bridge. Beyond a small river he saw red walls, gold onion domes, palaces of white stone — the Kremlin.

Pleasure boats with glass roofs slid lazily along the river, which was divided here by a long island. In the boats Stef could see brightly dressed people dancing. Then the crowd swept him onto the other bank, past the Aleksandrovsky Gardens and up a gentle rise. Here the throng divided; most people passed on, but some joined a long queue that had formed at a brick gatehouse.

Stef continued with the majority along the autumnal garden and the crenellated wall into Red Square. He stared like any tourist at a cathedral like a kif-head's dream and then, feeling tired and hungry, crossed the square and drifted into the archways of a huge building that filled the far side, a market of some sort crowded with shops and loudly bargaining people. At a stall that sold writing paper, Stef bought a small notebook, an envelope, and an object he had never seen before — a pen that emitted ink.

The building held eating places, too. Hungrily, Stef found himself a place at a small table in one of them and ordered *shchi* without knowing what cabbage was. Soon a bowl of hot greenish soup lay steaming before him, along with a sliced onion and a chunk of dense and delicious brown bread and sweet butter. It was the first time he'd ever tasted butter from a cow, since all the Earth's cattle had died in the Troubles. It had a subtle, complex flavor and an unctuous texture quite different from the manufactured stuff he knew.

He devoured it all, licked his fingers as the other diners were doing, and paid with a few of his rubles. Then, still sitting at the table, he laboriously wrote a few lines, tore out the page, and sealed it in an envelope which he addressed to Xian in care of Yama. He left the eating place smiling grimly; in case something went wrong, this note was another legacy he hoped to leave behind him.

He returned to Red Square to find that in his absence it had become almost unbearably beautiful. A light autumn snow had begun to fall, streetlights were coming on, and the bizarre cathedral of St. Basil floated in its own illumination, more than ever a dream.

Shadows, light and snow turned everything to magic. Strolling past were young people with faces as white and pink as dawn clouds, and among them stout men in astrakahns and elegant women in faux ermine. Old women were selling apples that could have been plucked from their own cheeks.

A little band began to play somewhere as Stef slowly retraced his steps, out of the square and up to a floodlit gate in the Kremlin wall. People were streaming in, all talking excitedly, and Stef followed.

Inside, he moved with difficulty through the throng gathering at a big, anonymous new building with the words DUMA OF THE RUSSIAN PEOPLE in gold letters above the doors. Guards in hats of faux fur were trying to keep a roadway open here, pushing people back but, to Stef's surprise, using no whips. Considering what he had always heard about the Tsars, the mildness of this government was astonishing. He circled the crowd, his mind now centered on Dyeva's hologram, searching faces of which there seemed no end, countless faces, all different, none hers.

Away from the Duma the Kremlin grounds were more open. In the last light, huge rooks wearing gray patches on their wings like shawls flew from one bare tree to another, cawing their complaints about the human invasion. Stef wandered into a small church like a glittering lacquered box. Gold-haloed saints ascended every wall and hung suspended in the red depths of the ceiling; ghostly notes of song showered down, although he could see nobody singing.

People knelt, prayed or simply stood and looked on. An old woman rose, crossed herself, and jostled Stef on her way out. Another and younger woman wearing a fur hat and a long coat rose and turned to go. Either Dyeva or her twin sister passed so close to Stef that he could have touched her.

After a stunned instant of surprise he followed, out into the dry fresh-falling snow, the lights and shadows of dusk. The rooks had settled into their nests. She didn't walk, she strode, eyes straight ahead. He followed her along a winding path, keeping one or two people between them. He was looking for a place to kill her, a dark corner, a moment of privacy.

Then he realized that he didn't need privacy. Left hand on the red button of the transponder, he gripped his weapon with his right, raising the barrel a little in his coat pocket. He would kill her in the open and escape where nobody could follow. He only had to make absolutely sure that this was his quarry. He stepped off the path, the dry snow crunched under his boots, he hastened, he was directly behind her.

She had stopped to watch a wedding party ending a day's celebration here in the Kremlin at dusk. Holding wine glasses were a pretty girl in voluminous white, her new husband in an uncomfortable-looking suit of black, and half a dozen friends. One of the friends stepped forward with a bottle of bubbling wine and filled their glasses. Everyone was laughing. They had picked up a street musician someplace, an old man with a primitive instrument of some sort that he crushed and stretched between his hands. He played wheezy music and the young people toasted the couple while onlookers clapped, laughed and wept.

"Dyeva," said Stef and she turned her head and looked at him.

Unquestionably it was the Tartar face he knew so well, with the high cheek-bones and the angled eyes. Her face didn't change, yet she knew instantly why he had come. Instead of pleading for her life, she said in Alspeke, in a low, urgent voice:

"Look at them! Look at them! Look at this world. Can you really let it destroy itself to save what we have — tyrants, fools, Darksiders, the White Chamber? These people are alive, they're free, they deserve to have a future. Whoever you are, take just one second before you kill me. Think about it!"

And for a lengthening instant Stef did. In fact, he had been thinking about it secretly for hours. To be here, now, seeing these people, this world — it wasn't theory anymore. Uncounted millions lived and breathed and wanted to keep on doing so. His own world seemed remote and for the moment unbelievable — the broken drains and babaku smells of Golden Horde Street, his dirty apartment and the kif pipe, Yama and his stinking guardian, his long day in the White Chamber, Lake Bai and the singsongers on the boat, the synthesizer and the *sisi* warbling the melody "This Dewdrop World."

For that instant he could have joined Crux himself. Then he thought of Dzhun and he was paralyzed by indecision. As he hesitated, Dyeva turned to face him squarely and he heard the soft sound *Phut!* as she shot him through her coat.

He felt — not pain, but an incredible, crushing pressure in his midsection. His upper body flew backward, almost separated from the rest of him and the back of his head struck the cold hard snowy ground. A last mechanical contraction of his right hand fired his pistol, sent the bullet up, up into the darkening overcast like a tiny missile. His left squeezed the red button, meaning: my job is finished, I have succeeded. Bring me home.

Dyeva turned and hastened away, boots squeaking in the fresh snow. People were gawking at the wedding party and almost a minute passed before she heard, by now far behind her, a single scream. She would never know that the reason was not only the sight of a dead man lying horribly mutilated in the snow, but the fact that, even as someone spotted him, he disappeared, evaporated into the gathering darkness. Yama had kept his word.

She plunged into the crowd before the Duma building, her mind running now on the scheduled arrival of the President and his cabinet for a debate on the Mongolian situation. Running also on the fact that such schedules were almost never kept. Running on the fact that she still had fifteen bullets, and that any one would be enough. Running on the importance of stopping this Minister Destruction that she had been hearing people on Ganesh curse since her childhood — the man who had given the order that ended their world.

No, she didn't believe in God any longer. But she had had to try once more to recapture her faith in the Cathedral of the Annunciation. Who could have imagined that she'd ever have a chance to pray there, in a building long since vaporized and its atoms embedded deep in the Kremlin Shield?

Well, the experiment had failed; she could not recapture her own faith, but she would insure that other people kept theirs. She would sacrifice herself as Christ had for the sins of the world. There was no heaven at the end of it, but this was how she wanted to die.

She squeezed herself through the crowd, murmuring apologies in her strangely accented Russian, a kind of Russian that wouldn't be invented, ever, if she could manage it. She wondered if her parents would still be born and meet and have a child and call it Maria. No, too unlikely; if they lived at all, they would meet other people and marry them. Everything would be different. She felt a strange, dark satisfaction in thinking that she would not merely die here in the Kremlin; in some sense, she would never have existed at all.

She had reached the front of the crowd, and stood pressed behind a bulky policeman. Fortunately, when the first gleaming limousine turned in through the Gate of the Savior and slid to a stop before the Duma, the policeman moved a little to get a good view of the notables. On the far side of the car, President Rostoff emerged and turned to wave at the crowd. On this side, a young and apparently nervous security man emerged and glanced briefly at Dyeva's face. Other security men appeared too, jumping from cars, stepping briskly through the snow.

Rostoff, instead of going inside, crossed behind his own car and came to the crowd, reaching out to shake hands. People were cheering, arms reaching out and waving like limbs at the edge of a forest in a windstorm. From a second limousine, Razumovsky approached, also smiling, but keeping a few steps back to avoid upstaging the President. Dyeva shifted the pistol in the deep pocket of her coat and prepared to fire.

Then a gaggle of odd-looking people ran up, carrying primitive cameras of some sort. A sudden spotlight flashed on the crowd and Dyeva was blinded by the light. The long barrel of the impact pistol slipped through the hole in her coat made by her last shot. Shielding her eyes, she aimed as well as she could at Razumovsky. The little sound *Phut!* vanished in the roar of the crowd.

But the young security man had spotted the gleam of metal, and without the slightest hesitation he shoved the President the wrong way, into the path of the exploding bullet. Suddenly half of Rostoff's large body was gone, shredded.

Unaware of the disaster, the security man raised his own right hand, which was holding the newest M91K police automatic, 7.8 mm and loaded with superteflon hollowpoints. The first of six bullets hit Dyeva. They were not impact ammo, but they were sufficient.

She toppled backward, firing a last around that skated upward and blew a meter-wide hole in the marble facing of the new Duma building. The chips were still flying as she hit the snow, feeling nothing but a strange lightness as if she had become a woman of air that would shortly disperse. She looked up into the faces of the security man and Minister Razumovsky as the two bent over her.

But you're supposed to be dead, she thought. And died.

Razumovsky glared down at her Tartar face.

"The goddamn Chinese did this!" he roared, and turned away.

Half a dozen people in the crowd were down, bleeding and crying for help, because the young security man and the others who had rushed to help him had managed to hit not only Dyeva but everyone near her as well. Razumovsky ignored all that, the screams, the confusion. Roughly he shook off the hands trying to drag him this way or that way to safety. Alone of them all, he knew exactly what he wanted to do.

He plunged into the President's armored limousine and shouted to the driver, "Get me out of here!"

While the driver, weeping and blinded by tears and lights, tried to find the gate, tried to force a way through the crowd without killing anybody else, Razumovsky took a key from around his neck and drove it into a lock in the back of the front seat. A small steel door fell open and he pulled out a red telephone.

"Razumovsky here!" he roared. "Chinese agents have wounded the President! I relay to you his exact words: 'We are at war! You will launch now!' Codeword: Ivan the Terrible."

He sank back on the upholstery and passed a shaking hand over his squashed-frog face. At least in dying the *glupetz* Rostoff had inadvertently chosen the right policy—for a change. Had he lived, who could tell what might have happened?

"Goddamn," said Oleary. "I still can't believe he managed it, all alone like that."

The Secret Committee had assembled to hear Yama's final report on Stef's mission to the past. Xian, Ugaitish, Hrka, Oleary—they were all there but Kathmann. Except for Xian—who already knew the story—the *fromazhi* were leaning breathlessly over the gilt Martian table, listening to the story of how their world had been saved.

"Well, here's the evidence," said Yama. "First, we recover Stef's body, dead, obviously shot by a modern weapon, *oké?* His own gun has been fired once. The world we live in does not vanish, but on the contrary looks as solid as ever, at least to me. Just to eliminate any doubts about what happened, we use the wormholer one more time. We pull back from Moscow, 360th day of 2091, an air sample which is full of intensely radioactive dust and ice particles.

"Now I ask you, Honored Grandees. What can we conclude, except that Stef and Dyeva killed each other, that with his last gasp, so to speak, he signaled us to recover him because his job was done, and that the Time of Troubles proceeded to happen on schedule?"

Xian turned to Yang, standing in the shadows, deference in every line of his big, weak body. "What do you think, Honored Professor?"

"I agree. The evidence is absolutely irrefutable, and I have spent my whole life evaluating evidence."

"Well, I guess we have to accept it," fretted Oleary. He still hoped to take back Stef's million, but he could see that it would be difficult now.

"I am obliged to add," Yama continued, "that a sealed envelope was found on Steffen's body containing a note to Solar System Controller Xian."

He glanced at her and she nodded.

"It reads as follows," said Yama, spreading a copy on the arm of the *shozit*.

> *Facing death, Dyeva states that Kathmann cooperated in the theft of the wormholer. He expected to win promotion by crushing the conspiracy afterward, but Crux was too clever for him. Ever since, he has been desperately trying to wipe out those few who know of his treason.*
>
> *Steffens Aleksandr*

The *fromazhi* drew a deep collective breath.

"Is it possible?" demanded Ugaitish. "The head of Earth Security? What could he hope to gain from assisting a conspiracy, then destroying it?"

"He told me once," said Yama, who had been waiting for this moment for many years, "that he dreamed of being Solar System Controller."

"Honored grandees," said Xian, "you must know that at first I, too, found this accusation hard to believe. But the evidence is great. The paper, ink and handwriting prove that Steffens wrote this note. In his own defense, Kathmann made the claim that Steffens was seeking revenge because he had been tortured. But Kathmann's own record of Steffens's interrogation certifies that the questioning was 'exceptionally gentle.' This was a troubling contradiction.

"We all know that Kathmann, in spite of his many virtues, was too zealous, too ambitious. I ordered him to bring me the scientist who stole the wormholer for questioning. The man had been beheaded. That seemed an extremely suspicious circumstance to me. Was Kathmann trying to ensure his silence? All the builders of the wormholer were also dead. I questioned the only two Crux prisoners who were still alive, but they were mere children and knew nothing — which was probably why they had kept their heads.

"In the end, to resolve the matter I ordered Kathmann into the White Chamber. With the needles in his spine, he made a full confession. Every statement made by Steffens in this note is true. Kathmann knew too many state secrets to be permitted to live, and so I had him beheaded."

She looked around at the others, as if waiting for a challenge. Yama smiled a little. Admiral Hrka remarked that he had never liked the fellow. Aside from that, Kathmann's harsh fate produced no comment whatever.

"Is there any other business, then?" asked Xian, preparing to end the meeting.

Yang had been waiting for this moment to step forward from the shadows. "Now that Crux is finished, Honored Grandees," he said smoothly, "I would suggest going public with the story and making Steffens a hero.

"The heroes we honor all lived a long time ago; they are almost mythic figures — indeed, some of them, like the Yellow Emperor, are entirely myths. But here we have a hero of today, one that people can identify with, one who brings the glory and splendor of the present world order home to the common man. It's true, of course," he added, "that certain aspects of Steffens's life will have to be edited for public consumption. But the same could be said of any other hero of history."

"Superb," cried Xian at once, ending any argument before it began. Raising a tiny, thin hand that looked with its many rings like a jeweled spider, she declared: "Steffens will be buried with full honors. Someone with talent will write his biography and Yang will sign it. Scenes from his life will be enacted on every mashina. A great tomb will be built — "

"Honored Solar System Controller," muttered Yama, "we've already cremated the body and disposed of the ashes."

"What difference does that make? Do you suppose Genghis Khan sleeps in what we call his grave? Now, *bistra, bistra!* — quick, quick! Get a move on. Remember that heroes are made, not born."

Professor Yang, smiling over the adoption of his idea, left the cabinet room with Yama.

"In some ways," he remarked, "the most intriguing supposition is that the world we live in has *always* been the consequence of the Crux conspiracy and its outcome. Wouldn't it be interesting, Honored Colonel, if time is, so to speak, absolutely relative—if this episode has been embedded in the past ever since 2091, and all our world is the long-term result of what, from our point of view, has only just happened?"

Yama, hurrying to carry out Xian's order, paused long enough to stare at Yang. "What complete nonsense," he growled.

Pending appointment of a replacement for Kathmann, Yama was combining Earth Central duties with his own. Most of his day was taken up with Stef in one way or another. Yama launched the process of glorification, then carried out a more personal duty: as he'd once promised Stef, he ordered the release of Iris and Ananda from the White Chamber. He did not see the young people, and so never knew that their brief stay beneath the Palace of Justice had turned their hair the same color as the tiled walls of their cells.

Weary and ready to go home, Yama was thinking of Hariko and his children when a piece of copy containing two lines of script was hand-delivered to his desk. Thus he learned that the woman Lata, last survivor of Crux on earth, had been tracked down at a village near Karakorum. She had committed suicide before the polizi and the Darksiders arrived and had left this note.

"It is all over," she wrote, "and I know it. This world endures as if protected by a god. But what sort of god would protect *this* world?"

Yama slid the paper into a port of his mashina.

"Copy, file, destroy," he said.

On the next Great Genghis Day, Government of the Universe Place was crowded with people. From every flagpole hung nine white faux yaktails in honor of the famous Unifier of Humankind. But the event of the day was not honoring Genghis—though President Mobutu burned incense on his grave—but the dedication of Stef's memorial.

As the veil over the statue fell, Dzhun and Selina stood together looking at an idealized Stef striding ever forward, holding an impact pistol in one hand and a globe symbolizing the world order in the other.

Since Dzhun was only semiliterate, Selina read the epitaph that Yang had composed: "Like the Great Khan in Courage and Like Jesus in Self-Sacrifice."

"Yang's been made a grandee, you know," Dzhun said. "They needed somebody to purge subversives from the University, and he just dropped into the slot. We're lucky to have him for a customer."

She had used the million Stef had left her, not to buy a cottage or get an education, but to open her own brothel. She called it House of Timeless Love. With clever Selina to manage it—and to serve a few select customers, such as the now famous, rich and powerful Yang—it had rapidly become the most popular of the newer houses, with capacity crowds every night.

Selina smiled down at her friend and employer.

"Anyway, the statue's nice. Of course he never walked stiff-legged like that. Stef just lounged around."

"I think I preferred him as he was," mused Dzhun. "Alive."

"You loved him, didn't you?"

"I guess so. I really don't know much about love. I know that I love you."

She and Selina had been sleeping together for years. Sometimes they made love, but sex wasn't really the point. After the night's work was done and all the customers were gone, they lay together for comfort, holding each other close.

"Can I ask you something, Dzhun?"

"Anything. Almost anything."

"How'd you get Stef to leave you all that money? Was it just telling him that you had a senator on the string?"

"That was part of it. But also I made up a sad story about myself and fed it to him. You know, in spite of everything he was sentimental. That's why he was thrown out of the Security Forces. I was working for the polizi then, keeping them informed about my customers. When I reported that Stef was working on an important secret project, I got a bonus. Kathmann himself told me about Stef's weakness," said Dzhun proudly. "Even way back then I had powerful friends, Selina."

"*Tu nespravimy*, Dzhun," said her friend, smiling and shaking her head. "You're incorrigible."

"What's that word mean?"

Selina told her. Dzhun smiled; she liked the sound of it.

"Well, honey, if you ask me, we live in an incorrigible world."

The cure for everything

SEVERNA PARK

Here's a disturbing look at an all-too-likely future, where, as usual, we don't know what we've got until we've lost it. . . .

New writer Severna Park has sold short fiction to markets such as Event Horizon, Sci Fiction, Realms of Fantasy, *and* Black Heart, Ivory Bones. *Her critically acclaimed novels include* Speaking Dreams, Hand of Prophecy, *and* The Annunciate; Speaking Dreams *and* The Annunciate *were finalists for the Lambda Literary Award. Coming up is a sequel to* The Annunciate, *called* Harbingers. *She lives in Frederick, Maryland, and maintains a web page at http://users.erols.com/feldsipe/index.htm.*

Maria was smoking damp cigarettes with Horace, taking a break in the humid evening, when the truck full of wild jungle Indians arrived from Ipiranga. She heard the truck before she saw it, laboring through the Xingu Forest Preserve.

"Are we expecting someone?" she said to Horace.

Horace shook his head, scratched his thin beard, and squinted into the forest. Diesel fumes drifted with the scent of churned earth and cigarette smoke. The truck revved higher and lumbered through the Xingu Indian Assimilation Center's main gates.

Except for the details of their face paint, the Indians behind the flatbed's fenced sides looked the same as all the other new arrivals; tired and scared in their own stoic way, packed together on narrow benches, everyone holding something—a baby, a drum, a cooking pot. Horace waved the driver to the right, down the hill toward Intake. Maria stared at the Indians and they stared back like she was a three-armed sideshow freak.

"Now you've scared the crap out of them," said Horace, who was the director of the *Projeto Brasileiro Nacional de Assimilação do Índio*. "They'll think this place is haunted."

"They should have called ahead," said Maria. "I'd be out of sight, like a good little ghost."

Horace ground his cigarette into the thin rainforest soil. "Go on down to the A/V trailer." he said. "I'll give you a call in a couple of minutes." He made an attempt to smooth his rough hair, and started after the truck.

Maria took a last drag on the cigarette and started in the opposite direction, toward the Audio/Visual trailer, where she could monitor what was going on in Intake without being seen. Horace was fluent in the major Amazonian dialects of Tupi-Guaraní, Arawak, and Ge, but Maria had a gut-level understanding that he didn't. She was the distant voice in his ear, mumbling advice into a microphone as he interviewed tribe after refugee tribe. She was the one picking out the nuances in language, guiding him as he spoke, like a conscience.

Or like a ghost. She glanced over her shoulder, but the truck and the Indians were out of sight. No matter where they were from, the Indians had some idea of how white people and black people looked, but you'd think they'd never seen an albino in their lives. Her strange eyes, her pale, translucent skin over African features. To most of them, she was an unknown and sometimes terrifying magical entity. To her . . . well . . . most of them were no more or less polite than anyone she'd ever met stateside.

She stopped to grind her cigarette into the dirt, leaned over to pick up the butt, and listened. Another engine. Not the heavy grind of a truck this time.

She started back toward the gate. In the treetops beyond Xingu's chain-link fence and scattered asphalt roofs, monkeys screamed and rushed through the branches like a visible wind. Headlights flickered between tree trunks and dense undergrowth and a Jeep lurched out of the forest. Bright red letters were stenciled over its hood: *Hiller Project.*

Maria waved the driver to a stop. He and his passenger were both wearing bright red jackets, with *Hiller Project* embroidered over the front pocket. The driver had a broad, almost Mexican face. The passenger was a black guy, deeply blue-black, like he was fresh off the boat from Nigeria. He gave Maria a funny look, but she knew what it was. He'd never seen an albino either.

"We're following the truck from Ipiranga," the black man said in Portuguese. His name was stenciled over his heart. *N'Lykli.*

She pointed down the dirt road where the overhead floodlights cut the descending dusk. "Intake's over there," she said in the same language. "You should have called ahead. You're lucky we've got space for them."

"Thanks," said N'Lykli, and the driver put the Jeep in gear.

"Hey," said Maria as they started to pull away. "What's a Hiller Project?"

Another cultural rescue group, she figured, but the black guy gave her a different funny look. She didn't recognize it and he didn't answer. The Jeep pulled away, jouncing down the rutted access road.

Maria groped in her pocket for another cigarette, took one out of the pack, then stuck it back in. Instead of heading for the A/V trailer, she followed them down the hill to Intake.

She found N'Lykli and the driver inside with Horace, arguing in Portuguese while four of Xingu's tribal staffers stood around listening, impassive in their various face paint, Xingu T-shirts, and khaki shorts.

"These people have to be isolated," the driver was saying. "They have to be isolated or we'll lose half of them to measles and the other half to the flu."

He seemed overly focused on this issue, even though Horace was nodding. Horace turned to one of the staffers and started to give instructions in the man's native Arawak. "Drive them down to Area C. Take the long way so you don't go past the Waura camp."

"No," said N'Lykli. "We'll drive them. You just show us where they can stay for the night."

Horace raised an eyebrow. "For the *night?*"

"We'll be gone in the morning," said N'Lykli. "We have permanent quarters set up for them south of here, in Xavantina."

Horace drew himself up. "Once they're on Xingu property, they're our responsibility. You can't just drop in and then take them somewhere else. This isn't a fucking motel."

The driver pulled a sheaf of papers out of his jacket and spread them on the table. Everything was stamped with official-looking seals and *Hiller Project* in red letters over the top of every page. "I have authorization."

"So do I," said Horace. "And mine's part of a big fat grant from *Plano de Desenvolvimento Econômico e Social* in Brazillia."

The driver glanced at his Hiller companion.

"Let me make a phone call," said N'Lykli. "We'll get this straightened out."

Horace snorted and waved him toward Maria. "She'll show you where it is."

"This way," said Maria.

It wasn't that Horace would kick the Indians out if they didn't have authorization. He'd kick out the Hiller whatever-the-fuck-that-was Project first, and hold onto the Indians until he knew where they were from and what they were doing on the back of a truck. Indians were shipped out of settlements all over Brazil as an act of mercy before the last of the tribe was gunned down by cattle ranchers, rubber tappers, or gold miners. Xingu's big fat grant was a sugar pill that the *Plano de Desenvolvimento* gave out with one hand while stripping away thousands of years of culture with the other. Horace knew it. Everyone knew it.

N'Lykli followed her across the compound, between swirls of floodlit mosquitoes, through the evening din of cicadas. The phone was on the other side of the reserve, and Maria slowed down to make him walk beside her.

"So what's a Hiller Project?" she said.

"Oh," he said, "we're part of a preservation coalition."

"Which one?" asked Maria. "Rainforest Agencies?"

"Something like that."

"You should be a little more specific." Maria jerked a thumb in Horace's direction. "Horace thinks Rainforest Agencies is a front for the World Bank, and they're not interested in preserving *anything*. If he finds out that's who you work for, you'll never get your little Indian friends out of here."

N'Lykli hesitated. "Okay. You've heard of International Pharmaceuticals?"

"They send biologists out with the shamans to collect medicinal plants."

"Right," he said. "IP underwrites part of our mission."

"You mean rainforest as medical resource?" Maria stopped. "So why're you taking Indians from Ipiranga to Xavantina? They won't know anything about the medicinal plants down there. Ipiranga's in an entirely different ecological zone."

He made a motion with his shoulders, a shrug, she thought, but it was more of a shudder. "There's a dam going up at Ipiranga," he said. "We had to relocate them."

"To Xavantina?" She couldn't think of anything down there except abandoned gold mines, maybe a rubber plantation or two. "Why can't you leave them with us?"

"Because they're . . . unique."

He was being so vague, so unforthcoming, she would have guessed that the entire tribe was going to be sold into gold-mining slavery, except that something in his tone said that he really cared about what happened to them.

"Unique?" said Maria. "You mean linguistically? Culturally?"

He stuck his hands in his pockets. He licked his lips. After a while he said, "Genetically."

That was a first. "Oh yeah?" said Maria. "How's that?"

"Ipiranga's an extremely isolated valley. If it wasn't for the dam, these people might not have been discovered for another century. The other tribes in the area told us they were just a fairy tale." He glanced at her. "We don't think there's been any new blood in the Ipiranga population for five hundred years."

Maria let out a doubtful laugh. "They must be completely inbred. And sterile."

"You'd think so," said N'Lykli. "But they've been very careful."

A whole slew of genetic consequences rose up in her mind. Mutants. Family insanities and nightmarish physical defects passed down the generations. She knew them all. "They'd have to have written records to keep so-and-so's nephew from marrying his mother's grand-niece."

"They have an oral tradition you wouldn't believe. Their children memorize family histories back two hundred generations. They *know* who they're not supposed to marry."

Maria blinked in the insect-laden night. "But they must have a few mistakes. Someone lies to their husband. Someone's got a girlfriend on the side—they can't be a hundred percent accurate."

"If they've made mistakes, none of them have survived. We haven't found any autism, or Down's." He finally gave her that three-armed sideshow freak look again. "Or Lucknow's."

Maria clenched her teeth, clenched her fists. "Excuse me?"

"Lucknow's Syndrome. Your albinism. That's what it is. Isn't it?"

She just stood there. She couldn't decide whether to sock him or start screaming. Not even Horace knew what *it* was called. No one was supposed to mention *it*. *It* was supposed to be as invisible as she was.

N'Lykli shifted uncomfortably. "If you have Lucknow's, your family must have originally been from the Ivory Coast. They were taken as slaves to South Carolina in the late 1700s and mixed with whites who were originally from County Cork in Ireland. That's the typical history for Lucknow's. It's a bad combination." He hesitated. "Unless you don't want children."

She stared at him. Her great-grandfather from South Carolina was "high yellow," as they said in those days to describe how dark he wasn't, referring not-so-subtly to the rapes of his grandmothers. His daughter's children turned out light-skinned and light eyed, all crazy in their heads. Only one survived and that was Maria's mother, the least deranged, who finally went for gene-testing and was told that her own freakishly albino daughter would bear monsters instead of grandchildren. That they would be squirming, mitten-handed imbeciles, white as maggots, dying as they exited the womb.

"Who the *hell* do you think you are?" whispered Maria.

"There's a cure," he said. "Or there will be." He made a vague gesture into the descending night, toward Intake. "International Pharmaceutical wants those people because their bloodlines are so carefully documented and so *clean*. There's a mutation in their genes—they all have it—it 'resets' the control regions in zygotic DNA. That means their genes can be used as templates to eliminate virtually any congenital illness—even aging. We've got an old lady who's a hundred years old and sharp as a whip. There's a twelve-year-old girl with the genes to wipe out leukemia." He moved closer. "We've got a guy who could be source for a hundred new vaccines. He's incredible—the cure for everything. But we'll lose them all if your boss keeps them here. And he can. He has the authority."

"Get on the phone to International Pharmaceutical," she said and heard her voice shaking. "Get them to twist his arm."

"I can't," he said. "This isn't a public project. We're not even supposed to be here. We were supposed to pick them up and get them down to the southern facility. We wouldn't have stopped except we spent a day fixing the truck." He spread his hands, like the plagues of the world, not just Lucknow's, would be on her shoulders if she refused to lie for him. "Help us," he said. "Tell your boss everything's fine in Xavantina."

She couldn't make herself say anything. She couldn't make herself believe him.

He moved even closer. "You won't be sorry," he said in a low voice. "Do it, and I'll make sure you won't ever be sorry."

She took him back to Intake and told Horace that Hiller seemed to be a legit operation, that there was a receiving area at Xavantina and it had been approved according to *Plano de Desenvolvimento* standards. Horace grunted and smoked and made more irritated pronouncements about Xingu as a cheap motel on the highway to Brazil's industrial future. At about one in the morning, he stubbed out his cigarette and went to bed, leaving Maria to lock up.

Maria showed N'Lykli and the Mexican driver where they could sleep, and then she walked down to Area C, to have a better look at The Cure for Everything.

Xingu's compounds would never make it into Frommer's, but to fleeing tribes, the split greenwood shelters, clean water, and firepits were five-star accommodations. The only fences were to keep the compound areas separated. Intertribal conflicts could survive bulldozers and rifles like nothing else.

Maria passed the Xingu guard, who squinted at her, then waved her on. Closer to Area C she was surprised to run into a second guard. A short guy—the truck driver, she realized—built like a brick and too bulky for his Hiller jacket.

His eyes widened at the sight of Maria and he crossed himself. "You can't come in here."

"I work here," snapped Maria.

"Everybody's sleeping," said the guard, but Maria took another step toward him, letting him get a good look at her spirit-pale face, and his resolve seemed to evaporate. "Germs," he said weakly. "Don't give them your germs."

"I've had all my shots," she said, and kept walking.

They weren't asleep. It was too dark to make out details, but from her shadowy hiding place, Maria could see seven or eight people sitting by the nearest fire, talking to each other. No different than a hundred other intakes. Exhausted little kids had been bundled into the shelters. The adults would watch for unknown dangers until sunrise.

Maria crouched in the leaves, invisible, and listened. Five hundred years of isolation would mean an unfathomable dialect. She might be able to catch a word or two, but the proof of the Hiller Project would be in what she could hear and not comprehend. She had the rest of the night to decide if N'Lykli was lying, and if she decided he was, she would tell Horace everything in the morning. She would tell him the exact name for her ghostliness and what N'Lykli had promised her. Horace would understand.

She squinted into the haze of wood smoke. The tone of the conversation around the fire had risen, like an argument. One young man made wide, angry gestures. Something flashed in his ear, a brilliant ruby red, and Maria thought she caught the word for *prisoners* in Tupi-Guarani.

Across from him, a remarkably old woman pounded a walking stick on the packed dirt. The fire showed her nearly-naked body—withered breasts and wiry muscles—striped here and there with yellow paint. And a scarlet glint in her ear.

The old woman pounded her walking stick even harder, raising puffs of dust. Flames leaped up, giving Maria a snapshot view of a half dozen elders with braided hair and feathers, the ruby glint in each earlobe. Their ancient faces focused on the young man's dissent. He shouted in a staccato burst of glottals and rising tones, closer to Chinese opera than any Amazon Basin language Maria had ever heard. The old woman made an unmistakably dismissive motion with both arms. Emphatic. The young man jumped to his feet and stalked off. The elders watched him go. The old woman glowered at the fire, and no one said another word.

In the dark, surrounded by mosquitoes and thick, damp heat, Maria eased out of her crouch. Bugs were crawling into her socks. Her left leg was cramping and she was holding her breath, but she could feel her body changing. She was becoming solid and brighter than she'd ever been before. Her life as a ghost was over. Right here. In this spot. Her invisibility and their isolation. Her scrupulously unconceived, mitten-handed mutant children, who had burrowed into her dreams for so many years, drifted around her, dispersing like smoke, and Maria felt the trees, the dirt, the insects and night birds—*everything*—hopeful and alive, and full of positive regeneration, for the first time in her life.

She got to her feet, wobbly with optimism, turned around and saw him.

He stared at her the way they all did. She stared back at his wide-set eyes and honest mouth. Yellow face paint and brilliant macaw feathers. His ruby earring wasn't jewelry at all, but a tiny digital sampler of some kind, ticking off combinations of numbers, pulsing as he breathed. She tried to tell herself he wasn't the one N'Lykli had told her about. That this wasn't the face and trim body of The Cure for Everything.

But it was.

My germs, she thought, and took an unsteady step backward.

He moved toward her and spoke in halting Portuguese. "You see me speak. You hear me."

She nodded.

He took a breath through his teeth. "Please. Take me away, *Jamarikuma*."

Another word with ancient, Tupi-Guaranian roots. *Jamarikuma*: a grandmother of powerful female spirits.

She turned around and ran.

She went to see N'Lykli. Pounded on his door and woke him up.

"Where are you really taking them?" she said. "There's nothing in Xavantina but a couple of bankrupt rubber plantations."

He hunched on the edge of the cot, covering himself with the sheet. "International Pharmaceutical has a facility there."

"Do those people *know* you're—you're *milking* them?"

His face made a defensive twitch. "We've explained what we need from them and they've discussed it. They all understand about the dam. They know why they can't stay in Ipiranga."

"Why do they think they're going to be prisoners?"

N'Lykli sat up straight. "Look. They're not captives. There're a few who don't like the idea, but we're not taking them against their will. We've been in contact with them for almost a decade. We even explained about Xingu and your assimilation programs. They didn't want anything to do with it. They don't want to be separated."

"We don't separate families."

"Can you relocate an entire tribe—eight hundred and seventy-four people—to a nice neighborhood in Brasilia?"

"But there's only—"

"This is the last group," he said. "We've been staging them into Xavantina for a month."

She sat down on the only chair in the room. "I can't even interview them to find out if any of what you're saying is true."

He shrugged again.

She took a breath. "So what am I supposed to do? Wait around until International Pharmaceutical announces a cure for Lucknow's?"

N'Lykli rubbed his chin. "You don't have to be cured of the syndrome to have normal children. You just need the right father."

Maria stared at him.

He looked down at the floor. "We don't just take blood samples. I can send you something in a couple of weeks. It'll be frozen and you'll have to use it right away. I'll send instructions . . ."

"You're going to send me *sperm?*"

"How else should I do it?" he said. "Would you rather make an appointment with him?"

"Oh, for *Christ's* sake!"

He watched her head for the door. "You're going to tell your boss what's going on?"

Maria stopped. Put her hands in her pockets and glared at him, the mosquito netting, the dank, bare room. *Jamarikuma.* Like hell.

"Goddamit," she said. "You'd better be out of here by daylight."

The Hiller Project truck pulled out at dawn, this time with the Jeep in the lead.

Maria stood out in full view, watching. N'Lykli gave her a half-salute and looked around nervously, probably for Horace. The Mexican driver gunned the engine, going too fast over the ruts and holes of the unpaved road.

The truck followed, angling for the open gate. In the back, every face turned to stare at her.

The Cures for Alzheimer's, Lucknow's, and all kinds of cancer made small gestures against spirits, turned to each other to whisper, but they didn't look frightened. They didn't look resigned to their fates. They looked like tired travelers who were sick of cheap motels, ready to be wherever they were going. Except for one.

The Cure for Everything lunged against the railing. "*Jamarikuma!*" He shouted high in his throat. "*Jamarikuma!*" He shook the wooden side rails as the truck lurched through the gates and down the hill. She could hear him yelling over the diesel rumble even when the truck was well out of sight.

She stood there in the gray sunlight, taking deep breaths of churned earth and fumes, and felt her body go vague again. It was sudden and strange, like a wind had blown through her.

She knew she should go down to Intake and tell Horace everything, but she was afraid to. It seemed sickeningly obvious now that she should have made the Hiller people stay. Even if what N'Lykli had told her was true, she should have gone over to the Indians arguing around their campfires and made them talk to her. If The Cure for Everything could speak a little Portuguese, so could a few of the others.

Was she *so* desperate in her ghostliness that she would betray herself like this, give up her job, her life, her colleagues and friends—*everything* for a cure? For frozen *sperm?*

Yes, she was that desperate. Yes, she was.

She turned away from the gate and the diminishing sounds of the truck. *It's too late*, she told herself, and felt the lie in that as well.

She drove off with the Toyota Land Cruiser without telling anyone, before the diesel stink of the Hiller truck was gone. The Toyota was the newest of the Xingu vehicles and the only one with a full tank. She plunged it down the muddy hill after the Hiller truck. There weren't that many ways to get to Xavantina.

She caught up with the truck in less than half an hour, but stayed out of sight, a klick or so behind. Xingu's rutted jungle access turned to a graded lumber trail, and she dropped even further back. When the scraggly trees gave way to burned stumps and abandoned timber, she gave herself more distance, until the Hiller truck was a speck behind the speck of the Jeep, forging along the muddy curves in the ruined hillsides.

She followed them through grim little settlements of displaced Indians and rubber tappers who lived in squalor downstream from the local plantations, past islands of pristine jungle where monkeys screamed at her and brilliant parrots burst out of the trees in clouds of pure color.

Fourteen hours from Xingu, long after the moon went down, the truck turned off the half-paved local Xavantina highway onto a dirt road along a narrow river. In the pitch blackness, it made a sharp right and came to a stop.

Maria pulled into the last stand of trees. Doors slammed and there was a brief silence. Then a bank of floodlights came on overhead and she could see the truck sitting by the Jeep in a cleared area at the foot of a high chain-link fence. The Indians peered out of the back, pointing into the darkness while N'Lykli pulled the gates open and the vehicles drove through.

There were no signs to identify the place. Maria hunched over the Toyota's steering wheel, stiff in her shoulders, thick in her head, tired beyond even the desire for coffee. She lit her last cigarette and dragged deep for energy and ideas as N'Lykli swung the gates shut, locked them, tugged on them, and vanished into the dark.

In a minute, the floods went out, leaving Maria with the glowing tip of her cigarette. She waited a while longer, turned on the dome light and crawled into the back of the car where the tool box was. She dug until she found a heavy-duty pair of wire cutters.

Inside the gate, the road deteriorated into a wasteland of bulldozed ruts. Weeds and young trees grew to shoulder height. Small animals scurried away as Maria groped through the dark. Bloodthirsty insects found her bare neck, her ankles, and the backs of her hands. Finally, she saw the glow of sulfur-colored floodlights, and at the top of the next rise, she got her first glimpse of the "facility."

A huddle of blocky, windowless buildings surrounded a fenced central court-yard. It had the look of an unfinished prison. Wire-topped fences glinted in the security floods.

She expected dogs, but didn't hear any. She made her way through the weeds expecting snakes, but decided that N'Lykli and his blood-sucking colleagues at Hiller had probably eliminated every poisonous thing for miles around—no accidental losses in their gene pool of cures. The whole idea made her furious—at *them* for such a blatant exploitation, and at herself for so badly needing what they'd found.

She circled the compound, trying to find an inconspicuous way to get into the inner courtyard, but the fences were new and some of them were electrified. When she had come almost all the way around to the front again, she found a lit row of barred windows on the ground floor of one of the blockhouses.

There was no one inside. The lights were dim, for security, not workers or visitors. Maria climbed up a hard dirt bank to the window sill and hung onto the bars with both hands.

Inside, modern desks and new computers lined one side of a huge white room. At the other end, there was a small lab with racks of glassware and a centrifuge. Color-coded gene charts covered the walls. Yellow lines braided into red, producing orange offspring. Bright pink Post-it notes followed one line and dead-ended with a handwritten note and an arrow drawn in black marker. She could read the print without effort: *Autism?*

Mitten-handed mutants. Ghostly spirit children.

She let herself down from the windowsill and crept through brittle grass to the edge of the wire fence.

Inside, she could see one end of the compound and the lights of the blockhouse beyond. Dark human shapes were silhouetted against small fires and she realized she'd expected them to be treated as inmates, locked up for the night and under constant guard. Instead she could smell the wood smoke and hear their muffled voices. Women laughing. A baby squalling, then shushed. Hands pattered on a drum.

She touched the fence with the back of her hand, testing for current.

Nothing.

She listened, but there was no alarm that she could hear.

Someone chanted a verse of a song. A chorus of children sang in answer. For the first time, Maria saw the enormity of what she was about to do.

The Cure for Everything. Not just Lucknow's.

She pulled out the cutters and started working on the fence. The gene chart. *Autism.* The way *his* voice had sounded, shrieking *Jamarikuma!* None of this was right.

She crawled through the hole in the fence and they saw her right away. The singing and conversation stopped. She got to her feet, brushed off her knees and went near enough to the closest fire to be seen, but not close enough to be threatening. The Cure for Everything gave Maria a quick, urgent nod but he didn't stand up. Around him, a few heads cocked in recognition of her face, her skin.

The withered old woman Maria had seen at Xingu hobbled over from one of the other fires, leaning on her walking stick. She frowned at Maria and started speaking in accented Portuguese.

"We saw you at Xingu. You're the Jamarikuma. What are you doing here?"

"I'm here to help," said Maria.

"Help us do what?" said the old woman.

"You don't have to stay in this place," said Maria. "If you do, you and your children and your grandchildren's children won't ever be allowed to leave."

The old woman—and half a dozen other older members of the tribe—glanced at the Cure. Not in a particularly friendly way.

"What's this all about?" said the old woman to the Cure, still in Portuguese. "You've got a spirit arguing for you now?"

He replied in their own language. To Maria he sounded sulky.

"Do you understand why you're here?" said Maria. "These people . . ." She gestured at the looming buildings. "They want your blood, your . . ." *Genes* might mean *souls* to them. "You have a—a talent to cure diseases," said Maria. "That's why they want your blood."

Guarded eyes stared back from around the fire.

The old woman nodded. "What's so bad about that?"

"You won't ever be able to go back home," said Maria.

The old woman snorted. "At home they were trying to shoot us." She spat into the fire. "We're afraid to go back there."

"But *here* we're animals." The Cure pushed himself to his feet. "We're *prisoners!*"

"We've had this discussion," said the old woman sharply and turned to Maria. "We made a decision months ago. We said he didn't have to stay if he didn't want to, but he stayed anyway, and now he's bringing in spirits to make an argument that no one else agrees with. We're safer right here than we've been for years. No one's shooting at us. So we have to wear their ugly jewelry." She touched the ruby sampler in her ear. "So we lose a little blood now and then. It's just a scratch."

"But you're in a cage," said Maria.

"I don't like that part," said the old woman. "But you have to admit, it's a big cage, and mostly it keeps the bandits and murderers out."

The Cure jabbed a finger at Maria, making his point in harsh staccato tones. Maria only caught the word *Xingu*.

The old woman eyed Maria. "What would happen to us at Xingu?"

"We'd teach you how to be part of the world outside," said Maria. "We'd show you what you need to know to be farmers, or to live in the city if that's what you want."

"Are there guns in the world outside?"

It was a patronizing question. Maria felt sweat break out at the small of her back. "You know there are."

"Would we all be able to stay together, the entire tribe?" asked the old woman.

"We do the best we can," said Maria. "Sometimes it isn't possible to keep everyone together, but we try."

The old woman made a wide gesture into the dark. "We didn't lose one single person on the trip. You're saying you can't guarantee that for us at Xingu, though. Is that right?"

"Right," said Maria.

"But we'd be free."

Maria didn't say anything.

The old woman made a sharp gesture. "It's time for the Jamarikuma spirit to leave. If that's what she actually is." She closed her eyes and began to hum, a spirit-dismissing song, Maria supposed, and she glanced at the Cure, who leaped to his feet.

"I am leaving. With the Jamarikuma."

The old woman nodded, still humming, as though she was glad he'd finally made up his mind.

The Cure took a step away from the fire. He walked—no, he sauntered around his silent friends, family, maybe even his wife. No one said anything and no one was shedding any tears. He came over to Maria and stood beside her.

"I will not come back," he said.

The old woman hummed a little louder, like she was covering his noise with hers.

When they got back to the Toyota, Maria unlocked the passenger side and let him in. He shut the door and she walked slowly around the back to give herself time to breathe. Her heart was pounding and her head felt empty and light, like she was dreaming. She leaned against the driver's side, just close enough to see his dim reflection in the side mirror. He was rubbing his sweaty face, hard, as though he could peel away his skin.

In that moment, she felt as though she could reach into the night, to just the right place and find an invisible door which would open into the next day. It was the results of a night with him that she wanted, she realized. He was like a prize she'd just won. For the first time, she wondered what his name was.

She pulled the driver's side open and got in beside him. She turned the key in the ignition and checked the rearview mirror as the dashboard lit up. All she could see of herself was a ghostly, indistinct shape.

"Is something wrong?" he asked.

"Everything's fine." She said and let the truck blunder forward into the insect-laden night.

Later, when the access road evened out to pavement, he put his hot palm on her thigh. She kept driving, watching how the headlights cut only so far ahead into the darkness. She stopped just before the main road, and without looking at him, reached out to touch his fingers.

"Are we going to Xingu?" he asked, like a child.

"No," she said. "I can't go back."

"Neither can I," he said, and let her kiss him. Here. And there.

The suspect Genome

PETER F. HAMILTON

Here's an absorbing and intricately plotted mystery set in a troubled future England, a story that expertly and effortlessly mixes two genres to produce a hybrid worthy of the best of either: a science fiction mystery full of surprises, where nothing is as it seems to be.

Prolific new British writer Peter F. Hamilton has sold to Interzone, In Dreams, New Worlds, Fears, *and elsewhere. He sold his first novel,* Mindstar Rising, *in 1993, and quickly followed it up with two sequels, A* Quantum Murder *and* The Nano Flower, *all detailing further adventures of Greg Mendel, who also features in "The Suspect Genome." Hamilton's first three books didn't attract a great deal of attention, on this side of the Atlantic, at least, but that changed dramatically with the publication of his next novel,* The Reality Dysfunction, *a huge modern Space Opera (it needed to be divided into two volumes for publication in the United States) that is itself only the start of a projected trilogy of staggering size and scope, the* Night's Dawn *trilogy.* The Reality Dysfunction *has been attracting the reviews and the acclaim that his prior novels did not, and has suddenly put Hamilton on the map, perhaps a potential rival for writers such as Dan Simmons, Iain Banks, Paul J. McAuley, Greg Benford, C. J. Cherryh, Stephen R. Donaldson, Colin Greenland, and other major players in the expanding subgenre of Modern Baroque Space Opera, an increasingly popular area these days. The subsequent novel in the trilogy,* The Neutronium Alchemist, *generated the same kind of excited critical buzz. Hamilton's most recent books include his first collection, A* Second Chance at Eden, *the third novel in the* Night's Dawn *trilogy,* The Naked God, *and a novella chapbook,* Watching Trees Grow.

One — The Dodgy Deal

▼

It was only quarter past nine on that particular Monday morning, but the September sun was already hot enough to soften the tarmac of Oakham's roads. The broad deep-tread tires of Richard Townsend's Mercedes were unaffected by the mildly adhesive quality of the surface, producing a sly purring sound as they crossed the spongy black surface.

Radio Rutland played as he drove. The station was still excited by the news about Byrne Tyler—the celebrity's death was the biggest thing to happen in the area all month. A newscaster was interviewing some detective about the lack of an arrest. The body had been found on Friday, and the police still had nothing.

Richard turned onto the High Street, and the road surface improved noticeably. The heart of the town was thriving again. Local shops were competing with the national brand-name stores that were muscling in on the central real estate, multiplying in the wake of the economic good times that had come to the town. Richard always regretted not having any interests in the new consumerism rush, but he'd been just too late to leap on that gravy train. Real money had been very short in the immediate aftermath of the PSP years, which was when the retail sector began its revival.

He drove into the Pillings Industrial Precinct, an area of small factories and warehouses at the outskirts of the town. Trim allotments down the right hand side of the road were planted with thick banana trees, their clumps of green fruit waving gently in the muggy breeze. The sturdy trunks came to a halt beside a sagging weed-webbed fence that sketched out a jumble of derelict land. All that remained of the factory that once stood there was a litter of shattered bricks and broken concrete footings half glimpsed among the tangle of nettles and rampant vines. A new sign had been pounded into the iron-hard ocher clay, proclaiming it to be Zone 7, and Ready For Renewal, a Rutland Council/Townsend Properties partnership.

Zone 7 was an embarrassment. It was the first site anyone saw when they entered the Pillings Precinct: a ramshackle remnant of the bad old days. The irony being Pillings was actually becoming quite a success story. Most of the original units, twentieth-century factories and builders' merchants, had been refurbished to house viable new businesses, while the contemporary zones, expanding out into the verdant cacao plantations that encircled the town, were sprouting the uniform blank sugar-cube structures of twenty-first-century construction. Seamless weather-resistant composite walls studded with mushroom-like air-conditioning vents, and jet-black solar-cell roofs. Whatever industry was conducted inside, it was securely masked by the standardized multipurpose facades. Even Richard wasn't sure what some of the companies did.

He parked the Merc outside his own offices, a small brick building recently renovated. Colm, his assistant, was already inside, going through the datapackages that had accumulated overnight on his desktop terminal.

"The architect for Zone 31 wants you to visit," he said as Richard walked in. "There's some problem with the floor reinforcements. And a Mr. Alan O'Hagen would like to see you. He suggested 10:30 this morning."

Richard paused. "Do I know him?"

Colm consulted his terminal. "We don't have any file on record. He said he may be interested in a zone."

"Ah." Richard smiled. "Fine, 10:30."

It was a typical morning spent juggling data. Builders, suppliers, clients, accountants, local planning officials; they all expected him to clear up the mess they were making of their own jobs. He'd spent a lot of his own money over the last four years, schmoozing and paying off the county and town councillors to get his partnership with the precinct project, and it had paid off. Townsend Properties was currently involved in developing eight of the zones, with architects working on plans for another three. Having the massive Event Horizon corporation open a memox processing facility on Zone 12 a year ago had been a real triumph for the town; other smaller corporations had immediately begun to nose around, eager for subcontracts. Quite how the council development officers managed to pull off that coup always baffled Richard. He'd never known a supposedly professional team quite as incompetent as the people who worked at Rutland Council. Every job he undertook was besieged by official delays and endless obstructionist revisions.

The man who walked in at 10:30 prompt wasn't quite what Richard had expected. He was in his late fifties, nothing like any of those eager young business types who normally came sniffing around the precinct. Alan O'Hagen wore a gray business suit with a pale purple tie. He had a sense of authority which made Richard automatically straighten up in his chair and reach to adjust his own tie. Even the man's handshake was carefully controlled, an impression of strength held in reserve.

"What can I do for you?" Richard asked as his visitor settled into the leather chair before the desk.

"My company." Alan O'Hagen held up a silver palmtop cybofax. Its key blinked with a tiny pink light as it squirted a datapackage into the desktop terminal. Richard scanned the information quickly.

"Firedrake Marketing? I'm afraid I've never heard of it."

O'Hagen smiled. "No reason you should. It's a small virtual company I own. I trade on-circuit, specializing in albums and multimedia drama games. I have some German software houses signed up, and a couple of African jazz bands who aren't well distributed in Europe. Naturally, I'd like to rectify that."

"Uh huh." Richard made an immediate guess about what kind of German software — the end of the PSP hadn't seen a total reversal of censorship in England. "So how does the Pillings Precinct fit in with all this?"

"I want Firedrake to become more than a virtual company. At the moment it consists of a circuit site with a few trial samples you can access, and an order form. I subcontract distribution and delivery to a mail-order company in Peterborough. After their fees, I'm not left with much in the way of profit. What I want to do is build up a distribution arm myself."

"I see." Richard made sure he wasn't grinning. It would appear predatory at this point. "And you'd like to build that distribution company here."

"It's a possibility."

"A very advantageous one for you. Event Horizon's memox plant would be next door, so there'd be no shortage of crystals, and we do have an excellent rail service to both Peterborough and Leicester. Not to mention a generous start-up tax allowance."

"Every industrial precinct does, these days," O'Hagen said. "Corby is offering a flat-rate construction loan for anyone starting on either of their new precincts."

Richard blanked his irritation at the mention of Corby. He'd lost three clients to their precinct developers in the last six weeks. "You'll find us a competitive match for any other precinct, I assure you."

"What about construction times?"

"That depends on the size of the operation you're looking for, of course."

"Nothing extravagant to start with, but I will require a zone with considerable potential for expansion if things take off."

"As I'm sure they will." Richard walked over to the precinct map pinned on the wall. "I have several zones I can offer you."

It took another two hours of cajoling before O'Hagen left. Richard had squirted just about every brochure and datapackage he'd got into the businessman's cybofax. He'd hate to play the man at poker; no hint of how keen he was had leaked from that impassive face. But the good news was that O'Hagen had invited Richard for dinner that night, suggesting the Lord Nelson restaurant in the Market Square.

After lunch, Richard drove to the courthouse in the town's old castle hall. Jodie Dobson, his solicitor, was waiting for him in the car park. In her mid-thirties, a junior partner in one of the local firms, she was more than capable when it came to corporate legal matters.

"We've got plenty of time," she said, gesturing to the ancient doors. "The land-registry clerk's only just finished his lunch."

"Fine." He paused. "I don't suppose you've heard of a company called Fire-drake?"

"Should I have?"

"Not really." He waved his cybofax. "I was checking their site this lunchtime. They sell a response formulator for interactives. Once you've plugged into a drama, it'll take your character wherever you want to go inside the arena. The plotlines will reconfigure to incorporate your movements and speech into the story. They're claiming a much better reaction time than other software."

"Sounds fairly standard to me."

"Yes, but it's not just for flatscreens, it can handle a total VR immersion. It's fully compatible with all the major multimedia formats; you can supplement it to whatever drama you buy."

"Why the interest?"

He shrugged and gestured her through the doorway. "I think it could be quite successful."

The old stone hall had a vaulted ceiling, and whitewashed plaster walls hung with hundreds of horseshoes. Prior to the Warming the hall had been little more than a historical tourist attraction, used only occasionally for a magistrate's court. Then in the aftermath of the seas flooding the Lincolnshire fens, the vast influx of refugees had more than doubled Rutland's population. The hall's legal activities had expanded to become full-time. Modern partitioning had been used to break up the rear of the hall into small office cubicles. Jodie and Richard maneuverd along a narrow corridor between the transparent sound-proofed walls. The Land Registry & Claims cubicle was barely large enough to hold the two of them as well as the clerk.

Jodie had the petition already prepared, and handed over the two memox crystals detailing the case, including the original farmer's title to the land. Richard, as the claimee, had to sign a host of papers verifying the action.

"Any idea when the case will be heard?" he asked.

"I'm sorry, Mr. Townsend." The clerk's hand fluttered over the pile of memox crystals and paper folders on his desk. "We have over eight hundred ownership cases filed in this court alone. The local PSP Land Rights allocation committee confiscated a lot of property."

"Yes, I appreciate that, but this is land for a commercial venture which will benefit many people in the town. It'll create jobs, and bring wealth into the area. Surely that warrants some additional attention."

"I would say yes," the clerk murmured diplomatically. "But it's not up to me."

"Nevertheless . . . I'd be grateful if you could point this out to the powers that be."

"I'll do what I can."

When they were back outside in the scorching sunlight Jodie frowned. "That was sailing close to the wind. You don't do backroom deals in a civic office."

"I'll bear it in mind. And you should remember that we need that leisure complex; your partnership will scoop up a big fee for steering it through the legal stages."

"I am aware of basic marketplace economics, thank you."

"Good. There's a lot of new industry moving into town right now. That means wealthy educated people looking for somewhere to relax, and prepared to pay for the privilege. Rutland Water is a fabulous commercial resource, which is tragically underused. Can you believe there's only three hotels on the shore?"

Jodie nudged him softly. He looked around to see a bicycle entering the castle hall grounds. It was Andy Broady peddling heavily, his ruddy young face glistening with sweat. Richard almost laughed out loud. Even in this weather the kibbutzniks still wore their thick dark dungarees.

Andy dismounted and leaned the bike against a wall. It was an ancient contraption of black steel tubes, with a wicker basket on the front of broad handlebars. The County Museum would be proud to possess a specimen like it.

Richard gave him a pleasant nod. Andy glared back furiously. For a moment Richard thought he might stalk over and swing a punch. Eventually, he pulled a bundle of papers out of the basket and made for the hall doors.

"My relocation offer stands," Richard said. "There's no need for either of us to go through this. It is my land."

"My father died this morning," Andy said. His voice was close to choking.

"I'm very sorry to hear that," Richard said.

"Accident, my arse!"

Richard kept his voice neutral. "I don't understand."

"Listen, you." Andy took a pace toward them, his finger raised. "Twenty years he worked that land. He kept the faith and taught it to all of us. God rewarded our labors with enough fruit and crops to feed ourselves. It's our home! We won't give it up."

"With all respect to your father, God didn't give you that land. The PSP did. They stole it from a family who were farming it a lot longer than twenty years, and didn't pay a penny in compensation. What kind of justice is that?"

"It's ours!" Andy was close to tears. "I've spent my life there."

Richard nearly said, *Time to move on, then*, but kept his sarcasm in check. It wouldn't do to get involved in a public fracas with some half-wit farm boy. Besides, the oaf was built like a combine harvester—solid power in a huge squat body. They stared at each other for a moment, then Andy hurried inside, rubbing the crucifix stitched to the front of his dungarees.

"Filing their counter claim, no doubt," Jodie said. "They'll appeal for post-acquisition compensation, you know. It's what I'd do in their situation."

"Fat lot of good that'll do them. I have full title."

"You'll have to let me see the plans for this leisure complex sometime. It must be quite something."

"It's a work of art. Most aesthetic."

"You mean, profitable."

He laughed. "What else?"

Alan O'Hagen had booked a table at the back of the Lord Nelson, where they were afforded some privacy. Richard enjoyed the small restaurant; it had tasteful antique decor, efficient service, and an excellent seafood menu. His ex-wife had always badgered him to take her, but he never had the money in those days. Now she was no longer a burden to him with her absurd middle-class a-fair-day's-work-for-a-fair-day's-pay ethic. Nothing worthwhile in this world came fair. The young waitress gave him a respectful smile as he came in. Success was the most succulent dish.

O'Hagen was waiting for him. Richard ordered a bottle of Australian Chardonnay from the wine list, almost the most expensive available. It was unusual for a client to buy him a meal, especially at this stage, and it made him wonder what kind of proposal O'Hagen was going to make.

"I want to take Zone 35," O'Hagen said. "However, I may have one small problem which I was wondering if you could help me with."

"Go on," Richard said. This was the part he enjoyed the most—the part, different every time, which had to be settled to make it all fall into place.

"The industrial unit will cost about half a million New Sterling to build and equip," O'Hagen said. "Firedrake is a viable concern, but I'm not going to get the capital backing from a bank to build a whole warehouse and mailing outfit from scratch. Not with that to offer as collateral on the deal."

"Firedrake can't be your only concern, surely?"

"It's not. But the kind of imports I've been dealing with in the past don't lend themselves to close examination. Besides, there's none of that money left."

"I see."

O'Hagen leaned over the table. "Look, the thing is this. At the moment Firedrake has a turnover of about 70,000 New Sterling per year. And that's just with one poxy site and not much advertising. Once my distribution arm is up and running I can expand the product range and the advertising. That'll start to generate enough income to pay off the kind of loan I'll need to get it started. I'm *this* close."

"I can see that, but . . ."

"Every business faces this point in the early years. It's a credibility gap, nothing more. I need the banks to take a favorable look at the proposal, that's all. England's economy is in a high boom stage right now, and it's going to last for a decade at least with this new giga-conductor Event Horizon has delivered. There's so much potential for expansion here, you know that. The banks are desperate for an excuse to invest in our companies."

"But have you got any kind of collateral you can offer the bank? Something concrete? Like you say, they're fairly flexible."

"I have one proposition. It's for you." He leaned in closer. "Become my partner in Firedrake. I'll sell you half of the shares."

"What?"

"It's simple. With your involvement, the bank is bound to approve the loan application. You're an established businessman; your development company is a success. With that kind of finance behind Firedrake, it couldn't fail."

"I'm sorry. It's my job to sell you part of the precinct, not the other way round. I'm not a buyer, Mr. O'Hagen."

"I'm not asking you to buy. I'm even prepared to pay you."

Richard carefully poured himself some more Chardonnay. "I don't follow."

"Look, what we're talking about here is credibility, right? I want financial credibility, and that's what I'll pay you for. You take a half share in Firedrake. It's not worth anything, there are only two shares, and they're valued at a pound each. I told you, it's a virtual company. Memory space on a mainframe, that's all. But if you combine its turnover with your company's involvement, we've got a valid application for an expansion loan. And you get another commercial unit built on the precinct, out of which you make a tidy profit. Nor will you be liable for Firedrake if—God forbid—it goes down the tube. The distribution operation will be a subsidiary which I own. There's no risk in it for you."

Richard hesitated. The idea almost made sense, and some of the arrangements he'd made on other deals were a lot less orthodox. "If I take a share in Firedrake, the banks will see what you're doing. That would help your credibility, and it would ruin mine."

"Yes. But if you'd taken that half share two years ago they'd be impressed. It would show that you'd been a part of a promising business for a decent period, and were now confident enough in it to expand."

"Hmm." Richard sat back and looked into that impassive face. O'Hagen was earnest, but certainly not pleading. "You mentioned payment. What kind of incentive would I have received to loan you my good name for the past two years?"

"I have a painting. It's a McCarthy, worth quite a bit. Not enough to trade in as collateral for a warehouse unit, you understand. But I could loan you that until Firedrake was earning enough to pay you back."

"How much is a bit?"

"Find the right collector, you should be able to get 20,000 for it."

Richard weighed it up. Twenty thousand for using his name and reputation to lever a loan from a bank for a deal in which he would profit. And costing one tiny blemish in record-keeping, a one-pound share and two years. To massage that kind of data you didn't even need to be an accountant . . . let alone a creative one. "I'd want to see Firedrake's accounts before I go any further," he said cautiously.

For the first time, there was a display of emotion on Alan O'Hagen's face as his lips moved into a small smile. "Come to my office tomorrow. My accountant will go over them with you."

Thistlemore Wood was a district on Peterborough's western sprawl, part of the industrial expansion which had turned the city into a commercial powerhouse in the post-Warning years. To south was an old park, now hosting an estate of hemispherical apartment blocks, silvery crescents rising up out of the grassland. The road Richard eased the Merc along was lined by closely planted maeosopis trees, their long branches curving into an arboreal arch above him. He had to slow on the edge of Thistlemore because a converter crew was at work on the road. Smoke was venting out of their big remoulder vehicle as it chewed up the cinder flecks the track was made from. An endless sheet of smooth thermo-hardened cellulose was extruded from its rear, a dark protective coating which sealed the raw earth away from pounding tires and searing sunlight. The crew diverted Richard around the vehicle, keeping him off the freshly laid surface. A couple of rickshaws came the other way, their riders clamping cloths over their noses as the smoke gushed around them.

The block where O'Hagen rented office space for Firedrake was eight stories high, its exterior white marble and copper glass. Satellite uplink antennae squatted on the roof inside their weather domes; an indicator of just how much data traffic the building handled. Richard pulled up in the visitors' car park, then took the lift to the sixth floor.

Firedrake had one employee. Apparently she did everything in the office: personal assistant, receptionist, site maintenance, made tea and coffee, handled communications. Like O'Hagen, she wasn't what Richard was expecting, but for very different reasons. She was small, though he quickly redefined that as compact. He didn't think she'd take very kindly to people who called her small. Every look was menacing, as if she were eyeing him up for a fight . . . a physical one. Her dress had short sleeves, showing arms scuffed with what looked like knife scars, and a tattoo: closed fist gripping a thorn cross, blood dripping.

After he'd given his name she reluctantly pressed her intercom button. "Mr. Townsend to see you," she growled.

"Thank you, Suzi," O'Hagen answered. "Send him in, please."

Her thumb jabbed at a door. "In there."

Richard went past her and found himself in Alan O'Hagen's office. "That's some secretary you've got there."

"She's cheap," O'Hagen replied with a grin. "She's also surprisingly efficient. And I don't get too many unwanted visitors barging in."

"I can imagine," Richard muttered.

O'Hagen indicated a woman who was standing at the side of his desk. "My accountant, Mrs. Jane Adams."

She gave Richard a curt nod. Her appearance was comfortable after the girl outside; she was in her late forties, dressed in a business suit, with white hair tidied in a neat short style.

"I understand you intend to invest in Firedrake," she said.

"That's what I'm here to decide."

"Very well." She gave O'Hagen a disapproving look. "I'm not sure I should be endorsing this kind of action."

"Jane, neither of us is getting any younger. If Firedrake works out the way we expect we'll have a decent nest-egg to sell to some kombinate or media prince. Hell, even Richard here might buy me out."

"Let's take it one step at a time, shall we," Richard said. "If I could see the accounts."

With one last reluctant look at O'Hagen, Mrs. Adams handed Richard a pair of memox crystals. "They're completely up to date," she said.

He put the first crystal into the slot on his cybofax and began scrolling down the columns of figures. O'Hagen had been optimistic rather than honest when he said the company's turnover was 70,000. This year was barely over sixty, and the year before scraped in at fifty. But it was an upward trend.

"I've already identified several new software products I'd like Firedrake to promote," O'Hagen was saying. "I should be able to sign exclusivity rights for the English market on the back of this expansion project."

"May I see the painting, please?" Richard asked.

"Sure." O'Hagen picked up a slim kelpboard-wrapped package from behind his desk. Richard had been expecting something larger. This was barely forty centimeters high, thirty wide. He slipped the thin kelpboard from the front. "What is it?" he asked. The painting was mostly sky sliced by a line of white cloud, with the mound of a hill rising out of the lower right corner. Hanging in the air like some bizarre obsidian dagger was an alien spaceship, or possibly an airborne neolithic monument.

"*View of a Hill and Clouds,*" O'Hagen said contentedly. "Remarkable, isn't it? It's from McCarthy's earlier phase, before he moved from oils to refractive sculpting."

"I see." Richard pulled the kelpboard wrapping back on. "I'd like to get it valued."

"Of course." O'Hagen smiled.

Richard took the painting to the Sotheby's office in Stamford on his way back from Thistlemore Wood. The assistant was appreciative when Richard told her he wanted it valued for his house-insurance policy. She took her time, checking its authenticity before giving him an estimate. Eighteen thousand New Sterling. Once again Mr. Alan O'Hagen was being financially optimistic. But all things considered, it wasn't a bad price for endorsing the Zone 35 development.

"I think we have an agreement," he told O'Hagen over the phone the next day.

There was a chuckle from the earpiece. "I thought you'd be able to appreciate a good deal. I'll get the paperwork over to you right away."

"Very well. I'll notify the precinct's banking consortium that I have another client."

Suzi turned up mid-afternoon carrying a small leather satchel. She opened it to produce a thin folder. There were two partnership agreement contracts to sign, both dated two years previously; even his signature counter-witness was filled in and dated. Mrs. Adams, he noted.

"It says here my partner in Firedrake is Newton Holdings," Richard said.

"Yeah. So?"

"I thought it was held by Mr. O'Hagen."

"Newton belongs to him; it does his imports. You want to call him?"

He couldn't meet her impatient antagonistic stare. "No." He signed the partnership contracts.

"Mr. O'Hagen said to say you can owe him the pound for the share," Suzi said. She gathered up one copy of the contract and handed him a share certificate with his name on it: again dated two years ago.

"Tell him that's very generous of him."

She scowled and marched out of the office. Richard glanced over the certificate again, then locked it and the partnership agreement in the wall safe.

Richard was having breakfast the next morning when the police arrived, hammering so hard on the door he thought they were trying to smash it down. He opened the door wearing just his dressing gown, blinking . . . partly from confusion at the team of eight armed uniformed officers standing on his front lawn, and partly at the bright morning sunlight.

The person knocking aggressively on his paintwork identified herself as Detective Amanda Patterson, holding her police card out for him to verify.

He didn't bother to show it to his cybofax. "I don't doubt who you are," he murmured. Three cars were parked on the street outside, their blue lights flashing insistently. Neighbors were pressed up against windows watching the drama. A Globecast camera crew lurked at the end of the drive, pointing their fat black lenses at him.

"Richard Townsend?" the detective demanded.

He put on a smile as polite as circumstances would allow. "Guilty of that, at least."

"Would you please accompany me to the station, sir. I have some questions for you."

"And if I refuse?"

"I will arrest you."

"For what, exactly?"

"Your suspected involvement in the murder of Byrne Tyler."

Richard stared at her in astonishment, then managed to gather some dignity. "I hate to ask you this in such a public arena." He indicated the camera crew. "But are you quite sure you have the right house?"

"Oh yes, sir. I have the right house. It's yours."

"Very well. May I at least get dressed first?"

"Yes, sir. One of my male colleagues will accompany you."

He gave a grunt of surprise as he realized just how serious she was. "I think I'd like my one phone call now as well."

"That's America's Miranda rights, sir. But you're certainly free to call a solicitor if you think you require one."

"I don't require one to establish my innocence," Richard snapped. "I simply wish to sue you into your grave. You have no idea how much trouble this mistake will bring down on your head."

Richard suspected the layout of the interview room at Oakham police station was deliberately designed to depress its occupants. Straight psychological assault on the subconscious. Drab light-brown walls shimmered harshly under the glare from the two biolum panels in the ceiling. The gray-steel desk in front of him vibrated softly, a cranky harmonic instigated by the buzzing air-conditioning grille.

He'd been in there for twenty minutes alone, dourly contemplating this ludicrous situation, before the door opened and Jodie Dobson came in.

"About time," he barked at her. "Can I go now?"

She gave him a sober look. "No, Richard. This isn't some case of mistaken identity. I've been talking to Detective Patterson, and they really do think you had something to do with Byrne Tyler's murder."

"That's insane! I've never even met him."

"I know, and I'm sure we can clear it up with a simple interview."

"I want that Patterson cow sued for doing this to me. They tipped off the news team. I'll have my face plastered all over the media. Do you know what kind of damage that'll do to me? Business is about trust, credibility. I can't believe this! She's ruined five years' hard work in five minutes. It was deliberate and malicious."

"It's not that bad. Listen, the quicker you're out and cleared, the quicker we can instigate damage limitation."

"I want her to make a public apology, starting with that news crew that was outside my bloody house."

"We can probably get that. But you'll need to cooperate. Fully."

"Fine, bring them on!" He caught the tone in her voice. "What do you mean?"

"They've brought in some kind of specialist they want to sit in on your interview. Greg Mandel, he's a gland psychic."

Richard hoped his flinch wasn't too visible. There were stories about gland psychics. Nothing a rational adult need concern themselves about, of course. Human psi ability was a strictly scientific field these days, quantified and researched. A bioware endocrine gland implanted in the brain released specific neurohormones to stimulate the ability. But . . . "Why do they want him to interview me?"

"*Help* interview you," Jodie stressed. "Apparently his speciality is sensing emotional states. In other words he'll know if you're lying."

"So if I just say that I didn't kill this Byrne Tyler, Mandel will know I'm being truthful?"

"That's the way it works."

"Okay. But I still want Patterson nailed afterward."

Richard gave Mandel a close look when he entered the interview room. Approaching middle age, but obviously in shape. The man's movements were very . . . precise moving the chair *just so* to sit on rather than casually pulling it out from the desk as most people would Richard supposed it was like a measure of confidence and Mandel seemed very self-assured. It was an attitude very similar to Alan O'Hagen's.

Amanda Patterson seated herself beside Mandel, and slotted a couple of matte-black memox crystals into the twin AV recording deck.

"Interview with Richard Townsend," Patterson said briskly. "Conducted by myself, Detective Patterson, with the assistance of CID advisory specialist Greg Mandel. Mr. Townsend has elected to have his solicitor present."

"I did not kill Byrne Tyler," Richard said. He stared at Mandel. "Is that true?"

"In as far as it goes," Mandel said.

"Thank you!" he sat back and fixed Patterson with a belligerent expression.

"However, I think we need to examine the subject in a little more detail before giving you a completely clean slate," Mandel said.

"If you must."

Mandel gave Patterson a small nod. She opened her cybofax and studied the display screen. "Are you are a partner in the Firedrake company, Mr. Townsend?" she asked.

"What?"

"A company called Firedrake, do you own half of the shares?"

"Well, yes. One share, fifty percent. But that's nothing to do with Byrne Tyler. It's a venture with a . . . a business colleague."

"Who is that?" Mandel asked.

"Not that it's anything to do with you or this murder enquiry, but his name is Alan O'Hagen."

"Interesting," Detective Patterson said. "The other listed shareholder in Firedrake is Newton Holdings."

"Well, yes, that's O'Hagen's company."

"No, Mr. Townsend. According to the companies register, Newton Holdings is owned by Byrne Tyler."

Richard gave Jodie a desperate look. She frowned.

Detective Patterson consulted her cybofax again. "You've been partners for two years, is that right?"

"I . . . I've been a partner with Mr. O'Hagen for two years, yes." He couldn't help the way his eyes glanced at Mandel. The psychic was watching him impassively. "Not Byrne Tyler. I've never met him. Never."

"Really?" Patterson's tone was highly skeptical. "Have you ever visited the Sotheby's office in Stamford?"

Richard hooked a finger around his shirt collar; the air-conditioning wasn't making any impression on the heat suddenly evaporating off his skin. O'Hagen! O'Hagen had scammed him. But how? He wasn't a fool, he hadn't paid O'Hagen any money, quite the opposite. The painting . . . Which the police obviously knew about. "Yes, I've been there."

"Recently?"

"Earlier this week actually. I think you know that, though, don't you? I was having an item of mine valued for insurance purposes."

"Was that item a painting?" Mandel asked.

"Yes."

"And didn't you also confirm its authenticity while you were there?"

"I suppose so, the assistant had to make sure it was genuine before she valued it. That's standard."

"And the painting definitely belongs to you?"

"It does."

Mandel turned to Patterson. "Well, that's true."

"Of course it is, I was given it some time ago by Mr. O'Hagen," Richard said. "It was a gift. He will confirm that."

"I shall be very interested in talking to this Mr. O'Hagen," Patterson said. "That's if you can ever produce him for us." She turned her cybofax around so Richard could see the screen, it held the image of *View of a Hill and Clouds*. "Is this the painting, Mr. Townsend?"

"Yes it is."

"For the record, *View of a Hill and Clouds* by Sean McCarthy belongs to Byrne Tyler. The artist was a friend of the deceased. It was stolen from his apartment, presumably at the same time that he was murdered."

"No," Richard hissed. "Look, okay, listen. I'd never even heard of Firedrake until this week. Taking me on as a partner was a way of proving its viability to the banks. O'Hagen wanted a loan from them, that was the only way he could get it. We fixed it to look like I'd been a partner for two years."

"Richard," Jodie warned.

"I'm being set up," he yelled at her. "Can't you see?"

"Set up for what?" Patterson asked; she sounded intrigued.

"Byrne Tyler's murder—that's what I'm in here for, isn't it? For Christ's sake. O'Hagen's rigged this so it looks like I was involved."

"Why would Mr. O'Hagen want to do that to you?"

"I don't fucking know. I've never met him before."

"Mr. Townsend."

Mandel's voice made Richard lurch upright. "Yes?"

"You've never killed anyone yourself, but did you ever pay a man to eliminate somebody for you?"

Richard gaped at the psychic. In his head a panicked voice was yelling *oh shit oh shit oh shit*. Mandel would be able to hear it, to taste the wretched knowledge. His own shock-induced paralysis was twisting the emotion to an excruciating level. He thought his head was going to burst open from the stress.

Mandel gave him a sad, knowing smile and said: "Guilty."

Two—A Suspicious Fall

Detective Amanda Patterson had never visited Bisbrooke before. It was a tiny village tucked away along the side of a deep valley just outside Uppingham. Unremarkable and uneventful even by Rutland's standards, which made it a contender for dullest place in Europe. Until today, that is, when one of the uniforms had responded to a semi-hysterical call from a cleaning agency operative, and confirmed the existence of a body with associated suspicious circumstances.

The unseasonal rain beat down heavily as she drove over from Oakham, turning the road into a dangerous skid-rink. Then she had almost missed the turning off the A47. As it happened, that was the least of her navigational worries.

"Call him again," she told Alison Weston. The probationary detective was sitting in the passenger seat beside her, squinting through the fogged-up windscreen trying to locate some landmark.

"No way. Uniform will crap themselves laughing at us if I ask for directions," Alison complained. "It's got to be here somewhere. There can't be more than five buildings in the whole godforsaken village."

Amanda let it go. Hailstones were falling with the rain now, their impacts making clacking sounds on the car's bodywork. She braked at yet another T-junction.

Bisbrooke was woven together by a lacework of roads barely wide enough for a single vehicle. They all curved sharply, making her nervous about oncoming cars, and they were all sunk into earthen gullies topped with hedges of thick bamboo that had been planted to replace the long-dead privet and hawthorn of the previous century. With the rain and hail pummeling the windscreen, it was perilously close to driving blind. The only clue they were even in the village was the occasional glimpse of ancient stone cottages and brick bungalows huddled at the end of gravelled drives.

"You must be able to see the church," she said. The address they had been given was in Church Lane.

Alison scanned the swaying tops of the bamboo shoots. "No." She gave her cybofax an instruction, and it produced a satnav map with their location given as a small pink dot. "Okay, try that one, down there on the left."

Amanda edged the car cautiously along the short stretch of road where Alison was pointing. The tarmac was reduced to a pair of tire tracks separated by a rich swathe of emerald moss.

"Finally!" The junction ahead had a small street sign for Church Lane; a white-painted iron rectangle almost overgrown by a flamboyant purple clematis. This road was even narrower. It led them past the village church, a squat building made from rust-colored stone that had long since been converted into accommodation units for refugee families.

The lane ran on past a big old farmhouse, and ended at a new building perched on the end of the village. Church Vista Apartments. Its design was pure Californian-Italian, completely out of place in the heart of rural England. Five luxury apartments sharing a single long building with a stable block and multi-port garage forming a courtyard at the rear. Climbing roses planted along the walls hadn't grown halfway up their trellises yet.

There was a tall security gate in the courtyard wall. Amanda held her police identity card up to the key, and it swung open for her. A police car and the cleaning agency van were parked on the cobbles beyond. Amanda drew up next to them. The rain was easing off.

They moved briskly over the cobbles to the door of apartment three. One of the uniforms was standing just inside, holding the heavy glass-and-wood door open. She didn't have to flash her card at him, as Rutland's police force was small enough for them all to know each other.

"Morning, Rex," she said as she hurried into the small hallway. He nodded politely as she shook the water from her jacket. "What have we got?"

"Definitely a corpse."

Alison slipped in and immediately blew her cheeks out. Her breath materialized in the air in front of her. "God, it's bloody freezing in here."

"Air-conditioning's on full," Rex said. "I left it that way, I'm afraid. Scene-of-crime, and all that."

"Good," Amanda muttered, not meaning it. The chill air was blowing over her wet clothes, giving her goosebumps.

Rex led them into the apartment. It was open-plan downstairs, a single space with white walls and terra-cotta tile flooring, Mexican blackwood cabinets and shelving were lined up around the edges. There were pictures hanging on every wall; prints, chalk and charcoal sketches, oils, watercolors, silver-patina photographs. Most of them featured young female nudes. Three big plump cream-colored leather settees formed a conversation area in the middle, surrounding a Persian rug. A woman in the cleaning agency's mauve tunic sat on one of the settees, looking shaken.

The front of the room was twice the height of the back. Wide wrought-iron stairs curved up to a balcony which ran the entire width, giving access to all the upstairs rooms. A sheer window wall in front of the balcony flooded the whole area with light.

The corpse lay at the foot of the stairs. A man in his mid-to-late twenties, wearing a pale gray dressing gown, his legs akimbo on the tiles, head twisted at a nasty angle. Some blood had dribbed from his nose. It was dry and flaking now.

There were three air-conditioning grilles set in the edge of the balcony. One of them was right above the corpse, blowing a stream of the frosty air directly over him.

"He fell down the stairs?" Alison asked.

"Looks like it," Rex said.

"So was it a fall, or a push?" Amanda wondered out loud.

"I had a quick look around upstairs," Rex said. "No sign of any struggle. The main bed's been used, but everything seems to be in place as far as I can tell."

Amanda wrinkled her nose up. There was a faint smell in the air, unpleasant and familiar. "How long's he been here?"

"Possibly a day," Rex said.

Alison gestured at the window wall. "And nobody saw him?"

"One-way glass," Amanda said. It had that slight give away gray tint. She stared through it, understanding why the apartments had been built here. The last of the rainclouds had drifted away, allowing the hot sun to shine down. It was a magnificent view out over the junction of two broad rolling grassland valleys. In the distance she could see an antique windmill, its wooden sail painted white. A long communal garden stretched out ahead of her, a paddock beyond that. There was a circular swimming pool twenty meters away, surrounded by a flagstone patio. Wooden-slat sun loungers were clustered around stripy parasols.

"All right," she said wearily. "Let's do the preliminary assessment."

Alison opened her cybofax. "When was the body discovered?"

"Approximately 8:45 this morning," Rex nodded toward the cleaning woman. "Helen?"

"That's right," the woman stammered. "I saw him — Mr. Tyler — as soon as I came in. I called the police right away."

Amanda pursed her lips and knelt down beside the body. The handsome face had quite a few resonances for her. Byrne Tyler. She remembered him mainly from *Marina Days*, a soap set amid Peterborough's yachting fraternity—though 90 percent of it was shot in the studio with the all-action boating sequences cooked on a graphics mainframe. That had been five or six years ago; Byrne played a teenage hunk crewman. But he had left and gone onto star in action-thriller dramas and interactives. Pretty bad ones if she remembered her tabloid gossip right. There would be media attention with this one.

She stood up. "Helen, was the door locked when you arrived?"

"Yes. And the alarm was on. I have the code, and my palm is one of the keys. Mr. Tyler was happy with that. He was a nice man. He always gave me a Christmas bonus.

"I'm sure he was lovely. Did you do all his cleaning?"

"Yes. Twice a week. Tuesday and Friday."

"Which means he could have been here since Tuesday. She rubbed her arms, trying to generate some warmth. "Rex, go see if the air-conditioning was set like this or it's glitched. Alison, look around for empty bottles, or anything else," she said pointedly. It could so easily be an accident. Drunk, stoned, or even sober, a fall could happen. And God knows what a showbiz type like Tyler would take for amusement in the privacy of his secluded secure home.

Amanda went upstairs to check the main bedroom. The door was open, revealing a huge circular waterbed with a black silk sheet over the mattress: there was no top sheet. An equally large mirror was fixed to the ceiling above it. She shook her head in bemusement at the stereotyping. Exactly the kind of seduction chamber a list celebrity sex symbol was expected to have. She remembered most of his scenes in *Marina Days* involved him being stripped to the waist, or wearing tight T-shirts.

Apart from the offensive decor, there was nothing overtly suspicious. A slower look and she realized the sheet was rumpled, pillows were scattered about. She stared. One person wouldn't mess up a bed that much, surely? On the bedside cabinet was a champagne bottle turned upside down in a silver ice bucket, a single cut-crystal flute beside it.

When she went back downstairs, Rex told her the air-conditioning was set at maximum. Alison was wearing plastic gloves; she held up a clear zip bag with a silver-plated infuser in it.

"Damn," Amanda grunted. "Okay, call the scene-of-crime team, and forensic. Let's find out exactly what happened here. And tell the uniform division we'll need help to cordon off the area."

Forty minutes later, Denzil Osborne drove up in the forensic team's white van. Alone. Amanda always found Denzil immensely reassuring. It was probably the phlegmatic way the forensic officer treated crime scenes when he arrived. Nothing ever fazed him.

"Where's the scene-of-crime team?" she asked as soon as he eased his huge frame out of the van.

"Vernon says he wants hard evidence there's been a crime before he'll authorize that kind of expense."

Amanda felt her cheeks reddening. All those orders she'd snapped out in front of Alison were making her look stupid now, empty wishes showing where the true authority in the police force lay. England's police had got rid of the PSP political officers observing their cases for ideological soundness, only for the New Conservatives to replace them all with accountants. She wasn't sure which was worse.

"And the uniform division?"

He winked broadly. "You've got Rex, haven't you?"

"Sod it," she snarled. "Come on, this way."

Denzil took one look at Byrne Tyler's sprawled body and said: "Ah yes, I see why you wanted forensic now. Of course, I'm no expert, but I think he may have fallen down the stairs."

She stuck her hands on her hips. "I want to know if he was pushed. I also want to know if he was even alive up on the balcony when it happened."

Denzil put his case on the floor beside Tyler, and lowered his bulk down next to it, wincing as his knees creaked.

"And you should lose some weight," she said.

"Come horizontal jogging with me—I'd lose kilos every night."

"That's sexual harassment." She just managed to keep a straight face in front of Alison.

He grinned wildly. "Yes please."

"Just tell me what happened here."

Denzil opened his case, revealing a plethora of specialist 'ware modules. He pulled on some tight plastic gloves before selecting a sensor wand which he waved over the dead man's face: then he stopped and peered closer. "Ah, a celebrity death. Best kind. Did you see his last? *Night Squad III: Descent of Angels.* Saving the world from card-carrying terrorists yet again. There was some cool helijets in that. They had nuclear-pumped X-ray lasers; cut clean thorough buildings."

Chuckling, Denzil resumed his scan of Tyler's face. "Shame about the air-conditioning," he said. "I can't work a simple temperature assessment on him."

"That's what made me wonder," Amanda said. "If he did get pushed then we won't be able to pinpoint the time very easily."

"Hmm. Maybe not pinpoint, but let's try something a little more detailed." Denzil replaced the sensor wand and took another cylinder from his case. It had a needle fifteen centimeters long protruding from one end, which Denzil slowly inserted into Tyler's abdomen then withdrew equally carefully. "Anything else immediately suspicious?"

Alison held up the zip bag with the infuser, and another bag with vials. "We think he was infusing this. Probably syntho."

"Where have you been, young lady? I'll have you know, it's dreampunch this season for the glitterati. Couple of levels up from syntho, it's supposed to stimulate your pleasure center and memories at the same time. Every hit a wet dream."

"Can you walk around when you're tripping it?" Alison asked.

"Okay, good point. They normally just crash out and drool a lot."

"I'll need DNA samples from the bed as well," Amanda said. "I think he had someone up there before he died."

Denzil gave her a curious look. "Vernon won't give you the budget for that kind of workover. I'm just authorized for a body analysis, determine cause of death, that kind of thing."

"Just do what you can for me, okay."

"Okay. CID's paying." The cylinder with the needle bleeped, and he consulted the graphics displayed on its screen. "According to cellular decay, he died sometime on Wednesday night, between 2200 hours and 1:30."

"That's a big window. Is that the best you can give me?"

"I always give you my best, Amanda. That's the preliminary, anyway. Let me get him into the lab and I can probably shave half an hour off that for you. The delay and this bloody arctic temperature doesn't help."

Amanda stood up and turned to Alison. "There's some reasonable security 'ware here. See what kind of records are available for this week, especially Wednesday evening. Rex, take a full statement from Helen, and let her go. And I want this place sealed as soon as the body's removed. We'll get authority to run a proper site examination eventually."

"You really think this was a murder?" Denzil asked.

"Too many things are wrong," Amanda said. "Somebody told me once: there's no such thing as coincidence."

Inspector Vernon Langley was putting his jacket on when Amanda walked into his small shabby office. He took one look at her, slumped his shoulders and groaned. "I'm due out for lunch," he said defensively.

"I was due a scene-of-crime team," she shot back.

"All right." He sat back behind his desk and waved her into a spare seat. "Amanda, you know we're severely restricted on how much we can spend on each case. Some syntho-head fell down stairs. Bag him up and notify the relatives."

"I think he was murdered."

Vernon grimaced. "Not the air-conditioning, please."

"Not by itself, no. But Denzil scanned the control box. No fingerprints. It had been wiped clean with a damp kitchen cloth."

"Means nothing. The cleaning lady could have done that on her last visit."

"Unlikely. Vernon, you just don't have the air-conditioning on that cold, not for days at a time. I also had Alison check the security 'ware. A car left at 23:13, Wednesday night—a Rover Ingalo registered to Claire Sullivan. It's loaded into Church Vista Apartments security list as an approved visitor for Byrne Tyler, so the gate opens automatically for it. Alison's mining the Home Office circuit for Sullivan now."

Vernon scratched at his chin. "I took a look at Denzil's preliminary file; time of death is very loose. This Sullivan woman will simply claim Tyler was alive when she left."

"Of course she will," Amanda said with a hint of irritation. "That doesn't mean we don't ask her."

Vernon looked unhappy.

"Oh, *come on*," she exclaimed.

"All right. I'll give you the time to interview her. But you don't get anything else without a positive result."

"Well, hey, thanks."

"I'm sorry, Amanda," he gave her a resigned smile. "Things just ain't what they used to be around here."

"Someone like Byrne Tyler is bound to have crime insurance coverage. We'll get the money to investigate properly. It won't even come out of your budget."

Vernon's mood darkened still further. "I'm sure he has coverage. Unlike seventy percent of the population."

Alison had tracked down Claire Sullivan's address, which was in Uppingham. She had also prepared quite a briefing file for Amanda, most of it mined from tabloid databases.

Amanda let the probationary detective drive to the Sullivan bungalow as she scanned the file on her cybofax. "Tyler was engaged to Tamzin Sullivan?"

"Yep, Claire's big sister. She's a model, got a contract with the Dermani house. Mainly on the back of the publicity she and Tyler were getting. They've hit the show-biz party trail extensively since the engagement was announced. You open your front door in the morning, and they'll be there for it. On their own, neither of them was important enough to get an image on the gossip 'casts; together they rate airtime. It helps that they have the same management agency."

Amanda looked at the image of Tamzin the screen was showing, posed for a Dermani advert, bracelet and earring accessories for a stupidly priced couture dress. The girl was beautiful, certainly, but it was a lofty beauty implying arrogance.

"So what's her little sister doing at her fiancé's house in the middle of the night?"

"One guess," Alison said dryly. "I always used to be jealous of my sister's boy-friends. And Byrne was no saint. I didn't load the real gutter-press reports for you, but they say he got fired from *Marina Days* because he couldn't leave the girls alone."

Amanda scrolled down the file to Claire. The girl was eighteen, a first-year medical student at DeMontfort University. Still living at home with her mother. The university fees were paid by her father as part of a child-maintenance agreement. He lived in Australia. Amanda skipped to the mother: Margina Sullivan.

Pre-judgment went against the nature of Amanda's training, but Margina's record made it difficult to avoid. She had three children, each with a different father each of whom was wealthy enough to support their offspring with independent schooling and an allowance. The Inland Revenue had no employment record for Margina Sullivan. Her tax returns (always filed late) listed a couple of small trust funds as her income source. She owned the bungalow in Uppingham where she lived along with Claire, Tamzin, and Daniel, her nine-year-old son; but her credit rating was dismal.

By the time they arrived at the address, an image of Margina had swollen into Amanda's mind, hardening like concrete: aging brittle harridan.

The Sullivan bungalow was just beyond the center of town, in the middle of a pleasant estate dominated by old evergreen pines which had survived the climate change. The wood and brick structure itself was well-maintained, with glossy paintwork and a roof of new solar panels, but the garden clearly hadn't seen any attention for years. Two cars were parked outside: a BMW so old it probably had a combustion engine, with flat tires and bleached paintwork hosting blooms of moss; next to it was a smart little scarlet and black Ingalo, a modern giga-conductor powered runabout that was proving popular as a first car for wealthy young trendies.

Margina Sullivan opened the door. Amanda assumed they had caught her going out; she was wearing some extravagant dress complemented by a white shawl cardigan. Heavy makeup labored to re-create the youthfulness of what was undeniably an attractive face. Not a single bottle-red hair was out of alignment from her iron-hard curled beret style. She put a hand theatrically on her chest when shown Amanda's police ID card and *oohed* breathlessly. The phoney concern changed to shock and barely concealed anger when Amanda regretfully informed her of Byrne Tyler's death. Margina hurried over to the drinks cabinet and poured herself a large Scotch.

"How am I going to tell Tamzin?" she gulped. Another shot of whiskey was poured. "God in heaven, what are we going to do? *Starlight* was paying for a bloody wedding exclusive, not a funeral."

A curious way of expressing grief, Amanda thought. She kept quiet, looking around the lounge. It was chintzy, with lavender cloths covering every table and sideboard, tassels dangling from their overhanging edges. Figurines from the kind of adverts found in the most downmarket weekend datatext channels stood on every surface. Tall, high-definition pictures of Tamzin looked down serenely from each wall, campaigns for a dozen different fashion products. Amanda would have liked to be dismissive, but the girl really was very beautiful. Healthy vitality was obviously The Look right now.

Claire and Daniel came in, wanting to know what was happening. Amanda studied the younger girl as her perturbed mother explained. Claire didn't have anything like her elder sister's poise, nor was there much resemblance—which was understandable enough. She had sandy hair rather than lush raven; her narrow face had a thin mouth instead of wide full lips; and her figure was a great deal fuller than that of the lean athlete. Nor was there any of Tamzin's ice-queen polish, just a mild sulkiness.

Daniel was different again . . . wide-eyed and cute, with a basin-cut mop of chestnut hair. Like every nine-year-old, he could not stay still. Even when told of Tyler's death he clung to his sister and shivered restlessly. The affection between the siblings was touching. It was Claire who soothed and comforted him rather than his mother. Amanda's attitude hardened still further when Margina went for yet another shot of whiskey.

"Where is Tamzin at the moment?" Alison asked.

"Paris," Margina sniffed. "She has a runway assignment tonight. I must call Colin at Hothouse—they're her agents; he can arrange for her to be flown home. We'll release a statement on the tragedy from here."

"A statement?"

"To the media," Margina said irritably. "Hothouse will see to it."

"Perhaps you should call the Hothouse people now," Amanda said. "In the meantime I have some questions which I need to ask Claire."

Margina gave her a puzzled glance. "What questions?"

Amanda steeled herself. This wasn't going to be pleasant. She could do the preliminary interview with the girl here or at the station. Either way, Margina, and after that Tamzin, would find out why. I'm not a social worker, she told herself. "We think Claire might have been the last person to see Mr. Tyler alive."

"Impossible," Margina insisted. "You said he died at home." She rounded on Claire. "What does she mean?"

The girl hung her head sullenly. "I saw Byrne on Wednesday evening."

"Why?"

"Because he was screwing me," Claire suddenly yelled. "All right? He'd been screwing me for months. How the hell do you think I bought my car? From the money my loving father gives me?" She burst into tears. Daniel hugged her tighter, and she gripped at him in reflex.

Margina's mouth opened. She stood absolutely still, staring at her daughter in disbelief. "You're lying. You little bitch. You're lying!"

"I am not!" Claire shouted back.

Amanda stepped between them, holding her hands up. "That's enough. Claire, you're going to have to come to the station with us."

The girl nodded.

"You could have ruined everything," Margina cried shrilly. "Everything! You stupid stupid bitch. You've got a whole university full of men to sleep around with. What the hell were you thinking of?"

"Don't you ever care about anyone but yourself? Ever? You don't know anything, you're just an ignorant old fraud."

"I said: enough," Amanda told them. "Mrs. Sullivan, we can arrange for a social case officer to counsel you and Tamzin if you would like."

Margina was still glaring at Claire, her breathing irregular. "Don't be absurd," she said contemptuously. "I'm not having a failed psychology graduate asking me impertinent questions as if I were some feeble-brained dole dependant. Colin will take care of everything we require."

"As you wish," Amanda said calmly.

Amanda decided to question the girl in her office rather than the station interview room. It was marginally less inhospitable. She got her a cup of tea, and even managed to find some biscuits in one of the desk drawers.

Claire didn't pay any attention, she sat with her head in her hands.

"Did you love him?" Amanda asked tenderly.

"Ha! Is that what you think?"

"I don't know. I'm asking."

"Of course I didn't love him." Her head came up abruptly, a worried expression on her face. "But I didn't kill him."

"Okay. So tell me why you were having a relationship with him?"

"It wasn't a relationship. He seduced me. I suppose. We'd gone to see Tamzin at a fashion show in Peterborough this Easter. He fixed it somehow that I was driven back home in his limo. It was just him and me. I'd had a lot to drink."

"Did he rape you?"

Claire gave a helpless grimace. "No. He was interested in me. That's never . . . Tamzin was always the one. She's *always* been the one. It's like she was born with two people's luck. Everything happens for her. She's so pretty and glamorous. Byrne Tyler was her boyfriend. I mean, *Byrne*. I used to watch him on *Marina Days*."

"So you were flattered, and it was exciting."

"Suppose so."

"And afterward? Then what happened?"

"He said he wanted to keep seeing me."

"You mean to have sex?"

Claire blushed and hung her head. "Yes."

"So you went back? Voluntarily?"

"Mum's really frightened, you know? You wouldn't be able to tell, not with her. She doesn't let anyone see. But she is. We don't have any money; mum's in debt to dozens of shops, just for food half the time. We can't get credit anywhere locally anymore—no bank will issue her with a card. Tamzin . . . well she can look after all of us. Since she met Byrne her career is really taking off. She earns tons of money."

"So what did Byrne Tyler tell you?"

"He said to just keep things going the way they were. That he'd never tell Tamzin as long as he was happy, and everything would stay the same."

"And he bought you the car?"

Yes. It was so I could drive out to Bisbrooke whenever he wanted me. He used to call me in the evenings, when Tamzin was away on an assignment. I'd tell mum I had late study at DeMontfort. It's not like she'd know any different."

"And you were there on Wednesday evening?"

"Yes," she whispered.

"When did you arrive?"

"About nine o'clock."

"And you left when?"

"Just after eleven."

"And Byrne Tyler was alive when you left?"

"Yes! I swear it. I left him in bed. I got dressed and went home."

"Was there anyone else there with you?"

"No. Just me."

"Claire, do you remember if it was cold in the apartment that night?"

"No. It never is. Byrne didn't like sheets or duvets on the bed. He always kept the bedroom warm enough so he didn't have to use them."

Amanda noted that in her cybofax. "Interesting. I need to know about the bedroom, I'm afraid. Did you have champagne up there that night?"

"Yes."

"We only found one glass. Isn't that a bit odd?"

"Oh." Claire looked hard at the top of the desk. "I have the glass. Byrne liked to . . . well, he poured some on me."

"I see. Did he say if he was meeting anyone else after you left?"

"No. Nothing like that."

"Had he met anyone before you arrived?"

"I don't know. He never said."

Amanda sighed, resisting the impulse to reach out and grip the girl's shoulder in reassurance. "Sounds like you've had a pretty rough few months."

"It wasn't that . . . I know it all sounds awful. He really liked me, though. You must think I'm some dreadful cheap tart."

"I don't think that at all. But what I'd like to do is refer you to a counsellor. I think you could do with someone to talk to right now."

"Maybe. Do I have to?"

"No. But I'd like you to think about it."

"I will. Can I go now?"

"Just about finished. I'll need a DNA sample from you to eliminate any traces we find at the apartment. After that you're free to go."

"Why do you need that?"

"Because this is now a murder investigation."

"Why is it murder?" Vernon asked.

"Claire claims the air-conditioning was operating normally when she left."

"Tyler could have changed it."

"We've been over this. That temperature isn't one you can live in. The only reason to change it is to fudge the time of the murder. And the controls were wiped. The murderer did that."

"All right, damnit. I've done some background data-work for you. He was insured by his management agenda and we now have reasonable doubt. I'll squirt the appropriate information off to them. We should get a response fairly quickly."

"Thank you. I'd like a scene-of-crime team to look at the apartment, and a full autopsy."

"I can give you that now."

"Great. I'll also need full access to all of Tyler's financial and personal data. Alison can start running it through some analysis programs."

"Okay, I'll have a magistrate sign the order this evening." Vernon fixed her with a thoughtful stare. "Did the girl do it?"

"She certainly had the motive. She was there around the time it happened. Unless we can put someone else at the scene, she's the obvious choice." She caught his troubled expression. "What?"

"I don't get it. She was smart enough to lower the temperature, so she must have realized everyone would find out she was sleeping with Tyler. Why not simply say he slipped, that it was an accident?"

"Guilt. Plain and simple. Trying to cover her tracks. You can see it in the way she talks. She's cautious about every word that comes out of her mouth, as if she'll give herself away just by speaking."

"Okay, Amanda, if you say so."

The next morning Amanda caught the Tyler story on Globecast's breakfast news. She was smoking an extremely illicit cigarette, trying to calm herself for the day to come. Tyler didn't rate much time: archive footage of him arriving at some glitzy party with Tamzin on his arm; the fact they were engaged, and she was believed to be flying home to be with her family; and a mention that the police investigation was ongoing, hinting that officers considered the circumstances unusual.

How do they find out so quickly? she wondered.

Amanda checked in at the station first, mainly to make sure there were no problems with Alison's analysis. The probationary detective gave her a grumpy look from behind her desk. Four terminal cubes were full of what looked like Inland Revenue datawork as she used her court access order to pull in details from his accountant, agent, solicitor and banks. Apparently Byrne Tyler's financial affairs were complex to the point of obscurity, not helped by the way showbusiness used accounting methods unknown to the rest of the human race. Amanda told her to concentrate on finding out if he had any large debts, and to confirm that he had bought the Ingalo for Claire.

With that part of the investigation on line she was ready to drive up to the apartment and supervise forensic's sweep. Vernon brought Mike Wilson to see her before she could get away. Wilson was from Crescent Insurance, who provided cover for Tyler. A real smoothy, she thought as they were introduced. Late thirties, in a smart blue-gray business suit at least two levels above a detective's price range, ginger hair neatly trimmed, a body he had kept in condition without being an obvious gym-rat. She didn't think he'd had any cosmetic alteration, his cheeks were slightly too puffy; but he certainly used too much aftershave.

"How much coverage did Tyler have?" she asked.

"His agency had taken out a full investigatory package," Mike Wilson said. "Whatever it takes to get the culprit into court and secure a conviction."

"Sounds good to me. Just give us your credit account details, we'll invoice you."

Wilson's smile was tolerant. "I'm afraid it's not that simple. We like to see first hand what our money is being spent on."

She gave Vernon a tight you're-kidding-me look. He smiled in retaliation. "Mike Wilson will be assigned to your team for the duration of the investigation."

"As what?"

"I have worked on a number of police cases," Wilson said. "I appreciate you don't want what you regard as outside interference—"

"Bloody right I don't."

"—however, the facts are that I can offer immediate access to considerable specialist resources such as forensic labs and database mining, which the police have to outsource anyway. And I'm certainly happy to finance any reasonable police deployment, like the scene of crime search. That goes without question."

"How active do you see your helpful role?"

"I only offer advice when I'm asked for it. It's your investigation, Detective."

Her terminal bleeped for attention. Mike Wilson and Vernon Langley watched expectantly. Without making too big a deal of it, Amanda sat behind her desk and pulled the call through. It was Denzil.

"I have good news and good news," he said. "From your point of view anyway, if not Byrne Tyler's."

"What did you find?"

"Narcotic toxicology was minimal, except for a very recent infusion of Laynon. Our boy was improving his bedtime performance that night, but nothing more. But there were plenty of residual traces. He's a regular and longtime user of several proscribed drugs. However he didn't have enough of anything in his bloodstream to impede locomotion or cause disorientation at the time he died."

"The champagne?"

"Minimal alcohol level, he couldn't have drunk more than half a glass."

"Thanks, Denzil. What else?"

"Dried saliva trails on his skin. And small scrapings of skin under two finger-nails."

"They must be from Claire." She glanced up at Mike Wilson, raising an eye-brow. He gave a small bow. "Run a DNA comparison for me, Denzil."

"Yeah, I heard we got money." His image vanished from the screen.

Wilson gave Vernon a meaningful look. "If it is the sister, the tabloid channels are going to have a feeding frenzy."

Amanda made an effort at conversation on the drive up to Bisbrooke. It wasn't that Wilson was unlikable; but her instinct was that he had no place on the investigation. Of course, intellectually, she appreciated his presence was due to social injustice rather than politics. External funding was a factor she would have to accept, especially in the future.

With the body gone and the air-conditioning back to normal, the apartment had lost its cheerless quality. Two scene-of-crime officers were moving methodi-cally through the ground floor, examining every surface with a variety of sensor wands. Rex was out in the courtyard, taking statements from the neighbors.

"What do you need to move for a prosecution?" Mike Wilson asked as they took a look at the cast-iron stairs.

"Basically, a lack of any other suspects. I expect the prosecution service will accept she changed the air-conditioning. She is a medical student, after all."

"So you'll interview his friends to see if anyone threatened him?"

"Friends, his agency, people he worked with. The usual. I'd love to try and track down his supplier, as well. But that would really cost you—they don't exactly rush out of the woodwork at times like these."

He gave a small grin. "I know."

"Previous case?"

"Crescent insures a lot of celebrity types. Having dealt with them before, I can see why we set the premiums so high."

"Really?" Amanda was wondering if he was going to let any gossip loose when her cybofax bleeped. Denzil's face appeared on the screen with an indecently malicious expression. "What?" she asked cautiously.

"The saliva is Claire's. The skin under the fingertips is not."

"Oh bugger," she groaned. Even so, some part of her was glad Claire had possibly been cleared. Although she was still convinced the girl was hiding some-thing. "Run a match through the central criminal records at the Home Office." She didn't even consult Mike Wilson with that one.

"Already running," Denzil said. "Plot getting thicker, huh?"

"Yeah, right." She ended the call.

Wilson was looking up at the top of the stairs. "So what do you think? Skin scrape from whoever pushed him."

"Looks that way. One last desperate grasp as he started to fall." She walked over to the red outline of the body on the terracotta tiles, and turned a full circle. "So what else have we got? No sign yet of a forced entry, which implies either the security 'ware let them through or it was a professional hit and they could burn through the system without a trace."

"Pushing someone off the top of the stairs isn't a widely used assassination method. It's heat-of-the-moment. Which fits."

"Fits what?"

"Someone turned up just after Claire left. A friend, or someone he knew. He let them in. There was an argument. It would also explain the air-conditioning. If it was a professional hit, then whoever did that wouldn't need to confuse the time of death, it wouldn't matter to them. For some reason, our murderer still cares about messing with the time."

"Still doesn't fit. If it was a friend, then the security 'ware would have an admissions record. There was nobody."

"We'd better have it checked very thoroughly, then. Get into the base management program and see if there's any sign of tampering."

Amanda nodded. "You have somebody who can do that?"

"Oh yes."

"While they're at it, make sure they enhance the surveillance picture of the Ingalo when it left, I'd like to confirm no one was inside along with Claire."

"Fair enough. What else do you need?"

She gestured out of the window wall. "Unless it was a real professional who yomped in over the fields, the only way to get here is to drive through the village. And believe me, that's not so easy. Bisbrooke is small, and confusing. The villagers would know all about strange cars. I want a door-to-door enquiry asking if any of them saw anything that night, any cars they didn't recognize, as well as full interviews with the neighboring apartments."

"That's a lot of labor-intensive groundwork. Could we just wait and see if the DNA register comes up with anything first?"

"Okay. We need the other angle anyway. This will give us some time."

"Other angle?"

"The motive, Mike. Personal, or financial, or professional jealousy, whatever . . . We need to start the good old-fashioned process of elimination. So, you get your expert here to examine the security 'ware, and I'll get back to the station and give Alison a hand with Tyler's finances."

It was late afternoon when Alison slapped a hand down on her terminal keyboard with a disgusted sigh, canceling a search program. "He doesn't have bloody finances, you've got to have money for that. All Tyler has are debts."

Which wasn't strictly true. Amanda glanced at Tyler's bank statement again. To think, she always worried about her monthly salary payment arriving in time to satisfy her standing orders and credit-card bill. Some people obviously operated on a higher plane. Although he owed close to quarter of a million New Sterling, the banks just kept extending his credit limit. Why he didn't pay it off she couldn't understand. His cashflow was more than adequate. Of course, neither she nor Alison could track down where half of the money actually came from, and in most cases where it went. One account at a bank in Peterborough was used just for withdrawing large sums of hard cash.

Amanda looked over at Mike Wilson who was studying some of the details himself. "I think we might justifiably request a qualified accountant at this point."

He ran a hand back through his hair, looking at a twisting column of numbers in one of the cubes with a perplexed expression. "I think you might be right."

Denzil came in and grinned at the blatant despondency in the room. "Having fun?"

"Always," Alison said sweetly.

"I have a positive result."

Amanda sat up fast. "What?"

"The skin scrape is definitely nobody we know of. No record of that DNA in the Home Office memory core. I even squirted the problem over to Interpol. They don't have it either. And before you ask, neither does the FBI." He gave Wilson an affable smile. "You'll get the bill tomorrow."

"I live for it."

"You want me to look elsewhere? Most countries will cooperate."

"I think we'll have to," Amanda said. "After all, that DNA is our murderer. Mike?"

"I agree. Although, I'd like to suggest widening the search parameters."

"How?"

"Organizations such as Interpol and the FBI simply store the DNA of known criminals. If it were a professional hit, I'd say search every police memory core on the planet. However, we favor the theory that this was a heat-of-the-moment killing, do we not?"

"I can go with that," she said.

"Then our murderer is unlikely to be listed."

"It was always a long shot, but what else can we do?" She pointed at the cubes full of financial datawork. "If we can find a motive, we can track the murderer that way."

"Crescent has a DNA-characteristics assembly program. I suggest we use that."

Denzil whistled quietly. "I'm impressed."

"I might be," Amanda said. "If I knew what you were talking about."

"The genes which make us what we are, are spaced out along the genome, the map of our DNA," Mike Wilson said. "Now that we know which site designates which protein or characteristic, like hair color or shape of the ear, it's possible to examine the genes which contribute to the facial features and see what that face will look like."

"You mean you can give me a picture of this person?" Amanda asked.

"Essentially, yes. We can then ask Tyler's friends and acquaintances if they recognize him . . . or her." He waved a hand at the busy terminal cubes. "Got to be easier than this, quicker, too. Crescent can also run standard comparison programs with the visual images stored in our data cores, and with the security departments of all the other companies we have reciprocal arrangements with. I think you'll find they're considerably more extensive than the criminal records held by governments. For a start, between us, the insurance companies have copies of every driving license issued in Europe. And we already decided the murderer drove to Bisbrooke."

Amanda studied him. This was suddenly too easy. Something was wrong, and she couldn't define it . . . apart from an intuitive distrust she had for the corporate machinator. And yet, he was helping. Solving the crime, in all probability. "How long will it take?"

"If we courier a sample of the DNA over to Crescent's lab in Oxford this evening, the program can crunch the genome overnight. We can have the picture by morning."

"Okay. Do it."

Amanda hated working Sundays. No way around it this week, though. And maybe, just maybe, she might get overtime, courtesy of Crescent.

When she arrived at the station there was an unusually large crowd of people in the main CID office for the time and day, uniform division as well as detectives. Alison gave Amanda a wry smile as she came in.

"The scene-of-crime team found something interesting," she said in a low voice, suggesting conspiracy. "No shortage of volunteers to go over this lot for us."

"What?" Amanda asked. She edged through the group to look at the flatscreen they were all absorbed with. It was a split-screen image, three viewpoints of the main bedroom in Byrne Tyler's apartment. Tyler himself was on the bed with a girl, their naked bodies writhing in animal passion.

Alison held up a carton full of memox crystals. "There's a lot of them. Over sixty."

"Okay." Amanda walked over to the AV player and switched it off. "That's enough. This is supposed to be a bloody police station, not a porno shop."

They moaned, one or two jeered, but nobody actually voiced a complaint. The group broke up, filing out of the CID office with sheepish grins and locker room chuckles.

"They found three cameras in there yesterday," Alison said. "Quite a professional recording setup. Looks like Tyler was something of an egotistical voyeur."

"Was he recording Wednesday night?" Amanda asked sharply. At least that explained why he didn't have a top sheet on his bed, she thought.

"No. Or at least, there was no memox of it. The AV recorder the cameras are rigged to was empty."

"Pity."

Alison rattled the carton. "Plenty more suspects: all the husbands and boyfriends."

The little black cylinders rolled about. Ten-hour capacity each. Amanda found herself doing mental arithmetic. Assuming they were even half-full, Tyler had been a very busy boy. Popular, too. "Is there an index?"

"Yes." Alison flourished a ziplock bag containing several sheets of paper. "In ink no less—I guess he didn't want to risk this list getting burned open by a hotrod. Mostly just first names, but he got some surnames as well; and they've all got dates. They go back over two years. There's quite a few personalities I recognize."

"Okay, scan the list in to your terminal and run the names through a search program. Then see if a visual-characteristics recognition program can identify the girls we don't have full names for. I want to know where all of them live, if they're married or have long-term partners, parents of the younger ones, that kind of thing. Oh, and check to see if the crystals are there."

Mike Wilson walked in past the last of the uniform division. His expression was bleak. "What did I miss?" he inquired.

"Tyler liked to record himself in bed," Alison said. "We found the crystals."

"Oh, shit. We'd better keep that quiet."

Amanda frowned. Not quite the response she expected. "I was planning on it," she said. "How did the DNA characteristics assembly go?"

He flipped open a shiny chrome Event Horizon executive cybofax and gave it an instruction. A young man's face appeared, light brown hair, greenish eyes, a thin nose, broad mouth. There was a small digital read-out in the corner of the screen saying: 18 YEARS. It started to wind forward. The man began to change, aging. Wrinkles appeared, the cheeks and neck thickened; the hairline receded, gray streaks appeared. The display finished at eighty years, showing a wizened face with shrunken cheeks plagued by liver spots, and wisps of silver-white hair.

"Denzil was right," Amanda said. "That's impressive. Just how accurate is it?"

"Perfectly accurate."

"You sound unhappy."

"There was no positive match."

"Are you sure?"

"Oh, we got hundreds of people who share eighty-five to ninety percent similarity. We just captured an image from every five years of his life and the computer ran a standard visual comparison reference program for each of them. In total we have access to pictures of two hundred twenty-five-million Caucasian males. Can you believe it? Nothing over ninety percent."

Amanda couldn't work out if she was disappointed or not. Mike Wilson had sounded so sure this was the solution, and now for all the astonishing technology and corporate data cores they had to revert to humble police work. "Give us the top twenty off your list, and we'll start to work through them, check if they knew Tyler, alibis, the usual. English residents to start with, please."

"Okay," he acknowledged the request with a subdued nod. "Who the hell did this? The only way this murderer could elude our programs is with major plastic surgery, changing his appearance."

"Someone in showbusiness, then," Alison said brightly.

"The percentage is a lot higher among celebrities than the rest of the population. They're always improving their appearance."

"Could be." Uncertainty was a strong presence in his voice.

"Alison, that can be your priority," Amanda said. "We'll turn Tyler's finances over to a professional accountant. That'll free us to interview friends and colleagues, see if any of them recognize this picture." Her finger tapped the cybofax screen. "I'll start with the Sullivans. You concentrate on his fellow celebrities."

Amanda was just going out the station door when she caught sight of a silhouette in the reception area, a man talking to the desk sergeant. "Greg?"

Greg Mandel turned round. His eyes narrowed for a second, then he grinned. "Amanda Patterson, right? Detective sergeant?"

She shook the hand he offered. "Detective, now."

"Congratulations."

"Thanks. So what are you doing here?"

"Checking on a vehicle accident. One of Eleanor's family was hurt."

"Oh, I'm sorry. Any luck?"

"None at all."

"Yeah, well, you know how the police force works. Traffic doesn't get the highest priority these days. Want me to pull any strings?"

"No. That's okay, thanks. I guess CID's pretty busy with the Tyler case. I saw it on the news."

"Yeah. It's my case, too." She glanced from Greg back to Mike Wilson who was standing waiting politely. Asking never hurt, she thought, and she'd had a reasonable relationship with Greg during an earlier case when he'd been appointed as a special adviser to Oakham's CID. "Look, Greg, I realize this probably isn't the best time to ask you, but the Tyler case is really a ball-breaker for me. We're hitting a lot of stone walls."

"Uh huh." Greg's expression became reluctant, trying to work out how to extricate himself.

"Just sit in on one interview, Greg, that's all I need. I've got a suspect I'm not sure about. How about it? You can cut straight through all the usual crap and tell me if she's on the level. We can even pay you a fee. Mike here is from Crescent Insurance, they're picking up the tab for Tyler."

Greg and Mike eyed each other suspiciously.

"What exactly is your field?" Mike asked.

"I have a gland," Greg said mildly.

Amanda enjoyed the discomfort leaking over Mike Wilson's face. She'd endured the same feeling the first time she met Greg; every guilty memory rushing to the front of her mind.

"I thought we'd cleared Claire?" Mike Wilson protested.

"She was at the apartment very close to the time," Amanda said. "And I know she's holding something back. That's why I need a psychic, to see where I'm going wrong. If I knew the right questions to ask her I bet we could take some big steps forward."

Mike Wilson clearly wanted to object; just didn't have the nerve.

"Detective's intuition, huh?" Greg asked.

"Must be catching," she told him spryly.

He consulted his watch. "Okay. I can give you an hour. But I'll have to call Eleanor first, let her know where I am."

She couldn't resist it. "Under the thumb, Greg—you?"

His smile was bright and proud. "Certainly am, I have two women in my life now. Christine is six months old."

"Oh, I didn't know. Congratulations."

"Thanks."

Amanda and Mike Wilson took it in turns to brief Greg on the case as they drove out to Uppingham. Just before they got to the roundabout with the A47 at Uppingham, Greg said: "I'd like to take a look at the apartment first."

"Why is that necessary?" Wilson asked.

"It's best if I can get a feel for the event," Greg said. "Sometimes my intuition can be quite strong. It might help with the interview."

They pulled up in Church Vista's courtyard. Greg got out and looked round, head tilted back slightly as if he was sniffing at the air. Wilson watched him, but didn't comment. There was a police seal on the door to apartment three, which Amanda's card opened.

Greg went over to the red outline at the foot of the stairs. "What was the result from the security 'ware?"

"As far as we can tell it's clean," Mike Wilson said. "If it was tampered with, then whoever did it covered their tracks perfectly."

"Hmm." Greg nodded and started to walk round, glancing at the coffee table with its spread of glossy art books.

"We've collected statements from all the neighbors now," Amanda said. "None of them heard or saw any other car arriving or departing that night. It was only Claire and the Ingalo. And we've received the enhanced images from the security camera by the gates. She was the only person in it coming in and out."

"Well, I can appreciate your problem," Greg said. He was walking along the wall, examining the pictures one at a time. "Circumstances make it look like a professional hit, but pushing Tyler down the stairs is strictly a chance killing."

"Tell me," Amanda muttered. "We know there was someone else here, we even know what they look like. But everything else we've got says it's Claire."

"Can I see the image you assembled from the genome data?"

Mike Wilson flipped open his cybofax and showed Greg the image while it ran through its eighteen-to-eighty lifecycle.

"Doesn't ring any psychic bells," Greg said. He stopped beside the smallest painting on the wall, a picture of a hill with a strange object in the air above it. "This is a bit out of place, isn't it?" The pictures on either side were colored chalk sketches of ballerinas clad only in tutus.

"Is that relevant?" Wilson asked as he slipped the cybofax back in his jacket pocket. He was beginning to sound more positive, overcoming his apprehension of the gland and its reputation.

"Probably not," Greg admitted. He led them up the stairs into the bedroom. The crime scene team had tagged the three cameras that were discreetly hidden within elaborate picture frames, the units no bigger than a coat button. Slender fiber-optic threads buried in the plaster linked them to an AV recorder deck in a chest of drawers.

"And you say there's no sign of a struggle?" Greg asked.

"No. The only thing messed up was the bed."

"Right." He stood in the door, looking at the top of the stairs. "If it was a professional hit, then the murderer could have waited until just after Claire had left, then thrown Tyler down the stairs. That would disguise the fact it was a hit, which would stop us looking for anyone else with a motive. Was Tyler alive when he fell?"

"The autopsy says yes. The impact snapped his neck, he was killed instantly."

"What about bruising or marks? If he was alive when he was forced to the stairs he would have put up some kind of struggle."

"No bruising," Amanda said.

"That doesn't necessarily follow," Mike Wilson said. "He'd only struggle if he realized what was happening. If the murderer made out he was a burglar and made him walk to the stairs with a gun to his head he wouldn't have fought back."

Greg pulled a face, looking from the bed to the stairs. "Yeah, this is all possible, but very tenuous. The simplest explanation is usually the correct one." He went over to the chest of drawers, and bent down to study the AV recorder, fingertips tracing the slender optical threads back into the skirting board. "How old is this place?"

"The apartment was finished two and a half years ago," Amanda said. "Tyler moved in just over two years ago."

"So he probably had it wired up then," Greg said. "How much did the apartment cost him?"

"Five hundred and fifty thousand New Sterling. There's over four hundred thousand outstanding on the mortgage. He was late with several payments."

"So he doesn't own it. I thought he was rich."

"By our standards he's loaded. But he had one hell of a lifestyle, and he didn't star in that many action interactives. Strictly C-list when it comes to the celebrity stakes. He's definitely short of hard cash."

Greg went over to the bed, running a hand along the edge of the mattress. "Did he make any recordings of himself with Claire?"

"I'm not sure," Amanda said. "Let me check if Alison's loaded the list in yet." She opened her cybofax and linked in to the station 'ware. "We're in luck, she's just finished it. Let's see . . . Yes, there's three crystals of Claire."

"When was the last one dated?"

"Three weeks ago."

"Why the interest?" Mike Wilson asked.

"That's a lot of recording time for one girl," Greg said. "And Claire doesn't come over here that often, or stay long when she does. That suggests he records every time. So why didn't he record last Wednesday night?"

"He did," Amanda said instinctively. She could see where he was going with this. "And the murderer took the memox crystal because he was caught by the cameras in here. Which implies that whoever the murderer is, he struck very quickly after Claire left. So close the recorder was still on."

"No messing," Greg said.

Tamzin Sullivan had returned home. When Amanda, Greg and Mike Wilson were shown into the bungalow, the bereaved girl was sitting in the lounge. To show her grief at the loss of her future husband she was wearing traditional black in the form of a less traditional micro dress with a deep scoop-top. Colin, from Hothouse, was fussing around with her mother while a seamstress made last minute adjustments to the shoulder straps, a makeup artist was finishing off the girl's face.

It was Claire who had answered the door and ushered them in. As soon as the sisters glanced at each other the atmosphere chilled to a level below that Tyler's apartment had ever reached. Daniel, who was lurking behind the sofa, shrank away from the visitors.

"This is not an appropriate time for you to be here," Margina said imperiously. "The *Starlight* crew will be here any minute."

"I apologize for interrupting you at what is undoubtedly a difficult time," Amanda said; it was her best official sympathy voice. She marveled she could manage to keep it irony-free. "But I'm afraid we do have some questions for Tamzin, and Claire again. We'll be brief."

Tamzin glanced at Colin, who gave a small nod.

"I'll help in whatever way I can," Tamzin said. "I want Byrne's murderer caught. Have you found the piece of scum yet?" Her gaze flicked pointedly to her sister.

"We have a possible suspect."

Mike Wilson showed her his cybofax, running the image. "Do you recognize this man? We think Byrne knew him."

Tamzin leaned forward with considerable interest, fabric straining. Amanda saw Wilson's glance slither helplessly down to her cleavage, and prayed hard no one else had seen.

"No. I don't."

He went onto show the image to Margina, Claire, and even Colin. They all said they had never seen the man before.

"What about threats?" Amanda asked. "Do you know if anyone was being abusive to him recently?"

"No," Tamzin said. "There was nothing like that. He did have a few crank callers, everyone as famous as us has them; but the agency screened them for him."

"I'd like a record of them, please," she told Colin.

"I'll get it squirted over to you," he promised.

"Thank you. Greg, anything you need to know?"

"The pictures in your fiancé's apartment are interesting," Greg said. "How long's he been buying them?"

Tamzin blinked, slightly baffled. "Since he moved in, I suppose. Byrne appreciated fine art, music, culture; he wasn't just an action hero, you know. He was friends with a lot of people in the media and arts. Inspiring people. He was even writing a script for a drama that we would star in together. Now that's talent."

"Yes, I'm sure. The pictures are all original, aren't they?"

"They're Byrne's *collection*," Tamzin said in pique. "Of course they're original."

"I see. Thanks."

Amanda had somehow expected more; she had seen Greg interview suspects before. When he didn't ask anything else, she said: "I'd like to talk to Claire alone for a moment, please."

Margina's face tightened in fury; she gave her youngest daughter a warning glare as she stalked out. Tamzin didn't even bother with that; she ignored everyone as she left. It was Colin who was left to take Daniel's hand and lead the lad away.

Claire slumped down petulantly into the sofa. She was wearing an oversize rouge T-shirt and baggy black jeans; cloaking while Tamzin exhibited. Always opposites. "Now what?"

"I really will be brief," Amanda said. "This is going to be personal, I'm sorry. Did you know about Tyler's obsession with recording events in his bedroom?"

"You've found the memox crystals?" Claire asked in a small voice.

"Yes, we did."

"I knew you would. Byrne liked me to watch them with him. He enjoyed the ones of him with famous people. There were a lot; actresses and singers, socialites, people like that. I know it was all wrong, but one more bad thing on top of all the rest didn't seem to matter much, not by then."

"Do you know if he was recording the pair of you that night?"

"I don't know. I knew he did sometimes. I didn't ask. I never wanted to think about stuff like that."

Amanda took a quick look at Greg, who was watching impassively. There was no clue as to what he saw with his sixth sense. "Thank you, Claire. I know that wasn't easy. I'd just like to go back to that night one more time. Did you see or hear anything unusual there?"

"No. I told you already, there was nothing different."

"Not even with Byrne—he wasn't acting oddly?"

"No."

"He didn't do anything that made you angry, or upset?"

"No! Why are you asking this? You think I did it, don't you? I didn't! I *didn't!* Tamzin thinks I did. Mum hates me. I didn't want any of this. You think I did?" Tears were starting to slide down her cheeks. She wiped at them with the back of a hand, sniffling loudly.

"Okay, Claire, I'm sorry. And you're sure you didn't recognize the man Mike showed you on the cybofax?"

"Yeah, I've never seen him. Who is he?"

"I wish we knew."

As soon as they all got back into Amanda's car, she turned to Greg. "Well?"

"Claire's telling the truth. She didn't kill him."

"God damn it! I'm sure she knows something about this."

"Not that I could sense. She certainly didn't recognize the killer's face, there was nothing odd about the apartment that night, and Byrne was behaving normally. You're going to have to come at it from a different angle."

"Shit." She faced forward and gripped the steering wheel. "It has to be someone with a big vicious grudge eating at them."

"The murderer knew all about the cameras," Greg said. "Not that Tyler exactly kept it a secret. That makes it more likely to be a jealous boyfriend or husband of some girl that Tyler's had up there."

"Then why the hell can't we find a match for his face?"

"We'll get him," Mike Wilson said. "It's just a question of time now."

"Yeah, right." She switched on the power cell, and drove off. "Sorry to waste your time, Greg."

"I don't think you did," he said cautiously. "There's something not quite right about the crime scene. Don't ask what, it's just a feeling. I just know something's wrong there. It might come to me later; these things normally take time to recognize. Can I give you a call?"

"Please!"

"Thanks. So what's your next step?"

"Work through his friends and acquaintances, and the girls on the crystals. See if any of them recognizes the murderer. Just a hell of a lot of datawork correlation, basically."

Making sense out of Byrne Tyler's twisted finances was one of Amanda's biggest priorities. She had emphasized that often enough to Vernon and Mike Wilson, both of whom assured her of their total agreement. But there was no accountant waiting for her on Monday morning when she arrived at the station. Mike Wilson was in full apology mode, explaining that the person he had asked to be assigned to the Tyler case was finishing off another audit. "But he'll have completed that by tomorrow at the latest."

"You mean he'll be here tomorrow?"

"I would assume so." He handed her a memox crystal. "Peace offering. This came in from Tyler's agency. It's an index of all his professional contacts, people he's worked with over the last eighteen months. They've also got records of his crankier fans."

Amanda gave the crystal a mistrustful glance; the number of people they were going to have to interview was expanding at an exponential rate. She went into the office to see what progress Alison had made identifying the girls on the memox crystals.

It was considerable. Amanda's eyebrows quirked several times as she ran down the list. For an ex-soap star he had an astonishing sex appeal. How he got to meet so many women in such a short time (during his engagement), and have such a success rate was beyond her. Sure he was boyishly handsome, and kept himself in top physical shape . . . They started to draw up an interview schedule. Most of it would have to be done over the phone; the preliminary inquiry, anyway.

Vernon called her into his office at 8:40, requesting a full briefing. He was appearing on Radio Rutland soon to explain the case to the public. The police station had been receiving a steady stream of requests from the media, which had doubled since *Starlight*'s interview and pictures of a mourning Tamzin had appeared on the datatext channels last night.

There wasn't much she could give him. They certainly weren't going to announce the failure of the characteristics assembly program to find the murderer. Vernon would just have to stick to confirming the investigation team was "progressing"; that anything else at this time could prejudice the case. He departed for the studio, fidgeting with his tie and collar.

Greg Mandel called her mid-morning, and asked to have a look around the apartment again. She agreed to meet him up there, glad for the break. The women on Alison's list that she'd called so far were uniformly apprehensive when they found out what the enquiry was about, brittle facades hiding real fear of discovery. It was a shabby process, leaving her feeling depressed and less than wholesome.

Greg's big EMC Ranger was waiting outside Church Vista's courtyard gates when she arrived.

"Any clue what you're looking for yet?" she asked when they went inside.

"Sorry, no. I guess I'm just here chasing phantoms." He tapped a finger on the rim of the glass and wood door leading out to the courtyard. "Logically, we ought to start with the point of entry. Do you have an idea where the murderer came in?"

Amanda flipped her cybofax open, and consulted the report from the scene-of-crime team. "No. According to the security 'ware logs, the main door here was opened at 21:12 hours with a duplicate card issued by Tyler, that's two minutes after the 'ware recorded the Ingalo driving in through the gates—which matches up with Claire's arrival. Then it was opened again at 23:09, from the inside, when she left."

"What's the security system like?"

"Good quality 'ware, standard application. All the doors and windows are wired up, and the log function records every time they open and close; motion and infrared sensors, voice codeword panic mode with a satellite link to a private watchdog company. I'd be happy here."

"Sounds foolproof." Greg walked across the ground floor to the big window wall. Broad patio doors were set into it, to the left of the stairs. "What about this one?"

"It's a manual lock, you can only open it from the inside. There isn't even a catch outside." Amanda glanced at the log again. "That was closed from 1900 hours onward." She followed after him as he went into the kitchen, which overlooked the courtyard. All the marble worktops were clean, there was nothing out of place, no food stains, tall glass storage pots of dried pasta unopened, spice jars full; even the line of potted ferns on the windowsill were aesthetic, healthy and well-watered. It was as though the whole place had been transplanted direct from a showroom. The band of windows above the sink had two sections which could open. Both had solid manual-key security bolts. Greg didn't even have to ask. "They haven't been opened for ages," she told him. "Not since June, actually."

There was a cloakroom next door; emerald-green ceramic tiles halfway up the walls, cool whitewashed plaster carrying on up to the ceiling. A hand basin at one end, toilet at the other with a small window just above it, four panes of fogged glass. Greg went over and looked at it. The top half of the frame was open a crack, its iron latch on the first notch. When he lifted the catch and pushed it open further the hinges creaked, protesting the movement.

"My cat couldn't get through that," Amanda said.

"Fat cat," Greg replied. "What about upstairs?"

Main bedroom, the bathroom, and both guest bedrooms all had wide windows equipped with security bolts. Out of the ten which opened, the security bolts were unfastened or loose on three, leaving just the standard latch to deter burglars.

"How would they get up to them?" Amanda asked skeptically when they finished checking the last guest bedroom.

"I've used wallwalker pads in my army days," Greg said. "And I'm not sure how strong those trellises outside are, maybe they'd act like a ladder."

"Security log says they stayed closed. You want me to run forensic checks on the external wall?"

"Not particularly. If you have the technical expertise to circumvent window sensors, then you can walk straight in through the main door."

Amanda's cybofax bleeped. She accepted a call from Mike Wilson. The accountant definitely wouldn't be available before Wednesday—did she want to wait, or get someone else in? One was available for Tuesday, but Wilson hadn't worked with him before. Amanda scratched irritably at her forehead; as Crescent was paying, she wanted results quickly, and, to her, one accountant was no different from any other. She said to get one in for Tuesday morning, first thing. It didn't matter who.

"No progress on finding a match for the murderer's face," Mike Wilson said. "And you won't believe how many of Tyler's showbiz pals have had discreet trips to the surgeon. It doesn't help our visual comparison programs."

She finished the call and went off to find Greg. He was downstairs again, crouching over the red body outline. "I've been thinking about motive," he said. "All we've come up with so far is jealously."

"The accountant's in tomorrow—maybe we'll find a big debtor."

"Could be, except the kind of debt that drives someone to kill isn't normally one you'll find on the books. And killing someone means you never get paid."

She glanced around at the paintings. Tyler had spent a lot of money on them, no matter how questionable his taste. "You think they stole something?"

"We know it had to be a professional who broke in here. It could have been someone trying to reclaim a debt the hard way. Maybe the death was an accident after all. What we have is a burglar who hadn't done enough research on his target to know Claire was making nighttime visits. I mean, they certainly kept it quiet enough. Tyler was awake when he wasn't supposed to be."

"Could be," she said.

"Crescent Insurance must have a list of his paintings; it's simple enough to check they're all here."

"Okay. We'll try that."

"Sorry I can't come up with anything more concrete." He made his way out, stopping to take one last look at the small odd painting. Frowning. Then left with a rueful wave.

Amanda used her cybofax to connect directly into Crescent's memory core, and requested Tyler's home contents file. Greg was wrong. All the insured paintings were there. Amazingly the most expensive one was *View of a Hill and Clouds*. She paused in front of it, not quite believing what she was seeing was worth 20,000 New Sterling. Art, she thought, just wasn't for people like her.

The accountant did arrive on Tuesday morning. He had brought three customized cybofaxes and a leather wallet full of memox crystals loaded with specialist financial analysis programs. His assiduous preparation, eagerness, and self-confidence did a lot to offset the fact that he looked about eighteen. Amanda assigned Alison to assist him.

Greg turned up at the station just before lunch. "I got your message about the paintings," he said. His manner was reticent, not like him at all.

"It was worth following up," she assured him. "I would have got around to doing it anyway."

"That feeling I had that something was out of kilter. I know what it is now. It's that small oil painting, the funny one with the flying saucer or whatever. I'm sure of it."

"What's wrong with it?"

"I don't know, but something is."

"I know it stands out from the others. But it turns out Tyler knew the artist: they went out partying together when McCarthy visited England a few years back. And believe it or not, it's the most expensive piece there."

"Ah." Greg began to look a lot more contented. "It's wrong, Amanda."

"How? It's still there, it wasn't stolen."

"You asked me in on this, remember?" he said gently. "I didn't think I'd have to convince you of all people about my gland all over again."

She stared at him for a minute while instinct, common sense, and fear of failure went thrashing about together in her head. In the end she decided he was worth the gamble; she had asked him in because she wanted that unique angle he could provide. Once, she'd heard Eleanor, his wife, call his talent a foresight equal to everyone else's hindsight.

"How do you want to handle it?" she asked in a martyred tone.

He grinned his thanks. "Somebody who knows what they're about needs to take a look at that painting. We should concentrate on the artist, too . . . get Alison to mine some background on him."

"Okay." She called Mike Wilson over.

"An art expert?" he asked cynically.

"Crescent must have a ton of them," Greg said. "Art fraud is pretty common. Insurance companies face it every day."

"We have them, yes, but . . ."

"An expert has told us something is wrong with the painting, and this is my investigation," she said, not too belligerently, but firmly enough to show him she wasn't going to compromise on this.

He held his hands up. "All right. But you only get three lives, not nine."

Hugh Snell wasn't exactly the scholarly old man with fraying tweed jacket and half-moon glasses that Amanda was expecting. When he turned up at Church Vista Apartments he was wearing a leather Harley Davidson jacket, a diamond stud through his nose, and five rings in his left ear. His elbow-length Mohican plume was dyed bright violet.

He took one look at Tyler's collection and laughed out loud. "Shit. He spent money on these? What a prat."

"Aren't they any good?" Amanda asked.

"My talent detector needle is simply quivering . . . on zero. One hates to speak ill of the dead, my dear, but if all he wanted was erotica, he should have torn the center pages out of a porno mag and framed them instead. This simply reeks of lower middle-class pretension. I know about him, I know nothing of the artists — they say nothing, they do nothing."

Mike Wilson indicated the McCarthy. "What about this one?"

Hugh Snell made a show of pulling a gold-rimmed monocle from his pocket. He held it daintily to his eye and examined the painting. "Yeah, good forgery."

Amanda smiled greedily. "Thanks, Greg."

"No problem."

"It's insured for twenty thousand," Wilson said.

"Alas my dear chap, you've been royally shafted."

"Are you sure?"

Hugh Snell gave him a pitying look. "Please don't flaunt your ignorance in public view, it's frightfully impolite. This isn't even a quality copy. Any halfway decent texture printer can churn out twenty of these per minute for you. Admittedly, it will fool the less well versed, but anyone in the trade would see it immediately."

"Makes sense," Amanda said. "The smallest and most valuable item, you could roll it up and carry it out in your pocket."

"Certainly could," Greg murmured.

"I owe you an apology, Mr. Mandel," Mike Wilson said.

"Not a problem," Greg assured him.

"Congratulations," Wilson said to Amanda. "So it was a burglary which went wrong, then. Which means it was a professional who broke in. That explains why we've been banging our heads against the wall."

"A pre-planned burglary, too, if he'd brought a forgery with him," she said. "I bet Tyler would never have noticed it had gone."

"Which means it was someone who knew Tyler had the McCarthy on his wall, and how much it was worth."

Amanda went up to the McCarthy; and gave it a happy smile. "I'll get forensics back to take a closer look at it," she said.

Three — Degrees of Guilt

Greg managed three hours of sleep before Christine decided it was time to begin another bright new day. His eyes blinked open as her cries began. Nothing in focus, mouth tasted foul, limbs too heavy to move. Classic symptoms — if only it were a hangover, that would mean he'd enjoyed some of last night.

"I'll get her," Eleanor grumbled.

The duvet was tugged across him as she clambered out of bed and went over to the cot. "Isn't it my turn?" he asked as the timber of the crying changed.

"Oh, who cares?" Eleanor snapped back. "I just want her to shut up."

He did the brave thing, and kept quiet. In his army days he'd gone without sleep for days at a time during some of the covert missions deep into enemy territory. Oh, to be back in those halcyon times. Christine could teach the Jihad Legion a thing or two about tenacity.

Eleanor started to change their daughter's nappy.

The doorbell rang. Greg knew he'd misheard that. When he squinted, the digital clock just made it into focus: 6:23. The bell went again. He and Eleanor stared at each other.

"Who the hell . . . ?"

Whoever they were, they started knocking.

The hall tiles were cold against his feet as he hopped over them to the front door. He managed to pull his dressing gown shut just before he flicked the lock over and pulled the door open. A young man with broad bull shoulders had his arm raised to knock again.

"What the bloody hell do you want?" Greg yelled. "Do you know what time it is?" Christine was wailing plaintively behind him.

The young man's defiance melted away into mild confusion. "Eleanor lives here doesn't she?"

"Yes." Greg noticed what the man was wearing, a pair of dark dungarees with a cross stitched on the front, blue wool shirt, sturdy black leather boots. It was his turn for a recoil; he hadn't seen a kibbutznik since the night he faced down Eleanor's father. "Who are you?" He ordered a tiny secretion from his gland, imagining a tiny mushroom squirt of white liquid scudding around his brain, neurohormones soaking into synaptic clefts. Actually, the physiological function was nothing like that; picturing it at all was a psychological quirk that most Mindstar Brigade veterans employed. There's no natural internal part of the human body which can be consciously activated; only muscles, and you can see that happen. So the mind copes by giving itself a picture of animation to explain the onrush of ethereal sensation. The result left him sensing an agitated haze of thoughts, entwined by grief. The man had forced himself to the Mandel farm against all kinds of deep-rooted doubts.

"I'm Andy," he said it as though puzzled that Greg didn't already know . . . as though his name explained away everything. "Andy Broady. Eleanor's brother."

Andy sat in a chair at the kitchen table, uncomfortable despite the cushion. He'd glanced around with a type of jealous surprise at the oak cupboards and tiled work surfaces. Greg followed his gaze with a mild embarrassment. The fittings were only a few years old, and Mrs. Owen came in to clean and help with Christine three times a week; but the room was still a mess. Baby bottles, washed and unwashed were all over the worktops, two linen baskets overflowing with clothes, packets of rusks, jars of puréed apple and other mushy, disgusting-tasting food were stacked in shop bags ready to be put away. Last night's plates and dishes were waiting on top of the dishwasher. Big, rainbow-colored fabric toys underfoot. Half the broad ash table was littered with the financial printouts which Eleanor had generated as she worked through summaries of the citrus grove crop and market sales.

Christine gurgled quietly in Andy's lap, and he looked down at his new niece with guilty surprise. His lips twitched with a tentative smile. He held her with the stiff terror of every bachelor, frightened that he'd drop her, or she'd start crying, or burp, or choke or . . .

"How old is she?"

"Coming up six months." Eleanor opened the dishwasher and retrieved three cups.

"She's lovely."

"Make me an offer, you can take her home with you today."

Andy's head came up in shock. Greg gave him a reassuring wink. Eleanor filled the cups from the Twinings carton and put them in the microwave. Greg never used to like instant tea, quietly fancying himself as a reasonable cook. These days everything was in convenience units.

Eleanor sat opposite her brother, and gave him a sympathetic look. "All right, what's happened, Andy?"

"Happened?"

"You wouldn't have come here otherwise."

He nodded reluctantly. "It's dad. There was an accident."

"Oh, shit." Eleanor let out a sigh, rubbing at her eyes. "How bad?"

"He was hit by a car. We took him back home, but he can't move. He hurts a lot, and he's hot . . . like with fever. Coughs blood. Other end, too."

"And of course he won't go to hospital."

Andy shook his head, too glum to speak.

She put her hand on his arm, squeezing reassuringly. "Who's looking after him?"

"Paddy, but he's not as good as you were at medicine and such. Don't have real training. Dad didn't want any of us to go to college for courses, not after you left. Said that all outside the kibbutz was an evil place, that it corrupts us." He gave Greg a nervous glance. "Said that the devil stole you away."

"I wasn't stolen, Andy; I was driven away. I saw what life can be like if you just have the courage to live it." Her hand moved to Greg. "And have a little help."

He kissed the top of her head. Andy's expression hardened.

"I'm not arguing with you Andy," she said. "But we're all free to make choices. Even you, because I know he didn't ask you to come up here today."

"So? Will you come and see him?"

"Yes, Andy, I'll come."

It was a funny kind of day to find the perfect definition of mixed feelings, Greg thought, but now here he was torn between complete disapproval and devotion. Didn't want Eleanor to go anywhere near the kibbutz, let alone back inside, and couldn't leave her to do it alone.

It didn't take long to drive to Egleton. The kibbutz was on the other side of the tiny village, on a flat expanse of land that bordered the road. One side of it was Rutland Water, a shoreline which ironically put only a short stretch of water between them and the Mandel farm's citrus groves on the peninsula. Close in miles, but not in time.

Eleanor had described the kibbutz to him often enough, there were even a few places on the farm where he could just make out their roofs over the top of the coconut palms they'd planted along their section of shore. Even so it came as a surprise. The buildings were all single-story, clumped together in three concentric rings with the church in the center. Long huts that were half house, half barn or stable. Unlike anything else built since the Warming, they didn't have glossy black solar-panel roofs, just flat wooden slates. Brick chimney stacks fumed wisps of gray wood smoke into the clear sky. Beyond the outermost ring, a pair of donkeys were harnessed to a wooden pole, circling a brick well-shaft, turning some incredibly primitive pump.

The fields surrounding the buildings were planted with corn, barley, maize and potatoes; dense clumps of kitchen vegetables in each one made them resemble oversized allotments. Some had fruit trees, small and wizened, with zigzag branches and dark-green glossy leaves. Greg drove the Ranger down a rough dirt track that indicated a boundary. They stopped at a gate in the maze of tall sturdy wooden fences which surrounded the buildings; paddocks and corrals containing goats, donkeys, cows, some elderly horses, llamas. Neither the crops nor the live-stock were genetically modified varieties, Greg noticed.

He busied himself unstrapping a sleeping Christine from her baby seat while Eleanor looked around her old home with pursed lips. She grunted abruptly, and pulled the first-aid case from the Ranger's boot, slamming it down. They made quite a spectacle walking to the Broady home through the dried mud which filled the space between the buildings, while dogs barked and giant black turkeys wad-dled away squawking loudly. Several children ran alongside, giggling and calling to Andy. They seemed well fed, Greg thought, though their clothes were all home-made and patched. The adults still milling among the buildings eyed them sus-piciously. Several must have recognized Eleanor; because they nudged each other and traded meaningful looks.

Eleanor didn't even hesitate when she reached the front door. Shoved it open and walked in. Greg and Andy followed. It was a single long room, brick oven with iron doors at one end, bed at the other, with a few simple pieces of furniture between. The walls were hung with pictures of Jesus and Mary. Windows had shutters rather than glass.

A pale figure lay on the bed, covered by a single thin blanket. Greg probably wouldn't have recognized Noel Broady. He'd only seen the old man once before, years ago, the night he met Eleanor. If any two people in the world were destined never to be friends, it was him and Noel.

Now though, that stubborn face was sunken and sweating. Grey hair had thinned out, several days' stubble furred his cheeks and chin, flecked with dry saliva.

His eyes flickered open and he turned his head at the commotion. A dismissive grunt. "I told that boy not to go bother you."

"Andy's not a boy anymore, father, he's a man who makes his own decisions. If he wants to tell me about you, he can do."

"Stubborn. Stubborn." He coughed, his shoulders quaking, and dropped his head back on the thin pillow. "Have you not yet learned God's humility, girl?"

"I respect God in my own way, father."

"By leaving us. By turning your back on Jesus and your family." His finger rose to point at Greg. "By lying with that abomination. You live in sin, you will drown in sin."

"Greg is my husband now, father. You were invited to the wedding."

"I would not despoil all I have taught my flock by giving you my blessing."

"Really?" Eleanor put the first-aid case on the floor, and opened it. She took out the diagnostic patch, and applied it to the side of her father's neck. He frowned his disapproval, but didn't resist.

"You have a granddaughter," she said in a milder tone. She began running a handheld deep-scan sensor along his arms, switching to his ribcage. A picture of his skeleton built up in the cube of her Event Horizon laptop terminal.

Noel's weak gaze moved to the bundle riding in Greg's papoose; for a moment surprise and a lonely smile lifted the exhaustion from his face.

"She's called Christine," Greg said, moving closer so he could see. Christine stirred, yawning, her little arms wiggling about.

"She looks handsome, a good strong child. I will pray for her." Talking was a big effort for him, the words wheezing out. He coughed again, dabbing a pink-stained handkerchief to his lips.

Eleanor took a breath, consulting the terminal cube again. Greg didn't need his gland to see how worried she was.

"Dad, you have to go to hospital."

"No."

"You've got broken bones, and there's a lot of internal damage, bleeding. You have to go."

"If God calls me, then I will go to Him. All things are written, all lives decreed."

"God gave us the knowledge to save ourselves . . . that's why we've got doctors and medicine. They're his gifts—are you going to throw them back in his face?"

"How well I remember these arguments. Always questioning and testing, you were. There are even some nights when I miss them." Noel gave her a thin smile. "How quickly you forget your scriptures. It was the serpent who gave us knowledge."

"Dad, please. It's really bad. I can't fix this sort of damage. You have to go to hospital. And quickly."

"I will not. Do not ask me again."

"Andy?" Eleanor appealed.

"Your brother's faith is strong, unlike yours. He respects all we have achieved, all we have built. Ours is a simple life, my dearest Eleanor. We live, and we believe. That is all. It is sufficient for any man. Everything else—this fast, plastic, electronic existence you have chosen—is the road to your own destruction. You can learn no values from it. It teaches you no respect for His glory."

"I value your life."

"As do I. And I have lived it true to myself. Would you take that dignity from me, even now? Would you punish me with your chemicals and mutilate me with your surgeon's laser scalpels?"

She turned to Greg, miserable and helpless. He put his arm around her, holding her tight. Noel was badly wrong about his own son, Greg sensed. Andy was desperate to intervene. There was a layer of fear and uncertainty running through his mind that was struggling to rise and express itself, held in check only by ingrained obedience. When he let his perception expand, Greg could feel a similar anxiety suffusing the entire kibbutz. It wasn't just shock and worry that their leader was harmed; some other affliction was gnawing at them.

"Well, I'm giving you some treatment anyway," Eleanor said defiantly. She bent down to the first-aid case, and began selecting vials for the infuser. "You can't run away from me."

Noel lay back, a degree of contentment showing. "The absence of pain is a strong temptation. I will succumb and pay my penance later."

Christine woke up and began her usual gurgle of interest at the world all around. "I'll take her out," Greg said. "Andy, could you give me a hand."

Andy gave his father an uncertain glance. Noel nodded permission.

Outside, Greg turned so that Christine was shielded from the bright rising sun. The kibbutz had resumed its normal routine of activity, interest in the visitors discarded. He looked across the collection of worn buildings with a kind of annoyed bemusement. Ten years of his life had been spent in active rebellion against an oppressive government, a decade of pain and death and blood so that people could once again have a chance to gather some dignity and improve their lives. And here on his own doorstep this group strove to return to medievalism at its worst, burdened by everlasting manual labor and in thrall to evangelical priests who could never accept anyone else was even entitled to a different point of view. A community where progress is evil.

The irony made him smile—something he would never have done before meeting Eleanor. A freedom fighter (now, anyway—after all, they were the ones writing the history files) appalled by the use to which his gift of freedom had been put. People . . . they're such a pain in the arse.

"He's gonna die, isn't he?"

Greg bounced Christine about, enjoying her happy grin at the motion. "Yes, Andy, I think he is." The young man knew it anyway, just needed to be told by someone else. As if saying it would make it so, would make it his fault.

"I can't believe it. Not him. He's so strong . . . where it counts, you know."

"Yeah, I know it. I had to face him down once. Toughest fight in my life."

"That's my father." Andy was on the point of tears.

"What happened?" Greg scanned the kibbutz again. "There's no cars here, no traffic."

Andy's arm was raised, pointing away over the fields toward the road. "There. We found him over there. Helped carry him back myself."

"Can you show me, please?"

They tramped over the sun-baked mud tracks, moving along the side of the tall fences, a long winding route. Andy was quiet as they walked. Nervous, Greg assumed, after years of being warned of the demon who had captured his big sister.

"This is where we found him," Andy said eventually.

They were on a stretch of track running between two of the fences. Two hundred meters away toward Oakham was a gate which opened onto the tiny road linking Egleton with the A6003: a hundred meters in the other direction it led out into a paddock with other tracks and footpaths spreading off over the kibbutz land, a regular motorway intersection.

Greg knelt down beside the fence where Andy indicated. A herd of cattle on the other side watched them idly, chewing on the few blades of grass they could find amid the buttercups. The three lower bars of the fence were splintered, bowing inward; and they were thick timber. It had taken a lot of force to cause that much damage. They had some short paint streaks along them, dark blue; a dusting of chrome flakes lay on the mud. Greg stood and tried to work out the angle of the impact. The car or whatever would have had to veer very sharply to dint the fence in such a fashion. It wasn't as though it would be swerving to avoid oncoming traffic.

"Was he right up against the fence?" Greg asked.

"Yeah, almost underneath it when we found him."

"Did he say what happened?"

"Not much. Just that the car was big, and it had its headlights on full. Then it hit him, he got trapped between it and the fence."

"Headlights? Was it nighttime?"

"No. It was early evening, still light."

"Did anyone else see it happen?"

"No. We started searching when he didn't turn up for evening chapel. It was dark by then; didn't find him till after ten."

"What about the car?" Greg indicated the gate onto the road. "It must have come from that direction, where was it going?"

"Don't know. Didn't come to us; haven't had no visitors for a while. We're the only ones that use this bit of track. It's the quickest way out to the road."

"What do you use on the road?"

"We've got bicycles. And a cart; horse pulls it to market most days. We sell vegetables and eggs. People still like fresh food instead of that chemical convenience packet rubbish."

"Okay, so the car must have reversed away and got back onto the road afterward. So was your father on a bike?"

"No." Andy shook his head ruefully. "He didn't even like them. Said: God gave us feet, didn't he? He always walked into town."

"Do you know what he was doing in town that day?"

"Gone to see the solicitor."

"What the hell did Noel want with a solicitor?"

"It's a bad business been happening here. A man came a month or so back. Said he wanted to build a leisure complex on the shore, right where we are. He offered us money, said that it wasn't really our land anyway and he'd help us find somewhere else to live. What kind of a man is that to disrespect us so? We built this place. It's ours by any law that's just and true."

"Right," Greg said. Now probably wasn't the best time to lecture Andy on the kind of abuses which the local PSP Land Rights committees had perpetrated against private landowners. Nevertheless, expelling a farmer from his land so it could be handed over to a tribe of Bible-thumpers was a minor violation compared to some of the practices he'd heard of. The Party had been overthrown in one final night of mass civil disobedience and well-planned acts of destruction by underground groups, but the problems it had created hadn't gone with it. "So what did Noel want with a solicitor?"

"He kept coming back, that man, after we said we wouldn't go. Said he'd have us evicted like so many cattle. Said everyone around here would be glad to see us go, that we were Party, so we'd best make it easy for ourselves. Dad wasn't having none of that. We have rights, he said. He went and found a solicitor who'd help us. Seeing as how we'd been here so long, we're entitled to appeal to the court for a ruling of post-acquisition compensation. Means we'd have to pay the farmer whose land it was. But that way we wouldn't have to leave. It would cost us plenty. We'd have to work hard to raise that much money, but we ain't afraid of hard work."

"I see." Greg looked down at the broken sections of fence, understanding now what had really happened here. "What is this man's name, the one who wants you off?"

"Richard Townsend, he's a property developer lives in Oakham."

"You think Townsend had my father run down?" Eleanor asked. They were sitting out on the farmhouse's newly laid patio, looking across the southern branch of Rutland Water. Citrus groves covered the peninsula's slope on both sides of the house's grounds, the young trees fluttering their silky verdant leaves in the breeze. Phalanxes of swans and signets glided past on the dark water, their serenity only occasionally broken by a speeding windsurfer.

"It's the obvious conclusion," Greg said bitterly. "Noel was the center of opposition, the one they all follow. Without him they might just keep the legal challenge going but their heart won't be in it. For all his flaws, he was bloody charismatic."

"You mean intimidating."

"Call it what you like; he was the one they looked to. And now . . ."

She closed her eyes, shuddering. "He won't last another day, Greg. I don't think it would make any difference now, even if we could get him into hospital."

She hadn't talked much about her father's condition since they had arrived back at the farmhouse at midday. The morning's events were taking time to assimilate. She had done what she could with the medicines in the first-aid kit, easing the worst of his pain. He had pretended indifference when she said she would return later. It didn't convince anyone. Her ambivalence was a long way from being resolved. It had been a very wide rift.

"Townsend won't have done it personally," Greg said. "There'll be a perfect alibi with plenty of witnesses while whoever he hired drove the car. But he won't be able to hide guilt from me during the interview."

"That won't work, darling," she said sadly. "It still takes a lot for a jury to be convinced by a psychic's evidence. And you're hardly impartial in this case. A novice barrister on her first case would have you thrown out of court."

"Okay. I accept that. We need some solid evidence to convict him."

"Where are you going to get that from? You don't even really know for certain that it was Townsend. You can hardly interrogate him privately and then tell the police what he's done and ask them to follow it up."

"The car is evidence," Greg said. "Andy called in an official hit-and-run report from Egleton's phonebox. I'll start with that."

Greg left Eleanor at the kibbutz next morning, and drove on into Oakham. It had been a couple of years since he'd visited the police station. The desk sergeant reacted with a stoicism verging on contempt when Greg asked him what progress had been made on the hit-and-run. "I'll check the file for you, but don't expect too much."

"The man it hit is my father-in-law. He's going to die from the injuries."

A squirt of information colored the sergeant's desktop terminal cube with flecks of light. "Sorry, sir. Whoever reported the incident didn't know what the vehicle was, nor when it happened. If we don't have anything to go on, we can't make enquiries. There's nothing to ask."

"Did anyone even go out there and check? He's dying! The driver of that vehicle has killed him."

The sergeant did manage to look reasonably embarrassed. "The nature of the injuries wasn't disclosed at the time, sir. It's not down here."

"Would it have made a difference?"

"The case would have been graded accordingly."

"Graded? What the fuck is graded?"

"We would have given the incident a higher priority, sir."

Greg bit back on his immediate reply. Shouting at the ranks wasn't going to solve anything—it was the generals not the squaddies who decide the campaign strategy. He paused, took a breath. "What about forensic? There are all sorts of marks out there, even some paint off the bodywork. Any decent forensic lab would be able to match the paint type with the manufacturer, at least get an idea of what kind of vehicle they were driving. Then you could start asking if anyone saw it."

"Yes, sir. Was the gentleman insured?"

"For what?"

"Crime investigation finance. It's becoming more necessary these days. Most companies offer it as part of their employment package along with health cover, pension, housing guarantee, that kind of thing. You see, the sort of investigation you're talking about launching will absorb a lot of our resources. The Rutland force has only limited civic funds. To be honest with you, successfully tracing the driver would be a long shot. The chief has to focus his budget on areas which have a good probability of bringing positive results."

"I don't believe this. He's a kibbutznik, he's not employed by some big-shot corporation. The only money they have comes from selling eggs at the market. But that doesn't mean he's not a citizen; he's entitled to time and attention from the police."

"Sorry, sir. I'm not trying to discourage you, just telling you the way it is these days. I don't want you to leave here with false hopes of us being able to launch a manhunt for the driver. And even if we did, a hit-and-run incident without a witness . . ." He shook his head. "Just about zero conviction rate."

"I can pay," Greg said. He pulled out his platinum Event Horizon card. "Just show me what I have to sign, and get that bloody forensic team out there."

"It's Sunday, sir. The assigned case officer won't be in until tomorrow, I'm afraid. You'll have to speak with him about upgrading the investigation status."

Greg wondered if they would have the resources to investigate a member of the public punching an officer inside the station. Tempting to find out.

"There are private forensic laboratories, sir," the desk sergeant said. "We have an approved list if you'd like to use one. Some of them are very good."

It was no good shouting. Greg could see he was trying to be helpful, after a fashion. At which point Amanda Patterson called out his name.

Greg put the two pints of Ruddles County down on the table. Mike Wilson gave his glass a wary look.

"Cheers," Greg said. After they had got back from the Sullivan bungalow, he had waited outside the police station until the insurance agent had come out, then invited him for a quiet drink at the Wheatsheaf pub just around the corner. So far, Wilson was curious enough not to offer resistance, but he was clearly worried.

"You can relax," Greg told him. "I used to be a private eye. I've worked on corporate cases before. I understand the need for discretion at times like this."

"Uh huh." Mike took a sip of his beer.

"I know who did it." From a psychic perspective, the jolt of surprise flashing into Wilson's mind was quite amusing. He only just managed to avoid it triggering a physical jerk. That spoke of good self-control. Greg wasn't surprised at that, it confirmed several things he had speculated about the man.

"Who? We didn't see anyone who matched that bloody genome image."

Greg folded his arms and smiled. "You don't need to know."

"Why the hell not?"

"I don't want them convicted."

"I see."

"Which is the same reason you were given this investigation, isn't it? Keep an eye on Amanda. Wise move by your company. I worked with her before. She's a smart girl. And a very good police officer. She won't make compromises."

"And you will?"

"When it suits me. And this certainly does."

"Crescent Insurance would be happy to consider an adequate remuneration for the time you've spent advising Oakham CID."

"You should research more. I'm already rich."

"What then?"

"Tell me what line of investigation Crescent wants avoiding, and I'll see if we can help each other."

Wilson took a slow sip, and eased back into his chair. "Okay. I'm actually on secondment to Crescent; my employer is Hothouse."

"Byrne Tyler's agency?"

"Yeah. Look, showbiz is not pretty, okay? We deal with images, illusions. That's what we sell: characters larger than life. To the general public, Byrne is some hot young chunk of meat with a six-pack stomach and the devil's smile. In the dramas all he's got to do is show off that body in some tough action sequences and blow away bad guys with his big gun. In real life we portray him as an It Guy; he goes to all the best parties, he dates the most beautiful actresses and models, he's friends with the older, real celebrities. That's what we're promoting here, the more he's in the 'casts, the more 'castworthy he is. Doesn't matter if it's private-life gossip, or reviews for his latest pile of interactive shit. We put him out there and shine a light on him for everyone to idolize and buy every tie-in funny-colored chocolate bar we can slam at them. We make money, and Byrne gets a bigger apartment and a better nose job. Unfortunately, in reality, he's some half-wit sink-estate boy from Walthamstow we uprooted and dropped in front of the cameras. That's a shock to anyone's system. Certainly for him it was. He couldn't tell where the image stopped and life began. He's got a syntho habit, a dream-punch habit, a sweet&sour habit . . . he even uses crack, for Christ's sake; he can barely remember his one-word catch-phrase, and his autograph isn't in joined-up writing. What I'm saying is, he needs—needed—a lot of agency management and handling to cope with his new existence, right down to potty-training level."

"You didn't like him."

"I've never met him. Like I said, this is showbusiness, with the emphasis on business. Byrne Tyler was an investment on Hothouse's part. And it was starting to go ripe. A year ago he was living on credit, and his career was nose-diving. Well, even that's okay. It's not exactly the first time that's happened to a celeb. We know how to handle that. We got him partway through detox therapy, paired him up with the gorgeous Tamzin, and together they're riding high. Bingo, we're back on track, he's being offered new interactives, she's getting runway assignments for the bigger couture houses."

"So you wrote a happy ending. So what's the problem?"

"The problem is the middle of the story. When his cash was low and no studio would touch him, he earned his living the oldest way you can. All those trophy wives who's husbands are so decrepit they can't even take Laynon anymore. Single trust-fund babes, except at their age they aren't babes any longer. Even supermodels who wanted a serious no-comebacks, no-involvement shagging one night. Tyler serviced them all."

"Let me guess. You pimped him."

"Our investment was going negative. We pointed people in the right direction. Nobody got hurt. It paid off."

"Except now he's dead. And he recorded all those women on that big waterbed of his."

"Stupid little prick." Wilson nodded remorsefully. "Was it one of them, some husband or boyfriend who found out?"

"No. You're in the clear."

"Hardly. Amanda Patterson is going to start phoning around that goddamn list he left behind. Look, he beds twenty rich and famous girls, and he's a superstud, a hero to the lads. Thirty and he's unbelievable . . . how the hell did he manage that? Fifty of the richest women in Europe night after night, and damn right nobody'll believe it can happen. There's going to be rumors; the media will start scratching round. We won't be able to keep a lid on it."

"Perfect," Greg said. "I can deliver someone who can take the rap for Tyler's death. Amanda will stop phoning your list, and go after him instead. The Tyler case will be closed, and the women involved can quietly apply to the police for the recordings to be wiped under the privacy act."

"Who is it?"

"A nasty little man called Richard Townsend."

"Never heard of him."

"No reason you should. But I'm going to need a motive to link him in with Tyler. What other failings did our late celebrity have?"

Gabriel Thompson was one of Greg's oldest friends, from his army days. Morgan Walshaw he knew pretty well, handling security for the biggest company there was: Event Horizon. Trustworthy and competent at exactly the level Greg needed. It helped that the two of them had taken a shine to each other after meeting on one of Greg's cases. They'd moved in together a few months later, living in a grand old terrace house in Stamford.

Greg phoned them as soon as he got back from his drink with Mike Wilson. They arrived together at the farmhouse as the sun was sinking behind Berrybut spinney on the far shore. Gabriel helped with Christine's bathtime, while Greg and Morgan tackled the menu from the Chinese take-away in Mill Street.

They wound up sitting in the conservatory with the cartons from the take-away on the big cedar table. Pink light drained away from the clouds bridging the horizon leaving a quiescent gloaming in its wake.

"I need a safeguard before I agree to this," Morgan said after Greg had finished talking. "I appreciate there's a lot of circumstantial evidence that Townsend had Noel Broady run down, but we don't know for certain."

"I'll get myself in on the preliminary interview," Greg said. "If I can see he's guilty of paying someone to run Noel over, will that be enough for you?"

"Yes," Morgan said. "I'll accept your word."

"If he's not?" Gabriel asked archly.

"Then we collapse the deal. It'll leave a nasty smell, but at least he walks away."

"Okay," she said. "So what's the link between him and Tyler?"

"Hothouse set up a virtual company for Tyler to sell his action dramas and interactives. I think there's even a best-of compilation from *Marina Days*."

"Compelling stuff," Gabriel muttered.

"Yeah, anyway. This company is called Firedrake, and Mike Wilson has agreed to sell Hothouse's half share. It's only a pound New Sterling, so they don't exactly lose out. All we have to do is convince Townsend to buy it, and back-date the agreement."

"Why?" Morgan asked.

"Tyler wasn't quite as stupid as you'd think. He was using the site to sell bootleg memox crystals of his own stuff. Any orders you place on the Firedrake site are supposed to go to the distribution company that's contracted to deal with all Hothouse's clients. Tyler, the clever little sod, rigged the site so that two thirds of the orders are redirected to a bootlegging operation that he's got an arrangement with. That way, instead of getting his half-percent royalty payment from the cover price of the genuine crystal, he gets fifty percent of the price from the bootleg. Cash only, non-taxable. Hothouse found out about it a month ago, and confronted Tyler. He claimed he knew nothing, and that some hotrod had hacked into the site and loaded the diversion instructions. As his engagement to Tamzin was starting to produce results, Hothouse overlooked it, and sorted the site out."

"So whoever his partner in Firedrake is, they're being ripped off by Tyler," Eleanor said. "Anyone examining the Firedrake site order log and comparing it to the legitimate distribution company's orders will see the missing sixty percent straight away. The partner in Firedrake will have a justifiable grudge against Tyler."

"What that partner will do is have Tyler's apartment broken into, and steal a painting that is of equal worth to the missing money. Unfortunately, Tyler was at home when the burglary happened, there was a brief struggle, and he got pushed downstairs. That makes whoever received the stolen painting an accessory to murder. It'll be the physical proof Amanda needs to nail him."

"Can you get us a painting out of the apartment?" Gabriel asked.

"I think so," Greg said. "I reviewed the Macmillan art encyclopedia database. We got lucky, the most valuable piece Tyler owns is also the smallest one. It should be easy enough to lift it."

"When do you want to start?" Morgan asked.

"Right away. See if you can get an appointment with Townsend tomorrow morning. Gabriel, you're going to be the accountant. You'll have to hire an office for us in Peterborough. It needs to be ready by Tuesday at the latest. Suzi will give you a hand."

"Suzi? You're kidding!"

"No way. I'm going to bring her in as your company's secretary. She'll be perfect as the courier for the swap—Townsend won't argue with her."

"Jesus wept. Okay, if you say so."

"What about the Firedrake site?" Morgan asked. "Won't Townsend be suspicious of me marketing the interactives of a dead celebrity?"

"You won't be selling Tyler's products," Greg said. "I've got Royan designing a completely new architecture for us; from midnight, Firedrake will be selling software products and obscure music acts. Once Townsend has bought in, we'll change it back."

Gabriel gave her glass of beer a quizzical glance, then smiled softly. "Sounds good to me."

Greg had been right about Amanda Patterson—she was a first-rate detective. As soon as Hugh Snell confirmed the McCarthy was a fake she redirected her team's effort to produce maximum results. Every art house and auctioneer in the country was squirted an immediate notification about the painting, and CID staff were told to get in touch with known fences and dealers. A reward was mentioned.

Of course, as Townsend was blissfully unaware he had anything to hide, Sotheby's in Stamford got back to Amanda less than two hours later. Richard Townsend was identified.

"Not the person who actually pushed Tyler," she said regretfully, as she compared his picture with the genome visualization. An undercover team was assigned to keep Townsend under surveillance.

Greg watched as she turned her team to establishing the link between Tyler and Townsend. It was the accountant who tracked down the partnership in Firedrake. After that it was plain sailing. The accountant worked well with Alison, running analysis programs through the virtual company's records. The distribution company made their order logs available.

By ten o'clock that evening they had it all worked out. Byrne Tyler was ripping off his Firedrake partner Townsend, who discovered what was happening. Knowing the money would never be paid over, a burglar was hired for a custom theft.

But there had been a flaw. Byrne Tyler was awake when the break-in occurred. There must have been a struggle.

Amanda took the case to Vernon at quarter past ten. He reviewed it, and authorized the arrest warrant.

Throughout the interview with Townsend, Greg had felt as if he was the one on trial. Not so far from the truth. He was the one who had brought them all together. The strain was twisting him up inside, having to wait patiently while Amanda asked questions which Townsend didn't understand, let alone have answers for. Finally, he could ask the one question that counted.

Physically, Townsend froze up. His hands gripped the armrests, sweat glistened on his brow as his mouth hung open. In his mind, horror and fright rose like ghouls to contaminate every thought.

"Guilty," Greg said. He hoped he hadn't sagged at the release of his own tension.

"Thank you, Mr. Mandel," Amanda said.

It was the tone which alarmed Greg. He hadn't been paying attention to the detective. Now he could sense the doubts rippling through her mind. She held his gaze steadily, and said: "I think we both need to take a break now. No doubt you'd like to consult with your solicitor, Mr. Townsend. Interview suspended." She switched the AV deck off. "Greg, a word, please."

"Sure."

As they left the interview room a frantic Townsend was whispering furiously to Jodie Dobson. Amanda went straight downstairs and out into the station's car park. She rounded on Greg. "What the hell is going on?"

"You were right about him, my question confirmed that."

"Oh, bollocks, Greg. He doesn't have a clue what's going on."

"He's guilty. I swear it, Amanda."

"Yeah?" She dug in her pocket and pulled out a cigarette.

"I thought they were illegal?"

"No. That's a common mistake. Usage just prohibits you from claiming National Health Service treatment. If you choose to make yourself ill, don't expect the state to pay to make you better. So given that smoking actually makes it illegal to go to an NHS hospital, it's easy to see how confused people can get over the actual wording of the law. And it suits the government to encourage that confusion."

"Are we talking in metaphors here?"

"I don't know, Greg. I don't know what's metaphor, what's confusion, and what's truth. But I'm bloody sure Townsend didn't have anything to do with Tyler's death. Detective's instinct, remember."

"The evidence points straight at him."

"Yes. With amazing clarity. Funny how that all fell together yesterday. Why yesterday? Why didn't we have it before?"

"We only discovered the painting had been taken yesterday."

"So we did. No, actually, you did. On the third visit. What's the matter, Greg— psychic power not what it used to be?"

"It's not an exact science."

"No, it isn't. But you're right. We're lucky to discover the painting. After all, it must have been stolen during a burglary, and that burglary must have been last Wednesday night. Because it couldn't have been taken afterward; no one else has been alone in Tyler's apartment since then, have they Greg? Alone downstairs while I was taking a stupid call from Mike bloody Wilson."

Greg spread his arms, trying not to show how alarmed he was getting. "A few seconds."

"How long does it take to switch something that small?"

"I wouldn't know."

"Neither does Richard Townsend. He claims he only received that painting yesterday."

"He claims. Do you think Alan O'Hagen can confirm that?"

"You know as well as I do I'll never get to ask that question. But my investigation only took off once every piece of the puzzle was dumped into Townsend's hands for me to find." She dropped the half-smoked cigarette and crunched it under her foot. "What the hell happened to you, Greg? You, I thought you, of all people were trustworthy. For Christ's sake, you fought the PSP for a decade while people like me hid behind our desks. This is the world you were fighting for. Are you surprised it's not perfection? Is that it? Do you have so little faith in the police, in me, that you have to fabricate all this crap to set up an innocent man? Who the hell are you protecting, Greg?"

"Amanda, I promise you, Townsend is not innocent. He is responsible for someone's death."

"But not Tyler. If I asked that in the interview room and he said no, what would you tell me, Greg? Would you tell me he's lying?"

"You have all the evidence you need. It will hold together in court without my testimony. He's an accessory to murder. He's responsible."

"And you couldn't prove it? Not for the real crime. That's it, isn't it? No proof. So you set him up for this."

Greg remained silent, wondering where all this shame he was suddenly feeling was coming from.

"Fine, Greg," she said. "You got your man. But what about Tyler's killer. He's still walking around loose. He got away with it, with murder. Tyler might not have been the best person in the world, but surely he deserves better than us turning our backs on him?"

"Tyler wasn't murdered. It was a genuine accident. Although, if he hadn't been the person he was, it wouldn't have happened."

"What do you mean?"

Greg slowly took his cybofax from his jacket pocket, and flipped it open. The face of Tyler's killer looked out blankly from the screen. Greg typed in a few simple instructions, altering the characteristics age-projection program. The face evolved again, but not running its standard eighteen-to-eighty cycle. This time it went back eight years. Daniel Sullivan stared out at Amanda.

"Oh, fuck," she whispered.

"He found out that Tyler was blackmailing his sister into having sex," Greg said. "So that night he sneaked into the Ingalo's boot. He must have got in through the cloakroom window, probably even saw them on the bed together. Tyler heard him moving around and went to investigate. Daniel pushed him. A little boy incensed at what he'd seen happen to the sister he loved."

"And she covered for him," Amanda said. "Turned down the air-conditioning, took the crystal from the AV deck, wiped his fingerprints, then drove him home."

"Yeah."

"You knew it all the minute you walked into the bungalow, didn't you?"

"That poor kid was so scared I'm just surprised no one else noticed him."

"I need another cigarette."

"You shouldn't. They'll kill you." He waited to see what she'd do.

She took the packet of twenty from her pocket, and after a long moment handed them to him. "You keep them, and don't tell the health police, huh?"

"I don't have time right now. I have to organize a funeral."

"Anyone I know?"

"My father-in-law. He died after a hit-and-run."

Amanda paused for a moment. "Take care, Greg."

"And you." He got into the Ranger, and drove out of the station car park. A last glance in the rearview mirror showed him Amanda squaring her shoulders, then marching back into the station.

The Raggle Taggle Gypsy-o
Michael Swanwick

Here's a story featuring characters who are literally larger than life, in which we're given a vivid and passionate look at the worlds behind the ordinary world we know. . . .

Michael Swanwick made his debut in 1980, and in the twenty-one years that have followed has established himself as one of SF's most prolific and consistently excellent writers at short lengths, as well as one of the premier novelists of his generation.

He has several times been a finalist for the Nebula Award, as well as for the World Fantasy Award and the John W. Campbell Award, and has won the Theodore Sturgeon Award and the Asimov's Readers Award poll. In 1991, his novel Stations of the Tide won him a Nebula Award as well, and in 1995 he won the World Fantasy Award for his story "Radio Waves." In the last two years, he's won back-to-back Hugo Awards—he won the Hugo in 1999 for his story "The Very Pulse of the Machine," and followed it up last year with another Hugo Award for his story "Scherzo with Tyrannosaur." His other books include his first novel, In the Drift, which was published in 1985, a novella-length book, Griffin's Egg, 1987's popular novel Vacuum Flowers, and a critically acclaimed fantasy novel The Iron Dragon's Daughter, which was a finalist for the World Fantasy Award and the Arthur C. Clarke Award (a rare distinction!). His most recent novel was Jack Faust, a sly reworking of the Faust legend that explores the unexpected impact of technology on society. He's just finished a new novel, featuring time travelers and hungry dinosaurs. His short fiction has been assembled in Gravity's Angels, A Geography of Unknown Lands, and in a collection of his collaborative short work with other writers, Slow Dancing Through Time. He's also published a collection of critical articles, The Postmodern Archipelago. His most recent books are three new collections, Moon Dogs, Puck Aleshire's Abecedary, and Tales of Old Earth. Swanwick lives in Philadelphia with his wife, Marianne Porter, and their son Sean.

Among twenty snowy mountains, the only moving thing was the eye of Crow. The sky was blue, and the air was cold. His beard was rimed with frost. The tangled road behind was black and dry and empty.

At last, satisfied that there was nobody coming after them, he put down his binoculars. The way down to the road was steep. He fell three times as he half pushed and half swam his way through the drifts. His truck waited for him, idling. He stamped his feet on the tarmac to clear the boot treads and climbed up on the cab.

Annie looked up as he opened the door. Her smile was warm and welcoming, but with just that little glint of man-fear first, brief as the green flash at sunset, gone so quickly you wouldn't see it if you didn't know to look. *That wasn't me, babe*, he wanted to tell her. *Nobody's ever going to hit you again.* But he said nothing. You could tell the goddamnedest lies, and who was there to stop you? Let her judge him by his deeds. Crow didn't much believe in words.

He sat down heavily, slamming the door. "Cold as hell out there," he commented. Then, "How are they doing?"

Annie shrugged. "They're hungry again."

"They're always hungry." But Crow pulled the wicker picnic hamper out from under the seat anyway. He took out a dead puppy and pulled back the slide window at the rear of the cab. Then, with a snap of his wrist, he tossed the morsel into the van.

The monsters in the back began fighting over the puppy, slamming each other against the walls, roaring in mindless rage.

"Competitive buggers." He yanked the brake and put the truck into gear.

They had the heat cranked up high for the sake of their cargo, and after a few minutes he began to sweat. He pulled off his gloves, biting the fingertips and jerking back his head, and laid them on the dash, alongside his wool cap. Then he unbuttoned his coat.

"Gimme a hand here, willya?" Annie held the sleeve so he could draw out his arm. He leaned forward and she pulled the coat free and tossed it aside. "Thanks," he said.

Annie said nothing. Her hands went to his lap and unzipped his pants. Crow felt his pecker harden. She undid his belt and yanked down his BVDs. Her mouth closed upon him. The truck rattled underneath them.

"Hey, babe, that ain't really safe."

"Safe." Her hand squeezed him so hard he almost asked her to stop. But thought better of it. "I didn't hook up with a thug like you so I could be *safe*."

She ran her tongue down his shaft and begun sucking on his nuts. Crow drew in his breath. What the hell, he figured, might as well go along for the ride. Only he'd still better keep an eye on the road. They were going down a series of switchbacks. Easy way to die.

He downshifted, and downshifted again.

It didn't take long before he spurted.

He came and groaned and stretched and felt inordinately happy. Annie's head came up from his lap. She was smiling impishly. He grinned back at her.

Then she mashed her face into his and was kissing him deeply, passionately, his jism salty on her tongue and her tongue sticky in his mouth, and he *couldn't see!* Terrified, he slammed his foot on the brake. He was blind and out of control on one of the twistiest and most dangerous roads in the universe. The tires screamed.

He pushed Annie away from him so hard the back of her head bounced off the rider-side window. The truck's front wheels went off the road. Empty sky swung up to fill the windshield. In a frenzy, he swung the wheel so sharply he thought for a second they were going to overturn. There was a hideous *crunch* that sounded like part of the frame hitting rock, and then they were jolting safely down the road again.

"God damn," Crow said flatly. "Don't you ever do that again." He was shaking. "You're fucking crazy!" he added, more emphatically.

"Your fly is unzipped," Annie said, amused.

He hastily tucked himself in. "Crazy."

"You want crazy? You so much as look at another woman and I'll show you crazy." She opened the glove compartment and dug out her packet of Kents. "I'm just the girl for you, boyo, and don't you forget it." She lit up and then opened the window a crack for ventilation. Mentholated smoke filled the cabin.

In a companionable wordlessness they drove on through the snow and the blinding sunlight, the cab warm, the motor humming, and the monsters screaming at their back.

For maybe fifty miles he drove, while Annie drowsed in the seat beside him. Then the steering got stiff and the wheel began to moan under his hands whenever he turned it. It was a long, low, mournful sound like whale-song.

Without opening her eyes, Annie said, "What kind of weird-shit station are you listening to? Can't you get us something better?"

"Ain't no radio out here, babe. Remember where we are."

She opened her eyes. "So what is it, then?"

"Steering fluid's low. I think maybe we sprung a leak back down the road, when we almost went off."

"What are we going to do about it?"

"I'm not sure there's much we *can* do."

At which exact moment they turned a bend in the road and saw a gas station ahead. Two sets of pumps, diesel, air, a Mini-Mart, and a garage. Various machines of dubious functionality rusting out back.

Crow slammed on the brakes. "*That* shouldn't be there." He knew that for a fact. Last time he'd been through, the road had been empty all the way through to Troy.

Annie finally opened her eyes. They were the greenest things Crow had ever seen. They reminded him of sunlight through jungle leaves, of moss-covered cathedrals, of a stone city he'd once been to, sunk in the shallow waters of the Caribbean. That had been a dangerous place, but no more dangerous than this slim and lovely lady beside him. After a minute, she simply said, "Ask if they do repairs."

Crow pulled up in front of the garage and honked the horn a few times. A hound-lean mechanic came out, wiping his hands on a rag. "Yah?"

"Lissen, Ace, we got us a situation here with our steering column. Think you can fix us up?"

The mechanic stared at him, unblinking, and said, "We're all out of fluid. I'll take a look at your underside, though."

While the man was on a creeper under the truck, Crow went to the crapper. Then he ambled around back of the garage. There was a window there. He snapped the latch, climbed in, and poked around.

When he strolled up front again, the mechanic was out from under the truck and Annie was leaning against one of the pumps, flirting with him. He liked it, Crow could tell. Hell, even faggots liked it when Annie flirted at them.

Annie went off to the ladies' when he walked up, and by the time she came back the mechanic was inside again. She raised her eyebrows and Crow said, "Bastard says he can't fix the leak and ain't got no fluid. Only I boosted two cases out a window and stashed 'em in a junker out back. Go in and distract him, while I get them into the truck."

Annie thrust her hands deep into the pockets of her leather jacket and twisted slightly from foot to foot. "I've got a better thought," she said quietly. "Kill him."

"Say what?"

"He's one of Eric's people."

"You sure of that?"

"Ninety percent sure. He's here. What else could he be?"

"Yeah, well, there's still that other ten percent."

Her face was a mask. "Why take chances?"

"Jesus." Crow shook his head. "Babe, sometimes you give me the creeps. I don't mind admitting that you do."

"Do you love me? Then kill him."

"Hey. Forget that bullshit. We been together long enough, you must know what I'm like, okay? I ain't killing nobody today. Now go into the convenience there and buy us ten minutes, eh? Distract the man."

He turned her around and gave her a shove toward the Mini-Mart. Her shoulders were stiff with anger, her bottom big and around in those tight leather pants. God, but he loved the way she looked in those things! His hand ached to give her a swat on the rump, just to see her scamper. Couldn't do that with Annie, though. Not now, not never. Just one more thing that bastard Eric had spoiled for others.

He had the truck loaded and the steering column topped up by the time Annie strode out of the Mini-Mart with a boom box and a stack of CDs. The mechanic trotted after her, toting up prices on a little pad. When he presented her with the total, she simply said, "Send the bill to my husband," and climbed into the cab.

With a curt, wordless nod, the man turned back toward the store.

"Got anymore doubts?" Annie asked coldly.

Crow cursed. He'd killed men in his time, but it wasn't anything he was proud of. And never what you'd call murder. He slammed down the back of the seat, to access the storage compartment. All his few possessions were in there, and little enough they were for such a hard life as he'd led. Some spare clothes. A basket of trinkets he'd picked up along the way. His guns.

Forty miles down the road, Annie was still fuming. Abruptly, she turned and slammed Crow in the side with her fist. Hard. She had a good punch for a woman. Keeping one hand on the wheel, he half-turned and tried to seize her hands in one enormous fist. She continued hitting him in the chest and face until he managed to nab them both.

"What?" he demanded, angrily.

"You should have killed him."

"Three handfuls of gold nuggets, babe. I dug 'em out of the Yukon with my own mitts. That's enough money to keep anybody's mouth shut."

"Oh mercy God! Not one of Eric's men. Depend upon it, yon whoreson caitiff was on the phone the very instant you were out of his sight."

"You don't know that kind of cheap-jack hustler the way I do—" Crow began. Which was—he knew it the instant the words left his mouth—exactly the wrong thing to say to Annie. Her lips went thin and her eyes went hard. Her words were bitter and curt. Before he knew it, they were yelling at each other.

Finally he had no choice but to pull over, put the truck in park, and settle things right there on the front seat.

Afterward, she put on a CD she liked, old ballads and shit, and kept on playing it over and over. One in particular made her smile at him, eyes sultry and full of love, whenever it came on.

> *It was upstairs downstairs the lady went*
> *Put on her suit of leather-o*
> *And there was a cry from around the door*
> *She's away wi' the raggle taggle gypsy-o*

To tell the truth, the music wasn't exactly to his taste. But that was what they liked back where Annie came from. She couldn't stand his music. Said it was just noise. But when he felt that smile and those eyes on him it was better than three nights in Tijuana with any other woman he'd ever met. So he didn't see any point in making a big thing out of it.

The wheel was starting to freeze up on them again. Crow was looking for a good place to pull off and dump in a few cans of fluid, when suddenly Annie shivered and sat up straight. She stared off into the distance, over the eternal mountains. "What is it?" he asked.

"I have a premonition."

"Of what?" He didn't much like her premonitions. They always came true.

"Something. Over there." She lifted her arm and pointed.

Two Basilisks lifted up over the mountains.

"Shit!"

He stepped on the gas. "Hold tight, babe. We're almost there. I think we can outrun 'em."

They came down the exit ramp with the steering column moaning and howling like a banshee. Crow had to put all his weight on the wheel to make it turn. Braking, he left the timeless lands.

And came out in Rome.

One instant they were on the exit ramp surrounded by lifeless mountains. The next they were pushing through narrow roads choked with donkey carts and toga-clad pedestrians. Crow brought the truck to a stop, and got out to add fluid.

The truck took up most of the road. People cursed and spat at him for being in their way. But nobody seemed to find anything unusual in the fact that he was driving an internal-combustion engine. They all took it in their stride.

It was wonderful how the timelines protected themselves against anachronisms by simply ignoring them. A theoretical physicist Crow had befriended in Babylon had called it "robust integrity." You could introduce the printing press into dynastic Egypt and six months later the device would be discarded and forgotten. Machine-gun the infant Charlemagne and within the year those who had been there would remember him having been stabbed. A century later every detail of his career as Emperor would be chronicled, documented, and revered, down to his dotage and death.

It hadn't made a lot of sense to Crow, but, "Live with it," the physicist had said, and staggered off in search of his great-great-five-hundred-times-great-grandmother with silver in his pocket and a demented gleam in his eye. So there it was.

Not an hour later, they arrived at the Coliseum and were sent around back to the tradesmen's entrance.

"*Ave*," Crow said to the guard there. "I want to talk to one of the—hey, Annie, what's Latin for animal wrangler?"

"Bestiarius."

"Yeah, that's it. Fella name of Carpophorus."

Carpophorus was delighted with his new pets. He watched eagerly as the truck was backed up to the cage. Two sparsores with grappling-hooks unlatched the truck doors and leaped back as eleven nightmares poured out of the truck. They were all teeth and claws and savage quickness. One of their number lay dead on the floor of the truck. Not bad for such a long haul.

"What are they?" Carpophorus asked, entranced.

"Deinonychi."

" 'Terrible-claws,' eh? Well, they fit the bill, all right." He thrust an arm between the bars, and then leaped back, chuckling, as two of the lithe young carnivores sprang at it. "Fast, too. Oh, Marcus *will* be pleased!"

"I'm glad you like 'em. Listen, we got a little trouble here with our steering column . . ."

"Down that ramp, to the right. Follow the signs. Tell Flamma I sent you." He turned back to the deinonychi, and musingly said, "Should they fight hoplomachi?

Or maybe dimachaeri?" Crow knew the terms; the former were warriors who fought in armor, the latter with two knives.

"Horses would be nice," a sparsore commented. "If you used andabatae, they'd be able to strike from above."

Carpophorus shook his head. "I have it! Those Norse bear-sarkers I've been saving for something special—what could be more special than this?"

It was a regular labyrinth under the Coliseum. They had everything down there: workshops, brothels, training rooms, even a garage. At the mention of Carpophorus' name, a mechanic dropped everything to check out their truck. They sat in the stands, munching on a head of lettuce and watching the gladiators practice. An hour later a slave came up to tell them it was fixed.

They bought a room at a tavern that evening and ordered the best meal in the house. Which turned out to be sow's udders stuffed with fried baby mice. They washed it down with a wine that tasted like turpentine and got drunk and screwed and fell asleep. At least, Annie did. Crow sat up for a time, thinking.

Was she going to wake up some morning in a cold barn or on a piss-stained mattress and miss her goose-down comforters, her satin sheets, and her liveried servants? She'd been nobility, after all, and the wife of a demiurge . . .

He hadn't meant to run off with anybody's wife. But when he and some buddies had showed up at Lord Eric's estates, intent upon their own plans, there Annie was. No man that liked women could look upon Annie and not want her. And Crow couldn't want something without trying to get it. Such was his nature—he couldn't alter it.

He'd met her in the gardens out by Lord Eric's menagerie. A minor tweak of the weather had been made, so that the drifts of snow were held back to make room for bright mounds of prehistoric orchids. "Th'art a ragged fellow indeed, sirrah," she'd said with cool amusement.

He'd come under guise of a musician at a time when Lord Eric was away for a few years monkeying with the physical constants of the universe or some such bullshit. The dinosaurs had been his target from the first, though he wasn't above boffing the boss's lady on the way out. But something about her made him want her for more than just the night. Then and there he swore to himself that he'd win her, fair and without deceit, and on his own terms. "These ain't rags, babe," he'd said, hooking his thumbs into his belt. "They're my colors."

They stayed in Rome for a week, and they didn't go to watch the games, though Annie—who was born in an era whose idea of entertainment included public executions and bear-baitings—wanted to. But the deinonychi were by all accounts a hit. Afterward, they collected their reward in the form of silver bars, "as many," Carpophorus gleefully quoted his sponsor, Marcus, as saying, "as the suspension of their truck will bear."

Marcus was a rich man from a good family and had political ambitions. Crow happened to know he'd be dead within the month, but he didn't bother mentioning the fact. Leave well enough alone, was his motto.

"Why did we wait around," Annie wanted to know afterward, "if we weren't going to watch?"

"To make sure it actually happened. Eric can't come in now and snatch back his dinos without creating a serious line paradox. As I read it, that's considered bad form for a Lord of Creation." They were on the streets of Rome again, slowed to a crawl by the density of human traffic. Crow leaned on the horn again and again.

They made a right turn and then another, and then the traffic was gone. Crow threw the transmission into second and stepped on the accelerator. They were back among the Mountains of Eternity. From here they could reach any historical era and even, should they wish, the vast stretches of time that came before and after. All the roads were clear, and there was nothing in their way.

Less than a month later, subjective time, they were biking down that same road, arguing. Annie was lobbying for him to get her a sidecar and Crow didn't think much of that idea at all.

"This here's my *hog*, goddamnit!" he explained. "I chopped her myself—you put a sidecar on it, it'll be all the fuck out of balance."

"Yeah, well, I hope you enjoy jerking off. Because my fucking ass is so goddamn sore that . . ."

He'd opened up the throttle to drown out what she was about to say when suddenly Annie was pounding on his back, screaming, "Pull over!"

Crow was still braking the Harley when she leaned over to the side and began to puke.

When she was done, Crow dug a Schlitz out of the saddlebags and popped the tab. Shakily, she accepted it. "What was it!" he asked.

Annie gargled and spat out the beer. "Another premonition—a muckle bad one, I trow." Then, "Hey. Who do I have to fuck to get a smoke around here?"

Crow lit up a Kent for her.

Midway through the cigarette, she shuddered again and went rigid. Her pupils shrank to pinpricks, and her eyes turned up in their sockets, so they were almost entirely white. The sort of thing that would've gotten her burned for a witch, back in good old sixteenth-c England.

She raised a hand, pointing. "Incoming. Five of them."

They were ugly fuckers, the Basilisks were: black, unornamented two-rotor jobs, and noisy too. You could hear them miles off.

Luckily, Annie's foresight had given Crow the time to pick out a good defensive position. Cliff face to their back, rocks to crouch behind, enough of an overhang they couldn't try anything from above. Enough room to stash the bike, just in case they came out of this one alive. There was a long, empty slope before them. Their pursuers would have to come running up it.

The formation of Basilisks thundered closer.

"Pay attention, babe," Crow said. "I'm gonna teach you a little guerrilla warfare."

He got out his rifle from its saddle sheath. It was a Savage 110 Tactical. Good sniper rifle. He knew this gun. He'd packed the shells himself. It was a reliable piece of machinery.

"This here's a trick I learned in a little jungle war you probably ain't never heard of. Hold out your thumb at arm's length, okay? Now you wait until the helicopter's as big as the thumb. That's when it's close enough you can shoot it down."

"Will that work?" she asked nervously.

"Hell, if the Cong could do it, so can I."

He took out three Basilisks before the others could sweep up and around and out of range again. It was damned fine shooting if he did say so himself. But then the survivors set down in the distant snow and disgorged at least thirty armed men. Which changed the odds somewhat.

Annie counted soldiers, and quietly said, "Crow . . ."

Crow held a finger to her lips.

"Don't you worry none about *me*. I'm a trickster, babe. I'm archetypal. Ain't none of them can touch the Man."

Annie kissed his finger and squeezed his hand. But by the look in her eyes, he could tell she knew he was lying. "They can make you suffer, though," she said. "Eric has an old enemy staked to a rock back at his estates. Vultures come and eat his intestines."

"That's his brother, actually." It was an ugly story, and he was just as glad when she didn't ask him to elaborate. "Hunker down, now. Here they come."

The troops came scattershot up the slope, running raggedly from cover to cover. Very professional. Crow settled himself down on his elbows, and raised his rifle. Not much wind. On a day like today, he ought to be able to hit a man at five hundred yards ten times out of ten. "Kiss your asses good-bye," he muttered.

He figured he'd take out half of them before they got close enough to throw a stasis grenade.

Lord Eric was a well-made man, tall and full of grace. He had the glint of power to him, was bold and fair of face. A touch of lace was at his wrist. His shirt was finest silk.

"Lady Anne," he said.

"Lord Eric."

"I have come to restore you to your home and station: to your lands, estates, gracious powers, and wide holdings. As well as to the bed of your devoted husband." His chariot rested in the snow behind him; he'd waited until all the dirty work was done before showing up.

"You are no longer my husband. I have cast my fortune with a better man than thou."

"That gypsy?" He afforded Crow the briefest and most dismissive of glances. " 'Tis no more than a common thief, scarce worth the hemp to hang him, the wood to burn him, the water to drown him, nor the earth to bury him. Yet he has made free with a someat trifle that is mine and mine alone to depose — I speak of your honor. So he must die. He must die, and thou be brought to heel, as obedient to my hand as my hawk, my hound, or my horse."

She spat at his feet. "Eat shit, asshole."

Lord Eric's elegant face went white. He drew back his fist to strike her.

Crow's hands were cuffed behind his back, and he couldn't free them. So he lurched suddenly forward, catching his captors and Eric by surprise, and took the blow on his own face. That sucker hurt, but he didn't let it show. With the biggest, meanest grin he could manage, he said, "See, there's the difference between you and me. You couldn't stop yourself from hurting her. I could."

"Think you so?" Lord Eric gestured and one of his men handed him a pair of gray kid gloves of finest Spanish leather. "I raised a mortal above her state. Four hundred years was she my consort. No more."

Fear entered Annie's eyes for the first time, though nobody who knew her less well than Crow could have told.

"I will strangle her myself," Eric said, pulling on the gloves. "She deserves no less honor, for she was once my wife."

The tiger cage was set up on a low dais; one focus of the large, oval room. Crow knew from tiger cages, but he'd never thought he'd wind up in one. Especially not in the middle of somebody's party.

Especially not at Annie's wake.

The living room was filled with demiurges and light laughter, cocaine and gin. Old Tezcatlipoca, who had been as good as a father to Crow in his time, seeing him, grimaced and shook his head. Now Crow regretted ever getting involved with Spaniards, however sensible an idea it had seemed at the time.

The powers and godlings who orbited the party, cocktails in hand, solitary and aloof as planets, included Lady Dale, who bestowed riches with one hand and lightnings from the other, and had a grudge against Crow for stealing her distaff; Lord Aubrey of the short and happy lives, who hated him for the sake of a friend; Lady Siff of the flames, whose attentions he had once scorned; and Reverend Wednesday, old father death himself, in clerical collar, stiff with disapproval at Crow's libertine ways.

He had no allies anywhere in this room.

Over there was Lord Taleisin, the demiurge of music, who, possibly alone of all this glittering assemblage, bore Crow no ill will. Crow figured it was because Tal had never learned the truth behind that business back in Crete.

He figured, too, there must be some way to turn that to his advantage.

"You look away from me every time I go by," Lord Taleisin said. "Yet I know of no offense you have given me, or I you."

"Just wanted to get your attention is all," Crow said. "Without any of the others suspecting it." His brow was set in angry lines but his words were soft and mild. "I been thinking about how I came to be. I mean, you guys are simply *there*, a part of the natural order of things. But us archetypes are created out of a million years of campfire tales and wishful lies. We're thrown up out of the collective unconscious. I got to wondering what would happen if somebody with access to that unconscious—you, for example—was to plant a few songs here and there."

"It could be done, possibly. Nothing's certain. But what would be the point?"

"How'd you like your brother's heart in a box?"

Lord Tal smiled urbanely. "Eric and I may not see eye to eye on everything, yet I cannot claim to hate him so as to wish the physical universe rendered uninhabitable."

"Not him. Your other brother."

Tal involuntarily glanced over his shoulder, toward the distant mountain, where a small dark figure lay tormented by vultures. The house had been built here with just that view in mind. "If it could be done, don't you think I'd've done it?" Leaving unsaid but understood: *How could you succeed where I have failed?*

"I'm the trickster, babe—remember? I'm the wild card, the unpredictable element, the unexpected event. I'm the blackfly under the saddle. I'm the ice on the O-rings. I am the *only* one who could do this for you."

Very quietly, Lord Taleisin said, "What sureties do you require?"

"Your word's good enough for me, pal. Just don't forget to spit in my face before you leave. It'll look better."

"Have fun," Lord Eric said, and left the room.

Eric's men worked Crow over good. They broke his ribs and kicked in his face. A couple of times they had to stop to get their breath back, they were laboring so hard. He had to give them credit, they put their backs into the work. But, like Crow himself, the entertainment was too boorish for its audience. Long before it was done, most of the partyers had left in boredom or disgust.

At last he groaned, and he died.

Well, what was a little thing like death to somebody like Crow? He was archetypal—the universe demanded that he exist. Kill him here-and-now and he'd be reborn there-and-then. It wouldn't be long before he was up and around again.

But not Annie.

No, that was the bitch of the thing. Annie was dead, and the odds were good she wasn't coming back.

Among twenty smog-choked cities, the only still thing was the eye of Crow. He leaned back, arms crossed, in the saddle of his Harley, staring at a certain door so hard he was almost surprised his gaze didn't burn a hole in it.

A martlet flew down from the sky and perched on the handlebars. It was a little bird, round-headed and short-beaked, with long sharp wings. Its eyes were two stars shining. "Hail!" it said.

"Hail, fire, and damnation," Crow growled. "Any results?"

"Lord Taleisin has done as you required, and salted the timelines with songs. In London, Nashville, and Azul-Tlon do they praise her beauty, and the steadfastness of her love. In a hundred guises and a thousand names is she exalted. From mammoth-bone medicine lodges to MTVirtual, they sing of Lady Anne, of the love that sacrifices all comfort, and of the price she gladly paid for it."

Still the door did not open.

"That's not what I asked, shit-for-brains. Did it work?"

"Perhaps." The bird cocked its head. "Perhaps not. I was told to caution you: Even at best, you will only have a now-and-again lady. Archetypes don't travel in pairs. If it works, your meetings will be like solar eclipses—primal, powerful, rare, and brief."

"Yeah, yeah."

The creature hesitated, and if a bird could be said to look abashed, then it looked strangely abashed. "I was also told that you would have something for me."

Without looking, Crow unstrapped his saddlebag and rummaged within. He removed a wooden heart-shaped box, tied up in string. "Here."

With a glorious burst of unearthly song, the martlet seized the string in its talons and, wings whirring, flew straight up into the sky. Crow did not look after it. He waited.

He waited until he was sure that the door would never open. Then he waited some more.

The door opened.

Out she came, in faded Levis, leather flight jacket, and a black halter top, sucking on a Kent menthol. She was looking as beautiful as the morning and as hard as nails. The sidewalk cringed under her high-heeled boots.

"Hey, babe," Crow said casually. "I got you a sidecar. See? It's lined with velvet and everything."

"Fuck that noise," Annie said and, climbing on behind him, hugged him so hard that his ribs creaked.

He kick-started the Harley and with a roar they pulled out into traffic. Crow cranked up the engine and popped a wheelie. Off they sped, down the road that leads everywhere and nowhere, to the past and the future, Tokyo and Short Pump, infinity and the corner store, with Annie laughing and unafraid, and Crow flying the black flag of himself.

Radiant green star

Lucius Shepard

Here's a powerful, darkly elegant, and high-intensity novella that takes us to the strange, haunted landscape of a high-tech future Vietnam for a study of hatred, compassion, betrayal, and redemption—and of the many different kinds of ghosts.

Lucius Shepard was one of the most popular, influential, and prolific of the new writers of the eighties and that decade and the decade that followed would see a steady stream of bizarre and powerfully compelling stories by Shepard, stories such as the landmark novella "R&R," which won him a Nebula Award in 1987, "The Jaguar Hunter," "Black Coral," "A Spanish Lesson," "The Man Who Painted the Dragon Griaule," "Shades," "A Traveller's Tale," "Human History," "How the Wind Spoke at Madaket," "Beast of the Heartland," "The Scalehunter's Beautiful Daughter," and "Barnacle Bill the Spacer," which won him a Hugo Award in 1993. In 1988, he picked up a World Fantasy Award for his monumental short-story collection The Jaguar Hunter, *following it in 1992 with a second World Fantasy Award for his second collection,* The Ends of the Earth. *Shepard's other books include the novels* Green Eyes, Kalimantan, *and* The Golden. *His most recent book is a new collection,* Barnacle Bill the Spacer, *and he's currently at work on a mainstream novel,* Family Values. *Born in Lynchburg, Virginia, he now lives in Vancouver, Washington.*

Several months before my thirteenth birthday, my mother visited me in a dream and explained why she had sent me to live with the circus seven years before. The dream was a Mitsubishi, I believe, its style that of the Moonflower series of biochips, which set the standard for pornography in those days; it had been programmed to activate once my testosterone production reached a certain level, and it featured a voluptuous Asian woman to whose body my mother had apparently grafted the image of her own face. I imagined she must have been in a desperate hurry and thus forced to use whatever materials fell to hand; yet, taking into account the Machiavellian intricacies of the family history, I later came to think that her decision to alter a pornographic chip might be intentional, designed to provoke Oedipal conflicts that would imbue her message with a heightened urgency.

In the dream, my mother told me that when I was eighteen I would come into the trust created by my maternal grandfather, a fortune that would make me the wealthiest man in Viet Nam. Were I to remain in her care, she feared my father would eventually coerce me into assigning control of the trust to him, whereupon he would have me killed. Sending me to live with her old friend Vang Ky was the one means she had of guaranteeing my safety. If all went as planned, I would have several years to consider whether it was in my best interests to claim the trust or to forswear it and continue my life in secure anonymity. She had faith that Vang would educate me in a fashion that would prepare me to arrive at the proper decision.

Needless to say, I woke from the dream in tears. Vang had informed me not long after my arrival at his door that my mother was dead, and that my father was likely responsible for her death; but this fresh evidence of his perfidy, and of her courage and sweetness, mingled though it was with the confusions of intense eroticism, renewed my bitterness and sharpened my sense of loss. I sat the rest of the night with only the eerie music of tree frogs to distract me from despair, which roiled about in my brain as if it were a species of sluggish life both separate from and inimical to my own.

The next morning, I sought out Vang and told him of the dream and asked what I should do. He was sitting at the desk in the tiny cluttered trailer that served as his home and office, going over the accounts: a frail man in his late sixties with close-cropped gray hair, dressed in a white open-collared shirt and green cotton trousers. He had a long face—especially long from cheekbones to jaw—and an almost feminine delicacy of feature, a combination of characteristics that lent him a sly, witchy look; but though he was capable of slyness, and though at times I suspected him of possessing supernatural powers, at least as regards his ability to ferret out my misdeeds, I perceived him at the time to be an inwardly directed soul who felt misused by the world and whose only interests, apart from the circus, were a love of books and calligraphy. He would occasionally take a pipe of opium, but was otherwise devoid of vices, and it strikes me now that while he had told me of his family and his career in government (he said he still maintained those connections), of a life replete with joys and passionate errors, he was now in the process of putting all that behind him and withdrawing from the world of the senses.

"You must study the situation," he said, shifting in his chair, a movement that shook the wall behind him, disturbing the leaflets stacked in the cabinet above his head and causing one to sail down toward the desk; he batted it away, and for an instant it floated in the air before me, as if held by the hand of a spirit, a detailed pastel rendering of a magnificent tent—a thousand times more magnificent than the one in which we performed—and a hand-lettered legend proclaiming the imminent arrival of the Radiant Green Star Circus.

"You must learn everything possible about your father and his associates," he went on. "Thus you will uncover his weaknesses and define his strengths. But first and foremost, you must continue to live. The man you become will determine how best to use the knowledge you have gained, and you mustn't allow the pursuit of your studies to rise to the level of obsession, or else his judgment will be clouded. Of course, this is easier to do in theory than in practice. But if you set about it in a measured way, you will succeed."

I asked how I should go about seeking the necessary information, and he gestured with his pen at another cabinet, one with a glass front containing scrapbooks and bundles of computer paper; beneath it, a marmalade cat was asleep atop a broken radio, which—along with framed photographs of his wife, daughter, and grandson, all killed, he'd told me, in an airline accident years before—rested on a chest of drawers.

"Start there," he said. "When you are done with those, my friends in the government will provide us with your father's financial records and other materials."

I took a cautious step toward the cabinet—stacks of magazines and newspapers and file boxes made the floor of the trailer difficult to negotiate—but Vang held up a hand to restrain me. "First," he said, "you must live. We will put aside a few hours each day for you to study, but before all else you are a member of my troupe. Do your chores. Afterward we will sit down together and make a schedule."

On the desk, in addition to his computer, were a cup of coffee topped with a mixture of sugar and egg, and a plastic dish bearing several slices of melon. He offered me a slice and sat with his hands steepled on his stomach, watching me eat. "Would you like time alone to honor your mother?" he asked. "I suppose we can manage without you for a morning."

"Not now," I told him. "Later, though . . ."

I finished the melon, laid the rind on his plate, and turned to the door, but he called me back.

"Philip," he said, "I cannot remedy the past, but I can assure you to a degree as to the future. I have made you my heir. One day the circus will be yours. Everything I own will be yours."

I peered at him, not quite certain that he meant what he said, even though his words had been plain.

"It may not seem a grand gift," he said. "But perhaps you will discover that it is more than it appears."

I thanked him effusively, but he grimaced and waved me to silence—he was not comfortable with displays of affection. Once again he told me to see to my chores.

"Attend to the major as soon as you're able," he said. "He had a difficult night. I know he would be grateful for your company."

Radiant Green Star was not a circus in the tradition of the spectacular traveling shows of the previous century. During my tenure, we never had more than eight performers and only a handful of exhibits, exotics that had been genetically altered in some fashion: a pair of miniature tigers with hands instead of paws, a monkey with a vocabulary of thirty-seven words, and the like. The entertainments we presented were unsophisticated; we could not compete with those available in Hanoi or Hue or Saigon, or, for that matter, those accessible in the villages. But the villagers perceived us as a link to a past they revered, and found in the crude charm of our performances a sop to their nostalgia—it was as if we carried the past with us, and we played to that illusion, keeping mainly to rural places that appeared on the surface to be part of another century. Even when the opportunity arose, Vang refused to play anywhere near large population centers because—he said—of the exorbitant bribes and licensing fees demanded by officials in such areas. Thus for the first eighteen years of my life, I did not venture into a city, and I came to know my country much as a tourist might, driving ceaselessly through it, isolated within the troupe. We traversed the north and central portions of Viet Nam in three battered methane-powered trucks, one of which towed Vang's trailer, and erected our tents in pastures and school yards and soccer fields, rarely staying anywhere longer than a few nights. On occasion, to accommodate a private celebration sponsored by a wealthy family, we would join forces with another troupe; but Vang was reluctant to participate in such events, because being surrounded by so many people caused our featured attraction to become agitated, thus imperiling his fragile health.

Even today the major remains a mystery to me. I have no idea if he was who he claimed to be; nor, I think, did *he* know—his statements concerning identity were usually vague and muddled, and the only point about which he was firm was that he had been orphaned as a young boy, raised by an uncle and aunt, and, being unmarried, was the last of his line. Further, it's unclear whether his claims were the product of actual memory, delusion, or implantation. For the benefit of our audiences, we let them stand as truth, and billed him as Major Martin Boyette, the last surviving POW of the American War, now well over a hundred years old and horribly disfigured, both conditions the result of experiments in genetic manipulation by means of viruses—this the opinion of a Hanoi physician who treated the major during a bout of illness. Since such unregulated experiments were performed with immoderate frequency throughout Southeast Asia after the turn of the century, it was not an unreasonable conclusion. Major Boyette himself had no recollection of the process that had rendered him so monstrous and—if one were to believe him—so long-lived.

We were camped that day near the village of Cam Lo, and the tent where the major was quartered had been set up at the edge of the jungle. He liked the jungle, liked its noise and shadow, the sense of enclosure it provided—he dreaded the prospect of being out in the open, so much so that whenever we escorted him to the main tent, we would walk with him, holding umbrellas to prevent him from seeing the sky and to shield him from the sight of god and man. But once inside the main tent, as if the formal structure of a performance neutralized his aversion to space and scrutiny, he showed himself pridefully, walking close to the bleachers, causing children to shy away and women to cover their eyes. His skin hung from his flesh in voluminous black folds (he was African-American), and when he raised his arms, the folds beneath them spread like the wings of a bat; his face, half-hidden by a layering of what appeared to be leather shawls, was the sort of uncanny face one might see emerging from a whorled pattern of bark, roughly human in form, yet animated by a force that seems hotter than the human soul, less self-aware. Bits of phosphorescence drifted in the darks of his eyes. His only clothing was a ragged gray shift, and he hobbled along with the aid of a staff cut from a sapling papaya—he might have been a prophet escaped after a term in hell, charred and magical and full of doom. But when he began to speak, relating stories from the American War, stories of ill-fated Viet Cong heroes and the supernatural forces whose aid they enlisted, all told in a deep rasping voice, his air of suffering and menace evaporated, and his ugliness became an intrinsic article of his power, as though he were a poet who had sacrificed superficial glamor for the ability to express more eloquently the beauty within. The audiences were won over, their alarm transformed to delight, and they saluted him with enthusiastic applause . . . but they never saw him as I did that morning: a decrepit hulk given to senile maundering and moments of bright terror when startled by a sound from outside the tent. Sitting in his own filth, too weak or too uncaring to move.

When I entered the tent, screwing up my face against the stench, he tucked his head into his shoulder and tried to shroud himself in the fetid folds of his skin. I talked softly, gentling him as I might a frightened animal, in order to persuade him to stand. Once he had heaved up to his feet, I bathed him, sloshing buckets of water over his convulsed surfaces; when at length I was satisfied that I'd done my best, I hauled in freshly cut boughs and made him a clean place to sit. Unsteadily, he lowered himself onto the boughs and started to eat from the bowl of rice and vegetables I had brought for his breakfast, using his fingers to mold bits of food into a ball and inserting it deep into his mouth—he often had difficulty swallowing.

"Is it good?" I asked. He made a growly noise of affirmation. In the half-dark, I could see the odd points of brilliance in his eyes.

I hated taking care of the major (this may have been the reason Vang put me in charge of him). His physical state repelled me, and though the American War had long since ceased to be a burning issue, I resented his purported historical reality—being half American, half Vietnamese, I felt doubly afflicted by the era he represented. But that morning, perhaps because my mother's message had inoculated me against my usual prejudices, he fascinated me. It was like watching a mythological creature feed, a chimera or a manticore, and I thought I perceived in him the soul of the inspired storyteller, the luminous half-inch of being that still burned behind the corroded ruin of his face.

"Do you know who I am?" I asked.

He swallowed and gazed at me with those haunted foxfire eyes. I repeated the question.

"Philip," he said tonelessly, giving equal value to both syllables, as if the name were a word he'd been taught but did not understand.

I wondered if he was—as Vang surmised—an ordinary man transformed into a monster, pumped full of glorious tales and false memories, all as a punishment for some unguessable crime or merely on a cruel whim. Or might he actually *be* who he claimed? A freak of history, a messenger from another time whose stories contained some core truth, just as the biochip had contained my mother's truth? All I knew for certain was that Vang had bought him from another circus, and that his previous owner had found him living in the jungle in the province of Quan Tri, kept alive by the charity of people from a nearby village who considered him the manifestation of a spirit.

Once he had finished his rice, I asked him to tell me about the war, and he launched into one of his mystical tales; but I stopped him, saying, "Tell me about the real war. The war you fought in."

He fell silent, and when at last he spoke, it was not in the resonant tones with which he entertained our audiences, but in an effortful whisper.

"We came to the firebase in . . . company strength. Tenth of May. Nineteen sixty-seven. The engineers had just finished construction and . . . and . . . there was still . . ." He paused to catch his breath. "The base was near the Laotian border. Overlooking a defoliated rubber plantation. Nothing but bare red earth in front of us . . . and wire. But at our rear . . . the jungle . . . it was too close. They brought in artillery to clear it. Lowered the batteries to full declension. The trees all toppled in the same direction . . . as if they'd been pushed down by the sweep . . . of an invisible hand."

His delivery, though still labored, grew less halting, and he made feeble gestures to illustrate the tale, movements that produced a faint slithering as folds of his skin rubbed together; the flickerings in his pupils grew more and more pronounced, and I half-believed his eyes were openings onto a battlefield at night, a place removed from us by miles and time.

"Because of the red dirt, the base was designated Firebase Ruby. But the dirt wasn't the color of rubies, it was the red of drying blood. For months we held the position with only token resistance. We'd expected serious opposition, and it was strange to sit there day after day with nothing to do except send out routine patrols. I tried to maintain discipline, but it was an impossible task. Everyone malingered. Drug use was rampant. If I'd gone by the book I could have brought charges against every man on the base. But what was the point? War was not truly being waged. We were engaged in a holding action. Policy was either directionless or misguided. And so I satisfied myself by maintaining a semblance of discipline as the summer heat and the monsoon melted away the men's resolve.

"October came, the rains slackened. There was no hint of increased enemy activity, but I had a feeling something big was on the horizon. I spoke to my battalion commander. He felt the same way. I was told we had intelligence suggesting that the enemy planned a fall and winter campaign building up to Tet. But no one took it seriously. I don't think I took it seriously myself. I was a professional soldier who'd been sitting idle for six months, and I was spoiling for a fight. I was so eager for engagement I failed to exercise good judgment. I ignored the signs, I . . . I refused . . . I . . ."

He broke off and pawed at something above him in the air—an apparition, perhaps; then he let out an anguished cry, covered his face with his hands, and began to shake like a man wracked by fever.

I sat with him until, exhausted, he lapsed into a fugue, staring dully at the ground. He was so perfectly still, if I had come across him in the jungle, I might have mistaken him for a root system that had assumed a hideous anthropomorphic shape. Only the glutinous surge of his breath opposed this impression. I didn't know what to think of his story. The plain style of its narration had been markedly different from that of his usual stories, and this lent it credibility; yet I recalled that whenever questioned about his identity, he would respond in a similar fashion. However, the ambiguous character of his personal tragedy did not diminish my new fascination with his mystery. It was as if I had been dusting a vase that rested on my mantelpiece, and, for the first time, I'd turned it over to inspect the bottom and found incised there a labyrinthine design, one that drew my eye inward along its black circuit, promising that should I be able to decipher the hidden character at its center, I would be granted a glimpse of something ultimately bleak and at the same time ultimately alluring. Not a secret, but rather the source of secrets. Not truth, but the ground upon which truth and its opposite were raised. I was a mere child—half a child, at any rate—thus I have no real understanding of how I arrived at this recognition, illusory though it may have been. But I can state with absolute surety why it seemed important at the time: I had a powerful sense of connection with the major, and, accompanying this, the presentiment that his mystery was somehow resonant with my own.

Except for my new program of study, researching my father's activities, and the enlarged parameters of my relationship with Major Boyette, whom I visited whenever I had the opportunity, over the next several years my days were much the same as ever, occupied by touring, performing (I functioned as a clown and an apprentice knife thrower), by all the tediums and pleasures that arose from life in Radiant Green Star. There were, of course, other changes. Vang grew increasingly frail and withdrawn, the major's psychological state deteriorated, and four members of the troupe left and were replaced. We gained two new acrobats, Kim and Kai, pretty Korean sisters aged seven and ten respectively—orphans trained by another circus—and Tranh, a middle-aged, moonfaced man whose potbelly did not hamper in the slightest his energetic tumbling and pratfalls. But to my mind, the most notable of the replacements was Vang's niece, Tan, a slim, quiet girl from Hue with whom I immediately fell in love.

Tan was nearly seventeen when she joined us, a year older than I, an age difference that seemed unbridgeable to my teenage sensibilities. Her shining black hair hung to her waist, her skin was the color of sandalwood dusted with gold, and her face was a perfect cameo in which the demure and the sensual commingled. Her father had been in failing health, and both he and his wife had been uploaded into a virtual community hosted by the Sony AI—Tan had then become her uncle's ward. She had no actual performing skills, but dressed in glittery revealing costumes, she danced and took part in comic skits and served as one of the targets for our knife thrower, a taciturn young man named Dat who was billed as James Bond Cochise. Dat's other target, Mei, a chunky girl of Taiwanese extraction who also served as the troupe's physician, having some knowledge of herbal medicine, would come prancing out and stand at the board, and Dat would plant his knives within a centimeter of her flesh; but when Tan took her place, he would exercise extreme caution and set the knives no closer than seven or eight inches away, a contrast that amused our audiences no end.

For months after her arrival, I hardly spoke to Tan, and then only for some utilitarian purpose; I was too shy to manage a normal conversation. I wished with all my heart that I was eighteen and a man, with the manly confidence that, I assumed, naturally flowed from having attained the age. As things stood I was condemned by my utter lack of self-confidence to admire her from afar, to imagine conversations and other intimacies, to burn with all the frustration of unrequited lust. But then, one afternoon, while I sat in the grass outside Vang's trailer, poring over some papers dealing with my father's investments, she approached, wearing loose black trousers and a white blouse, and asked what I was doing.

"I see you reading every day," she said. "You are so dedicated to your studies. Are you preparing for the university?"

We had set up our tents outside Bien Pho, a village some sixty miles south of Hanoi, on the grassy bank of a wide, meandering river whose water showed black beneath a pewter sky. Dark green conical hills with rocky out-cropping hemmed in the spot, and it was shaded here and there by smallish trees with crooked trunks and puffs of foliage at the ends of their corkscrew branches. The main tent had been erected at the base of the nearest hill and displayed atop it a pennant bearing the starry emblem of our troupe. Everyone else was inside, getting ready for the night's performance. It was a brooding yet tranquil scene, like a painting on an ancient Chinese scroll, but I noticed none of it—the world had shrunk to the bubble of grass and air that enclosed the two of us.

Tan sat beside me, crossed her legs in a half-lotus, and I caught her scent. Not perfume, but the natural musky yield of her flesh. I did my best to explain the purpose of my studies, the words rushing out as if I were unburdening myself of an awful secret. Which was more-or-less the case. No one apart from Vang knew what I was doing, and because his position relative to the task was tutelary, not that of a confidante, I felt oppressed, isolated by the responsibility I bore. Now it seemed that by disclosing the sad facts bracketing my life, I was acting to reduce their power over me. And so, hoping to exorcise them completely, I told her about my father.

"His name is William Ferrance," I said, hastening to add that I'd taken Ky for my own surname. "His father emigrated to Asia in the Nineties, during the onset of *doi moi* (this the Vietnamese equivalent of *perestroika*), and made a fortune in Saigon, adapting fleets of taxis to methane power. His son—my father—expanded the family interests. He invested in a number of construction projects, all of which lost money. He was in trouble financially when he married my mother, and he used her money to fund a casino in Danang. That allowed him to recoup most of his losses. Since then, he's established connections with the triads, Malaysian gambling syndicates, and the Bamboo Union in Taiwan. He's become an influential man, but his money's tied up. He has no room to maneuver. Should he gain control of my grandfather's estate, he'll be a very dangerous man."

"But this is so impersonal," Tan said. "Have you no memories of him?"

"Hazy ones," I said. "From all I can gather, he never took much interest in me . . . except as a potential tool. The truth is, I can scarcely remember my mother. Just the occasional moment. How she looked standing at a window. The sound of her voice when she sang. And I have a general impression of the person she was. Nothing more."

Tan looked off toward the river; some of the village children were chasing each other along the bank, and a cargo boat with a yellow sail was coming into view around the bend. "I wonder," she said. "Is it worse to remember those who've gone, or not to remember them?"

I guessed she was thinking about her parents, and I wanted to say something helpful, but the concept of uploading an intelligence, a personality, was so foreign to me, I was afraid of appearing foolish.

"I can see my mother and father whenever I want," Tan said, lowering her gaze to the grass. "I can go to a Sony office anywhere in the world and summon them with a code. When they appear they look like themselves, they sound like themselves, but I know it's not them. The things they say are always . . . appropriate. But something is missing. Some energy, some quality." She glanced up at me, and, looking into her beautiful dark eyes, I felt giddy, almost weightless. "Something dies," she went on. "I know it! We're not just electrical impulses, we can't be sucked up into a machine and live. Something dies, something important. What goes into the machine is nothing. It's only a colored shadow of what we are."

"I don't have much experience with computers," I said.

"But you've experienced life!" She touched the back of my hand. "Can't you feel it within you? I don't know what to call it . . . a soul? I don't know . . ."

It seemed then I could feel the presence of the thing she spoke of moving in my chest, my blood, going all through me, attached to my mind, my flesh, by an unfathomable connection, existing inside me the way breath exists inside a flute, breeding the brief, pretty life of a note, a unique tone, and then passing on into the ocean of the air. Whenever I think of Tan, how she looked that morning, I'm able to feel that delicate, tremulous thing, both temporary and eternal, hovering in the same space I occupy.

"This is too serious," she said. "I'm sorry. I've been thinking about my parents more than I should." She shook back the fall of her hair, put on a smile. "Do you play chess?"

"No," I admitted.

"You must learn! A knowledge of the game will help if you intend to wage war against your father." A regretful expression crossed her face, as if she thought she'd spoken out of turn. "Even if you don't . . . I mean . . ." Flustered, she waved her hands to dispel the awkwardness of the moment. "It's fun," she said. "I'll teach you."

I did not make a good chess player, I was far too distracted by the presence of my teacher to heed her lessons. But I'm grateful to the game, for through the movements of knights and queens, through my clumsiness and her patience, through hours of sitting with our heads bent close together, our hearts grew close. We were never merely friends—from that initial conversation on, it was apparent that we would someday take the next step in exploring our relationship, and I rarely felt any anxiety in this regard; I knew that when Tan was ready, she would tell me. For the time being, we enjoyed a kind of amplified friendship, spending our leisure moments together, our physical contact limited to hand-holding and kisses on the cheek. This is not to say that I always succeeded in conforming to those limits. Once as we lay atop Vang's trailer, watching the stars, I was overcome by her scent, the warmth of her shoulder against mine, and I propped myself up on an elbow and kissed her on the mouth. She responded, and I stealthily unbuttoned her blouse, exposing her breasts. Before I could proceed further, she sat bolt upright, holding her blouse closed, and gave me a injured look; then she slid down from the trailer and walked off into the dark, leaving me in a state of dismay and painful arousal. I slept little that night, worried that I had done permanent damage to the relationship; but the next day she acted as if nothing had happened, and we went on as before, except that I now wanted her more than ever.

Vang, however, was not so forgiving. How he knew I had taken liberties with his niece, I'm not sure — it may have been simply an incidence of his intuitive abilities; I cannot imagine that Tan told him. Whatever his sources, after our performance the next night he came into the main tent where I was practicing with my knives, hurling them into a sheet of plywood upon which the red outline of a human figure had been painted, and asked if my respect for him had dwindled to the point that I would dishonor his sister's daughter.

He was sitting in the first row of the bleachers, leaning back, resting his elbows on the row behind him, gazing at me with distaste. I was infuriated by this casual indictment, and rather than answer immediately I threw another knife, placing it between the outline's arm and its waist. I walked to the board, yanked the blade free, and said without turning to him, "I haven't dishonored her."

"But surely that is your intent," he said.

Unable to contain my anger, I spun about to face him. "Were you never young? Have you never been in love?"

"Love." He let out a dry chuckle. "If you are in love, perhaps you would care to enlighten me as to its nature."

I would have liked to tell him how I felt about Tan, to explain the sense of security I found with her, the varieties of tenderness, the niceties of my concern for her, the thousand nuances of longing, the intricate complicity of our two hearts and the complex specificity of my desire, for though I wanted to lose myself in the turns of her body, I also wanted to celebrate her, enliven her, to draw out of her the sadness that sometimes weighed her down, and to have her leach my sadness from me as well — I knew this was possible for us. But I was too young and too angry to articulate these things.

"Do you love your mother?" Vang asked, and before I could respond, he said, "You have admitted that you have but a few disjointed memories of her. And, of course, a dream. Yet you have chosen to devote yourself to pursuing the dictates of that dream, to making a life that honors your mother's wishes. That is love. How can you compare this to your infatuation with Tan?"

Frustrated, I cast my eyes up to the billow of patched gray canvas overhead, to the metal rings at the peak from which Kai and Kim were nightly suspended. When I looked back to Vang, I saw that he had gotten to his feet.

"Think on it," he said. "If the time comes when you can regard Tan with the same devotion, well . . ." He made a subtle dismissive gesture with his fingers that suggested this was an unlikely prospect.

I turned to the board and hefted another knife. The target suddenly appeared evil in its anonymity, a dangerous creature with a wood-grain face and bloodred skin, and as I drew back my arm, my anger at Vang merged with the greater anger I felt at the anonymous forces that had shaped my life, and I buried the knife dead center of the head — it took all my strength to work the blade free. Glancing up, I was surprised to see Vang watching from the entrance. I had assumed that, having spoken his piece, he had returned to his trailer. He stood there for a few seconds, giving no overt sign of his mood, but I had the impression he was pleased.

When she had no other duties, Tan would assist me with my chores: feeding the exotics, cleaning out their cages, and, though she did not relish his company, helping me care for the major. I must confess I was coming to enjoy my visits with him less and less; I still felt a connection to him, and I remained curious as to the particulars of his past, but his mental slippage had grown so pronounced, it was difficult to be around him. Frequently he insisted on trying to relate the story of Firebase Ruby, but he always lapsed into terror and grief at the same point he had previously broken off the narrative. It seemed that this was a tale he was making up, not one he had been taught or programmed to tell, and that his mind was no longer capable of other than fragmentary invention. But one afternoon, as we were finishing up in his tent, he began to tell the story again, this time starting at the place where he had previously faltered, speaking without hesitancy in the deep, raspy voice he used while performing.

"It came to be October," he said. "The rains slackened, the snakes kept to their holes during the day, and the spiderwebs were not so thick with victims as they'd been during the monsoon. I began to have a feeling that something ominous was on the horizon, and when I communicated this sense of things to my superiors, I was told that according to intelligence, an intensification of enemy activity was expected, leading up to what was presumed to be a major offensive during the celebration of Tet. But I gave no real weight to either my feeling or to the intelligence reports. I was a professional soldier, and for six months I'd been engaged in nothing more than sitting in a bunker and surveying a wasteland of red dirt and razor wire. I was spoiling for a fight."

He was sitting on a nest of palm fronds, drenched in a spill of buttery light — we had partially unzipped the roof of the tent in order to increase ventilation — and it looked as if the fronds were an island adrift in a dark void and he a spiritual being who had been scorched and twisted by some cosmic fire, marooned in eternal emptiness.

"The evening of the Fourteenth, I sent out the usual patrols and retired to my bunker. I sat at my desk reading a paperback novel and drinking whiskey. After a time, I put down the book and began a letter to my wife. I was tipsy, and instead of the usual sentimental lines designed to make her feel secure, I let my feelings pour onto the paper, writing about the lack of discipline, my fears concerning the enemy, my disgust at the way the war was being prosecuted. I told her how much I hated Viet Nam. The ubiquitous corruption, the stupidity of the South Vietnamese government. The smell of fish sauce, the poisonous greens of the jungle. Everything. The goddamn place had been a battlefield so long, it was good for nothing else. I kept drinking, and the liquor eroded my remaining inhibitions. I told her about the treachery and ineptitude of the ARVN forces, about the fuckups on our side who called themselves generals."

"I was still writing when, around twenty-one hundred hours, something distracted me. I'm not sure what it was. A noise . . . or maybe a vibration. But I knew something had happened. I stepped out into the corridor and heard a cry. Then the crackling of small arms fire. I grabbed my rifle and ran outside. The VC were inside the wire. In the perimeter lights I saw dozens of diminutive men and women in black pajamas scurrying about, white stars sputtering from the muzzles of their weapons. I cut down several of them. I couldn't think how they had gotten through the wire and the minefields without alerting the sentries, but then, as I continued to fire, I spotted a man's head pop up out of the ground and realized that they had tunneled in. All that slow uneventful summer, they'd been busy beneath the surface of the earth, secretive as termites."

At this juncture the major fell prey once again to emotional collapse, and I prepared myself for the arduous process of helping him recover; but Tan kneeled beside him, took his hand, and said, "Martin? Martin, listen to me."

No one ever used the major's Christian name, except to introduce him to an audience, and I didn't doubt that it had been a long time since a woman had addressed him with tenderness. He abruptly stopped his shaking, as if the nerves that had betrayed him had been severed, and stared wonderingly at Tan. White pinprick suns flickered and died in the deep places behind his eyes.

"Where are you from, Martin?" she asked, and the major, in a dazed tone, replied, "Oakland . . . Oakland, California. But I was born up in Santa Cruz."

"Santa Cruz." Tan gave the name a bell-like reading. "Is it beautiful in Santa Cruz? It sounds like a beautiful place."

"Yeah . . . it's kinda pretty. There's old-growth redwoods not far from town. And there's the ocean. It's real pretty along the ocean."

To my amazement, Tan and the major began to carry on a coherent—albeit simplistic—conversation, and I realized that he had never spoken in this fashion before. His syntax had an uncustomary informality, and his voice held the trace of an accent. I thought that Tan's gentle approach must have penetrated his tormented psyche, either reaching the submerged individual, the real Martin Boyette, or else encountering a fresh layer of delusion. It was curious to hear him talk about such commonplace subjects as foggy weather and jazz music and Mexican food, all of which he claimed could be found in good supply in Santa Cruz. Though his usual nervous tics were in evidence, a new placidity showed in his face. But, of course this state of affairs didn't last.

"I can't," he said, taking a sudden turn from the subject at hand; he shook his head, dragging folds of skin across his neck and shoulders, "I can't go back anymore. I can't go back there."

"Don't be upset, Martin," Tan said. "There's no reason for you to worry. We'll stay with you, we'll . . ."

"I don't want you to stay." He tucked his head into his shoulder so his face was hidden by a bulge of skin. "I got to get back doin' what I was doin'."

"What's that?" I asked him. "What were you doing?"

A muffled rhythmic grunting issued from his throat—laughter that went on too long to be an expression of simple mirth. It swelled in volume, trebled in pitch, becoming a signature of instability.

"I'm figurin' it all out," he said. "That's what I'm doin'. Jus' you go away now."

"Figuring out what?" I asked, intrigued by the possibility—however unlikely—that the major might have a mental life other than the chaotic, that his apparent incoherence was merely an incidental byproduct of concentration, like the smoke that rises from a leaf upon which a beam of sunlight has been focused.

He made no reply, and Tan touched my hand, signaling that we should leave.

As I ducked through the tent flap, behind me the major said, "I can't go back there, and I can't be here. So jus' where's that leave me, y'know?"

Exactly what the major meant by this cryptic statement was unclear, but his words stirred something in me, reawakened me to internal conflicts that had been pushed aside by my studies and my involvement with Tan. When I had arrived to take up residence at Green Star, I was in a state of emotional upheaval, frightened, confused, longing for my mother. Yet even after I calmed down, I was troubled by the feeling that I had lost my place in the world, and it seemed this was not just a consequence of having been uprooted from my family, but that I had always felt this way, that the turbulence of my emotions had been a cloud obscuring what was a constant strain in my life. This was due in part to my mixed heritage. Though the taint associated with the children of Vietnamese mothers and American fathers (dust children, they had once been called) had dissipated since the end of the war, it had not done so entirely, and wherever the circus traveled. I would encounter people who, upon noticing the lightness of my skin and the shape of my eyes, expressed scorn and kept their distance. Further fueling this apprehension was the paucity of my memories deriving from the years before I had come to live with Vang. Whenever Tan spoke about her childhood, she brought up friends, birthdays, uncles and cousins, trips to Saigon, dances, hundreds of details and incidents that caused my own memory to appear grossly underpopulated by comparison. Trauma was to blame, I reckoned. The shock of my mother's abandonment, however well-intended, had ripped open my mental storehouse and scattered the contents. That and the fact that I had been six when I left home and thus hadn't had time to accumulate the sort of cohesive memories that lent color to Tan's stories of Hue. But explaining it away did not lessen my discomfort, and I became fixated on the belief that no matter the nature of the freakish lightning that had sheared away my past, I would never find a cure for the sense of dislocation it had provoked, only medicines that would suppress the symptoms and mask the disease—and, that being so masked, it would grow stronger, immune to treatment, until eventually I would be possessed by it, incapable of feeling at home anywhere.

I had no remedy for these anxieties other than to throw myself with greater intensity into my studies, and with this increase in intensity came a concomitant increase in anger. I would sit at Vang's computer, gazing at photographs of my father, imagining violent resolutions to our story. I doubted that he would recognize me; I favored my mother and bore little resemblance to him, a genetic blessing for which I was grateful: he was not particularly handsome, though he was imposing, standing nearly six and a half feet tall and weighing—according to a recent medical report—two hundred and sixty-four pounds, giving the impression not of a fat man, but a massive one. His large squarish head was kept shaved, and on his left cheek was the dark blue and green tattoo of his corporate emblem—a flying fish—ringed by three smaller tattoos denoting various of his business associations. At the base of his skull was an oblong silver plate beneath which lay a number of ports allowing him direct access to a computer. Whenever he posed for a picture, he affected what I assumed he would consider a look of hauteur, but the smallness of his eyes (grayish blue) and nose and mouth in contrast to the largeness of his face caused them to be limited in their capacity to convey character and emotional temperature, rather like the features on a distant planet seen through a telescope, and as a result this particular expression came across as prim. In less formal photographs, taken in the company of one or another of his sexual partners, predominantly women, he was quite obviously intoxicated.

He owned an old French Colonial in Saigon, but spent the bulk of his time at his house in Binh Khoi, one of the flower towns—communities built at the turn of the century, intended to provide privacy and comfort for well-to-do Vietnamese whose sexual preferences did not conform to communist morality. Now that communism—if not the concept of sexual morality itself—had become quaint, a colorful patch of history dressed up with theme-park neatness to amuse the tourists, it would seem that these communities no longer had any reason to exist; yet exist they did. Their citizenry had come to comprise a kind of gay aristocracy that defined styles, set trends, and wielded significant political power. Though they maintained a rigid exclusivity, and though my father's bisexuality was motivated to a great degree—I believe—by concerns of business and status, he had managed to cajole and bribe his way into Binh Khoi, and as best I could determine, he was sincere in his attachment to the place.

The pictures taken at Binh Khoi rankled me the most—I hated to see him laughing and smiling. I would stare at those photographs, my emotions overheating, until it seemed I could focus rage into a beam and destroy any object upon which I turned my gaze. My eventual decision, I thought, would be easy to make. Anger and history, the history of his violence and greed, were making it for me, building a spiritual momentum impossible to stop. When the time came, I would avenge my mother and claim my inheritance. I knew exactly how to go about the task. My father feared no one less powerful than himself—if such a person moved against him, they would be the target of terrible reprisals—and he recognized the futility of trying to fend off an assassination attempt by anyone more powerful; thus his security was good, yet not impenetrable. The uniqueness of my situation lay in the fact that if I were able to kill him, I would as a consequence become more powerful than he or any of his connections; and so, without the least hesitancy, I began to plan his murder both in Binh Khoi and Saigon— I had schematics detailing the security systems of both homes. But in the midst of crafting the means of his death, I lost track of events that were in the process of altering the conditions attendant upon my decision.

One night not long after my seventeenth birthday, I was working at the computer in the trailer, when Vang entered and lowered himself carefully in the chair opposite me, first shooing away the marmalade cat who had been sleeping there. He wore a threadbare gray cardigan and the striped trousers from an old suit, and carried a thin folder bound in plastic. I was preoccupied with tracking my father's movements via his banking records and I acknowledged Vang's presence with a nod. He sat without speaking a while and finally said, "Forgive my intrusion, but would you be so kind as to allow me a minute of your time."

I realized he was angry, but my own anger took precedence. It was not just that

I was furious with my father; I had grown weary of Vang's distant manner, his goading, his incessant demands for respect in face of his lack of respect for me. "What do you want?" I asked without looking away from the screen.

He tossed the folder onto the desk. "Your task has become more problematic."

The folder contained the personnel file of an attractive woman named Phuong Anh Nguyen whom my father had hired as a bodyguard. Much of the data concerned her considerable expertise with weapons and her reaction times, which were remarkable — it was apparent that she had been bred for her occupation, genetically enhanced. According to the file her senses were so acute, she could detect shifts in the heat patterns of the brain, subtle changes in blood pressure, heart rate, pupillary dilation, speech, all the telltales that would betray the presence of a potential assassin. The information concerning her personal life was skimpy. Though Vietnamese, she had been born in China, and had spent her life until the age of sixteen behind the walls of a private security agency, where she had received her training. Serving a variety of employers, she had killed sixteen men and women over the next five years. Several months before, she had bought out her contract from the security agency and signed on long-term with my father. Like him, she was bisexual, and, also like him, the majority of her partners were women.

I glanced up from the file to find Vang studying me with an expectant air. "Well," he said, "what do you think?"

"She's not bad-looking," I said.

He folded his arms, made a disgusted noise.

"All right." I turned the pages of the file. "My father's upgrading his security. That means he's looking ahead to bigger things. Preparing for the day when he can claim my trust."

"Is that all you're able to extract from the document?"

From outside came voices, laughter. They passed, faded. Mei, I thought, and Tranh. It was a cool night, the air heavy with the scent of rain. The door was cracked open, and I could see darkness and thin streamers of fog. "What else is there?" I asked.

"Use your mind, won't you?" Vang let his head tip forward and closed his eyes — a formal notice of his exasperation. "Phuong would require a vast sum in order to pay off her contract. Several million, at least. Her wage is a good one, but even if she lived in poverty, which she does not, it would take her a decade or more to save sufficient funds. Where might she obtain such a sum?"

I had no idea.

"From her new employer, of course," Vang said.

"My father doesn't have that kind of money lying around."

"It seems he does. Only a very wealthy man could afford such a servant as Phuong Anh Nguyen."

I took mental stock of my father's finances, but was unable to recall an excess of cash.

"It's safe to say the money did not come from your father's business enterprises," said Vang. "We have good information on them. So we may assume he either stole it or coerced someone else into stealing it." The cat jumped up into his lap, began kneading his abdomen. "Rather than taxing your brain further," he went on, "I'll tell you what I believe has happened. He's tapped into your trust. It's much too large to be managed by one individual, and it's quite possible he's succeeded in corrupting one of the officers in charge."

"You can't be sure of that."

"No, but I intend to contact my government friends and suggest an investigation of the trust. If your father has done what I suspect, it will prevent him from doing more damage." The cat had settled on his lap; he stroked its head. "But the trust is not the problem. Even if your father has stolen from it, he can't have taken much more than was necessary to secure this woman's services. Otherwise the man who gave me this"—he gestured at the folder—"would have detected evidence of other expenditures. There'll be more than enough left to make you a powerful man. Phuong Anh Nguyen is the problem. You'll have to kill her first."

The loopy cry of a night bird cut the silence. Someone with a flashlight was crossing the pasture where the trailer rested, the beam of light slicing through layers of fog, sweeping over shrubs and patches of grass. I suggested that one woman shouldn't pose that much of a problem, no matter how efficient she was at violence.

Vang closed his eyes again. "You have not witnessed this kind of professional in action. They're fearless, totally dedicated to their work. They develop a sixth sense concerning their clients; they bond with them. You'll need to be circumspect in dealing with her."

"Perhaps she's beyond my capacity to deal with," I said after a pause. "Perhaps I'm simply too thickheaded. I should probably let it all go and devote myself to Green Star."

"Do as you see fit."

Vang's expression did not shift from its stoic cast, but it appeared to harden, and I could tell that he was startled. I instructed the computer to sleep and leaned back, bracing one foot against the side of the desk. "There's no need for pretense," I said. "I know you want me to kill him. I just don't understand why."

I waited for him to respond, and when he did not, I said, "You were my mother's friend—that's reason enough to wish him dead, I suppose. But I've never felt that you were *my* friend. You've given me . . . everything. Life. A place to live. A purpose. Yet whenever I try to thank you, you dismiss it out of hand. I used to think this was because you were shy, because you were embarrassed by displays of emotion. Now, I'm not sure. Sometimes it seems you find my gratitude repugnant . . . or embarrassing in a way that has nothing to do with shyness. It's as if"—I struggled to collect my thoughts "—as if you have some reason for hating my father that you haven't told me. One you're ashamed to admit. Or maybe it's something else, some piece of information you have that gives you a different perspective on the situation."

Being honest with him was both exhilarating and frightening—I felt as though I were violating a taboo—and after this speech I was left breathless and disoriented, unsure of everything I'd said, though I'd been thoroughly convinced of its truth when I said it. "I'm sorry," I told him. "I've no right to doubt you."

He started to make a gesture of dismissal such as was his habit when uncomfortable with a conversation, but caught himself and petted the cat instead. "Despite the differences in our stations, I was very close to your mother," he said.

"And to your grandfather. No longer having a family of my own, I made them into a surrogate. When they died, one after the other . . . you see, your grandfather's presence, his wealth, protected your mother, and once he was gone, your father had no qualms against misusing her." He blew out a breath, like a horse, through his lips. "When they died, I lost my heart. I'd lost so much already, I was unable to bear the sorrow I felt. I retreated from the world, I rejected my emotions. In effect, I shut myself down." He put a hand to his forehead, covering his eyes. I could see he was upset, and I felt badly that I had caused these old griefs to wound him again. "I know you have suffered as a result," he went on. "You've grown up without the affection of a parent, and that is a cruel condition. I wish I could change that. I wish I could change the way I am, but the idea of risking myself, of having everything ripped away from me a third time . . . it's unbearable." His hand began to tremble; he clenched it into a fist, pressed it against the bridge of his nose. "It is I who should apologize to you. Please, forgive me."

I assured him that he need not ask for forgiveness, I honored and respected him. I had the urge to tell him I loved him, and at that moment I did—I believed now that in loving my family, in carrying out my mother's wishes, he had established his love for me. Hoping to distract him from his grief, I asked him to tell me about my grandfather, a man concerning whom I knew next to nothing, only that he had been remarkably successful in business.

Vang seemed startled by the question, but after taking a second to compose himself, he said, "I'm not sure you would have approved of him. He was a strong man, and strong men often sacrifice much that ordinary men hold dear in order to achieve their ends. But he loved your mother, and he loved you."

This was not the sort of detail I'd been seeking, but it was plain that Vang was still gripped by emotion, and I decided it would be best to leave him alone. As I passed behind him, I laid a hand on his shoulder. He twitched, as if burned by the touch, and I thought he might respond by covering my hand with his own. But he only nodded and made a humming noise deep in his throat. I stood there for a few beats, wishing I could think of something else to say; then I bid him good night and went off into the darkness to look for Tan.

One morning, about a month after this conversation, in the little seaside town of Vung Tao, Dat quit the circus following an argument with Vang, and I was forced that same evening to assume the role of James Bond Cochise. The prospect of performing the entire act in public—I had previously made token appearances along with Dat—gave rise to some anxiety, but I was confident in my skill. Tan took in Dat's tuxedo jacket a bit, so it would hang nicely, and helped me paint my face with Native American designs, and when Vang announced me, standing at the center of our single ring and extolling my legendary virtues into a microphone, I strode into the rich yellow glow of the tent, the warmth smelling of sawdust and cowshit (a small herd had been foraging on the spot before we arrived), with my arms overhead, flourishing the belt that held my hatchets and knives, and enjoying the applause. All seven rows of the bleachers were full, the audience consisting of resort workers, fishermen and their families, with a smattering of tourists, mainly backpackers, but also a group of immensely fat Russian women who had been transported from a hotel farther along the beach in cycles pedaled by diminutive Vietnamese men. They were in a good mood, thanks to a comic skit in which Tan played a farm girl and Tranh a village buffoon hopelessly in love with her, his lust manifested by a telescoping rod that could spring outward to a length of fourteen inches and was belted to his hips beneath a pair of baggy trousers.

Mei, dressed in a red sequined costume that pushed up her breasts and squeezed the tops of her chubby thighs like sausage ends, assumed a spread-eagled position in front of the board, and the crowd fell silent. Sitting in a wooden chair at ring center, Vang switched on the music, the theme from a venerable James Bond film. I displayed a knife to the bleachers, took my mark, and sent the blade hurtling toward Mei, planting it solidly in the wood an inch above her head. The first four or five throws were perfect, outlining Mei's head and shoulders. The crowd oohed and ahhed each time the blade sank into the board. Supremely confident now, I flung the knives as I whirled and ducked, pretending to dodge the gunshots embedded in the theme music, throwing from a crouch, on my stomach, leaping—but then I made the slightest of missteps, and the knife I hurled flashed so close to Mei, it nicked the fleshy portion of her upper arm. She shrieked and staggered away from the board, holding the injury. She remained stock-still for an instant, fixing me with a look of anguish, then bolted for the entrance. The crowd was stunned. Vang jumped up, the microphone dangling from his hand. For a second or two, I was rooted to the spot, not certain what to do. The bombastic music isolated me as surely as if it were a fence, and when Tranh shut it off, the fence collapsed, and I felt the pressure of a thousand eyes upon me. Unable to withstand it, I followed Mei out into the night.

The main tent had been erected atop a dune overlooking a bay and a stretch of sandy beach. It was a warm, windy night, and as I emerged from the tent the tall grasses cresting the dune were blown flat by a gust. From behind me, Vang's amplified voice sounded above the rush of the wind and the heavier beat of the surf, urging the audience to stay seated, the show would continue momentarily. The moon was almost full, but it hung behind the clouds, edging an alp of cumulus with silver, and I couldn't find Mei at first. Then the moon sailed clear, paving a glittering avenue across the black water, touching the plumes of combers with phosphorous, brightening the sand, and I spotted Mei—recognizable by her red costume—and two other figures on the beach some thirty feet below; they appeared to be ministering to her.

I started down the face of the dune, slipped in the loose sand and fell. As I scrambled to my feet, I saw Tan struggling up the slope toward me. She caught at the lapels of my tuxedo for balance, nearly causing me to fall again, and we swayed together; holding each other upright. She wore a nylon jacket over her costume, which was like Mei's in every respect but one—it was a shade of peacock blue spangled with silver stars. Her shining hair was gathered at the nape of her neck, crystal earrings sparkled in the lobes of her ears, her dark eyes brimmed with light. She looked made of light, an illusion that would fade once the clouds regrouped about the moon. But the thing that most affected me was not her beauty. Moment to moment, that was something of which I was always aware, how she flowed between states of beauty, shifting from schoolgirl to seductress to serious young woman, and now this starry incarnation materialized before me, the devi of a world that existed only for this precise second. . . . No, it was her calmness that affected me most. It poured over me, coursing around and through me, and even before she spoke, not mentioning what had happened to Mei, as if it were not a potentially fatal accident, a confidence-destroyer that would cause me to falter whenever I picked up a knife—even before that I was convinced by her unruffled manner that everything was as usual, there had been a slight disruption of routine, and now we should go back into the tent because Vang was running out of jokes to tell.

"Mei . . ." I said as we clambered over the crest of the dune, and Tan said, "It's not even a scratch." She took my arm and guided me toward the entrance, walking briskly yet unhurriedly.

I felt I'd been hypnotized—not by a sonorous voice or the pendulum swing of a shiny object, but by a heightened awareness of the ordinary, the steady pulse of time, all the background rhythms of the universe. I was filled with an immaculate calm, distant from the crowd and the booming music. It seemed that I wasn't throwing the knives so much as I was fitting them into slots and letting the turning of the earth whisk them away to thud and quiver in the board, creating a figure of steel slightly larger than the figure of soft brown flesh and peacock blue silk it contained. Dat had never received such applause—I think the crowd believed Mei's injury had been a trick designed to heighten suspense, and they showed their enthusiasm by standing as Tan and I took our bows and walked together through the entranceway. Once outside, she pressed herself against me, kissed my cheek, and said she would see me later. Then she went off toward the rear of the tent to change for the finale.

Under normal circumstances, I would have gone to help with the major, but on this occasion, feeling disconnected and now, bereft of Tan's soothing influence, upset at having injured Mei, I wandered along the top of the dune until I came to a gully choked with grasses that afforded protection from the wind, which was still gusting hard, filling the air with grit. I sat down amidst the grass and looked off along the curve of the beach. About fifteen meters to the north, the sand gave out into a narrow shingle and the land planed upward into low hills thick with vegetation. Half-hidden by the foliage was a row of small houses with sloping tiled roofs and open porches; they stood close to the sea, and chutes of yellow light spilled from their windows to illuminate the wavelets beneath. The moon was high, no longer silvery, resembling instead a piece of bloated bone china mottled with dark splotches, and, appearing to lie directly beneath it among a hammock of coconut palms was a pink stucco castle that guarded the point of the bay: the hotel where the tourists who had attended our performance were staying. I could make out antlike shapes scurrying back and forth on the brightly lit crescent of sand in front of it, and I heard a faint music shredded by the wind. The water beyond the break was black as opium.

My thoughts turned not to the accident with Mei, but to how I had performed with Tan. The act had passed quickly, a flurry of knives and light, yet now I recalled details: the coolness of the metal between my fingers; Vang watching anxiously off to the side; a fiery glint on a hatchet blade tumbling toward a spot between Tan's legs. My most significant memory, however, was of her eyes. How they had seemed to beam instructions, orchestrating my movements, so forceful that I'd imagined she was capable of deflecting a blade if my aim proved errant. Given my emotional investment in her, my absolute faith—though we'd never discussed it—in our future together, it was easy to believe she had that kind of power over me. Easy to believe, and somewhat troublesome, for it struck me that we were not equals, we couldn't be as long as she controlled every facet of the relationship. And having concluded this, as if the conclusion were the end of all possible logics concerning the subject, my mind slowed and became mired in despondency.

I'm not certain how long I had been sitting when Tan came walking down the beach, brushing windblown hair from her eyes. She had on a man's short-sleeved shirt and a pair of loose-fitting shorts, and was carrying a blanket. I was hidden from her by the grass, and I was at such a remove from things, not comfortable with but accepting of my solitude, I was half-inclined to let her pass; but then she stopped and called my name, and I, by reflex, responded. She spotted me and picked up her pace. When she reached my side she said without a hint of reproval, merely as if stating a fact, "You went so far. I wasn't sure I'd find you." She spread the blanket on the sand and encouraged me to join her on it. I felt guilty at having had clinical thoughts about her and our relationship—to put this sort of practical construction on what I tended to view as a magical union, a thing of fate and dharma, seemed unworthy, and as a consequence I was at a loss for words. The wind began to blow in a long unbroken stream off the water, and she shivered. I asked if she would like to put on my tuxedo jacket. She said, "No." The line of her mouth tightened, and with a sudden movement, she looked away from me, half-turning her upper body. I thought I must have done something to annoy her, and this so unnerved me, I didn't immediately notice that she was unbuttoning her shirt. She shrugged out of it, held it balled against her chest for a moment, then set it aside; she glanced at me over her shoulder, engaging my eyes. I could tell her usual calm was returning—I could almost see her filling with it—and I realized then that this calmness of hers was not hers alone, it was ours, a byproduct of our trust in one another, and what had happened in the main tent had not been a case of her controlling me, saving me from panic, but had been the two of us channeling each other's strength, converting nervousness and fear to certainty and precision. Just as we were doing now.

I kissed her mouth, her small breasts, exulting in their salty aftertaste of brine and dried sweat. Then I drew her down onto the blanket, and what followed, despite clumsiness and flashes of insecurity, was somehow both fierce and chaste, the natural culmination of two years of longing, of unspoken treaties and accommodations. Afterward, pressed together, wrapped in the silk and warmth of spent splendor, whispering the old yet never less than astonishing secrets and promises, saying things that had long gone unsaid, I remember thinking that I would do anything for her. This was not an abstract thought, not simply the atavistic reaction of a man new to a feeling of mastery, though I can't deny that was in me—the sexual and the violent break from the same spring—but was an understanding founded on a considered appreciation of the trials I might have to overcome and the blood I might have to shed in order to keep her safe in a world where wife-murder was a crime for profit and patricide an act of self-defense. It's strange to recall with what a profound sense of reverence I accepted the idea that I was now willing to engage in every sort of human behavior, ranging from the self-sacrificial to the self-gratifying to the perpetration of acts so abhorrent that, once committed, they would harrow me until the end of my days.

At dawn the clouds closed in, the wind died, and the sea lay flat. Now and again a weak sun penetrated the overcast, causing the water to glisten like an expanse of freshly applied gray paint. We climbed to the top of the dune and sat with our arms around each other, not wanting to return to the circus, to break the elastic of the long moment stretching backward into night. The unstirring grass, the energyless water and dead sky, made it appear that time itself had been becalmed. The beach in front of the pink hotel was littered with debris, deserted. You might have thought that our lovemaking had succeeded in emptying the world. But soon we caught sight of Tranh and Mei walking toward us across the dune, Kim and Kai skipping along behind. All were dressed in shorts and shirts, and Tranh carried a net shopping bag that—I saw as he lurched up, stumbling in the sand—contained mineral water and sandwiches.

"What have you kids been up to?" he asked, displaying an exaggerated degree of concern.

Mei punched him on the arm, and, after glancing back and forth between us, as if he suddenly understood the situation, Tranh put on a shocked face and covered his mouth with a hand. Giggling, Kai and Kim went scampering down onto the beach. Mei tugged at Tranh's shirt, but he ignored her and sank onto his knees beside me. "I bet you're hungry," he said, and his round face was split by a gaptoothed grin. He thrust a sandwich wrapped in a paper napkin at me. "Better eat! You're probably going to need your strength."

With an apologetic look in Tan's direction, Mei kneeled beside him; she unwrapped sandwiches and opened two bottles of water. She caught my eye, frowned, pointed to her arm, and shook her forefinger as she might have done with a mischievous child. "Next time don't dance around so much," she said, and pretended to sprinkle something on one of the sandwiches. "Or else one night I'll put special herbs in your dinner." Tranh kept peering at Tan, then at me, grinning, nodding, and finally, with a laugh, Tan pushed him onto his back. Down by the water Kai and Kim were tossing pebbles into the sea with girlish ineptitude. Mei called to them and they came running, their braids bouncing; they threw themselves bellyfirst onto the sand, squirmed up to sitting positions, and began gobbling sandwiches.

"Don't eat so fast!" Mei cautioned. "You'll get sick."

Kim, the younger of the sisters, squinched her face at Mei and shoved half the sandwich into her mouth. Tranh contorted his features so his lips nearly touched his nose, and Kim laughed so hard she sprayed bits of bread and fried fish. Tan told her that this was not ladylike. Both girls sat up straight, nibbled their sandwiches—they took it to heart whenever Tan spoke to them about being ladies.

"Didn't you bring anything beside fish?" I asked, inspecting the filling of my sandwich.

"I guess we should have brought oysters," said Tranh. "Maybe some rhinoceros horn, some . . ."

"That stuff's for old guys like you," I told him. "Me, I just need peanut butter."

After we had done eating, Tranh lay back with his head in Mei's lap and told a story about a talking lizard that had convinced a farmer it was the Buddha. Kim and Kai cuddled together, sleepy from their feast. Tan leaned into the notch of my shoulder, and I put my arm around her. It came to me then, not suddenly, but gradually, as if I were being immersed in the knowledge like a man lowering his body into a warm bath, that for the first time in my life—all the life I could remember—I was at home. These people were my family, and the sense of dislocation that had burdened me all those years had evaporated. I closed my eyes and buried my face in Tan's hair, trying to hold onto the feeling, to seal it inside my head so I would never forget it.

Two men in T-shirts and bathing suits came walking along the water's edge in our direction. When they reached the dune they climbed up to where we were sitting. Both were not much older than I, and judging by their fleshiness and soft features, I presumed them to be Americans, a judgment confirmed when the taller of the two, a fellow with a heavy jaw and hundreds of white beads threaded on the strings of his long black hair, lending him a savage appearance, said, "You guys are with that tent show, right?"

Mei, who did not care for Americans, stared meanly at him, but Tranh, who habitually viewed them as potential sources of income, told him that we were, indeed, performers with the circus. Kai and Kim whispered and giggled, and Tranh asked the American what his friend—skinnier, beadless, dull-eyed and open-mouthed, with a complicated headset covering his scalp—was studying.

"Parasailing. We're going parasailing . . . if there's ever any wind and the program doesn't screw up. I woulda left him at the house, but the program's fucked. Didn't want his ass convulsing." He extracted a sectioned strip of plastic from his shirt pocket; each square of plastic held a gelatin capsule shaped like a cut gem and filled with blue fluid. "Wanna brighten your day?" He dangled the strip as if tempting us with a treat. When no one accepted his offer, he shrugged, returned the strip to his pocket; he glanced down at me. "Hey, that shit with the knives . . . that was part of the fucking plan! Especially when you went benihana on Little Plum Blossom." He jerked his thumb at Mei and then stood nodding, gazing at the sea, as if receiving a transmission from that quarter. "Okay," he said. "Okay. It could be the drugs, but the trusty inner voice is telling me my foreign ways seem ludicrous . . . perhaps even offensive. It well may be that I am somewhat ludicrous. And I'm pretty torched, so I have to assume I've been offensive."

Tranh made to deny this, Mei grunted, Kim and Kai looked puzzled, and Tan asked the American if he was on vacation.

"Thank you," he said to Tan. "Beautiful lady. I am always grateful for the gift of courtesy. No, my friend and I—and two others—are playing at the hotel. We're musicians." He took out his wallet, which had been hinged over the waist of his trunks, and removed from it a thin gold square the size of a postage stamp; he handed it to Tan. "Have you seen these? They're new . . . souvenir things, like. They just play once, but it'll give you a taste. Press your finger on it until it you hear the sound. Then don't touch it again—they get extremely hot."

Tan started to do as he instructed but he said, "No, wait till we're gone. I want to imagine you enjoyed hearing it. If you do, come on down to the hotel after you're finished tonight. You'll be my guests."

"Is it one of your songs?" I asked, curious about him now that he had turned out to be more complicated than he first appeared.

He said, yes, it was an original composition.

"What's it called?" Tranh asked.

"We haven't named it yet," said the American; then, after a pause: "What's the name of your circus?"

Almost as one we said, "Radiant Green Star."

"Perfect," said the American.

Once the two men were out of earshot, Tan pressed her fingertip to the gold square, and soon a throbbing music issued forth, simply structured yet intricately layered by synthesizers, horns, guitars, densely figured by theme and subtle counter-theme, both insinuating and urgent. Kai and Kim stood and danced with one another. Tranh bobbed his head, tapped his foot, and even Mei was charmed, swaying, her eyes closed. Tan kissed me, and we watched a thin white smoke trickle upward from the square, which itself began to shrink, and I thought how amazing it was that things were often not what they seemed, and what a strange confluence of possibilities it had taken to bring all the troupe together—and the six of us *were* the entire troupe, for Vang was never really part of us even when he was there, and though the major was rarely with us, he was always there, a shadow in the corners of our minds. . . . How magical and ineluctable a thing it was for us all to be together at the precise place and time when a man—a rather unprepossessing man at that—walked up from a deserted beach and presented us with a golden square imprinted with a song that he named for our circus, a song that so accurately evoked the mixture of the commonplace and the exotic that characterized life in Radiant Green Star, music that was like smoke, rising up for a few perfect moments, and then vanishing with the wind.

Had Vang asked me at any point during the months that followed to tell him about love, I might have spoken for hours, answering him not with definitions, principles, or homilies, but specific instances, moments, and anecdotes. I was happy. Despite the gloomy nature of my soul, I could think of no word that better described how I felt. Though I continued to study my father, to follow his comings and goings, his business maneuvers and social interactions, I now believed that I would never seek to confront him, never try to claim my inheritance. I had all I needed to live, and I only wanted to keep those I loved safe and free from worry.

Tan and I did not bother to hide our relationship, and I expected Vang to rail at me for my transgression. I half-expected him to drive me away from the circus— indeed, I prepared for that eventuality. But he never said a word. I did notice a certain cooling of the atmosphere. He snapped at me more often and on occasion refused to speak; yet that was the extent of his anger. I didn't know how to take this. Either, I thought, he had overstated his concern for Tan or else he had simply accepted the inevitable. That explanation didn't satisfy me, however. I suspected that he might have something more important on his mind, something so weighty that my involvement with his niece seemed a triviality by comparison. And one day, some seven months after Tan and I became lovers, my suspicions were proved correct.

I went to the trailer at mid-afternoon, thinking Vang would be in town. We were camped at the edge of a hardwood forest on a cleared acre of red dirt near Buon Ma Thuot in the Central Highlands, not far from the Cambodian border. Vang usually spent the day before a performance putting up posters, and I had intended to work on the computer; but when I entered, I saw him standing by his desk, folding a shirt, a suitcase open on the chair beside him. I asked what he was doing and he handed me a thick envelope; inside were the licenses and deeds of ownership relating to the circus and its property. "I've signed everything over," he said. "If you have any problems, contact my lawyer."

"I don't understand," I said, dumfounded. "You're leaving?"

He bent to the suitcase and laid the folded shirt inside it. "You can move into the trailer tonight. You and Tan. She'll be able to put it in order. I suppose you've noticed that she's almost morbidly neat." He straightened, pressed his hand against his lower back as if stricken by a pain. "The accounts, the bookings for next year . . . it's all in the computer. Everything else . . ." He gestured at the cabinets on the walls. "You remember where things are."

I couldn't get a grasp on the situation, overwhelmed by the thought that I was now responsible for Green Star, by the fact that the man who for years had been the only consistent presence in my life was about to walk out the door forever. "Why are you leaving?"

He turned to me, frowning. "If you must know, I'm ill."

"But why would you want to leave? We'll just . . ."

"I'm not going to recover," he said flatly.

I peered at him, trying to detect the signs of his mortality, but he looked no thinner, no grayer, than he had for some time. I felt the stirrings of a reaction that I knew he would not want to see, and I tamped down my emotions. "We can care for you here," I said.

He began to fold another shirt. "I plan to join my sister and her husband in what they insist upon calling—" he clicked his tongue against his teeth "—Heaven."

I recalled the talks I'd had with Tan in which she had decried the process of uploading the intelligence, the personality. If the old man was dying, there was no real risk involved. Still, the concept of such a mechanical transmogrification did not sit well with me.

"Have you nothing to say on the subject?" he asked. "Tan was quite voluble."

"You've told her, then?"

"Of course." He inspected the tail of the shirt he'd been folding, and finding a hole, cast it aside. "We've said our goodbyes."

He continued to putter about, and as I watched him shuffling among the stacks of magazines and newspapers, kicking file boxes and books aside, dust rising wherever he set his hand, a tightness in my chest began to loosen, to work its way up into my throat. I went to the door and stood looking out, seeing nothing, letting the strong sunlight harden the glaze of my feelings. When I turned back, he was standing close to me, suitcase in hand. He held out a folded piece of paper and said, "This is the code by which you can contact me once I've been . . ." He laughed dryly. "Processed, I imagine, would be the appropriate verb. At any rate, I hope you will let me know what you decide concerning your father."

It was in my mind to tell him that I had no intention of contending with my father, but I thought that this would disappoint him, and I merely said that I would do as he asked. We stood facing one another, the air thick with unspoken feelings, with vibrations that communicated an entire history comprised of such mute, awkward moments. "If I'm to have a last walk in the sun," he said at length, "you'll have to let me pass."

That at the end of his days he viewed me only as a minor impediment—it angered me. But I reminded myself that this was all the sentiment of which he was capable. Without asking permission, I embraced him. He patted me lightly on the back and said, "I know you'll take care of things." And with that, he pushed past me and walked off in the direction of the town, vanishing behind one of the parked trucks.

I went into the rear of the trailer, into the partitioned cubicle where Vang slept, and sat down on his bunk. His pillowcase bore a silk-screened image of a beautiful Vietnamese woman and the words HONEY LADY KEEP YOU COM-FORT EVERY NIGHT. In the cabinet beside his bed were a broken clock, a small plaster bust of Ho Chi Minh, a few books, several pieces of hard candy, and a plastic key chain in the shape of a butterfly. The meagerness of the life these items described caught at my emotions, and I thought I might weep, but it was as if by assuming Vang's position as the owner of Green Star, I had undergone a corresponding reduction in my natural responses, and I remained dry-eyed. I felt strangely aloof from myself, connected to the life of my mind and body by a tube along which impressions of the world around me were now and then transmitted. Looking back on my years with Vang, I could make no sense of them. He had nurtured and educated me, yet the sum of all that effort—not given cohesion by the glue of affection—came to scraps of memory no more illustrative of a com-prehensible whole than were the memories of my mother. They had substance, yet no flavor . . . none, that is, except for a dusty gray aftertaste that I associated with disappointment and loss.

I didn't feel like talking to anyone, and for want of anything else to do, I went to the desk and started inspecting the accounts, working through dusk and into the night. When I had satisfied myself that all was in order, I turned to the book-ings. Nothing out of the ordinary. The usual villages, the occasional festival. But when I accessed the bookings for the month of March, I saw that during the week of the seventeenth through the twenty-third—the latter date just ten days from my birthday—we were scheduled to perform in Binh Khoi.

I thought this must be a mistake—Vang had probably been thinking of Binh Khoi and my father while recording a new booking and had inadvertently put down the wrong name. But when I called up the contract, I found that no mistake had been made. We were to be paid a great deal of money, sufficient to guarantee a profitable year, but I doubted that Vang's actions had been motivated by our financial needs. He must, I thought, have seen the way things were going with Tan and me, and he must have realized that I would never risk her in order to avenge a crime committed nearly two decades before—thus he had decided to force a confrontation between me and my father. I was furious, and my first impulse was to break the contract; but after I had calmed down I realized that doing so would put us all at risk—the citizens of Binh Khoi were not known for their generosity or flexibility, and if I were to renege on Vang's agreement they would surely pursue the matter in the courts. I would have no chance of winning a judgment. The only thing to do was to play the festival and steel myself to ignore the presence of my father. Perhaps he would be elsewhere, or, even if he was in residence, perhaps he would not attend our little show. Whatever the circumstances, I swore I would not be caught in this trap, and when my eighteenth birthday arrived I would go to the nearest Sony office and take great pleasure in telling Vang—whatever was left of him—that his scheme had failed.

I was still sitting there, trying to comprehend whether or not by contracting the engagement, Vang hoped to provide me with a basis for an informed decision, or if his interests were purely self-serving, when Tan stepped into the trailer. She had on a sleeveless plaid smock, the garment she wore whenever she was cleaning, and it was evident that she'd been crying—the skin beneath her eyes was puffy and red. But she had regained her composure, and she listened patiently, perched on the edge of the desk, while I told her all I'd been thinking about Vang and what he had done to us.

"Maybe it's for the best," she said after I had run down. "This way you'll be sure you've done what you had to do."

I was startled by her reaction. "Are you saying that you think I should kill my father . . . that I should even entertain the possibility?"

She shrugged. "That's for you to decide."

"I've decided already," I said.

"Then there's not a problem."

The studied neutrality of her attitude puzzled me. "You don't think I'll stand by my decision, do you?"

She put a hand to her brow, hiding her face—a gesture that reminded me of Vang. "I don't think you have decided, and I don't think you should . . . not until you see your father." She pinched a fold of skin above the bridge of her nose, then looked up at me. "Let's not talk about this now."

We sat silently for half a minute or thereabouts, each following the path of our own thoughts; then she wrinkled up her nose and said, "It smells bad in here. Do you want to get some air?"

We climbed onto the roof of the trailer and sat gazing at the shadowy line of the forest to the west, the main tent bulking up above it, and a sky so thick with stars that the familiar constellations were assimilated into new and busier cosmic designs: a Buddha face with a diamond on its brow, a tiger's head, a palm tree—constructions of sparkling pinlights against a midnight blue canvas stretched from horizon to horizon. The wind brought the scent of sweet rot and the less pervasive odor of someone's cooking. Somebody switched on a radio in the main tent; a Chinese orchestra whined and jangled. I felt I was sixteen again, that Tan and I had just met, and I thought perhaps we had chosen to occupy this place where we spent so many hours before we were lovers, because here we could banish the daunting pressures of the present, the threat of the future, and be children again. But although those days were scarcely two years removed, we had forever shattered the comforting illusions and frustrating limitations of childhood. I lay back on the aluminum roof, which still held a faint warmth of the day, and Tan hitched up her smock about her waist and mounted me, bracing her hands on my chest as I slipped inside her. Framed by the crowded stars, features made mysterious by the cowl of her hair, she seemed as distant and unreal as the imagined creatures of my zodiac; but this illusion, too, was shattered as she began to rock her hips with an accomplished passion and lifted her face to the sky, transfigured by a look of exalted, almost agonized yearning, like one of those Renaissance angels marooned on a scrap of painted cloud who has just witnessed something amazing pass over-head, a miracle of glowing promise too perfect to hold in the mind. She shook her head wildly when she came, her hair flying all to one side so that it resembled in shape the pennant flying on the main tent, a dark signal of release, and then collapsed against my chest. I held onto her hips, continuing to thrust until the knot of heat in my groin shuddered out of me, leaving a residue of black peace into which the last shreds of my thought were subsumed.

The sweat dried on our skin, and still we lay there, both — I believed — aware that once we went down from the roof, the world would close around us, restore us to its troubled spin. Someone changed stations on the radio, bringing in a Cambodian program — a cooler, wispier music played. A cough sounded close by the trailer, and I raised myself to an elbow, wanting to see who it was. The major was making his way with painful slowness across the cleared ground, leaning on his staff. In the starlight his grotesque shape was lent a certain anonymity — he might have been a figure in a fantasy game, an old down-at-heels magician shrouded in a heavy, ragged cloak, or a beggar on a quest. He shuffled a few steps more, and then, shaking with effort, sank to his knees. For several seconds he remained motionless, then he scooped a handful of the red dirt and held it up to his face. And I recalled that Buon Ma Thuot was near the location of his fictive — or if not fictive, ill-remembered — firebase. Firebase Ruby. Built upon the red dirt of a defoliated plantation.

Tan sat up beside me and whispered, "What's he doing?"

I put a finger to my lips, urging her to silence; I was convinced that the major would not expose himself to the terror of the open sky unless moved by some equally terrifying inner force, and I hoped he might do something that would illuminate the underpinnings of his mystery.

He let the dirt sift through his fingers and struggled to stand. Failed and sagged onto his haunches. His head fell back, and he held a spread-fingered hand up to it as if trying to shield himself from the starlight. His quavery voice ran out of him like a shredded battle flag. "Turn back!" he said. "Oh, God! God! Turn back!"

During the next four months, I had little opportunity to brood over the prospect of meeting my father. Dealing with the minutiae of Green Star's daily operation took most of my energy and hours, and whenever I had a few minutes respite, Tan was there to fill them. So it was that by the time we arrived in Binh Khoi, I had made scarcely any progress in adjusting to the possibility that I might soon come face-to-face with the man who had killed my mother.

In one aspect, Binh Khoi was the perfect venue for us, since the town affected the same conceit as the circus, being designed to resemble a fragment of another time. It was situated near the Pass of the Ocean Clouds in the Truong Son Mountains some forty kilometers north of Danang, and many of the homes there were afforded a view of green hills declining toward the Coastal Plain. On the morning we arrived those same hills were half-submerged in thick white fog, the plain was totally obscured, and a pale mist had infiltrated the narrow streets, casting an air of ominous enchantment over the place. The oldest of the houses had been built no more than fifty years before, yet they were all similar to nineteenth century houses that still existed in certain sections of Hanoi: two and three stories tall and fashioned of stone, painted dull yellow and gray and various other sober hues, with sharply sloping roofs of dark green tile and compounds hidden by high walls and shaded by bougainvillea, papaya, and banana trees. Except for street lights in the main square and pedestrians in bright eccentric clothing, we might have been driving through a hill station during the 1800s; but I knew that hidden behind this antiquated façade were state-of-the-art security systems that could have vaporized us had we not been cleared to enter.

The most unusual thing about Binh Khoi was its silence. I'd never been in a place where people lived in any considerable quantity that was so hushed, devoid of the stew of sounds natural to a human environment. No hens squabbling or dogs yipping, no whining motor scooters or humming cars, no children at play. In only one area was there anything approximating normal activity and noise: the marketplace, which occupied an unpaved street leading off the square. Here men and women in coolie hats hunkered beside baskets of jackfruit, chilies, garlic, custard apples, durians, geckos, and dried fish; meat and caged puppies and monkeys and innumerable other foodstuffs were sold in canvas-roofed stalls; and the shoppers, mostly male couples, haggled with the vendors, occasionally venting their dismay at the prices . . . this despite the fact that any one of them could have bought everything in the market without blinking. Though the troupe shared their immersion in a contrived past, I found the depth of their pretense alarming and somewhat perverse. As I maneuvered the truck cautiously through the press, they peered incuriously at me through the windows—faces rendered exotic and nearly unreadable by tattoos and implants and caps of silver wire and winking light that appeared to be woven into their hair—and I thought I could feel their amusement at the shabby counterfeit we offered of their more elegantly realized illusion. I believe I might have hated them for the fashionable play they made of arguing over minuscule sums with the poor vendors, for the triviality of spirit this mockery implied, if I had not already hated them so completely for being my father's friends and colleagues.

At the end of the street, beyond the last building, lay a grassy field bordered by a low whitewashed wall. Strings of light bulbs linked the banana trees and palms that grew close to the wall on three sides, and I noticed several paths leading off into the jungle that were lit in the same fashion. On the fourth side, beyond the wall, the land dropped off into a notch, now choked with fog, and on the far side of the notch, perhaps fifty yards away, a massive hill with a sheer rock face and the ruins of an old temple atop it lifted from the fog, looming above the field— it was such a dramatic sight and so completely free of mist, every palm frond articulated, every vine-enlaced crevice and knob of dark, discolored stone showing clear, that I wondered if it might be a clever projection, another element of Binh Khoi's decor.

We spent the morning and early afternoon setting up, and once I was satisfied that everything was in readiness, I sought out Tan, thinking we might go for a walk; but she was engaged in altering Kai's costume. I wandered into the main tent and busied myself by making sure the sawdust had been spread evenly. Kai was swinging high above on a rope suspended from the metal ring at the top of the tent, and one of our miniature tigers had climbed a second rope and was clinging to it by its furry hands, batting at her playfully whenever she swooped near. Tranh and Mei were playing cards in the bleachers, and Kim was walking hand-in-hand with our talking monkey, chattering away as if the creature could understand her—now and then it would turn its white face to her and squeak in response, saying "I love you" and "I'm hungry" and other equally non-responsive phrases. I stood by the entranceway, feeling rather paternal toward my little family gathered under the lights, and I was just considering whether or not I should return to the trailer and see if Tan had finished, when a baritone voice sounded behind me, saying, "Where can I find Vang Ky?"

My father was standing with hands in pockets a few feet away, wearing black trousers and a gray shirt of some shiny material. He looked softer and heavier than he did in his photographs, and the flying fish tattoo on his cheek was now sur-rounded by more than half-a-dozen tiny emblems denoting his business connec-tions. With his immense head, his shaved skull gleaming in the hot lights, he himself seemed the emblem of some monumental and soul-less concern. At his shoulder, over a foot shorter than he, was a striking Vietnamese woman with long straight hair, dressed in tight black slacks and a matching tunic: Phuong Ahn Nguyen. She was staring at me intently.

Stunned, I managed to get out that Vang was no longer with the circus, and my father said, "How can that be? He's the owner, isn't he?"

Shock was giving way to anger, anger so fulminant I could barely contain it. My hands trembled. If I'd had one of my knives to hand, I would have plunged it without a thought into his chest. I did the best I could to conceal my mood and told him what had become of Vang; but it seemed that as I catalogued each new detail of his face and body—a frown line, a reddened ear lobe, a crease in his fleshy neck—a vial of some furious chemical was tipped over and added to the mix of my blood.

"Goddamn it!" he said, casting his eyes up to the canvas; he appeared distraught. "Shit!" He glanced down at me. "Have you got his access code? It's never the same once they go to Heaven. I'm not sure they really know what's going on. But I guess it's my only option."

"I doubt he'd approve of my giving the code to a stranger," I told him.

"We're not strangers," he said. "Vang was my father-in-law. We had a falling-out after my wife died. I hoped having the circus here for a week, I'd be able to persuade him to sit down and talk. There's no reason for us to be at odds."

I suppose the most astonishing thing he said was that Vang was his father-in-law, and thus my grandfather. I didn't know what to make of that; I could think of no reason he might have for lying, yet it raised a number of troubling questions.

But his last statement, his implicit denial of responsibility for my mother's death . . . it had come so easily to his lips! Hatred flowered in me like a cold star, acting to calm me, allowing me to exert a measure of control over my anger.

Phoung stepped forward and put a hand on my chest; my heart pounded against the pressure of her palm. "Is anything wrong?" she asked.

"I'm . . . surprised," I said. "That's all. I didn't realize Vang had a son-in-law."

Her make-up was severe, her lips painted a dark mauve, her eyes shaded by the same color, but in the fineness of her features and the long oval shape of her face, she bore a slight resemblance to Tan.

"Why are you angry?" she asked.

My father eased her aside. "It's all right. I came on pretty strong—he's got every right to be angry. Why don't the two of us . . . what's your name, kid?"

"Dat," I said, though I was tempted to tell him the truth.

"Dat and I will have a talk," he said to Phuong. "I'll meet you back at the house."

We went outside, and Phuong, displaying more than a little reluctance, headed off in the general direction of the trailer. It was going on dusk and the fog was closing in. The many-colored bulbs strung in the trees close to the wall and lining the paths had been turned on; each bulb was englobed by a fuzzy halo, and altogether they imbued the encroaching jungle with an eerily festive air, as if the spirits lost in the dark green tangles were planning a party. We stood beside the wall, beneath the great hill rising from the shifting fogbank, and my father tried to convince me to hand over the code. When I refused he offered money, and when I refused his money he glared at me and said, "Maybe you don't get it. I really need the code. What's it going to take for you to give it to me?"

"Perhaps it's you who doesn't get it," I said. "If Vang wanted you to have the code he would have given it to you. But he gave it to *me*, and to no one else. I consider that a trust, and I won't break it unless he signifies that I should."

He looked off into the jungle, ran a hand across his scalp, and made a frustrated noise. I doubted he was experienced at rejection, and though it didn't satisfy my anger, it pleased me to have rejected him. Finally he laughed. "Either you're a hell of a businessman or an honorable man. Or maybe you're both. That's a scary notion." He shook his head in what I took for amiable acceptance. "Why not call Vang? Ask him if he'd mind having a talk with me."

I didn't understand how this was possible.

"What sort of computer do you own?" he asked.

I told him and he said, "That won't do it. Tell you what. Come over to my house tonight after your show. You can use my computer to contact him. I'll pay for your time."

I was suddenly suspicious. He seemed to be offering himself to me, making himself vulnerable, and I did not believe that was in his nature. His desire to contact Vang might be a charade. What if he had discovered my identity and was luring me into a trap?

"I don't know if I can get away," I said. "It may have to be in the morning."

He looked displeased, but said, "Very well." He fingered a business card from his pocket, gave it to me. "My address." Then he pressed what appeared to be a crystal button into my hand. "Don't lose it. Carry it with you whenever you come. If you don't, you'll be picked up on the street and taken somewhere quite unpleasant."

As soon as he was out of sight I hurried over to the trailer, intending to sort things out with Tan. She was outside, sitting on a folding chair, framed by a spill of hazy yellow light from the door. Her head was down, and her blouse was torn, the top two buttons missing. I asked what was wrong; she shook her head and would not meet my eyes. But when I persisted she said, "That woman . . . the one who works for your father . . ."

"Phuong? Did she hurt you?"

She kept her head down, but I could see her chin quivering. "I was coming to find you, and I ran into her. She started talking to me. I thought she was just being friendly, but then she tried to kiss me. And when I resisted" — she displayed the tear in her blouse — "she did this." She gathered herself. "She wants me to be with her tonight. If I refuse, she says she'll make trouble for us."

It would have been impossible for me to hate my father more, but this new insult, this threat to Tan, perfected it, added a finishing color, like the last brush stroke applied to a masterpiece. I stood a moment gazing off toward the hill — it seemed I had inside me an analog to that forbidding shape, something equally stony and vast. I led Tan into the trailer, sat her down at the desk, and made her tea; then I repeated all my father had said. "Is it possible," I asked, "that Vang is my grandfather?"

She held the teacup in both hands, blew on the steaming liquid and took a sip. "I don't know. My family has always been secretive. All my parents told me was that Vang was once a wealthy man with a loving family, and that he had lost everything."

"If he is my grandfather," I said, "then we're cousins."

She set down the cup and stared dolefully into it as if she saw in its depths an inescapable resolution. "I don't care. If we were brother and sister, I wouldn't care."

I pulled her up, put my arms around her, and she pressed herself against me. I felt that I was at the center of an enormously complicated knot, too diminutive to be able to see all its loops and twists. If Vang was my grandfather, why had he treated me with such coldness? Perhaps my mother's death had deadened his heart, perhaps that explained it. But knowing that Tan and I were cousins, wouldn't he have told us the truth when he saw how close we were becoming? Or was he so old-fashioned that the idea of an intimate union between cousins didn't bother him? The most reasonable explanation was that my father had lied. I saw that now, saw it with absolute clarity. It was the only possibility that made sense. And if he had lied, it followed that he knew who I was. And if he knew who I was . . .

"I have to kill him," I said. "Tonight . . . it has to be tonight."

I was prepared to justify the decision, to explain why a course of inaction would be a greater risk, to lay out all the potentials of the situation for Tan to analyze, but she pushed me away, just enough so that she could see my face, and said, "You can't do it alone. That woman's a professional assassin." She rested her forehead against mine. "I'll help you."

"That's ridiculous! If I . . ."

"Listen to me, Philip! She can read physical signs, she can tell if someone's angry. If they're anxious. Well, she'll expect me to be angry. And anxious. She'll think it's just resentment . . . nerves. I'll be able to get close to her."

"And kill her? Will you be able to kill her?"

Tan broke from the embrace and went to stand at the doorway, gazing out at the fog. Her hair had come unbound, spilling down over her shoulders and back, the ribbon that had tied it dangling like a bright blue river winding across a ground of black silk.

"I'll ask Mei to give me something. She has herbs that will induce sleep." She glanced back at me. "There are things you can do to insure our safety once your father's dead. We should discuss them now."

I was amazed by her coolness, how easily she had made the transition from being distraught. "I can't ask you to do this," I said.

"You're not asking—I'm volunteering." I detected a note of sad distraction in her voice. "You'd do as much for me."

"Of course, but if it weren't for me, you wouldn't be involved in this."

"If it weren't for you," she said, the sadness even more evident in her tone, "I'd have no involvements at all."

The first part of the show that evening, the entrance of the troupe to march music, Mei leading the way, wearing a red and white majorette's uniform, twirling—and frequently dropping—a baton, the tigers gamboling at her heels; then two comic skits; then Kai and Kim whirling and spinning aloft in their gold and sequined costumes, tumbling through the air happy as birds; then another skit and Tranh's clownish juggling, pretending to be drunk and making improbable catches as he tumbled, rolled, and staggered about . . . all this was received by the predominantly male audience with a degree of ironic detachment. They laughed at Mei, they whispered and smirked during the skits, they stared dispassionately at Kim and Kai, and they jeered Tranh. It was plain that they had come to belittle us, that doing so validated their sense of superiority. I registered their reactions, but was so absorbed in thinking about what was to happen later, they seemed unreal, unimportant, and it took all my discipline to focus on my own act, a performance punctuated by a knife hurled from behind me that struck home between Tan's legs. There was a burst of enthusiastic cheers, and I turned to see Phuong some thirty feet away, taking a bow in the bleachers—it was she who had thrown the knife. She looked at me and shrugged, with that gesture dismissing my poor skills, and lifted her arms to receive the building applause. I searched the area around her for my father, but he was nowhere to be seen.

The audience remained abuzz, pleased that one of their own had achieved this victory, but when the major entered, led in by Mei and Tranh, they fell silent at the sight of his dark, convulsed figure. Leaning on his staff, he hobbled along the edge of the bleachers, looking into this and that face as if hoping to find a familiar one, and then, moving to the center of the ring, he began to tell the story of Firebase Ruby. I was alarmed at first, but his delivery was eloquent, lyrical, not the plainspoken style in which he had originally couched the tale, and the audience was enthralled. When he came to tell of the letter he had written his wife detailing his hatred of all things Vietnamese, an uneasy muttering arose from the bleachers and rapt expressions turned to scowls; but then he was past that point, and as he described the Viet Cong assault, his listeners settled back and seemed once again riveted by his words.

"In the phosphor light of the hanging flares," he said, "I saw the bloodred ground spread out before me. Beyond the head-high hedgerows of coiled steel wire, black-clad men and women coursed from the jungle, myriad and quick as ants, and, inside the wire, emerging from their secret warrens, more sprouted from the earth like the demon yield of some infernal rain. All around me, my men were dying, and even in the midst of fear, I felt myself the object of a great calm observance, as if the tiny necklace-strung images of the Buddha the enemy held in their mouths when they attacked had been empowered to summon their ribbed original, and somewhere up above the flares, an enormous face had been conjured from the dark matter of the sky and was gazing down with serene approval.

"We could not hold the position long—that was clear. But I had no intention of surrendering. Drunk on whiskey and adrenaline, I was consumed by the thought of death, my own and others', and though I was afraid, I acted less out of fear than from the madness of battle and a kind of communion with death, a desire to make death grow and flourish and triumph. I retreated into the communications bunker and ordered the corporal in charge to call for an air strike on the coordinates of Firebase Ruby. When he balked I put a pistol to his head until he had obeyed. Then I emptied a clip into the radio so no one could countermand me."

The major bowed his head and spread his arms, as though preparing for a supreme display of magic; then his resonant voice sounded forth again, like the voice of a beast speaking from a cave, rough from the bones that have torn its throat. His eyes were chunks of phosphorous burning in the bark of a rotting log.

"When the explosions began, I was firing from a sandbagged position atop the communications bunker. The VC pouring from the jungle slowed their advance, milled about, and those inside the wire looked up in terror to see the jets screaming overhead, so low I could make out the stars on their wings. Victory was stitched across the sky in rocket trails. Gouts of flame gouged the red dirt, opening the tunnels to the air. The detonations began to blend one into the other, and the ground shook like a sheet of plywood under the pounding of a hammer. Clouds of marbled fire and smoke boiled across the earth, rising to form a dreadful second sky of orange and black, and I came to my feet, fearful yet delighted, astonished by the enormity of the destruction I had called down. Then I was knocked flat. Sandbags fell across my legs, a body flung from God knows where landed on my back, driving the breath from me, and in the instant before consciousness fled, I caught the rich stink of napalm.

"In the morning I awoke and saw a bloody, jawless face with staring blue eyes pressed close to mine, looking as if it were still trying to convey a last desperate message. I clawed my way from beneath the corpse and staggered upright to find myself the lord of a killed land, of a raw, red scar littered with corpses in the midst of a charcoaled forest. I went down from the bunker and wandered among the dead. From every quarter issued the droning of flies. Everywhere lay arms, legs, and grisly relics I could not identify. I was numb, I had no feeling apart from a pale satisfaction at having survived. But as I wandered among the dead, taking notice of the awful intimacies death had imposed: a dozen child-sized bodies huddled in a crater, anonymous as a nest of scorched beetles; a horribly burned woman with buttocks exposed reaching out a clawed hand to touch the lips of a disembodied head—these and a hundred other such scenes brought home the truth that I was their author. It wasn't guilt I felt then. Guilt was irrelevant. We were all guilty, the dead and the living, the good and those who had abandoned God. Guilt is our inevitable portion of the world's great trouble. No, it was the recognition that at the moment when I knew the war was lost—my share of it, at least—I chose not to cut my losses but to align myself with a force so base and negative that we refuse to admit its place in human nature and dress it in mystical clothing and call it Satan or Shiva so as to separate it from ourselves. Perhaps this sort of choice is a soldier's virtue, but I can no longer view it in that light." He tapped his chest with the tip of his staff. "Though I will never say that my enemies were just, there is justice in what I have endured since that day. All men sin, all men do evil. And evil shows itself in our faces." Here he aimed the staff at the audience and tracked it from face to face, as if highlighting the misdeeds imprinted on each. "What you see of me now is not the man I was, but the thing I became at the instant I made my choice. Take from my story what you will, but understand this: I am unique only in that the judgment of my days is inscribed not merely on my face, but upon every inch of my body. We are all of us monsters waiting to be summoned forth by a moment of madness and pride."

As Tranh and I led him from the tent, across the damp grass, the major was excited, almost incoherently so, not by the acclaim he had received, but because he had managed to complete his story. He plucked at my sleeve, babbling, bobbing his head, but I paid him no mind, concerned about Tan, whom I had seen talking to Phuong in the bleachers. And when she came running from the main tent, a windbreaker thrown over her costume, I forgot him entirely.

"We're not going directly back to the house," she said. "She wants to take me to a club on the square. I don't know when we'll get to your father's."

"Maybe this isn't such a good idea. I think we should wait until morning."

"It's all right," she said. "Go to the house and as soon as you've dealt with your father, do exactly what I told you. When you hear us enter the house, stay out of sight. Don't do a thing until I come and get you. Understand?"

"I don't know," I said, perplexed at the way she had taken charge.

"Please!" She grabbed me by the lapels. "Promise you'll do as I say! Please!"

I promised, but as I watched her run off into the dark I had a resurgence of my old sense of dislocation, and though I had not truly listened to the major's story, having been occupied with my own troubles, the sound of him sputtering and chortling behind me, gloating over the treasure of his recovered memory, his invention, whatever it was, caused me to wonder then about the nature of my own choice, and the story that I might someday tell.

My father's house was on Yen Phu Street—two stories of pocked gray stone with green vented shutters and a green door with a knocker carved in the shape of a water buffalo's head. I arrived shortly after midnight and stood in the lee of the high whitewashed wall that enclosed his compound. The fog had been cut by a steady drizzle, and no pedestrians were about. Light slanted from the vents of a shuttered upstairs window, and beneath it was parked a bicycle in whose basket rested a dozen white lilies, their stems wrapped in butcher paper. I imagined that my father had ridden the bicycle to market and had forgotten to retrieve the flowers after carrying his other purchases inside. They seemed omenical in their glossy pallor, a sterile emblem of the bloody work ahead.

The idea of killing my father held no terrors for me — I had performed the act in my mind hundreds of times, I'd conceived its every element — and as I stood there I felt the past accumulating at my back like the cars of a train stretching for eighteen years, building from my mother's death to the shuddering engine of the moment I was soon to inhabit. All the misgivings that earlier had nagged at me melted away, like fog before rain. I was secure in my hatred and in the knowledge that I had no choice, that my father was a menace who would never fade.

I crossed the street, knocked, and after a few seconds he admitted me into a brightly lit alcove with a darkened room opening off to the right. He was dressed in a voluminous robe of green silk, and as he proceeded me up the stairway to the left of the alcove, the sight of his bell-like shape and bald head with the silver plate collaring the base of his skull . . . these things along with the odor of jasmine incense led me to imagine that I was being escorted to an audience with some mysterious religious figure by one of his eunuch priests. At the head of the stair was a narrow white room furnished with two padded chrome chairs, a wall screen, and, at the far end, a desk bearing papers, an ornamental vase, an old-fashioned letter opener, and a foot-high gilt and bronze Buddha. My father sat down in one of the chairs, triggered the wall screen's computer mode with a penlight, and set about accessing the Sony AI, working through various menus, all the while chatting away, saying he was sorry he'd missed our show, he hoped to attend the following night, and how was I enjoying my stay in Binh Khoi, it often seemed an unfriendly place to newcomers, but by week's end I'd feel right at home. I had brought no weapon, assuming that his security would detect it. The letter opener, I thought, would do the job. But my hand fell instead to the Buddha. It would be cleaner, I decided. A single blow. I picked it up, hefted it. I had anticipated that when the moment arrived, I would want to make myself known to my father, to relish his shock and dismay; but I understood that was no longer important, and I only wanted him to die. In any case, since he likely knew the truth about me, the dramatic scene I'd envisioned would be greatly diminished.

"That's Thai. Fifteenth century," he said, nodding at the statue, then returned his attention to the screen. "Beautiful, isn't it?"

"Very," I said.

Then, without a thought, all thinking necessary having already been done, and the deed itself merely an automatic function, the final surge of an eighteen-year-long momentum, I stepped behind him and swung the statue at the back of his head. I expected to hear a crack but the sound of impact was plush, muffled, such as might be caused by the flat of one's hand striking a pillow. He let out an explosive grunt, toppled with a twisting motion against the wall, ending up on his side, facing outward. There was so much blood, I assumed he must be dead. But then he groaned, his eyes blinked open, and he struggled to his knees. I saw that

I'd hit the silver plate at the base of his skull. Blood was flowing out around the plate, but it had protected him from mortal damage. His robe had fallen open, and with his pale mottled belly bulging from the green silk and the blood streaking his neck, his smallish features knitted in pain and perplexity, he looked gross and clownishly pitiable. He held up an unsteady hand to block a second blow. His mouth worked, and he said "Wait . . ." or "What. . . ." Which, I can't be sure. But I was in no mood either to wait or to explain myself. A clean death might not have affected me so deeply, but that I had made of a whole healthy life this repellent half-dead thing wobbling at my feet—it assaulted my moral foundation, it washed the romantic tint of revenge from the simple, terrible act of slaughter, and when I struck at him again, this time smashing the statue down two-handed onto the top of his skull, I was charged with the kind of fear that afflicts a child when he more or less by accident wounds a bird with a stone and seeks to hide the act from God by tossing his victim onto an ash heap. My father sagged onto his back, blood gushing from his nose and mouth. I caught a whiff of feces and staggered away, dropping the Buddha. Now that my purpose had been accomplished, like a bee dying from having stung its enemy, I felt drained of poison, full of dull surprise that there had been no more rewarding result.

The penlight had rolled beneath the second chair. I picked it up, and, following Tan's instructions, I used the computer to contact a security agency in Danang. A blond woman with a brittle manner appeared on the screen and asked my business. I explained my circumstances, not bothering to characterize the murder as anything other than it was—the size of my trust would guarantee my legal immunity—and also provided her with the number of Vang's lawyer, as well as some particulars concerning the trust, thereby establishing my bona fides. The woman vanished, her image replaced by a shifting pattern of pastel colors, and, after several minutes, this in turn was replaced by a contract form with a glowing blue patch at the bottom to which I pressed the ball of my thumb. The woman reappeared, much more solicitous now, and cautioned me to remain where I was. She assured me that an armed force would be at the house within the hour. As an afterthought she advised me to wipe the blood from my face.

The presence of the body—its meat reality—made me uncomfortable. I picked up the letter opener and went down the stairs and groped my way across the unlit room off the alcove and found a chair in a corner from which I could see the door. Sitting alone in the darkness amplified the torpor that had pervaded me, and though I sensed certain unsettling dissonances surrounding what had just taken place, I was not sufficiently alert to consider them as other than aggravations. I had been sitting there for perhaps ten minutes when the door opened and Phuong, laughing, stepped into the alcove with Tan behind her, wearing a blue skirt and checkered blouse. She kicked the door shut, pushed Tan against the wall, and began to kiss her, running a hand up under her skirt. Then her head snapped around, and although I didn't believe she could see in the dark, she stared directly at me.

Before I could react, before I could be sure that Phuong had detected me, Tan struck her beneath the jaw with the heel of her left hand, driving her against the opposite wall, and followed this with a kick to the stomach. Phuong rolled away and up into a crouch. She cried out my father's name: "William!" Whether in warning or—recognizing what had happened—in grief, I cannot say. Then the two women began to fight. It lasted no more than half a minute, but their speed and eerie grace were incredible to see: like watching two long-fingered witches dancing in a bright patch of weakened gravity and casting violent spells. Dazed by Tan's initial blows, Phuong went on the defensive, but soon she recovered and started to hold her own. I remembered the letter opener in my hand. The thing was poorly balanced and Phuong's quickness made the timing hard to judge, but then she paused, preparing to launch an attack, and I flung the opener, lodging it squarely between her shoulderblades. Not a mortal wound—the blade was too dull to bite deep—but a distracting one. She shrieked, tried to reach the opener, and, as she reeled to the side, Tan came up behind her and broke her neck with a savage twist. She let the body fall and walked toward me, a shadow in the darkened room. It seemed impossible that she was the same woman I had known on the beach at Vung Tau, and I felt a spark of fear.

"Are you all right?" she asked, stopping a few feet away.

"All right?" I laughed. "What's going on here?"

She gave no reply, and I said, "Apparently you decided against using Mei's herbs."

"If you had done as I asked, if you'd stayed clear, it might not have been necessary to kill her." She came another step forward. "Have you called for security?"

I nodded. "Did you learn to fight like that in Hue?"

"In China," she said.

"At a private security company. Like Phuong."

"Yes."

"Then it would follow that you're not Vang's niece."

"But I am," she said. "He used the last of his fortune to have me trained so I could protect you. He was a bitter man . . . to have used his family so."

"And I suppose sleeping with me falls under the umbrella of protection." She kneeled beside the chair, put a hand on my neck, and gazed at me entreatingly. "I love you, Philip. I would do anything for you. How can you doubt it?"

I was moved by her sincerity, but I could not help but treat her coldly. It was as if a valve had been twisted shut to block the flow of my emotions. "That's right," I said. "Vang told me that your kind were conditioned to bond with their clients."

I watched the words hit home, a wounded expression washing across her features, then fading, like a ripple caused by a pebble dropped into a still pond. "Is that so important?" she asked. "Does it alter the fact that you fell in love with me?"

I ignored this, yet I was tempted to tell her, No, it did not. "If you were trained to protect me, why did Vang discourage our relationship?"

She got to her feet, her face unreadable, and went a few paces toward the alcove; she appeared to be staring at Phuong's body, lying crumpled in the light. "There was a time when I think he wanted me for himself. That may explain it."

"Did Phuong really accost you?" I asked. "Or was that . . .

"I've never lied to you. I've deceived you by not revealing everything I knew about Vang," she said. "But I was bound to obey him in that. As you said, I've been conditioned."

I had other questions, but I could not frame one of them. The silence of the house seemed to breed a faint humming, and I became oppressed by the idea that Tan and I were living analogs of the two corpses, that the wealth I was soon to receive as a consequence of our actions would lead us to a pass wherein we would someday lie dead in separate rooms of a silent house, while two creatures like ourselves but younger would stand apart from one another in fretful isolation, pondering their future. I wanted to dispossess myself of this notion, to contrive a more potent reality, and I crossed the room to Tan and turned her to face me. She refused to meet my eyes, but I tipped up her chin and kissed her. A lover's kiss. I touched her breasts—a treasuring touch. But despite the sweet affirmation and openness of the kiss, I think it also served a formal purpose, the sealing of a bargain whose terms we did not fully understand.

Six months and a bit after my eighteenth birthday, I was sitting in a room in the Sony offices in Saigon, a windowless space with black walls and carpet and silver-framed photographs of scenes along the Perfume River and in the South China Sea, when Vang flickered into being against the far wall. I thought I must seem to him, as he seemed to me, like a visitation, a figure from another time manifested in a dream. He appeared no different than he had on the day he left the circus— thin and gray-haired, dressed in care-worn clothing—and his attitude toward me was, as ever, distant. I told him what had happened in Binh Khoi, and he said, "I presumed you would have more trouble with William. Of course he thought he had leverage over me—he thought he had Tan in his clutches. So he let his guard down. He believed he had nothing to fear."

His logic was overly simplistic, but rather than pursue this, I asked the question foremost on my mind: why had he not told me that he was my grandfather? I had uncovered quite a lot about my past in the process of familiarizing myself with Vang's affairs, but I wanted to hear it all.

"Because I'm *not* your grandfather," he said. "I was William's father-in-law, but . . ." He shot me an amused look. "I should have thought you would have understood all this by now."

I saw no humor in the situation. "Explain it to me."

"As you wish." He paced away from me, stopped to inspect one of the framed photographs. "William engineered the death of my wife, my daughter, and my grandson in a plane crash. Once he had isolated me, he challenged my mental competency, intending to take over my business concerns. To thwart him, I faked my suicide. It was a very convincing fake. I used a body I'd had cloned to supply me with organs. I kept enough money to support Green Star and to pay for Tan's training. The rest you know."

"Not so," I said. "You haven't told me who I am."

"Ah, yes." He turned from the photograph and smiled pleasantly at me. "I suppose that would interest you. Your mother's name was Tuyet. Tuyet Su Vanh. She was an actress in various pornographic media. The woman you saw in your dream—that was she. We had a relationship for several years, then we drifted apart. Not long before I lost my family, she came to me and told me she was dying. One of the mutated HIVs. She said she'd borne a child by me. A son. She begged me to take care of you. I didn't believe her, of course. But she had given me pleasure, so I set up a trust for you. A small one."

"And then you decided to use me."

"William had undermined my authority to the extent that I could not confront him directly. I needed an arrow to aim at his heart. I told your mother that if she cooperated with me I'd adopt you, place my fortune in the trust, and make you my heir. She gave permission to have your memory wiped. I wanted you empty so I could fill you with my purpose. After you were re-educated, she helped construct some fragmentary memories that were implanted by means of a biochip. Nonetheless, you were a difficult child to mold. I couldn't be certain that you would seek William out, and so, since I was old and tired and likely not far from Heaven, I decided to feign an illness and withdraw. This allowed me to arrange a confrontation without risk to myself."

I should have hated Vang, but after six months of running his businesses, of viewing the world from a position of governance and control, I understood him far too well to hate—though at that moment, understanding the dispassionate requisites and protocols of such a position seemed as harsh a form of judgment as the most bitter of hatreds. "What happened to my mother?" I asked.

"I arranged for her to receive terminal care in an Australian hospital."

"And her claim that I was your biological son. . . . did you investigate it?"

"Why should I? It didn't matter. A man in my position could not acknowledge an illegitimate child, and once I had made my decision to abdicate my old life, it mattered even less. If it has any meaning for you, there are medical records you can access."

"I think I'd prefer it to remain a mystery," I told him.

"You've no reason to be angry at me," he said. "I've made you wealthy. And what did it cost? A few memories."

I shifted in my chair, steepled my hands on my stomach. "Are you convinced that my . . . that William had your family killed? He seemed to think there had been a misunderstanding."

"That was a charade! If you're asking whether or not I had proof—of course I didn't. William knew how to disguise his hand."

"So everything you did was based solely on the grounds of your suspicions."

"No! It was based on my knowledge of the man!" His tone softened. "What does it matter? Only William and I knew the truth, and he is dead. If you doubt me, if you pursue this further, you'll never be able to satisfy yourself."

"I suppose you're right," I said, getting to my feet.

"Are you leaving already?" He wore an aggrieved expression. "I was hoping you'd tell me about Tan . . . and Green Star. What has happened with my little circus?"

"Tan is well. As for Green Star, I gave it to Mei and Tranh."

I opened the door, and Vang made a gesture of restraint. "Stay a while longer, Philip. Please. You and Tan are the only people with whom I have an emotional connection. It heartens me to spend time with you."

Hearing him describe our relationship in these terms gave me pause. I recalled the conversation in which Tan had asserted that something central to the idea of life died when one was uploaded into Heaven—Vang's uncharacteristic claim to an emotional debt caused me to think that he might well be, as she'd described her parents, a colored shadow, a cunningly contrived representation of the original. I hoped that this was not the case; I hoped that he was alive in every respect.

"I have to go," I said. "Business, you understand. But I have some news that may be of interest to you."

"Oh?" he said eagerly. "Tell me."

"I've invested heavily in Sony, and through negotiation I've arranged for one of your old companies—Intertech of Hanoi—to be placed in charge of overseeing the virtual environment. I would expect you're soon going to see some changes in your particular part of Heaven."

He seemed nonplussed, then a look of alarm dawned on his face. "What are you going to do?"

"Me? Not a thing." I smiled, and the act of smiling weakened my emotional restraint—a business skill I had not yet perfected—and let anger roughen my voice. "It's much more agreeable to have your dirty work handled by others, don't you think?"

On occasion, Tan and I manage to rekindle an intimacy that reminds us of the days when we first were lovers, but these occasions never last for long, and our relationship is plagued by the lapses into neutrality or—worse—indifference that tend to plague any two people who have spent ten years in each other's company. In our case these lapses are often accompanied by bouts of self-destructive behavior. It seems we're punishing ourselves for having experienced what we consider an undeserved happiness. Even our most honest infidelities are inclined to be of the degrading sort. I understand this. The beach at Vung Tau, once the foundation of our union, has been replaced by a night on Yen Phu Street in Binh Khoi, and no edifice built upon such imperfect stone could be other than cracked and deficient. Nonetheless, we both realize that whatever our portion of contentment in this world, we are fated to seek it together.

From time to time, I receive a communication from Vang. He does not look well, and his tone is always desperate, cajoling. I tell myself that I should relent and restore him to the afterlife for which he contracted; but I am not highly motivated in that regard. If there truly is something that dies when one ascends to Heaven, I fear it has already died in me, and I blame Vang for this.

Seven years after my talk with Vang, Tan and I attended a performance of the circus in the village of Loc Noi. There was a new James Bond Cochise, Kai and Kim had become pretty teenagers, both Tranh and Mei were thinner, but otherwise things were much the same. We sat in the main tent after the show and reminisced. The troupe—Mei in particular—were unnerved by my bodyguards, but all in all, it was a pleasant reunion.

After a while I excused myself and went to see the major. He was huddled in his tent, visible by the weird flickerings in his eyes . . . though as my vision adapted to the dark, I was able to make out the cowled shape of his head against the canvas backdrop. Tranh had told me he did not expect the major to live much longer, and now that I was close to him, I found that his infirmity was palpable, I could hear it in his labored breath. I asked if he knew who I was, and he replied without inflection, as he had so many years before, "Philip." I'd hoped that he would be more forthcoming, because I still felt akin to him, related through the cryptic character of our separate histories, and I thought that he might once have sensed that kinship, that he'd had some diffuse knowledge of the choices I confronted, and had designed the story of Firebase Ruby for my benefit, shaping it as a cautionary tale—one I'd failed to heed. But perhaps I'd read too much into what was sheer coincidence. I touched his hand, and his breath caught, then shuddered forth, heavy as a sob. All that remained for him were a few stories, a few hours in the light. I tried to think of something I could do to ease his last days, but I knew death was the only mercy that could mend him.

Mei invited Tan and me to spend the night in the trailer—for old times' sake, she said—and we were of no mind to refuse. We both yearned for those old times, despite neither of us believing that we could recapture them. Watching Tan prepare for bed, it seemed to me that she had grown too vivid for the drab surroundings, her beauty become too cultivated and too lush. But when she slipped in beside me, when we began to make love on that creaky bunk, the years fell away and she felt like a girl in my arms, tremulous and new to such customs, and I was newly awakened to her charms. She drifted off to sleep afterward with her head on my chest, and as I lay there trying to quiet my breath so not to wake her, it came to me that future and past were joined in the darkness that enclosed us, two black rivers flowing together, and I understood that while the circus would go its own way in the morning and we would go ours, those rivers, too, were forever joined—we shared a confluence and a wandering course, and a moment proof against the world's denial, and we would always be a troupe, Kim and Kai, Mei and Tranh, Tan and I, and the major . . . that living ghost who, like myself, was the figment of a tragic past he never knew, or—if, indeed, he knew it—with which he could never come to terms. It was a bond that could not save us, from either our enemies or ourselves, but it held out a hope of simple glory, a promise truer than Heaven. Illusory or not, all our wars would continue until their cause was long-forgotten under the banner of Radiant Green Star.

great wall of mars

ALASTAIR REYNOLDS

Here's a relentless, wildly inventive, pyrotechnic thriller, paced like a run-away freight train, that takes us to Mars for a mission of peace that instead leads us ever deeper into the heart of war . . .

New writer Alastair Reynolds is a frequent contributor to Interzone, *and has also sold to* Asimov's Science Fiction, Spectrum SF, *and elsewhere. His first novel,* Revelation Space, *is being widely hailed as one of the major SF books of the year; coming up is a sequel,* Chasm City. *A professional scientist with a Ph.D. in astronomy, he comes from Wales, but lives in the Netherlands, where he works for the European Space Agency.*

Y ou realize you might die down there," said Warren.

Nevil Clavain looked into his brother's one good eye; the one the Conjoiners had left him with after the battle of Tharsis Bulge. "Yes, I know," he said. "But if there's another war, we might all die. I'd rather take that risk, if there's a chance for peace."

Warren shook his head, slowly and patiently. "No matter how many times we've been over this, you just don't seem to get it, do you? There can't ever be any kind of peace while they're still down there. That's what you don't understand, Nevil. The only long-term solution here is . . ." he trailed off.

"Go on," Clavain goaded. "Say it. Genocide."

Warren might have been about to answer when there was a bustle of activity down the docking tube, at the far end from the waiting spacecraft. Through the door Clavain saw a throng of media people, then someone gliding through them, fielding questions with only the curtest of answers. That was Sandra Voi, the Demarchist woman who would be coming with him to Mars.

"It's not genocide when they're just a faction, not an ethnically distinct race," Warren said, before Voi was within earshot.

"What is it, then?"

"I don't know. Prudence?"

Voi approached. She bore herself stiffly, her face a mask of quiet resignation.

Her ship had only just docked from Circum-Jove, after a three-week transit at maximum burn. During that time the prospects for a peaceful resolution of the current crisis had steadily deteriorated.

"Welcome to Deimos," Warren said.

"Marshalls," she said, addressing both of them. "I wish the circumstances were better. Let's get straight to business. Warren; how long do you think we have to find a solution?"

"Not long. If Galiana maintains the pattern she's been following for the last six months, we're due another escape attempt in . . ." Warren glanced at a readout buried in his cuff. "About three days. If she does try and get another shuttle off Mars, we'll really have no option but to escalate."

They all knew what that would mean: a military strike against the Conjoiner nest.

"You've tolerated her attempts so far," Voi said. "And each time you've successfully destroyed her ship with all the people in it. The net risk of a successful breakout hasn't increased. So why retaliate now?"

"It's very simple. After each violation we issued Galiana with a stronger warning than the one before. Our last was absolute and final."

"You'll be in violation of treaty if you attack."

Warren's smile was one of quiet triumph. "Not quite, Sandra. You may not be completely conversant with the treaty's fine print, but we've discovered that it allows us to storm Galiana's nest without breaking any terms. The technical phrase is a police action, I believe."

Clavain saw that Voi was momentarily lost for words. That was hardly surprising. The treaty between the Coalition and the Conjoiners—which Voi's neutral Demarchists had helped draft—was the longest document in existence, apart from some obscure, computer-generated mathematical proofs. It was supposed to be watertight, though only machines had ever read it from beginning to end, and only machines had ever stood a chance of finding the kind of loophole which Warren was now brandishing.

"No . . ." she said. "There's some mistake."

"I'm afraid he's right," Clavain said. "I've seen the natural-language summaries, and there's no doubt about the legality of a police action. But it needn't come to that. I'm sure I can persuade Galiana not to make another escape attempt."

"But if we should fail?" Voi looked at Warren now. "Nevil and myself could still be on Mars in three days."

"Don't be, is my advice."

Disgusted, Voi turned and stepped into the green cool of the shuttle. Clavain was left alone with his brother for a moment. Warren fingered the leathery patch over his ruined eye with the chrome gauntlet of his prosthetic arm, as if to remind Clavain of what the war had cost him; how little love he had for the enemy, even now.

"We haven't got a chance of succeeding, have we?" Clavain said. "We're only going down there so you can say you explored all avenues of negotiation before sending in the troops. You actually want another damned war."

"Don't be so defeatist," Warren said, shaking his head sadly, forever the older brother disappointed at his sibling's failings. "It really doesn't become you."

"It's not me who's defeatist," Clavain said.

"No; of course not. Just do your best, little brother."

Warren extended his hand for his brother to shake. Hesitating, Clavain looked again into his brother's good eye. What he saw there was an interrogator's eye: as pale, colorless and cold as a midwinter sun. There was hatred in it. Warren despised Clavain's pacifism; Clavain's belief that any kind of peace, even a peace which consisted only of stumbling episodes of mistrust between crises, was always better than war. That schism had fractured any lingering fraternal feelings they might have retained. Now, when Warren reminded Clavain that they were brothers, he never entirely concealed the disgust in his voice.

"You misjudge me," Clavain whispered, before quietly shaking Warren's hand.

"No; I honestly don't think I do."

Clavain stepped through the airlock just before it sphinctered shut. Voi had already buckled herself in; she had a glazed look now, as if staring into infinity. Clavain guessed she was uploading a copy of the treaty through her implants, scrolling it across her visual field, trying to find the loophole; probably running a global search for any references to police actions.

The ship recognized Clavain, its interior shivering to his preferences. The green was closer to turquoise now; the readouts and controls minimalist in layout, displaying only the most mission-critical systems. Though the shuttle was the tiniest peacetime vessel Clavain had been in, it was a cathedral compared to the dropships he had flown during the war; so small that they were assembled around their occupants like Medieval armor before a joust.

"Don't worry about the treaty," Clavain said. "I promise you Warren won't get his chance to apply that loophole."

Voi snapped out of her trance irritatedly. "You'd better be right, Nevil. Is it me, or is your brother hoping we fail?" She was speaking Quebecois French now; Clavain shifting mental gears to follow her. "If my people discover that there's a hidden agenda here, there'll be hell to pay."

"The Conjoiners gave Warren plenty of reasons to hate them after the battle of the Bulge," Clavain said. "And he's a tactician, not a field specialist. After the cease-fire my knowledge of worms was even more valuable than before, so I had a role. But Warren's skills were a lot less transferable."

"So that gives him a right to edge us closer to another war?" The way Voi spoke, it was as if her own side had not been neutral in the last exchange. But Clavain knew she was right. If hostilities between the Conjoiners and the Coalition reignited, the Demarchy would not be able to stand aside as they had fifteen years ago. And it was anyone's guess how they would align themselves.

"There won't be war."

"And if you can't reason with Galiana? Or are you going to play on your personal connection?"

"I was just her prisoner, that's all." Clavain took the controls—Voi said piloting was a bore—and unlatched the shuttle from Deimos. They dropped away at a tangent to the rotation of the equatorial ring which girdled the moon, instantly in free-fall. Clavain sketched a porthole in the wall with his fingertip, outlining a rectangle which instantly became transparent.

For a moment he saw his reflection in the glass: older than he felt he had any right to look, the gray beard and hair making him look ancient rather than patriarchal; a man deeply wearied by recent circumstance. With some relief he darkened the cabin so that he could see Deimos, dwindling at surprising speed. The higher of the two Martian moons was a dark, bristling lump, infested with armaments, belted by the bright, window-studded band of the moving ring. For the last nine years, Deimos was all that he had known, but now he could encompass it within the arc of his fist.

"Not just her prisoner," Voi said. "No one else came back sane from the Conjoiners. She never even tried to infect you with her machines."

"No, she didn't. But only because the timing was on my side." Clavain was reciting an old argument now; as much for his own benefit as Voi's. "I was the only prisoner she had. She was losing the war by then; one more recruit to her side wouldn't have made any real difference. The terms of cease-fire were being thrashed out and she knew she could buy herself favors by releasing me unharmed. There was something else, too. Conjoiners weren't supposed to be capable of anything so primitive as mercy. They were spiders, as far as we were concerned. Galiana's act threw a wrench into our thinking. It divided alliances within the high command. If she hadn't released me, they might well have nuked her out of existence."

"So there was absolutely nothing personal?"

"No," Clavain said. "There was nothing personal about it at all."

Voi nodded, without in any way suggesting that she actually believed him. It was a skill some women had honed to perfection, Clavain thought.

Of course, he respected Voi completely. She had been one of the first human beings to enter Europa's ocean, decades back. Now they were planning fabulous cities under the ice; efforts which she had spearheaded. Demarchist society was supposedly flat in structure, non-hierarchical; but someone of Voi's brilliance ascended through echelons of her own making. She had been instrumental in brokering the peace between the Conjoiners and Clavain's own Coalition. That was why she was coming along now: Galiana had only agreed to Clavain's mission provided he was accompanied by a neutral observer, and Voi had been the obvious choice. Respect was easy. Trust, however, was harder: it required that Clavain ignore the fact that, with her head dotted with implants, the Demarchist woman's condition was not very far removed from that of the enemy.

The descent to Mars was hard and steep.

Once or twice they were queried by the automated tracking systems of the satellite interdiction network. Dark weapons hovering in Mars-synchronous orbit above the nest locked onto the ship for a few instants, magnetic railguns powering up, before the shuttle's diplomatic nature was established and it was allowed to proceed. The Interdiction was very efficient; as well it might be, given that Clavain had designed much of it himself. In fifteen years no ship had entered or left the Martian atmosphere, nor had any surface vehicle ever escaped from Galiana's nest.

"There she is," Clavain said, as the Great Wall rose over the horizon.

"Why do you call 'it' a 'she'?" Voi asked. "I never felt the urge to personalize it, and I designed it. Besides . . . even if it was alive once, it's dead now."

She was right, but the Wall was still awesome to behold. Seen from orbit, it was a pale, circular ring on the surface of Mars, two thousand kilometers wide. Like a coral atoll, it entrapped its own weather system; a disk of bluer air, flecked with creamy white clouds which stopped abruptly at the boundary.

Once, hundreds of communities had sheltered inside that cell of warm, thick, oxygen-rich atmosphere. The Wall was the most audacious and visible of Voi's projects. The logic had been inescapable: a means to avoid the millennia-long timescales needed to terraform Mars via such conventional schemes as cometary bombardment or ice-cap thawing. Instead of modifying the whole atmosphere at once, the Wall allowed the initial effort to be concentrated in a relatively small region, at first only a thousand kilometers across. There were no craters deep enough, so the Wall had been completely artificial: a vast ring-shaped atmospheric dam designed to move slowly outward, encompassing ever more surface area at a rate of a twenty kilometers per year. The Wall needed to be very tall because the low Martian gravity meant that the column of atmosphere was higher for a fixed surface pressure than on Earth. The ramparts were hundreds of meters thick, dark as glacial ice, sinking great taproots deep into the lithosphere to harvest the ores needed for the Wall's continual growth. Yet two hundred kilometers higher the wall was a diaphanously thin membrane only microns wide; completely invisible except when rare optical effects made it hang like a frozen aurora against the stars. Eco-engineers had invaded the Wall's liveable area with terran genestocks deftly altered in orbital labs. Flora and fauna had moved out in vivacious waves, lapping eagerly against the constraints of the Wall.

But the Wall was dead.

It had stopped growing during the war, hit by some sort of viral weapon which crippled its replicating subsystems, and now even the ecosystem within it was failing; the atmosphere cooling, oxygen bleeding into space, pressure declining inevitably toward the Martian norm of one seven-thousandth of an atmosphere.

He wondered how it must look to Voi; whether in any sense she saw it as her murdered child.

"I'm sorry that we had to kill it," Clavain said. He was about to add that it been the kind of act which war normalized, but decided that the statement would have sounded hopelessly defensive.

"You needn't apologize," Voi said. "It was only machinery. I'm surprised it's lasted as long as it has, frankly. There must still be some residual damage-repair capability. We Demarchists build for posterity, you know."

Yes, and it worried his own side. There was talk of challenging the Demarchist supremacy in the outer solar system; perhaps even an attempt to gain a Coalition foothold around Jupiter.

They skimmed the top of the Wall and punched through the thickening layers of atmosphere within it, the shuttle's hull morphing to an arrowhead shape. The ground had an arid, bleached look to it, dotted here and there by ruined shacks, broken domes, gutted vehicles or shot-down shuttles. There were patches of shallow-rooted, mainly dark-red tundra vegetation; cotton grass, saxifrage, arctic poppies and lichen. Clavain knew each species by its distinct infrared signature, but many of the plants were in recession now that the imported bird species had died. Ice lay in great silver swathes, and what few expanses of open water remained were warmed by buried thermopiles. Elsewhere there were whole zones which had reverted to almost sterile permafrost. It could have been a kind of paradise, Clavain thought, if the war had not ruined everything. Yet what had happened here could only be a foretaste of the devastation that would follow across the system, on Earth as well as Mars, if another war was allowed to happen.

"Do you see the nest yet?" Voi asked.

"Wait a second," Clavain said, requesting a head-up display which boxed the nest. "That's it. A nice fat thermal signature too. Nothing else for miles around— nothing inhabited, anyway."

"Yes. I see it now."

The Conjoiner nest lay a third of the way from the Wall's edge, not far from the footslopes of Arsia Mons. The entire encampment was only a kilometer across, circled by a dyke which was piled high with regolith dust on one side. The area within the Great Wall was large enough to have an appreciable weather system: spanning enough Martian latitude for significant coriolis effects; enough longitude for diurnal warming and cooling to cause thermal currents.

He could see the nest much more clearly now; details leaping out of the haze.

Its external layout was crushingly familiar. Clavain's side had been studying the nest from the vantage point of Deimos ever since the cease-fire. Phobos, with its lower orbit, would have been even better, of course—but there was no helping that, and perhaps the Phobos problem might actually prove useful in his negoti-ations with Galiana. She was somewhere in the nest, he knew: somewhere beneath the twenty varyingly sized domes emplaced within the rim, linked together by pressurized tunnels or merged at their boundaries like soap bubbles. The nest extended several tens of levels beneath the Martian surface maybe deeper.

"How many people do you think are inside?" Voi said.

"Nine hundred or so," said Clavain. "That's an estimate based on my experi-ences as a prisoner, and the hundred or so who've died trying to escape since. The rest, I have to say, is pretty much guesswork."

"Our estimates aren't dissimilar. A thousand or less here, and perhaps another three or four spread across the system in smaller nests. I know your side thinks we have better intelligence than that, but it happens not to be the case."

"Actually, I believe you." The shuttle's airframe was flexing around them, morphing to a low-altitude profile with wide, batlike wings.

"I was just hoping you might have some clue as to why Galiana keeps wasting valuable lives with escape attempts."

Voi shrugged. "Maybe to her the lives aren't anywhere near as valuable as you'd like to think."

"Do you honestly think that?"

"I don't think we can begin to guess the thinking of a true hive-mind society, Clavain. Even from a Demarchist standpoint."

There was a chirp from the console; Galiana signaling them. Clavain opened the channel allocated for Coalition-Conjoiner diplomacy.

"Nevil Clavain?" he heard.

"Yes." He tried to sound as calm as possible. "I'm with Sandra Voi. We're ready to land as soon as you show us where."

"Okay," Galiana said. "Vector your ship toward the westerly rim wall. And please, be careful."

"Thank you. Any particular reason for the caution?"

"Just be quick about it, Nevil."

They banked over the nest, shedding height until they were skimming only a few tens of meters above the weatherworn Martian surface. A wide rectangular door had opened in the concrete dyke, revealing a hangar bay aglow with yellow lights.

"That must be where Galiana launches her shuttles from," Clavain whispered. "We always thought there must be some kind of opening on the west side of the rim, but we never had a good view of it before."

"Which still doesn't tell us why she does it," Voi said.

The console chirped again—the link poor even though they were so close. "Nose up," Galiana said. "You're too low and slow. Get some altitude or the worms will lock onto you."

"You're telling me there are worms here?" Clavain said.

"I thought you were the worm expert, Nevil."

He nosed the shuttle up, but fractionally too late. Ahead of them something coiled out of the ground with lightning speed, metallic jaws opening in its blunt, armored head. He recognized the type immediately: Ouroborus class. Worms of this form still infested a hundred niches across the system. Not quite as smart as the type infesting Phobos, but still adequately dangerous.

"Shit," Voi said, her veneer of Demarchist cool cracking for an instant.

"You said it," Clavain answered.

The Ouroborus passed underneath and then there was a spine-jarring series of bumps as the jaws tore into the shuttle's belly. Clavain felt the shuttle lurch down sickeningly; no longer a flying thing but an exercise in ballistics. The cool, minimalist turquoise interior shifted liquidly into an emergency configuration; damage readouts competing for attention with weapons status options. Their seats ballooned around them.

"Hold on," he said. "We're going down."

Voi's calm returned. "Do you think we can reach the rim in time?"

"Not a cat in hell's chance." He wrestled with the controls all the same, but it was no good. The ground was coming up fast and hard. "I wish Galiana had warned us a bit sooner . . ."

"I think she thought we already knew."

They hit. It was harder than Clavain had been expecting, but the shuttle stayed in one piece and the seat cushioned him from the worst of the impact. They skidded for a few meters and then nosed up against a sandbank. Through the window Clavain saw the white worm racing toward them with undulating waves of its segmented robot body.

"I think we're finished," Voi said.

"Not quite," Clavain said. "You're not going to like this, but . . . Biting his tongue he brought the shuttle's hidden weapons online. An aiming scope plunged down from the ceiling; he brought his eyes to it and locked crosshairs onto the Ouroborus. Just like old times . . .

"Damn you," Voi said. "This was meant to be an unarmed mission!"

"You're welcome to lodge a formal complaint."

Clavain fired, the hull shaking from the recoil. Through the side window they watched the white worm blow apart into stubby segments. The parts wriggled beneath the dust.

"Good shooting," Voi said, almost grudgingly. "Is it dead?"

"For now," Clavain said. "It'll take several hours for the segments to fuse back into a functional worm."

"Good," Voi said, pushing herself out of her seat. "But there will be a formal complaint, take my word."

"Maybe you'd rather the worm ate us?"

"I just hate duplicity, Clavain."

He tried the radio again. "Galiana? We're down—the ship's history—but we're both unharmed."

"Thank God." Old verbal mannerisms died hard, even among the Conjoined. "But you can't stay where you are. There are more worms in the area. Do you think you can make it overland to the nest?"

"It's only two hundred meters," Voi said. "It shouldn't be a problem."

Two hundred meters, yes—but two hundred meters across treacherous, pot-holed ground riddled with enough soft depressions to hide a dozen worms. And then they would have to climb up the rim's side to reach the entrance to the hangar bay; ten or fifteen meters above the soil.

"Let's hope it isn't," Clavain said.

He unbuckled, feeling light-headed as he stood for the first time in Martian gravity. He had adapted entirely too well to the one-gee of the Deimos ring, constructed for the comfort of Earthside tacticians. He went to the emergency locker and found a mask which slivered eagerly across his face; another for Voi. They plugged in air-tanks and went to the shuttle's door. This time when it sphinc-tered open there was a glistening membrane stretched across the doorway, a re-cently licensed item of Demarchist technology. Clavain pushed through the membrane and the stuff enveloped him with a wet, sucking sound. By the time he hit the dirt the membrane had hardened itself around his soles and had begun to contour itself with ribs and accordioned joints, even though it stayed transparent.

Voi came behind him, gaining her own m-suit.

They loped away from the crashed shuttle, toward the dyke. The worms would be locking onto their seismic patterns already, if there were any nearby. They might be more interested in the shuttle for now, but that was nothing they could count on. Clavain knew the behavior of worms intimately, knew the major routines which drove them; but that expertise did not guarantee his survival. It had almost failed him in Phobos.

The mask felt clammy against his face. The air at the base of the Great Wall was technically breathable even now, but there seemed no point in taking chances when speed was of the essence. His feet scuffed through the topsoil, and while he seemed to be crossing ground, the dyke obstinately refused to come any closer. It was larger than it looked from the crash; the distance further.

"Another worm," Voi said.

White coils erupted through sand to the west. The Ouroborus was making undulating progress toward them, zig-zagging with predatory calm, knowing that it could afford to take its time. In the tunnels of Phobos, they had never had the luxury of knowing when a worm was close. They struck from ambush, quick as pythons.

"Run," Clavain said.

Dark figures appeared in the opening high in the rimwall. A rope-ladder unfurled down the side of the structure. Clavain, making for the base of it, made no effort to quieten his footfalls. He knew that the worm almost certainly had a lock on him by now.

He looked back.

The worm paused by the downed shuttle, then smashed its diamond-jawed head into the ship, impaling the hull on its body. The worm reared up, wearing the ship like a garland. Then it shivered and the ship flew apart like a rotten carcass. The worm returned its attention to Clavain and Voi. Like a sidewinder it pulled its thirty-meter long body from the sand and rolled toward them on wheeling coils.

Clavain reached the base of the ladder.

Once, he could have ascended the ladder with his arms alone, in one-gee, but now the ladder felt alive beneath his feet. He began to climb, then realized that the ground was dropping away much faster than he was passing rungs. The Conjoiners were hauling him aloft.

He looked back in time to see Voi stumble.

"Sandra! No!"

She made to stand up, but it was too late by then. As the worm descended on her, Clavain could do nothing but turn his gaze away and pray for her death to be quick. If it had to be meaningless, he thought, at least let it be swift.

Then he started thinking about his own survival. "Faster!" he shouted, but the mask reduced his voice to a panicked muffle. He had forgotten to assign the ship's radio frequency to the suit.

The worm thrashed against the base of the wall, then began to rear up, its maw opening beneath him; a diamond-ringed orifice like the drill of a tunnelling machine. Then something eye-hurtingly bright cut into the worm's hide. Craning his neck, Clavain saw a group of Conjoiners kneeling over the lip of the opening, aiming guns downward. The worm writhed in intense robotic irritation. Across the sand, he could see the coils of other worms coming closer. There must have been dozens ringing the nest. No wonder Galiana's people had made so few attempts to leave by land.

They had hauled him within ten meters of safety. The injured worm showed cybernetic workings where its hide had been flensed away by weapons impacts. Enraged, it flung itself against the rim wall, chipping off scabs of concrete the size of boulders. Clavain felt the vibration of each impact through the wall as he was dragged upward.

The worm hit again and the wall shook more violently than before. To his horror, Clavain watched one of the Conjoiners lose his footing and tumble over the edge of the rim toward him. Time oozed to a crawl. The falling man was almost upon him. Without thinking, Clavain hugged closer to the wall, locking his limbs around the ladder. Suddenly, he had seized the man by the arm. Even in Martian gravity, even allowing for the Conjoiner's willowy build, the impact almost sent both of them toward the Ouroborus. Clavain felt his bones pop out of location, tearing at gristle, but he managed to keep his grip on both the Conjoiner and the ladder.

Conjoiners breathed the air at the base of the Wall without difficulty. The man wore only lightweight clothes, gray silk pajamas belted at the waist. With his sunken cheeks and bald skull, the man's Martian physique lent him a cadaverous look. Yet somehow he had managed not to drop his gun, still holding it in his other hand.

"Let me go," the man said.

Below, the worm inched higher despite the harm the Conjoiners had inflicted on it. "No," Clavain said, through clenched teeth and the distorting membrane of his mask. "I'm not letting you go."

"You've no option." The man's voice was placid. "They can't haul both of us up fast enough, Clavain."

Clavain looked into the Conjoiner's face, trying to judge the man's age. Thirty, perhaps — maybe not even that, since the cadaverous look probably made him seem older than he really was. Clavain was easily twice his age; had surely lived a richer life; had comfortably cheated death on three or four previous occasions.

"I'm the one who should die, not you."

"No," the Conjoiner said. "They'd find a way to blame your death on us. They'd make it a pretext for war." Without any fuss the man pointed the gun at his own head and blew his brains out.

As much in shock as recognition that the man's life was no longer his to save, Clavain released his grip. The dead man tumbled down the rim wall, into the mouth of the worm which had just killed Sandra Voi.

Numb, Clavain allowed himself to be pulled to safety.

When the armored door to the hangar was shut the Conjoiners attacked his m-suit with enzymic sprays. The sprays digested the fabric in seconds, leaving Clavain wheezing in a pool of slime. Then a pair of Conjoiners helped him unsteadily to his feet and waited patiently while he caught his breath from the mask. Through tears of exhaustion he saw that the hangar was racked full of half-assembled spacecraft; skeletal geodesic shark-shapes designed to punch out of an atmosphere, fast.

"Sandra Voi is dead," he said, removing the mask to speak.

There was no way the Conjoiners could not have seen this for themselves, but it seemed inhuman not to acknowledge what had happened.

"I know," Galiana said. "But at least you survived."

He thought of the man falling into the Ouroborus. "I'm sorry about your . . ." But then trailed off, because for all his depth of knowledge concerning the Conjoiners, he had no idea what the appropriate term was.

"You placed your life in danger in trying to save him."

"He didn't have to die."

Galiana nodded sagely. "No; in all likelihood he didn't. But the risk to yourself was too great. You heard what he said. Your death would be made to seem our fault; justification for a pre-emptive strike against our nest. Even the Demarchists would turn against us if we were seen to murder a diplomat."

Taking another suck from the mask, he looked into her face. He had spoken to her over low-bandwidth video-links, but only in person was it obvious that Galiana had hardly aged in fifteen years. A decade and a half of habitual expression should have engraved existing lines deeper into her face—but Conjoiners were not known for their habits of expression. Galiana had seen little sunlight in the intervening time, cooped here in the nest, and Martian gravity was much kinder to bone structure than the one-gee of Deimos. She still had the cruel beauty he remembered from his time as a prisoner. The only real evidence of aging lay in the filaments of gray threading her hair; raven-black when she had been his captor.

"Why didn't you warn us about the worms?"

"Warn you?" For the first time something like doubt crossed her face, but it was only fleeting. "We assumed you were fully aware of the Ouroborus infestation. Those worms have been dormant—waiting—for years, but they've always been there. It was only when I saw how low your approach was that I realized . . ."

"That we might not have known?"

Worms were area-denial devices; autonomous prey-seeking mines. The war had left many pockets of the solar system still riddled with active worms. The machines were intelligent, in a one-dimensional way. Nobody ever admitted to deploying them and it was usually impossible to convince them that the war was over and that they should quietly deactivate.

"After what happened to you in Phobos," Galiana said, "I assumed there was nothing you needed to be taught about worms."

He never liked thinking about Phobos: the pain was still too deeply engraved. But if it had not been for the injuries he had sustained there he would never have been sent to Deimos to recuperate; would never have been recruited into his brother's intelligence wing to study the Conjoiners. Out of that phase of deep immersion in everything concerning the enemy had come his peacetime role as negotiator—and now diplomat—on the eve of another war. Everything was circular, ultimately. And now Phobos was central to his thinking because he saw it as a way out of the impasse—maybe the last chance for peace. But it was too soon to put his idea to Galiana. He was not even sure the mission could still continue, after what had happened.

"We're safe now, I take it?"

"Yes; we can repair the damage to the dyke. Mostly, we can ignore their presence."

"We should have been warned. Look, I need to talk to my brother."

"Warren? Of course. It's easily arranged."

They walked out of the hangar; away from the half-assembled ships. Somewhere deeper in the nest, Clavain knew, was a factory where the components for the ships were made, mined out of Mars or winnowed from the fabric of the nest. The Conjoiners managed to launch one every six weeks or so; had been doing so for six months. Not one of the ships had ever managed to escape the Martian atmosphere before being shot down . . . but sooner or later he would have to ask Galiana why she persisted with this provocative folly.

Now, though, was not the time—even if, by Warren's estimate, he only had three days before Galiana's next provocation.

The air elsewhere in the nest was thicker and warmer than in the hangar, which meant he could dispense with the mask. Galiana took him down a short, gray-walled, metallic corridor which ended in a circular room containing a console. He recognized the room from the times he had spoken to Galiana from Deimos. Galiana showed him how to use the system then left him in privacy while he established a connection with Deimos.

Warren's face soon appeared on a screen, thick with pixels like an impressionist portrait. Conjoiners were only allowed to send kilobytes a second to other parts of the system. Much of that bandwidth was now being sucked up by this one video link.

"You've heard, I take it," Clavain said.

Warren nodded, his face ashen. "We had a pretty good view from orbit, of course. Enough to see that Voi didn't make it. Poor woman. We were reasonably sure you survived, but it's good to have it confirmed."

"Do you want me to abandon the mission?"

Warren's hesitation was more than just time-lag. "No . . . I thought about it, of course, and high command agrees with me. Voi's death was tragic—no escaping that. But she was only along as a neutral observer. If Galiana consents for you to stay, I suggest you do so."

"But you still say I only have three days?"

"That's up to Galiana, isn't it? Have you learned much?"

"You must be kidding. I've seen shuttles ready for launch, that's all. I haven't raised the Phobos proposal, either. The timing wasn't exactly ideal, after what happened to Voi."

"Yes. If only we'd known about that Ouroborus infestation."

Clavain leaned closer to the screen. "Yes. Why the hell didn't we? Galiana assumed that we would, and I don't blame her for that. We've had the nest under constant surveillance for fifteen years. Surely in all that time we'd have seen evidence of the worms?"

"You'd have thought so, wouldn't you?"

"Meaning what?"

"Meaning, maybe the worms weren't always there."

Conscious that there could be nothing private about this conversation—but unwilling to drop the thread—Clavain said: "You think the Conjoiners put them there to ambush us?"

"I'm saying we shouldn't disregard any possibility, no matter how unpalatable."

"Galiana would never do something like that."

"No, I wouldn't." She had just stepped back into the room. "And I'm disappointed that you'd even debate the possibility."

Clavain terminated the link with Deimos. "Eavesdropping's not a very nice habit, you know."

"What did you expect me to do?"

"Show some trust? Or is that too much of a stretch?"

"I never had to trust you when you were my prisoner," Galiana said. "That made our relationship infinitely simpler. Our roles were completely defined."

"And now? If you distrust me so completely, why did you ever agree to my visit? Plenty of other specialists could have come in my place. You could even have refused any dialogue."

"Voi's people pressured us to allow your visit," Galiana said. "Just as they pressured your side into delaying hostilities a little longer."

"Is that all?"

She hesitated slightly now. "I . . . knew you."

"Knew me? Is that how you sum up a year of imprisonment? What about the thousands of conversations we had; the times when we put aside our differences to talk about something other than the damned war? You kept me sane, Galiana. I've never forgotten that. It's why I've risked my life to come here and talk you out of another provocation."

"It's completely different now."

"Of course!" He forced himself not to shout. "Of course it's different. But not fundamentally. We can still build on that bond of trust and find a way out of this crisis."

"But does your side really want a way out of it?"

He did not answer her immediately; wary of what the truth might mean. "I'm not sure. But I'm also not sure you do, or else you wouldn't keep pushing your luck." Something snapped inside him and he asked the question he had meant to ask in a million better ways. "Why do you keep doing it, Galiana? Why do you keep launching those ships when you know they'll be shot down as soon as they leave the nest?"

Her eyes locked onto his own, unflinchingly. "Because we can. Because sooner or later one will succeed."

Clavain nodded. It was exactly the sort of thing he had feared she would say.

She led him through more gray-walled corridors, descending several levels deeper into the nest. Light poured from snaking strips embedded into the walls like arteries. It was possible that the snaking design was decorative, but Clavain thought it much more likely that the strips had simply grown that way, expressing biological algorithms. There was no evidence that the Conjoiners had attempted to enliven their surroundings; to render them in any sense human.

"It's a terrible risk you're running," Clavain said.

"And the status quo is intolerable. I've every desire to avoid another war, but if it came to one, we'd at least have the chance to break these shackles."

"If you didn't get exterminated first . . ."

"We'd avoid that. In any case, fear plays no part in our thinking. You saw the man accept his fate on the dyke, when he understood that your death would harm us more than his own. He altered his state of mind to one of total acceptance."

"Fine. That makes it all right, then."

She halted. They were alone in one of the snakingly lit corridors; he had seen no other Conjoiners since the hangar. "It's not that we regard individual lives as worthless, any more than you would willingly sacrifice a limb. But now that we're part of something larger . . ."

"Transenlightenment, you mean?"

It was the Conjoiners' term for the state of neural communion they shared, mediated by the machines swarming in their skulls. Whereas Demarchists used implants to facilitate real-time democracy, Conjoiners used them to share sensory data, memories—even conscious thought itself. That was what had precipitated the war. Back in 2190 half of humanity had been hooked into the system-wide data nets via neural implants. Then the Conjoiner experiments had exceeded some threshold, unleashing a transforming virus into the nets. Implants had begun to change, infecting millions of minds with the templates of Conjoiner thought. Instantly the infected had become the enemy. Earth and the other inner planets had always been more conservative, preferring to access the nets via traditional media.

Once they saw communities on Mars and in the asteroid belts fall prey to the Conjoiner phenomenon, the Coalition powers hurriedly pooled their resources to prevent the spread reaching their own states. The Demarchists, out around the gas giants, had managed to get firewalls up before many of their habitats were lost. They had chosen neutrality while the Coalition tried to contain—some said sterilize—zones of Conjoiner takeover. Within three years—after some of the bloodiest battles in human experience—the Conjoiners had been pushed back to a clutch of hideaways dotted around the system. Yet all along they professed a kind of puzzled bemusement that their spread was being resisted. After all, no one who had been assimilated seemed to regret it. Quite the contrary. The few prisoners whom the Conjoiners had reluctantly returned to their pre-infection state had sought every means to return to the fold. Some had even chosen suicide rather than be denied Transenlightenment. Like acolytes given a vision of heaven, they devoted their entire waking existence to the search for another glimpse.

"Transenlightenment blurs our sense of self," Galiana said. "When the man elected to die, the sacrifice was not absolute for him. He understood that much of what he was had already achieved preservation among the rest of us."

"But he was just one man. What about the hundred lives you've thrown away with your escape attempts? We know—we've counted the bodies."

"Replacements can always be cloned."

Clavain hoped that he hid his disgust satisfactorily. Among his people the very notion of cloning was an unspeakable atrocity; redolent with horror. To Galiana it would be just another technique in her arsenal. "But you don't clone, do you? And you're losing people. We thought there would be nine hundred of you in this nest, but that was a gross overestimate, wasn't it?"

"You haven't seen much yet," Galiana said.

"No, but this place smells deserted. You can't hide absence, Galiana. I bet there aren't more than a hundred of you left here."

"You're wrong," Galiana said. "We have cloning technology, but we've hardly ever used it. What would be the point? We don't aspire to genetic unity, no matter what your propagandists think. The pursuit of optima leads only to local minima. We honor our errors. We actively seek persistent disequilibrium."

"Right." The last thing he needed now was a dose of Conjoiner rhetoric. "So where the hell is everyone?"

In a while he had part of the answer, if not the whole of it. At the end of the maze of corridors—far under Mars now—Galiana brought him to a nursery.

It was shockingly unlike his expectations. Not only did it not match what he had imagined from the vantage point of Deimos, but it jarred against his predictions based on what he had seen so far of the nest. In Deimos, he had assumed a Conjoiner nursery would be a place of grim medical efficiency; all gleaming machines with babies plugged in like peripherals, like a monstrously productive doll factory. Within the nest, he had revised his model to allow for the depleted numbers of Conjoiners. If there was a nursery, it was obviously not very productive. Fewer babies, then—but still a vision of hulking gray machines, bathed in snaking light.

The nursery was nothing like that.

The huge room Galiana showed him was almost painfully bright and cheerful; a child's fantasy of friendly shapes and primary colors. The walls and ceiling projected a holographic sky: infinite blue and billowing clouds of heavenly white. The floor was an undulating mat of synthetic grass forming hillocks and meadows. There were banks of flowers and forests of bonsai trees. There were robot animals: fabulous birds and rabbits just slightly too anthropomorphic to fool Clavain. They were like the animals in children's books; big-eyed and happy-looking. Toys were scattered on the grass.

And there were children. They numbered between forty and fifty; spanning by his estimate ages from a few months to six or seven standard years. Some were crawling among the rabbits; other, older children were gathered around tree stumps whose sheered-off surfaces flickered rapidly with images, underlighting their faces. They were talking among themselves, giggling or singing. He counted perhaps half a dozen adult Conjoiners kneeling among the children. The children's clothes were a headache of bright, clashing colors and patterns. The Conjoiners crouched among them like ravens. Yet the children seemed at ease with them, listening attentively when the adults had something to say.

"This isn't what you thought it would be like, is it?"

"No . . . not at all." There seemed no point lying to her. "We thought you'd raise your young in a simplified version of the machine-generated environment you experience."

"In the early days that's more or less what we did." Subtly, Galiana's tone of voice had changed. "Do you know why chimpanzees are less intelligent than humans?"

He blinked at the change of tack. "I don't know—are their brains smaller?"

"Yes—but a dolphin's brain is larger, and they're scarcely more intelligent than dogs." Galiana stooped next to a vacant tree stump. Without seeming to do anything, she made a diagram of mammal brain anatomies appear on the trunk's upper surface, then sketched her finger across the relevant parts. "It's not overall brain volume that counts so much as the developmental history. The difference in brain volume between a neonatal chimp and an adult is only about twenty percent. By the time the chimp receives any data from beyond the womb, there's almost no plasticity left to use. Similarly, dolphins are born with almost their complete repertoire of adult behavior already hardwired. A human brain, on the other hand, keeps growing through years of learning. We inverted that thinking. If data received during post-natal growth was so crucial to intelligence, perhaps we could boost our intelligence even further by intervening during the earliest phases of brain development."

"In the womb?"

"Yes." Now she made the tree-trunk show a human embryo running through cycles of cell-division, until the faint fold of a rudimentary spinal nerve began to form, nubbed with the tiniest of emergent minds. Droves of subcellular machines swarmed in, invading the nascent nervous system. Then the embryo's development slammed forward, until Clavain was looking at an unborn human baby.

"What happened?"

"It was a grave error," Galiana said. "Instead of enhancing normal neural development, we impaired it terribly. All we ended up with were various manifestations of savant syndrome."

Clavain looked around him. "Then you let these kids develop normally?"

"More or less. There's no family structure, of course, but then again there are plenty of human and primate societies where the family is less important in child development than the cohort group. So far we haven't seen any pathologies."

Clavain watched as one of the older children was escorted out of the grassy room, through a door in the sky. When the Conjoiner reached the door the child hesitated, tugging against the man's gentle insistence. The child looked back for a moment, then followed the man through the gap.

"Where's that child going?"

"To the next stage of its development."

Clavain wondered what were the chances of him seeing the nursery just as one of the children was being promoted. Small, he judged—unless there was a crash program to rush as many of them through as quickly as possible. As he thought about this, Galiana took him into another part of the nursery. While this room was smaller and dourer it was still more colorful than any other part of the nest he had seen before the grassy room. The walls were a mosaic of crowded, intermingling displays, teeming with moving images and rapidly scrolling text. He saw a herd of zebra stampeding through the core of a neutron star. Elsewhere an octopus squirted ink at the face of a twentieth-century despot. Other display facets rose from the floor like Japanese paper screens, flooded with data. Children—up to early teenagers—sat on soft black toadstools next to the screens in little groups, debating. A few musical instruments lay around unused: holoclaviers and air-guitars. Some of the children had gray bands around their eyes and were poking their fingers through the interstices of abstract structures, exploring the dragon-infested waters of mathematical space. Clavain could see what they were manipulating on the flat screens: shapes that made his head hurt even in two dimensions.

"They're nearly there," Clavain said. "The machines are outside their heads, but not for long. When does it happen?"

"Soon; very soon."

"You're rushing them, aren't you? Trying to get as many children Conjoined as you can. What are you planning?"

"Something . . . has arisen, that's all. The timing of your arrival is either very bad or very fortunate, depending on your point of view." Before he could query her, Galiana added: "Clavain; I want you to meet someone."

"Who?"

"Someone very precious to us."

She took him through a series of child-proof doors until they reached a small circular room. The walls and ceiling were veined gray; tranquil after what he had seen in the last place. A child sat cross-legged on the floor in the middle of the room. Clavain estimated the girl's age as ten standard years—perhaps fractionally older. But she did not respond to Clavain's presence in any way an adult, or even a normal child, would have. She just kept on doing the thing she had been doing when they stepped inside, as if they were not really present at all. It was not at all clear what she was doing. Her hands moved before her in slow, precise gestures. It was as if she were playing a holoclavier or working a phantom puppet show. Now and then she would pivot around until she was facing another direction and carry on doing the hand movements.

"Her name's Felka," Galiana said.

"Hello, Felka . . ." He waited for a response, but none came. "I can see there's something wrong with her."

"She was one of the savants. Felka developed with machines in her head. She was the last to be born before we realized our failure."

Something about Felka disturbed him. Perhaps it was the way she carried on regardless, engrossed in an activity to which she seemed to attribute the utmost significance, yet which had to be without any sane purpose.

"She doesn't seem aware of us."

"Her deficits are severe," Galiana said. "She has no interest in other human beings. She has prosopagnosia; the inability to distinguish faces. We all seem alike to her. Can you imagine something more strange than that?"

He tried, and failed. Life from Felka's viewpoint must have been a nightmarish thing, surrounded by identical clones whose inner lives she could not begin to grasp. No wonder she seemed so engrossed in her game.

"Why is she so precious to you?" Clavain asked, not really wanting to know the answer.

"She's keeping us alive," Galiana said.

Of course, he asked Galiana what she meant by that. Galiana's only response was to tell him that he was not yet ready to be shown the answer.

"And what exactly would it take for me to reach that stage?"

"A simple procedure."

Oh yes, he understood that part well enough. Just a few machines in the right parts of his brain and the truth could be his. Politely, doing his best to mask his distaste, Clavain declined. Fortunately, Galiana did not press the point, for the time had arrived for the meeting he had been promised before his arrival on Mars.

He watched a subset of the nest file into the conference room. Galiana was their leader only inasmuch as she had founded the lab here from which the original experiment had sprung and was accorded some respect deriving from seniority. She was also the most obvious spokesperson among them. They all had areas of expertise which could not be easily shared among other Conjoined; very distinct from the hive-mind of identical clones which still figured in the Coalition's propaganda. If the nest was in any way like an ant colony, then it was an ant colony in which every ant fulfilled a distinct role from all the others. Naturally, no individual could be solely entrusted with a particular skill essential to the nest— that would have been dangerous over-specialization—but neither had individuality been completely subsumed into the group mind.

The conference room must have dated back to the days when the nest was a research outpost, or even earlier, when it was some kind of mining base in the early 2100s. It was much too big for the dour handful of Conjoiners who stood around the main table. Tactical readouts around the table showed the build-up of strike forces above the Martian exclusion zone; probable drop trajectories for ground-force deployment.

"Nevil Clavain," Galiana said, introducing him to the others. Everyone sat down. "I'm just sorry that Sandra Voi can't be with us now. We all feel the tragedy of her death. But perhaps out of this terrible event we can find some common ground. Nevil; before you came here you told us you had a proposal for a peaceful resolution to the crisis."

"I'd really like to hear it," one of the others murmured audibly.

Clavain's throat was dry. Diplomatically, this was quicksand. "My proposal concerns Phobos . . ."

"Go on."

"I was injured there," he said. "Very badly. Our attempt to clean out the worm infestation failed and I lost some good friends. That makes it personal between me and the worms. But I'd accept anyone's help to finish them off."

Galiana glanced quickly at her compatriots before answering. "A joint assault operation?"

"It could work."

"Yes . . ." Galiana seemed lost momentarily. "I suppose it could be a way out of the impasse. Our own attempt failed too—and the interdiction's stopped us from trying again." Again, she seemed to fall into reverie. "But who would really benefit from the flushing out of Phobos? We'd still be quarantined here."

Clavain leaned forward. "A cooperative gesture might be exactly the thing to lead to a relaxation in the terms of the interdiction. But don't think of it in those terms. Think instead of reducing the current threat from the worms."

"Threat?"

Clavain nodded. "It's possible that you haven't noticed." He leaned forward, elbows on the table. "We're concerned about the Phobos worms. They've begun altering the moon's orbit. The shift is tiny at the moment, but too large to be anything other than deliberate."

Galiana looked away from him for an instant, as if weighing her options. Then said: "We were aware of this, but you weren't to know that."

Gratitude?

He had assumed the worms' activity could not have escaped Galiana. "We've seen odd behavior from other worm infestations across the system; things that begin to look like emergent intelligence. But never anything this purposeful. This infestation must have come from a batch with some subroutines we never even guessed about. Do you have any ideas about what they might be up to?"

Again, there was the briefest of hesitations, as if she was communing with her compatriots for the right response. Then she nodded toward a male Conjoiner sitting opposite her, Clavain guessing that the gesture was entirely for his benefit. His hair was black and curly; his face as smooth and untroubled by expression as Galiana's, with something of the same beautifully symmetrical bone structure.

"This is Remontoire," said Galiana. "He's our specialist on the Phobos situation."

Remontoire nodded politely. "In answer to your question, we currently have no viable theories as to what they're doing, but we do know one thing. They're raising the apocentre of the moon's orbit." Apocentre, Clavain knew, was the Martian equivalent of apogee for an object orbiting Earth: the point of highest altitude in an elliptical orbit. Remontoire continued, his voice as preternaturally calm as a parent reading slowly to a child. "The natural orbit of Phobos is actually inside the Roche limit for a gravitationally bound moon; Phobos is raising a tidal bulge on Mars but, because of friction, the bulge can't quite keep up with Phobos. It's causing Phobos to spiral slowly closer to Mars, by about two meters a century. In a few tens of millions of years, what's left of the moon will crash into Mars."

"You think the worms are elevating the orbit to avoid a cataclysm so far in the future?"

"I don't know," Remontoire said. "I suppose the orbital alterations could also be a by-product of some less meaningful worm activity."

"I agree," Clavain said. "But the danger remains. If the worms can elevate the moon's apocentre—even accidentally—we can assume they also have the means to lower its pericentre. They could drop Phobos on top of your nest. Does that scare you sufficiently that you'd consider cooperation with the Coalition?"

Galiana steepled her fingers before her face; a human gesture of deep concentration which her time as a Conjoiner had not quite eroded. Clavain could almost feel the web of thought looming in the room; ghostly strands of cognition reaching between each Conjoiner at the table, and beyond into the nest proper.

"A winning team, is that your idea?"

"It's got to be better than war," Clavain said. "Hasn't it?"

Galiana might have been about to answer him when her face grew troubled. Clavain saw the wave of discomposure sweep over the others almost simultaneously. Something told him that it was nothing to do with his proposal.

Around the table, half the display facets switched automatically over to another channel. The face that Clavain was looking at was much like his own, except that the face on the screen was missing an eye. It was his brother. Warren was overlaid with the official insignia of the Coalition and a dozen system-wide media cartels.

He was in the middle of a speech. ". . . express my shock," Warren said. "Or, for that matter, my outrage. It's not just that they've murdered a valued colleague and deeply experienced member of my team. They've murdered my brother."

Clavain felt the deepest of chills. "What is this?"

"A live transmission from Deimos," Galiana breathed. "It's going out to all the nets; right out to the trans-Pluto habitats."

"What they did was an act of unspeakable treachery," Warren said. "Nothing less than the premeditated, cold-blooded murder of a peace envoy." And then a video clip sprang up to replace Warren. The image must have been snapped from Deimos or one of the interdiction satellites. It showed Clavain's shuttle, lying in the dust close to the dyke. He watched the Ouroborus destroy the shuttle, then saw the image zoom in on himself and Voi, running for sanctuary. The Ouroborus took Voi. But this time there was no ladder lowered down for him. Instead, he saw weapon-beams scythe out from the nest toward him, knocking him to the ground. Horribly wounded, he tried to get up, to crawl a few inches nearer to his tormentors, but the worm was already upon him.

He watched himself get eaten.

Warren was back again. "The worms around the nest were a Conjoiner trap. My brother's death must have been planned days—maybe even weeks—in advance." His face glistened with a wave of military composure. "There can only be one outcome from such an action—something the Conjoiners must have well understood. For months they've been goading us toward hostile action." He paused, then nodded at an unseen audience. "Well now they're going to get it. In fact, our response has already commenced."

"Dear God, no," Clavain said, but the evidence was all there now; all around the table he could see the updating orbital spread of the Coalition's dropships, knifing down toward Mars.

"I think it's war," Galiana said.

Conjoiners stormed onto the roof of the nest, taking up defensive positions around the domes and the dyke's edge. Most of them carried the same guns which they had used against the Ouroborus. Smaller numbers were setting up automatic cannon on tripods. One or two were manhandling large anti-assault weapons into position. Most of it was war-surplus. Fifteen years ago the Conjoiners had avoided extinction by deploying weapons of awesome ferocity—but those ship-to-ship armaments were too simply too destructive to use against a nearby foe. Now it would be more visceral; closer to the primal templates of combat, and none of what the Conjoiners were marshalling would be much use against the kind of assault Warren had prepared, Clavain knew. They could slow an attack, but not much more than that.

Galiana had given him another breather mask, made him don lightweight chameleoflage armor, and then forced him to carry one of the smaller guns. The gun felt alien in his hands; something he had never expected to carry again. The only possible justification for carrying it was to use it against his brother's forces—against his own side.

Could he do that?

It was clear that Warren had betrayed him; he had surely been aware of the worms around the nest. So his brother was capable not just of contempt, but of treacherous murder. For the first time, Clavain felt genuine hatred for Warren. He must have hoped that the worms would destroy the shuttle completely and kill Clavain and Voi in the process. It must have pained him to see Clavain make it to the dyke . . . pained him even more when Clavain called to talk about the tragedy. But Warren's larger plan had not been affected. The diplomatic link between the nest and Deimos was secure—even the Demarchists had no immediate access to it. So Clavain's call from the surface could be quietly ignored; spysat imagery doctored to make it seem that he had never reached the dyke . . . had in fact been repelled by Conjoiner treachery. Inevitably the Demarchists would unravel the deception given time . . . but if Warren's plan succeeded, they would all be embroiled in war long before then. That, thought Clavain, was all that Warren had ever wanted.

Two brothers, Clavain thought. In many ways so alike. Both had embraced war once, but like a fickle lover Clavain had wearied of its glories. He had not even been injured as severely as Warren . . . but perhaps that was the point, too. Warren needed another war to avenge what one had stolen from him.

Clavain despised and pitied him in equal measure.

He searched for the safety clip on the gun. The rifle, now that he studied it more closely, was not all that different from those he had used during the war. The readout said the ammo-cell was fully charged.

He looked into the sky.

The attack wave broke orbit hard and steep above the Wall; five hundred fireballs screeching toward the nest. The insertion scorched inches of ablative armor from most of the ships; fried a few others which came in just fractionally too hard. Clavain knew that was how it was happening: he had studied possible attack scenarios for years, the range of outcomes burned indelibly into his memory.

The anti-assault guns were already working—locking onto the plasma trails as they flowered overhead, swinging down to find the tiny spark of heat at the head, computing refraction paths for laser pulses, spitting death into the sky. The unlucky ships flared a white that hurt the back of the eye and rained down in a billion dulling sparks. A dozen—then a dozen more. Maybe fifty in total before the guns could no longer acquire targets. It was nowhere near enough. Clavain's memory of the simulations told him that at least four hundred units of the attack wave would survive both re-entry and the Conjoiner's heavy defenses.

Nothing that Galiana could do would make any difference.

And that had always been the paradox. Galiana was capable of running the same simulations. She must always have known that her provocations would bring down something she could never hope to defeat.

Something that was always going to destroy her.

The surviving members of the wave were levelling out now, commencing long, ground-hugging runs from all directions. Cocooned in their dropships, the soldiers would be suffering punishing gee-loads . . . but it was nothing they were not engineered to withstand; half their cardiovascular systems were augmented by the only kinds of implant the Coalition tolerated.

The first of the wave came arcing in at supersonic speeds. All around, worms struggled to snatch them out of the sky, but mostly they were too slow to catch the dropships. Galiana's people manned their cannon positions and did their best to fend off what they could. Clavain clutched his gun, not firing yet. Best to save his ammo-cell power for a target he stood a chance of injuring.

Above, the first dropships made hairpin turns, nosing suicidally down toward the nest. Then they fractured cleanly apart, revealing falling pilots clad in bulbous armor. Just before the moment of impact each pilot exploded into a mass of black shock-absorbing balloons, looking something like a blackberry, bouncing across the nest before the balloons deflated just as swiftly and the pilot was left standing on the ground. By then the pilot—now properly a soldier—would have a comprehensive computer-generated map of the nest's nooks and crannies; enemy positions graphed in realtime from the down-looking spysats.

Clavain fell behind the curve of a dome before the nearest soldier got a lock onto him. The firefight was beginning now. He had to hand it to Galiana's people—they were fighting like devils. And they were at least as well coordinated as the attackers. But their weapons and armor were simply inadequate. Chameleoflage was only truly effective against a solitary enemy, or a massed enemy moving in from a common direction. With Coalition forces surrounding him, Clavain's suit was going crazy to trying to match itself against every background, like a chameleon in a house of mirrors.

The sky overhead looked strange now—darkening purple. And the purple was spreading in a mist across the nest. Galiana had deployed some kind of chemical smoke screen: infrared and optically opaque, he guessed. It would occlude the spysats and might be primed to adhere only to enemy chameleoflage. That had never been in Warren's simulations. Galiana had just given herself the slightest of edges.

A soldier stepped out of the mist, the obscene darkness of a gun muzzle trained on Clavain. His chameleoflage armor was dappled with vivid purple patches, ruining its stealthiness. The man fired, but his discharge wasted itself against Clavain's armor. Clavain returned the compliment, dropping his compatriot. What he had done, he thought, was not technically treason. Not yet. All he had done was act in self-preservation.

The man was wounded, but not yet dead. Clavain stepped through the purple haze and knelt down beside the soldier. He tried not to look at the man's wound.

"Can you hear me?" he said. There was no answer from the man, but beneath his visor, Clavain thought he saw the man's lips shape a sound. The man was just a kid—hardly old enough to remember much of the last war. "There's something you have to know," Clavain continued. "Do you realize who I am?" He wondered how recognizable he was, under the breather mask. Then something made him relent. He could tell the man he was Nevil Clavain—but what would that achieve? The soldier would be dead in minutes; maybe sooner than that. Nothing would be served by the soldier knowing that the basis for his attack was a lie; that he would not in fact be laying down his life for a just cause. The universe could be spared a single callous act.

"It's all right," Clavain said, turning away from his victim.

And then moved deeper into the nest, to see who else he could kill before the odds took him.

But the odds never did.

"You always were lucky," Galiana said, leaning over him. They were somewhere underground again—deep in the nest. A medical area, by the look of things. He was on a bed, fully clothed apart from the outer layer of chameleoflage armor. The room was gray and kettle-shaped, ringed by a circular balcony.

"What happened?"

"You took a head wound, but you'll survive."

He groped for the right question. "What about Warren's attack?"

"We endured three waves. We took casualties, of course."

Around the circumference of the balcony were thirty or so gray couches, slightly recessed into archways studded with gray medical equipment. They were all occupied. There were more Conjoiners in this room than he had seen so far in one place. Some of them looked very close to death.

Clavain reached up and examined his head, gingerly. There was some dried blood on the scalp, matted with his hair; some numbness, but it could have been a lot worse. He felt normal — no memory drop-outs or aphasia. When he made to stand from the bed, his body obeyed his will with only a tinge of dizziness.

"Warren won't stop at just three waves, Galiana."

"I know." She paused. "We know there'll be more."

He walked to the railing on the inner side of the balcony and looked over the edge. He had expected to see something — some chunk of incomprehensible surgical equipment, perhaps — but the middle of the room was only an empty, smooth-walled, gray pit. He shivered. The air was colder than any part of the nest he had visited so far, with a medicinal tang which reminded him of the convalescence ward on Deimos. What made him shiver even more was the realization that some of the injured — some of the dead — were barely older than the children he had visited only hours ago. Perhaps some of them were those children, conscripted from the nursery since his visit, uploaded with fighting reflexes through their new implants.

"What are you going to do? You know you can't win. Warren lost only a tiny fraction of his available force in those waves. You look like you've lost half your nest."

"It's much worse than that," Galiana said.

"What do you mean?"

"You're not quite ready yet. But I can show you in a moment."

He felt colder than ever now. "What do you mean, not quite ready?"

Galiana looked deep into his eyes now. "You took a serious head wound, Clavain. The entry wound was small, but the internal bleeding . . . it would have killed you, had we not intervened." Before he could ask the inevitable question she answered it for him. "We injected a small cluster of medichines into your head. They undid the damage very easily. But it seemed provident to allow them to grow."

"You've put replicators in my head?"

"You needn't sound so horrified. They're already growing — spreading out and interfacing with your existing neural circuitry — but the total volume of glial mass that they will consume is tiny: only a few cubic millimeters in total, across your entire brain."

He wondered if she was calling his bluff. "I don't feel anything."

"You won't — not for a minute or so." Now she pointed into the empty pit in the middle of the room. "Stand here and look into the air."

"There's nothing there."

But as soon as he had spoken, he knew he was wrong. There was something in the pit. He blinked and directed his attention somewhere else, but when he returned his gaze to the pit, the thing he imagined he had seen — milky, spectral — was still there, and becoming sharper and brighter by the second. It was a three-dimensional structure, as complex as an exercise in protein-folding. A tangle of loops and connecting branches and nodes and tunnels, embedded in a ghostly red matrix.

Suddenly he saw it for what it was: a map of the nest, dug into Mars. Just as the Coalition had suspected, the base was deeper than the original structure; far more extensive, reaching deeper down but much further out than anyone had imagined. Clavain made a mental effort to retain some of what he was seeing in his mind, the intelligence-gathering reflex stronger than the conscious knowledge that he would never see Deimos again.

"The medichines in your brain have interfaced with your visual cortex," Galiana said. "That's the first step on the road to Transenlightenment. Now you're privy to the machine-generated imagery encoded by the fields through which we move—most of it, anyway."

"Tell me this wasn't planned, Galiana. Tell me you weren't intending to put machines in me at the first opportunity."

"No; I wasn't planning it. But nor was I going to let your phobias stop me from saving your life."

The image grew in complexity. Glowing nodes of light appeared in the tunnels, some moving slowly through the network.

"What are they?"

"You're seeing the locations of the Conjoiners," Galiana said. "Are there as many as you imagined?"

Clavain judged that there were no more than seventy lights in the whole complex now. He searched for a cluster which would identify the room where he stood. There: twenty-odd bright lights, accompanied by one much fainter. Himself, of course. There were few people near the top of the nest—the attack must have collapsed half the tunnels, or maybe Galiana had deliberately sealed entrances herself.

"Where is everyone? Where are the children?"

"Most of the children are gone now." She paused. "You were right to guess that we were rushing them to Transenlightenment, Clavain."

"Why?"

"Because it's the only way out of here."

The image changed again. Now each of the bright lights was connected to another by a shimmering filament. The topology of the network was constantly shifting, like a pattern seen in a kaleidoscope. Occasionally, too swiftly for Clavain to be sure, it shifted toward a mandala of elusive symmetry, only to dissolve into the flickering chaos of the ever-changing network. He studied Galiana's node and saw that—even as she was speaking to him—her mind was in constant rapport with the rest of the nest.

Now something very bright appeared in the middle of the image, like a tiny star, against which the shimmering network paled almost to invisibility. "The network is abstracted now," Galiana said. "The bright light represents its totality: the unity of Transenlightenment. Watch."

He watched. The bright light—beautiful and alluring as anything Clavain had ever imagined—was extending a ray toward the isolated node which represented himself. The ray was extending itself through the map, coming closer by the second.

"The new structures in your mind are nearing maturity," Galiana said. "When the ray touches you, you will experience partial integration with the rest of us. Prepare yourself, Nevil."

Her words were unnecessary. His fingers were already clenched sweating on the railing as the light inched closer and engulfed his node.

"I should hate you for this," Clavain said.

"Why don't you? Hate's always the easier option."

"Because . . ." Because it made no difference now. His old life was over. He reached out for Galiana, needing some anchor against what was about to hit him. Galiana squeezed his hand and an instant later he knew something of Transenlightenment. The experience was shocking; not because it was painful or fearful, but because it was profoundly and totally new. He was literally thinking in ways that had not been possible microseconds earlier.

Afterward, when Clavain tried to imagine how he might describe it, he found that words were never going to be adequate for the task. And that was no surprise: evolution had shaped language to convey many concepts, but going from a single to a networked topology of self was not among them. But if he could not convey the core of the experience, he could at least skirt its essence with metaphor. It was like standing on the shore of an ocean, being engulfed by a wave taller than himself. For a moment he sought the surface; tried to keep the water from his lungs. But there happened not to be a surface. What had consumed him extended infinitely in all directions. He could only submit to it. Yet as the moments slipped by it turned from something terrifying in its unfamiliarity to something he could begin to adapt to; something that even began in the tiniest way to seem comforting. Even then he glimpsed that it was only a shadow of what Galiana was experiencing every instant of her life.

"All right," Galiana said. "That's enough for now."

The fullness of Transenlightenment retreated, like a fading vision of Godhead. What he was left with was purely sensory; no longer any direct rapport with the others. His state of mind came crashing back to normality.

"Are you all right, Nevil?"

"Yes . . ." His mouth was dry. "Yes; I think so."

"Look around you."

He did.

The room had changed completely. So had everyone in it.

His head reeling, Clavain walked in light. The formerly gray walls oozed beguiling patterns; as if a dark forest had suddenly become enchanted. Information hung in veils in the air; icons and diagrams and numbers clustering around the beds of the injured, thinning out into the general space like fantastically delicate neon sculptures. As he walked toward the icons they darted out of his way, mocking him like schools of brilliant fish. Sometimes they seemed to sing, or tickle the back of his nose with half-familiar smells.

"You can perceive things now," Galiana said. "But none of it will mean much to you. You'd need years of education, or deeper neural machinery for that— building cognitive layers. We read all this almost subliminally."

Galiana was dressed differently now. He could still see the vague shape of her gray outfit, but layered around it were billowing skeins of light, unravelling at their edges into chains of Boolean logic. Icons danced in her hair like angels. He could see, faintly, the web of thought linking her with the other Conjoiners.

She was inhumanly beautiful.

"You said things were much worse," Clavain said. "Are you ready to show me now?"

She took him to see Felka again, passing on the way through deserted nursery rooms, populated now only by bewildered mechanical animals. Felka was the only child left in the nursery.

Clavain had been deeply disturbed by Felka when he had seen her before, but not for any reason he could easily express. Something about the purposefulness of what she did; performed with ferocious concentration, as if the fate of creation hung on the outcome of her game. Felka and her surroundings had not changed at all since his visit. The room was still austere to the point of oppressiveness. Felka looked the same. In every respect it was as if only an instant had passed since their meeting; as if the onset of war and the assaults against the nest—the battle of which this was only an interlude—were only figments from someone else's troubling dream; nothing that need concern Felka in her devotion to the task at hand.

And what the task was awed Clavain.

Before he had watched her make strange gestures in front of her. Now the machines in his head revealed the purpose that those gestures served. Around Felka—cordoning her like a barricade—was a ghostly representation of the Great Wall.

She was doing something to it.

It was not a scale representation, Clavain knew. The Wall looked much higher here in relation to its diameter. And the surface was not the nearly invisible membrane of the real thing, but something like etched glass. The etchwork was a filigree of lines and junctions, descending down to smaller and smaller scales in fractal steps, until the blur of detail was too fine for his eyes to discriminate. It was shifting and altering color, and Felka was responding to these alterations with what he now saw was frightening efficiency. It was as if the color changes warned of some malignancy in part of the Wall, and by touching it—expressing some tactile code—Felka was able to restructure the etchwork to block and neutralize the malignancy before it spread.

"I don't understand," Clavain said. "I thought we destroyed the Wall; completely killed its systems."

"No," Galiana said. "You only ever injured it. Stopped it from growing, and from managing its own repair-processes correctly . . . but you never truly killed it."

Sandra Voi had guessed, Clavain realized. She had wondered how the Wall had survived this long.

Galiana told him the rest—how they had managed to establish control pathways to the Wall from the nest, fifteen years earlier—optical cables sunk deep below the worm zone. "We stabilized the Wall's degradation with software running on dumb machines," she said. "But when Felka was born we found that she managed the task just as efficiently as the computers; in some ways better than they ever did. In fact, she seemed to thrive on it. It was as if in the Wall she found . . ." Galiana trailed off. "I was going to say a friend."

"Why don't you?"

"Because the Wall's just a machine. Which means if Felka recognized kinship . . . what would that make her?"

"Someone lonely, that's all." Clavain watched the girl's motions. "She seems faster than before. Is that possible?"

"I told you things were worse than before. She's having to work harder to hold the Wall together."

"Warren must have attacked it." Clavain said. "The possibility of knocking down the Wall always figured in our contingency plans for another war. I just never thought it would happen so soon." Then he looked at Felka. Maybe it was imagination but she seemed to be working even faster than when he had entered the room; not just since his last visit. "How long do you think she can keep it together?"

"Not much longer," Galiana said. "As a matter of fact I think she's already failing."

It was true. Now that he looked closely at the ghost Wall he saw that the upper edge was not the mathematically smooth ring it should have been; that there were scores of tiny ragged bites eating down from the top. Felka's activities were increasingly directed to these opening cracks in the structure; instructing the crippled structure to divert energy and raw materials to these critical failure points. Clavain knew that the distant processes Felka directed were awesome. Within the Wall lay a lymphatic system whose peristaltic feed-pipes ranged in size from meters across to the submicroscopic; flowing with myriad tiny repair machines. Felka chose where to send those machines; her hand gestures establishing pathways between damage points and the factories sunk into the Wall's ramparts which made the required types of machine. For more than a decade, Galiana said, Felka had kept the Wall from crumbling—but for most of that time her adversary had been only natural decay and accidental damage. It was a different game now that the Wall had been attacked again. It was not one she could ever win.

Felka's movements were swifter; less fluid. Her face remained impassive, but in the quickening way that her eyes darted from point to point it was possible to read the first hints of panic. No surprise, either: the deepest cracks in the structure now reached a quarter of the way to the surface, and they were too wide to be repaired. The Wall was unzipping along those flaws. Cubic kilometers of atmosphere would be howling out through the openings. The loss of pressure would be immeasurably slow at first, for near the top the trapped cylinder of atmosphere was only fractionally thicker than the rest of the Martian atmosphere. But only at first . . .

"We have to get deeper," Clavain said. "Once the Wall goes, we won't have a chance in hell if we're anywhere near the surface. It'll be like the worst tornado in history."

"What will your brother do? Will he nuke us?"

"No; I don't think so. He'll want to get hold of any technologies you've hidden away. He'll wait until the dust storms have died down, then he'll raid the nest with a hundred times as many troops as you've seen so far. You won't be able to resist, Galiana. If you're lucky you may just survive long enough to be taken prisoner."

"There won't be any prisoners," Galiana said.

"You're planning to die fighting?"

"No. And mass suicide doesn't figure in our plans either. Neither will be necessary. By the time your brother reaches here, there won't be anyone left in the nest."

Clavain thought of the worms encircling the area; how small were the chances of reaching any kind of safety if it involved getting past them. "Secret tunnels under the worm zone, is that it? I hope you're serious."

"I'm deadly serious," Galiana said. "And yes, there is a secret tunnel. The other children have already gone through it now. But it doesn't lead under the worm zone."

"Where, then?"

"Somewhere a lot further away."

When they passed through the medical center again it was empty, save for a few swan-necked robots patiently waiting for further casualties. They had left Felka behind tending the Wall, her hands a manic blur as she tried to slow the rate of collapse. Clavain had tried to make her come with them, but Galiana had told him he was wasting his time: that she would sooner die than be parted from the Wall.

"You don't understand," Galiana said. "You're placing too much humanity behind her eyes. Keeping the Wall alive is the single most important fact of her universe — more important than love, pain, death — anything you or I would consider definitively human."

"Then what happens to her when the Wall dies?"

"Her life ends," Galiana said.

Reluctantly he had left without her, the taste of shame in his mouth. Rationally it made sense: without Felka's help the Wall would collapse much sooner and there was a good chance all their lives would end; not just that of the haunted girl. How deep would they have to go before they were safe from the suction of the escaping atmosphere? Would any part of the nest be safe?

The regions through which they were descending now were as cold and gray as any Clavain had seen. There were no entoptic generators buried in these walls to supply visual information to the implants Galiana had put in his head, and even her own aura of light was gone. They only met a few other Conjoiners, and they seemed to be moving in the same general direction; down to the nest's basement levels. This was unknown territory to Clavain.

Where was Galiana taking him?

"If you had an escape route all along, why did you wait so long before sending the children through it?"

"I told you, we couldn't bring them to Transenlightenment too soon. The older they were, the better," Galiana said. "Now though . . ."

"There was no waiting any longer, was there?"

Eventually they reached a chamber with the same echoing acoustics as the topside hangar. The chamber was dark except for a few pools of light, but in the shadows Clavain made out discarded excavation equipment and freight pallets; cranes and de-activated robots. The air smelled of ozone. Something was still going on here.

"Is this the factory where you make the shuttles?" Clavain said.

"We manufactured parts of them here, yes," Galiana said. "But that was a side-industry."

"Of what?"

"The tunnel, of course." Galiana made more lights come on. At the far end of the chamber—they were walking toward it—waited a series of cylindrical things with pointed ends; like huge bullets. They rested on rails, one after the other. The tip of the very first bullet was next to a dark hole in the wall. Clavain was about to say something when there was a sudden loud buzz and the first bullet slammed into the hole. The other bullets—there were three of them now—eased slowly forward and halted. Conjoiners were waiting to board them.

He remembered what Galiana had said about no one being left behind.

"What am I seeing here?"

"A way out of the nest," Galiana said. "And a way off Mars, though I suppose you figured that part for yourself."

"There is no way off Mars," Clavain said. "The interdiction guarantees that. Haven't you learned that with your shuttles?"

"The shuttles were only ever a diversionary tactic," Galiana said. "They made your side think we were still striving to escape, whereas our true escape route was already fully operational."

"A pretty desperate diversion."

"Not really. I lied to you when I said we didn't clone. We did—but only to produce brain-dead corpses. The shuttles were full of corpses before we ever launched them."

For the first time since leaving Deimos Clavain smiled, amused at the sheer obliquity of Galiana's thinking.

"Of course, there was another function," she said. "The shuttles provoked your side into a direct attack against the nest."

"So this was deliberate all along?"

"Yes. We needed to draw your side's attention; to concentrate your military presence in low-orbit, near the nest. Of course we were hoping the offensive would come later than it did . . . but we reckoned without Warren's conspiracy."

"Then you are planning something."

"Yes." The next bullet slammed into the wall, ozone crackling from its linear induction rails. Now only two remained. "We can talk later. There isn't much time now." She projected an image into his visual field: the Wall, now veined by titanic fractures down half its length. "It's collapsing."

"And Felka?"

"She's still trying to save it."

He looked at the Conjoiners boarding the leading bullet; tried to imagine where they were going. Was it to any kind of sanctuary he might recognize—or to something so beyond his experience that it might as well be death? Did he have the nerve to find out? Perhaps. He had nothing to lose now, after all; he could certainly not return home. But if he was going to follow Galiana's exodus, it could not be with the sense of shame he now felt in abandoning Felka.

The answer, when it came, was simple. "I'm going back for her. If you can't wait for me, don't. But don't try and stop me doing this."

Galiana looked at him, shaking her head slowly. "She won't thank you for saving her life, Clavain."

"Maybe not now," he said.

He had the feeling he was running back into a burning building. Given what Galiana had said about the girl's deficiencies—that by any reasonable definition she was hardly more than an automaton—what he was doing was very likely pointless, if not suicidal. But if he turned his back on her, he would become something even less than human himself. He had misread Galiana badly when she said the girl was precious to them. He had assumed some bond of affection . . . whereas what Galiana meant was that the girl was precious in the sense of a vital component. Now—with the nest being abandoned—the component had no further use. Did that make Galiana as cold as a machine herself—or was she just being unfailingly realistic? He found the nursery after only one or two false turns, and then Felka's room. The implants Galiana had given him were again throwing phantom images into the air. Felka sat within the crumbling circle of the Wall. Great fissures now reached to the surface of Mars. Shards of the Wall, as big as icebergs, had fractured away and now lay like vast sheets of broken glass across the regolith.

She was losing, and now she knew it. This was not just some more difficult phase of the game. This was something she could never win, and her realization was now plainly evident in her face. She was still moving her arms frantically, but her face was red now, locked into a petulant scowl of anger and fear.

For the first time, she seemed to notice him.

Something had broken through her shell, Clavain thought. For the first time in years, something was happening that was beyond her control; something that threatened to destroy the neat, geometric universe she had made for herself. She might not have distinguished his face from all the other people who came to see her, but she surely recognized something . . . that now the adult world was bigger than she was, and it was only from the adult world that any kind of salvation could come.

Then she did something that shocked him beyond words. She looked deep into his eyes and reached out a hand.

But there was nothing he could do to help her.

Later—it seemed hours, but in fact could only have been tens of minutes—Clavain found that he was able to breathe normally again. They had escaped Mars now; Galiana, Felka and himself, riding the last bullet.

And they were still alive.

The bullet's vacuum-filled tunnel cut deep into Mars; a shallow arc bending under the crust before rising again, two thousand kilometers away, well beyond the Wall, where the atmosphere was as thin as ever. For the Conjoiners, boring the tunnel had not been especially difficult. Such engineering would have been impossible on a planet that had plate tectonics, but beneath its lithosphere Mars was geologically quiet. They had not even had to worry about tailings. What they excavated, they compressed and fused and used to line the tunnel, maintaining rigidity against awesome pressure with some trick of piezo-electricity. In the tunnel, the bullet accelerated continuously at three gees for six minutes. Their seats had tilted back and wrapped around them, applying pressure to the legs to maintain bloodflow to the head. Even so, it was hard to think, let alone move, but Clavain knew that it was no worse than what the earliest space explorers had endured climbing away from Earth. And he had undergone similar tortures during the war, in combat insertions.

They were moving at ten kilometers a second when they reached the surface again, exiting via a camouflaged trapdoor. For a moment the atmosphere snatched at them . . . but almost as soon as Clavain had registered the deceleration, it was over. The surface of Mars was dropping below them very quickly indeed.

In half a minute, they were in true space.

"The Interdiction's sensor web can't track us," Galiana said. "You placed your best spy-sats directly over the nest. That was a mistake, Clavain — even though we did our best to reinforce your thinking with the shuttle launches. But now we're well outside your sensor footprint."

Clavain nodded. "But that won't help us once we're far from the surface. Then, we'll just look like another ship trying to reach deep space. The web may be late locking onto us, but it'll still get us in the end."

"It would," Galiana said. "If deep space was where we were going."

Felka stirred next to him. She had withdrawn into some kind of catatonia. Separation from the Wall had undermined her entire existence; now she was free-falling through an abyss of meaninglessness. Perhaps, Clavain, thought, she would fall forever. If that was the case, he had only brought forward her fate. Was that much of a cruelty? Perhaps he was deluding himself, but with time, was it out of the question that Galiana's machines could undo the harm they had inflicted ten years earlier? Surely they could try. It depended, of course, on where exactly they were headed. One of the system's other Conjoiner nests had been Clavain's initial guess — even though it seemed unlikely that they would ever survive the crossing. At ten klicks per second it would take years . . .

"Where are you taking us?" he asked.

Galiana issued some neural command which made the bullet seem to become transparent.

"There," she said.

Something lay distantly ahead. Galiana made the forward view zoom in, until the object was much clearer.

Dark — misshapen. Like Deimos without fortifications.

"Phobos," Clavain said, wonderingly. "We're going to Phobos."

"Yes," Galiana said.

"But the worms —"

"Don't exist anymore." She spoke with the same tutorly patience with which Remontoire had addressed him on the same subject not long before. "Your attempt to oust the worms failed. You assumed our subsequent attempt failed . . . but that was only what we wanted you to think."

For a moment he was lost for words. "You've had people in Phobos all along?"

"Ever since the cease-fire, yes. They've been quite busy, too."

Phobos altered. Layers of it were peeled away, revealing the glittering device which lay hidden in its heart, poised and ready for flight. Clavain had never seen anything like it, but the nature of the thing was instantly obvious. He was looking at something wonderful; something which had never existed before in the whole of human experience.

He was looking at a starship.

"We'll be leaving soon," Galiana said. "They'll try and stop us, of course. But now that their forces are concentrated near the surface, they won't succeed. We'll leave Phobos and Mars behind, and send messages to the other nests. If they can break out and meet us, we'll take them as well. We'll leave this whole system behind."

"Where are you going?"

"Shouldn't that be where are we going? You're coming with us, after all." She paused. "There are a number of candidate systems. Our choice will depend on the trajectory the Coalition forces upon us."

"What about the Demarchists?"

"They won't stop us." It was said with total assurance — implying, what? That the Demarchy knew of this ship? Perhaps. It had long been rumored that the Demarchists and the Conjoiners were closer than they admitted.

Clavain thought of something. "What about the worms' altering the orbit?"

"That was our doing," Galiana said. "We couldn't help it. Every time we send up one of these canisters, we nudge Phobos into a different orbit. Even after we sent up a thousand canisters, the effect was tiny — we changed Phobos's velocity by less than one tenth of a millimeter per second — but there was no way to hide it." Then she paused and looked at Clavain with something like apprehension. "We'll be arriving in two hundred seconds. Do you want to live?"

"I'm sorry?"

"Think about it. The tube in Mars was two thousand kilometers long, which allowed us to spread the acceleration over six minutes. Even then it was three gees. But there simply isn't room for anything like that in Phobos. We'll be slowing down much more abruptly."

Clavain felt the hairs on the back of his neck prickle. "How much more abruptly?"

"Complete deceleration in one fifth of a second." She let that sink home. "That's around five thousand gees."

"I can't survive that."

"No; you can't. Not now, anyway. But there are machines in your head now. If you allow it, there's time for them to establish a structural web across your brain. We'll flood the cabin with foam. We'll all die temporarily, but there won't be anything they can't fix in Phobos."

"It won't just be a structural web, will it? I'll be like you, then. There won't be any difference between us."

"You'll become Conjoined, yes." Galiana offered the faintest of smiles. "The procedure is reversible. It's just that no one's ever wanted to go back."

"And you still tell me none of this was planned?"

"No; but I don't expect you to believe me. For what it's worth, though . . . you're a good man, Nevil. The Transenlightenment could use you. Maybe at the back of my mind . . . at the back of our mind . . ."

"You always hoped it might come to this?"

Galiana smiled.

He looked at Phobos. Even without Galiana's magnification, it was clearly bigger. They would be arriving very shortly. He would have liked longer to think about it, but the one thing not on his side now was time. Then he looked at Felka, and wondered which of them was about to embark on the stranger journey. Felka's search for meaning in a universe without her beloved Wall, or his passage into Transenlightenment? Neither would necessarily be easy. But together, perhaps, they might even find a way to help each other. That was all he could hope for now.

Clavain nodded assent, ready for the loom of machines to embrace his mind.

He was ready to defect.

milo and sylvie

ELIOT FINTUSHEL

Eliot Fintushel made his first sale in 1993, to tomorrow *magazine. Since then, he has become a regular in* Asimov's Science Fiction, *with a large number of sales there, has appeared in* Amazing, Science Fiction Age, Crank!, Aboriginal SF, *and other markets, and is beginning to attract attention from cognoscenti as one of the most original and inventive writers to enter the genre in many years, worthy to be ranked among other prac- titioners of the fast-paced* Wild And Crazy *gonzo modern tall tale such as R. A. Lafferty, Howard Waldrop, and Neal Barrett, Jr. Fintushel, a baker's son from Rochester, New York, is a performer and teacher of mask theater and mime, has won the National Endowment for the Arts' Solo Performer Award twice, and now lives in Santa Rosa, California.*

Here, in something of a change of pace for him (although still wry, funny, and almost extravagantly inventive), a story to me reminiscent of Theodore Sturgeon at his poetic best, he takes a lyrical, tender, and bitter- sweet look at an odd relationship between two very peculiar people.

Everything has its portion of smell," Milo said. His skin and bones were en- throned in a plush, gold club chair facing the doctor's more severe straight-back with the cabriole legs. Milo strummed his fingers nervously against the insides of his thighs as he looked around the room, richly dark, with scrolled woodwork, diplomas in gilded frames hanging on the wall behind the doctor's mahogany rolltop next to the heavily curtained window. He could smell the doctor's after- shave. He could smell the last client too, a woman, a large woman, a sweating carnivore with drugstore perfume.

"Smell?" Doctor Devore always looked worried. Inquisitive and worried—the look was like a high trump, drawing out all your best cards before you had planned to play them. He had white, curly hair. He wore sweaters and baggy pants that made him look like a rag doll. He was old. His cheeks and jowls sagged like the folds of drapery beside him. He wore thick, wire-rimmed glasses that made his tired eyes look bigger and even more plaintive. He was small, a midget, almost; one got over that quickly, though, because he never acted short.

"It's something my sister used to say."

"Why?"

"I don't remember." Like so much else. Milo moved too quickly for memories to adhere, or for sleep for that matter, except in evanescent snatches. Memories, sleep, *haunted* him. They were never invited guests. His sister's name, for example, which he did not remember, did not remember, *did not remember*, was death to pronounce or even think of.

There was a long pause. Devore was trying to use the silence to suck something out of him—*horror vacui*—but it didn't work. Milo had a practiced grip. The things he had to hold down bucked harder than this shrink.

Dr. Devore broke the silence: "Have you been sleeping any better?"

"Yes."

"Taking the prescription, hmm?"

"Yes." That was a trade-off. The pills let him sleep dreamlessly for longer spells, but with the danger that his grip would loosen.

"Let's talk about one of your dreams. Do you have one you want to talk about?"

Grudgingly, Milo said, "Yes." Could he snatch the cheese and escape the wire?

"Go ahead."

"It's dark. The fog is rolling in."

"Where are *you?*" Devore said. Milo began to cry. "That's all right. Just let the tears come. You don't have to answer right away, you know?"

"I have another dream."

"Okay . . ."

"A Dumpster. One of those big, steel Dumpsters full of scraps and garbage. A car runs into it."

"Are you driving the car?"

"You don't get it!" Milo hooked one thumb over the side of his pants and tugged down the waist, hiking up his shirt so that Dr. Devore could see his hip. "It was all smashed up! Everything was steaming and sputtering and dripping."

"What are you showing me? Are you telling me you hurt yourself? I don't see any marks, Milo—we're talking about a dream, yes?"

"Yeah. That was while I was in the waiting room just now. I dozed off."

"You dreamed that you hurt your hip in a car crash, is that it?"

"No, no! The fender, the hood, the engine! That's what was hurt!" Milo began crying again. "I'm a monster, that's all! Give me some more medicine! Give me something stronger! I can't hold on much longer!"

Dr. Devore paused. "Milo, when the car crashed into the Dumpster, where were *you?*"

"I have another dream," Milo blurted. He was angry, like a small child choking back tears to shout his malediction.

"Let's stay with the last one . . ."

"A window shatters."

"That's all?"

"That's all." Milo felt his skin and skull shattering like glass. He was collapsing into his own pelvis and lacerating the soft tissue of his remaining viscera—but it was the dream. He shouted too loudly, as if trying to be heard against the roar of a hurricane. "It hurts!"

"The glass hits you?"

"No."

"I don't think I follow, Milo. In all these dreams, where are you?"

"The fog, the Dumpster and the car, the window . . ." Milo clamped his bony fingers around the scrolls at the edges of his armchair as if it were an electric chair. He stared straight ahead, straight through Dr. Devore, focusing on ghosts three thousand miles distant, waving from the past like dead men from the ports of a sunken ship.

Devore interrupted him. "Don't say anymore if you don't want to, Milo." Milo froze, then slumped back into the chair. Dr. Devore was standing up, hands on his sacrum, arching back and stretching his neck from side to side. It made a little crackling sound. "Anyway, our hour is about up. This was good, Milo. This was very good. You shared some of your dreams with me. We talked a little about your sleep problem, and about your sister . . ."

"I didn't tell you anything about my sister."

"Right. We've got to get you to relax, you know? I am going to increase your chlorpromazine. Your house parents will give you the tablets in the morning and at night. I'll talk to them about it. You shouldn't worry. Just try to do the best you can, you know? And keep track of those dreams for me, will you, Milo?"

"Yeah, sure."

Dr. Devore stood before Milo, waiting for him to get up. He had set up his psychic vacuum pump again, to suck Milo out of the club chair and get rid of him, Milo thought. Devore needed his beauty sleep.

Milo stood, turned, and walked out the door without saying thank you or good-bye. The waiting room was empty. Milo crossed the waiting room, opened the hall door and shut it again without going through. He waited thirty seconds, then returned to Dr. Devore's office door and cupped his ear against it.

He heard Devore part the drapes and open one of the windows; it shuddered and squeaked against the casement. Then he heard the rolltop clack open, and Devore spoke into his tape recorder:

"Milo is on the verge of finding out. He would have blurted it out just now if I hadn't stopped him. It would be most inopportune for him to know everything just now. I think the best course would be to slow him down. The thorazine should help, but we can't rely on it. This is a tricky business. If he's too tight, something fatigues inside him and he manifests in spite of himself; if he's too loose, of course, he changes. Can't leave him at the home much longer the way things are going. Somebody's sure to see something, and what happens next may be out of my control. Get Sylvie in there, that's the only way. Remember to call Sylvie tonight, now, soon.

"Oh, yes! He said the thing about smell again, but he doesn't seem to understand what it means—which is good. There's a little time . . . God! I've got to take a nap. My knees are buckling."

The machine clicked off. Milo heard Devore stretch and yawn, then the rustle of clothing peeling off, the two chairs scraping the floor as Devore pushed them together. A moment later he was snoring.

The little machine! The box sheathed in perforated black leather hiding inside Dr. Devore's rolltop with all of Milo's secrets! Like the totemic soul of a primitive:

a pouch, a feather, or a whittled doll secreted in a hollow log, proof against soul-snatching demons and enemies. Only, the demon was *in possession* of Milo's soul.

There was a fake window in the waiting room, drapery with a solid wall behind it, and opposite that, a print of some famous painting, a different one every time Milo visited. Sometimes, in fact, it was different when he left than it had been when he arrived; Devore must have paid someone he never saw to slip in and change it periodically, like a diaper service. Mondrian to Dalí, Manet to Munch or an anonymous Byzantine, each with a brass name tag on an ornate frame, while Milo conveyed his soul, via Devore, to the skin-covered box! Just now, it was a Chinese painting of a warrior monkey standing on a cloud in a great, plumed hat, brandishing a cudgel.

Milo tiptoed away from the door, hid behind the drapes and waited. He made quite a perceptible bulge there, but he was relying on Devore's drowsiness to get by with it. Being caught might not be so bad either. The way they looked at you then, at the home or at school, cross as it was, felt a lot like love.

It was hard to tell how much time had passed, because there was no daylight in there, but it seemed like a long time, and Milo had not had his thorazine. Below his stomach, inside the habitual knot, an older knot was beginning to ache. Aches in aches, Milo stood flush to the wall, breathing dust behind the drapery.

At last, he ventured out. The snoring had stopped. He pressed his ear to the door and heard nothing. What did he look like dreaming, the little man who harvested Milo's dreams? Milo turned the knob, degree by degree, soundlessly, until it stopped; then he pulled the door ajar and peeked in.

Impossibly, the room was empty. Devore was gone. The club chair and the cabriole chair were still pushed together in the center of the room to form an odd, uncomfortable bed. Milo strode in and slammed the door behind him, as if to test, to make sure his senses hadn't fooled him, that Devore was actually absent. Nothing stirred. There was no other way out except the window, which was actually open, but the office was six stories up.

Milo squinted and cocked his head like a cat listening for rats in the wall. However he had managed it, Devore was not there. Maybe, unawares, Milo had dozed standing up, and Devore had simply left through the waiting room. Milo went to the rolltop and pulled it open. The tape recorder was there. He opened it and took out the cassette. It had Milo's name on it, a cassette all to himself. He put it back in the machine and rewound.

The last rays of sunlight to skirt the top of the building across the street shone through a crystal suspended from the window sash, splashing rainbows on the office wall. As the land breeze breathed it back and forth, the crystal shook and spun, whirling colors about the room. Milo had never before seen Dr. Devore's crystal or the rainbows. So there was a dance in the old bagface yet!

The prism clacked against the shivering glass. The tape whirred, then stopped. Milo pressed PLAY:

> "Milo Smith. *Smith* not his real name. An assigned name. Nobody knows his real name. First name's probably *Milo*, though. Fourteen. Sporadically guilty of many relatively minor offenses such as disorderly conduct, battery against other children, petty thefts, and so on. Fre-

quently truant. Has been under state guardianship in group homes for about seven years. Generally shy and withdrawn, presents as extremely nervous, with many obsessive mannerisms. Plays his cards close to the chest, this one.

"Referred because of violent, disturbing dreams, waking other boys. Also some evidence of self-inflicted wounds. Chronic sleeplessness, nervosity. Looks like a mess, sunken eyes, thin as a rail, reminds me of the old photos of liberated camps at Auschwitz, Bergen-Belsen, Dachau. All he needs is the striped pants and a star of David.

"Seemed like he came in, then just waited for the hour to end. But he came in! Why? Something going on here. Okayed chlorpromazine for now. Next week . . . ?"

Milo PAUSED to think that one over. Why *had* he come? Nobody could force him. Nobody could hurt him. He hurt himself so badly already, just squeezing and squeezing to stay in control, that there was nothing worse to threaten Milo with. He stretched out on the two armchairs, cradling the tape recorder in his arms like a teddy bear. Think it over: *why?*

Outside the window, the street lamps flicked on. Milo had dozed off, he didn't know for how long, but it was dark. Unusual, dangerous, to sleep so long. Luckily, there had been no dream. There was still a rainbow on the wall — that was a new one! Milo walked to the window and passed his hand in front of the crystal.

That explained it; the crystal was a prop. The rainbow didn't move. It was somehow painted on the wall, painted no doubt over the real rainbow, the one from the crystal at the rainbow moment, sunset behind the MacCauly Building. Funny he'd never noticed it, but he always sat with his back to that wall, and when he came in or left this room, he always had a lot on his mind, or a lot to keep out of his mind.

PLAY:
". . . I want to remind myself here that Sylvie has come up with a way of using Zorn's Lemma for shape-shifting. She finds the maximal element of all the upper bounds of the chains in the shape she's departing from . . ."

STOP. REWIND. PLAY:
". . . shape-shifting . . ."

REWIND. PLAY:
". . . shape-shifting . . ."

STOP.
Below, a car drove by with its windows rolled down and the radio blasting, about a hound dog. . . . The old song faded out of hearing, along with the clatter of a dragging muffler. Then there were voices and honking horns. The theater crowd was arriving. Milo stared up at the rainbow on the wall, dimly aglow in the shadowy light of neon from outside.

PLAY:
". . . Why do I always think of Sylvie when I think of Milo? Could he be like *us?*"

STOP. REWIND. PLAY:
". . . Could he be like *us?*"

There was a click, then static, an intentional erasure or else a dumb mistake: the wrong button pressed, the machine dropped, or just old, stretched tape. Then it resumed:

"Now I know something about Milo Smith. *I know what he's doing here, with me.* Once he trusted me enough to start describing those dreams of his, it came together for me—the odd inanimate object romances, the animal reveries, the sensations of bodiless flight, his deep terror; and the physical evidences, like fairy dust on the dreamer's bedclothes in the old folk tales.

"But it's hardly time for Milo to be told anything. First we have to build up the psychic *container.* If he were to realize it now, it would blast him to pieces. Sylvie went through the same sort of thing, but Milo's got the additional problem of this distorted, secret past.

"My approach has been all wrong. I mustn't precipitate any sudden epiphanies. More chlorpromazine. Slow, careful work. Test the ground before each step, Devore, or you'll land the both of you in a dark hole. If the state won't keep paying, screw them! Call it a charity case. God knows, there's plenty in it *for me!*"

STOP. REWIND. PLAY:
". . . plenty in it *for me!*"

STOP. REWIND. PLAY:
". . . plenty in it *for me!*"

STOP.

"Dr. Devore?"—a voice out in the corridor. "Dr. Devore? Dr. Devore? Security, Dr. Devore! You in there, sir?" A rapping at the outer door. Fumbling for keys.

The knot in the knot in Milo's belly tightened further. He had to get up to ease the pain. He padded to the office door and peeked into the waiting room. The only light in there was the gray-green light that leaked out the door when he opened it, light through the office window from the lamps and signs on the street and the buildings nearby—and the glow of the wall rainbow reflected in the corner of Milo's eye. In the dark of the waiting room Milo saw what must have been an afterimage of the rainbow, as if it were a small animal that had sneaked out ahead of him through the office door.

Except for the rainbow, the waiting room was empty now, but Milo must have been dead-out dozing before, because the painting had been changed again.

Someone must have gone in and out of the waiting room without waking him. The monkey warrior was gone. Instead, it was Munch's screamer on the screaming bridge, the air and river screaming.

He heard the key in the lock. For a moment, Milo had a sense of déjà vu, the feeling that the turning key was himself. He shut himself in the office again, his heart pounding. Suddenly, to his astonishment, he heard Dr. Devore's voice in the waiting room: "No, wait. I'm sorry. I'll open it for you. I must have fallen asleep."

The sneak! Everybody wants a piece of me. Milo ran to the open window, swung his feet over the ledge—it was a long way down—and listened. He yanked Devore's crystal off the sash by the string that held it, and he threw it out the window. A tiny, occasional glint, it plummeted six stories and shattered on a curbstone.

". . . plenty in it for me!"

He stared at the rainbow wall—all dark. No rainbow. Probably, it was Milo's own shadow blocking the window light from shining on it. He heard the hallway door opening. The voice outside went up nearly an octave: "Oh. Sorry, Doctor. I just had to check. I thought I heard somebody in here. I mean, I *thought* it was you, but I had to make sure."

"No problem. I'm *glad* you checked. It might *not* have been me, after all. I might have been somebody else."

"Right. Everything okay then, right?"

"Right. And I have a weapon, remember?"

"I remember. I still don't think it's a good idea."

"I do."

"You're the doctor."

The door clicked shut. The inner door opened. Milo jumped.

"Can you fly like that all the time, or was it just some kind of crazy fluke?" The big kid speared one of Milo's fries—"You mind?"—and shoveled it on in. He was only an inch taller than Milo, if that, but the swagger made it six. He never stopped talking except to swallow. "Because if you can do that whenever you want to, little man, I've got a proposition for you."

They sat in a corner of the big, greasy restaurant. The light there was like bleach, harsh and merciless. Cadaverous chain smokers sucked coffee and talked to themselves, silently or aloud. With one hand, a lean, gap-toothed Okie was rocking her toddler's walker, while, with the other, finger by finger, she managed a hot-dog bun oozing green. At the next table, three college students discussed Heidegger over meatloaf. The proprietor, Aristotle Jitsi, sweet-talked a girlfriend on the phone pinched between his ear and shoulder, while he scraped the grill.

The big kid wore a bowler hat and a black leather jacket, the overcoat kind favored by suave Italian street toughs, not the motorcycle kind. He had drawstring pants on, loose, with wide vertical stripes, red and white. His shoes were black leather Danskins—a rope walker? A ballet dancer? The ensemble didn't make much sense. "Well? Can you?"

Milo mopped up ketchup with a crust of his grilled cheese, then didn't eat it. He pushed the whole plate of French fries toward the big kid. "I don't know what happened. . . . Thanks, I'm not hungry anymore." Milo sneaked a look down at his own clothes. He never knew what he was wearing until he looked: T-shirt, faded jeans, sneakers, the cowboy belt they gave him last year on his birthday— lassoed Brahma bull buckle.

"You weren't trying to kill yourself, were you?"

"No."

"I think you could do it again. I think you've got some kind of a talent. I was just walking by, and I saw you whistling down like a dropped bomb. I heard the thud. I just about threw up. Then I ran up, and there you were, folding in your wings. Are they wings? Where did you get them? Do you make 'em? Your wings and that furry stuff you tucked away somewhere. For aerodynamics, right? Come on! I'm in the show business, little man. I could do something for you. Tell me some stuff. . . . How about a piece of pie?"

Milo got up from the table and looked around for an exit.

"Hey, sit back down. I'm not done with you. Where you going, anyway? I bet you got no place to stay. Look at you. I can get you a place to stay, no sweat, no charge, but talk to me, little man, talk to me."

Milo started to walk, but a twinge in his calves stopped him. He didn't know what to do with his legs anymore. He felt like an unmagnetized compass. Where to go? Not the group home—they'd ship him back to Devore! Outside of that, one place seemed as good as another. He could live *here*, talking to himself, breathing cigarettes, eating grease. He could die *here*, rocking some toddler in a walker, waiting for his teeth to rot.

"Come back," the big kid said. "I'll buy you a piece of pie. I'm rich as Croesus. I'm in the show business."

Milo sat down. "But I don't feel like talking. I don't know what happened, honest. Some guy was after me. He thought I had something he wanted, but I don't have anything. Do I look like I have anything?"

"What about those wings, boy? Those must be something to have."

"Do I look like I have any secret pockets on me?" Milo lifted his arms up over his head. "You must have been seeing things. I just landed lucky."

"No, I don't think so. Something's fishy here, little man, but I don't care. I like you. I live off fishy, anyway. Look at this." The big kid pulled a card out of his inner vest pocket and spun it across the table in front of Milo:

*** M O O N * A N D * S T A R S ***
Spectacles, Phantasmagoria, Puppets
for
Festivals, Conventions, Parties,
Theatrical Events, Promotions
Of Every Conceivable Variety!!!
by
S. VERDUCCI, MASTER SHOWMAN
(Equidecomposabilization Services Available
to Select Clientele)

"What's *equidecohoozits?*"

"That's a sort of code word, little man. People who need it generally know that word; when they see it on my card, they know that I can supply it. It's a sort of a side line."

"What does it mean?"

The big kid leaned across the table and spoke to Milo in a low voice. He watched Milo as he spoke, as if to measure Milo's response, word by word. "Look here, suppose you got two balls, okay? A great big one and a little bitsy one, both of them thick as a brick. Suppose I told you I had a way of taking the bitsy one apart and putting it back together so it was just as big as the great biggy, or making the biggy into a bitsy without adding or taking away a single atom? You reckon that would be handy?"

"That's what Dede wanted to know!" Milo started in his chair as if he'd touched a high power line. He hadn't spoken or thought that name for eight years. He coughed, trying to hide his shock, but the big kid hadn't missed it.

"Who's Dede?"

"I don't know. Just somebody. I told you, I don't feel like talking."

"Is she some kind of a brain?"

"She was my sister. Leave it alone, okay?"

"Okay, okay!" the big kid said. "I got brains in my family too—brains and weirdoes, take your pick. I'm the only *normal* one . . . Look at the back of the card." Milo had to tilt the card to catch the light just so, but then he saw—there was a rainbow across it. "I'm a puppeteer, little man. I'm S. Verducci, traveling showman: MOON & STARS, Inc. And I want you to work with me. What do you say to that? You'll be rich as Croesus, too."

"I don't know. You gonna put me up for the night?"

"Didn't I say so? Let's go. You're tired, huh? Wait—pie?"

"No."

"So what's your name?"

"Milo."

"Okay, Milo, follow me. Follow me, flying boy." S. Verducci dropped a silver dollar into his glass of water, which was still full. He picked up a crushed, empty hard-pack of Marlboros from the floor, tore off one side and placed it over the top of the glass. Then, holding the cardboard there, he inverted the glass on the table and slipped the cardboard out. The silver dollar was at the bottom of an upside-down glass of water. "Don't you love it? Let the waiter earn his tip, huh? It's okay—Jitsi likes me."

Milo followed S. Verducci past the coffee hounds, the welfare mothers, the college brains—a hooker moving in—and past the counter, to the door.

"Bye-bye Jitsi, you old poisoner!" S. Verducci said.

"Bye-bye, Moon and Stars!"

Out the door into the breezy evening.

They walked twenty blocks, increasingly dark, increasingly run-down. Milo spied Dede watching from behind trash cans, though he was careful not to look. She disguised herself as a pimp cruising by in a vintage Cadillac. Her telescope was trained on Milo from a tenement window. And Devore was with her. He was small. He could hide anywhere, even behind fire hydrants maybe, or down below a sewer grate, phoning Milo's position in to Dede, who had a cop's uniform, a patrol car and a gun. Devore had a gun, too. He'd said so.

Don't think about Dede. There was a way to unthink things, to hold them in the blind spot. All it took was a knot in your stomach—and insomnia. *Don't think about . . . who?*

They came to a sooty storefront to which S. Verducci had a key. Stenciled across one large bay window in bold cursive were the words, "THE GRASS AND TREES." Underneath that: "Coffee and Conversation." There was a faint red light inside. S. Verducci turned the key in the lock and pushed open the door. The hinges squeaked. The casement groaned. A wonderful smell of wisteria flowed out.

"Everything has its portion of smell," Milo said.

"Anaxagoras!" said S. Verducci. "Smell, scent, essence, *sentience!* Everything is everywhere. Nothing's as solid as it seems! That's my whole business, little man! How did *you* know that?"

"My sister used to say it, that's all."

They walked past round tables with chairs on top of them. At the back, they turned a tight corner, and Verducci flicked on a light. They were at the top of a staircase leading to the basement. "Come on." He led Milo into a sort of black box theater downstairs, with a dozen transplanted church pews around a square platform. There was a large canopied bed onstage. "You can sleep here. I'll sleep upstairs. There's a toilet around the corner. I'll leave the light on at the top of the stairwell so you don't get totally spooked. See you in the morning, champ."

S. Verducci pulled off the bowler. He shook his head, and a stream of brown hair tumbled down to his waist.

"You're a girl!" Milo said.

"Sure. What did you think?"

"What does the 'S' stand for?"

"Sylvie. Sweet dreams, little man." She climbed the stairs, leaving Milo alone, in the cellar, in the dark.

Dede at the library on a Saturday morning, Milo in her lap with a Dr. Seuss. He peers up at the book she's reading, sees diagrams that look like envelopes folded funny and ones like globes with twisted meridians. There are letters Dede says are Greek and words she says are German. One Hebrew letter: aleph. Aleph with a tiny *zero*. Aleph with a tiny *one*. And a lazy eight: infinity.

"Is this how you do it, Milo?" Dede whispers. She doesn't expect an answer. At home Mama is washing her hands. Washing her hands and washing her hands.

Suddenly he is in the dark cellar at *The Grass and Trees* again, the air swarming with hypnagogic images, red and green, intricate, impenetrable geometries. He feels that he has just screamed, but nothing stirs. He rubs himself all over to make sure he is a human being. He checks his skin for fur, his shoulder blades for wings.

Sylvie's in cahoots with Devore—the thought, like a sudden needle, pierces him, as he remembers where he is.

He falls asleep again, and when he blows out the candles, seven of them plus one for good luck, all at once he finds himself on the wrong side of his lips. He is a puff of air eddying around the flames. It only lasts a second. Then all the candles are out. He smiles, but everyone else is screaming. Some of the children cover their eyes. "What's wrong?" Milo says. Dede is watching with intense curiosity. Curiosity and desire.

Mama hasn't seen it. Mama is in the kitchen washing the sink over and over. Papa's eyes are bulging, his mouth hangs open, and his muscles are drawn so tight he looks like a starved alley cat. "What did you do? What the hell kind of trick is that?" He licks his lips and scans the room with a wild look. "Never mind! Never mind!" He runs to the door, then runs back, clenching and unclenching his fists. "I didn't see nothing." He shakes one of the guests. "Shut up! Shut up! Everything's okay!" They all stop crying, terrified. "Am I right, Milo? Am I right?"

"Yes, Papa."

"That was a mean, dumb trick, Milo. What, did you sneak under the table and back, huh? Don't you ever let me see you do that again." Milo won't.

"What's the matter?" Sylvie, in her striped pants and a sleeveless undershirt, was standing silhouetted at the cellar door. Scant light from the stairway bathed her like earthshine on a slight, crescent moon.

"Huh?" He sat up. He had been lying fully clothed on top of the covers.

"You shouted. What's the matter? Scared of the dark? Tell me. Don't be ashamed." She walked toward him. Dim, reflected light played on her bare shoulders, through a tangle of hair. A moment of brighter light on one collarbone, as she brushed the hair away, made Milo lift his gaze to the soft, simple curve of her face, the broad forehead, the gentle slope of her nose, and her full lips. The thin fabric of the undershirt hung away from her torso, down from the peaks of her small breasts, and light diffused through the undershirt, shadowing her breasts like X rays. Then she blended into the teeming dark nearer Milo's bed.

"Stay away."

"You think I'm gonna rape you or something? There's a little blue light I was gonna turn on behind the stage. The techy uses it to see what he's doing when he runs cues. Or maybe you'd like a couple of Kliegs. The control board is back there. I was gonna fiddle with it for you. Don't bother to say thank you."

"Okay. Put on the blue light. Don't touch me, though."

"You're a pip, you know that?"

Milo clutched the covers around him and crouched under the canopy while Sylvie walked past him, barely visible in the deepening shadow toward the back of the room. She was just a glint, now and then, a hint of skin, a wrinkle of fabric, disjointed patches of shifting light. Milo heard a click, blue light spilled faintly around the edge of a curtain, then the curtain was pulled back, and the black room filled with blue objects and blue air. It was as if the tide had gone out, leaving jetsam draped with blue algae on blue sand.

"Okay?" she said.

"Okay . . . did I really scream?"

"Yeah."

"It wasn't the dark. I'm not afraid of the dark. But this is better. Thank you."

"Sure thing. Okay now?" She was crossing the room, making a wide arc around the stage, weaving through the chairs.

"Yeah . . . hey!" Milo called to her as she started to mount the stairs again.

"What?"

"Why's there a bed onstage?"

"Don't ask." She trudged upstairs again. Milo heard her scuffling around, then slumping down and groaning quickly into slumber.

In cahoots. Definitely in cahoots. Milo whispered to himself, "I'm going to watch her. I'm going to find out about her. Her and Devore. They're up to something. They think I'm dumb, but I'm going to fool them."

No thorazine tonight. His muscles itched in places he couldn't reach to scratch. Every time he closed his eyes, he was deeply asleep; if he winked them open again, it was as if he'd been out for hours. Every sensum was thick with Devore's malevolence and Sylvie's conspiracy. Like a bombarded infantryman: "Keep a tight ass, Milo," he told himself.

Then Dede was cradling him in her lap, saying, "Everything is made of numbers, Milo. That's what Pythagoras said. Whatever you are, honey, something's the same, see? But what? Is it numbers? Euclid's all wet; there's no *congruence* between a little boy and a BankAmerica Mastercard, is there? No *similarity*, like angles and stuff. They're not even the same *genus* of topological space, because you got holes through your head and your butt and your little winkie, but a charge card's all connected everywhere.

"Something's the same though, because you go from this to that and back again, and whatever you are, you're *you*, aren't you? So how do you do it?"

"Why do you care, Dede?"

"You do such nice things for me, Milo, when you do those change-ums, I never want it to stop. I gotta figure out what's going on, so we don't lose you." She turns pages so furiously, a few of them rip. The librarian says something, but Dede pays no attention. "Maybe it has something to do with equideco . . ."

From upstairs: "Hey! You okay?"

"What?"

"You were screaming again."

"Sorry!"

There was no sunlight in the cellar, and therefore no time, just blue. Milo slept and woke like a subway car surfacing and descending through a dark metropolis. He got up to find the toilet. He stumbled past the control board "backstage," a closet with massive, ancient rheostats, a clipboard on a string, empty Coke bottles, and dust. Passing beyond the sphere of the backstage light, Milo knew where he was by the sound of his footsteps. They echoed more sharply as he reached the tiled room.

The bathroom door was held open by a mop bucket full of dirty water. On its scummy surface there were rainbows. Daylight leaked in through the bathroom window. Milo walked into the light and relieved himself into a urinal. The daylight, the tinkle, the morning breeze, were like a benediction. He walked out past the rainbows, the dimmers, and the stage, to the stairway. He smelled bacon.

He started up the stairs, when a gigantic crow peeked into the stairway from above, cawed a few times and said, in a high, scratchy voice, "Soup's on, little man!" Milo stumbled three steps backward.

Then Sylvie's face appeared next to the crow's. She continued, in the crow's voice, "Eggs and toast for humans! *Pictures* of eggs and toast for the puppets!" Then she thrust out one arm, at the end of it a puppet made of five or six tiny men in trench coats—one puppet with multiple jaws that moved together: "*Hiss! Boo!*"

"Oh shut up," Sylvie said, "or I'll give you a picture of angleworms to eat." She pulled out of sight, her puppets with her. A second later the tiny men reappeared. "*Angleworms!*" they shuddered. "We're not partial to *angleworms!*" They scooted off.

The walls upstairs were covered with posters, masks, hand puppets, and marionettes, from minuscule to elephantine, hanging by hooks and wire. There were posters for wassail consorts, pantomimes, plays by people named Beckett, Ionesco, Tzara, Artaud, old cigarette ads enameled in three colors, embossed on tin; also a wall-sized photograph of a man gleefully smiling as he leapt, birdlike, from a high window onto the street below—a bicyclist trundling past, unawares. "SAUT DANS LA VIDE," it said underneath. "LEAP INTO NOTHINGNESS," Sylvie explained.

Among the masks there were bug-eyed Balinese demons with teeth like tusks; there were lions' heads, monkeys, frogs, grotesque insects, the mask of a beautiful girl with a skull mask nested underneath, also a variety of clown noses and Swiss carnival masks, larval, exaggerated, alive, that Sylvie said she had received from a "business associate" in Basel. And the puppets: the huge crow and the little men back on their hooks already, mustached villains with black hats, Punch and Judy, Orlando Furioso in a plumed helmet, and also a variety of animals and inanimate objects. There was a printing press puppet, a city block whose tenement windows were mouths, a sky with star eyes and the moon for a mouth, a mountain, a lock and key, a long-legged airplane, and a truck with teeth under its hood, among many still stranger.

Everything has its portion of smell. Sylvie had taken down the chairs from one round table and was laying down two steaming dishes of eggs and toast. Several flies accompanied her, and when Milo approached, they found their way to his face and neck. He slapped at them.

"Don't," Sylvie said. "Those are friends of mine, Eric and Mehitabel. The small one is Beulah. Leave them alone. They're from upstate."

"Are you for real?"

"I'm a vegetarian, okay?"

"What about the pig? I smelled bacon."

"Nope. I can't help what kind of grease is caked on the burner. That's the owner's, not mine. Pull up and chow down, little man. We've got a day ahead of us."

Milo sat. Sylvie poured them both coffee. "You're strange," Milo said.

"Strange is good. I like strange."

"You're not rich. Not if you sleep in *this* place."

"Did I say I was rich, Milo?"

"Rich as Croesus."

"No, you got me wrong." Sylvie squeegeed egg yolk with her toast and folded the toast into her mouth. "Rich in creases, that's what I said. My costume gets all creased sleeping here under the tables, see? Rich in creases, is what I said. It's a Biblical locution."

"Sure. Who owns this place, if *you* don't?" Milo nibbled at his toast, played with the spoon in his coffee. Nonchalant—*that's the ticket.*

"The Grass and Trees? Some guy you don't know."

"You work for him?" Bet it's Devore, he thought.

"Hell, no. This is a *fellowship* I got here. No strings attached. Guy appreciates my artistic ability, see? Why aren't you eating? Miss the meat?"

"No."

"Well?"

He started on the eggs, and then he couldn't stop. He ravened the toast and licked the plate. Sylvie poured him some more coffee. "Hurry it up, though. We got a gig the other side of town."

"We?"

Sylvie shooed Milo from the table, cleared it, and had him put the chairs back up and sweep while she did the dishes. She ducked behind a counter into a small enclosure covered with green striped awning, and fished out two black suitcases. She handed one of them to Milo. "Wait a minute." Sylvie unlatched her case and pulled out a collapsible top hat, flattened to a disk. She contrived to blow on it, while flexing it just so, and it popped open. She twirled the hat between her fingers so that it wound up on Milo's head. He flinched. She grabbed her bowler from behind the counter and twirled it onto her own head the same way. "See? It's just business, little man. Now you're with *me.* Moon and Stars!"

That's what was stenciled on the suitcases, too:

*** M O O N *

on hers,

A N D * S T A R S ***

on his.

"Do I have to wear the hat?" he said.

"Sure you do! It suits you, too. Isn't it neat how it changes . . ." She pushed ahead of him to unlock and open the door, and he thought he heard her say, ". . . just like you?"

They only spent a few minutes in daylight, and Sylvie led Milo underground again, this time into the subways. They sat side by side in the strobing, shaking car with the suitcases on their laps; it was awkward, but Sylvie insisted they carry them that way. She also insisted that Milo sit on her left and that they hold the suitcases with the lettering facing out:

MOON* . . . AND*STARS

"Free advertising," she said. No one looked. No one *ever* looked on the subway. If they looked, it meant trouble. Anything could happen down there, Milo learned; a baby could be born, water could spring from a stone, the Four Horsemen of the Apocalypse could thunder from a businessman's lapel, and everybody would turn their page of *Newsweek* or the *Enquirer* or the *New York Times* and keep their eyes down and their elbows close to their hips.

"What were you doing on the street where I fell yesterday?" Milo said between Manchester Avenue and Lafayette Park. *Make it sound like ordinary conversation.* "You were right below there, weren't you?"

"It was listed in my ephemeris: 'Boy falling out of the sky northeast of the MacCauly Building.' "

"Come on, Sylvie."

Sylvie shifted uncomfortably on the crowded bench. "Hey! You're the mystery man, not me, champ. I was going someplace, that's all. Do you have to take up so much room?"

Milo scrunched himself farther into the end of the bench. "Have you ever been up there in that building where I fell from?"

"Where you *flew* from, you mean? Maybe. Yeah. Why? Yeah." She looked away. *Don't push too hard. She already knows I'm suspicious. She probably thinks I've seen her up there, and she's cooking up an excuse right now.*

"I might have a client up there, I think, if it's the building I'm thinking of," Sylvie said.

"Equidecohoozits?"

"No. Well, sort of. Paintings. Copies of the Masters. Subscription service. It's another sideline. I got a *couple* of clients like that in that block. What were *you* doing up there?"

"Seeing a shrink."

"You crazy?"

"Just nervous. I have trouble sleeping, like."

"You're telling me!"

"What do you mean?"

The train stopped. Sylvie slid sideways into Milo, then righted herself as the doors slid open and two women rushed in, business executives, briefcases under their arms, talking about wheat futures. They grabbed a stanchion and braced themselves. The doors clapped shut, and the train lurched forward.

"What did you mean?" Milo said.

"You kept me up half the night, screaming and talking in your sleep."

"More than the once? What did I say?"

"Who cares? Stick with me, Milo. I'll teach you how to sleep. . . . Let's move to the next car. I don't like those two ladies."

"Did I say something about Dede?"

"Every damn thing you say is about Dede, Milo. Get up and let's go to the next car. They're looking at me."

One of the execs was edging closer. "Moon and Stars? Hey, Moon and Stars! I want to talk to you! I've got another deal. Hey!" There was a quality of pleading in the woman's voice. Sylvie shoved Milo through the passage to the next car, and then the next, brutalizing whoever blocked the way and letting them curse.

"I hate that," she said at last. "I did something for her when I was still green, and now she won't leave me alone."

"What do you mean, everything I say is about Dede?"

"It's a big city, Milo. You can say whatever you like."

The train stopped. They squeezed out, pinched between the shoulders of a dozen workers, shoppers, and students, only some of whom, in the subterranean light, looked human. Milo dutifully clutched his suitcase handle, clutched it so hard it made him think of the way he was clutching something else, in his belly, clutching so deep and so hard for so long that he had stopped thinking of it as something he *did*; instead it had come to seem like something he suffered. They climbed up into a broad, cobbled square separated by a massive archway from a sunlit park.

Sylvie walked briskly. Milo quickened his pace to stay abreast. They passed through the arch, across a meadow the size of a football field, and down a dirt pathway through a clump of trees, until they came in sight of a picnic shelter.

"This is it," she said. "Employee picnic. Dingsboomps, Incorporated or something. Full payment on day of performance. Watch this."

A few children were running toward them from the shelter. As they came within badgering distance, Milo, hanging back a few yards, saw Sylvie's suitcase stop in midair while Sylvie herself kept walking, still holding on. Like a tugboat trying to pull the shoreline out to sea, Sylvie suddenly was yanked back. The children giggled. Sylvie scowled. She pulled at the case. It wouldn't budge. She pushed it. She leaned against it. The children fell down laughing.

Between her teeth, she said to Milo, "Kick it."

"Huh?"

"Kick it."

Milo kicked it. The case flew forward, tumbling Sylvie to the ground. Milo rushed to help her.

"You ass," she said. "This is *part* of it. Give me your hand." Befuddled, he did it. Sylvie grabbed, pulling Milo down on top of her, sputtering and flailing. "Whoa!" she said—theatrically. The children howled. They ran to the shelter to get their friends.

Milo lay face down, blinking and huffing, on top of Sylvie, face up, laughing. "You'll do," she said. His chest was on top of her chest. He could feel the breasts inside her smock. His legs were on top of hers. Her hair, the little of it that spilled out of the bowler when she tumbled, was in his face.

He scrambled to his feet, tucked his shirt in, wiped his face, recovered the fallen top hat. Sylvie got up. They picked up the suitcases and walked.

"Why do you dress like a boy?" he said.

"Showbiz, little man. It's all showbiz. Why do you?"

Sylvie found the Dingsboomps honcho and set up where he told her to. Inside the "AND * STARS ***" suitcase there were plastic pipes, tent poles, and colored nylon sheets with sleeves sewn along the hems for the poles and pipes to make a frame. It took fifteen minutes to erect the puppet stage, five of them to shoo away the children and grab back joints and dinguses they'd boosted from Milo's suitcase.

Once the puppet stage was up, Sylvie was ruthless about keeping kids away. "This is our space, see?" she said to Milo, stooping low in the red light filtering through the nylon. She was hanging puppets and props on hooks backstage. "Nobody but showfolk here, Milo. If Mr. Dingsboomps comes back here, we boot him. If it's the President of the United States, we boot him. If it's God Almighty with Saint Peter and Saint Paul . . . what?"

"Huh?"

"What do we *do?*" she said, exasperated.

"We boot 'em," Milo said.

"That's right. You gotta draw the line, Milo. You see what I mean?" She thrust her arm in and out of a few of the puppets hanging upside-down below the stage, practicing transitions. "Go find the guy in the suit and tell him we're ready. Then come back here with me. Got it?"

"Yuh!" Milo ran.

Sylvie's puppet show was a Chinese folk tale: Stone Monkey. Milo crouched low and handed her things when she clucked, scowled or elbowed him. He watched, fascinated.

First, the initial phases of the creation of the universe were enacted: 129,000 years in twelve parts (sixty seconds each) represented by cacophonously squabbling puppets of mouse, bull, tiger, hare, dragon, serpent, horse, goat, monkey, cock, dog, and pig. After another twenty-seven thousand years, Sylvie's *Pan Gui* smithereened the Enormous Vagueness (a gelatinous blob manipulated by rods and strings). At last, halfway through the show, Stone Monkey was born atop the Mountain of Flowers and Fruit from a rock that Sylvie reported, in the wavering voice of an Ancient Taoist Sage, to be precisely thirty-six feet five inches in height and twenty-four feet in circumference.

Rascally Stone Monkey terrorized Heaven and Earth, absconding with various elixirs, virtuous gems, and magic weapons from the Jade Emperor — and anybody else who got in his way. In the end, on a bet with Buddha, he pissed on the Five Pillars at the End of the Universe — some children applauded, some booed, some giggled nervously — but they turned out to be the Buddha's fingers. Big Bud grabbed up poor Monkey and imprisoned him in a mountain of iron. Curtain.

The instant the curtain fell, Sylvie said, "Get the money." In a louder voice, she announced, "Children or others coming within two feet of the puppet stage will be shot," and she started taking everything apart.

Always, they slept and breakfasted at *The Grass and Trees.* Supper at Jitsi's. They did shows a few times a week at places all over town, indoors and out: libraries, loading docks, the beach, the park, a historical society, some rec centers and settlement houses, street fairs, block parties, and a hospital or two. "If they knew what I was," Sylvie said, "they'd never hire me. But I look like your clean-cut American kid, now don't I?"

"So what *are* you, Sylvie?" Milo would say.

"Oh, go fish! When are you gonna show me those wings?"

"Go fish, yourself!"

Milo learned the setup routine and could strike quicker than Sylvie after a while. He started doing a few puppets, notably Lord Buddha and, in Sylvie's "Trash Show," a bilious Dumpster named Hector. He did chores like filling Monkey's rubber bladder with water for the piss scene, and velcroing the Enormous Vagueness back together after Pan Gui *decomposed* it. He learned what to say to Sylvie's patrons, how to accept their money or put them off when they were late setting up.

He enjoyed himself. He got a little sun tan. His ribs stopped showing. The hollows around his eyes disappeared. He got to know Jitsi, who called him "Little Man," because that's what he heard Sylvie call him.

Sylvie paid Milo part of her take, fivers at first, then tens and an occasional twenty. When they busked, he got half the hat. "For street work," she said, "we're strictly partners." He liked that.

After the first week or so, Milo forgot about investigating the Devore-Sylvie connection. It just didn't seem so important anymore. When Sylvie disappeared, on off days, without explanation or apology, Milo took himself to the zoo, the beach, or the museum. There was never anyone at *The Grass and Trees* except Milo and Sylvie — and the Monkey King. The owner was on vacation, she said.

Milo would be settling into his fitful night's sleep, or would wake at an unknown hour — all the hours were dark down there — and hear the Monkey King cudgeling Lord Erlang. "Take that, you shriveled pus bag!" He would creep sometimes to the foot of the stairs to hear it better.

"You can't fool me, you imbecilic macaque!" Sylvie blustered *basso profundo*, then squealed as Monkey: "Kowtow, pig-face, or I'll knock you silly!"

One night Sylvie surprised him by shouting, in her own voice, "Come on up here, Milo. I know you're awake. You might as well help me with the chase sequence."

He walked upstairs and saw Sylvie's puppet theater set up in one of the bay windows, facing in. It was lit eerily from inside — bloodred. The puppet theater had been transformed into a weird temple with rows of fluted columns (papier-mâché) and stained glass windows (cellophane). The God Erlang, frightening in the red light, appeared in full battle array, carrying a huge lance, huge, that is, in proportion to his own size of ten inches or so.

Suddenly, the opening of the puppet stage closed in on itself. The carpet Erlang stood on lapped at him like a tongue, the columns gnashed like teeth, the proscenium was like a lip smacking against the apron. Erlang barely managed to wedge the theater space open with his lance.

"It's Monkey's mouth, Milo," Sylvie said. She left Erlang there, his head drooping lifelessly on his chain mail. "He's equideco'ed into a temple, get it?"

"First, Monkey turns into a sparrow and Erlang turns into a kite. Then Monkey is a fish, and Erlang is a fish-hawk. When Monkey changes to a water-snake, Erlang turns into a red-crested gray crane. What can Monkey do? He turns into a bustard. Look." She showed him a thin-billed, long-legged plop of a bird-puppet, with an enlarged face retaining a few essentials of Stone Monkey. "That's the lowest. A bustard'll let anything hump it — even crows. Promise me you won't ever be a bustard, flying boy."

"Huh?"

"Anyway, Erlang shoots him then. So he takes off and turns himself into this temple. See? This flagpole is Monkey's tail, only I haven't Sobo-glued the hair on yet. This whole thing *here* is Monkey's mouth. The windows are his eyes. But Erlang is onto him. He threatens to break the window panes. That would blind old Monkey."

"It's great, Sylvie! How did you do that?"

"Adhesives," she said. "Everything is adhesives, Milo, in the show business any-ways: duct tape, hot glue, velcro, rivets — this is like my catechism, see? — stuff inside other stuff all over the place. I wanna start doing this story in a week. Sound okay?"

"Teach me."

"That's all I wanted to hear." She led him behind the puppet stage, into the heart of the red glow, and started to fill his hands with odd things.

"Sylvie . . ." he said.

"Yeah?"

"How can Monkey do all that? I mean, what is he supposed to be that he can change into stuff that way?"

She stopped what she was doing and looked at Milo. There was nothing in the entire world outside this small ball of red light, Monkey's mouth, the jumble of props and puppets, the window glass behind them — "and Conversation and Coffee . . ." — Milo's eyes, Sylvie's eyes, each other's eyes in each other's eyes. "He's a *shape-shifter*, Milo. A *shape-shifter*."

Inside himself, Milo squeezed: not a tightening, but a pushing together, the way he might squeeze the string together on both sides of a knot, to let more slack in for the undoing. There was no thought before him, but a sort of déjà vu. "Dede . . ." he said.

". . . Sylvie, you mean."

"*Sylvie*, I feel like I want to tell you something."

"I don't think so," she said. "We've got a lot of lines to learn here, a lot of cues to get down. Hold this." She handed him Monkey's Gold-Banded As-You-Will Cudgel, Weight 13,500 Pounds. She got up and switched on the overhead light. It was a cheap chandelier. The crystals dangled and made little rainbows on Lord Erlang, the puppet heads, masks and posters on the walls, "SAUT DANS LA VIDE," and all. They went to work.

There were never any customers, no coffee, no conversation; day after day, the chairs never came off the tables except for Sylvie and Milo. Once, an exterminator showed up with a gas mask, a heavy cylinder, and a spray gun that looked like a sci-fi blaster; Sylvie nearly beat him unconscious, shoving him back out the door, while he waved his Service Orders in pink and blue and protected his private parts.

"Over my dead body," she said.

"Vegetarian!" Milo shook his head.

"They might be Stone Monkey, flying boy. They might be Franz frigging Kafka. How the hell do you know who the cockroaches are? Go kill, if you want to." She stalked out and didn't come back until the dark of the next morning, when she woke him to borrow some cash. It took Milo two days to feel that he had made it up to her.

The fifth week, she taught him how to sleep. She whispered to him in the dark. He let her onto the stage, but not too close: "Milo, there's a bowl at the bottom of your belly, a big bowl—can you feel it?"

"Uh huh."

"Well; every time you take a breath, like, the bowl kind of fills up with air. Doesn't that feel good?"

"I guess."

"And every time you breathe out, it kind of steams off, like soup steaming into cold air, see? You don't have to do a thing, little man. Just feel that bowl fill up, and then feel the steam float off it. Watch how it goes out your mouth and nose, and then feel the air coming in there again. Over and over. Because it feels good, that's all. If you start thinking about something, just go back to the bowl again. Nobody's keeping track. You don't have to get past *one*. Just one . . . one . . . one— see? That's the *real* way to count. All those other numbers are a lot of crap. Then, if it's night, you fall asleep, and if it's day, you keep awake. Get it?"

"I'll try it, Sylvie, but I'm scared."

"Tell me about it, sky-jumper boy. Scared!"

"How old are you?" he asked, staring at her with sudden intensity.

"A million."

"Come on, Sylvie!"

"Seventeen," she said.

"I'm fifteen. We're practically the same."

"Dream on, little man."

"Do you have a boyfriend?"

"No."

"Did you ever . . . ?"

"Yes." Suddenly she took his hand. "Not yet, Milo. It's too soon. But I feel it too. I think it might happen. Don't push, okay?"

"Okay."

She cocked her head at him and bit her lip in a way that melted whatever of Milo remained solid before Sylvie. "What do you see when you look at me, Milo?"

"A girl—what do you mean?"

"When you see the moon and stars, maybe it'll be time then . . ."

"Sylvie, I want to tell you something about myself."

She looked away. "I gotta go somewhere. Tell me when I get back. . . . Do you have any money? I'm a little short."

At the beach that day, lying in the sun on a hulk of driftwood, sand dusting his face, fine sea air puffing his shirt and filling his lungs like a sail, Milo breathed. Water welled, sucked, and whispered around him. Waves lapped. The bowl filled and emptied. Thoughts came and went. Inside him, a knot loosened.

Dede was saying, "Milo, how can you be so small?" *She* was *big*. She was the Jolly Green Giant. She was King Kong, Mount Everest, the Moon. He felt that he was looking at her the wrong way through a microscope. She flipped him, and he came up heads. She laughed. "I mean, where's the rest of you, Milo? Don't worry, I won't spend you. I wonder what Galileo would say about this. He's the one who figured out how there are as many square numbers as there are numbers, baby. 1, 2, 3, 4, 5, . . . or 1, 4, 9, 16, 25 . . . for each of each there's one of the other—*savvy?*—even though the one bunch looks bigger, even though the one bunch is *a part of* the other. Is that how it is for you, Milo?" She tickled him on the eagle's breast. "Lots or little, somehow you're still my little Milo. Don't you *lose* something when you turn to a quarter? Don't you *get* something when you turn to a blimp? How *do* you do those change-ums?"

The bowl filled, the bowl emptied. The sea. The wind. A knot inside him came undone. "I'm a *shape-shifter!*"

The sky darkened. The lake began to glow so intensely blue-green, seething in its basin, that it seemed more emotion than liquid. Strati knit the sky shut. Thunder. Milo climbed down from the log, brushed the sand off and started running. He was supposed to meet Sylvie in front of the bathhouse for a show in the old carousel enclosure.

"When the great world horse pisses, it rains," Dede had told him once. "Everything is transformations—it says so here in the Upanishads. Wanna hear more?"

"No." It had frightened him.

Now, just as in Dede's Upanishads, the rain broke like piss from a tight bladder. It sprayed down. The world horse whinnied. Its eyes flashed. The sand was speckled then splotched then rutted, and Milo was spattered with wet sand, splashing, pool to pool, toward the bathhouse. Then the hail began to fall. His scalp tickled. His hair sparkled with hail. When he brushed the tiny hail stones out, his hair *crunched.*

It only lasted a few moments, and the drumming of rain and hail subsided. He could hear the waves again, breathing back and forth far behind him, and the flag by the bathhouse flapping like a faltering conversation.

Sylvie was pacing back and forth between two pillars at the top of the bathhouse steps, just under the eaves of the roof, protected from the downpour. The broad stone steps were littered with tiny hailstones that crackled under Milo's feet.

"Sylvie!" he shouted. "I've got to tell you something. You've got to listen."

"Look, I'm in a hurry, Milo. There's a guy waiting on me inside there, and then we still have that show to do."

"But Sylvie . . ."

A tall wiry man in a Hawaiian shirt strolled out of the men's door across the landing from Sylvie and Milo. He was balding but meticulously groomed and greased, with sideburns down to his long, heavy jaw. His fingers were covered with rings. "Hey, what's the holdup *now?* My client is getting impatient."

Sylvie turned toward him. "One minute. Just wait inside. I never let you down yet, did I?"

"Okiedokie." He ducked back in.

"Listen, Milo." Sylvie was slightly trembling. So was Milo, but Sylvie wasn't wet. "I'm going to leave in a second, but I need you to stay here. You gotta go in where Lenny is and give him something for me—a box with some stuff inside. Watch him, Milo. Watch that he's careful with the thing I leave him, okay?"

"Sure, Sylvie . . ."

"Listen. The guy he's with will do some stuff—it won't take long—and then Lenny'll give you some money. And he'll give you the box back. Make sure you get that box back and everything in it. *Mint.* Understand?" She handed him something. She had to push it into his hand, because at first he didn't see it, he had been focusing so intently on Sylvie's eyes. It was an ice pick.

He didn't know what to make of it at first. "Sylvie?"

"You won't have to use it, don't worry. It's just in case. You might have to *show* it to him—that's the worst it could get. Then he would give you everything and run. Lenny's not brave like you, jumper boy. Believe me, I know Lenny."

Milo put the ice pick under his shirt, inside his belt.

"Let Lenny leave. Just stay there by the showers. Make sure he's gone. Make sure nobody's around. If anybody's around, wait till they're gone. Put the box down on a bench. Come out to the door, and wait. I'll meet you there in less than a minute, guaranteed." She took a deep breath and huffed it out.

"Okay," she said, strictly business now, all the tension turned to purpose. "Turn around, Milo. I gotta do something you can't see. Then I'll split, and I'll leave the package there for you to take in to Lenny. Just turn around, count to twenty, then do what I told you. Get it?"

"Yes, Sylvie."

"You're soaking wet, you jerk." She smiled and tousled his hair. "Don't you know to come in out of the rain?" Then she pushed his shoulder to make him turn.

"One, two . . ." rain dripping from the eaves. His teeth chattered a little. At twenty, he turned around and Sylvie was gone. There was a hat box on the landing, bound with a red ribbon. Milo picked it up and carried it across the landing and in through the men's door, hugging it closely to his chest with both arms. The ice pick pricked his thigh a little when he stepped, but it didn't hurt much.

He didn't see anyone at first. He was standing in a large, echoey dome with arched passages leading off every sixty degrees or so. The sound of slowly dripping water boomed all around him. He stood near the center trying to figure out which way to go, when he heard a voice: "Psst! Hey, kid! This way!" Milo followed the voice as well as he could.

Moving into one of the small passageways, the quality of sound changed so abruptly that he felt someone had boxed his ears. Or else he was walking inside a sea shell, or inside the labyrinth of his own ear. The passage opened into a small, concrete courtyard with showers along the perimeter and a few benches near the middle. The hard floor sloped down toward a drain in the center. Milo looked up. The sky was the color of iron. He was cold.

Suddenly Lenny was at his side. "Surprised you, huh?" He had come from a shower stall beside the entrance. "I had to take a leak. Mr. Jones used the regular facilities. He'll be right here. . . . You a pal of Sylvie's? She never used you before."

Milo heard steps echoing behind him. He turned and backed out of the way, toward the benches. Mr. Jones was a thick, crewcut man with a flaccid face. He wore a stiff, white short-sleeved shirt that fairly glowed in the stormy light. He squinted and cocked his head at the sight of Milo. "This isn't a girl."

Lenny laughed. "So what? So she sent an associate. You'll notice he's got the merchandise."

Jones rolled his eyes. He looked disgusted. "That ain't all he's got, Lenny."

"Huh?"

"This associate here has got a weapon in his belt," Jones said. Milo looked down around the hat box to his waist. The soaked shirt was bunched around the handle of the ice pick. Jones stepped toward Milo and extended one hand, palm up. "Give."

"Come on, kid," Lenny said. "You don't need that. We trust each other here. God! I'm sorry, Mr. Jones. The kid doesn't know how we do business, is all."

"Sure. So give."

Milo didn't move. He looked back and forth between Lenny and Mr. Jones. For some reason, he didn't feel worried about them. He was worried about something else. Something Lenny had said.

"Sylvie doesn't *use* me."

Lenny smiled. "Tough. Very tough. Very impressive. Okay. Sylvie doesn't *use* you. Just give Mr. Jones the knife."

"It's an ice pick," Milo said. He looked straight at Jones. "And I'm keeping it. Sylvie didn't say anything about giving it to you — unless you try to cheat me."

"He's a *kid*, for crissakes!" Lenny laid a hand on Mr. Jones's shoulder. Mr. Jones kept his hand extended and his eyes straight on Milo. "Nobody's got anything to gain by violence here, am I right? Let's just do our business and adjourn. Okay, Mr. Jones?"

Jones nodded slowly. "*I'm* not impressed. I'm not *pleased*. But we'll let it go, because I respect Lenny, and because I think this little boy would lose his lunch before he pricked anybody with that steel dick. Also, I have a gun. . . . So, let's see the goods."

Jones stepped back. Lenny gave Milo a sheepish look. Facing Milo, so Jones couldn't see, Lenny mouthed the words: "He doesn't have any gun." Lenny shrugged. Milo held out the box to Mr. Jones. Jones took it from Milo and carried it to one of the benches, where he laid it down and undid the ribbon.

Lenny stayed a few feet back with Milo. "You're wet, kid. Quite a downpour, huh?"

"Don't get the box wet," Milo said to Jones. The wooden bench was damp. Jones shot him a black look and snarled something under his breath. Jones lifted the cover from the round box and laid it down on the bench beside the box itself. He reached in and pulled out a roll of cash. He fanned it, then removed the rubber band around it, pulled out one of the bills and held it at arm's length to look it over. He did the same thing with a few others, turning them over, flapping them and pulling them out with a snap. Then Mr. Jones took a magnifying glass from his pocket and examined one of the bills more closely.

He returned the magnifying glass to his pants pocket. He stacked the bills together and bound them with the rubber band again. He put the cash back into the box, closed it and tied the ribbon with the same sort of bow it had had before.

"So?" said Lenny.

Mr. Jones handed the box back to Milo and smiled. He turned to Lenny. "It's crap."

"What do you mean, it's crap? You can't tell me this is crap. This is the work of a goddam artist. Uncle fucking Sam himself couldn't tell this stuff from the real thing."

"I can. It's crap."

"You're trying to weasel a better deal out of me, aren't you, Harold? You said if this passed muster you'd front me the ten thou. I told you I could guarantee delivery of the rest in two weeks. Okay, you said. Two weeks, you said. Ten thou up front on approval, you said."

"*On approval.*"

"There's nothing wrong with this job. I'm telling you Sylvie's guy is an artist. He's a Da Vinci, Harold. Nothing's wrong with it. What's wrong with it?"

"It's off, that's all. The border's off. The weave is funny. We won't work with it. Find another distributor—it's your funeral."

"Somebody's supposed to give me some money," Milo said.

Jones turned on him, laughing. His face was like bread dough being folded and kneaded. His lips curled back, showing the gums, big and pink, like a horse's. "What, are you gonna pull out your ice pick now? You an artist too? You gonna make me into an ice sculpture, kid? You guys are a million laughs."

Jones walked into the passage to the main chamber.

"Harold!" Lenny turned his head to shout after him, but didn't *move* an inch. He looked beaten. "Harold! Hey! Wait a minute here! Harold . . . Shit!"

"Are you gonna give me the money?" Milo asked Lenny.

"You're a real piece of work, kid, you and that bitch of a sister you got."

"She's not my sister."

"Give me the box. Screw Mr. Jones. I'll find another Mr. Jones."

"I'm supposed to take the box back to Sylvie. You're supposed to pay me."

Lenny grabbed at the hat box. Milo swung it out of his reach.

"I don't need this, kid," Lenny said. "I don't need your whore sister either, not after this. She screwed up. Give me the damn box. I'll pay her when I get *my* advance, see? This is supposed to be our sample. This is supposed to buy me a little time while our printer gets his act together. You see how many people you're holding up here, kid? Me, the printer, the printer's family, *my* family . . ." He was walking forward as Milo walked back, between the benches, toward the far showers. ". . . and Sylvie too. She's got no use for it, without I get some dough on it for her. Now, *gimme.*"

Milo was backed against a wall under a shower head. Lenny took another swipe at the box. Milo reached back and turned on the shower, spraying Lenny full in the face. Milo grabbed the ice pick from his belt. The point gouged Milo's own stomach, and his soaked shirt reddened. He looked down, uttered a small cry of surprise, and dropped the ice pick.

Lenny stopped sputtering and flailing. He stood still, with the spray pelting his face and plastering his sparse hair down in absurd curls. He stared at the blood welling up along Milo's belt. He stepped back out of the shower. "Oh, God, what a mess! Kid, you keep it. You keep the damn paper. Tell Sylvie she screwed up. Oh, God! Equidecomposabullshit! I musta been outa my gourd! Tell her this is the last time she does a job for anybody east of Topeka. And get a doctor, kid!" He turned and ran.

"She's not my sister," Milo said. He turned off the shower. There was a shallow pool of red before him, pushed outward by the force of the spray and streaming back again toward the drain behind his heels. Like a drunkard navigating one sensum at a time, Milo looked at his right arm and saw that the hat box was still cradled there, soaked; then he found his feet and walked back to the benches, trailing bloody water.

He laid the box down on a bench. He started back toward the main chamber, but as soon as he entered the passageway, the air filled with bright Paisleys, and he found himself on his knees, gasping. He pulled up his shirt to look underneath. He could see the lip of the wound, where blood oozed. "It's not so bad," he said. He slumped down onto his buttocks. He was about to black out, but he forced himself awake. He rolled onto all fours, then stood up, a little at a time. He leaned his shoulder against the wall of the passage and slid along, like a child pulling himself along the gutter of a swimming pool.

He was halfway down the passage when he heard Sylvie's voice behind him, in the courtyard, among the showers. "Milo! Milo, what happened? Whose blood is this?"

He started to say "Dede's," but stopped it before his tongue left his palate. *Dede's blood!* He looked at his fingers, and for a moment he thought that they were bloody claws . . .

> Dede lies before him, all bloody. Her spasms are like the jerks of a severed frog leg. He looks at his fingers. The claws are just now retracting into his fingertips, the carpal pad receding into a palm, the fur on his forearm turning into the slightest blond down. He cries, and his chin shudders into a gelatinous ooze, pulling upward, shortening, then hardening again, as the fangs recede with a squeak, shrinking into his gums and out of sight. "Dede! Dede! Did I do what you wanted? Dede!" He looks around for help. His knees have softened and recongealed to face the right direction now. The boy he was supposed to kill for Dede, the one who wouldn't be her lover, is gone. The door has been thrown open and Milo can hear running down the street. "Dede, please say something!" He looks at his bloody fingers . . .

"Mine, Sylvie," he said. "It's *my* blood!" There was something hilarious about it. He started to laugh. He turned to look back toward the showers, back to where Sylvie's voice had come from. The bit of sky he saw had cleared. There was a bright rainbow arching above the concrete wall, blue to red, and a fainter one above it, red to blue. He took one step toward the courtyard, and *everything* went red, then black.

"I'm a shape-shifter, Sylvie."

"You dope!" She was changing the dressing again. Her face hovered above him. She was biting her lip. He could see that she was working hard not to cry.

"Where are we?" He was lying on a bed made of two chairs pushed together and covered with a white sheet. He had been undressed. He lay naked under another sheet.

"Someplace, that's all. I took you to a doctor. It's the first time in my whole life I missed a booking, and it's *your* fault, little man."

"Did I tell you what happened?"

"Yeah. Who needs those crooks, anyway?" She kissed him on the forehead. "Milo . . . you were a champ. I can't believe how brave you are. I'm sorry I put you in that spot."

"I'm a shape-shifter, Sylvie. I remember everything. I breathed, and I remembered my sister, Dede. I did stuff for her. I was keys and credit cards and . . . *money* . . ." He stopped talking. Then he said it again: "The money!"

Sylvie looked away. "I'm sorry." The room was dark behind her.

"It was *you!*"

Sylvie shrugged.

"You were the money!" Milo said.

"I do stuff for Lenny sometimes. He had a press going somewhere, all set to turn out fifties, hundreds, deluxe items, Milo, really good work, but they needed some front money. I provided Lenny with a sample, is all. Like a grant application, see? They weren't ready to print yet. He was just supposed to show it and collect the advance. Then he pays me. Anyway, that was the idea."

"Was that Lenny *Zorn?*"

"What?" Sylvie looked at him with a slightly shocked expression, like a hoer who has struck an unexpected rock in a well-cultivated field. "Lenny *who* . . . ? Wait a minute. How do you know about that? You mean *Zorn's Lemma*, don't you? How did you hear about Zorn's Lemma?" She stared at him, her mouth hanging open. Slowly, it closed. Her brows descended. She grabbed Milo's arm. "You little rat! What do you think you are, some kind of a damned *spy?* You were listening in on me and the doctor, weren't you? You knew the whole time, didn't you?"

"*You're* a shape-shifter, too," Milo said, "you and Devore! What do you want from me?"

"God damn you, Milo! What is it with you? You think I want to hurt you? You think I want to use you? What the hell do I need you for? I'm rich as fucking Croesus!"

"You *already* used me, Sylvie. You nearly got me killed. Why?"

"I needed some money, damn it, that's all. And *you're* the one who nearly got you killed. You stabbed yourself, for pity's sake! It was a simple setup. Failsafe!"

"You blew the borders, Sylvie. The guy said they were fuzzy."

"Well, it couldn't be *perfect*, could it? The guy would think it was regular dough. You think you could do better?"

Milo knew fifty-dollar bills pretty well. Sylvie insisted on cash from her puppet show patrons, and Milo had been doing most of the collecting lately. They often paid with a fifty, which was a headache for Sylvie to break, but easy for the sponsors to carry. In his mind, Milo could see a fifty dollar bill as clearly as he could see his own hand. He could *look* right through it and all around it, on both sides. He felt the pattern of ink on its surface as if it were a network of varicose veins. He felt the rough surface like a hairy pelt, like his own hairy pelt.

Suddenly, he felt the sheets collapse around him, his skin shrivel and implode. He felt as if he were becoming all tongue, and the tongue was sucking an unripe fruit that sucked back at him, drying him out till he winked out of existence entirely. It was very quiet, very dark, very still. *Milo* was gone. There was only a vague *electricity*, a tension, slight at first, but it became more and more irritating, until it was unbearable. Then he burst into mundane awareness again, like a frogman bursting above the surface, gasping, shocked by the sudden light and air.

"Damn you," Sylvie was saying. "Don't you ever, *ever* do that again."

"Don't tell him *that*," a low voice said from behind Sylvie. A door had opened. Light poured in. Someone was walking in, silhouetted in the doorway. Milo could see only that he was a small man and, from the light flashing from his head, that he wore glasses. "His father told him that once. He won't like to hear that, will you, Milo? Tell the truth now, Sylvie. Was he any good?"

Sylvie was fuming. She swallowed. She breathed. She calmed herself for the small man's sake. "He's fabulous. I've never seen anything like it."

"That's what I figured." The man came closer and put his hand on Sylvie's shoulder. "You know who I am, don't you, Milo?"

"Sure," Milo said. "You're Dr. Devore."

"That's right, Milo. I don't know much *materia medica* anymore, but I can still do first aid okay. How's the belly?"

"I'm all right. Do you own *The Grass and Trees*?"

"You're a smart boy, Milo. We don't want to hurt you. We don't want to use you. In fact, it's exactly the opposite, you know?"

Now he made out the drapes, the rolltop, the chairs he lay on. "I jumped out that window. I was a bat. I flew down."

"I didn't expect that," Devore said. "I didn't know you were still here. I wasn't in a position to know *anything* at that moment."

"The doctor was a *rainbow*," Sylvie said.

Devore clucked his tongue. "Ach! My small talent!"

"But you called Sylvie," Milo said.

"Yes, I had already called her to tell her about you, you know? She was on her way here when she saw you fly down. She improvised."

Milo started to tremble. He shut his eyes, then forced them open again. "Sylvie, Dr. Devore, there's something I remembered from a long time ago . . ."

Devore cut in, "You don't have to tell us this, Milo. You don't have to say anything you're not ready to say . . ."

"I killed my sister. I killed Dede." He began to sob.

Sylvie kissed him on the forehead and cradled his head in her arms. "It wasn't you, little man. It was a mountain lion. You were a little boy! You couldn't control it! You didn't know anything! Dede was an *operator*! She would have used you up and thrown you away like an old Kleenex!"

Devore spoke in his low, soothing voice, the voice that held Milo just this side of panic when he retold his dreams. "We knew, Milo. All that talking in your sleep! We followed the leads. We traced your history, well, up until you disappeared, after your sister's death.

"Milo, you were no more at fault for Dede's death than you were for wrecking that car in your dream about the Dumpster. For a child as young as you were then, shape-shifting is the same as dreaming, you know? It's all make-believe!"

"She was my big sister! She took care of me!" Milo's face, like his throat, was tightening into a knot. "She read to me. She tucked me in at night."

Sylvie shook her head. "Milo! Milo!"

All at once, it was too much—the arch of Sylvie's brow, Dr. Devore's sad smile, the sweet warmth of Sylvie's hand stroking his head. Milo braved the pain in his stomach and bolted upright. "I'm no good! I'm some kind of monster, is all! You don't understand!"

Sylvie tried to hold him, but he swung his legs over the side of the makeshift bed and pulled away from her. He flinched and started to double over, then braced himself and ran to the window, clutching the sheet about him. Devore followed him.

Milo pressed his forehead against the glass. "She wanted me to kill that guy. It wasn't the first time. The guy wouldn't do what she wanted. I was the only one who always did what she wanted—except just that once. I didn't mean to kill her, though!"

"You didn't kill her, you jerk!" Sylvie was crying too now. "It was the goddamn mountain lion, Milo! It wasn't your fault!"

Milo pushed open the window and leaned out. He let his head hang, panting, dripping tears. Tears slid down his nose and cheeks and chin. "I could jump. I deserve it."

Devore's hand on his shoulder. "You already tried that, Milo. Inside you, you're too smart, you're too good to do that to yourself. When you jump, Milo, you fly! In your heart you know you must live. Dede *used* you, Milo. You protected yourself."

"Why are you so good to me? Nobody's ever been so good to me!" He turned around, trusting them to see his face, so ugly, he thought, with tears and spasms of grief.

"We just want to look out for you, Milo." Sylvie cupped his cheek, wet with tears, in the palm of her hand, and all at once his ugliness vanished: he didn't look like anything, he was only this touch, this gazing into Sylvie's gaze. It wasn't a shape-shifter's trick but the most human thing he had ever felt.

"We all look out for one another," she said. "We're all finding out what we are, what we can do."

Like a knot pulled free, Milo's breath shuddered once, then steadied. The sheet wrapped around him opened slightly: his movement had irritated the wound, and blood trickled below the dressing.

"Take a good look, Sylvie," Devore said, "and next time you need pin money, ask me."

"I said I was sorry," she said, "and I meant it. But I can't be told what to do, not by you, not by anybody. I got my own plans, you know. Your fellowship won't take me to Edinburgh for the Fringe Festival or Amsterdam for the Festival of Fools or to the Carnival in Venice or any of those other big venues that are goddam dying to experience the Moon and Stars!" Devore half-smiled, looked down, and shook his head.

Milo blinked. For a split second, Dede was there, pale and doughy. She was lingering in the corner with a hangdog look. She wasn't as big as Milo used to think, nor as subtle. As his big sister, then as a nameless forbidden dream, she had been mighty: volcanoes, oceans, storming skies, or a hot dry wind. Now she was just a shadow. "You used me, Dede! I was just a baby, and you were my big sister! Oh, Dede, you shouldn't have done that! That wasn't right!" Bookish, wan, small-hearted, eaten up by jealousy and desire, she simply faded from view.

Milo had been whispering to himself, he realized. He caught Sylvie and De-vore's eyes on him; they looked away, embarrassed for him perhaps, but Milo didn't mind that they had heard him. *We all look out for one another,* Sylvie had said. *We!* There were others like him! Milo breathed. Milo breathed. He was *innocent.*

He felt like someone suddenly waking after a long fever and rummaging for food. "Tell me about the painting in the waiting room. Is it . . . *somebody?*"

"Yes," said Devore. "I guess you'd have to say so. At least, she *was* somebody. She seems to be caught in there, like Narcissus staring into the lake. We can't get her back. Maybe she doesn't *want* to come back."

Milo shut his eyes; tears streamed down his cheeks.

Sylvie squeezed his hand. "Milo . . . ?"

"I was caught like that, Sylvie. I belonged to Dede, even though she was dead. She said I'd be all hers forever."

"Milo, you're going to be all *yours* forever," said Devore. "We're going to see to it. We're going to teach you everything. And you're going to teach us, too."

"Yes, I will." Milo took Sylvie's other hand in his. He looked at her, then at Devore, then Sylvie again. He had the extraordinary sensation of recognizing *him-self* behind their eyes. "I love you, both of you!" he blurted out.

Sylvie smiled. Her face sparkled so, he thought he was looking at the moon and stars.

snowball in Hell

BRIAN STABLEFORD

*Critically acclaimed British "hard-science" writer Brian Stableford is the
author of more than thirty books, including* Cradle of the Sun, The Blind
Worm, Days of Glory, In the Kingdom of the Beasts, Day of Wrath, The
Halcyon Drift, The Paradox of the Sets, The Realms of Tartarus, The
Empire of Fear, The Angel of Pain, *and* The Carnival of Destruction,
Serpent's Blood, *and* Inherit the Earth. *His short fiction has been collected
in* Sexual Chemistry: Sardonic Tales of the Genetic Revolution. *His non-
fiction books include* The Sociology of Science Fiction, *and, with David
Langford,* The Third Millennium: A History of the World AD 2000–3000.
*His acclaimed novella "Les Fleurs du Mal" was a finalist for the Hugo
Award in 1994. His most recent books are the novels* The Fountains of
Youth *and* Architects of Emortality. *A biologist and sociologist by training,
Stableford lives in Reading, England.*

*Stableford may have written more about how the ongoing revolutions in
biological and genetic science will change the very nature of humanity itself
than any other writer of the last decade. Here he takes a penetrating look
at what really makes us human — and comes to a few conclusions that may
surprise you.*

From the very beginning I had a niggling feeling that the operation was going
to go wrong, but I put it down to nerves. Scientific advisors to the Home Office
rarely get a chance to take part in Special Branch operations, and I always knew
that it would be my first and last opportunity to be part of a real Boy's Own
adventure.

I calmed my anxieties by telling myself that the police must know what they
were doing. The plan looked so neat and tidy when it was laid out on the map
with colored dots: blue for the lower ranks, red for the Armed Response Unit,
green for the likes of yours truly and black for the senior Special Branch officers
who were supervising and coordinating the whole thing. We deeply resented the
fact that the reports from the surveillance team had been carefully censored, ac-

cording to the sacred principle of NEED TO KNOW, but there seemed to be no obvious reason to suppose that the raid itself wouldn't go like clockwork.

"But what are they actually supposed to have *done*, exactly?" one of my juniors was reckless enough to ask.

"If we knew *exactly*," came the inevitable withering reply, "we wouldn't need to include you in the operation, would we?"

I could tell from the reports we had been allowed to see that the so-called investigation into the experiments at Hollinghurst Manor had been a committee product, and that no one had ever had a clear idea exactly what was going on. Warrants for surveillance had been obtained on the grounds that the Branch's GE-Crime Unit had "compelling reasons" to suspect that Drs. Hemans, Rawlingford, and Bradby were using "human genetic material" in the creation of "transgenic animals," but it was mostly speculation. What they really had to go on was gossip and rumor, and the rumors in question seemed to me to be suspiciously akin to the urban legends that had sprung up everywhere since the tabloids' yuck factor campaign had finally forced the government to pass stringent laws controlling the uses of genetic engineering and to set up the GE-Crime Unit to enforce them. Once it existed, the Unit had to do *something* to justify its budget, and its senior staff obviously reckoned that whatever was going on at Hollinghurst Manor had to be yucky enough to allow them to get that invaluable first goal on the great scoresheet.

It seemed to me that the whole affair had always had a faint air of surreal absurdity about it. The illegal experiments that Hemans and his fellows were alleged by rumor to be conducting were unfortunately conducive to silly jokes, ranging from lame references to flying pigs to covert references to the raid as the Boar War. Even the Home Office joined in the jokey name game; it was some idiot undersecretary who decided to code-name the "target" Animal Farm, borrowing the most popular of the derisory nicknames it had accumulated during the surveillance. It was, alas, my own people who took some delight in explaining to anyone who would listen why the people inside had allegedly taken to calling the project "Commoner's Isle." (It was because the place where the ambitious scientist had conducted his unsuccessful experiment in H. G. Wells's *The Island of Doctor Moreau* had been called Noble's Isle.) When the inspector in charge of the Armed Response Unit assured us at the final briefing that the people in the manor didn't have a snowball's chance in hell of getting past his men he couldn't understand why the men from the ministry snickered. (In *Animal Farm*, Snowball is the idealist who gets purged by the ruthless Napoleon.)

In a sense, the inspector was right. When the Animal Farmers found out that they were being raided and ran like hell they *didn't* have a snowball's chance in hell of getting past his men. Unfortunately, that didn't make them stop running and give up.

The part of the plan that included me involved uniformed policemen smashing their way through the main door and making as many arrests as possible while my people went for the computers and any paper files that were still around. We didn't expect to get all the records out—we'd been told at the briefing that Hemans, Rawlingford, and Bradby would probably start crunching diskettes and reformatting hard disks as soon as they were roused from sleep—but we figured that there'd be more than enough left to salvage. They were scientists, after all; keeping backup files ought to have been second nature to them.

Unfortunately, it wasn't that simple. The Animal Farmers didn't bother with shredding and reformatting; they just torched the place. Nobody had thought to give us gas-masks, and the fumes that met us in the corridors of the manor were so foul and instantly dizzying that we should have known that they were toxic and turned back immediately. Actually, that was what most of my colleagues did. I was the only thoroughly stupid one. I kept on going, determined to get to the office that was my designated objective. It was hopeless—but it was my one and only Boy's Own adventure and I hadn't been trained to an adequate sense of self-preservation. I was just on the point of blacking out when I heard shots fired in the woods, and realized just how badly awry the operation had gone.

I would certainly have died if I hadn't been pulled out of the fume-filled corridor—and by the time my own team got around to noticing that I was missing it was far too late for *them* to do anything constructive. It was the Animal Farmers who saved me—not the scientists who had actually set up the illegal experiments, but a handful of lesser beings who'd turned back when the shooting started in the hope of finding a safer way out on the other side of the house.

I woke up with a terrible headache and stinging eyes, coughing weakly. It felt for a minute or two as though my lungs had been so badly scorched that I could no longer draw sufficient oxygen from the warm and musty air that I drew into them—but that, mercifully, was an illusion born of distress.

I managed to crack open my weeping eyes just long enough to perceive that it was too dark to see what was happening, then shut them tight and hoped that the pain would go away.

Somebody lifted my head and pressed a cup of water to my lips. I managed to take a few sips, and decided not to protest when a female voice said: "He's okay."

While I lay there collecting myself a different female voice said: "It's no good. There's no way out up there. As the fire draws air upward our supply's being renewed via the tunnel to the old icehouse, but there's no way through the grilles. They haven't been opened in half a century and the locks are rusted solid. Hemans should have taken care of them years ago. He should have known that this would happen one day."

"There's a hacksaw in the toolbox," a male voice put in. "If we get to work right away . . ."

"They were *shooting*, Ed," the second female told him. "They're trying to wipe us out, just like Bradby always said they would. They don't even want to ask the questions, let alone hear the answers. They just want us dead. Even if we could get to the lakeside, they're probably waiting for us. We wouldn't stand a chance."

"What chance have we got if we wait here, Ali?" Ed replied. "Even if the fire burns all day tomorrow, they'll come to pick over the ruins as soon as they can. If they're still in the woods by then, they'll certainly be all around what's left of the house. The tunnel's our only chance. If we can just get to Brighton, to a crowd. Then London . . . we can pass, Ali. I know we can. We can hide."

I wanted to tell them that nobody wanted to shoot them, that they'd be fine if they sat tight until it was safe to go upstairs and then surrendered, but I knew that they wouldn't believe me. What on earth had made them so paranoid? And why had the ARU men opened fire?

"Ed's right," said the female who'd given me the water to drink. "If they have the icehouse covered, we're dead—but all the exits upstairs will still be useless when the fire dies down. We have to start work on the grilles. Somebody ought to watch this one, though—he's not badly hurt. If he doesn't come at us, he'll give us away."

"We should have left him where he was," Ed opined, bitterly. "He's not going to be any use as a hostage, is he?"

"He wouldn't be any use as a corpse," the unnamed female retorted. "He'd just be an excuse for branding us as murderers, justifying the ethnic cleansing."

Ethnic cleansing! What on earth had Bradby been telling them? And who the hell were they, anyway? I couldn't help jumping to the obvious conclusion, but I refused to entertain it. I was supposed to be a scientist, not some sucker who'd swallow any urban legend that happened along.

"We don't know that the others who came in with him all got out," Ali pointed out.

"No, we don't," the other female admitted, "but we did know that he hadn't. If we'd left him where he went down, it *would* have been murder."

"It would have been suicide," said Ed, "But Kath's right, Ali. They'd have *called* it murder. They'll have to justify the shooting somehow."

I coughed again, partly because I needed to and partly because I wanted to remind them that I had a voice too, even if I hadn't yet obtained sufficient control of it to formulate meaningful utterances.

"You'd better stay with him, Ali," the male voice said. "If he gets aggressive, hit him with this."

At that stage, I could only guess what "this" might be—some time passed before I was able to make out that it was an axe—but I wasn't about to make any trouble. I was still trying to convince myself that I hadn't breathed in enough poison to be mortally hurt, and that I hadn't done sufficient damage to my lungs to prejudice my long-term ability to breathe. I heard two sets of feet moving away across a stone floor, and I forced myself to relax, collecting myself together by slow degrees.

Eventually, I felt well enough to begin to feel angry. I stopped being grateful for being alive and started resenting the fact that I had come so close to dying. Setting the fire had been an act of pure spite on the part of the mad scientists. People like me—law-abiding geneticists, that is—had collaborated with the Home Office in drawing up the careful legislation which presumably defined whatever the Animal Farmers were doing as unacceptable, but they had simply been too arrogant to comply with the law. On top of that, it seemed, they had taken the view that if we wouldn't countenance the research then we couldn't have the results. They had obviously decided that if they had to go to jail, they'd take all their hard-won understanding with them—and woe betide anyone who got in their way.

Once I began to get angry, I didn't stop. If Hemans and Co. really had been transplanting human genes into the embryos of pigs in order to turn out simulacra of human beings, it was unforgivable, and the murderous fire was piling injury on insult. I'd never been convinced that the Animal Farmers *had* done what Special Branch said they'd done—I'd gone through the doors of Commoner's Isle still wondering whether it was all going to turn out to be a big mistake, exaggerated out of all proportion—but the fact that the place had been torched with such alacrity suggested that they must have done *something* that they were desperate to conceal.

Unless, of course, that was what we were *supposed* to think. There was still a possibility that we were all being taken for a ride—that it was all a game, intended to discredit the GE-Crime Unit and the Home Office advisors before they began to get their act together.

While I lay there being angry, it occurred to me that I might be in a uniquely good position to find out exactly what the Animal Farmers were *really* up to.

When I was finally confident that I could hold a conversation, I had already formulated my plan of campaign.

"Is Ali short for Alison?" I asked. I was able to open my eyes by then, and they had accustomed themselves to the near-darkness sufficiently to let me see that the person standing guard over me was a blond teenager, perhaps fourteen or fifteen years of age. She was too young to be a lab assistant, so I seized upon the hypothesis that she was probably someone's daughter. We had been warned that some of the live-in staff at the manor had children, but we hadn't expected them to be abandoned when the shit hit the fan.

"Alice," she informed me, stiffly.

"As in Wonderland?" I quipped, hoping to help her relax.

"As in *Through the Looking Glass*," she retorted. It didn't seem to be worthwhile asking her what the difference was.

"I'm Stephen Hitchens," I told her. "I'm not a policeman—I'm a geneticist, currently employed as an advisor to the Home Office."

"Bully for you," she said, dryly. I wondered whether she might be older than she looked—maybe sixteen or seventeen—but I concluded in the end that natural insolence, like puberty, probably arrived ahead of its time nowadays.

"Why did the scientists set fire to the house, Alice?" I asked.

"Why did armed police surround it?" she countered.

"None of this is your fault, or mine," I assured her. "I was just trying to recover the records of the experiments the scientists had done. They should have made sure that you were safe before they started the fire. They're not your friends, Alice. Did your parents work for Dr. Hemans?"

"In a manner of speaking," she told me, as if relishing a hidden irony.

"What manner of speaking?" I demanded, although I could hardly help seeing the obvious implication. If she wasn't the child of someone on the staff, she had to be one of the experimental subjects—or, I reminded myself, someone *pretending* to be one of the experimental subjects.

"The kind of work you do in a sty," she replied, casually confirming the inference she must have known I'd take. "The kind of work where your pay arrives in a trough."

If it was true, then she certainly had come from Wonderland—but was it

true? Wasn't it far more likely to be a lie, a carefully constructed bluff? Was it
to hear this, I wondered, that I had been hauled out of the corridor and brought
down here into near-darkness? Could the Animal Farmers be using me, trying
to convince me that they had achieved far, far more than they had? If so, what
should my policy be? Should I run with the bluff and let her make her pitch,
or challenge her and refuse to believe that she was anything but what she appeared to be?

"You're telling me that you're not human?" I said, just to make sure that she
wasn't just making a joke. I knew as soon as I'd said it that I'd framed the rhetor-
ical question wrongly. What she'd actually told me was that her parents weren't
human.

"Like hell I am," she said. Like Snowball in hell, I couldn't help thinking. Play
along, I told myself. Find out what she has to say.

"So you think you're human," I conceded. "You can certainly pass for it,
probably in a far brighter light than this—but if your parents really were pigs,
you must understand that other people might not see things the same way." As
I said *that* I realized that her creators or drama-coaches—must already have put
it in much stronger terms. That was why Ed and Kath had been so paranoid
about the possibility of being shot down—that and the fact that the ARU really
had opened fire.

"I know what I see when I look in a mirror," Alice told me, perhaps to make
sure that I'd understood how clever her reference to *Through the Looking Glass*
was. "It's not the image of itself that's important, of course—it's the fact that there's
an eye to see it. A human I—and I don't mean e-y-e."

Cogito, ergo sum, she might have said, if she—or whoever had written her
script—hadn't been so anxious about the need to stay viewer-friendly. I hadn't
enough anger left to prevent me from wondering whether Special Branch might
always have known exactly how human Animal Farmers' experimental subjects
looked, and whether their senior officers might have taken it upon themselves to
decide that the ministry didn't need to know until the shooting was well and truly
over. If they had, and my captors knew it—or even if they hadn't and my captors
merely believed it—I might be in deeper trouble than I thought.

"What about Ed and Kath?" I asked. "Are they like you?"

They're human," Alice assured me, in a tone that left little doubt as to what
kind of human she was talking about. She was telling me, in her own perverse
way, that they were the kind of humans who were made as well as born: the kind
which started off as a fertilized ovum in a sow's belly before the genetic engineers
got to work.

Dr. Moreau had remade beasts in his own image by means of surgery, but
modern scientists had much cleverer means at their disposal—and the degree of
success they might be expected to achieve was far greater. I had to remind myself
again that all of this could be a bluff run by a thoroughly human child, and that
I was only playing along to see how the story would go.

Alice had relaxed a little since she first started talking, but the way she held her
shadowed head and the way she gripped the axe she'd been ordered to hit me
with if I got out of line suggested that she wasn't about to get careless. Now that
she'd made her first impression, she was busy reminding herself that she was stuck

in a cellar beneath a burning building with a man who might be dangerous. All in all, philosophical discussion seemed the safest way to build a modicum of trust.

"You think you're human because you have a human mind: because you're self-aware?" I said, earnestly—trying with all my might to sound like the dull and harmless scientist I actually was (and am).

"All animals are self-aware," Alice replied, calmly. "I'm aware that I'm human. I love and respect my fellow men, no matter what the circumstances of their birth may have been."

"How do you feel about pigs?" I asked.

"I love and respect them too," she replied. "Even the ones which aren't human. I don't eat pork—or any other meat, come to that. How do you feel about pigs, Dr. Hitchens?"

I eat pork, I also eat bacon, and all kinds of other meat, but it didn't seem diplomatic to talk about that. "I don't think pigs are human, Alice," I told her. "I don't think they can become human, even with the aid of transplanted genes."

Her answer to that certainly wasn't the kind of answer I'd have expected from an ordinary teenager, or even an extraordinary one. "How did humans become humans, Dr. Hitchens?" she asked me. "A handful of extra genes, obligingly de-livered up by mutation, do you suppose? Perhaps—but perhaps not. Just because a human and a chimpanzee only share ninety-nine per cent of their genes, it doesn't neccessarily follow that the variant one per cent are solely responsible for the differences. Even if they are, it's not a matter of different protein-making stocks. It's a matter of *control*. The one per cent is almost entirely homeotic." She might have been parroting something Hemans or one of his coworkers had said, but I didn't think so. She seemed confident that she was making sense, and that she understood that import of her argument—but she hesitated, just in case I didn't.

"Go on," I said, interestedly. The invitation was enough to set her off with the bit between her pearly, neatly aligned teeth.

"Most of what it took to turn apes into men," she told me, as if it were a matter of absolute certainty, "was a handful of modifications to the ways in which genes were switched on and off as the cells of the developing embryo became specialized. You don't need dozens of extra genes to grow a bigger brain. All you need is for a few more unspecialized cells to become brain cells. You don't need dozens of extra genes to make a clever hand or to stand upright, either. What you need is for the cells that differentiate into bone and muscle to distribute themselves in slightly different ways within the developing embryo. Becoming human isn't so very difficult, once you get the hang of it. Cows could do it. Sheep too. Lions and tigers, horses and elephants, dolphins and seals. Dogs, probably; cats, maybe; rats perhaps; birds probably not. You have to get right down to snakes and sharks before you can say that there's no chance at all. We all start out as eggs, Dr. Hitchens, and every egg that can make a pig or a donkey or a goat can probably make a human, if it only invests enough effort in shaping the brain and the hand and the backbone. That may be an unsettling thought, but it's true."

It *was* an unsettling thought. I had already thought it, and it had already un-settled me—but the fact that Alice was prepared to confront me with it, perhaps on behalf of Hemans, Rawlingford, and Bradby, but more probably on her own initiative, was even more unsettling.

I reminded myself again that it might be a lie, a careful hoax intended to persuade me, falsely, that the men from Commoner's Isle had mastered godlike powers—but if it was, it was beginning to work.

"Would you like to live as other humans do, Alice?" I asked, ostentatiously leading with my chin. "Would you like to go to school, to university, to get a job, to get married one day and have children of your own?"

"I do live as other humans do," she replied, blandly refusing to see what I was getting at. "I've been to school. I expect that I'll do all the other things when the time comes." Her tone said that she didn't expect any such thing—that she expected to be pursued and captured, shot at worst and imprisoned at best. Her tone told me that she expected to have to fight for her life, let alone her entitlements as a human being, and that she wasn't about to take any bullshit from me while she had an axe in her hands.

"I'm not sure that you'll be allowed to do anything that other teenagers routinely do, Alice," I admitted, figuring that it was best to pose as the honest man I really am. "The scientists who shaped your brain, hand and backbone were breaking the law. That's not your fault, of course, but the fact remains that you're the product of illegal genetic engineering. The law doesn't consider you to be a human being—nor do the vast majority of human beings. All the things you hope you'll be able to do depend on the willingness of human society to admit you as a member, and that willingness simply isn't there. There's a sense, you see, in which it isn't enough just to define yourself as human—it's for human society as a whole to decide who belongs to it and who doesn't."

"No, it isn't," she replied, promptly. "White people once refused to define black people as human, and German gentiles once refused to define Jews as human, but that didn't make the black people or the Jews any less human than they were. The only people who became less human because of those refusals were the people who tried to deny humanity to others. They were the ones who were refusing to love and respect their fellow men, the ones who weren't acting morally."

She was carrying the argument better than any fourteen-year-old should have been able to, and she wasn't trying to conceal the fact. I couldn't help wondering whether that might be a mistake, if she ever got the chance to plead her case before a wider audience. Nobody loves a smartarse, especially if the smartarse is a jumped-up pig. If you want to pass for human, you can't afford to be too good at it—and, as Alice had stubbornly insisted on pointing out, real humans frequently aren't very good at it at all.

"Do you think the scientists who made you were acting morally?" I asked. "They knew what kind of world they were bringing you into. They knew what would happen—to you as well as to them—when they were found out, and they must have known that they'd eventually be found out."

"I could understand a slave who was reluctant to bear children who would also be slaves," Alice replied, "but I can also understand those who didn't refuse. They knew that they were human, and that their children were human too, and they had to hope that the fact would one day be recognized. To have refused to bear children would have been giving in to evil, consenting to its effects."

"Why do you think the men who made you destroyed their records, Alice?" I asked. "Why do you think they were so eager to burn them that they endangered your life—not to mention mine?" Because they didn't want anyone to know the true extent of their success, I told myself. Because they wanted to be able to run this bluff.

"Because they wanted to be able to use their knowledge as a bargaining chip," Alice said. "For our benefit as well as their own. If you'd got the records, you'd have put a stop to everything. Because you didn't, we still have something up our sleeves." She seemed to think that it was a reasonably good argument—which implied that in spite of all her hard-won sophistication she really was the mere child she appeared to be.

Theoretically, I thought, an animal embryo modified to replicate human form ought to develop as neotenously as a human embryo, and an animal brain modified to accommodate all that a human brain could accommodate ought not to be educated anymore rapidly. If so, Alice shouldn't be any cleverer than a fully human child reared in similarly exceptional circumstances—but without access to her school records, I knew that it would be dangerous to take too much for granted, or too little.

"No one will bargain with them, Alice," I lied. "They broke the law, and they'll be punished. Perhaps it's best if their discoveries are lost. That way, no one will be able to repeat their error."

"That's silly, Dr. Hitchens," Alice said, calmly. "If it's a mystery, that will just make more people interested in solving it. And if it's not so very difficult to solve . . ."

She left it there, as if it were some kind of threat. She was still trying to convince me, in her own subtle fashion, that my world had just ended and that another had just begun, and that if she and all her fugitive kind were slaughtered by the ARU's guns they would be martyrs to a great and unstoppable cause.

"Have you read *The Island of Dr. Moreau*, Alice?" I asked.

"Yes," she said.

"What do you think of it?"

"It's a parable. It tells us that it takes more than a little cosmetic surgery and a few memorized laws to make people—any people—human. That's true. Whether humans are born or made, the test of their humanity is their behavior, their love and respect for their fellow humans."

"How many naturally born humans would pass that test, do you think?" I asked.

"I have no idea," she replied. "Lots, I hope."

"Would I pass it?" I asked.

"I have to hope so," she said, casually, "don't I, Dr. Hitchens? But I don't actually know. What do you think?"

"There wasn't supposed to be any shooting," I told her. "The police were supposed to put everyone under arrest. If your makers hadn't set fire to the house and told everyone to scatter and run, no one would have been hurt. Then, the matter of your humanity could have been decided in a proper and reasonable manner."

I hoped that I was telling the truth, but I had a niggling feeling that the plan to which I'd been admitted wasn't the whole one. The GE-Crime Unit *had* called up the Armed Response Unit.

"Well," said Alice, "that isn't the way things worked out, is it? It seems to me that the matter of our humanity, as you put it, has already been decided. You'll never be sure, of course, that you've got us all. Even if Ed and Kath can't get to the old icehouse, and even if they run into the police when they do, you'll never be sure how many of us got out under the noses of your surveillance unit before they figured out that the apparently obvious wasn't necessarily true."

She was definitely feeding me a line there, but I couldn't tell whether she was feeding it to me because it was false, or because it was true. I thought the time had come for me to make a grab for the axe and take control of the situation. I was probably right—or would have been, if I'd actually succeeded.

I suppose, on reflection, that I was lucky she only swiped me with the flat of the blade. If she'd hit me that hard with the edge, she could easily have fractured my skull.

When I woke up again I was in a hospital bed. My head wasn't aching anymore and my eyes weren't stinging, but I felt spaced-out and bleary. It took a few minutes for me to remember where I might have been, if things had worked out differently.

I learned, in due course, that the fire brigade had found me while searching the cellars for survivors and had handed me over to the paramedics before midnight. Unfortunately, the medication they'd fed me ensured that I didn't wake up again until thirty-six hours later, so I'd missed all of the official postmortems as well as the remainder of the action—but the urgency with which the Unit moved to debrief me reassured me that the adventure still had a long way to run.

"There were three of them," I told Inspector Headley. "I only saw one of them, and it was too dark to see her features clearly. She had blond hair, cut to shoulder length, and very even teeth that caught what little light there was when she smiled. I couldn't swear that I'd be able to recognize her again, dead or alive. Her name was Alice. She called the others Ed and Kath. They were trying to reach an old icehouse on the edge of the lake, but the tunnel had been blocked off. Did you get them?"

"What else did they tell you?" Inspector Headley countered, jesuitically.

That wasn't a game I intended to play. "Did you get them?" I repeated.

"No," he conceded, reluctantly. "But the tunnel was still blocked off—had been for the best part of a century. Nobody got out that way."

"But you didn't pick up three stragglers in the house?"

"No," he admitted, "but if you'll pardon my pointing it out, Dr. Hitchens, I'm the one who's supposed to be debriefing you. Yes, they *could* have been piglets— and no, we wouldn't have believed that if we hadn't had the autopsy reports your colleagues carried out on the ones we shot. Personally, I'd have passed every one of the corpses as human, and I wasn't the only one who wouldn't believe otherwise until your colleagues came back to us with the results of the DNA-tests—but we didn't capture any of the piglets alive. Now, would you mind telling me exactly what happened to you?"

"Not at all," I said. "But there's one thing I need to know. Was the shooting always part of the plan? Did you always intend to kill the children?"

He seemed genuinely shocked. "Of course not," he said. "They wouldn't stop. They just kept on running. They *were* warned."

The problem was, I knew, that they'd already been warned. They'd had far too many warnings for their own good.

I recited the whole story, in as much detail as I could remember, into Headley's tape-recorder. I watched his expression becoming more troubled as I spoke, and I gathered that Special Branch were just as confused as I was as to what might be real and what might be bluff.

"This has turned into a real can of worms," he told me, when he'd switched the recorder off. "We don't know how many of the piglets might be missing. We've been waist-deep in lawyers ever since we got Hemans and his friends under lock and key, including lawyers claiming to represent your fugitive friend and her alleged litter-mates."

"How many died?" I asked.

"Only seven," he said, so weakly that it was obvious that seven was either far too many or far too few. "Three of them were real humans. Unfortunate, but it *was* their own fault. I think they wanted us to shoot, to put us in the wrong. I think Hemans told those kids to keep running no matter what because he *knew* that some of them would be killed. Cynical bastard."

I had already told him that Bradby had warned his experimental subjects that an attempt might be made to wipe them out, but I wasn't convinced that the warning had been cynical. It seemed to me that he might have been honestly concerned, and rightly so. If Alice and the others *had* got away . . .

"We might not find it easy to prove in court that the other four *weren't* real humans," I told Headley, although that news must already have been broken to him. "Did the DNA-tests throw up any evidence that they were transgenics?"

Headley shook his head. He seemed to understand the implications of the question. Transplanting human genes into animals was clearly and manifestly illegal, but if Alice had told me the truth, that wasn't what had been done to her. If Alice really was a pig through and through, genetically speaking, then there was a slim possibility that Hemans' lawyers could argue that what he and his colleagues had done wasn't illegal at all. And if Alice was as human as she seemed to be in every respect except genetically, her lawyers might have a field day trying to establish exactly what the law might and ought to mean by "human"—assuming that the Unit ever caught up with her.

Whatever had been intended, it was obvious that the raid had been a colossal cock-up. It would be up to the minister to pull everyone's irons out of the fire, and to look at the broader implications of what we now knew. Men like me were the minister's eyes and brains, so it would be up to us to figure out what the real implications of the Animal Farm fiasco might be. Governments had been brought down by matters of a far more trivial nature and it was too late to hope that the situation could be contained. The cat was already out of the bag—or the pig from the poke.

Headley admitted, when I questioned him further, that without the records that had gone up in smoke, there was no way to know for sure how many experimental "piglets" there had been. They had always been kept inside, away from the prying eyes of the surveillance team, who wouldn't have recognized them for what they were if and when they'd caught glimpses of them. Their creators and the piglets themselves knew the real number, but no one would ever know whether any figure they might offer was to be trusted. Now that we knew for sure that the piglets could pass for human, at least while they were still alive and kicking, we had to consider the possibility that some of them already were passing, in Brighton or in London, or anywhere at all.

If my evidence could be taken at face value, at least three piglets had escaped. Headley told me that other debriefings had produced evidence that at least two more, both female, might have evaded their pursuers in the woods behind the manor house. He was enough of an intellectual to understand my observation that it added up to a better breeding population than God had placed in Eden or Lot had led from Sodom.

As a scientist, of course, I wasn't at all sure of that—engineered organisms hardly ever breed true, and it was perfectly possible that even if the ersatz girls could produce offspring, the offspring in question might have snouts and tails—but we had to consider the worst possible case. Bringing human-seeming babies out of a sow's womb might sound no more likely than making silk purses out of sow's ears, but we had moved into unknown territory, scientifically speaking. What did I know, given that I had never dabbled in illicit experimentation? What did any of us know, unless and until Hemans, Rawlingford, and Bradby condescended to enlighten us?

I suppose that I was lucky to be kept on the project, given that I'd ended up in hospital, but I was needed. I'd been brought in to analyze data, not to conduct interrogations, but the changed circumstances necessitated my taking a new role. My conversation with Alice had put me one up on my colleagues, so I was hustled out of the hospital with a bagful of pills as soon as the doctors could be persuaded to let me go.

"We haven't charged them yet," Headley explained to me, while I was being taken to the police station where Hemans, Rawlingford, and Bradby were to be questioned. "At the moment, they're supposed to be cooperating voluntarily with our enquiries. We're keeping in mind the possibility of charging them with arson, kidnapping and child molesting, but we want to see how they and their lawyers are going to play it before we go in hard. If they're prepared to come clean and tell us where their backed-up data is—assuming they do have backups some-where—we might still be able to tidy up the mess."

It seemed like a reasonable assumption to me, although I wasn't sure how reasonable our mad scientists would prove to be.

I went into the interview with Hemans thinking that I was the only one on our side who'd actually thought the matter through, and the only one to have grasped the full complexity of the issue. I thought that I might be approaching the high-point of my career—a taller peak than I had ever dreamed of scaling—if only I could keep my wits about me.

The interview was being videotaped, of course, but the tape wouldn't be admissible in court.

I couldn't measure the exact combination of emotions that mingled in Hemans' expression as he looked at me, but there was at least a little contempt and at least a little distaste. I couldn't understand that. When I'd first met Hemans, way back in '06, he'd been working in the public sector himself, helping to tidy up the loose ends of the Human Genome Project—but even before the HGP had delivered its treasure, its workers were being sucked into private enterprise. Comparative genomics was supposed to be the next big thing. I didn't hold it against Hemans that he had jumped ship, and I couldn't see any reason why he'd hold it against me that I hadn't.

It was obvious by '06 that the attempts that had been made to patent human gene sequences and develop diagnostic kits based on HGP sequencing data wouldn't bear much commercial fruit in the immediate future, because they'd be tied up in the courts for years. The precedents for patenting animal genes had, however, been established by the Harvard oncomouse and all the disease-models that had followed in its wake. Given that all mammals had homologues for at least ninety-five percent of human genes, the obvious thing for ambitious biotech companies to do was to steer around the moral minefield by concentrating their immediate efforts on what could be done with animals. Pigs were already contributing organs for xenotransplantation, so they were a natural target for sequencing and potential exploitation, and there was nothing surprising in the fact that Hemans and his coworkers had decided to concentrate their efforts in that direction. What was surprising, though—and disturbing—was that they'd decided to cross the line that the European Court had drawn regarding the uses to which human genes could be put. What was even more surprising, to me—and even more disturbing—was that the way Hemans looked at me when I sat down to question him showed not the slightest trace of guilt or shame. That made me wary, and wariness made me even more punctilious than usual.

"First of all, Dr. Hemans," I said, carefully, "I've been asked to apologize on behalf of His Majesty's Government for the unfortunate deaths which occurred during the course of the police raid on Hollinghurst Manor. The police had reason to believe that a serious breach of the law had taken place, and they were proceeding in full accordance with the law, but they deeply regret the fact that so many of those fleeing the building refused to stop when challenged, forcing the Armed Response Unit to open fire."

"Never mind the bullshit, Hitchens," he countered, curling his lip disdainfully. "Are they going to charge us, and if so, what with?"

"Okay," I said, easing my tone according to plan, in order to imply—falsely, and perhaps not very convincingly—that there would be no more bullshit. "They haven't decided yet whether to charge you, or with what. There are several different schools of thought. As soon as they catch up with one of the escapers—and they will—the hawks will want to move. You have until then to make your offer, if you have one to make."

"Aren't you the one who's supposed to be making offers?" Hemans countered.

"No," I said. "I'm not. You're the one who knows whether the experiments being carried out at Hollinghurst Manor were illegal, and to what extent. You're the one who knows the identities of the children who were living in the house, and the extent of the irregularities surrounding the registration of their births, their schooling, and whatever else might come up. If you want to offer explanations and excuses before the police draw their own conclusions, you'd best do it quickly."

He didn't laugh, but he didn't seem to be intimidated either. "You must have determined the identities of the ones you killed," he said.

"On the contrary," I replied, carefully. "The police haven't been able to match the bodies with any public records or any missing persons. That is, in itself, cause for concern. There is no record of any application for the custody of any children having been made by you or any of your colleagues, so the police are completely at a loss to understand how they came to be resident in the house—or why, given that they were resident in the house, they don't appear to have attended school or to be registered with a doctor, or . . ."

"This is a waste of time," Hemans interrupted. "If you're just going to pretend that you don't know anything, I think I'll wait for the formal interrogation, when my lawyer can decide how little I ought to say."

"I spoke to one of the children in the aftermath of the fire," I told him, abruptly. "She seemed to believe that she wasn't the product of a human womb. Did you tell her that?"

"We told her the truth about her origins," he answered.

"And what was the truth?" I asked.

"That she was the product of a scientific experiment."

"An illegal experiment?"

"Certainly not. Neither I nor any of my colleagues has ever transplanted any human genes into any other animal. We have been exceedingly careful to work within the existing law."

"But you haven't published any of your work," I pointed out. "You haven't applied for any patents. Even by private sector standards, that's unusually secretive."

"We haven't published because the work wasn't complete," Hemans retorted, "and now, thanks to your murderous interference, it never will be. We haven't applied for any patents because we aren't ready. Not that it's any of your business—or anyone else's. Rawley, Brad, and I were able to finance this project ourselves."

"The police didn't set fire to the house," I pointed out. "It isn't their fault that your equipment and records were destroyed. You did that yourselves."

"No, we didn't," Hemans lied. "The fire was an accident—the result of the confusion generated by the raid."

"Your work wasn't merely self-funded," I pointed out, not wishing to pursue that particular red herring. "It was clandestine. You've made every possible effort to keep it secret. You seem to have been using children as experimental subjects—children of whom there is no official record of any kind. Even if they were your own children, that would be illegal. If they aren't . . . there's a great deal that requires explanation."

"And you already know what the explanation is, so we'd make better progress if you cut to the chase."

"I'm sorry," I said, "but I don't know any such thing. I don't know that the story the girl gave me was anything but a pack of lies, cooked up to make your work seem much more successful than it was. We can't interrogate the dead, so we have no way to know whether the individuals identified by genetic fingerprinting as pigs in human form were capable of speech, let alone rational thought. I'm certain in my own mind that the scene in the cellar was staged—how else would the three of them have been able to disappear, given that the exit they were ostensibly aiming for was blocked?"

"Maybe they found another," Hemans said. "Who did you talk to?"

"She called herself Alice."

"We all called her Alice," he assured me. "She's not among the dead, then? And she did get away from the gunmen?"

"They *will* find her," I told him. "Whoever and whatever she is, she can't hide. Wherever she went, there'll be a trail. This is the twenty-first century. *Nobody* can hide for long."

"That includes the people chasing her," he pointed out. "It's one thing to surround a house in the middle of a wood for one night only, and quite another to conduct a nationwide manhunt for weeks on end. How many are you looking for?"

"How many were there?"

He still didn't smile, but he knew that that was one of the best cards he held up his sleeve. If we'd been fooled into thinking there were at least seven, when there were really only four, we might keep searching for a long time—and he was right about the difficulty of hiding a nationwide manhunt, whether that was the right word for it or not.

"Why did you do it?" I asked him, abruptly. "It's such a strange thing to attempt. Why did you even *try?*"

"You're a geneticist yourself, Dr. Hitchens," he replied. "You, of all people, should understand."

I thought I did. I thought that now was the time to show him that I did. "If you really did do it," I said, "I can only conclude that it was by accident. I can't imagine that you had the least idea when you started out just how successful your experiment in Applied Homeotics would be. I can only suppose that you started out trying to figure out what the limits of embryonic plasticity were, and that you wouldn't have dared to superimpose a human anatomical template on the pig embryos if you had realized that it would work so spectacularly. Once you found out what the babies were actually capable of, you must have been thrown into a quandary, unable to decide what to do next—so you simply carried on, monitoring their development in secret, not knowing when or how to stop. You must have been grateful when the police finally made their move, taking the matter out of your hands."

He looked at me with what seemed to me to be a new respect. "You keep saying *if*," he pointed out, "but you don't really believe there's an if, do you? You know perfectly well that Alice is the real thing."

"I don't *know* it," I told him, truthfully. "You're the one that *knows*. How clever is she, do you think?"

"Not so very clever," he told me feigning slight reluctance. "Precocious, but not so very far from the norm. Only human. But her parents *were* pigs, Dr. Hitchens. We did do it—and we're prepared to defend ourselves in any court you care to haul us into. We're prepared to defend it all the way. I like your label, by the way. *Applied Homeotics* sounds so much more dignified than Brad's *homeoboxing*. If you know that that's what it is, you must also know that it isn't going to go away. Not now."

Hemans didn't just mean that he and his colleagues were prepared to defend the legality of their experiment and the merits of their new biotechnology. He meant that they were prepared to defend the humanity of its first products. Maybe he *was* just a little bit grateful to have his hand forced, but he had decided long ago exactly how he would play it when the forcing started. He might have fallen into a godlike role by accident, but he had accepted the responsibility that went with it. Our side hadn't, yet. Our side had gone in blind and trigger-happy. That wasn't my fault, but I'd have to carry the can along with everyone else if things continued to get more and more screwed-up.

"I also know that it can't be *merely* a matter of tweaking development times," I said. "Pigs may have homologues of ninety-eight point six percent of human genes, but that still isn't enough. Whatever you told Alice, you had to make up a sub-stantial fraction of the remainder. Maybe you copied the sequences from a contig library, used YACs to multiply them and then delivered them into the embryo by retrovirus, but that doesn't make it legal. Human sequences are human sequences, even if you build them base by base, and when you transplanted them into pig embryos you broke the law."

"We didn't transplant anything," Hemans insisted. "We didn't break any laws. Put us in the dock and we'll prove it. But you don't want to do that, do you?"

"That depends," I hedged—but his lip curled again, and I knew that I had to play the game more openly than that. "You have to give me more," I went on. "You have to give me some idea of what you actually did, if you didn't transplant the human sequences."

"Why should I?" he countered, bluntly.

I wasn't speaking for myself, but I had to make the offer. "Because we might still be able to put this thing away," I told him. "We might not be able to unmake the discovery, but we might be able to save ourselves from its consequences, at least for a while."

"No," he said, wearily as well as firmly. "We can't. We thought about it—Rawley, Brad and I—but we decided that we couldn't. We're not policemen, Dr. Hitchens, we're not politicians and we're not lawyers. We couldn't put it away, and we still can't. Not because it wouldn't do any good, although it wouldn't, but because it simply wouldn't be right. We're not going to cooperate, Dr. Hitchens. We're not going to take it to the bitter end. They're human, and every ovum produced by every animal on our farms and in our zoos is potentially human. That's the way it is, and we can't just ignore the fact. We can't make any deal that doesn't make the whole matter public."

"You were the ones who never published," I pointed out. "You were the ones who kept on working in secret."

"It *wasn't finished*," he told me. I was sure that he wasn't trying to wriggle out of it.

"If you're telling the truth," I told him, "it never will be. But you still have to convince me of that."

He was still looking at me with faint disgust, because of what he thought I'd become, but in the end he had to loosen up. Like me, he didn't have any alternative.

Even when we'd reviewed the tape and gone through it step by step, the senior Special branch men and most of the Home Office staff still didn't get it.

"Okay," said the Unit's top man, "so the one you talked to was smart and kind of cute—but she isn't ever going to get to court, let alone to daytime TV. She's a pig. An animal. We *can* send her to the slaughterhouse. We can get rid of them all, if we decide that's the appropriate thing to do."

"We wouldn't necessarily have to go that far," one of the junior ministers put in. "Once people know what she really is, that will color everyone's view of her. It doesn't matter how cute or clever she is, nobody is going to make out a serious case for making anymore like her. Let's not throw the baby out with the bathwater here."

What he meant, of course, was "let's not throw the bathwater out with the baby." He figured that there might be useful purposes to which the technics might be put—secret purposes, of course, if the legal advisors decided that the whole area was legally out of bounds, but government-approvable purposes nevertheless. He was thinking about designing ultra-smart animals for use as spies and soldiers. He'd probably been a fan of the wrong kind of comic books in his youth. He wasn't thinking Boy's Own adventures; he was thinking *Reality is What You Can Get Away With.*

The permanent under-secretary knew better, of course. "She was right about the records," he observed, reflectively. "The fact that we failed to recover them makes it a mystery. As soon as the rumor spreads that you can turn animal embryos into passable human beings with standard equipment and a chicken-feed budget, everybody and his cousin will be curious to know how it's done. We left it far too late to make our move—and I'm talking years, not weeks. We should have applied the new laws as soon as we had reason to believe that they'd been broken."

"Without the records," I said, quietly, "there's no way to be sure that even the new laws *have* been broken. And that makes it an even better mystery."

"She's a *pig*, Hitchens," the plain-speaking policeman pointed out. "She's a pig that looks like a little girl. If that isn't illegal genetic engineering, what is?"

"If Hemans is telling the truth," I said, "Applied Homeotics isn't genetic engineering in the legal sense at all. He had to make up most of the missing one point four percent somehow, but if he'd simply tried to transplant or import it he'd probably have failed in exactly the same way that most other attempts to transplant whole blocks of genes have failed. Assuming that what he told me was true—and I'm inclined to believe him—his way is *much* better, and it's not against the law. If this ever gets to court, we might have to hope that the backup records really have been destroyed—because if they haven't, and Hemans, Rawlingford, and Bradby can use them to mount a successful defense, we're going to look really stupid."

"That won't happen," the permanent under-secretary said. "If they want any kind of life after acquittal, they'll make a deal. They'll give us their secrets *and* they'll sign a nondisclosure agreement. The real question is whether other people will be able to duplicate their work anyhow, guided by the knowledge — or even the rumor — that it's *possible*."

"Who but the wackos would want to?" asked the chief inspector. "Do you really think the world is full of people who want to turn out imitation human beings? Even the worst kinds of animal liberation lunatics aren't about to start clamoring for every piglet's right to walk on two legs and wear a dress. This is the real world. Some animals are a hell of a lot more equal than others, and we're them, and that's the way it's going to stay."

It was time to cut through the bullshit to the real heart of the matter. "You're not taking Alice seriously enough," I told them. "You haven't listened properly to what she and Hemans said. Suppose she's right. Suppose she isn't a pig pretending to be a human. Suppose she really is a human."

"She's not," the policeman said, flatly. "Genetically, she's a pig. End of story."

"According to her," I pointed out, "genetics doesn't enter into it. Human is as human does — and her brothers and sisters were the ones who got gunned down because they didn't believe that their fellow men would open fire on a bunch of unarmed children. Without her school records, and until she consents to be tested again, we can only guess at her IQ, but on the evidence of my conversation and Hemans' assurances I'd be willing to bet that it's a little bit higher than the average teenager's. You haven't yet begun to consider the implications of that fact."

"*If* pigs in human form are smarter than real humans, that's all the more reason for making sure that all the world's pigs stay in their sties," the man from Special Branch insisted. The minister was content to listen, for the time being.

"If Hemans is telling the truth," I went on, disregarding the policeman's interruption, "he and his colleagues didn't need to transplant any genes to make her human. DNA analysis of the dead bodies supports that contention. The difference between a human being and a chimpanzee, as Alice pointed out, is very small. The most important differences are in the homeotic genes — the genes that control the expression of other genes, thus determining which cells in a developing embryo are going to specialize as liver cells or as neurons, and how the structures built out of specialized cells are going to be laid out within an anatomical frame. If you have an alternative control mechanism which can take over the work of those controlling genes, they become redundant — and as long as the embryo you're working with has the stocks of genes required to make all the specialized kinds of cell you need, you can make any kind of an embryo grow into any form you required. You could make human beings out of pigs and cows, tigers and elephants, exactly as Alice said — and *vice versa*."

"That's bullshit," the policeman said. "You've said all along that they had to make up the difference. We have to have the extra genes that make us human."

"That's true," I agreed, wondering how simple I could make it, and how simple I'd need to make it before he could understand. "And until today I'd assumed, just as you had, that the extra genes would have to be transplanted, or that they'd have to synthesized from library DNA and imported — but that almost never works with whole sets of genes, because mere possession of a gene is only part of the story. You have to control its expression — and that's what Applied Homeotics is all about. We've become so accustomed to genetic engineering by transplantation that we've lost sight of other approaches—but Hemans and his friends are lateral thinkers. We didn't get to be human by having genes transplanted into us—we *grew* the new genes *in situ*. Only a few million of the three billion base pairs in the human genome are actually expressed, but it's an insult to the rest to call it junk DNA, the way we used to. Most of it is satellite repeat sequences, but in between the satellites there are hundreds of thousands of truncated genes and pseudogenes, all of them in a constant state of crossgenerational flux because of transposon activity.

"Pigs may only have homologues of ninety-eight point six percent of our genes, but they also have homologues of almost all the protogenes making up the difference. Those protogenes are not only present within the pig genome, they're mostly in the right sites. Hemans, Rawlingford, and Bradby didn't need to transplant any human DNA—all they had to do was tweak the pig DNA that was already in place. And as Alice said when she had me trapped in Wonderland, if you can do it to a pig, you can do it to a cow—and given that the common ancestor relating us to rats and bats seems to be more recent than the one relating us to pigs, you can probably do it to a hundred or a thousand other species."

"It still sounds like bullshit to me," the policeman repeated, as if he were some obstinate DNA satellite hopelessly intent on taking over an entire genome.

"You may not like its implications, Chief Inspector," I said, tiredly, "but that's not enough to make it bullshit. I don't know *exactly* how Hemans did it, because he isn't going to tell us until he gets some guarantees, but I already know how I'd go about trying to copy the trick, now that I know that it can be done. Transforming and activating the protogenes is probably the easy part, given that every sequencer in the world is avid to learn how to write as well as read the language of the bases. I'm pretty sure I could figure out a way to do that. If I could also figure out a way to delay an embryo's phylotypic stage—that's the moment at which the control of an embryo's development is transferred from the maternal environment to the embryo's own genes—I might be able to stop the homeotic genes kicking in at all. Given that the onset of the phylotypic stage is much later in some species than others, that doesn't seem be any great hurdle to leap. A careful inspection of the research Hemans, Rawlingford, and Bradby published before they got together at Hollinghurst Manor suggests that they were probably using human maternal tissue as a mediator in the embryonic induction process. That's not genetic engineering, of course—there's no law against interspecific transplantation of mature tissues or the use of human somatic cells in tissue cultures. Believe me, sir: Applied Homeotics is a whole new field of biotechnology. None of the existing rules apply."

"So you're telling me that every fucking farm animal in the realm—not to mention every household pet—is potentially human?" The Special Branch man was looking at me with as much contempt and distaste as Hemans had, but with even less justification.

"No," I said, patiently. "I'm telling you that the embryos they produce as parents are now potentially human. It still adds a whole new dimension to the ethics of animal usage, but we don't yet know how far that dimension extends. We can be reasonably sure that birds and reptiles don't have the required stocks of protein-template genes, and some of the smaller mammals probably don't have them either, but the question of where the limits of potential metamorphosis actually lie is a minor one. The point is that unless we're the victims of a monstrous hoax, humanity is determined almost entirely by the development of the embryo. If so, Hemans is right. Alice and all her kind are as human as you or I. An even more important question, of course, is what this kind of technology might allow us to make of human beings."

I paused for effect, but nobody jumped in with an exclamation of astonishment. They were all waiting, guardedly, to see what came next.

"We, after all, are merely *nature's* humans," I told them. "We're a product of the rough-and-ready process of natural selection, and control of the expression of *our* genes has been left to other genes. Homeotic genes were never an ideal solution to the problem of embryo-formation — they were just the best improvisation that DNA could come up with on its own. Alice's humanity is the product of relatively unskilled artifice — and the evidence we've so far seen suggests that relatively unskilled artifice might already be the slightly better maker of men. If it isn't, then it certainly will be, just as soon as we bring our ingenuity fully to bear on the problem.

"The genie's out of the bottle, gentlemen. We can pass all the laws we like against the genetic engineering of human beings, and we can make sure if we care to that what Hemans, Rawlingford, and Bradby have actually done to pig embryos will in future fall within the scope of those laws — but that won't alter the fact that human beings and the world they have made are imperfect in more ways than any of us would care to count, and that Hemans, Rawlingford, and Bradby have found a new way to allow us to set to work on those imperfections. If Alice is telling the truth, we've already passed through the looking-glass, and there's no way back. You might be able to stop the animals walking and talking, but you won't be able to stop the people. If a mere pig can be a better human than any of us, *imagine what our own children might become, with the proper assistance!*"

The minister and his junior nodded gravely, but that was just the legacy of good schooling by their image-consultants. The chief inspector looked dumbfounded. The permanent under-secretary was the only one who was keeping up, after his own crude fashion. "You're talking about building a Master Race," he said reflexively. If in doubt, hoist a scarecrow.

"I'm talking about D-I-Y supermen," I told him, frankly. "I'm talking about something that can be done with standard equipment on a chicken-feed budget, after a little bit of practice on the family pet. I'm talking anarchy, not mad dictators. If you intend to make a deal with the Three Musketeers, you need to know what cards they're holding. It's still conceivable that they're bluffing, and that Alice was just feeding us a line, but I can't believe that — and if they're *not* bluffing, the old world has already ended. The GE-Crime Unit will catch up with the runaways eventually, but it's already too late. Their story has been told, and *will* be told, again and again and again."

Nobody told me I was crazy. The policeman might have lacked imagination, but he wasn't stupid enough to continue to argue that his reflexive prejudices were worth more than my educated judgment. "We could still shoot the lot," he muttered—but he knew, deep down, that it wouldn't do the trick, even if that option could be put back on the agenda.

"What *can* we do?" asked the permanent under-secretary, who had already moved reluctantly onto the next stage.

I knew that it wouldn't be easy to persuade him, but nobody ever said that working for the Home Office was going to be easy. The instinct of government is to govern, to take control, to keep as tight a hold on the reins as humanly possible.

"Basically," I said, "we have two options. We can be Napoleon, or we can be Snowball. Neither way will be easy—in fact, I suspect that all hell has already been let loose—so I figure that we might as well try to do the right thing. For once in our lives, let's not even try to stand in the way of progress. I know you're not going to be grateful for the advice, but my vote is that we simply let them all go and let them get on with it."

"Let public opinion take care of them, you mean," the junior minister said, still trying his damnedest to misunderstand. "Let the mob take care of them, the way they take care of child molesters."

"No," I said. "I mean, let artifice take its course. Let the pioneers of Applied Homeotics do what they have to, and what they can. Even the pigs."

It *wasn't* easy to persuade them, but Hemans and his collaborators had a battery of lawyers on their side as well as reason and stubbornness, and in the end, the situation simply wasn't governable, even by the government. Eventually, I made them see that.

They weren't grateful, of course, but I never expected them to be. Sometimes, you just have to settle for being right.

By the time I saw Alice again she was twenty-two and famous, although she never went anywhere without her bodyguards. She came to my lab to see what I was working on, and to thank me for the small part I had played in winning her precarious freedom.

"You did save my life," I pointed out, when we'd done the tour and had time to reflect.

"That was Ed and Kath," she admitted. "They were the ones who picked you up and dragged you down the stairs. All I did was hit you with the axe when you tried to grab it."

"But you hit me with the flat bit, not the edge," I said. "If you'd hit me with the edge, I'd be dead—and so, I suspect, would you."

"They really wanted to kill us all," she said, as if it were still very hard for her to comprehend.

"Only some of them—and only because they didn't understand," I told her, hoping that it was the truth. "None of us understood, not even Hemans, Rawlingford, and Bradby, although they'd had longer to think about it than anybody else. None of us really understood what it meant to be human, because we'd never had to explore the limits of the argument before—and none of us understood what scope there was for us to be more than human. We simply didn't realize how easy it is to be creative, once you have the basic stock of protein-producing genes—

and protogenes—to work with. Maybe we should have, given what we knew about the diversity of Earthly species and the unreliability of mutation as a means of change, but we didn't. We needed a lesson to bring it home to us. How does it feel to be accepted as human just as the species is becoming obsolete?"

"My children will have the same chances as anyone else's," she pointed out. I wasn't so sure about that. She was now as human as anyone else, in law as well as in fact, but there were an awful lot of people who hadn't yet conceded the point. *My* children, on the other hand, really would have opportunities of which I had never dreamed ten years before; the people who wanted to reserve the privileges of creativity to imaginary gods wouldn't be able to stop me making sure of that.

"I was sorry to hear about Hemans," I said. Hemans had been taken out by a sniper eight months before. I had no reason to think that he and Alice were particularly close, but it seemed only polite to offer my condolences.

"Me too," she said. "It always upsets me to hear about my friends being shot."

"What happened at the manor really wasn't a conspiracy," I told her, although I'd never been *entirely* sure. "It was a genuine mistake. It's in the nature of Armed Response Units that they sometimes make mistakes, especially when they're working in the dark."

"I remember Dr. Hemans saying the same thing, afterward," she admitted. "But some mistakes work out better than others, don't they?" She wasn't talking about the wayward ways of mutation. She was talking about the freak of chance that made me go on when I should have turned back, and the one that had made Ed and Kath pause to pull me out of the fume-filled corridor and down the cellar steps to safety. She was talking about the freak of chance that had made me go on when things got tough at the Home Office, blowing my career in government in order to make sure that nobody could put a lid on it even for a little while, and that the government couldn't even make a convincing show of governing the unfolding situation. She was talking about the mistake that Hemans and his colleagues had made when they decided to try something wildly ambitious, and found that it succeeded far too well. She was talking about the fact that science proceeds by trial and error, and that the errors sometimes turn out to be far more important than the intentions.

"Yes they do," I agreed. "If that weren't the case, progress wouldn't be possible at all. But it is. In spite of the fact that every significant advance in biotechnology is seen by the vast majority of horrified onlookers as a hideous perversion, we do make progress. We keep on passing through the looking glass, finding new worlds and new selves."

"You've been practicing," she said. "Do you really think you can talk yourself back into the corridors of power?"

"Not a snowball's chance in hell," I admitted. "But I did my bit for the revolution when I had the chance—and there aren't many of nature's humans who can say that, are there?"

"There never used to be," Alice admitted. "But things are different now. Human history is only just beginning."

on the orion line

STEPHEN BAXTER

Here's a harrowing look at the proposition that a soldier's first duty is to survive, *especially when trapped behind enemy lines, especially when those "enemy lines" are in the depths of interstellar space, thousands of light-years from Earth, and you have no ship, no shelter, and only a quickly dwindling supply of air. In those circumstances, you do anything you have to do to survive—if you're strong enough to actually do it, that is!*

Like many of his colleagues here at the beginning of a new century— Greg Egan comes to mind, as do people like Paul J. McAuley, Michael Swanwick, Iain Banks, Bruce Sterling, Pat Cadigan, Brian Stableford, Gregory Benford, Ian McDonald, Gwyneth Jones, Vernor Vinge, Greg Bear, David Marusek, Geoff Ryman, and a half dozen others—British writer Stephen Baxter has been engaged for the last ten years or so with the task of revitalizing and reinventing the "hard-science" story for a new generation of readers, producing work on the Cutting Edge of science which bristles with weird new ideas and often takes place against vistas of almost outrageously cosmic scope.

Baxter made his first sale to Interzone *in 1987, and since then has become one of that magazine's most frequent contributors, as well as making sales to* Asimov's Science Fiction, Science Fiction Age, Zenith, New Worlds, *and elsewhere. He's one of the most prolific new writers in science fiction, and is rapidly becoming one of the most popular and acclaimed of them as well. Baxter's first novel,* Raft, *was released in 1991 to wide and enthusiastic response, and was rapidly followed by other well-received novels such as* Timelike Infinity, Anti-Ice, Flux, *and the H. G. Wells pastiche—a sequel to* The Time Machine—The Time Ships, *which won both the John W. Campbell Memorial Award and the Philip K. Dick Award. His other books include the novels,* Voyage, Titan, Moonseed, *and the three books of the* Mammoth *sequence, and the collections* Vacuum Diagrams: Stories of the Xeelee Sequence *and* Traces. *His most recent books are the novels* Manifold: Time, Manifold: Space, *and a novel written in collaboration with Arthur C. Clarke,* The Light of Other Days.

The *Brief Life Burns Brightly* broke out of the fleet. We were chasing down a Ghost cruiser, and we were closing.

The lifedome of the *Brightly* was transparent, so it was as if Captain Teid in her big chair, and her officers and their equipment clusters — and a few low-grade tars like me — were just floating in space. The light was subtle, coming from a nearby cluster of hot young stars, and from the rivers of sparking lights that made up the fleet formation we had just left, and beyond *that* from the sparking of novae. This was the Orion Line — six thousand light years from Earth and a thousand lights long, a front that spread right along the inner edge of the Orion Spiral Arm — and the stellar explosions marked battles that must have concluded years ago.

And, not a handful of klicks away, the Ghost cruiser slid across space, running for home. The cruiser was a rough egg-shape of silvered rope. Hundreds of Ghosts clung to the rope. You could see them slithering this way and that, not affected at all by the emptiness around them.

The Ghosts' destination was a small, old yellow star. Pael, our tame Academician, had identified it as a fortress star from some kind of strangeness in its light. But up close you don't need to be an Academician to spot a fortress. From the *Brightly* I could see with my unaided eyes that the star had a pale blue cage around it — an open lattice with struts half a million kilometers long — thrown there by the Ghosts, for their own purposes.

I had a lot of time to watch all this. I was just a tar. I was fifteen years old.

My duties at that moment were non-specific. I was supposed to stand to, and render assistance any way that was required — most likely with basic medical attention should we go into combat. Right now the only one of us tars actually working was Halle, who was chasing down a pool of vomit sicked up by Pael, the Academician, the only non-Navy personnel on the bridge.

The action on the *Brightly* wasn't like you see in Virtual shows. The atmosphere was calm, quiet, competent. All you could hear was the murmur of voices, from the crew and the equipment, and the hiss of recycling air. No drama: it was like an operating theater.

There was a soft warning chime.

The captain raised an arm and called over Academician Pael, First Officer Till, and Jeru, the commissary assigned to the ship. They huddled close, conferring — apparently arguing. I saw the way flickering nova light reflected from Jeru's shaven head.

I felt my heart beat harder.

Everybody knew what the chime meant: that we were approaching the fortress cordon. Either we would break off, or we would chase the Ghost cruiser inside its invisible fortress. And everybody knew that no Navy ship that had ever penetrated a fortress cordon, ten light-minutes from the central star, had come back out again.

One way or the other, it would all be resolved soon.

Captain Teid cut short the debate. She leaned forward and addressed the crew. Her voice, cast through the ship, was friendly, like a cadre leader whispering in your ear. "You can all see we can't catch that swarm of Ghosts this side of the cordon. And you all know the hazard of crossing a cordon. But if we're ever going to break this blockade of theirs we have to find a way to bust open those forts. So we're going in anyhow. Stand by your stations."

There was a half-hearted cheer.

I caught Halle's eye. She grinned at me. She pointed at the captain, closed her fist and made a pumping movement. I admired her sentiment but she wasn't being too accurate, anatomically speaking, so I raised my middle finger and jiggled it back and forth.

It took a slap on the back of the head from Jeru, the commissary, to put a stop to that. "Little morons," she growled.

"Sorry, sir—"

I got another slap for the apology. Jeru was a tall, stocky woman, dressed in the bland monastic robes said to date from the time of the founding of the Commission for Historical Truth a thousand years ago. But rumor was she'd seen plenty of combat action of her own before joining the Commission, and such was her physical strength and speed of reflex I could well believe it.

As we neared the cordon the Academician, Pael, started a gloomy count-down. The slow geometry of Ghost cruiser and tinsel-wrapped fortress star swiveled across the crowded sky.

Everybody went quiet.

The darkest time is always just before the action starts. Even if you can see or hear what is going on, all you do is think. What was going to happen to us when we crossed that intangible border? Would a fleet of Ghost ships materialize all around us? Would some mysterious weapon simply blast us out of the sky?

I caught the eye of First Officer Till. He was a veteran of twenty years; his scalp had been burned away in some ancient close-run combat, long before I was born, and he wore a crown of scar tissue with pride.

"Let's do it, tar," he growled.

All the fear went away. I was overwhelmed by a feeling of togetherness, of us all being in this crap together. I had no thought of dying. Just: let's get through this.

"Yes, *sir!*"

Pael finished his countdown.

All the lights went out. Detonating stars wheeled.

And the ship exploded.

I was thrown into darkness. Air howled. Emergency bulkheads scythed past me, and I could hear people scream.

I slammed into the curving hull, nose pressed against the stars.

I bounced off and drifted. The inertial suspension was out, then. I thought I could smell blood—probably my own.

I could see the Ghost ship, a tangle of rope and silver baubles, tingling with highlights from the fortress star. We were still closing.

But I could also see shards of shattered lifedome, a sputtering drive unit. The shards were bits of the *Brightly*. It had gone, all gone, in a fraction of a second.

"Let's do it," I murmured.

Maybe I was out of it for a while.

Somebody grabbed my ankle and tugged me down. There was a competent slap on my cheek, enough to make me focus.

"Case. Can you hear me?"

It was First Officer Till. Even in the swimming starlight that burned-off scalp was unmistakable.

I glanced around. There were four of us here: Till, Commissary Jeru, Academician Pael, me. We were huddled up against what looked like the stump of the First Officer's console. I realized that the gale of venting air had stopped. I was back inside a hull with integrity, then—

"Case!"

"I—yes, sir."

"Report."

I touched my lip; my hand came away bloody. At a time like that it's your duty to report your injuries, honestly and fully. Nobody needs a hero who turns out not to be able to function. "I think I'm all right. I may have a concussion."

"Good enough. Strap down." Till handed me a length of rope.

I saw that the others had tied themselves to struts. I did the same.

Till, with practiced ease, swam away into the air, I guessed looking for other survivors.

Academician Pael was trying to curl into a ball. He couldn't even speak. The tears just rolled out of his eyes. I stared at the way big globules welled up and drifted away into the air, glimmering.

The action had been over in seconds. All a bit sudden for an earthworm, I guess.

Nearby, I saw, trapped under one of the emergency bulkheads, there was a pair of legs—just that. The rest of the body must have been chopped away, gone drifting off with the rest of the debris from *Brightly*. But I recognized those legs, from a garish pink stripe on the sole of the right boot. That had been Halle. She was the only girl I had ever screwed, I thought—and more than likely, given the situation, the only girl I ever would get to screw.

I couldn't figure out how I felt about that.

Jeru was watching me. "Tar—do you think we should all be frightened for ourselves, like the Academician?" Her accent was strong, unidentifiable.

"No, sir."

"No." Jeru studied Pael with contempt. "We are in a yacht, Academician. Something has happened to the *Brightly*. The 'dome was designed to break up into yachts like this." She sniffed. "We have air, and it isn't foul yet." She winked at me. "Maybe we can do a little damage to the Ghosts before we die, tar. What do you think?"

I grinned. "Yes, sir."

Pael lifted his head and stared at me with salt water eyes. "Lethe. You people are monsters." His accent was gentle, a lilt. "Even such a child as this. You embrace death—"

Jeru grabbed Pael's jaw in a massive hand, and pinched the joint until he squealed. "Captain Teid grabbed you, Academician; she threw you here, into the yacht, before the bulkhead came down. I saw it. If she hadn't taken the time to do that, she would have made it herself. Was *she* a monster? Did *she* embrace death?" And she pushed Pael's face away.

For some reason I hadn't thought about the rest of the crew until that moment. I guess I have a limited imagination. Now, I felt adrift. The captain—dead?

I said, "Excuse me, Commissary. How many other yachts got out?"

"None," she said steadily, making sure I had no illusions. "Just this one. They died doing their duty, tar. Like the captain."

Of course she was right, and I felt a little better. Whatever his character, Pael was too valuable not to save. As for me, I had survived through sheer blind chance, through being in the right place when the walls came down: if the captain had been close, her duty would have been to pull me out of the way and take my place. It isn't a question of human values but of economics: a *lot* more is invested in the training and experience of a Captain Teid—or a Pael—than in *me*.

But Pael seemed more confused than I was.

First Officer Till came bustling back with a heap of equipment. "Put these on." He handed out pressure suits. They were what we called slime suits in training: lightweight skinsuits, running off a backpack of gen-enged algae. "Move it," said Till. "Impact with the Ghost cruiser in four minutes. We don't have any power; there's nothing we can do but ride it out."

I crammed my legs into my suit.

Jeru complied, stripping off her robe to reveal a hard, scarred body. But she was frowning. "Why not heavier armor?"

For answer, Till picked out a gravity-wave handgun from the gear he had retrieved. Without pausing he held it to Pael's head and pushed the fire button.

Pael twitched.

Till said, "See? Nothing is working. Nothing but bio systems, it seems." He threw the gun aside.

Pael closed his eyes, breathing hard.

Till said to me, "Test your comms."

I closed up my hood and faceplate and began intoning, "One, two, three..." I could hear nothing.

Till began tapping at our backpacks, resetting the systems. His hood started to glow with transient, pale blue symbols. And then, scratchily, his voice started to come through. "... Five, six, seven—can you hear me, tar?"

"Yes, sir."

The symbols were bioluminescent. There were receptors on all our suits— photoreceptors, simple eyes—which could "read" the messages scrawled on our companions' suits. It was a backup system meant for use in environments where anything higher-tech would be a liability. But obviously it would only work as long as we were in line of sight.

"That will make life harder," Jeru said. Oddly, mediated by software, she was easier to understand.

Till shrugged. "You take it as it comes." Briskly, he began to hand out more gear. "These are basic field belt kits. There's some medical stuff: a suture kit, scalpel blades, blood-giving sets. You wear these syrettes around your neck, Academician. They contain painkillers, various gen-enged med-viruses . . . no, you wear it *outside* your suit, Pael, so you can reach it. You'll find valve inlets here, on your sleeve, and here, on the leg." Now came weapons. "We should carry handguns, just in case they start working, but be ready with these." He handed out combat knives.

Pael shrank back.

"Take the knife, Academician. You can shave off that ugly beard, if nothing else."

I laughed out loud, and was rewarded with a wink from Till.

I took a knife. It was a heavy chunk of steel, solid and reassuring. I tucked it in my belt. I was starting to feel a whole lot better.

"Two minutes to impact," Jeru said. I didn't have a working chronometer; she must have been counting the seconds.

"Seal up." Till began to check the integrity of Pael's suit; Jeru and I helped each other. Face seal, glove seal, boot seal, pressure check. Water check, oh-two flow, cee-oh-two scrub . . .

When we were sealed I risked poking my head above Till's chair.

The Ghost ship filled space. The craft was kilometers across, big enough to have dwarfed the poor, doomed *Brief Life Burns Brightly*. It was a tangle of silvery rope of depthless complexity, occluding the stars and the warring fleets. Bulky equipment pods were suspended in the tangle.

And everywhere there were Silver Ghosts, sliding like beads of mercury. I could see how the yacht's emergency lights were returning crimson highlights from the featureless hides of Ghosts, so they looked like sprays of blood droplets across that shining perfection.

"Ten seconds," Till called. "Brace."

Suddenly silver ropes thick as tree trunks were all around us, looming out of the sky.

And we were thrown into chaos again.

I heard a grind of twisted metal, a scream of air. The hull popped open like an eggshell. The last of our air fled in a gush of ice crystals, and the only sound I could hear was my own breathing.

The crumpling hull soaked up some of our momentum.

But then the base of the yacht hit, and it hit hard.

The chair was wrenched out of my grasp, and I was hurled upward. There was a sudden pain in my left arm. I couldn't help but cry out.

I reached the limit of my tether and rebounded. The jolt sent further waves of pain through my arm. From up there, I could see the others were clustered around the base of the First Officer's chair, which had collapsed.

I looked up. We had stuck like a dart in the outer layers of the Ghost ship. There were shining threads arcing all around us, as if a huge net had scooped us up.

Jeru grabbed me and pulled me down. She jarred my bad arm, and I winced.

But she ignored me, and went back to working on Till. He was under the fallen chair.

Pael started to take a syrette of dope from the sachet around his neck.

Jeru knocked his hand away. "You always use the casualty's," she hissed. "Never your own."

Pael looked hurt, rebuffed. "Why?"

I could answer that. "Because the chances are you'll need your own in a minute."

Jeru stabbed a syrette into Till's arm.

Pael was staring at me through his faceplate with wide, frightened eyes. "You've broken your arm."

Looking closely at the arm for the first time, I saw that it was bent back at an impossible angle. I couldn't believe it, even through the pain. I'd never bust so much as a finger, all the way through training.

Now Till jerked, a kind of miniature convulsion, and a big bubble of spit and blood blew out of his lips. Then the bubble popped, and his limbs went loose.

Jeru sat back, breathing hard. She said, "Okay. Okay. How did he put it?—You take it as it comes." She looked around, at me, Pael. I could see she was trembling, which scared me. She said, "Now we move. We have to find an LUP. A lying-up point, Academician. A place to hole up."

I said, "The First Officer—"

"Is dead." She glanced at Pael. "Now it's just the three of us. We won't be able to avoid each other anymore, Pael."

Pael stared back, eyes empty.

Jeru looked at me, and for a second her expression softened. "A broken neck. Till broke his neck, tar."

Another death, just like that: just for a heartbeat that was too much for me.

Jeru said briskly, "Do your duty, tar. Help the worm."

I snapped back. "Yes, sir." I grabbed Pael's unresisting arm.

Led by Jeru, we began to move, the three of us, away from the crumpled wreck of our yacht, deep into the alien tangle of a Silver Ghost cruiser.

We found our LUP.

It was just a hollow in a somewhat denser tangle of silvery ropes, but it afforded us some cover, and it seemed to be away from the main concentration of Ghosts. We were still open to the vacuum—as the whole cruiser seemed to be—and I realized then that I wouldn't be getting out of this suit for a while.

As soon as we picked the LUP, Jeru made us take up positions in an all-around defense, covering a 360-degree arc.

Then we did nothing, absolutely nothing, for ten minutes.

It was SOP, standard operating procedure, and I was impressed. You've just come out of all the chaos of the destruction of the *Brightly* and the crash of the yacht, a frenzy of activity. Now you have to give your body a chance to adjust to the new environment, to the sounds and smells and sights.

Only here, there was nothing to smell but my own sweat and piss, nothing to hear but my ragged breathing. And my arm was hurting like hell.

To occupy my mind I concentrated on getting my night vision working. Your eyes take a while to adjust to the darkness — forty-five minutes before they are fully effective — but you are already seeing better after five. I could see stars through the chinks in the wiry metallic brush around me, the flares of distant novae, and the reassuring lights of our fleet. But a Ghost ship is a dark place, a mess of shadows and smeared-out reflections. It was going to be easy to get spooked here.

When the ten minutes were done, Academician Pael started bleating, but Jeru ignored him and came straight over to me. She got hold of my busted arm and started to feel the bone. "So," she said briskly. "What's your name, tar?"

"Case, sir."

"What do you think of your new quarters?"

"Where do I eat?"

She grinned. "Turn off your comms," she said.

I complied.

Without warning she pulled my arm, hard. I was glad she couldn't hear how I howled.

She pulled a canister out of her belt and squirted gunk over my arm; it was semi-sentient and snuggled into place, setting as a hard cast around my injury. When I was healed the cast would fall away of its own accord.

She motioned me to turn on my comms again, and held up a syrette.

"I don't need that."

"Don't be brave, tar. It will help your bones knit."

"Sir, there's a rumor that stuff makes you impotent." I felt stupid even as I said it.

Jeru laughed out loud, and just grabbed my arm. "Anyhow it's the First Officer's, and he doesn't need it anymore, does he?"

I couldn't argue with that; I accepted the injection. The pain started ebbing almost immediately.

Jeru pulled a tactical beacon out of her belt kit. It was a thumb-sized orange cylinder. "I'm going to try to signal the fleet. I'll work my way out of this tangle; even if the beacon is working we might be shielded in here." Pael started to protest, but she shut him up. I sensed I had been thrown into the middle of an ongoing conflict between them. "Case, you're on stag. And show this *worm* what's in his kit. I'll come back the same way I go. All right?"

"Yes." More SOP.

She slid away through silvery threads.

I lodged myself in the tangle and started to go through the stuff in the belt kits Till had fetched for us. There was water, rehydration salts, and compressed food, all to be delivered to spigots inside our sealed hoods. We had power packs the size of my thumbnail, but they were as dead as the rest of the kit. There was a lot of low-tech gear meant to prolong survival in a variety of situations, such as a magnetic compass, a heliograph, a thumb saw, a magnifying glass, pitons, and spindles of rope, even fishing line.

I had to show Pael how his suit functioned as a lavatory. The trick is just to let go; a slime suit recycles most of what you give it, and compresses the rest. That's not to say it's comfortable. I've never yet worn a suit that was good at absorbing odors. I bet no suit designer spent more than an hour in one of her own creations.

I felt fine.

The wreck, the hammer-blow deaths one after the other—none of it was far beneath the surface of my mind. But that's where it stayed, for now; as long as I had the next task to focus on, and the next after that, I could keep moving forward. The time to let it all hit you is after the show.

I guess Pael had never been trained like that.

He was a thin, spindly man, his eyes sunk in black shadow, and his ridiculous red beard was crammed up inside his faceplate. Now that the great crises were over, his energy seemed to have drained away, and his functioning was slowing to a crawl. He looked almost comical as he pawed at his useless bits of kit.

After a time he said, "Case, is it?"

"Yes, sir."

"Are you from Earth, child?"

"No. I—"

He ignored me. "The Academies are based on Earth. Did you know that, child? But they do admit a few off-worlders."

I glimpsed a lifetime of outsider resentment. But I couldn't care less. Also I wasn't a child. I asked cautiously, "Where are you from, sir?"

He sighed. "It's 51 Pegasi. I-B."

I'd never heard of it. "What kind of place is that? Is it near Earth?"

"Is everything measured relative to Earth . . . ? Not very far. My home world was one of the first extra-solar planets to be discovered—or at least, the primary is. I grew up on a moon. The primary is a hot Jupiter."

I knew what *that* meant: a giant planet huddled close to its parent star.

He looked up at me. "Where you grew up, could you see the sky?"

"No—"

"I could. And the sky was full of sails. That close to the sun, solar sails work efficiently, you see. I used to watch them at night, schooners with sails hundreds of kilometers wide, tacking this way and that in the light. But you can't see the sky from Earth—not from the Academy bunkers anyhow."

"Then why did you go there?"

"I didn't have a choice." He laughed, hollowly. "I was doomed by being smart. That is why your precious commissary despises me so much, you see. I have been taught to think—and we can't have that, can we . . . ?"

I turned away from him and shut up. Jeru wasn't "my" commissary, and this sure wasn't my argument. Besides, Pael gave me the creeps. I've always been wary of people who knew too much about science and technology. With a weapon, all you want to know is how it works, what kind of energy or ammunition it needs, and what to do when it goes wrong. People who know all the technical background and the statistics are usually covering up their own failings; it is experience of use that counts.

But this was no loudmouth weapons tech. This was an Academician: one of humanity's elite scientists. I felt I had no point of contact with him at all.

I looked out through the tangle, trying to see the fleet's sliding, glimmering lanes of light.

There was motion in the tangle. I turned that way, motioning Pael to keep still and silent, and got hold of my knife in my good hand.

Jeru came bustling back, exactly the way she had left. She nodded approvingly at my alertness. "Not a peep out of the beacon."

Pael said, "You realize our time here is limited."

I asked, "The suits?"

"He means the star," Jeru said heavily. "Case, fortress stars seem to be unstable. When the Ghosts throw up their cordon, the stars don't last long before going pop."

Pael shrugged. "We have hours, a few days at most."

Jeru said, "Well, we're going to have to get out, beyond the fortress cordon, so we can signal the fleet. That or find a way to collapse the cordon altogether."

Pael laughed hollowly. "And how do you propose we do that?"

Jeru glared. "Isn't it your role to tell me, Academician?"

Pael leaned back and closed his eyes. "Not for the first time, you're being ridiculous."

Jeru growled. She turned to me. "You. What do *you* know about the Ghosts?"

I said, "They come from someplace cold. That's why they are wrapped up in silvery shells. You can't bring a Ghost down with laser fire because of those shells. They're perfectly reflective."

Pael said, "Not perfectly. They are based on a Planck-zero effect. . . . About one part in a billion of incident energy is absorbed."

I hesitated. "They say the Ghosts experiment on people."

Pael sneered. "Lies put about by your Commission for Historical Truth, Commissary. To demonize an opponent is a tactic as old as mankind."

Jeru wasn't perturbed. "Then why don't you put young Case right? How *do* the Ghosts go about their business?"

Pael said, "The Silver Ghosts tinker with the laws of physics."

I looked to Jeru; she shrugged.

Pael tried to explain. It was all to do with quagma.

Quagma is the state of matter that emerged from the Big bang. Matter; when raised to sufficiently high temperatures, melts into a magma of quarks—a quagma. And at such temperatures the four fundamental forces of physics unify into a single superforce. When quagma is allowed to cool and expand its binding superforce decomposes into four sub-forces.

To my surprise, I understood some of this. The principle of the GUTdrive, which powers intrasystem ships like *Brief Life Burns Brightly*, is related.

Anyhow, by controlling the superforce decomposition, you can select the ratio between those forces. And those ratios govern the fundamental constants of physics.

Something like that.

Pael said, "That marvelous reflective coating of theirs is an example. Each Ghost is surrounded by a thin layer of space in which a fundamental number called the Planck constant is significantly lower than elsewhere. Thus, quantum effects are collapsed. . . . Because the energy carried by a photon, a particle of light, is proportional to the Planck constant, an incoming photon must shed most of its energy when it hits the shell—hence the reflectivity."

"All right," Jeru said. "So what are they doing here?"

Pael sighed. "The fortress star seems to be surrounded by an open shell of quagma and exotic matter. We surmise that the Ghosts have blown a bubble around each star, a space-time volume in which the laws of physics are—tweaked."

"And that's why our equipment failed."

"Presumably," said Pael, with cold sarcasm.

I asked, "What do the Ghosts want? Why do they do all this stuff?"

Pael studied me. "You are trained to kill them, and they don't even tell you that?"

Jeru just glowered.

Pael said, "The Ghosts were not shaped by competitive evolution. They are symbiotic creatures; they derive from life-forms that huddled into cooperative collectives as their world turned cold. And they seem to be motivated—not by expansion and the acquisition of territory for its own sake, as we are—but by a desire to understand the fine-tuning of the universe. *Why are we here?* You see, young tar, there is only a narrow range of the constants of physics within which life of *any* sort is possible. We think the Ghosts are studying this question by pushing at the boundaries—by tinkering with the laws that sustain and contain us all."

Jeru said, "An enemy who can deploy the laws of physics as a weapon is formidable. But in the long run, we will out-compete the Ghosts."

Pael said bleakly, "Ah, the evolutionary destiny of mankind. How dismal. But we lived in peace with the Ghosts, under the Raoul Accords, for a thousand years. We are so different, with disparate motivations—why should there be a clash, anymore than between two species of birds in the same garden?"

I'd never seen birds, or a garden, so that passed me by.

Jeru glared. She said at last, "Let's return to practicalities. *How* do their fortresses work?" When Pael didn't reply, she snapped, "Academician, you've been *inside* a fortress cordon for an hour already and you haven't made a single fresh observation?"

Acidly, Pael demanded, "What would you have me do?"

Jeru nodded at me. "What have *you* seen, tar?"

"Our instruments and weapons don't work," I said promptly. "The *Brightly* exploded. I broke my arm."

Jeru said, "Till snapped his neck also." She flexed her hand within her glove. "What would make our bones more brittle? Anything else?"

I shrugged.

Pael admitted, "I do feel somewhat warm."

Jeru asked, "Could these body changes be relevant?"

"I don't see how."

"Then figure it out."

"I have no equipment."

Jeru dumped spare gear—weapons, beacons—in his lap. "You have your eyes, your hands and your mind. Improvise." She turned to me. "As for you, tar, let's do a little infil. We still need to find a way off this scow."

I glanced doubtfully at Pael. "There's nobody to stand on stag."

Jeru said, "I know. But there are only three of us." She grasped Pael's shoulder, hard. "Keep your eyes open, Academician. We'll come back the same way we left. So you'll know it's us. Do you understand?"

Pael shrugged her away, focusing on the gadgets on his lap.

I looked at him doubtfully. It seemed to me a whole platoon of Ghosts could have come down on him without his even noticing. But Jeru was right; there was nothing more we could do.

She studied me, fingered my arm. "You up to this?"

"I'm fine, sir."

"You are lucky. A good war comes along once in a lifetime. And this is your war, tar."

That sounded like parade-ground pep talk, and I responded in kind. "Can I have your rations, sir? You won't be needing them soon." I mimed digging a grave.

She grinned back fiercely. "Yeah. When your turn comes, slit your suit and let the farts out before I take it off your stiffening corpse—"

Pael's voice was trembling. "You really are monsters."

I shared a glance with Jeru. But we shut up, for fear of upsetting the earthworm further.

I grasped my fighting knife, and we slid away into the dark.

What we were hoping to find was some equivalent of a bridge. Even if we succeeded, I couldn't imagine what we'd do next. Anyhow, we had to try.

We slid through the tangle. Ghost cable stuff is tough, even to a knife blade. But it is reasonably flexible; you can just push it aside if you get stuck, although we tried to avoid doing that for fear of leaving a sign.

We used standard patrolling SOP, adapted for the circumstance. We would move for ten or fifteen minutes, clambering through the tangle, and then take a break for five minutes. I'd sip water—I was getting hot—and maybe nibble on a glucose tab, check on my arm, and pull the suit around me to get comfortable again. It's the way to do it. If you just push yourself on and on you run down your reserves and end up in no fit state to achieve the goal anyhow.

And all the while I was trying to keep up my all-around awareness, protecting my dark adaptation, and making appreciations. How far away is Jeru? What if an attack comes from in front, behind, above, below, left or right? Where can I find cover?

I began to build up an impression of the Ghost cruiser. It was a rough egg-shape, a couple of kilometers long, and basically a mass of the anonymous silvery cable. There were chambers and platforms and instruments stuck as if at random into the tangle, like food fragments in an old man's beard. I guess it makes for a flexible, easily modified configuration. Where the tangle was a little less thick, I glimpsed a more substantial core, a cylinder running along the axis of the craft. Perhaps it was the drive unit. I wondered if it was functioning; perhaps the Ghost equipment was designed to adapt to the changed conditions inside the fortress cordon.

There were Ghosts all over the craft.

They drifted over and through the tangle, following pathways invisible to us. Or they would cluster in little knots on the tangle. We couldn't tell what they were doing or saying. To human eyes a Silver Ghost is just a silvery sphere, visible only by reflection like a hole cut out of space, and without specialist equipment it is impossible even to tell one from another.

We kept out of sight. But I was sure the Ghosts must have spotted us, or were at least tracking our movements. After all we'd crash-landed in their ship. But they made no overt moves toward us.

We reached the outer hull, the place the cabling ran out, and dug back into the tangle a little way to stay out of sight.

I got an unimpeded view of the stars.

Still those nova firecrackers went off all over the sky; still those young stars glared like lanterns. It seemed to me the fortress's central, enclosed star looked a little brighter, hotter than it had been. I made a mental note to report that to the Academician.

But the most striking sight was the fleet.

Over a volume light-months wide, countless craft slid silently across the sky. They were organized in a complex network of corridors filling three-dimensional space: rivers of light gushed this way and that, their different colors denoting different classes and sizes of vessel. And, here and there, denser knots of color and light sparked, irregular flares in the orderly flows. They were places where human ships were engaging the enemy, places where people were fighting and dying.

It was a magnificent sight. But it was a big, empty sky, and the nearest sun was that eerie dwarf enclosed in its spooky blue net, a long way away, and there was movement in three dimensions, above me, below me, all around me. . . .

I found the fingers of my good hand had locked themselves around a sliver of the tangle.

Jeru grabbed my wrist and shook my arm until I was able to let go. She kept hold of my arm, her eyes locked on mine. *I have you. You won't fall.* Then she pulled me into a dense knot of the tangle, shutting out the sky.

She huddled close to me, so the bio lights of our suits wouldn't show far. Her eyes were pale blue, like windows. "You aren't used to being outside, are you, tar?"

"I'm sorry, Commissary. I've been trained—"

"You're still human. We all have weak points. The trick is to know them and allow for them. Where are you from?"

I managed a grin. "Mercury. Caloris Planitia." Mercury is a ball of iron at the bottom of the sun's gravity well. It is an iron mine, and an exotic matter factory, with a sun like a lid hanging over it. Most of the surface is given over to solar power collectors. It is a place of tunnels and warrens, where kids compete with the rats.

"And that's why you joined up? To get away?"

"I was drafted."

"Come on," she scoffed. "On a place like Mercury there are ways to hide. Are you a romantic, tar? You wanted to see the stars?"

"No," I said bluntly. "Life is more useful here."

She studied me. "A brief life should burn brightly—eh, tar?"

"Yes, sir."

"I came from Deneb," she said. "Do you know it?"

"No."

"Sixteen hundred light years from Earth — a system settled some four centuries after the start of the Third Expansion. It is quite different from the solar system. It is — organized. By the time the first ships reached Deneb, the mechanics of exploitation had become efficient. From preliminary exploration to working ship-yards and daughter colonies in less than a century. . . . Deneb's resources — its planets and asteroids and comets, even the star itself — have been mined to fund fresh colonizing waves, the greater Expansion — and, of course, to support the war with the Ghosts."

She swept her hand over the sky. "Think of it, tar. The Third Expansion: be-tween here and Sol, across six thousand light years — nothing but mankind, the fruit of a thousand years of world-building. And all of it linked by economics. Older systems like Deneb, their resources spent — even the solar system itself — are supported by a flow of goods and materials inward from the growing periphery of the Expansion. There are trade lanes spanning thousands of light years, lanes that never leave human territory, plied by vast schooners kilometers wide. But now the Ghosts are in our way. And *that's* what we're fighting for!"

"Yes, sir."

She eyed me. "You ready to go on?"

"Yes."

We began to make our way forward again, just under the tangle, still following patrol SOP.

I was glad to be moving again. I've never been comfortable talking personally — and for sure not with a Commissary. But I suppose even Commissaries need to talk.

Jeru spotted a file of the Ghosts moving in a crocodile, like so many schoolchil-dren, toward the head of the ship. It was the most purposeful activity we'd seen so far, so we followed them.

After a couple of hundred meters the Ghosts began to duck down into the tangle, out of our sight. We followed them in.

Maybe fifty meters deep, we came to a large enclosed chamber, a smooth bean-shaped pod that would have been big enough to enclose our yacht. The surface appeared to be semi-transparent, perhaps designed to let in sunlight. I could see shadowy shapes moving within.

Ghosts were clustered around the pod's hull, brushing its surface.

Jeru beckoned, and we worked our way through the tangle toward the far end of the pod, where the density of the Ghosts seemed to be lowest.

We slithered to the surface of the pod. There were sucker pads on our palms and toes to help us grip. We began crawling along the length of the pod, ducking flat when we saw Ghosts loom into view. It was like climbing over a glass ceiling.

The pod was pressurized. At one end of the pod a big ball of mud hung in the air, brown and viscous. It seemed to be heated from within; it was slowly boiling, with big sticky bubbles of vapor crowding its surface, and I saw how it was laced with purple and red smears. There is no convection in zero gravity, of course. Maybe the Ghosts were using pumps to drive the flow of vapor.

Tubes led off from the mud ball to the hull of the pod. Ghosts clustered there, sucking up the purple gunk from the mud.

We figured it out in bioluminescent "whispers." The Ghosts were *feeding*. Their home world is too small to have retained much internal warmth, but, deep beneath their frozen oceans or in the dark of their rocks, a little primordial geotherm heat must leak out still, driving fountains of minerals dragged up from the depths. And, as at the bottom of Earth's oceans, on those minerals and the slow leak of heat, life-forms feed. And the Ghosts feed on *them*.

So this mud ball was a field kitchen. I peered down at purplish slime, a gourmet meal for Ghosts, and I didn't envy them.

There was nothing for us here. Jeru beckoned me again, and we slithered further forward.

The next section of the pod was . . . strange.

It was a chamber full of sparkling, silvery saucer-shapes, like smaller, flattened-out Ghosts, perhaps. They fizzed through the air or crawled over each other or jammed themselves together into great wadded balls that would hold for a few seconds and then collapse, their component parts squirming off for some new adventure elsewhere. I could see there were feeding tubes on the walls, and one or two Ghosts drifted among the saucer things, like an adult in a yard of squabbling children.

There was a subtle shadow before me.

I looked up, and found myself staring at my own reflection — an angled head, an open mouth, a sprawled body — folded over, fish-eye style, just centimeters from my nose.

It was a Ghost. It bobbed massively before me.

I pushed myself away from the hull, slowly. I grabbed hold of the nearest tangle branch with my good hand. I knew I couldn't reach for my knife, which was tucked into my belt at my back. And I couldn't see Jeru anywhere. It might be that the Ghosts had taken her already. Either way I couldn't call her, or even look for her, for fear of giving her away.

The Ghost had a heavy-looking belt wrapped around its equator. I had to assume that those complex knots of equipment were weapons. Aside from its belt, the Ghost was quite featureless: it might have been stationary, or spinning at a hundred revolutions a minute. I stared at its hide, trying to understand that there was a layer in there like a separate universe, where the laws of physics had been tweaked. But all I could see was my own scared face looking back at me.

And then Jeru fell on the Ghost from above, limbs splayed, knives glinting in both hands. I could see she was yelling — mouth open, eyes wide — but she fell in utter silence, her comms disabled.

Flexing her body like a whip, she rammed both knives into the Ghost's hide — if I took that belt to be its equator, somewhere near its north pole. The Ghost pulsated, complex ripples chasing across its surface. But Jeru did a handstand and reached up with her legs to the tangle above, and anchored herself there.

The Ghost began to spin, trying to throw Jeru off. But she held her grip on the tangle, and kept the knives thrust in its hide, and all the Ghost succeeded in doing was opening up twin gashes, right across its upper section. Steam pulsed out, and I glimpsed redness within.

For long seconds I just hung there, frozen.

You're trained to mount the proper reaction to an enemy assault. But it all vaporizes when you're faced with a ton of spinning, pulsing monster, and you're armed with nothing but a knife. You just want to make yourself as small as possible; maybe it will all go away. But in the end you know it won't, that something has to be done.

So I pulled out my own knife and launched myself at that north pole area.

I started to make cross-cuts between Jeru's gashes. Ghost skin is tough, like thick rubber, but easy to cut if you have the anchorage. Soon I had loosened flaps and lids of skin, and I started pulling them away, exposing a deep redness within. Steam gushed out, sparkling to ice.

Jeru let go of her perch and joined me. We clung with our fingers and hands to the gashes we'd made, and we cut and slashed and dug; though the Ghost spun crazily, it couldn't shake us loose. Soon we were hauling out great warm mounds of meat—ropes like entrails, pulsing slabs like a human's liver or heart. At first ice crystals spurted all around us, but as the Ghost lost the heat it had hoarded all its life, that thin wind died, and frost began to gather on the cut and torn flesh.

At last Jeru pushed my shoulder, and we both drifted away from the Ghost. It was still spinning, but I could see that the spin was nothing but dead momentum; the Ghost had lost its heat, and its life.

Jeru and I faced each other.

I said breathlessly, "I never heard of anyone in hand-to-hand with a Ghost before."

"Neither did I. Lethe," she said, inspecting her hand. "I think I cracked a finger."

It wasn't funny. But Jeru stared at me, and I stared back, and then we both started to laugh, and our slime suits pulsed with pink and blue icons.

"He stood his ground," I said.

"Yes. Maybe he thought we were threatening the nursery."

"The place with the silver saucers?"

She looked at me quizzically. "Ghosts are symbiotes, tar. That looked to me like a nursery for Ghost hides. Independent entities."

I had never thought of Ghosts having young. I had not thought of the Ghost we had killed as a mother protecting its young. I'm not a deep thinker now, and wasn't then; but it was not, for me, a comfortable thought.

But then Jeru started to move. "Come on, tar. Back to work." She anchored her legs in the tangle and began to grab at the still-rotating Ghost carcass, trying to slow its spin.

I anchored likewise and began to help her. The Ghost was massive, the size of a major piece of machinery, and it had built up respectable momentum; at first I couldn't grab hold of the skin flaps that spun past my hand. As we labored I became aware I was getting uncomfortably hot. The light that seeped into the tangle from that caged sun seemed to be getting stronger by the minute.

But as we worked those uneasy thoughts soon dissipated.

At last we got the Ghost under control. Briskly Jeru stripped it of its kit belt, and we began to cram the baggy corpse as deep as we could into the surrounding tangle. It was a grisly job. As the Ghost crumpled further, more of its innards, stiffening now, came pushing out of the holes we'd given it in its hide, and I had to keep from gagging as the foul stuff came pushing out into my face.

At last it was done—as best we could manage it, anyhow.

Jeru's faceplate was smeared with black and red. She was sweating hard, her face pink. But she was grinning, and she had a trophy, the Ghost belt around her shoulders. We began to make our way back, following the same SOP as before.

When we got back to our lying-up point, we found Academician Pael was in trouble.

Pael had curled up in a ball, his hands over his face. We pulled him open. His eyes were closed, his face blotched pink, and his faceplate dripped with condensation.

He was surrounded by gadgets stuck in the tangle—including parts from what looked like a broken-open starbreaker handgun; I recognized prisms and mirrors and diffraction gratings. Well, unless he woke up, he wouldn't be able to tell us what he had been doing here.

Jeru glanced around. The light of the fortress's central star had gotten a *lot* stronger. Our lying-up point was now bathed in light—and heat—with the surrounding tangle offering very little shelter. "Any ideas, tar?"

I felt the exhilaration of our infil drain away. "No, sir."

Jeru's face, bathed in sweat, showed tension. I noticed she was favoring her left hand. She'd mentioned, back at the nursery pod, that she'd cracked a finger, but had said nothing about it since—nor did she give it any time now. "All right." She dumped the Ghost equipment belt and took a deep draft of water from her hood spigot. "Tar, you're on stag. Try to keep Pael in the shade of your body. And if he wakes up, *ask him what he's found out.*"

"Yes, sir."

"Good."

And then she was gone, melting into the complex shadows of the tangle as if she'd been born to these conditions.

I found a place where I could keep up 360-degree vision, and offer a little of my shadow to Pael—not that I imagined it helped much.

I had nothing to do but wait.

As the Ghost ship followed its own mysterious course, the light dapples that came filtering through the tangle shifted and evolved. Clinging to the tangle, I thought I could feel vibration: a slow, deep harmonization that pulsed through the ship's giant structure. I wondered if I was hearing the deep voices of Ghosts, calling to each other from one end of their mighty ship to another. It all served to remind me that everything in my environment, *everything*, was alien, and I was very far from home.

I tried to count my heartbeat, my breaths; I tried to figure out how long a second was. "A thousand and one. A thousand and two . . ." Keeping time is a basic human trait; time provides a basic orientation, and keeps you mentally sharp and in touch with reality. But I kept losing count.

And all my efforts failed to stop darker thoughts creeping into my head.

During a drama like the contact with the Ghost, you don't realize what's happening to you because your body blanks it out; on some level you know you just don't have time to deal with it. Now I had stopped moving, the aches and pains of the last few hours started crowding in on me. I was still sore in my head and back and, of course, my busted arm. I could feel deep bruises, maybe cuts, on my gloved hands where I had hauled at my knife, and I felt as if I had wrenched my good shoulder. One of my toes was throbbing ominously: I wondered if I had cracked another bone, here in this weird environment in which my skeleton had become as brittle as an old man's. I was chafed at my groin and armpits and knees and ankles and elbows, my skin rubbed raw. I was used to suits; normally I'm tougher than that.

The shafts of sunlight on my back were working on me too; it felt as if I was lying underneath the elements of an oven. I had a headache, a deep sick feeling in the pit of my stomach, a ringing in my ears, and a persistent ring of blackness around my eyes. Maybe I was just exhausted, dehydrated; maybe it was more than that.

I started to think back over my operation with Jeru, and the regrets began.

Okay, I'd stood my ground when confronted by the Ghost and not betrayed Jeru's position. But when she launched her attack I'd hesitated, for those crucial few seconds. Maybe if I'd been tougher the commissary wouldn't find herself hauling through the tangle, alone, with a busted finger distracting her with pain signals.

Our training is comprehensive. You're taught to expect that kind of hindsight torture, in the quiet moments, and to discount it—or, better yet, learn from it. But, effectively alone in that metallic alien forest, I wasn't finding my training was offering much perspective.

And, worse, I started to think ahead. Always a mistake.

I couldn't believe that the Academician and his reluctant gadgetry were going to achieve anything significant. And for all the excitement of our infil, we hadn't found anything resembling a bridge or any vulnerable point we could attack, and all we'd come back with was a belt of field kit we didn't even understand.

For the first time I began to consider seriously the possibility that I wasn't going to live through this—that I was going to die when my suit gave up or the sun went pop, whichever came first, in no more than a few hours.

A *brief life burns brightly*. That's what you're taught. Longevity makes you conservative, fearful, selfish. Humans made that mistake before, and we finished up a subject race. Live fast and furiously, for *you* aren't important—all that matters is what you can do for the species.

But I didn't want to die.

If I never returned to Mercury again I wouldn't shed a tear. But I had a life now, in the Navy. And then there were my buddies: the people I'd trained and served with, people like Halle—even Jeru. Having found fellowship for the first time in my life, I didn't want to lose it so quickly, and fall into the darkness alone—especially if it was to be for *nothing*.

But maybe I wasn't going to get a choice.

After an unmeasured time, Jeru returned. She was hauling a silvery blanket. It was Ghost hide. She started to shake it out.

I dropped down to help her. "You went back to the one we killed—"

"—and skinned him," she said, breathless. "I just scraped off the crap with a knife. The Planck-zero layer peels away easily. And look . . ." she made a quick incision in the glimmering sheet with her knife. Then she put the two edges together again, ran her finger along the seam, and showed me the result. I couldn't even see where the cut had been. "Self-sealing, self-healing," she said. "Remember that, tar."

"Yes, sir."

We started to rig the punctured, splayed-out hide as a rough canopy over our LUP, blocking as much of the sunlight as possible from Pael. A few slivers of frozen flesh still clung to the hide, but mostly it was like working with a fine, light metallic foil.

In the sudden shade, Pael was starting to stir. His moans were translated to stark bioluminescent icons.

"Help him," Jeru snapped. "Make him drink." And while I did that she dug into the med kit on her belt and started to spray cast material around the fingers of her left hand.

"It's the speed of light," Pael said. He was huddled in a corner of our LUP, his legs tucked against his chest. His voice must have been feeble; the bioluminescent sigils on his suit were fragmentary and came with possible variants extrapolated by the translator software.

"Tell us," Jeru said, relatively gently.

"The Ghosts have found a way to *change* lightspeed in this fortress. In fact to increase it." He began talking again about quagma and physics constants and the rolled-up dimensions of spacetime, but Jeru waved that away irritably.

"How do you *know* this?"

Pael began tinkering with his prisms and gratings. "I took your advice, Commissary." He beckoned to me. "Come see, child."

I saw that a shaft of red light, split out and deflected by his prism, shone through a diffraction grating and cast an angular pattern of dots and lines on a scrap of smooth plastic behind.

"You see?" His eyes searched my face.

"I'm sorry, sir."

"The wavelength of the light has changed. It has been increased. Red light should have a wavelength, oh, a fifth shorter than that indicated by this pattern."

I was struggling to understand. I held up my hand. "Shouldn't the green of this glove turn yellow, or blue . . . ?"

Pael sighed. "No. Because the color you see depends, not on the wavelength of a photon, but on its energy. Conservation of energy still applies, even where the Ghosts are tinkering. So each photon carries as much energy as before—and evokes the same 'color.' Since a photon's energy is proportional to its frequency, that means frequencies are left unchanged. But since lightspeed is equal to frequency multiplied by wavelength, an increase in wavelength implies—"

"An increase in lightspeed," said Jeru.

"Yes."

I didn't follow much of that. I turned and looked up at the light that leaked around our Ghost-hide canopy. "So we see the same colors. The light of that star gets here a little faster. What difference does it make?"

Pael shook his head. "Child, a fundamental constant like lightspeed is embedded in the deep structure of our universe. Lightspeed is part of the ratio known as the fine structure constant." He started babbling about the charge on the electron, but Jeru cut him off.

She said, "Case, the fine structure constant is a measure of the strength of an electric or magnetic force."

I could follow that much. "And if you increase lightspeed—"

"You *reduce* the strength of the force." Pael raised himself. "Consider this. Human bodies are held together by molecular binding energy—electromagnetic forces. Here, electrons are more loosely bound to atoms; the atoms in a molecule are more loosely bound to each other." He rapped on the cast on my arm. "And so your bones are more brittle, your skin more easy to pierce or chafe. Do you see? You too are embedded in spacetime, my young friend. You too are affected by the Ghosts' tinkering. And because lightspeed in this infernal pocket continues to increase—as far as I can tell from these poor experiments—you are becoming more fragile every second."

It was a strange, eerie thought: that something so basic in my universe could be manipulated. I put my arms around my chest and shuddered.

"Other effects," Pael went on bleakly. "The density of matter is dropping. Perhaps our structure will eventually begin to crumble. And dissociation temperatures are reduced."

Jeru snapped, "What does that mean?"

"Melting and boiling points are reduced. No wonder we are overheating. It is intriguing that bio systems have proven rather more robust than electromechanical ones. But if we don't get out of here soon, our blood will start to boil. . . ."

"Enough," Jeru said. "What of the star?"

"A star is a mass of gas with a tendency to collapse under its own gravity. But heat, supplied by fusion reactions in the core, creates gas and radiation pressures that push outward, counteracting gravity."

"And if the fine structure constant changes—"

"Then the balance is lost. Commissary, as gravity begins to win its ancient battle, the fortress star has become more luminous—it is burning faster. That explains the observations we made from outside the cordon. But this cannot last."

"The novae," I said.

"Yes. The explosions, layers of the star blasted into space, are a symptom of destabilized stars seeking a new balance. The rate at which *our* star is approaching that catastrophic moment fits with the lightspeed drift I have observed." He smiled and closed his eyes. "A single cause predicating so many effects. It is all rather pleasing, in an aesthetic way."

Jeru said, "At least we know how the ship was destroyed. Every control system is mediated by finely tuned electromagnetic effects. Everything must have gone crazy at once. . . ."

We figured it out. The *Brief Life Burns Brightly* had been a classic GUTship, of a design that hasn't changed in its essentials for thousands of years. The lifedome, a tough translucent bubble, contained the crew of twenty. The 'dome was connected by a spine a klick long to a GUTdrive engine pod.

When we crossed the cordon boundary—when all the bridge lights failed—the control systems went down, and all the pod's superforce energy must have tried to escape at once. The spine of the ship had thrust itself up into the lifedome, like a nail rammed into a skull.

Pael said dreamily, "If lightspeed were a tad faster, throughout the universe, then hydrogen could not fuse to helium. There would only be hydrogen: no fusion to power stars, no chemistry. Conversely if lightspeed were a little lower, hydrogen would fuse too easily, and there would be *no* hydrogen, nothing to make stars— or water. You see how critical it all is? No doubt the Ghosts' science of fine-tuning is advancing considerably here on the Orion Line, even as it serves its trivial defensive purpose . . ."

Jeru glared at him, her contempt obvious. "We must take this piece of intelligence back to the Commission. If the Ghosts can survive and function in these fast-light bubbles of theirs, so can we. We may be at the pivot of history, gentlemen."

I knew she was right. The primary duty of the Commission for Historical Truth is to gather and deploy intelligence about the enemy. And so *my* primary duty, and Pael's, was now to help Jeru get this piece of data back to her organization.

But Pael was mocking her.

"Not for ourselves, but for the species. Is that the line, Commissary? You are so grandiose. And yet you blunder around in comical ignorance. Even your quixotic quest aboard this cruiser was futile. There probably is no bridge on this ship. The Ghosts' entire morphology, their evolutionary design, is based on the notion of cooperation, of symbiosis; why should a Ghost ship have a metaphoric *head*? And as for the trophy you have returned—" He held up the belt of Ghost artifacts. "There are no weapons here. These are sensors, tools. There is nothing here capable of producing a significant energy discharge. This is less threatening than a bow and arrow." He let go of the belt; it drifted away. "The Ghost wasn't trying to kill you. It was blocking you. Which is a classic Ghost tactic."

Jeru's face was stony. "It was in our way. That is sufficient reason for destroying it."

Pael shook his head. "Minds like yours will destroy *us*, Commissary."

Jeru stared at him with suspicion. Then she said, "*You have a way.* Don't you, Academician? A way to get us out of here."

He tried to face her down, but her will was stronger, and he averted his eyes.

Jeru said heavily, "Regardless of the fact that three lives are at stake—does duty mean nothing to you, Academician? You are an intelligent man. Can you not see that this is a war of human destiny?"

Pael laughed. "Destiny—or economics?"

I looked from one to the other, dismayed, baffled. I thought we should be doing less yapping and more fighting.

Pael said, watching me, "You see, child, as long as the explorers and the mining fleets and the colony ships are pushing outward, as long as the Third Expansion is growing, our economy works. The riches can continue to flow inward, into the mined-out systems, feeding a vast horde of humanity who have become more populous than the stars themselves. But as soon as that growth falters . . ."

Jeru was silent.

I understood some of this. The Third Expansion had reached all the way to the inner edge of our spiral arm of the galaxy. Now the first colony ships were attempting to make their way across the void to the next arm.

Our arm, the Orion Arm, is really just a shingle, a short arc. But the Sagittarius Arm is one of the galaxy's dominant features. For example, it contains a huge region of star-birth, one of the largest in the galaxy, immense clouds of gas and dust capable of producing millions of stars each. It was a prize indeed.

But that is where the Silver Ghosts live.

When it appeared that our inexorable expansion was threatening not just their own mysterious projects but their home system, the Ghosts began, for the first time, to resist us.

They had formed a blockade, called by human strategists the Orion Line: a thick sheet of fortress stars, right across the inner edge of the Orion Arm, places the Navy and the colony ships couldn't follow. It was a devastatingly effective ploy.

This was a war of colonization, of world-building. For a thousand years we had been spreading steadily from star to star, using the resources of one system to explore, terraform and populate the worlds of the next. With too deep a break in that chain of exploitation, the enterprise broke down.

And so the Ghosts had been able to hold up human expansion for fifty years.

Pael said, "We are already choking. There have already been wars, young Case: human fighting human, as the inner systems starve. All the Ghosts have to do is wait for us to destroy ourselves, and free them to continue their own rather more worthy projects."

Jeru floated down before him. "Academician, listen to me. Growing up at Deneb, I saw the great schooners in the sky, bringing the interstellar riches that kept my people alive. I was intelligent enough to see the logic of history—that we must maintain the Expansion, *because there is no choice*. And that is why I joined the armed forces, and later the Commission for Historical Truth. For I understood the dreadful truth which the Commission cradles. And that is why we must labor every day to maintain the unity and purpose of mankind. For if we falter we die; as simple as that."

"Commissary, your creed of mankind's evolutionary destiny condemns our own kind to become a swarm of children, granted a few moments of loving and breeding and dying, before being cast into futile war." Pael glanced at me.

"But," Jeru said, "it is a creed that has bound us together for a thousand years. It is a creed that binds uncounted trillions of human beings across thousands of light years. It is a creed that binds a humanity so diverse it appears to be undergoing speciation. . . . Are you strong enough to defy such a creed now? Come, Academician. None of us *chooses* to be born in the middle of a war. We must all do our best for each other, for other human beings; what else is there?"

I touched Pael's shoulder; he flinched away. "Academician—is Jeru right? Is there a way we can live through this?"

Pael shuddered. Jeru hovered over him.

"Yes," Pael said at last. "Yes, there is a way."

The idea turned out to be simple.

And the plan Jeru and I devised to implement it was even simpler. It was based on a single assumption: Ghosts aren't aggressive. It was ugly, I'll admit that, and I could see why it would distress a squeamish earthworm like Pael. But sometimes there are no good choices.

Jeru and I took a few minutes to rest up, check over our suits and our various injuries, and to make ourselves comfortable. Then, following patrol SOP once more, we made our way back to the pod of immature hides.

We came out of the tangle and drifted down to that translucent hull. We tried to keep away from concentrations of Ghosts, but we made no real effort to conceal ourselves. There was little point, after all; the Ghosts would know all about us, and what we intended, soon enough.

We hammered pitons into the pliable hull, and fixed rope to anchor ourselves. Then we took our knives and started to saw our way through the hull.

As soon as we started, the Ghosts began to gather around us, like vast antibodies.

They just hovered there, eerie faceless baubles drifting as if in vacuum breezes. But as I stared up at a dozen distorted reflections of my own skinny face, I felt an unreasonable loathing rise up in me. Maybe you could think of them as a family banding together to protect their young. I didn't care; a lifetime's carefully designed hatred isn't thrown off so easily. I went at my work with a will.

Jeru got through the pod hull first.

The air gushed out in a fast-condensing fountain. The baby hides fluttered, their distress obvious. And the Ghosts began to cluster around Jeru, like huge light globes.

Jeru glanced at me. "Keep working, tar."

"Yes, sir."

In another couple of minutes I was through. The air pressure was already dropping. It dwindled to nothing when we cut a big door-sized flap in that roof. Anchoring ourselves with the ropes, we rolled that lid back, opening the roof wide. A few last wisps of vapor came curling around our heads, ice fragments sparkling.

The hide babies convulsed. Immature, they could not survive the sudden vacuum, intended as their ultimate environment. But the way they died made it easy for us.

The silvery hides came flapping up out of the hole in the roof, one by one. We just grabbed each one—like grabbing hold of a billowing sheet—and we speared it with a knife, and threaded it on a length of rope. All we had to do was sit there and wait for them to come. There were hundreds of them, and we were kept busy.

I hadn't expected the adult Ghosts to sit through that, non-aggressive or not; and I was proved right. Soon they were clustering all around me, vast silvery bellies looming. A Ghost is massive and solid, and it packs a lot of inertia; if one hits you in the back you know about it. Soon they were nudging me hard enough to knock me flat against the roof, over and over. Once I was wrenched so hard against my tethering rope it felt as if I had cracked another bone or two in my foot.

And, meanwhile, I was starting to feel a lot worse: dizzy, nauseous, overheated. It was getting harder to get back upright each time after being knocked down. I was growing weaker fast; I imagined the tiny molecules of my body falling apart in this Ghost-polluted space.

For the first time I began to believe we were going to fail.

But then, quite suddenly, the Ghosts backed off. When they were clear of me, I saw they were clustering around Jeru.

She was standing on the hull, her feet tangled up in rope, and she had knives in both hands. She was slashing crazily at the Ghosts, and at the baby hides that came flapping past her, making no attempt to capture them now, simply cutting and destroying whatever she could reach. I could see that one arm was hanging awkwardly—maybe it was dislocated, or even broken—but she kept on slicing regardless.

And the Ghosts were clustering around her, huge silver spheres crushing her frail, battling human form.

She was sacrificing herself to save me—just as Captain Teid, in the last moments of the *Brightly*, had given herself to save Pael. And *my* duty was to complete the job.

I stabbed and threaded, over and over, as the flimsy hides came tumbling out of that hole, slowly dying.

At last no more hides came.

I looked up, blinking to get the salt sweat out of my eyes. A few hides were still tumbling around the interior of the pod, but they were inert and out of my reach. Others had evaded us and gotten stuck in the tangle of the ship's structure, too far and too scattered to make them worth pursuing further. What I had got would have to suffice.

I started to make my way out of there, back through the tangle, to the location of our wrecked yacht, where I hoped Pael would be waiting.

I looked back once. I couldn't help it. The Ghosts were still clustered over the ripped pod roof. Somewhere in there, whatever was left of Jeru was still fighting.

I had an impulse, almost overpowering, to go back to her. No human being should die alone. But I knew I had to get out of there, to complete the mission, to make her sacrifice worthwhile.

So I got.

Pael and I finished the job at the outer hull of the Ghost cruiser.

Stripping the hides turned out to be as easy as Jeru had described. Fitting together the Planck-zero sheets was simple too—you just line them up and seal them with a thumb. I got on with that, sewing the hides together into a sail, while Pael worked on a rigging of lengths of rope, all fixed to a deck panel from the wreck of the yacht. He was fast and efficient: Pael, after all, came from a world where everybody goes solar sailing on their vacations.

We worked steadily, for hours.

I ignored the varying aches and chafes, the increasing pain in my head and chest and stomach, the throbbing of a broken arm that hadn't healed, the agony of cracked bones in my foot. And we didn't talk about anything but the task in hand. Pael didn't ask what had become of Jeru, not once; it was as if he had anticipated the commissary's fate.

We were undisturbed by the Ghosts through all of this.

I tried not to think about whatever emotions churned within those silvered carapaces, what despairing debates might chatter on invisible wavelengths. I was, after all, trying to complete a mission. And I had been exhausted even before I got back to Pael. I just kept going, ignoring my fatigue, focusing on the task.

I was surprised to find it was done.

We had made a sail hundreds of meters across, stitched together from the invisibly thin immature Ghost hide. It was roughly circular, and it was connected by a dozen lengths of fine rope to struts on the panel we had wrenched out of the wreck. The sail lay across space, languid ripples crossing its glimmering surface.

Pael showed me how to work the thing. "Pull this rope, or this . . ." the great patchwork sail twitched in response to his commands. "I've set it so you shouldn't have to try anything fancy, like tacking. The boat will just sail out, hopefully, to the cordon perimeter. If you need to lose the sail, just cut the ropes."

I was taking in all this automatically. It made sense for both of us to know how to operate our little yacht. But then I started to pick up the subtext of what he was saying.

Before I knew what he was doing he had shoved me onto the deck panel, and pushed it away from the Ghost ship. His strength was surprising.

I watched him recede. He clung wistfully to a bit of tangle. I couldn't summon the strength to figure out a way to cross the widening gap. But my suit could read his, as clear as day.

"Where I grew up, the sky was full of sails . . ."

"Why, Academician?"

"You will go further and faster without my mass to haul. And besides—our lives are short enough; we should preserve the young. Don't you think?"

I had no idea what he was talking about. Pael was much more valuable than I was; I was the one who should have been left behind. He had shamed himself.

Complex glyphs criss-crossed his suit. "Keep out of the direct sunlight. It is growing more intense, of course. That will help you. . . ."

And then he ducked out of sight, back into the tangle. The Ghost ship was receding now, closing over into its vast egg shape, the detail of the tangle becoming lost to my blurred vision.

The sail above me slowly billowed, filling up with the light of the brightening sun. Pael had designed his improvised craft well; the rigging lines were all taut, and I could see no rips or creases in the silvery fabric.

I clung to my bit of decking and sought shade.

Twelve hours later, I reached an invisible radius where the tactical beacon in my pocket started to howl with a whine that filled my headset. My suit's auxiliary systems cut in and I found myself breathing fresh air.

A little after that, a set of lights ducked out of the streaming lanes of the fleet, and plunged toward me, growing brighter. At last it resolved into a golden bullet shape adorned with a blue-green tetrahedron, the sigil of free humanity. It was a supply ship called *The Dominance of Primates*.

And a little after *that*, as a Ghost fleet fled their fortress, the star exploded.

As soon as I had completed my formal report to the ship's commissary—and I was able to check out of the *Dominance's* sick bay—I asked to see the captain.

I walked up to the bridge. My story had got around, and the various med patches I sported added to my heroic mythos. So I had to run the gauntlet of the crew—"You're supposed to be dead, I impounded your back pay and slept with your mother already"—and was greeted by what seems to be the universal gesture of recognition of one tar to another, the clenched fist pumping up and down around an imaginary penis.

But anything more respectful just wouldn't feel normal.

The captain turned out to be a grizzled veteran type with a vast laser burn scar on one cheek. She reminded me of First Officer Till.

I told her I wanted to return to active duty as soon as my health allowed.

She looked me up and down. "Are you sure, tar? You have a lot of options. Young as you are, you've made your contribution to the Expansion. You can go home."

"Sir, and do what?"

She shrugged. "Farm. Mine. Raise babies. Whatever earthworms do. Or you can join the Commission for Historical Truth."

"Me, a commissary?"

"You've been there, tar. You've been in among the Ghosts, and come out again—with a bit of intelligence more important than anything the Commission has come up with in fifty years. Are you *sure* you want to face action again?"

I thought it over.

I remembered how Jeru and Pael had argued. It had been an unwelcome perspective, for me. I was in a war that had nothing to do with me, trapped by what Jeru had called the logic of history. But then, I bet that's been true of most of humanity through our long and bloody history. All you can do is live your life, and grasp your moment in the light—and stand by your comrades.

A farmer—me? And I could never be smart enough for the Commission. No, I had no doubts.

"A brief life burns brightly, sir."

Lethe, the captain looked like she had a lump in her throat. "Do I take that as a yes, tar?"

I stood straight, ignoring the twinges of my injuries. "Yes, *sir!*"

oracle

GREG EGAN

Looking back at the century that's just ended, it's obvious that Australian writer Greg Egan was one of the Big New Names to emerge in SF in the nineties, and is probably one of the most significant talents to enter the field in the last several decades. Already one of the most widely known of all Australian genre writers, Egan may well be the best new "hard-science" writer to enter the field since Greg Bear, and is still growing in range, power, and sophistication. In the last few years, he has become a frequent contributor to Interzone *and* Asimov's Science Fiction, *and has made sales as well as to* Pulphouse, Analog, Aurealis, Eidolon, *and elsewhere; many of his stories have also appeared in various "Best of the Year" series, and he was on the Hugo final ballot in 1995 for his story "Cocoon," which won the Ditmar Award and the Asimov's Readers Award. He won the Hugo Award in 1999 for his novella "Oceanic." His first novel,* Quarantine, *appeared in 1992; his second novel,* Permutation City, *won the John W. Campbell Memorial Award in 1994. His other books include the novels,* Distress *and* Diaspora, *and three collections of his short fiction,* Axiomatic, Luminous, *and* Our Lady of Chernobyl. *His most recent book is a major new novel,* Teranesia. *He has a web site at http://www.netspace.netau/^gregegan/.*

In the strange and eloquent story that follows, he takes us to a slightly altered version of our own familiar Earth in the days just after World War II, for a memorable battle of ideas between two of the smartest humans alive—a deceptively quiet battle, fought with words broadcast over the radio, that could nevertheless change our view of the universe forever . . . and perhaps even change the universe itself.

1

On his eighteenth day in the tiger cage, Robert Stoney began to lose hope of emerging unscathed.

He'd woken a dozen times throughout the night with an overwhelming need to stretch his back and limbs, and none of the useful compromise positions he'd discovered in his first few days—the least-worst solutions to the geometrical problem of his confinement—had been able to dull his sense of panic. He'd been in far more pain in the second week, suffering cramps that felt as if the muscles of his legs were dying on the bone, but these new spasms had come from somewhere deeper, powered by a sense of urgency that revolved entirely around his own awareness of his situation.

That was what frightened him. Sometimes he could find ways to minimize his discomfort, sometimes he couldn't, but he'd been clinging to the thought that, in the end, all these fuckers could ever do was hurt him. That wasn't true, though. They could make him ache for freedom in the middle of the night, the way he might have ached with grief, or love. He'd always cherished the understanding that his self was a whole, his mind and body indivisible. But he'd failed to appreciate the corollary: through his body, they could touch every part of him. Change every part of him.

Morning brought a fresh torment: hay fever. The house was somewhere deep in the countryside, with nothing to be heard in the middle of the day but bird song. June had always been his worst month for hay fever, but in Manchester it had been tolerable. As he ate breakfast, mucus dripped from his face into the bowl of lukewarm oats they'd given him. He stanched the flow with the back of his hand, but suffered a moment of shuddering revulsion when he couldn't find a way to reposition himself to wipe his hand clean on his trousers. Soon he'd need to empty his bowels. They supplied him with a chamber pot whenever he asked, but they always waited two or three hours before removing it. The smell was bad enough, but the fact that it took up space in the cage was worse.

Toward the middle of the morning, Peter Quint came to see him. "How are we today, Prof?" Robert didn't reply. Since the day Quint had responded with a puzzled frown to the suggestion that he had an appropriate name for a spook, Robert had tried to make at least one fresh joke at the man's expense every time they met, a petty but satisfying indulgence. But now his mind was blank, and, in retrospect the whole exercise seemed like an insane distraction, as bizarre and futile as scoring philosophical points against some predatory animal while it gnawed on his leg.

"Many happy returns," Quint said cheerfully.

Robert took care to betray no surprise. He'd never lost track of the days, but he'd stopped thinking in terms of the calendar date; it simply wasn't relevant. Back in the real world, to have forgotten his own birthday would have been considered a benign eccentricity. Here it would be taken as proof of his deterioration, and imminent surrender.

If he was cracking, he could at least choose the point of fissure. He spoke as calmly as he could, without looking up. "You know I almost qualified for the Olympic marathon, back in forty-eight? If I hadn't done my hip in just before the trials, I might have competed." He tried a self-deprecating laugh. "I suppose I was never really much of an athlete. But I'm only forty-six. I'm not ready for a wheelchair yet." The words did help: he could beg this way without breaking down completely, expressing an honest fear without revealing how much deeper the threat of damage went.

He continued, with a measured note of plaintiveness that he hoped sounded like an appeal to fairness. "I just can't bear the thought of being crippled. All I'm asking is that you let me stand upright. Let me keep my health."

Quint was silent for a moment, then he replied with a tone of thoughtful sympathy. "It's unnatural, isn't it? Living like this: bent over, twisted, day after day. Living in an unnatural way is always going to harm you. I'm glad you can finally see that."

Robert was tired; it took several seconds for the meaning to sink in. *It was that crude, that obvious?* They'd locked him in this cage, for all this time . . . as a kind of ham-fisted *metaphor* for his crimes?

He almost burst out laughing, but he contained himself. "I don't suppose you know Franz Kafka?"

"Kafka?" Quint could never hide his voracity for names. "One of your Commie chums, is he?"

"I very much doubt that he was ever a Marxist."

Quint was disappointed, but prepared to make do with second best. "One of the other kind, then?"

Robert pretended to be pondering the question. "On balance, I suspect that's not too likely either."

"So why bring his name up?"

"I have a feeling he would have admired your methods, that's all. He was quite the connoisseur."

"Hmm." Quint sounded suspicious, but not entirely unflattered.

Robert had first set eyes on Quint in February of 1952. His house had been burgled the week before, and Arthur, a young man he'd been seeing since Christmas, had confessed to Robert that he'd given an acquaintance the address. Perhaps the two of them had planned to rob him, and Arthur had backed out at the last moment. In any case, Robert had gone to the police with an unlikely story about spotting the culprit in a pub, trying to sell an electric razor of the same make and model as the one taken from his house. No one could be charged on such flimsy evidence, so Robert had had no qualms about the consequences if Arthur had turned out to be lying. He'd simply hoped to prompt an investigation that might turn up something more tangible.

The following day, the CID had paid Robert a visit. The man he'd accused was known to the police, and fingerprints taken on the day of the burglary matched the prints they had on file. However, at the time Robert claimed to have seen him in the pub, he'd been in custody already on an entirely different charge.

The detectives had wanted to know why he'd lied. To spare himself the embarrassment, Robert had explained, of spelling out the true source of his information. Why was that embarrassing?

"I'm involved with the informant."

One detective, Mr. Wills, had asked matter-of-factly, "What exactly does that entail, sir?" And Robert—in a burst of frankness, as if honesty itself was sure to be rewarded—had told him every detail. He'd known it was still technically illegal, of course. But then, so was playing football on Easter Sunday. It could hardly be treated as a serious crime, like burglary.

The police had strung him along for hours, gathering as much information as they could before disabusing him of this misconception. They hadn't charged him immediately; they'd needed a statement from Arthur first. But then Quint had materialized the next morning, and spelled out the choices very starkly. Three years in prison, with hard labor. Or Robert could resume his war-time work—for just one day a week, as a handsomely paid consultant to Quint's branch of the secret service—and the charges would quietly vanish.

At first, he'd told Quint to let the courts do their worst. He'd been angry enough to want to take a stand against the preposterous law, and whatever his feelings for Arthur, Quint had suggested—gloatingly, as if it strengthened his case—that the younger, working-class man would be treated far more leniently than Robert, having been led astray by someone whose duty was to set an example for the lower orders. Three years in prison was an unsettling prospect, but it would not have been the end of the world; the Mark I had changed the way he worked, but he could still function with nothing but a pencil and paper, if necessary. Even if they'd had him breaking rocks from dawn to dusk, he probably would have been able to daydream productively, and for all Quint's scaremongering he'd doubted it would come to that.

At some point, though, in the twenty-four hours Quint had given him to reach a decision, he'd lost his nerve. By granting the spooks their one day a week, he could avoid all the fuss and disruption of a trial. And though his work at the time—modeling embryological development—had been as challenging as anything he'd done in his life, he hadn't been immune to pangs of nostalgia for the old days, when the fate of whole fleets of battleships had rested on finding the most efficient way to extract logical contradictions from a bank of rotating wheels.

The trouble with giving in to extortion was, *it proved that you could be bought.* Never mind that the Russians could hardly have offered to intervene with the Manchester constabulary next time he needed to be rescued. Never mind that he would scarcely have cared if an enemy agent had threatened to send such comprehensive evidence to the newspapers that there'd be no prospect of his patrons saving him again. He'd lost any chance to proclaim that what he did in bed with another willing partner was not an issue of national security; by saying yes to Quint, he'd made it one. By choosing to be corrupted once, he'd brought the whole torrent of clichés and paranoia down upon his head: he was vulnerable to blackmail, an easy target for entrapment, perfidious by nature. He might as well have posed *in flagrante delicto* with Guy Burgess on the steps of the Kremlin.

It wouldn't have mattered if Quint and his masters had merely decided that they couldn't trust him. The problem was—some six years after recruiting him, with no reason to believe that he had ever breached security in any way—they'd convinced themselves that they could neither continue to employ him, nor safely leave him in peace, until they'd rid him of the trait they'd used to control him in the first place.

Robert went through the painful, complicated process of rearranging his body so he could look Quint in the eye. "You know, if it was legal there'd be nothing to worry about, would there? Why don't you devote some of your considerable Machiavellian talents to that end? Blackmail a few politicians. Set up a Royal Commission. It would only take you a couple of years. Then we could all get on with our real jobs."

Quint blinked at him, more startled than outraged. "You might as well say that we should legalize treason!"

Robert opened his mouth to reply, then decided not to waste his breath. Quint wasn't expressing a moral opinion. He simply meant that a world in which fewer people's lives were ruled by the constant fear of discovery was hardly one that a man in his profession would wish to hasten into existence.

When Robert was alone again, the time dragged. His hay fever worsened, until he was sneezing and gagging almost continuously; even with freedom of movement and an endless supply of the softest linen handkerchiefs, he would have been reduced to abject misery. Gradually, though, he grew more adept at dealing with the symptoms, delegating the task to some barely conscious part of himself. By the middle of the afternoon—covered in filth, eyes almost swollen shut—he finally managed to turn his mind back to his work.

For the past four years, he'd been immersed in particle physics. He'd been following the field on and off since before the war, but the paper by Yang and Mills in '54, in which they'd generalized Maxwell's equations for electromagnetism to apply to the strong nuclear force, had jolted him into action.

After several false starts, he believed he'd discovered a useful way to cast gravity into the same form. In general relativity, if you carried a four-dimensional velocity vector around a loop that enclosed a curved region of spacetime, it came back rotated—a phenomenon highly reminiscent of the way more abstract vectors behaved in nuclear physics. In both cases, the rotations could be treated algebraically, and the traditional way to get a handle on this was to make use of a set of matrices of complex numbers whose relationships mimicked the algebra in question. Hermann Weyl had catalogued most of the possibilities back in the twenties and thirties.

In spacetime, there were six distinct ways you could rotate an object: you could turn it around any of three perpendicular axes in space, or you could boost its velocity in any of the same three directions. These two kinds of rotation were complementary, or "dual" to each other, with the ordinary rotations only affecting coordinates that were untouched by the corresponding boost, and *vice versa*. This meant that you could rotate something around, say, the x-axis, and speed it up in the same direction, without the two processes interfering.

When Robert had tried applying the Yang-Mills approach to gravity in the obvious way, he'd floundered. It was only when he'd shifted the algebra of rotations into a new, strangely skewed guise that the mathematics had begun to fall into place. Inspired by a trick that particle physicists used to construct fields with left- or right-handed spin, he'd combined every rotation with its own dual multiplied by i, the square root of minus one. The result was a set of rotations in four *complex* dimensions, rather than the four real ones of ordinary spacetime, but the relationships between them preserved the original algebra.

Demanding that these "self-dual" rotations satisfy Einstein's equations turned out to be equivalent to ordinary general relativity, but the process leading to a quantum-mechanical version of the theory became dramatically simpler. Robert still had no idea how to interpret this, but as a purely formal trick it worked spectacularly well—and when the mathematics fell into place like that, it had to mean *something*.

He spent several hours pondering old results, turning them over in his mind's eye, rechecking and reimagining everything in the hope of forging some new connection. Making no progress, but there'd always been days like that. It was a triumph merely to spend this much time doing what he would have done back in the real world—however mundane, or even frustrating, the same activity might have been in its original setting.

By evening, though, the victory began to seem hollow. He hadn't lost his wits entirely, but he was frozen, stunted. He might as well have whiled away the hours reciting the base-32 multiplication table in Baudot code, just to prove that he still remembered it.

As the room filled with shadows, his powers of concentration deserted him completely. His hay fever had abated, but he was too tired to think, and in too much pain to sleep. This wasn't Russia, they couldn't hold him forever; he simply had to wear them down with his patience. *But when, exactly, would they have to let him go?* And how much more patient could *Quint* be, with no pain, no terror, to erode his determination?

The moon rose, casting a patch of light on the far wall; hunched over, he couldn't see it directly, but it silvered the gray at his feet, and changed his whole sense of the space around him. The cavernous room mocking his confinement reminded him of nights he'd spent lying awake in the dormitory at Sherborne. A public school education did have one great advantage: however miserable you were afterward, you could always take comfort in the knowledge that life would never be quite as bad again.

"This room smells of mathematics! Go out and fetch a disinfectant spray!" That had been his form-master's idea of showing what a civilized man he was: contempt for that loathsome subject, the stuff of engineering and other low trades. And as for Robert's chemistry experiments, like the beautiful color-changing iodate reaction he'd learned from Chris's brother—

Robert felt a familiar ache in the pit of his stomach. *Not now. I can't afford this now.* But the whole thing swept over him, unwanted, unbidden. He used to meet Chris in the library on Wednesdays; for months, that had been the only time they could spend together. Robert had been fifteen then, Chris a year older. If Chris had been plain, he still would have shone like a creature from another world. No one else in Sherborne had read Eddington on relativity, Hardy on mathematics. No one else's horizons stretched beyond rugby, sadism, and the dimly satisfying prospect of reading classic at Oxford, then vanishing into the maw of the civil service.

They had never touched, never kissed. While half the school had been indulging in passionless sodomy—as a rather literal-minded substitute for the much too difficult task of imagining women—Robert had been too shy even to declare his feelings. Too shy, and too afraid that they might not be reciprocated. It hadn't mattered. To have a friend like Chris had been enough.

In December of 1929, they'd both sat the exams for Trinity College, Cambridge. Chris had won a scholarship; Robert hadn't. He'd reconciled himself to their separation, and prepared for one more year at Sherborne without the one person who'd made it bearable. Chris would be following happily in the footsteps of Newton; just thinking of that would be some consolation.

Chris never made it to Cambridge. In February, after six days in agony, he'd died of bovine tuberculosis.

Robert wept silently, angry with himself because he knew that half his wretchedness was just self-pity, exploiting his grief as a disguise. He had to stay honest; once every source of unhappiness in his life melted together and became indistinguishable, he'd be like a cowed animal, with no sense of the past or the future. Ready to do anything to get out of the cage.

If he hadn't yet reached that point, he was close. It would only take a few more nights like the last one. Drifting off in the hope of a few minutes' blankness, to find that sleep itself shone a colder light on everything. Drifting off, then waking with a sense of loss so extreme it was like suffocation.

A woman's voice spoke from the darkness in front of him. "Get off your knees!"

Robert wondered if he was hallucinating. He'd heard no one approach across the creaky floorboards.

The voice said nothing more. Robert rearranged his body so he could look up from the floor. There was a woman he'd never seen before, standing a few feet away.

She'd sounded angry, but as he studied her face in the moonlight through the slits of his swollen eyes, he realized that her anger was directed, not at him, but at his condition. She gazed at him with an expression of horror and outrage, as if she'd chanced upon him being held like this in some respectable neighbor's basement, rather than an MI6 facility. Maybe she was one of the staff employed in the upkeep of the house, but had no idea what went on here? Surely those people were vetted and supervised, though, and threatened with life imprisonment if they ever set foot outside their prescribed domains.

For one surreal moment, Robert wondered if Quint had sent her to seduce him. It would not have been the strangest thing they'd tried. But she radiated such fierce self-assurance—such a sense of confidence that she could speak with the authority of her convictions, and expect to be heeded—that he knew she could never have been chosen for the role. No one in Her Majesty's government would consider self-assurance an attractive quality in a woman.

He said, "Throw me the key, and I'll show you my Roger Bannister impression."

She shook her head. "You don't need a key. Those days are over."

Robert started with fright. *There were no bars between them.* But the cage couldn't have vanished before his eyes; she must have removed it while he'd been lost in his reverie. He'd gone through the whole painful exercise of turning to face her as if he were still confined, without even noticing.

Removed it how?

He wiped his eyes, shivering at the dizzying prospect of freedom. "Who are you?" An agent for the Russians, sent to liberate him from his own side? She'd have to be a zealot, then, or strangely naive, to view his torture with such wide-eyed innocence.

She stepped forward, then reached down and took his hand. "Do you think you can walk?" Her grip was firm, and her skin was cool and dry. She was completely unafraid; she might have been a good Samaritan in a public street helping an old man to his feet after a fall—not an intruder helping a threat to national security break out of therapeutic detention, at the risk of being shot on sight.

"I'm not even sure I can stand." Robert steeled himself; maybe this woman was a trained assassin, but it would be too much to presume that if he cried out in pain and brought guards rushing in, she could still extricate him without raising a sweat. "You haven't answered my question."

"My name's Helen." She smiled and hoisted him to his feet, looking at once like a compassionate child pulling open the jaws of a hunter's cruel trap, and a very powerful, very intelligent carnivore contemplating its own strength. "I've come to change everything."

Robert said, "Oh, good."

Robert found that he could hobble; it was painful and undignified, but at least he didn't have to be carried. Helen led him through the house; lights showed from some of the rooms, but there were no voices, no footsteps save their own, no signs of life at all. When they reached the tradesmen's entrance, she unbolted the door, revealing a moonlit garden.

"Did you kill everyone?" he whispered. He'd made far too much noise to have come this far unmolested. Much as he had reason to despise his captors, mass-murder on his behalf was a lot to take in.

Helen cringed. "What a revolting idea! It's hard to believe sometimes, how uncivilized you are."

"You mean the British?"

"All of you!"

"I must say, your accent's rather good."

"I watched a lot of cinema," she explained. "Mostly Ealing comedies. You never know how much that will help, though."

"Quite."

They crossed the garden, heading for a wooden gate in the hedge. Since murder was strictly for imperialists, Robert could only assume that she'd managed to drug everyone.

The gate was unlocked. Outside the grounds, a cobbled lane ran past the hedge, leading into forest. Robert was barefoot, but the stones weren't cold, and the slight unevenness of the path was welcome, restoring circulation to the soles of his feet.

As they walked, he took stock of his situation. He was out of captivity, thanks entirely to this woman. Sooner or later he was going to have to confront her agenda.

He said, "I'm not leaving the country."

Helen murmured assent, as if he'd passed a casual remark about the weather.

"And I'm not going to discuss my work with you."

"Fine."

Robert stopped and stared at her. She said, "Put your arm across my shoulders."

He complied; she was exactly the right height to support him comfortably. He said, "You're not a Soviet agent, are you?"

Helen was amused. "Is that really what you thought?"

"I'm not all that quick on my feet tonight."

"No." They began walking together. Helen said, "There's a train station about three kilometers away. You can get cleaned up, rest there until morning, and decide where you want to go."

"Won't the station be the first place they'll look?"

"They won't be looking anywhere for a while."

The moon was high above the trees. The two of them could not have made a more conspicuous couple: a sensibly dressed, quite striking young woman, supporting a filthy, ragged tramp. If a villager cycled past, the best they could hope for was being mistaken for an alcoholic father and his martyred daughter.

Martyred, all right: she moved so efficiently, despite the burden, that any onlooker would assume she'd been doing this for years. Robert tried altering his gait slightly, subtly changing the timing of his steps to see if he could make her falter, but Helen adapted instantly. If she knew she was being tested, though, she kept it to herself.

Finally he said, "What did you do with the cage?"

"I time-reversed it."

Hairs stood up on the back of his neck. Even assuming that she could do such a thing, it wasn't at all clear to him how that could have stopped the bars from scattering light and interacting with his body. It should merely have turned electrons into positions, and killed them both in a shower of gamma rays.

That conjuring trick wasn't his most pressing concern, though. "I can only think of three places you might have come from," he said.

Helen nodded, as if she'd put herself in his shoes and catalogued the possibilities. "Rule out one; the other two are both right."

She was not from an extrasolar planet. Even if her civilization possessed some means of viewing Ealing comedies from a distance of light years, she was far too sensitive to his specific human concerns.

She was from the future, but not his own.

She was from the future of another Everett branch.

He turned to her. "No paradoxes."

She smiled, deciphering his shorthand immediately. "That's right. It's physically impossible to travel into your own past, unless you've made exacting preparations to ensure compatible boundary conditions. That *can* be achieved, in a controlled laboratory setting—but in the field it would be like trying to balance ten thousand elephants in an inverted pyramid, while the bottom one rode a unicycle: excruciatingly difficult, and entirely pointless."

Robert was tongue-tied for several seconds, a horde of questions battling for access to his vocal chords. "But how do you travel into the past at all?"

"It will take a while to bring you up to speed completely, but if you want the short answer: you've already stumbled on one of the clues. I read your paper in *Physical Review*, and it's correct as far as it goes. Quantum gravity involves four complex dimensions, but the only classical solutions—the only geometries that remain in phase under slight perturbations—have curvature that's either *self-dual*, or *anti-self-dual*. Those are the only stationary points of the action, for the complete Lagrangian. And both solutions appear, from the inside, to contain only four real dimensions.

"It's meaningless to ask which sector we're in, but we might as well call it self-dual. In that case, the anti-self-dual solutions have an arrow of time running backward compared to ours."

"Why?" As he blurted out the question, Robert wondered if he sounded like an impatient child to her. But if she suddenly vanished back into thin air, he'd have far fewer regrets for making a fool of himself this way than if he'd maintained a façade of sophisticated nonchalance.

Helen said, "Ultimately, that's related to spin. And it's down to the mass of the neutrino that we can tunnel between sectors. But I'll need to draw you some diagrams and equations to explain it all properly."

Robert didn't press her for more; he had no choice but to trust that she wouldn't desert him. He staggered on in silence, a wonderful ache of anticipation building in his chest. If someone had put this situation to him hypothetically, he would have piously insisted that he'd prefer to toil on at his own pace. But despite the satisfaction it had given him on the few occasions when he'd made genuine discoveries himself, what mattered in the end was understanding as much as you could, *however* you could. Better to ransack the past and the future than go through life in a state of willful ignorance.

"You said you've come to change things?"

She nodded. "I can't predict the future here, of course, but there are pitfalls in my own past that I can help you avoid. In my twentieth century, people discovered things too slowly. Everything changed much too slowly. Between us, I think we can speed things up."

Robert was silent for a while, contemplating the magnitude of what she was proposing. Then he said, "It's a pity you didn't come sooner. In this branch, about twenty years ago — "

Helen cut him off. "I know. We had the same war. The same Holocaust, the same Soviet death toll. But we've yet to be able to avert that, anywhere. You can never do anything in just one history — even the most focused intervention happens across a broad 'ribbon' of strands. When we try to reach back to the thirties and forties, the ribbon overlaps with its own past to such a degree that all the worst horrors are *faits accompli*. We can't shoot *any* version of Adolf Hitler, because we can't shrink the ribbon to the point where none of us would be shooting ourselves in the back. All we've ever managed are minor interventions, like sending projectiles back to the Blitz, saving a few lives by deflecting bombs."

"What, knocking them into the Thames?"

"No, that would have been too risky. We did some modeling, and the safest thing turned out to be diverting them onto big, empty buildings: Westminster Abbey, Saint Paul's Cathedral."

The station came into view ahead of them. Helen said, "What do you think? Do you want to head back to Manchester?"

Robert hadn't given the question much thought. Quint could track him down anywhere, but the more people he had around him, the less vulnerable he'd be. In his house in Wilmslow he'd be there for the taking.

"I still have rooms at Cambridge," he said tentatively.

"Good idea."

"What are your own plans?"

Helen turned to him. "I thought I'd stay with you." She smiled at the expression on his face. "Don't worry, I'll give you plenty of privacy. And if people want to make assumptions, let them. You already have a scandalous reputation; you might as well see it branch out in new directions."

Robert said wryly, "I'm afraid it doesn't quite work that way. They'd throw us out immediately."

Helen snorted. "They could try."

"You may have defeated MI6, but you haven't dealt with Cambridge porters." The reality of the situation washed over him anew at the thought of her in his study, writing out the equations for time travel on the blackboard. "*Why me?* I can appreciate that you'd want to make contact with someone who could understand how you came here — but why not Everett, or Yang, or Feynman? Compared to Feynman, I'm a dilettante."

Helen said, "Maybe. But you have an equally practical bent, and you'll learn fast enough."

There had to be more to it than that: thousands of people would have been capable of absorbing her lessons just as rapidly. "The physics you've hinted at — in your past, did I discover all that?"

"No. Your *Physical Review* paper helped me track you down here, but in my own history that was never published." There was a flicker of disquiet in her eyes, as if she had far greater disappointments in store on that subject.

Robert didn't care much either way; if anything, the less his alter ego had achieved, the less he'd be troubled by jealousy.

"Then what was it, that made you choose me?"

"You really haven't guessed?" Helen took his free hand and held the fingers to her face; it was a tender gesture, but much more like a daughter's than a lover's. "It's a warm night. No one's skin should be this cold."

Robert gazed into her dark eyes, as playful as any human's, as serious, as proud. Given the chance, perhaps any decent person would have plucked him from Quint's grasp. But only one kind would feel a special obligation, as if they were repaying an ancient debt.

He said, "You're a machine."

2

John Hamilton, Professor of Medieval and Renaissance English at Magdalene College, Cambridge, read the last letter in the morning's pile of fan mail with a growing sense of satisfaction.

The letter was from a young American, a twelve-year-old girl in Boston. It opened in the usual way, declaring how much pleasure his books had given her, before going onto list her favorite scenes and characters. As ever, Jack was delighted that the stories had touched someone deeply enough to prompt them to respond this way. But it was the final paragraph that was by far the most gratifying:

> However much other children might tease me, or grown-ups too when I'm older, I will NEVER, EVER stop believing in the Kingdom of Nescia. Sarah stopped believing, and she was locked out of the King-

dom forever. At first that made me cry, and I couldn't sleep all night because I was afraid I might stop believing myself one day. But I understand now that it's good to be afraid, because it will help me keep people from changing my mind. And if you're not willing to believe in magic lands, of course you can't enter them. There's nothing even Belvedere himself can do to save you, then.

Jack refilled and lit his pipe, then reread the letter. This was his vindication: the proof that through his books he could touch a young mind, and plant the seed of faith in fertile ground. It made all the scorn of his jealous, stuck-up colleagues fade into insignificance. Children understood the power of stories, the reality of myth, the need to believe in something beyond the dismal gray farce of the material world.

It wasn't a truth that could be revealed the "adult" way: through scholarship, or reason. Least of all through philosophy, as Elizabeth Anscombe had shown him on that awful night at the Socratic Club. A devout Christian herself, Anscombe had nonetheless taken all the arguments against materialism from his popular book, *Signs and Wonders*, and trampled them into the ground. It had been an unfair match from the start: Anscombe was a professional philosopher, steeped in the work of everyone from Aquinas to Wittgenstein; Jack knew the history of ideas in medieval Europe intimately, but he'd lost interest in modern philosophy once it had been invaded by fashionable positivists. And *Signs and Wonders* had never been intended as a scholarly work; it had been good enough to pass muster with a sympathetic lay readership, but trying to defend his admittedly rough-and-ready mixture of common sense and useful shortcuts to faith against Anscombe's merciless analysis had made him feel like a country yokel stammering in front of a bishop.

Ten years later, he still burned with resentment at the humiliation she'd put him through, but he was grateful for the lesson she'd taught him. His earlier books, and his radio talks, had not been a complete waste of time—but the harpy's triumph had shown him just how pitiful human reason was when it came to the great questions. He'd begun working on the stories of Nescia years before, but it was only when the dust had settled on his most painful defeat that he'd finally recognized his true calling.

He removed his pipe, stood, and turned to face Oxford. "Kiss my arse, Elizabeth!" he growled happily, waving the letter at her. This was a wonderful omen. It was going to be a very good day.

There was a knock at the door of his study.

"Come."

It was his brother, William. Jack was puzzled—he hadn't even realized Willie was in town—but he nodded a greeting and motioned at the couch opposite his desk.

Willie sat, his face flushed from the stairs, frowning. After a moment he said, "This chap Stoney."

"Hmm?" Jack was only half listening as he sorted papers on his desk. He knew from long experience that Willie would take forever to get to the point.

"Did some kind of hush-hush work during the war, apparently."

"Who did?"

"Robert Stoney. Mathematician. Used to be up at Manchester, but he's a Fellow of Kings, and now he's back in Cambridge. Did some kind of secret war work. Same thing as Malcolm Muggeridge, apparently. No one's allowed to say what."

Jack looked up, amused. He'd heard rumors about Muggeridge, but they all revolved around the business of analyzing intercepted German radio messages. What conceivable use would a mathematician have been, for that? Sharpening pencils for the intelligence analysts, presumably.

"What about him, Willie?" Jack asked patiently.

Willie continued reluctantly, as if he was confessing to something mildly immoral. "I paid him a visit yesterday. Place called the Cavendish. Old army friend of mine has a brother who works there. Got the whole tour."

"I know the Cavendish. What's there to see?"

"He's doing things, Jack. *Impossible things.*"

"Impossible?"

"Looking inside people. Putting it on a screen, like a television."

Jack sighed. "Taking X rays?"

Willie snapped back angrily, "I'm not a fool; I know what an X ray looks like. This is different. You can see the blood flow. You can watch your heartbeating. You can follow a sensation through the nerves from . . . fingertip to brain. He says, soon he'll be able to watch a thought in motion."

"Nonsense." Jack scowled. "So he's invented some gadget, some fancy kind of X-ray machine. What are you so agitated about?"

Willie shook his head gravely. "There's more. That's just the tip of the iceberg. He's only been back in Cambridge a year, and already the place is overflowing with . . . wonders." He used the word begrudgingly, as if he had no choice, but was afraid of conveying more approval than he intended.

Jack was beginning to feel a distinct sense of unease.

"What exactly is it you want me to do?" he asked.

Willie replied plainly, "Go and see for yourself. Go and see what he's up to."

The Cavendish Laboratory was a mid-Victorian building, designed to resemble something considerably older and grander. It housed the entire Department of Physics, complete with lecture theaters; the place was swarming with noisy undergraduates. Jack had had no trouble arranging a tour: he'd simply telephoned Stoney and expressed his curiosity, and no more substantial reason had been required.

Stoney had been allocated three adjoining rooms at the back of the building, and the "spin resonance imager" occupied most of the first. Jack obligingly placed his arm between the coils, then almost jerked it out in fright when the strange, transected view of his muscles and veins appeared on the picture tube. He wondered if it could be some kind of hoax, but he clenched his fist slowly and watched the image do the same, then made several unpredictable movements that it mimicked equally well.

"I can show you individual blood cells, if you like," Stoney offered cheerfully.

Jack shook his head; his current, unmagnified flaying was quite enough to take in.

Stoney hesitated, then added awkwardly, "You might want to talk to your doctor at some point. It's just that, your bone density's rather—" He pointed to a chart on the screen beside the image. "Well, it's quite a bit below the normal range."

Jack withdrew his arm. He'd already been diagnosed with osteoporosis, and he'd welcomed the news: it meant that he'd taken a small part of Joyce's illness—the weakness in her bones—into his own body. God was allowing him to suffer a little in her stead.

If Joyce were to step between these coils, what might that reveal? But there'd be nothing to add to her diagnosis. Besides, if he kept up his prayers, and kept up both their spirits, in time her remission would blossom from an uncertain reprieve into a fully fledged cure.

He said, "How does this work?"

"In a strong magnetic field, some of the atomic nuclei and electrons in your body are free to align themselves in various ways with the field." Stoney must have seen Jack's eyes beginning to glaze over; he quickly changed tack. "Think of it as being like setting a whole lot of spinning tops whirling, as vigorously as possible, then listening carefully as they slow down and tip over. For the atoms in your body, that's enough to give some clues as to what kind of molecule, and what kind of tissue, they're in. The machine listens to atoms in different places by changing the way it combines all the signals from billions of tiny antennae. It's like a whispering gallery where we can play with the time that signals take to travel from different places, moving the focus back and forth through any part of your body, thousands of times a second."

Jack pondered this explanation. Though it sounded complicated, in principle it wasn't that much stranger than X rays.

"The physics itself is old hat," Stoney continued, "but for imaging, you need a very strong magnetic field, and you need to make sense of all the data you've gathered. Nevill Mott made the superconducting alloys for the magnets. And I managed to persuade Rosalind Franklin from Birkbeck to collaborate with us, to help perfect the fabrication process for the computing circuits. We cross-link lots of little Y-shaped DNA fragments, then selectively coat them with metal; Rosalind worked out a way to use X-ray crystallography for quality control. We paid her back with a purpose-built computer that will let her solve hydrated protein struc-tures in real time, once she gets her hands on a bright enough X-ray source." He held up a small, unprepossessing object, rimmed with protruding gold wires. "Each logic gate is roughly a hundred Ångstroms cubed, and we grow them in three-dimensional arrays. That's a million, million, million switches in the palm of my hand."

Jack didn't know how to respond to this claim. Even when he couldn't quite follow the man there was something mesmerizing about his ramblings, like a cross between William Blake and nursery talk.

"If computers don't excite you, we're doing all kinds of other things with DNA." Stoney ushered him into the next room, which was full of glassware, and seedlings in pots beneath strip lights. Two assistants seated at a bench were toiling over microscopes; another was dispensing fluids into test tubes with a device that looked like an overgrown eye-dropper.

"There are a dozen new species of rice, corn, and wheat here. They all have at least double the protein and mineral content of existing crops, and each one uses a different biochemical repertoire to protect itself against insects and fungi. Farmers have to get away from monocultures; it leaves them too vulnerable to disease, and too dependent on chemical pesticides."

Jack said, "You've bred these? All these new varieties, in a matter of months?"

"No, no! Instead of hunting down the heritable traits we needed in the wild, and struggling for years to produce cross-breeds bearing all of them, we designed every trait from scratch. Then we manufactured DNA that would make the tools the plants need, and inserted it into their germ cells."

Jack demanded angrily, "Who are you to say what a plant needs?"

Stoney shook his head innocently. "I took my advice from agricultural scientists, who took their advice from farmers. They know what pests and blights they're up against. Food crops are as artificial as Pekinese. Nature didn't hand them to us on a plate, and if they're not working as well as we need them to, nature isn't going to fix them for us."

Jack glowered at him, but said nothing. He was beginning to understand why Willie had sent him here. The man came across as an enthusiastic tinkerer, but there was a breath-taking arrogance lurking behind the boyish exterior.

Stoney explained a collaboration he'd brokered between scientists in Cairo, Bogotá, London, and Calcutta, to develop vaccines for polio, smallpox, malaria, typhoid, yellow fever, tuberculosis, influenza, and leprosy. Some were the first of their kind; others were intended as replacements for existing vaccines. "It's important that we create antigens without culturing the pathogens in animal cells that might themselves harbor viruses. The teams are all looking at variants on a simple, cheap technique that involves putting antigen genes into harmless bacteria that will double as delivery vehicles and adjuvants, then freeze-drying them into spores that can survive tropical heat without refrigeration."

Jack was slightly mollified; this all sounded highly admirable. What business Stoney had instructing doctors on vaccines was another question. Presumably his jargon made sense to them, but when exactly had this mathematician acquired the training to make even the most modest suggestions on the topic?

"You're having a remarkably productive year," he observed.

Stoney smiled. "The muse comes and goes for all of us. But I'm really just the catalyst in most of this. I've been lucky enough to find some people—here in Cambridge, and further afield—who've been willing to chance their arm on some wild ideas. They've done the real work." He gestured toward the next room. "My own pet projects are through here."

The third room was full of electronic gadgets, wired up to picture tubes displaying both phosphorescent words and images resembling engineering blueprints come to life. In the middle of one bench, incongruously, sat a large cage containing several hamsters.

Stoney fiddled with one of the gadgets, and a face like a stylized drawing of a mask appeared on an adjacent screen. The mask looked around the room, then said, "Good morning, Robert. Good morning, Professor Hamilton."

Jack said, "You had someone record those words?"

The mask replied, "No, Robert showed me photographs of all the teaching staff at Cambridge. If I see anyone I know from the photographs, I greet them." The face was crudely rendered, but the hollow eyes seemed to meet Jack's. Stoney explained, "It has no idea what it's saying, of course. It's just an exercise in face and voice recognition."

Jack responded stiffly, "Of course."

Stoney motioned to Jack to approach and examine the hamster cage. He obliged him. There were two adult animals, presumably a breeding pair. Two pink young were suckling from the mother, who reclined in a bed of straw.

"Look closely," Stoney urged him. Jack peered into the nest, then cried out an obscenity and backed away.

One of the young was exactly what it seemed. The other was a machine, wrapped in ersatz skin, with a nozzle clamped to the warm teat.

"That's the most monstrous thing that I've ever seen!" Jack's whole body was trembling. "What possible reason could you have to do that?"

Stoney laughed and made a reassuring gesture, as if his guest were a nervous child recoiling from a harmless toy. "It's not hurting her! And the point is to discover what it takes for the mother to accept it. To 'reproduce one's kind' means having some set of parameters as to what that *is*. Scent, and some aspects of appearance, are important cues in this case, but through trial and error I've also pinned down a set of behaviors that lets the simulacrum pass through every stage of the life cycle. An acceptable child, an acceptable sibling, an acceptable mate."

Jack stared at him, nauseated. "These animals fuck your machines?"

Stoney was apologetic. "Yes, but hamsters will fuck anything. I'll really have to shift to a more discerning species, in order to test that properly."

Jack struggled to regain his composure. "What on Earth possessed you, to do this?"

"In the long run," Stoney said mildly, "I believe this is something we're going to need to understand far better than we do at present. Now that we can map the structures of the brain in fine detail, and match its raw complexity with our computers, it's only a matter of a decade or so before we build machines that think.

"That in itself will be a vast endeavor, but I want to ensure that it's not stillborn from the start. There's not much point creating the most marvelous children in history, only to find that some awful mammalian instinct drives us to strangle them at birth."

Jack sat in his study drinking whiskey. He'd telephoned Joyce after dinner, and they'd chatted for a while, but it wasn't the same as being with her. The weekends never came soon enough, and by Tuesday or Wednesday any sense of reassurance he'd gained from seeing her had slipped away entirely.

It was almost midnight now. After speaking to Joyce, he'd spent three more hours on the telephone, finding out what he could about Stoney. Milking his connections, such as they were; Jack had only been at Cambridge for five years, so he was still very much an outsider. Not that he'd ever been admitted into any inner circles back at Oxford: he'd always belonged to a small, quiet group of dissenters against the tide of fashion. Whatever else might be said about the Tiddlywinks, they'd never had their hands on the levers of academic power.

A year ago, while on sabbatical in Germany, Stoney had resigned suddenly from a position he'd held at Manchester for a decade. He'd returned to Cambridge, despite having no official posting to take up. He'd started collaborating informally with various people at the Cavendish, until the head of the place, Mott, had invented a job description for him, and given him a modest salary, the three rooms Jack had seen, and some students to assist him.

Stoney's colleagues were uniformly amazed by his spate of successful inventions. Though none of his gadgets were based on entirely new science, his skill at seeing straight to the heart of existing theories and plucking some practical consequence from them was unprecedented. Jack had expected some jealous back-stabbing, but no one seemed to have a bad word to say about Stoney. He was willing to turn his scientific Midas touch to the service of anyone who approached him, and it sounded to Jack as if every would-be skeptic or enemy had been bought off with some rewarding insight into their own field.

Stoney's personal life was rather murkier. Half of Jack's informants were convinced that the man was a confirmed pansy, but others spoke of a beautiful, mysterious woman named Helen, with whom he was plainly on intimate terms.

Jack emptied his glass and stared out across the courtyard. *Was it pride, to wonder if he might have received some kind of prophetic vision?* Fifteen years earlier, when he'd written *The Broken Planet*, he'd imagined that he'd merely been satirizing the hubris of modern science. His portrait of the evil forces behind the sardonically named Laboratory Overseeing Various Experiments had been intended as a deadly serious metaphor, but he'd never expected to find himself wondering if real fallen angels were whispering secrets in the ears of a Cambridge don.

How many times, though, had he told his readers that the devil's greatest victory had been convincing the world that he did not exist? The devil was *not* a metaphor, a mere symbol of human weakness: he was a real, scheming presence, acting in time, acting in the world, as much as God Himself.

And hadn't Faustus's damnation been sealed by the most beautiful woman of all time: Helen of Troy?

Jack's skin crawled. He'd once written a humorous newspaper column called "Letters from a Demon," in which a Senior Tempter offered advice to a less experienced colleague on the best means to lead the faithful astray. Even that had been an exhausting, almost corrupting experience; adopting the necessary point of view, however whimsically, had made him feel that he was withering inside. The thought that a cross between the *Faustbuch* and *The Broken Planet* might be coming to life around him was too terrifying to contemplate. He was no hero out of his own fiction—not even a mildmannered Cedric Duffy, let alone a modern Pendragon. And he did not believe that Merlin would rise from the woods to bring chaos to that hubristic Tower of Babel, the Cavendish Laboratory.

Nevertheless, if he was the only person in England who suspected Stoney's true source of inspiration, who *else* would act?

Jack poured himself another glass. There was nothing to be gained by procrastinating. He would not be able to rest until he knew what he was facing: a vain, foolish overgrown boy who was having a run of good luck—or a vain, foolish overgrown boy who had sold his soul and imperiled all humanity.

"A *Satanist?* You're accusing me of being a Satanist?"

Stoney tugged angrily at his dressing gown; he'd been in bed when Jack had pounded on the door. Given the hour, it had been remarkably civil of him to accept a visitor at all, and he appeared so genuinely affronted now that Jack was almost prepared to apologize and slink away. He said, "I had to ask you—"

"You have to be doubly foolish to be a Satanist," Stoney muttered.

"Doubly?"

"Not only do you need to believe all the nonsense of Christian theology, you then have to turn around and back the preordained, guaranteed-to-fail, absolutely futile *losing side*." He held up his hand, as if he believed he'd anticipated the only possible objection to this remark, and wished to spare Jack the trouble of wasting his breath by uttering it. "I *know*, some people claim it's all really about some pre-Christian deity: Mercury, or Pan—guff like that. But assuming that we're not talking about some complicated mislabeling of objects of worship, I really can't think of anything more insulting. You're comparing me to someone like . . . *Huysmans*, who was basically just a very dim Catholic."

Stoney folded his arms and settled back on the couch, waiting for Jack's response.

Jack's head was thick from the whiskey; he wasn't at all sure how to take this. It was the kind of smart-arsed undergraduate drivel he might have expected from any smug atheist—but then, short of a confession, exactly what kind of reply would have constituted evidence of guilt? *If you'd sold your soul to the devil, what lie would you tell in place of the truth?* Had he seriously believed that Stoney would claim to be a devout churchgoer, as if that were the best possible answer to put Jack off the scent?

He had to concentrate on things he'd seen with his own eyes, facts that could not be denied.

"You're plotting to overthrow nature, bending the world to the will of man."

Stoney sighed. "Not at all. More refined technology will help us tread more *lightly*. We have to cut back on pollution and pesticides as rapidly as possible. Or do you want to live in a world where all the animals are born as hermaphrodites, and half the Pacific islands disappear in storms?"

"Don't try telling me that you're some kind of guardian of the animal kingdom! You want to replace us all with machines!"

"Does every Zulu or Tibetan who gives birth to a child, and wants the best for it, threaten you in the same way?"

Jack bristled. "I'm not a racist. A Zulu or Tibetan had a *soul*."

Stoney groaned and put his head in his hands. "It's half past one in the morning! Can't we have this debate some other time?"

Someone banged on the door. Stoney looked up, disbelieving. "What is this? Grand Central Station?"

He crossed to the door and opened it. A disheveled, unshaven man pushed his way into the room. "Quint? What a pleasant—"

The intruder grabbed Stoney and slammed him against the wall. Jack exhaled with surprise. Quint turned bloodshot eyes on him.

"Who the fuck are you?"

"John Hamilton. Who the fuck are you?"

"Never you mind. Just stay put." He jerked Stoney's arm up behind his back with one hand, while grinding his face into the wall with the other. "You're mine now, you piece of shit. No one's going to protect you this time."

Stoney addressed Jack through a mouth squashed against the masonry. "Dith ith Pether Quinth, my own perthonal thpook. I did make a Fauthtian bargain. But with thtrictly temporal—"

"Shut up!" Quint pulled a gun from his jacket and held it to Stoney's head.

Jack said, "Steady on."

"Just how far do your connections go?" Quint screamed. "I've had memos disappear, sources clam up—and now my superiors are treating *me* like some kind of traitor! Well, don't worry: when I'm through with you, I'll have the names of the entire network." He turned to address Jack again. "And don't *you* think you're going anywhere."

Stoney said, "Leave him out of dith. He'th at Magdalene. You mutht know by now: all the thpieth are at Trinity."

Jack was shaken by the sight of Quint waving his gun around, but the implications of this drama came as something of a relief. Stoney's ideas must have had their genesis in some secret war-time research project. He hadn't made a deal with the devil after all, but he'd broken the Official Secrets Act, and now he was paying the price.

Stoney flexed his body and knocked Quint backward. Quint staggered, but didn't fall; he raised his arm menacingly, but there was no gun in his hand. Jack looked around to see where it had fallen, but he couldn't spot it anywhere. Stoney landed a kick squarely in Quint's testicles; barefoot, but Quint wailed with pain. A second kick sent him sprawling.

Stoney called out, "Luke? *Luke!* Would you come and give me a hand?"

A solidly built man with tattooed forearms emerged from Stoney's bedroom, yawning and tugging his braces into place. At the sight of Quint, he groaned. "Not again!"

Stoney said, "I'm sorry."

Luke shrugged stoically. The two of them managed to grab hold of Quint, then they dragged him struggling out the door. Jack waited a few seconds, then searched the floor for the gun. But it wasn't anywhere in sight, and it hadn't slid under the furniture; none of the crevices where it might have ended up were so dark that it would have been lost in shadow. It was not in the room at all.

Jack went to the window and watched the three men cross the courtyard, half expecting to witness an assassination. But Stoney and his lover merely lifted Quint into the air between them, and tossed him into a shallow, rather slimy-looking pond.

Jack spent the ensuing days in a state of turmoil. He wasn't ready to confide in anyone until he could frame his suspicions clearly, and the events in Stoney's rooms were difficult to interpret unambiguously. He couldn't state with absolute certainty that Quint's gun had vanished before his eyes. But surely the fact that Stoney was walking free proved that he was receiving supernatural protection? And Quint himself, confused and demoralized, had certainly had the appearance of a man who'd been demonically confounded at every turn.

If this was true, though, Stoney must have bought more with his soul than immunity from worldly authority. *The knowledge itself* had to be Satanic in origin, as the legend of Faustus described it. Tollers had been right, in his great essay "Mythopoesis": myths were remnants of man's pre-lapsarian capacity to apprehend, directly, the great truths of the world. Why else would they resonate in the imagination, and survive from generation to generation?

By Friday, a sense of urgency gripped him. He couldn't take his confusion back to Potter's Barn, back to Joyce and the boys. This had to be resolved, if only in his own mind, before he returned to his family.

With Wagner on the gramophone, he sat and meditated on the challenge he was facing. Stoney had to be thwarted, but how? Jack had always said that the Church of England — apparently so quaint and harmless, a Church of cake stalls and kindly spinsters — was like a fearsome army in the eyes of Satan. But even if his master were quaking in Hell, it would take more than a few stern words from a bicycling vicar to force Stoney to abandon his obscene plans.

But Stoney's intentions, in themselves, didn't matter. He'd been granted the power to dazzle and seduce, but not to force his will upon the populace. What mattered was how his plans were viewed by others. And the way to stop him was to open people's eyes to the true emptiness of his apparent cornucopia.

The more he thought and prayed about it, the more certain Jack became that he'd discerned the task required of him. No denunciation from the pulpits would suffice; people wouldn't turn down the fruits of Stoney's damnation on the mere say-so of the Church. Why would anyone reject such lustrous gifts, without a carefully reasoned argument?

Jack had been humiliated once, defeated once, trying to expose the barrenness of materialism. But might that not have been a form of preparation? He'd been badly mauled by Anscombe, but she'd made an infinitely gentler enemy than the one he now confronted. He had suffered from her taunts — but what was *suffering*, if not the chisel God used to shape his children into their true selves?

His role was clear, now. He would find Stoney's intellectual Achilles' heel, and expose it to the world.

He would debate him.

3

Robert gazed at the blackboard for a full minute, then started laughing with delight. "That's so beautiful!"

"Isn't it?" Helen put down the chalk and joined him on the couch. "Any more symmetry, and nothing would happen: the universe would be full of crystalline blankness. Any less, and it would all be uncorrelated noise."

Over the months, in a series of tutorials, Helen had led him through a small part of the century of physics that had separated them at their first meeting, down to the purely algebraic structures that lay beneath spacetime and matter. Mathematics catalogued everything that was not self-contradictory; within that vast inventory, physics was an island of structures rich enough to contain their own beholders.

Robert sat and mentally reviewed everything he'd learned, trying to apprehend as much as he could in a single image. As he did, a part of him waited fearfully for a sense of disappointment, a sense of anticlimax. *He might never see more deeply into the nature of the world. In this direction, at least, there was nothing more to be discovered.*

But anticlimax was impossible. To become jaded with *this* was impossible. However familiar he became with the algebra of the universe, it would never grow less marvelous.

Finally he asked, "Are there other islands?" Not merely other histories, sharing the same underlying basis, but other realities entirely.

"I suspect so," Helen replied. "People have mapped some possibilities. I don't know how that could ever be confirmed, though."

Robert shook his head, sated. "I won't even think about that. I need to come down to Earth for a while." He stretched his arms and leaned back, still grinning.

Helen said, "Where's Luke today? He usually shows up by now, to drag you out into the sunshine."

The question wiped the smile from Robert's face. "Apparently I make poor company. Being insufficiently fanatical about darts and football."

"He's left you?" Helen reached over and squeezed his hand sympathetically. A little mockingly, too.

Robert was annoyed; she never said anything, but he always felt that she was judging him. "You think I should grow up, don't you? Find someone more like myself. Some kind of *soulmate*." He'd meant the word to sound sardonic, but it emerged rather differently.

"It's your life," she said.

A year before, that would have been a laughable claim, but it was almost the truth now. There was a de facto moratorium on prosecutions, while the recently acquired genetic and neurological evidence was being assessed by a parliamentary subcommittee. Robert had helped plant the seeds of the campaign, but he'd played no real part in it; other people had taken up the cause. In a matter of months, it was possible that Quint's cage would be smashed, at least for everyone in Britain.

The prospect filled him with a kind of vertigo. He might have broken the laws at every opportunity, but they had still molded him. The cage might not have left him crippled, but he'd be lying to himself if he denied that he'd been stunted.

He said, "Is that what happened, in your past? I ended up in some . . . lifelong partnership?" As he spoke the words, his mouth went dry, and he was suddenly afraid that the answer would be yes. *With Chris. The life he'd missed out on was a life of happiness with Chris.*

"No."

"Then . . . what?" he pleaded. "What did I do? How did I live?" He caught himself, suddenly self-conscious, but added, "You can't blame me for being curious."

Helen said gently, "You don't want to know what you can't change. All of that is part of your own causal past now, as much as it is of mine."

"If it's part of my own history," Robert countered, "don't I deserve to know it? This man wasn't me, but he brought you to me."

Helen considered this. "You accept that he was someone else? Not someone whose actions you're responsible for?"

"Of course."

She said, "There was a trial, in 1952. For 'Gross Indecency contrary to Section 11 of the Criminal Amendment Act of 1885.' He wasn't imprisoned, but the court ordered hormone treatments."

"*Hormone treatments?*" Robert laughed. "What—testosterone, to make him more of a man?"

"No, estrogen. Which in men reduces the sex drive. There are side-effects, of course. Gynecomorphism, among other things."

Robert felt physically sick.*They'd chemically castrated him, with drugs that had made him sprout breasts*. Of all the bizarre abuse to which he'd been subjected, nothing had been as horrifying as that.

Helen continued, "The treatment lasted six months, and the effects were all temporary. But two years later, he took his own life. It was never clear exactly why."

Robert absorbed this in silence. He didn't want to know anything more.

After a while, he said, "How do you bear it? Knowing that in some branch or other, every possible form of humiliation is being inflicted on someone?"

Helen said, "I don't *bear it*. I change it. That's why I'm here."

Robert bowed his head. "I know. And I'm grateful that our histories collided. But . . . how many histories *don't?*" He struggled to find an example, though it was almost too painful to contemplate; since their first conversation, it was a topic he'd deliberately pushed to the back of his mind. "There's not just an unchangeable Auschwitz in each of our pasts, there are an astronomical number of others— along with an astronomical number of things that are even worse."

Helen said bluntly, "That's not true."

"What?" Robert looked up at her, startled.

She walked to the blackboard and erased it. "Auschwitz has happened, for both of us, and no one I'm aware of has ever prevented it—but that doesn't mean that *nobody* stops it, anywhere." She began sketching a network of fine lines on the blackboard. "You and I are having this conversation in countless microhistories—sequences of events where various different things happen with subatomic particles throughout the universe—but that's irrelevant to us, we can't tell those strands apart, so we might as well treat them all as one history." She pressed the chalk down hard to make a thick streak that covered everything she'd drawn. "The quantum decoherence people call this 'coarse graining.' Summing over all these indistinguishable details is what gives rise to classical physics in the first place.

"Now, 'the two of us' would have first met in many perceivably different coarse-grained histories—and furthermore, you've since diverged by making different choices, and experiencing different external possibilities, after those events." She sketched two intersecting ribbons of coarse-grained histories, and then showed each history diverging further.

"World War II and the Holocaust certainly happened in both of *our* pasts — but that's no proof that the total is so vast that it might as well be infinite. Remember, what stops us successfully intervening is the fact that we're reaching back to a point where some of the parallel interventions start to bite their own tail. So when we fail, it can't be counted twice: it's just confirming what we already know."

Robert protested, "But what about all the versions of thirties Europe that don't happen to lie in either your past or mine? Just because we have no direct evidence for a Holocaust in those branches, that hardly makes it unlikely."

Helen said, "Not unlikely *per se*, without intervention. But not fixed in stone either. We'll keep trying, refining the technology, until we can reach branches where there's no overlap with our own past in the thirties. And there must be other, separate ribbons of intervention that happen in histories we can never even know about."

Robert was elated. He'd imagined himself clinging to a rock of improbable good fortune in an infinite sea of suffering — struggling to pretend, for the sake of his own sanity, that the rock was all there was. But what lay around him was not inevitably worse; it was merely unknown. In time, he might even play a part in ensuring that every last tragedy was *not* repeated across billions of worlds.

He reexamined the diagram. "Hang on. Intervention doesn't end divergence, though, does it? You reached *us*, a year ago, but in at least some of the histories spreading out from that moment, won't we still have suffered all kinds of disasters, and reacted in all kinds of self-defeating ways?"

"Yes," Helen conceded, "but fewer than you might think. If you merely listed every sequence of events that superficially appeared to have a nonzero probability, you'd end up with a staggering catalog of absurdist tragedies. But when you calculate everything more carefully, and take account of Planck-scale effects, it turns out to be nowhere near as bad. There are *no* coarse-grained histories where boulders assemble themselves out of dust and rain from the sky, or everyone in London or Madras goes mad and slaughters their children. Most macroscopic systems end up being quite robust — people included. Across histories, the range of natural disasters, human stupidity, and sheer bad luck isn't overwhelmingly greater than the range you're aware of from this history alone."

Robert laughed. "And that's not bad enough?"

"Oh, it is. But that's the best thing about the form I've taken."

"I'm sorry?"

Helen tipped her head and regarded him with an expression of disappointment. "You know, you're still not as quick on your feet as I'd expected."

Robert's face burned, but then he realized what he'd missed, and his resentment vanished.

"*You don't diverge?* Your hardware is designed to end the process? Your environment, your surroundings, will still split you into different histories — but on a coarse-grained level, you don't contribute to the process yourself?"

"That's right."

Robert was speechless. Even after a year, she could still toss him a hand grenade like this.

Helen said, "I can't help living in many worlds; that's beyond my control. But I do know that I'm one person. Faced with a choice that puts me on a knife-edge, I know I won't split and take every path."

Robert hugged himself, suddenly cold. "Like I do. Like I have. Like all of us poor creatures of flesh."

Helen came and sat beside him. "Even that's not irrevocable. Once you've taken this form — if that's what you choose — you can meet your other selves, reverse some of the scatter. Give some a chance to undo what they've done."

This time, Robert grasped her meaning at once. "Gather myself together? Make myself whole?"

Helen shrugged. "If it's what you want. If you see it that way."

He stared back at her, disoriented. Touching the bedrock of physics was one thing, but this possibility was too much to take in.

Someone knocked on the study door. The two of them exchanged wary glances, but it wasn't Quint, back for more punishment. It was a porter bearing a telegram.

When the man had left, Robert opened the envelope.

"Bad news?" Helen asked.

He shook his head. "Not a death in the family, if that's what you meant. It's from John Hamilton. He's challenging me to a debate. On the topic 'Can a Machine Think?' "

"What, at some university function?"

"No. On the BBC: Four weeks from tomorrow." He looked up. "Do you think I should do it?"

"Radio or television?"

Robert reread the message. "Television."

Helen smiled. "Definitely. I'll give you some tips."

"On the subject?"

"No! That would be cheating." She eyed him appraisingly. "You can start by throwing out your electric razor. Get rid of the permanent five o'clock shadow."

Robert was hurt. "Some people find that quite attractive."

Helen replied firmly, "Trust me on this."

The BBC sent a car to take Robert down to London. Helen sat beside him in the back seat.

"Are you nervous?" she asked.

"Nothing that an hour of throwing up won't cure."

Hamilton had suggested a live broadcast, "to keep things interesting," and the producer had agreed. Robert had never been on television; he'd taken part in a couple of radio discussions on the future of computing, back when the Mark I had first come into use, but even those had been taped.

Hamilton's choice of topic had surprised him at first, but in retrospect it seemed quite shrewd. A debate on the proposition that "Modern Science is the Devil's Work" would have brought howls of laughter from all but the most pious viewers, whereas the purely metaphorical claim that "Modern Science is a Faustian Pact" would have had the entire audience nodding sagely in agreement, while carrying no implications whatsoever. If you weren't going to take the whole dire fairy tale literally, everything was "a Faustian Pact" in some sufficiently watered-down sense: everything had a potential downside, and this was as pointless to assert as it was easy to demonstrate.

Robert had met considerable incredulity, though, when he'd explained to journalists where his own research was leading. To date, the press had treated him as a kind of eccentric British Edison, churning out inventions of indisputable utility, and no one seemed to find it at all surprising or alarming that he was also, frankly, a bit of a loon. But Hamilton would have a chance to exploit, and reshape, that perception. If Robert insisted on defending his goal of creating machine intelligence, not as an amusing hobby that might have been chosen by a public relations firm to make him appear endearingly daft, but as both the ultimate vindication of materialist science and the logical endpoint of most of his life's work, Hamilton could use a victory tonight to cast doubt on everything Robert had done, and everything he symbolized. By asking, not at all rhetorically, "Where will this all end?," he was inviting Robert to step forward and hang himself with the answer.

The traffic was heavy for a Sunday evening, and they arrived at the Shepherd's Bush studios with only fifteen minutes until the broadcast. Hamilton had been collected by a separate car, from his family home near Oxford. As they crossed the studio, Robert spotted him, conversing intensely with a dark-haired young man.

He whispered to Helen, "Do you know who that is, with Hamilton?"

She followed his gaze, then smiled cryptically. Robert said, "What? Do you recognize him from somewhere?"

"Yes, but I'll tell you later."

As the makeup woman applied powder, Helen ran through her long list of rules again. "Don't stare into the camera, or you'll look like you're peddling soap powder. But don't avert your eyes. You don't want to look shifty."

The makeup woman whispered to Robert, "Everyone's an expert."

"Annoying, isn't it?" he confided.

Michael Polanyi, an academic philosopher who was well-known to the public after presenting a series of radio talks, had agreed to moderate the debate. Polanyi popped into the makeup room, accompanied by the producer; they chatted with Robert for a couple of minutes, setting him at ease and reminding him of the procedure they'd be following.

They'd only just left him when the floor manager appeared. "We need you in the studio now, please, Professor." Robert followed her, and Helen pursued him part of the way. "Breathe slowly and deeply," she urged him.

"As if *you'd* know!" he snapped.

Robert shook hands with Hamilton, then took his seat on one side of the podium. Hamilton's young adviser had retreated into the shadows; Robert glanced back to see Helen watching from a similar position. It was like a duel: they both had seconds. The floor manager pointed out the studio monitor, and, as Robert watched, it was switched between the feeds from two cameras: a wide shot of the whole set, and a closer view of the podium, including the small blackboard on a stand beside it. He'd once asked Helen whether television had progressed to far greater levels of sophistication in her branch of the future, once the pioneering days were left behind, but the question had left her uncharacteristically tongue-tied.

The floor manager retreated behind the cameras, called for silence, then counted down from ten, mouthing the final numbers.

The broadcast began with an introduction from Polanyi: concise, witty, and nonpartisan. Then Hamilton stepped up to the podium. Robert watched him directly while the wide-angle view was being transmitted, so as not to appear rude or distracted. He only turned to the monitor when he was no longer visible himself.

"Can a machine think?" Hamilton began. "My intuition tells me: *no*. My heart tells me: *no*. I'm sure that most of you feel the same way. But that's not enough, is it? In this day and age, we aren't allowed to rely on our hearts for anything. We need something scientific. We need some kind of *proof*.

"Some years ago, I took part in a debate at Oxford University. The issue then was not whether machines might behave like people, but whether people themselves might *be* mere machines. Materialists, you see, claim that we are all just a collection of purposeless atoms, colliding at random. Everything we do, everything we feel, everything we say, comes down to some sequence of events that might as well be the spinning of cogs, or the opening and closing of electrical relays.

"To me, this was self-evidently false. What point could there be, I argued, in even conversing with a materialist? By his own admission, the words that came out of his mouth would be the result of nothing but a mindless, mechanical process! By his own theory, he could have no reason to think that those words would be the truth! Only believers in a transcendent human soul could claim any interest in the truth."

Hamilton nodded slowly, a penitent's gesture. "I was wrong, and I was put in my place. This might be self-evident to *me*, and it might be self-evident to *you*, but it's certainly not what philosophers call an 'analytical truth': it's not actually a nonsense, a contradiction in terms, to believe that we are mere machines. There might, there just *might*, be some reason why the words that emerge from a materialist's mouth are truthful, despite their origins lying entirely in unthinking matter.

"There might." Hamilton smiled wistfully. "I had to concede that possibility, because I only had my instinct, my gut feeling, to tell me otherwise.

"But the reason I only had my instinct to guide me was because I'd failed to learn of an event that had taken place many years before. A discovery made in 1930, by an Austrian mathematician named Kurt Gödel."

Robert felt a shiver of excitement run down his spine. He'd been afraid that the whole contest would degenerate into theology, with Hamilton invoking Aquinas all night — or Aristotle, at best. But it looked as if his mysterious adviser had dragged him into the twentieth century, and they were going to have a chance to debate the real issues after all.

"What is it that we *know* Professor Stoney's computers can do, and do well?" Hamilton continued. "Arithmetic! In a fraction of a second, they can add up a million numbers. Once we've told them, very precisely, what calculations to perform, they'll complete them in the blink of an eye — even if those calculations would take you or me a lifetime.

"But do these machines *understand* what it is they're doing? Professor Stoney says, 'Not yet. Not right now. Give them time. Rome wasn't built in a day.'" Hamilton nodded thoughtfully. "Perhaps that's fair. His computers are only a few years old. They're just babies. Why should they understand anything, so soon?

"But let's stop and think about this a bit more carefully. A computer, as it stands today, is simply a machine that does arithmetic, and Professor Stoney isn't proposing that they're going to sprout new kinds of brains all on their own. Nor is he proposing *giving* them anything really new. He can already let them look at the world with television cameras, turning the pictures into a stream of numbers describing the brightness of different points on the screen . . . on which the computer can then perform *arithmetic*. He can already let them speak to us with a special kind of loudspeaker, to which the computer feeds a stream of numbers to describe how loud the sound should be . . . a stream of numbers produced by more *arithmetic*.

"So the world can come into the computer, as numbers, and words can emerge, as numbers too. All Professor Stoney hopes to add to his computers is a 'cleverer' way to do the arithmetic that takes the first set of numbers and churns out the second. It's that 'clever arithmetic,' he tells us, that will make these machines think."

Hamilton folded his arms and paused for a moment. "What are we to make of this? Can *doing arithmetic*, and nothing more, be enough to let a machine *understand* anything? My instinct certainly tells me no, but who am I that you should trust my instinct?

"So, let's narrow down the question of understanding, and to be scrupulously fair, let's put it in the most favorable light possible for Professor Stoney. If there's one thing a computer *ought* to be able to understand—as well as us, if not better— it's arithmetic itself. If a computer could think at all, it would surely be able to grasp the nature of its own best talent.

"The question, then, comes down to this: can you *describe* all of arithmetic, *using* nothing but arithmetic? Thirty years ago—long before Professor Stoney and his computers came along—Professor Gödel asked himself exactly that question.

"Now, you might be wondering how anyone could even *begin* to describe the rules of arithmetic, using nothing but arithmetic itself." Hamilton turned to the blackboard, picked up the chalk, and wrote two lines:

$$\text{If } x + z = y + z$$
$$\text{then } x = y$$

"This is an important rule, but it's written in symbols, not numbers, because it has to be true for *every* number, every x, y, and z. But Professor Gödel had a clever idea: why not use a code, like spies use, where every symbol is assigned a number?" Hamilton wrote:

$$\text{The code for "a" is 1.}$$
$$\text{The code for "b" is 2.}$$

"And so on. You can have a code for every letter of the alphabet, and for all the other symbols needed for arithmetic: plus signs, equals signs, that kind of thing. Telegrams are sent this way every day, with a code called the Baudot code, so there's really nothing strange or sinister about it.

"All the rules of arithmetic that we learned at school can be written with a carefully chosen set of symbols, which can then be translated into numbers. Every question as to what does or does not *follow from* those rules can then be seen anew, as a question about numbers. If *this* line follows from *this* one," Hamilton indicated the two lines of the cancellation rule, "we can see it in the relationship between their code numbers. We can judge each inference, and declare it valid or not, purely by doing arithmetic.

"So, given *any* proposition at all about arithmetic — such as the claim that 'there are infinitely many prime numbers' — we can restate the notion that we have a proof for that claim in terms of code numbers. If the code number for our claim is x, we can say 'There is a number p, ending with the code number x, that passes our test for being the code number of a valid proof.' "

Hamilton took a visible breath.

"In 1930, Professor Gödel used this scheme to do something rather ingenious." He wrote on the blackboard:

There DOES NOT EXIST a number p meeting the following condition:
p is the code number of a valid proof of this claim.

"Here is a claim about arithmetic, about numbers. It has to be either true or false. So let's start by supposing that it happens to be true. Then there *is no* number p that is the code number for a proof of this claim. So this is a true statement about arithmetic, but it can't be proved merely by *doing* arithmetic!"

Hamilton smiled. "If you don't catch on immediately, don't worry; when I first heard this argument from a young friend of mine, it took a while for the meaning to sink in. But remember: the only hope a computer has for understanding *any-thing* is by doing arithmetic, and we've just found a statement that *cannot* be proved with mere arithmetic.

"Is this statement really true, though? We mustn't jump to conclusions, we mustn't damn the machines too hastily. Suppose this claim is false! Since it claims there is no number p that is the code number of its own proof, to be false there would have to be such a number, after all. And that number would encode the 'proof' of an acknowledged falsehood!"

Hamilton spread his arms triumphantly. "You and I, like every schoolboy, know that you can't prove a falsehood from sound premises — and if the premises of arithmetic aren't sound, what is? So *we* know, as a matter of certainty, that this statement is true.

"Professor Gödel was the first to see this, but with a little help and perseverance, any educated person can follow in his footsteps. A *machine could never do that.* We might divulge to a machine our own knowledge of this fact, offering it as something to be taken on trust, but the machine could neither stumble on this truth for itself, nor truly comprehend it when we offered it as a gift.

"You and I *understand* arithmetic, in a way that no electronic calculator ever will. What hope has a machine, then, of moving beyond its own most favorable milieu and comprehending any wider truth?

"None at all, ladies and gentlemen. Though this detour into mathematics might have seemed arcane to you, it has served a very down-to-Earth purpose. It has proved — beyond refutation by even the most ardent materialist or the most pedantic philosopher — what we common folk knew all along: no machine will ever think."

Hamilton took his seat. For a moment, Robert was simply exhilarated; coached or not, Hamilton had grasped the essential features of the incompleteness proof, and presented them to a lay audience. What might have been a night of shadow-boxing—with no blows connecting, and nothing for the audience to judge but two solo performances in separate arenas—had turned into a genuine clash of ideas.

As Polanyi introduced him and he walked to the podium, Robert realized that his usual shyness and self-consciousness had evaporated. He was filled with an altogether different kind of tension: he sensed more acutely than ever what was at stake.

When he reached the podium, he adopted the posture of someone about to begin a prepared speech, but then he caught himself, as if he'd forgotten something. "Bear with me for a moment." He walked around to the far side of the blackboard and quickly wrote a few words on it, upside-down. Then he resumed his place.

"Can a machine think? Professor Hamilton would like us to believe that he's settled the issue once and for all, by coming up with a statement that *we* know is true, but a particular machine—programmed to explore the theorems of arithmetic in a certain rigid way—would never be able to produce. Well . . . we all have our limitations." He flipped the blackboard over to reveal what he'd written on the opposite side:

If Robert Stoney speaks these words, he will NOT be telling the truth.

He waited a few beats, then continued.

"What I'd like to explore, though, is not so much a question of limitations, as of opportunities. How exactly is it that we've all ended up with this mysterious ability to know that Gödel's statement is true? Where does this advantage, this great insight, come from? From our souls? From some immaterial entity that no machine could ever possess? Is that the only possible source, the only conceivable explanation? Or might it come from something a little less ethereal?

"As Professor Hamilton explained, we believe Gödel's statement is true because we trust the rules of arithmetic not to lead us into contradictions and falsehoods. But where does that trust come from? How does it arise?"

Robert turned the blackboard back to Hamilton's side, and pointed to the cancellation rule. "If x plus z equals y plus z, then x equals y. Why is this so *reasonable*? We might not learn to put it quite like this until we're in our teens, but if you showed a young child two boxes—without revealing their contents—added an equal number of shells, or stones, or pieces of fruit to both, and then let the child look inside to see that each box now contained the same number of items, it wouldn't take any formal education for the child to understand that the two boxes must have held the same number of things to begin with.

"The child knows, we all know, how a certain kind of object behaves. Our lives are steeped in direct experience of whole numbers: whole numbers of coins, stamps, pebbles, birds, cats, sheep, buses. If I tried to persuade a six-year-old that I could put three stones in a box, remove one of them, and be left with four . . . he'd simply laugh at me. Why? It's not merely that he's sure to have taken one

thing away from three to get two, on many prior occasions. Even a child understands that some things that appear reliable will eventually fail: a toy that works
perfectly, day after day, for a month or a year, can still break. But not arithmetic,
not taking one from three. He can't even picture *that* failing. Once you've lived
in the world, once you've seen how it works, the failure of arithmetic becomes
unimaginable.

"Professor Hamilton suggests that this is down to our souls. But what would he
say about a child reared in a world of water and mist, never in the company of
more than one person at a time, never taught to count on his fingers and toes. I
doubt that such a child would possess the same certainty that you and I have, as
to the impossibility of arithmetic ever leading him astray. To banish whole numbers entirely from his world would require very strange surroundings, and a level
of deprivation amounting to cruelty, but would that be enough to rob a child of
his *soul?*

"A computer, programmed to pursue arithmetic as Professor Hamilton has described, is subject to far more deprivation than that child. If I'd been raised with
my hands and feet tied, my head in a sack, and someone shouting orders at me,
I doubt that I'd have much grasp of reality—and I'd still be better prepared for
the task than such a computer. It's a great mercy that a machine treated that way
wouldn't be able to think: if it could, the shackles we'd placed upon it would be
criminally oppressive!

"But that's hardly the fault of the computer, or a revelation of some irreparable
flaw in its nature. If we want to judge the potential of our machines with any
degree of honesty, we have to play fair with them, not saddle them with restrictions
that we'd never dream of imposing on ourselves. There really is no point comparing an eagle with a spanner, or a gazelle with a washing machine: it's our jets
that fly and our cars that run, albeit in quite different ways than any animal.

"*Thought* is sure to be far harder to achieve than those other skills, and to do
so we might need to mimic the natural world far more closely. But I believe that
once a machine is endowed with facilities resembling the inborn tools for learning
that we all have as our birthright, and is set free to learn the way a child learns,
through experience, observation, trial and error, hunches and failures—instead of
being handed a list of instructions that it has no choice but to obey—we will
finally be in a position to compare like with like.

"When that happens, and we can meet and talk and argue with these machines—about arithmetic, or any other topic—there'll be no need to take the
word of Professor Gödel, or Professor Hamilton, or myself, for anything. We'll
invite them down to the local pub, and interrogate them in person. And if we
play fair with them, we'll use the same experience and judgment we use with any
friend, or guest, or stranger, to decide for ourselves whether or not they can think."

The BBC put on a lavish assortment of wine and cheese in a small room off the
studio. Robert ended up in a heated argument with Polanyi, who revealed himself
to be firmly on the negative side, while Helen flirted shamelessly with Hamilton's
young friend, who turned out to have a Ph.D. in algebraic geometry from Cambridge; he must have completed the degree just before Robert had come back

from Manchester. After exchanging some polite formalities with Hamilton, Robert kept his distance, sensing that any further contact would not be welcome.

An hour later, though, after getting lost in the maze of corridors on his way back from the toilets, Robert came across Hamilton sitting alone in the studio, weeping.

He almost backed away in silence, but Hamilton looked up and saw him. With their eyes locked, it was impossible to retreat.

Robert said, "It's your wife?" He'd heard that she'd been seriously ill, but the gossip had included a miraculous recovery. Some friend of the family had lain hands on her a year ago, and she'd gone into remission.

Hamilton said, "She's dying."

Robert approached and sat beside him. "From what?"

"Breast cancer. It's spread throughout her body. Into her bones, into her lungs, into her liver." He sobbed again, a helpless spasm, then caught himself angrily. "*Suffering is the chisel God uses to shape us.* What kind of idiot comes up with a line like that?"

Robert said, "I'll talk to a friend of mine, an oncologist at Guy's Hospital. He's doing a trial of a new genetic treatment."

Hamilton stared at him. "One of your *miracle cures?*"

"No, no. I mean, only very indirectly."

Hamilton said angrily, "She won't take your poison."

Robert almost snapped back: *She won't? Or you won't let her?* But it was an unfair question. In some marriages, the lines blurred. It was not for him to judge the way the two of them faced this together.

"They go away in order to be with us in a new way, even closer than before." Hamilton spoke the words like a defiant incantation, a declaration of faith that would ward off temptation, whether or not he entirely believed it.

Robert was silent for a while, then he said, "I lost someone close to me, when I was a boy. And I thought the same thing. I thought he was still with me, for a long time afterward. Guiding me. Encouraging me." It was hard to get the words out; he hadn't spoken about this to anyone for almost thirty years. "I dreamed up a whole theory to explain it, in which 'souls' used quantum uncertainty to control the body during life, and communicate with the living after death, without breaking any laws of physics. The kind of thing every science-minded seventeen-year-old probably stumbles on, and takes seriously for a couple of weeks, before realizing how nonsensical it is. But I had a good reason not to see the flaws, so I clung to it for almost two years. Because I missed him so much, it took me that long to understand what I was doing, how I was deceiving myself."

Hamilton said pointedly, "If you'd not tried to explain it, you might never have lost him. He might still be with you now."

Robert thought about this. "I'm glad he's not, though. It wouldn't be fair to either of us."

Hamilton shuddered. "Then you can't have loved him very much, can you?" He put his head in his arms. "Just fuck off, now, will you?"

Robert said, "What exactly would it take, to prove to you that I'm not in league with the devil?"

Hamilton turned red eyes on him and announced triumphantly, "Nothing will do that! I saw what happened to Quint's gun!"

Robert sighed. "That was a conjuring trick. Stage magic, not black magic."

"Oh yes? Show me how it's done, then. Teach me how to do it, so I can impress my friends."

"It's rather technical. It would take all night."

Hamilton laughed humorlessly. "You can't deceive me. I saw through you from the start."

"Do you think X rays are Satanic? Penicillin?"

"Don't treat me like a fool. There's no comparison."

"*Why not?* Everything I've helped develop is part of the same continuum. I've read some of your writing on medieval culture, and you're always berating modern commentators for presenting it as unsophisticated. No one really thought the Earth was flat. No one really treated every novelty as witchcraft. So why view any of my work any differently than a fourteenth-century man would view twentieth-century medicine?"

Hamilton replied, "If a fourteenth-century man was suddenly faced with twentieth-century medicine, don't you think he'd be entitled to wonder how it had been revealed to his contemporaries?"

Robert shifted uneasily on his chair. Helen hadn't sworn him to secrecy, but he'd agreed with her view: it was better to wait, to spread the knowledge that would ground an understanding of what had happened, before revealing any details of the contact between branches.

But this man's wife was dying, needlessly. And Robert was tired of keeping secrets. Some wars required it, but others were better won with honesty.

He said, "I know you hate H. G. Wells. But what if he was right, about one little thing?"

Robert told him everything, glossing over the technicalities but leaving out nothing substantial. Hamilton listened without interrupting, gripped by a kind of unwilling fascination. His expression shifted from hostile to incredulous, but there were also hints of begrudging amazement, as if he could at least appreciate some of the beauty and complexity of the picture Robert was painting.

But when Robert had finished, Hamilton said merely, "You're a grand liar, Stoney. But what else should I expect, from the King of Lies?"

Robert was in a somber mood on the drive back to Cambridge. The encounter with Hamilton had depressed him, and the question of who'd swayed the nation in the debate seemed remote and abstract in comparison.

Helen had taken a house in the suburbs, rather than inviting scandal by cohabiting with him, though her frequent visits to his rooms seemed to have had almost the same effect. Robert walked her to the door.

"I think it went well, don't you?" she said.

"I suppose so."

"I'm leaving tonight," she added casually. "This is goodbye."

"What?" Robert was staggered. "Everything's still up in the air! I still need you!"

She shook her head. "You have all the tools you need, all the clues. And plenty of local allies. There's nothing truly urgent I could tell you, now, that you couldn't find out just as quickly on your own."

Robert pleaded with her, but her mind was made up. The driver beeped the horn; Robert gestured to him impatiently.

"You know, my breath's frosting visibly," he said, "and you're producing nothing. You really ought to be more careful."

She laughed. "It's a bit late to worry about that."

"Where will you go? Back home? Or off to twist another branch?"

"Another branch. But there's something I'm planning to do on the way."

"What's that?"

"Do you remember once, you wrote about an Oracle? A machine that could solve the halting problem?"

"Of course." Given a device that could tell you in advance whether a given computer program would halt, or go on running forever, you'd be able to prove or disprove any theorem whatsoever about the integers: the Goldbach conjecture, Fermat's Last Theorem, anything. You'd simply show this "Oracle" a program that would loop through all the integers, testing every possible set of values and only halting if it came to a set that violated the conjecture. You'd never need to run the program itself; the Oracle's verdict on whether or not it halted would be enough.

Such a device might or might not be possible, but Robert had proved more than twenty years before that no ordinary computer, however ingeniously programmed, would suffice. If program H could always tell you in a finite time whether or not program X would halt, you could tack on a small addition to H to create program Z, which perversely and deliberately went into an infinite loop whenever it examined a program that halted. If Z examined itself, it would either halt eventually, or run forever. But either possibility contradicted the alleged powers of program H: if Z actually ran forever, it would be because H had claimed that it wouldn't, and *vice versa*. Program H could not exist.

"Time travel," Helen said, "gives me a chance to become an Oracle. There's a way to exploit the inability to change your own past, a way to squeeze an infinite number of timelike paths — none of them closed, but some of them arbitrarily near to it — into a finite physical system. Once you do that, you can solve the halting problem."

"How?" Robert's mind was racing. "And once you've done that . . . what about higher cardinalities? An Oracle for Oracles, able to test conjectures about the real numbers?"

Helen smiled enigmatically. "The first problem should only take you forty or fifty years to solve. As for the rest," she pulled away from him, moving into the darkness of the hallway, "what makes you think I know the answer myself?" She blew him a kiss, then vanished from sight.

Robert took a step toward her, but the hallway was empty.

He walked back to the car, sad and exalted, his heart pounding.

The driver asked wearily, "Where to now, sir?"

Robert said, "Further up, and further in."

4

The night after the funeral, Jack paced the house until three A.M. When would it be bearable? *When?* She'd shown more strength and courage, dying, than he felt within himself right now. But she'd share it with him, in the weeks to come. She'd share it with them all.

In bed, in the darkness, he tried to sense her presence around him. But it was forced, it was premature. It was one thing to have faith that she was watching over him, but quite another to expect to be spared every trace of grief, every trace of pain.

He waited for sleep. He needed to get some rest before dawn, or how would he face her children in the morning?

Gradually, he became aware of someone standing in the darkness at the foot of the bed. As he examined and reexamined the shadows, he formed a clear image of the apparition's face.

It was his own. Younger, happier, surer of himself.

Jack sat up. "What do you want?"

"I want you to come with me." The figure approached; Jack recoiled, and it halted.

"Come with you, where?" Jack demanded.

"To a place where she's waiting."

Jack shook his head. "No. I don't believe you. She said she'd come for me herself, when it was time. She said she'd guide me."

"She didn't understand, then," the apparition insisted gently. "She didn't know I could fetch you myself. Do you think I'd send her in my place? Do you think I'd shirk the task?"

Jack searched the smiling, supplicatory face. "Who are you?" *His own soul, in Heaven, remade?* Was this a gift God offered everyone? To meet, before death, the very thing you would become — if you so chose? So that even this would be an act of free will?

The apparition said, "Stoney persuaded me to let his friend treat Joyce. We lived on, together. More than a century has passed. And now we want you to join us."

Jack choked with horror. "No! This is a trick! *You're the Devil!*"

The thing replied mildly, "There is no Devil. And no God, either. Just people. But I promise you: people with the powers of gods are kinder than any god we ever imagined."

Jack covered his face. "Leave me be." He whispered fervent prayers, and waited. It was a test, a moment of vulnerability, but God wouldn't leave him naked like this, face-to-face with the Enemy, for longer than he could endure.

He uncovered his face. The thing was still with him.

It said, "Do you remember, when your faith came to you? The sense of a shield around you melting away, like armor you'd worn to keep God at bay?"

"Yes." Jack acknowledged the truth defiantly; he wasn't frightened that this abomination could see into his past, into his heart.

"That took strength: to admit that you needed God. But it takes the same kind of strength, again, to understand that *some needs can never be met*. I can't promise you Heaven. We have no disease, we have no war, we have no poverty. But we have to find our own love, our own goodness. There is no final word of comfort. We only have each other."

Jack didn't reply; this blasphemous fantasy wasn't even worth challenging. He said, "I know you're lying. Do you really imagine that I'd leave the boys alone here?"

"They'd go back to America, back to their father. How many years do you think you'd have with them, if you stay? They've already lost their mother. It would be easier for them now, a single clean break."

Jack shouted angrily, "Get out of my house!"

The thing came closer, and sat on the bed. It put a hand on his shoulder. Jack sobbed, "Help me!" But he didn't know whose aid he was invoking anymore.

"Do you remember the scene in *The Seat of Oak*? When the Harpy traps everyone in her cave underground, and tries to convince them that there is no Nescia? Only this drab underworld is real, she tells them. Everything else they think they've seen was just make-believe." Jack's own young face smiled nostalgically. "And we had dear old Shrugweight reply: he didn't think much of this so-called 'real world' of hers. And even if she was right, since four little children could make up a better world, he'd rather go on pretending that their imaginary one was real.

"But we had it all upside down! The real world is richer, and stranger, and more beautiful than anything ever imagined. Milton, Dante, John the Divine are the ones who trapped you in a drab, gray underworld. That's where you are now. But if you give me your hand, I can pull you out."

Jack's chest was bursting. *He couldn't lose his faith. He'd kept it through worse than this. He'd kept it through every torture and indignity God had inflicted on his wife's frail body. No one could take it from him now.* He crooned to himself, "In my time of trouble, He will find me."

The cool hand tightened its grip on his shoulder. "You can be with her, now. Just say the word, and you will become a part of me. I will take you inside me, and you will see through my eyes, and we will travel back to the world where she still lives."

Jack wept openly. "Leave me in peace! Just leave me to mourn her!"

The thing nodded sadly. "If that's what you want."

"I do! Go!"

"When I'm sure."

Suddenly, Jack thought back to the long rant Stoney had delivered in the studio. Every choice went every way, Stoney had claimed. No decision could ever be final.

"Now I know you're lying!" he shouted triumphantly. "If you believed everything Stoney told you, how could my choice ever mean a thing? I would always say yes to you, and I would always say no! It would all be the same!"

The apparition replied solemnly, "While I'm here with you, touching you, *you can't be divided*. Your choice will count."

Jack wiped his eyes, and gazed into its face. It seemed to believe every word it was speaking. What if this truly was his metaphysical twin, speaking as honestly as he could, and not merely the Devil in a mask? Perhaps there was a grain of truth in Stoney's awful vision; perhaps this was another version of himself, a living person who honestly believed that the two of them shared a history.

Then it was a visitor sent by God, to humble him. To teach him compassion toward Stoney. To show Jack that he, too, with a little less faith, and a little more pride, might have been damned forever.

Jack stretched out a hand and touched the face of this poor lost soul. *There, but for the grace of God, go I.*

He said, "I've made my choice. Now leave me."

author's note:

Where the lives of the fictional characters of this story parallel those of real historical figures, I've drawn on biographies by Andrew Hodges and A. N. Wilson. The self-dual formulation of general relativity was discovered by Abhay Ashtekar in 1986, and has since led to ground-breaking developments in quantum gravity, but the implications drawn from it here are fanciful.

obsidian Harvest

Rick Cook & Ernest Hogan

Rick Cook is a frequent contributor to Analog, and has also sold fiction to
New Destinies, Sword and Sorceress, and elsewhere. His many novels in-
clude Wizard's Bane, The Wizardry Compiled, The Wizardry Consulted,
The Wizardry Cursed, The Wizardry Quested, The Wiz Biz (an omnibus
volume of the first two titles in the Wiz series), Limbo System, and Mall
Purchase Night. He lives in Phoenix, Arizona.

Ernest Hogan has sold stories to Analog, Amazing, New Pathways, Se-
miotext(e), Last Wave, Pulphouse, and Science Fiction Age. His novels
include Cortez on Jupiter and High Aztech.

In the flamboyant, colorful, and hugely entertaining story that follows,
audaciously mixing the mystery genre with the Alternate History tale, they
join forces to take a hard-boiled Private Eye down some Mean Streets much
meaner, much weirder, and much more profoundly dangerous, than any
ever seen by Philip Marlowe or Sam Spade . . .

I have always liked you, my boy," Uncle Tlaloc rumbled. He smiled at me,
showing a row of jade-inlaid teeth.

I nodded politely, sipped my bitter chocolate and listened to my head throb. I
wondered what the old bastard had in store for me this time.

Classical music keened and thumped to a crescendo on the main floor of the
Hummingbird's Palace as the tone-deaf current object of Uncle Tlaloc's affections
belted out the line about the unhappy ending of the romance between Smoking
Mountain and White Lady. She didn't even come near the high note. In the old
days they skinned singers for performances like that. But times change and the
world decays as cycles end; so she smiled, bowed and received enthusiastic applause as she blushed through her yellow skin dye. The combination of the blush
and the dye made her look more jaundiced than attractive.

The pungent mixture of tobacco and drug smoke stung my eyes as it blended with
the piney-sweet reek of burning copal incense, almost hiding the odors of spices, citrus flowers — and a hint of stale urine creeping in from the privy in back.

Uncle Tlaloc, as fat and ugly as his Rain God namesake, leaned back in his chair, the one with Death carved beneath his right hand and the Earth Monster beneath his left. "In fact I consider you more of a nephew than an employee."

Something bad. Whenever Uncle went into that almost-a-relative routine it meant he had something especially nasty in store for me.

He signaled the kneeling pulque girl, and she glided forward to refill his cup. Her eardrums had been pierced so she could not hear, but he kept silent until she had withdrawn, as noiselessly as she had come.

He glanced around conspiratorially and leaned forward toward where I knelt at his feet, took a hefty swig of pulque out of the skull he used for a chalice and belched malodorously. "I have a small task for you."

"I am yours to command, Lord Uncle."

"Your cousin, Ninedeer . . ."

About as bad as it can fucking get!

"I know him, Uncle-tzin." My voice betrayed nothing.

"He is an acolyte of the Death Master, I believe."

"So I have heard."

"The Death Master has—something—in his temple. I would like to know how it came to die and whatever else your cousin might know about it."

"Am I permitted to know what this thing is, Uncle-tzin?"

Uncle Tlaloc paused, as if considering whether to tell me, and leaned even closer.

"It is a huetlacoatl. An important one."

It was raining when I stepped out of the Hummingbird's Palace, a soft, warm drizzle that felt like Tlaloc Himself was pissing on me. Just like his whoreson namesake inside. I pulled my cloak tighter around me, fingering the single row of featherwork at the neck of my cape. Hummingbird feathers, the mark of a warrior, of the war god, Left-Handed Hummingbird Himself, and hence an inalienable symbol of nobility. Of course, the greater nobles supplemented hummingbird feathers with the plumes of the quetzal, symbol of Lord Quetzalcoatl; but it had been a while since I had any dealings with the nobility, minor or otherwise.

It had been a good deal longer since I had dealt with any of my clansmen. My relatives and I would much rather it stayed that way. But Uncle Tlaloc commanded, and his word was the closest thing there was to law down in English Town. I stepped over a sleeping beggar on the sidewalk, threw back my head, squared my shoulders, and marched off toward the Death Master's temple—every inch a Child of the Hummingbird on his way to his destiny on the Field of Flowers.

The guards at the Temple Precinct passed me on the strength of my cloak, the clan tattoo on my cheeks—and my bearing. None of Uncle's other employees could have entered the sacred quarter of the Atlnahuac so easily, which was why the old bastard had chosen me for this job.

The Death Master's temple was at the far end of the sacred quarter, close to the bay and downwind of the major temples. I strolled easily and unremarked among the other nobles, priests, and servants who were out at this hour. Floodlights cast the painted and carved friezes in garish light. Here and there neon tubes outlined the temples on top of the pyramids in reds, the color of fresh blood, and purples, the shade of clotted blood. It was different—harsher—than I remembered, and yet I knew the sacred quarter hadn't changed.

Ninedeer hadn't changed either. He was as thin and gangly as I remembered him. Adulthood hadn't cured his weak chin, and the elaborate jade lip plug he affected only heightened the deficiency. We had never particularly liked each other.

"I didn't expect to ever see you again," he said when a temple servant ushered me into his presence.

I cast an arm at the stone tables behind him and the draped burdens a few of them bore. "Working here? Surely I would have thought you'd expect me to turn up sooner or later."

The years had done as much to improve his sense of humor as they had to improve his jawline. "I didn't expect to see you alive," he amended. "You're not even supposed to be here."

I smiled in the way I had learned since I had been with Uncle Tlaloc. "You could call the guards and have me sent away," I said mildly. "Of course, then I would have to seek you elsewhere to conduct our business."

His expression told me that rumors about what had happened to the last relative who crossed me had leaked into clan gossip. "What do you want?" he asked sullenly.

"I want a look at one of your charges," I said. "And I want to know what you can tell me about it."

"It? You mean an animal?" That was possible, of course. The Death Master's duties included collecting the bodies of animals who had died in the city, as well as dead humans, sacrificial victims, and executed criminals. But he knew damn well it wasn't any animal, and his voice showed it.

"I mean the huetlacoatl."

Ninedeer flinched as if I had slapped him. "No! Absolutely not."

I leaned against the wall in an attitude of exaggerated ease. "One way or another, cousin. One way or another."

He hesitated, weighed his alternatives, and decided it would be better to give me what I wanted now. He shrugged, gestured, and led me down a short corridor. The room at the end was narrow and low, but cleaner than the main receiving chamber. There were sweet herbs strewn on the floor and the gas torches gave a steady, bright light. Normally a room like this would be used to receive the bodies of high nobles and other important functionaries. What lay on the table now was not a noble, and perhaps not a functionary, but it was clearly important.

"Make it quick," he said as we entered the chamber. "They are coming for the body soon."

I gestured and Ninedeer flung back the red cotton sheet that draped the corpse.

The thing on the slab was man-sized and had walked on two legs. Beyond that there was little enough resemblance to a human. The skin was greenish-gray, shading to fishbelly white between the legs. The head had a prominent muzzle filled with sharp teeth made for tearing. The huge middle claw on each foot was drawn back in the rigor of death. The hands were more delicate and supple, but were frozen in a raking gesture. The corpse lay half on its side because its tail would not let it lie on its back.

Huetlacoatl, the old Serpent Lords, mysterious inhabitants of Viru, the continent to the south. In spite of hundreds of years of trading, raiding, and occasional open warfare, and in spite of the fact that they had a trading post on an island in the bay, I had never seen one in the flesh before.

"Satisfied?" Ninedeer demanded and made to re-cover the body.

I frowned and gestured him away. The corpse was split from the crotch almost to the neck. There were other wounds on the body, stab wounds to the upper chest showing how the creature had died, and a dark line around the neck that I took to be the bruise left by a garrotte.

I pointed to the gaping wound and cocked my eye at Ninedeer. "It was done after he was dead," he admitted. "At least if the thing works like a human being or an animal. The heart—or whatever kept its soul—had stopped pumping."

"Is the heart still there?"

"Quetzalcoatl, yes!" Ninedeer exclaimed, wide-eyed. "As least as best the Death Master can tell. This one wasn't sacrificed, if that's your meaning."

I bent down to examine one of the three-fingered hands with its raking talons. "Any blood?"

"No. Nor on the big claw on the foot, either. Now will you please get out of here?"

"Shortly. Now what else can you tell me?"

"Nothing. Go away." I didn't need to be a spirit reader to follow his thoughts. As a lesser noble and scion of a Reed clan, I had every right to be here. But my clan membership, and my life, were the only things they had not taken from me when they cast me out. And in spite of a clansman's theoretical rights, I doubted the authorities would appreciate even a clansman in good standing poking around something as sensitive as a dead huetlacoatl. If I were found here they might not spare my life this time. But whatever they did to me, Ninedeer would be in trouble, and that was all he cared about.

Since Ninedeer put more value on his record than I did on my life, the rest was easy. "I've got all night, you know."

Ninedeer ground his teeth. "It was done where it was found, in the alley. At least if these things bleed the way animals do."

That made sense. A deserted alley was as good as any other place for such butchery. I reached down and examined the hem of the thing's drab cotton cloak. "What's this?"

He shifted from one foot to the other. "I don't know. Honestly, I don't."

I held the hem to my nose and sniffed, trying to drown out the snake stink. "Candle grease." I dropped it and looked the body over. Whoever had done this had stood over the thing for a while.

Ninedeer was almost dancing with impatience. "The Speakers to the Huetlacoatl will be here any minute to retrieve the body. If they find you here it will be hard on both of us."

"No sweet herbs and winding sheet?"

"We do not know what the huetlacoatls' customs are on these things. Now *go!*"

There wasn't much else to learn there, so I went. I stood in the shadows across from the Death Master's temple for a while, under a carved Earth Monster that protected me from most of the rain, while I thought about what my cousin had told me. I wasn't ready to return to the Hummingbird's Palace. Uncle Tlaloc likes complete reports, not mysteries.

The first mystery was how the thing had died. A fight among the huetlacoatl? Possibly. They were supposed to kill by disemboweling with the ripping claws on their feet, but the wound had been made from the bottom up, not the top down. What's more, the flesh was sliced neatly, not torn as by a claw. And the marks of the garrotte and the stab wounds to the chest suggested human assistance, at least.

Not for the first time I wondered what Uncle Tlaloc was doing sticking his nose in this business. That in itself suggested human involvement.

So, assume the huetlacoatl had been killed by men. It had taken several of them, one to hold it by the garrotte around its neck and more to stab it—probably two more, at least, judging from the stab wounds.

Then why had humans gone to all that trouble to kill a huetlacoatl? True, they were unpopular—so unpopular they seldom left their treaty island in the bay and almost always traveled with an escort of human guards. Yet, there was neither sign nor mention of any guards. Was this one out on privy business?

The swish of rubber tires on rain-slick pavement made me step back further into the shadows. A land steamer, long, low, and as black as the polished jet in Lady Death's necklace, pulled up to the entrance to Death Master's temple. Steam hissed from the beneath the hood as the door swung open. A door too wide and low. Four heavily cloaked and hooded figures emerged silently; the first three as a group, followed after a moment by the fourth.

The three were human, in spite of their elaborate guise and stiff-legged walk. The fourth was not. It was fluid where the others were stiff, strutting where they were jerky, and completely natural where they were studied. It leaned forward and picked its feet high under the muffling cloak. The portal to the temple swung open and the four vanished silently inside.

So. Whatever this was, it was important enough to bring out a huetlacoatl in addition to the Speakers. I knew virtually nothing about huetlacoatl clans, but I did know they weren't noted for family feeling. Clearly it wasn't sentiment that had brought this one along with its human servants. This was looking more and more interesting.

Within minutes the portal opened again and the cloaked figures emerged, a human in the lead, then Lord Huetlacoatl; and then the others, carrying a wrapped bundle between them. The huetlacoatl entered the land steamer first, followed by the burden bearers and the third man. As the door silently closed, the land steamer belched once and then swished off into the night.

I turned and headed back toward the dock area, but not to the Hummingbird's Palace. The night was young enough. The storm clouds were clearing to reveal the dull, starless night sky over the blackened waters of the bay. The colossal statue of the Storm Goddess on the quay smiled at me with chipped teeth and weathered lips. The city of Atlnahuac provided other avenues to explore.

The Serpent's Court was no Hummingbird's Palace. It was garishly modern where the Palace was determinedly antique. Tinny modern music coming out of a beat-up horned machine grated the nerves and set the mood. Its clientele was way down the scale as well, but Uncle Tlaloc's word carried weight here and some of the clients might prove useful.

I paused in the entrance alcove and shook the rain off my hat as the blast of the air conditioning chilled me in my rain-soaked cloak. I scanned the room for a useful face.

There weren't many possibilities. The watchmen from the evening shift had finished their drinks and had gone home long ago, and the night shift would not end until dawn. The other patrons, criminals, whores, and hangers-on, couldn't help me. The only one who looked likely was Sevenrain, sitting by himself in the corner. Not my first choice, but he would do.

Sevenrain was well into his fourth decade, with lines on his face, scars cutting through the tattoos on his arms and chest, and the burly, slightly bloated build of a man who likes corn beer too much and exercise too little. A sneer formed on his face as I crossed the room.

"Well, young lordling," he said just a little too loudly as I approached. "You honor us with your presence."

I gave it back to him with a condescending nod. "The honor is mine entirely, oh estimable hound of men," I lisped in a parody of a noble accent. "Allow me a small token of my appreciation by purchasing your next pot of beer."

He glared at me as I sat down next to him, trying to decide if the game was worth continuing. He apparently remembered what had happened the last time he had pursued it—or who I still worked for—and decided it wasn't.

"What in the Nine Hells do you want?" he growled.

"Just a few minutes conversation, and perhaps a chance to show my gratitude afterward." Sevenrain knew damn well whose gratitude might be shown; and so, probably, did everyone else in the bar who was at all interested. But better not to mention such things.

I shifted my stool so no one else could see my lips move. "There was a killing today down in the warehouse district."

"Quetzalcoatl's dick! Do you expect me to remember every miserable person who gets his throat slit in my precinct?"

"I didn't say it was a person." I said softly.

His face froze. "Yeah," he mumbled. "There was one of those."

"Where exactly?"

His eyes darted left and right, but his lips hardly moved at all. "Behind the warehouses off the English Docks. Between the third and fourth one."

"Time?"

"Found it an hour before dawn. Not one of our people, a sailor looking for a place to puke." His face split in a mirthless grin. "Puked his fucking guts out when he saw."

"Any leads?"

A longer pause this time. "No. No one saw anything. No one heard anything. Nothing at the scene but that—and a big puddle of sailor puke."

I nodded. "You'll send word if you learn anything more?"

"I'll see it reaches the right ears." Meaning he wasn't going to take a chance on me cutting him out of Uncle's generosity.

I nodded and rose, flipping a coin down onto the table so that the silver rang loudly on the stone top. "For your refreshment, my good man," I lisped and swaggered out to the metaphorical sound of grinding teeth behind me.

The night was heavy with the Storm Goddess' moist, salty breath. I could feel more than the usual number of disease spirits floating in the air. My sweat soaked my bed. I threw off the blanket. Sleep was impossible on nights like this.

My eyes caught something. I strained to see it in the darkness. There was a figure at the door, walking toward the foot of my bed.

I wanted to run. I wanted to reach for the sword by my pillow. But I couldn't move. I couldn't even breathe.

The figure knelt at the foot of my bed. It picked up the box I kept there. When it opened the box, a cold, green light was released that lit up its skinless face.

Skinless, not fleshless. The eyes, muscles, and other meat of the body were still present. It was a flayed man. Of course, there was only one flayed man of great significance in my life.

I looked into the lidless eyes, and recognized them. The color of watery chocolate.

"Smoke?"

I couldn't tell if he was smiling. He didn't have lips.

"I've come to visit my skin," he said. "A night like this can be cold to one without skin."

"How sweet."

His teeth glistened in the green light. "I also came to remind you that your life grew in my death as corn grows in the death of the Corn God."

"My life. How marvelous."

"And to remind you that you could be the one who walks at night without his skin."

He snapped the box shut. The light was gone. I was alone.

Shaking, I crawled to the foot of the bed. I could barely see in the moonlight from the window, but I could feel that the layer of grime on the box had not been disturbed. No one had touched the box. Smoke was not here. It was a dream.

I had only looked into the box at Smoke's skin once, when Uncle Tlaloc gave it to me after he had saved what was left of my life. I haven't been able to make myself open it and look at the dried and neatly folded, tattooed skin since.

"The thing you desire most," Uncle had said when he presented me the box with his own hands. And he was right—then. Then I desired nothing more than Smoke's slow, painful death for leading me into shame and abandoning me to save himself. But like most of Uncle Tlaloc's gifts, this one had two edges, and a point keener than obsidian. By killing my enemy in such a fashion, he cut me off from any possibility of return to my former life. By presenting the skin to me, he tied me inexorably to the deed. And he reminded me, oh so subtly, who held the power of life and death in English Town.

Smoke did not return that night, but my dreams were uneasy and peopled with things I would rather forget. I awoke bolt upright, clutching a dagger before I realized that someone had nudged the foot of my bed. It was my man, Uo, standing over me, impassive despite the knife in my hand. "One to see you," he said as soon as he was sure I was awake.

"Who?"

He shrugged. "She is veiled."

"Weapons?"

His flat peasant face didn't change expression. "A high-born lady."

My visitor was standing in the middle of my front room, arms at her sides and rigid, as if to touch anything was to contaminate herself. Her mantle bore a single conservative row of embroidery which proclaimed her status without specifying her clan.

"My Lady."

She turned to face me, cotton mantle still over her head. Her eyes were large and dark, but not crossed enough to be truly beautiful. Like the eyes of another woman, from a long time ago. The memory grabbed at my gut with chilled talons.

"Are we alone?" she asked when my servant had withdrawn. I nodded and she dropped her mantle, showing her face.

She was handsome without being beautiful. Her skull was not flattened in the Frog fashion. Her hair was lustrous, her lip plug small like the jade spools in her ears. On her chin were the four lines of a high-class married lady. It took me a second to put the picture together and recognize her.

"Well, at least you are not drunk," she remarked.

"Threeflower?"

"*Lady* Threeflower." Her voice was hard and cold. She would not unbend an inch.

"And how may I serve the gracious lady?"

Her eyes flashed. Once, in another life, she was the elder sister of the one I was supposed to marry. Now what was she?

"Ninedeer told of meeting you."

"I am not surprised my cousin could not keep the news to himself. But was that enough to bring you running to me?"

She snorted. "Let us say he reminded me of your existence." She stressed the last word as if I were actually dead. Which, I suppose I was, from her viewpoint.

"Then what brings you to English Town?"

"A relative. Fourflower."

Oh ho. A gambling debt perhaps, and Threeflower using our past connection to charm her way out of it? That didn't seem right. "I do not know the lady."

"She was hardly a child when you left." Again that emphasis.

By now I was sick of her attitude, sick of the things she represented, and sick of the skinless face of Smoke floating in my mind. I softened my voice. "My Lady, you obviously want something. Will insulting me help you to gain your end?"

A pause. "You are correct," she said, suddenly coldly gracious. "I am trying to *find* Fourflower. She disappeared three days ago, seemingly kidnapped at the Forest Market."

"Seemingly?"

"Her maid heard a muffled scream, and when she turned her mistress was gone."

I cocked an eyebrow at her and she flushed. "The maid was questioned very thoroughly. She held to her story to the end."

"Then Fourflower probably has been kidnapped."

Lady Threeflower glared at me. "I wish her return."

"Then I would suggest contacting a go-between. I can give you a name . . ."

"The go-betweens say they know nothing of the matter," she cut in.

That stopped me. Kidnapping was an old, if not honorable, profession, and one of the reasons the nobles kept their women and children close. But there was an order to these things, a procedure. And that called for the approach to be made through a go-between.

"Three days, you said?"

"Mid-morning on the day of the Ocelot last." Plenty of time for a go-between to contact the family.

Mentally I ran down the list of possibilities. The most obvious one was that the snatch team had bungled the job and the girl was dead. Or perhaps this was an unusually complicated bit of business. Someone had dropped the ball, or the girl's other relatives had been contacted and were keeping it quiet. Too many things could have happened.

"Was Fourflower important?"

"She was of the line of the Emperor Montezuma Himself."

Which was a polite way of saying she was very well-born and had nothing else. No position, no title of her own, no fortune, and no prospects. A cousin-companion to Threeflower, perhaps chosen for her name, and ranking little higher than a servant. But a young noblewoman could become attached to such a one. Especially if her blood sister was a beautiful, faithless, empty-headed ninny. I broke that train of thought off sharply.

"Then there is more to this than you think. Best you go home and await word."

"I want her found!"

"Do you think I can snap my fingers and conjure her here for you?"

"I think you can contact your friends who kidnap."

"They are my associates, not my friends, and they only kidnap for ransom." A thought came. "Was Fourflower pretty?"

"Very," she snapped, and the color drained from her cheeks as she caught the implication. "I suppose you know brothel keepers as well," she said with cold fury.

"Many of them," I said and smiled at her discomfiture. "But none of the ones I know would be foolish enough to kidnap a high-born maid off the streets in broad daylight." *Not unless they were very well paid,* I thought, *and well enough protected not to fear Uncle Tlaloc and his peers.* But word of something that big should have gotten around. This was beginning to sound interesting.

"Did she have lovers?"

"She was untouched," Threeflower said. "The maid confirmed that before she died."

"A flirtation, then?"

"I would have known even that."

"So." I was silent for a long time.

"I will pay well for Fourflower's safe return," Threeflower said.

"Undoubtedly, Lady. But I will be honest with you. I doubt very much the child is still alive."

"Then I will pay for her killers."

If the girl had died in a bungled kidnapping, the head of the ring would gladly give the skins of her killers as a peace offering and pay wergild besides.

"I will see what I can discover."

She nodded, reached beneath her mantle and tossed something at me. I dodged instinctively, and the deerskin pouch hit the floor with the metallic clink.

"That will do for a start, I think."

I kicked the pouch back to the hem of her skirt. "I am not doing this for money," I told her.

She smiled for the first time. "You shall have nothing else of me. My husband cannot restore you and I would not ask it of him even if he could."

"You misread me," I said coldly.

"I read you well enough to know that in an age when things were done properly you would have been killed instead of merely banished."

"And in an age when things were done properly you would be whipped naked from one temple plaza to the next for visiting a man not a relative, unescorted, and at night." I looked at her speculatively. "That could still happen, you know."

She snorted, threw her mantle over her head and stalked out. Uo must have met her at the door because I did not hear it slam as she left. I was already reaching for the tequila.

It was late the next afternoon when I awoke with a pounding head, a foul taste in my mouth, and a sourness in the pit of my stomach that was more than physical. Twice in two days I had had to deal with ghosts from my former life and that was two times too many.

I dressed in a clean tunic and cloak, bolted down a cold tamale that settled in my stomach like a lump of basalt, and hurried out. It was not long until the market gates would close, and there was someone I wanted to see, as much for my own peace of mind as anything else.

The streets about the Fireflower Market were thronged with porters, slaves, housewives, and their maids. Here and there were caged parrots with their mouths open, hanging their wormlike tongues as if they were dying of thirst. A barefoot Frog girl, barely old enough to be married, blocked my way to the entrance. She was holding a baby who had wooden blocks tied to his skull to make it slope like the forehead of a reptile, but she broke off her plea as we were pressed back against the wall to make way for a green-plumed noble and his retinue.

I followed in his convenient wake, being forced to pause only twice, as he stopped to watch the tiny daughter of a featherworker delicately plucking the feathers off of a skewered hummingbird with thin bone tweezers; and then as he paused by the tattooist, who was beating the line that would make a young man's pretty face look as if it were covered with scales. Around us, the busy market was beginning to clear out. A few of the vendors had already shut their stalls, and here and there sweepers were at work. I dove into the maze of twisty lanes between the stalls, checked my bearings once, and pulled up before a narrow doorway hidden by a reed mat which still bore the stained and weary outline of a jaguar.

"Who comes?" A voice croaked as I thrust aside the matting and stepped through the door into the darkness.

"A pilgrim seeking wisdom from Mother Jaguar," I answered. There was a shifting sound behind me, as if someone had just relaxed, and perhaps lowered a weapon.

"Enter then and be welcome," the voice called, stronger this time. I stepped through the second doorway, thrust aside a cotton curtain and came face to face with Mother Jaguar.

She was kneeling at a low clay altar table, casting and recasting knucklebones too small for a deer or a pig. "Sit, my son," she said in a voice that was stronger and younger than the one which had greeted me at the door. "What do you seek?"

She didn't look up until I tossed three silver coins onto the table next to the knucklebones. She was ancient, but her eyes were black and sharp as obsidian points in her wrinkled, tattooed face.

"There is a maid named Fourflower, a high-born maid," I began. "It is said she was stolen from the marketplace on the day of the Ocelot, last. Her family seeks her and would be grateful for any aid."

Mother Jaguar nodded. "I have heard this story, but I know nothing of such a maid or such a stealing. Nor do any of my ones in the world of spirits know of such a thing."

"A kidnapping for private reasons then? Perhaps lust?"

Mother Jaguar cast the bones again and shook her head. "I and my spirits know nothing," she repeated.

I nodded. If you paid Mother Jaguar for information, and if she took your money, then she would tell you the truth. Which meant that neither Mother nor any of her kind knew anything about what had happened to Fourflower.

"Thank you for your wisdom," I said and rose to go.

"Your money," Mother Jaguar said.

I tossed a fourth coin on the table. "It is yours. I asked, and you gave of your wisdom. It is not a fault that the answer was other than I hoped." I turned to pass through the curtain.

"Wait," Mother Jaguar said. I turned and she cast the bones, once, twice, and again, while I waited.

"Your maid is not the only one so taken," Mother Jaguar said at last. "There have been several others, all of impeccable lineage, but perhaps not favored by fortune."

"All maids?"

"Some maids, some boys, a few unmarried men and women, perhaps a hand count in all. All in the last two cycles of days."

"Who?"

"No one knows. Nor why." She turned again to her casting and the coins vanished from the altar as if by magic.

Uncle Tlaloc was impassive when I told him what I had found out about the kidnapping that evening.

It was still early and Uncle was drinking maté rather than alcohol. He took a last long pull on the gourd through his golden straw as I finished my report. "Diverting perhaps," he rumbled, "but I fail to see why it should be of concern to us."

I frowned. "There are ransoms, Uncle."

He waved that away. "Assuming they are alive."

"They aren't?"

"The odds are strongly against it. Besides, I understand the Emperor's Shadow has taken an interest in the matter."

I started to ask why, realized it was a stupid question and closed my mouth. Kidnapped humans could be sacrificed, especially ones of little note but of excellent lineage. And, of course, it was treason for anyone other than the Emperor or the Imperial Priests to conduct a human sacrifice, since it implied a relationship to the Gods which was the Emperor's alone. Yes, the Emperor's Shadow would investigate a thing like that. And the Emperor's Shadow was very bad news indeed.

"Uncle, do you think this is somehow related to the matter of the huetlacoatl?"

"It was not sacrificed, you said. Besides the Emperor's Shadow has shown no interest in that matter." He shifted his position on his great chair and sucked the gourd dry noisily. "No, I think for now we can consider such a connection unlikely.

"Meanwhile, my boy, I have another job for you. One that might shed some light on — the other matter."

I leaned against the low stone railing with the midafternoon sun behind me and looked down upon the former lords of creation.

Not far away, a howler monkey bellowed and a jaguar cried.

Long ago, the Hero Twins, Quetzalcoatl and Tezcatlipoca, slew the water monster Cipactli. They made the world out of its mangled carcass, and human creation began. Before that, these, or ones like them, had ruled the Earth.

For their evil, lust, and impiety, the Gods had sent fire from the sky, and their rule had ended. Only on the southern continent, hidden behind a veil of storms, did they remain as a warning to men of the power and majesty of the Gods.

Or so the story went. Personally, I thought that if the Gods allowed man to continue, they owed the huetlacoatls an apology.

There were four of them in the pit below me, picking at the mass of greenery in the mangers on the walls. When one of them stretched erect, its head came to within a few feet of the parapet. And these were not the biggest of the huetlacoatls, only two-legged browsers that walked with their bodies nearly horizontal and their tails straight out behind them. One of them lifted its head, with leaves dripping from its jaws, and cocked an incurious eye at me. For an instant, I wondered what the old lords of creation thought of the new. Then it dropped its gaze and went back to the manger.

That was about the closest I'd come to an insight in the course of a long, tedious afternoon at the Imperial Menagerie. Uncle Tlaloc wanted more information, and I'd hoped for something that would give me an idea, anything, about the murder of the huetlacoatl from studying the other creatures of the Viru.

I'd seen big huetlacoatls and bigger ones. Ones that were big and ferocious enough to be demigods, and ones that were ponderous and stupid. Apparently the southern continent was overrun with the things in all sorts of nightmare shapes. But nothing I saw gave me insight.

It was a rare sunny day, and the menagerie was thronged with nobility and their servants. There was even a fair sprinkling of commoners, admitted by "special dispensation"—actually a small bribe to the keepers. The commoners were wearing their feast day best and the nobles the bright mantles appropriate to their stations. The people were far more colorful than the huetlacoatls, and a lot more interesting than tanks of water monsters, and cages of woolly beasts of the distant north.

I forced my attention back to the huetlacoatls below me, but as I turned something flew past my shoulder into the huetlacoatl pit. They shifted and honked nervously. Then a hand of bananas landed close to the first object, a red-and-green mango. I turned to see four or five other people crowding up against the rail, male and female and most dressed in the plain tunics of commoners. They were chanting prayers and throwing fruit into the pit like worshipers at a shrine. Some of them were rocking back and forth with their eyes closed, as if in ecstasy.

Two of the menagerie attendants came running up, shouting at the congregation and waving their staffs of office. They laid into the little group of worshipers with the heavy mahogany sticks, sending them scattering and screaming. One guard struck a young woman across the kidneys. The woman stumbled toward me, and the attendant caught her a glancing blow on the side of the head. The woman tried to run, but the guard was almost on top of her, striking again and again with his stick.

I waited until she staggered by me and casually shifted my stance. The guard tripped over my foot and went sprawling face-first into the dirt. While he was down, I took the young woman's arm and motioned toward the alley between the pens with my eyes. In spite of the blood running down her cheek she smiled and darted off. I turned my attention to helping the attendant to his feet. By the time he shook off my ministrations, the girl and the others had vanished.

Meanwhile, other attendants had entered the pit and were busy gathering up the offerings. They scurried among the huetlacoatls' huge clawed feet, ducking beneath the great tails to grab the smashed remnants of fruit. The huetlacoatls were still nervous and any second I expected to see an attendant smashed as flat as that first mango.

There was a low whistle over my right shoulder. All four of the beasts below me jerked upright as if on a string. Their heads swiveled toward me and they pushed closer to the wall. Instinctively I took a step back and groped under my cloak for my sword.

"It's all right," someone said. I turned and there was an old man. He was wearing a dirty cloak with the three lines of feathers of the middle nobility and leaning on a heavy, carved stick. "They're just looking for me. Aren't you, my pretties?" At the sound of his voice all the huetlacoatls began to whistle and hiss.

He stumped to the parapet and looked down. The animals pressed against the wall and craned their necks even higher. He leaned out at a dangerous angle and reached down with his stick to scratch the tallest ones on their muzzles. "How are we today?" he crooned. "All healthy and happy?" The smaller ones were making little leaps to try to bring their muzzles within range of his cane.

"Magnificent, aren't they?" he asked without taking his eyes from them. "I'm their mother, you know." He glanced sideways to see if the statement had the desired effect.

"It must have been a difficult labor, Uncle."

He cackled at the thought. All the while the cane tip kept caressing the monsters in the pit.

"I raised them from eggs," he said as he straightened up to the audible disappointment of his "children." "I was the first thing they saw when they hatched and I stayed with them night and day when they were in the nest, fed them chewed-up leaves. When they were older they followed me everywhere. Oh yes, they are my children."

"You know them well? The huetlacoatls, I mean."

His face cracked into an improbable smile. "As well as anyone. I am Foureagle, the keeper of the Emperor's animals."

"What can you tell me about the huetlacoatls?"

"More than you want to know, young one. Or would believe if I told you."

"Would you share your wisdom with me," I made a quick mental judgment, "over a bowl of pulque?"

Again the smile. "Lead on, young sir."

A grog seller had his cart, brightly painted with many portraits of Lady Mayahuel, the inventor of the sacred drink, just outside the gates of the menagerie. I purchased a couple of gourds, received a perfunctory blessing, and Foureagle and I settled in the shade with our backs to the wall. The old man took a long, deep pull, wiped his mouth and sighed lustily.

"Those damn fools," he said, jerking his head to indicate where the fruit-throwers had been. "They don't understand that those beasts can't digest fruit. It makes them sick."

"Is that why they throw it?"

He snorted. "They think they are worshiping them, making offerings to the avatars of their gods. What they're really doing is killing the poor things—if we don't stop them." He took another swig from his gourd. "All this whoring after new gods, young sir. No good can come of it."

I nodded gravely, as if the old man had said something profound. "But of the huetlacoatls themselves, what can you tell me of them?"

"Ah," he sighed and took another pull. "They thrive only down on Viru, you know," he said by way of a beginning. "Only there. They do not do well here, just as man does not prosper there."

"The ones here," I gestured to the menagerie behind us, "seem to do well enough."

"Only because we care for them," the old man said. "It took generations for us to learn how to do so. There are many kinds, and each has subtly different needs. That pen the duckbills are in, for example: it would not do for the longnecks, nor the spike-tails. And if you tried to keep the big meat-eaters in there, they'd be out and among the visitors in less than a day-cycle." Another pull on the gourd. "Those meat-eaters can jump."

"Do they share a common language?"

Again the cackle. "The ones here? They are mere beasts. The huetlacoatl version of deer and jaguar. Only the talking huetlacoatls are intelligent in the way of man."

Shit! An afternoon wasted. I had never thought of the huetlacoatls as intelligent in the sense that men are intelligent, but I assumed they were more than beasts.

"They were unknown to us until we reached the southern lands," said Foureagle. "They are big, powerful, and strange, so men try to worship them."

"Do they ever sacrifice them?"

The old man snorted. "Here? To what end? Their blood will not aid our corn, nor can their deaths help keep the balance with our Gods. They are of an older creation, a different order of magic, if you believe in such things."

"So you have never heard of one being sacrificed?"

"On this continent? Never."

"I have heard it said that they carry powerful medicine within them. Valuable medicine."

The old man looked at me sharply. "Who told you such nonsense? Inside a huetlacoatl is nothing but bone, guts, and muscle, just like a deer, or a man. I should know. I have seen the inside of enough of all of them."

"Nothing worth cutting one open for, then?"

Again the sharp look. "I did not say that. There is knowledge to be gained."

A kind of divination? "Knowledge of the future?"

"Shit, no! Knowledge of the huetlacoatls. How they work. And how they are related to us."

"We are relatives?"

"Not close. They are closer to lizards and snakes, and closer yet to crocodiles and birds. But yes, we are related as all animals are related." He sucked his gourd dry and looked at me expectantly.

"Allow me to provide you with another," I said, rising to return to the vendor's cart for fresh gourds of the milky brew.

While the vendor refilled the gourds, I pondered what Foureagle had told me. By the time I returned I had my new line of questions framed and ready.

"It is said," I began when the old man raised his nose from the gourd again, "that a priest can tell the future from the entrails of a deer." *Or a man.* "Could a priest not do the same from the entrails of one of these?"

"It is said that in England men are born with prehensile toes to better grip the earth so that they may not fall off it," he retorted. "Even those who believe such things know that like calls to like. Better to read the entrails of a chicken, unless you wish to know what portends on the southern continent."

"And yet . . ."

"And yet you seek after phantoms," the old man said, pouring the last of his pulque on the ground and levering himself erect. "You treat these things as if they were supernatural, not of this world. They are not, I can assure you. They are of the same world and the same flesh as we are. Older, it is true. Far older, but there is nothing miraculous to be had from them. Now I thank you for your generosity, young sir, but if you will excuse me I will seek a quiet place to piss."

I had just debarked from a water taxi and gone perhaps two streets back toward the Hummingbird's Palace when I realized I was being followed. A single man, far enough back not to be obvious and no apparent threat. I loosened my sword in its scabbard under the cover of adjusting my cloak and continued on without breaking stride.

It could be I was simply being shadowed for some reason, I told myself. After all, no one would risk Uncle Tlaloc's wrath by attacking me while I was about his business. *Yeah, right.*

I made two blocks more when there was a low whistle from behind me and three more men glided out of the darkness. All were stubby, thick-set, and muffled in coarse black cloaks. Gray turbans were tied about their heads and adjusted to hide their faces and painted to look like death-heads.

I turned to face the one to my left, fumbling under my cloak as if for my sword. The man hung back and our eyes locked. I sensed rather than heard his companions rushing me.

At just the proper moment I thrust backward through my cloak and into the body of the man behind. Then I sidestepped, slashed at the man on my right. That made him jump back and left me free to concentrate on the one to my left for just a split second. A quick upward slash and I felt my blade bite flesh and scrape along bone. He grasped his arm and reeled away while I turned to take on the man on my right as he closed in, sword held hilt low for a finishing thrust.

With a single motion, I swept my cloak off and tossed it at his head, sidestepping toward him as I moved. He dodged away from the cloak, but he was still off balance when I stepped in and split his skull.

I turned to put my back to the wall and looked around. The one with the arm wound was pattering off down the street. The one with the split skull was dead and the third man would soon join him. Now he was rolling on the ground and clutching his belly. My follower, the one who had whistled, had disappeared.

I was breathing hard, and my hands were shaking so badly I could hardly re-sheathe my sword. *Damn! And that was my second-best cloak.* The blood had soaked into the featherwork and there was no way to get it clean. I left it behind as a calling card and, with a final look up and down the streets, hurried off to the Hummingbird's Palace. Uncle Tlaloc doesn't like it when a messenger is late, and it takes more than an attack by three men to deflect his displeasure.

After delivering my report to Uncle Tlaloc, I sat in the bar at the Hummingbird's

Palace, sipping snow wine and keeping my back to the wall while I tried to figure out my next move.

Uncle Tlaloc had been much amused and mildly interested by my adventure with the Silver Skulls. I was much less amused and a lot more interested. Obviously, someone wanted me dead even more than usual. Badly enough to hire one of English Town's strong-arm gangs to try to take me out. But who? Who had I seriously annoyed recently? Three-flower? Unlikely. Certainly this wasn't connected to my errand for Uncle Tlaloc.

And anyway I couldn't imagine anyone in English Town setting the Silver Skulls on me. They were the best-known of the muscle gangs, but the local opinion was they were much better at making threats and breaking knees than killing people. Which implied that my enemy was someone with more money than knowledge. Which brought me back to Lady Threeflower, but that was ridiculous.

The Emperor's Shadow? Even more ridiculous. If they wanted me dead, I'd be dead. It would be an accident, a fair duel, the work of mysterious unknowns, or perhaps at the hands of the Death Master, but it would not be done by a bunch like the Silver Skulls. A warning from the Emperor's Shadow then? No, that was too paranoid even for English Town.

The one thing I was sure of was that I didn't like all this attention. Not only would I have to watch my back with more than usual care, but I'd probably have to pay wergild to the Silver Skulls for the men I had killed. And I'd have to replace my feathered cloak.

I sipped my wine and thought about my tailor for a while. Certainly a more pleasant subject than the Emperor's Shadow, or the Silver Skulls.

I was wandering the streets through a dark, starless night. Disease spirits floated through the air, brushing by me as they passed.

A dark alley filled with rapid, delicate noise. A blue hummingbird was fighting with a black butterfly. The noise of battle grew louder and louder. I ran away.

Then a rubber ball came bouncing toward me. I was about to hit it with my hip, the way I would try to play the sacred ball game as a boy. The ball suddenly stopped bouncing.

It wasn't a ball anymore. It was Smoke's skinless head.

"Who are you disappointing this time, Lucky?" it asked.

And a voice said, "Lucky, over here!" I knew that voice. All too well.

I found myself in the neighborhood where I grew up, where I am forbidden ever to return.

Turning to look, I saw Twoocelot. She was standing in the doorway of a rotting Frog-style hut. She wore a bride's dress, but her lips were painted black like a prostitute's.

"Lucky, where have you been all these years?" She asked. Her eyes were so much friendlier than her older sister's.

I tried hard to politely look away. "You know. I know. We're not supposed to talk about it."

"Am I so horrible? Do you prefer my sister Threeflower?"

"No."

She stepped close to me. There was something wrong with her face. Her skin hung slack, like a limp mask.

"Why do you look at me like that? Am I so ugly?" She grabbed a handful of the skin hanging from her face, pulled and tore it away. Underneath was her sister, Threeflower.

"You miss the old days, and your old life, don't you?" She sneered. "You wish that you could have been a gentleman, instead of a thug!"

"I am what the Gods made me to be." I turned to go.

"Lucky," her soft voice called. Something about it stopped me in my tracks. I thought my heart was going to explode. Against my will, I looked over my shoulder at Threeflower.

"Are you really? Do the Gods make us, or do we make ourselves?" Her skin rippled, became blotchy and bloated. Flesh-eating worms emerged like long pimples and ate away her face; except for her teeth, which grew long and rearranged themselves until she had the face of a huetlacoatl.

The next day started in the same way as the day before—which is to say late in the afternoon in a fog of leftover alcohol. No visit from Threeflower, of course. I waited until my reflexes were back together, even if my head wasn't, before I ventured out. Between the padded cotton tunic and the light mail shirt over it, a regular tunic over that, and a rain cloak on top of it all, I was seriously overdressed for the wet season, but I still felt better for it.

I stepped out of my building with all my senses on full alert. The way was thronged. There were overdressed merchants with retinues like nobles, too-well-dressed individuals whose professions weren't immediately apparent but obviously unsavory. There were slaves staggering under burdens, house servants whose tunics clashed with each other and the brightly tiled walls of the houses. On the corner a vendor was hawking fruit juices from a cart. All perfectly normal and all guaranteed to put my nerves on edge this day.

I moved along at a leisurely amble with my stomach going tight every time someone moved past me or I passed the mouth of an alley. I had gone two blocks like this when someone called my name.

"Hsst. Sir Lucky." Beside me was a boy perhaps ten years old wearing a dirty yellow tunic that marked him as someone's not-too-important house servant.

"I know someone who's got something for you," he hissed without moving his lips. His eyes were darting around and his head swiveled from side to side as if looking for eavesdroppers. Obviously he was enjoying this.

I wasn't, so I gave him my best supercilious stare. "Who might that be?"

"Oh, a beautiful lady who misses your company." The line was the standard panderer's come-on but he flashed a sign with the hand hidden between our bodies. The sign of the jaguar.

"Not in the market," I said gruffly. "Go away." I raised my hand as if to strike him and he grinned and vanished into crowd. I resumed my leisurely pace and at the next corner I turned right and headed for the market.

The gates were closed by the time I got there, but Mother Jaguar wasn't hard to find. There is a dive called the Vulture's Rest on the street of third-rate wine shops and fourth-rate brothels that runs along the market wall near where Mother Jaguar has her divining business. As usual, Mother was in a tiny nook in the back, well hidden from the doorway and doubtless close to one of her many bolt holes.

"I found something that might interest you," she said without looking as I slid in across from her.

"Any words of the wise woman are as spring rain on my ears." She cackled and pressed her hand into mine beneath the table. I felt her make the sign for gold.

Without comment I withdrew my hand, and slid out my other hand bearing three gold pieces beneath the table.

Mother's head sank upon her withered breasts and she seemed to drop into sleep, or a trance. I waited as she rocked back and forth and her breathing steadied.

"One of those has been found," she mumbled in her reedy trance voice.

My lips barely moved. "Ransomed?"

"Dead, quite dead," she keened softly. "In the street of warehouses behind the English Docks. A man of most excellent family, of the Watermonster Clan, and most excellent prospects."

Meaning he was well-born, but otherwise unremarkable, and had reached at least middle age without accomplishing anything of note.

"How was he found?" I asked thinking of the huetlacoatl.

"By the smell," Mother Jaguar intoned. "The smell of those who die slowly. His belly had been slit, and days ago."

"Sacrificed?"

"Who knows? Who knows?" Mother Jaguar wailed softly. Then she dropped her voice even lower. "Others came and took him even before the Death Master arrived. Shadows fell and the poor man vanished forever."

"Forever," she repeated even more faintly and pitched forward onto the table, seemingly unconscious.

"Thank you for your wisdom, Mother." I said loudly enough to be overheard. And, rising from the table, I placed three more gold coins upon it.

I was even more nervous when I left the Vulture's Rest than I had been when I went in. I didn't have to ask who the shadows were, or who had taken the body, or why the Emperor's Shadow was interested in the death of a very minor noble. The slit belly implied he had been sacrificed.

I thought briefly of Lady Threeflower and what had likely become of her friend. Then I thought in more detail about the effect this was likely to have on my career and longevity. Being interested in anything that involved the Emperor's Shadow was not a positive career move, to say nothing of its possible effect on your lifespan. I suspected the only reason Mother Jaguar had the courage to tell me about it was that the story was all over English Town. I just hoped my interest in the matter wasn't.

I considered my options and the more I thought about them, the more convinced I became that this was a time to spend a quiet evening at home. That wouldn't help me if the Emperor's Shadow came after me, but it was the last place my other enemies would expect to find me at this time of night. Besides, if I decided a sudden retirement to the country was in my best interest,

I'd need items that were at home, such as gold and a certain casket that sat near my bed.

Lady Threeflower was waiting for me in my chambers. She kept her mantle over her face but I knew her by her carriage.

"Is there news of Fourflower?" she asked without preamble.

"None, my lady."

"I had heard," she stopped and gathered herself. "I had heard that someone was found today. Someone who had been taken."

"It was not her, Lady. It was a man." I debated telling her how he had been found—or what the implications were for Fourflower.

She sighed deeply, as if a weight had been lifted from her. "There is one other matter," she said. "My lord husband found out about my visit to you. He is extremely angry, and he may seek vengeance on you."

So that was it! "He already has, lady." My smile was one part irony and one part relief.

She cocked an eyebrow. "I take it he was not successful?"

"Let's say he caused me a certain amount of uncertainty, cost me the price of a new cloak, and probably the out-of-pocket cost of a couple of back-alley thugs, but overall it was little enough."

"Nevertheless, I shall repay you," she said, reaching beneath her mantle.

There was something in the way she moved that made me reach out and jerk the mantle from her face. One eye was purple black and nearly swollen shut. There were livid spots on her neck where someone's fingers had dug into her pale flesh.

"I think," I said slowly, "I would rather be recompensed of your lord husband."

Her chin came up and her dark eyes flashed. "You would see me shamed, then. Does it please you? Does it excite you?" With a jerk she loosened the pin at her shoulder and her mantle and dress cascaded to the floor. "Here. Would you like to see all of what my lord husband did to me?"

I averted my eyes but I still had a glimpse of matronly hips and full breasts, the brown nipples crisscrossed with lash marks. There were other lash marks on her flat stomach and down the sides of her thighs. "I'm sorry."

"What is between a man and wife is no business of anyone else, especially not a clanless brigand," she said, stooping to gather her garments. There was a rustle as she replaced them. "You have served me and I have paid you. Now it is at an end between us."

Even if I had my full clan rank Threeflower would have been too proud to accept help.

Besides, I recognized bitterly, she was right. She knew the risk she ran in coming to me in the first place and so did I. She had been caught and paid the price. It was not my affair.

The tequila pot was empty, so I slept badly that night.

"Ah, Lucky my boy," Uncle Tlaloc rumbled when I showed up at the Hummingbird's Palace the next afternoon. "We have a request for the pleasure of your company." My stomach clinched at the words.

"A high-born lady, I hope." At least he hadn't used the nephew routine, so how bad could it be?

Uncle sighed gustily. "Nothing so romantic, I am afraid. This is from a priest — of sorts." He caught my look. "Oh, not one of your relatives, I can assure you," he said, holding up a flipperlike hand. "At least not one close enough to claim the relationship, but with the way you nobles intermarry, who can say?"

I cocked an eyebrow at my mentor and employer.

"I do not know why," Uncle said. "He simply asked, very politely, to see you." Then he reached out and took a sip from his skull mug. "Life is so charmingly full of surprises, is it not?"

Personally my life had been way too full of surprises recently, and none of them pleasant. But I smiled and took my leave as if Uncle had done me the greatest of favors. The first rule in this game is never let them see you sweat. The second rule is never let them see you bleed.

The Cloud Villas were on the other side of the city, so I took a water taxi for the first part of the trip, and then a cable car up into the hills. Once, a long time ago, the area had been a suburb, a pleasant retreat beyond the city walls for nobles seeking refuge from the heat and insects of summer. Then, as the Empire tightened its grip and clan warfare was sublimated into other channels, the wealthy and noble began to live here year around. Now those seeking a summer refuge used the distant mountains, only a few hours away by steam train. Proximity to the Great Plaza and the invention of air-conditioning had drawn the nobles back to their compounds and the wealthy had found it more convenient to live closer to their businesses. So the neighborhood had filled up with smaller houses and less important residents and the big houses had been divided into apartments or put to other uses.

The temple had started life as a nobleman's mansion, or more likely two or three adjacent mansions. It had been knitted together with a glazed brick exterior, brilliant bloodred around the bottom and sunburst yellow on top. There was an elaborate frieze about two-thirds of the way up the side and the wall was subtly shaded to represent a stepped pyramid rather than a flat surface. A set of four broad stone steps led up to the recessed space in front of the door, flanked by two life-size carvings. The two muscular servants in feathered cloaks who stood by the oversized carved doors bore no weapons, but they were guards nonetheless.

The place looked like a child's picture of a temple. Awesome and splendid, but overdone. I'd seen worse, such as the Whore's Temple to Tlazolteotl, down in English Town, but this place spoke of dark old gods put to bright new uses in a way I found unsettling.

A temple virgin guided me from the door, down a maze of halls and up a flight of inside stairs to a rooftop pavilion where my host awaited.

Toltectecuhtli was large, paunchy, middle-aged, and as much of a mixture as the temple he presided over. His head was flattened, Frog-fashion, until he looked like a painting on a Frog temple wall rather than a human being. His lip and ears had been pierced for the heavy jade spools the Frogs favored, but the holes were empty. He wore a green-feathered short cloak that covered his shoulders and came within a finger's breadth of being blasphemy against the priests of Quetzalcoatl. His tunic was snowy white set off with gold bangles and a stomacher of lizard skin, and a beaten gold pectoral depicting Lord Quetzalcoatl hung from his neck. His eyes were permanently crossed but that didn't add to his beauty. The whole effect combined the barbaric, foreign, and modern in a way that was not in the least laughable. He sat rigid as a statue on a carved stool, staring out over the rooftops at the city and the bay beyond.

Wordlessly he gestured me to a seat on the step below him, and wordlessly I took it. He kept his gaze on the horizon as I kept mine on him. Although he never turned his face toward me I got the feeling he was sizing me up just as carefully as I was sizing up him.

"Tworabbit," he said at last, in a voice as distant as his gaze. The name startled me. It was my natal name and should have been my everyday name, save that it was notoriously unlucky.

"I am called Lucky," I said quietly.

He turned and suddenly focused hard and sharp as a hunting hawk on me. That unblinking crossed stare gave me the feeling he could see all the way inside me to the black nodules of my inmost soul. A nice trick, that stare.

"Do not discard what you are," he said sharply. "For it is what you are in the beginning that determines what you will become in the end."

"If the fates allow."

"Ah yes, fate." He was silent for an instant. "You represent a noble branch of a fine clan," he continued. "Brought low by unfortunate circumstances."

I said nothing. If this one was trying to unsettle me . . . well, I had been played upon by masters.

"I owe you thanks," he said at last. "You helped someone two days ago."

I shrugged. "The attendant was clumsy. He tripped over his own feet."

"Still, thanks are in order. And a seeker of wisdom you have become."

I shrugged. "Anything that turns a profit."

"Don't lie to me," he snapped. "Profit is not what drives you."

"Not entirely," I said as I thought of the small casket beside my bed.

He smiled in a particularly unsettling manner. "Nor revenge either, much as you would like that believed. No, you seek wisdom, albeit you do not do so wisely."

I licked my lips and wondered where this one got his information. "What would be the wise way to seek wisdom?"

"There is no wise way," he said. "Wise ways are for cowards, fools, and those who do not seek to know. Wisdom is found by treading unwise paths."

I wondered if the extreme skull binding had affected his brain somehow. This "priest" appeared more than half mad, but if it was madness it was combined with an unusual force of character.

"The cycle closes, Tworabbit," he said. "Venus will not cross the sun thrice before the Monkey Baktun draws to a close."

"The cycle dies as all things must." It was the first thing that came into my mind.

He made a dismissive gesture. "That it dies is unimportant. How it is reborn is all that matters. For that is in our hands. Each time the cycle turns we have it in our power to re-create the world entire. To bring together the elements that are tearing our world apart and to form them together as a potter forms clay. To temper them in the fires of the end times until the new world emerges whole and unbroken."

"I had thought that was in the hands of the Gods," I said carefully.

"The Gods do not play dice with the world," the priest said sharply. "They show man the path and each cycle they offer him the chance anew to take it. That we do not is our own doing."

This conversation had started off peculiar and it had gotten weirder and weirder. "You wished to see me," I said, hoping to force the talk back to a path that made sense.

Again that stare like a cross-eyed hawk. "And I have seen you. The cycle turns, Tworabbit, and neither you nor I can escape our place upon the calendar stone of fate. Now is the time to weld together all the elements so they may be mixed as potter's clay."

This part vaguely reminded me of some of the street-corner priests of the English Quarter. "You mean nobles and commoners?"

"Oh, more than that, Tworabbit. Far more than that. Nobles, commoners, Reeds and Frogs, Englishmen and others, yes, even the huetlacoatl. To create a thing transcending anything the world has ever seen. A new being for a new cycle."

"That would be a thing to be seen," I said as neutrally as I could.

"And it will be seen, Tworabbit, if we all play the parts we are destined to play."

This wasn't just weird anymore. It had started to remind me of those conversations one had with one's age mates at noble parties. Conversations where nothing was stated, no matter how bright the surface, and much was implied: threats, offers, information swapping, all wrapped up in inconsequential talk. Only here I didn't know the language or understand symbolism. Was I being offered something? Was I being threatened? Was I being pumped for information? It was like one of those dreams where Smoke came to talk to me about his skin. Just as bizarre and just as menacing.

"If we are destined to, then we shall play those parts." Not much in the way of snappy repartee, but it was the best I could do without knowing what the hell was going on here.

This time the stare held me even longer, as if Toltectecuhtli tried to pin me to my cushion by the force of his eyes. "See that you play your part well, Tworabbit. Play it well indeed."

"Forgive me, uncle, but I do not know what my part is."

"That is because your part is ignorance, Tworabbit. Cling to that ignorance. Cherish it. Profess it to all who ask. That is your part."

Then he looked back out over the sea and I waited for him to speak again until the temple virgin touched my shoulder to tell me the interview was at an end.

As I left the temple, I paused at the bottom of the stairs. The frieze showed a polyglot of symbols. There was Quetzalcoatl in both his Reed and Frog aspects. There were human forms representing all ranks and stations. There were signs of the zodiac and the glyph for the end of the cycle. And mixed in with it all were stylized huetlacoatls, running, walking, commanding, and lying in repose. Here and there were the conventional symbols for the burden of time, but instead of burdens or the traditional monsters, these glazed brick figures of humans were locked in the embrace of huetlacoatls. There was something vaguely erotic about their posture, and much more that bordered on the obscene.

As I made my way down the street to the cable car stop, I pondered Toltecte-cuhtli and his religion. New religions weren't anything out of the ordinary, especially here in the south where the Mexica Reeds mixed with the native Frogs and the regime of the priests was not as strict as it was back in the Valley of Anahuac by the shores of the Lakes of Mexico. I had heard vaguely of the Toltec and his followers, but I had classed them as another huetlacoatl-worshiping cult. Wrong. Even though Toltec was definitely concerned with the huetlacoatls, he was not a huetlacoatl worshiper. It was a lot more complex than that and tied in with the coming end of the cycle.

If I had more than my usual share of luck I might live to see the end of the cycle. It was two hand-spans of fingers and a finger away. Not the Great Cycle, when the Universe is re-created, but the smallest of the great cycles, the Baktun, or 394 and a half English years. Baktun 13, the Grass Baktun. A time when the world, or man's part of it, was traditionally broken apart and remade new. I was no student of religion, much less of ephemeral cults, but I couldn't ever remember one that tied the huetlacoatls to the end of the cycle before.

Every cycle's end brought with it prophecies of doom of one sort or another. In the time of the Emperor Montezuma they had seemed fulfilled when the first English had landed and stirred rebellion among the subject tribes. But the English had succumbed to the Empire's might and when the English came again years later it was the English English, not the Spanish English, and they built English Town as traders rather than conquerors. Eventually Montezuma's successor, Montezuma V, *the* Emperor Montezuma of popular legend, had welded the empire together even more firmly than it had been before the coming of the English.

Aside from that, the end of cycles had passed with only the usual quota of wars, plagues, and rebellions to mark them. Or so they taught in the schools of the nobles. Each time, the new cycle began with the lighting of the sacred fire atop the Grand Pyramid at the Great Plaza on the shores of the Lakes of Mexico. The Emperor was reconfirmed and life continued, largely unchanged from one cycle to the next. Only the unofficial cults changed as the old ones were discredited when the predicted miracles and wonders didn't appear.

Since leaving my old life I found the common folk saw matters differently. To them the end of a cycle marked a profound change, a chance to strike the world's balance anew—and by implication to ease the lot of the commoners.

But only by implication. Even here in the tolerant South, the priests would not countenance a cult that spread unrest or criticized the divinely inspired order of things. Still, was it such an odd notion that the world as we knew was it coming to an end? Was the Empire as strong or the Emperor as vigilant as He had been? Was there more unrest, more muttering in the cities and banditry in the countryside? Was there more injustice and less punishment for it? Was it really such a strange notion that Reeds and Frogs, nobles and commoners, and yes, even huetlacoatls, might somehow be combined into something new and better for the next cycle?

That thought was still with me when I hailed a water taxi to take me back through the increasingly noisome canals to the English Quarter.

Uncle Tlaloc kept me waiting for nearly four hours at the Hummingbird's Palace before he heard my report. Not that there was anything to report, but I didn't want Uncle getting ideas about my meeting with Toltectecuhtli.

When he finally got around to me he heard me out with a bored expression and waved me away without a word, a sign he wasn't pleased. I didn't bother to finish my last drink and headed for home. It was raining again, and I felt as if all three worlds were pissing on me.

The hall was dark when I reached my apartment building. Not terribly unusual. The gas torch at the end was old and cranky and so was the porter who was supposed to see to it. But tonight it struck me wrong. I pressed myself against the wall and drew my sword. Then I sidled down the corridor with my back to the wall, silently testing every door behind me as I went.

They were all securely locked, but mine wasn't. I pressed flatter against the wall beside the door and reached out with my sword to work the latch. The door swung open noiselessly. Which meant something was really wrong. I deliberately left the hinges unoiled.

The apartment was dimly lit by the gas lamp at its lowest setting. I wasn't about to go stumbling about in the semi-dark, so I reached over and turned the light full on.

Shit. The apartment was a mess. The cushions had been slit, items pulled off shelves and scattered on the floor, the shelves themselves had been moved. A low table was upended, as if someone had searched the base.

I made straight for the bedroom. Everything there was in disarray, except the box at the foot of the bed. It was sitting just as I had left it—almost.

I'm very particular about that box. It is arranged just so with a hair clasped in the front corner between the lid and the box. Whoever had searched it had gotten it almost right. The box was within a finger-breadth of where I had left it, the angle was almost right. The hair was missing, having fallen out unnoticed when the box was opened.

I turned away, damning myself for keeping such a thing in the first place. Then I realized I hadn't seen my servant Uo, or his body, anywhere. With my sword still drawn, I went looking.

I found him on his pallet by the kitchen fire, alive, amazingly enough. He barely stirred when I kicked him and a brief examination showed he was drugged. From the looks of it there'd be no information to be gotten out of him before morning.

I went back to the front room, turned the table right side up, pulled up one of the least-damaged cushions, and got out the tequila jug. I needed to settle my nerves, but most of all I needed to think.

Whoever did this wasn't a personal enemy. That the skin was still in its box told me that. No, this was business, and obviously that business involved something I was supposed to have. It wasn't the skin and it wasn't money—although my strong-box had been cleaned out. So what was it?

I thought back to the priest's words. That my part in the changing of the cycles was ignorance. That I was to cling to ignorance, profess ignorance and cherish it. *Screw that!* I was sure as hell ignorant, but this kind of ignorance was likely to get me killed. The obvious conclusion for whoever searched my apartment was that I'd been clever about hiding whatever it was. Their next obvious action was to grab me and question me. I doubted very seriously they'd take "I don't know" for an answer—not unless I said it with my dying breath.

By this time the tequila was half gone and so was I. I braced a chair against the door to prevent unwelcome night visitors, kicked Uo again to see if he was any closer to waking, and when he obviously wasn't, I staggered off to bed.

Sleep ended abruptly. I felt the presence of someone's eyes and breath on me. It was not my servant. "Smoke?" I mumbled. There was no answer. A stranger had been in my room, over my bed, like a disease-ridden spirit coming in an open window. I was not in the mood for another nightmare. My spine from neck to tailbone became unnaturally cold. I did not move.

Dawn was breaking. The light of fallen warriors accompanying the Sun on today's arc through the sky filtered in weakly through the mosquito netting. After some intense staring into empty space, my eyes adjusted to the half-light.

Then some of the neighborhood roosters crowed inharmoniously. My nerves were scrambled, but I was wide awake.

Carefully, I let my eye dart about the room. No one was there. Nothing lurking in the corners or shadows.

I felt that *something* was near. It had to be almost touching me.

There is a time-honored method of revenge in which poisonous insects or reptiles are placed inside a person's body through the sorcerer's art. If skill at sorcery is lacking, the cruder method of simply putting a small deadly creature in a person's bed will do. In these times, among those who deal in not-so-flowery wars between clans, the later, cruder method is preferred.

My sleep was deep, but restless. I was tangled in my sheet. With a slow, deep breath I tried to relax all my muscles without moving them too much, raised my head, looked with my eyes, felt with the entire surface of my skin.

I saw and felt nothing, and almost breathed a hearty sigh of relief. Then something glinted in light that grew slowly brighter. Something shiny sparkled. It was close to me. Near my face. Close to my heart.

There, precariously balanced on the knot of sheets under my chin was a delicate work of the carver's art that horrified me. It was a butterfly, masterfully carved of black volcanic glass. A real obsidian butterfly, a manifestation of the goddess of nocturnal visions. The Emperor's Shadow, in the tradition of the poet-emperors of old, used this fragile, razor-sharp metaphor as a warning.

Popular knowledge says that if you are careful and take the obsidian butterfly off your body, pick it up and set it aside without breaking it or cutting yourself, you are destined to live. To cut yourself or to break the delicate symbol meant you are doomed.

I remembered how my mother was always telling me to be careful, and how my carelessness finally disappointed her for good. With an agonizing effort, I pulled a hand free of the sheets. The butterfly, teetered, and slipped between a fold of cloth. I carefully reached for it, aiming my fingers at the flat surface of the wings.

"Holy Shit!" I screamed as the edge of one of those black, transparent wings bit into a fingertip. Instinctively, I jerked back my hand. As if alive, the butterfly soared across the room, to shatter into spray of black crystal against the wall.

I sprang from bed, sucked the blood from my finger like a thirsty god, and thought, They may call me Lucky, but there's no question that I was born on the second day of the Rabbit.

Uncle Tlaloc wasn't drinking when he summoned me into his presence. That was a very bad sign.

As I knelt before him I felt his eyes boring into the back of my head. He didn't bid me to rise and sit as usual. He just kept looking at me like an ocelot looks at a baby bird it can't decide whether to play with or just eat right away.

"I understand there was some excitement at your quarters last night," he said at last.

His face didn't change while I told him the story.

"It sounds as if someone wants something you have," Uncle Tlaloc said mildly.

"So it would seem, Uncle-tzin."

"What?" His voice had the sting of a cracking whip. "What is it they seek?"

"On my grave, Uncle, I do not. . . ."

"What did you take from the huetlacoatl?" he roared. I flinched from the sound.

"Nothing, Uncle. I swear it. Ask Ninedeer, if you do not believe me."

"Others are already asking," Uncle said slowly. "Your cousin Ninedeer was taken yesterday. By the Emperor's Shadow, apparently. It seems His Imperial Majesty has decided to interest himself in the matter of the huetlacoatl's death after all."

I realized I was sweating in spite of the air-conditioning. Sweat had already soaked the armpits of my cotton tunic and was starting to trickle down my chest and back. This could probably get worse, but right now I couldn't imagine how.

He looked at me again in a way that wasn't at all settling. "It is not unknown," he said softly, "for someone to try to keep something back if the prize is rich enough."

I remembered what had happened to those people—the ones Uncle Tlaloc had chosen to make an example of—and shuddered. There are worse fates than being slowly flayed alive.

"Uncle-tzin, I swear to you that I hold nothing back. On my own grave I swear it."

Uncle was looking at me in a way that indicated that might not just be a metaphor. Then he leaned back, rested one hand on Death and the other on the Earth Monster and smiled in a way that was totally unsettling.

"And I believe you, my boy. You swear you do not have this thing, whatever it is, and of course you would never lie to me."

"Of course not, Uncle," I croaked.

"So the matter is closed," he said with the same terrifying geniality. "But, nephew . . ."

"Yes, Uncle?"

"If you do find this thing, you will tell your old uncle, will you not?"

"Of course, Uncle. Absolutely." He gestured at me and I backed away, still on my knees.

I wandered the streets, examining the gathering clouds and play of light on the waters of the bay. There wasn't any place I was going. There also wasn't anybody I could talk to. People who seem to know anything about this mess keep ending up dead.

On a busy corner an old man with the matted hair of a traditional priest was holding out a limp, obviously drugged, rattlesnake. When he saw me, he practically shoved it in my face.

"For only one small gold coin," he said in a voice that had been destroyed by years of exposure to sacred smokes, "I will let you pet the noble serpent who warns before striking, the brother to the Feathered Serpent who gave us our law and culture. It will bring you good luck."

The snake's face was close to mine. Its mouth opened, and its fangs slipped out of their sheaths. All the while, its tail and rattle hung limp, probably because of the drug.

"I don't know, unwashed one," I replied without slowing down. "Your friend looks like he may make an exception and rattle after he bites me."

"Blasphemer!" The old man screamed as walked away. "The Gods will punish you!"

"I know, I know," I said and turned away.

The problem was, that I didn't know. At least about just what it was that everyone seemed to think I had. I'm an axe, a sweeper, not a sneak-thief. And what is it that I could have slipped under my cloak and smuggled out of the Death Master's, and to my apartment or some secret location? What could be that important? And why would it be on the body of a dead huetlacoatl?

Or maybe it was *in* the body. . . .

The thought was too disgusting to pursue. Besides, the hairs standing on the back of my neck told me that I was being pursued. The old geezer with groggy rattlesnake was still glaring at me. And his weren't the only eyes on me. People on the street looked away when I looked at them, but I could tell that they were aware of me. Every window and corner made me nervous.

I put my hand on the hilt of my sword. Somehow it did not make me feel secure.

Suddenly, I felt the need to flee. There were too many people. I couldn't sort out who—if anybody—I should be looking out for. I walked faster, until I was just short of a run.

I glanced into some deserted alleys. Unfortunately, they were too deserted. Someone could be cornered, killed, left in a pile of garbage, and not be found for days, flayed by the rats and scavengers that feed off corpses.

Then someone grabbed my sword arm. Something else struck the back of my head. Everything went white hot, then dead black.

The sound of conch trumpets filled the air. It was the long, deep tone that announces the approach of a hurricane. Near the English Docks, the great statue of the Storm Goddess looked at me and licked her ragged, stone lips with a pink, fleshy tongue. The water withdrew, back toward the southern continent, leaving ships to sink into the muck on the seafloor. I ran toward higher ground.

The city was deserted. The only signs of life were cages containing parrots that had been reduced to skeletons, and the ants that were picking away at the last remaining bits of meat. Was I asleep when the city was evacuated? No one was in the streets. Nothing moved except for the debris that flew about in the winds.

The clouds boiled. There was a rumbling deep in the earth that echoed through my bones and across the sky. The wind grew stronger, making a noise like the mother of all disease spirits.

Then it rained. The things that pelted me and the empty streets were not raindrops, but eggs. When they hit the ground, they cracked open, leaking a steaming purple fluid and revealing the tiny bodies of creatures that looked almost human.

"Earthmonster, devour me!" I screamed.

"Be calm, Lucky." It was Mother Jaguar. "Things will be all right. Look." She held out a polished obsidian mirror.

I looked into it, and saw myself. My skin hung loosely around my face. Grabbing a handful, I tore it away. Underneath I had a huetlacoatl snout.

"Face your destiny, Tworabbit," said Toltectecuhrli, who was suddenly holding the mirror. As I looked into the mirror I was plunged into darkness. Pungent smoke curled up and I coughed at the vile snake scent.

"He wakens," came a voice from far, far away.

Then the world reeled, the hood was yanked from my head, and I was blinking in the light.

My first thought was that this wasn't the doing of Threeflower's husband. Then where I was actually sank in.

The room was low, gloomy, and damp. The gas torches were turned too low for me to see the extent. The furniture was uncomfortably low as well. Uncomfortable for humans, at least. There were three men standing before me and one more crouched down in the background. Correction: There was one more *something* crouched down behind them, but it wasn't human. It was a huetlacoatl, the first intelligent one I had ever seen — alive, that is.

"We want the body," one of the Speakers said abruptly.

"What?"

"The body of the slain one. We want the rest of it. Come. Do not waste the Great One's time. Give it to us." One of the other three had turned to the huetlacoatl and croaked and squeaked at it as if translating. I couldn't see the huetlacoatl well enough to make out its expression and that was probably just as well.

"You have the body," I said.

This was translated and produced a roar from the huetlacoatl.

"All of it," the Speaker cried. "We must have all of it."

"But it wasn't sacrificed. It was all there."

"*Lies!*" the Speaker screamed. "You think you can lie to us because we do not torture like animals. But we will have the truth and we will have the treasures of the line, the rest of the Great One's body."

I thought fast. Ninedeer had said that all the parts of the body were there. They must mean something else, something that was on the body. An insignia of rank perhaps. That made sense in light of Uncle Tlaloc's comment about something being taken from the body. Some priests referred to the sacred objects they wore as part of themselves. And there were stories that the huetlacoatls adorned themselves with rare and costly jewels—as well as less pleasant things. The Speakers were notoriously hard to communicate with, but it made sense.

"Describe this thing to me. The thing that was missing from the Great One's body."

The translation produced another roar from the huetlacoatl and I thought the Speaker would explode, the way he turned red and puffed up. "The treasures of the line," he screamed. "The things that make the Great Ones. We must have them now!"

Treasures. Multiple. Then several things had been taken from the body. I tried to remember if there were any spots on the dead one's cloak where something might have been torn off. Or perhaps they had been attached directly to the skin and that was why it had been cut up.

The huetlacoatl spoke for the first time except in response to the translator: a long collection of hisses, squeaks, and squeals that ended with a clash of teeth like a gunshot. All three of the Speakers turned toward the creature and froze in identical postures, one foot in front, bowing forward from the waist and the right fist pressed to the forehead.

"We waste the Great One's time," the Speaker spat as he turned back to me. "If an animal you act, then an animal you shall be treated."

"We are civilized," the Speaker snapped. "We do not offer ourselves in the marketplace for food."

I wondered just what it was the huetlacoatls were trading for—or what they thought they were trading for. "But it is meet that our enemies be hunted in a civilized manner, to expiate their crimes." He gestured to the slaves holding my arms, turned and strode away with me being dragged after him.

"There!" the Speaker gestured over a balcony and down to a courtyard below.

At first I couldn't see anything but a flagged stone yard with a water trough. Then there was a "wheeping" sound from beneath the balcony, and another, and another. Then four huetlacoatls came bounding into the court, wheeping and craning their necks to see what was on the balcony.

There was nothing to give me scale, so it took me a minute to realize these huetlacoatls were smaller than usual. It took me a minute longer to infer from their clumsy movements and their tussling that these were immature huetlacoatls. As a group they were as cute as a nest of baby rattlesnakes. Only I didn't think they had the high ethical standards of rattlesnakes. And I didn't like the way they were looking up at me and wheeping expectantly.

"We tie you by your arms," the Speaker said. "Then we lower you down so the young can practice hunting. Just your feet and ankles and first, then your legs. So you may reconsider your theft from the Great Ones."

Well, at least I'll be able to kick the little bastards' teeth in. Not much comfort, but you take what you can find.

The Speaker leaned close. "Only first we break your legs so you cannot hurt the little Great Ones."

I was digesting this information and trying desperately to come up with a plausible lie when a huetlacoatl whistled so high that it almost hurt. I managed to twist around in the slaves' grip and see that a new group of humans had entered the room.

There were six of them, cloaked in gray, with gray hoods drawn over the heads, and gray masks covering their faces. I'd never seen that outfit before, but I knew what it was. It was the closest thing to a uniform ever worn by the Emperor's Shadow.

There was a long palaver between the Speaker and one of the Shadows. I divided my attention between trying to overhear them and listening to the plaintive cries of the young huetlacoatls below me, who obviously weren't used to waiting for their supper. Finally, after an extended, involved discussion, the adult huetlacoatl made a slashing gesture and a steamwhistle bellow. The Speakers bowed and stepped aside, letting the Emperor's Shadow have me. Personally, I would have preferred the huetlacoatls, but my wishes didn't count for a whore's fart.

Another hood, another journey, but this time I was awake. I know we walked for a ways, there was a boat ride across the bay, a slower, smellier ride through the city's canals, and then more walking. No one spoke, and the ones who held me never loosened their grip.

This time when the hood came off I was in a low-ceilinged room with stone beneath my feet. There was a single blinding light shining in my eyes. I squinted and tried to twist my head away but the ones behind me forced me to look straight ahead.

"Young sir," came a voice from the darkness, "you must learn to associate with more wholesome companions." He hobbled into the light and I saw it was old Foureagle, the menagerie keeper. "If you consort with those who want to be huetlacoatls, evil will befall you."

"What about the company you keep? What's a tender of caged beasts doing with the Emperor's Shadow?" I remembered his remark about having seen the insides of a lot of people and tried not to show it.

He smiled. "A man is many things. It not only keeps life interesting, but it is necessary in times such as these." I decided I had liked the old man a lot better when we were sucking down pulque outside the menagerie. I also realized I had gone fishing for information on a very sensitive matter by questioning a high officer of the Emperor's Shadow. *Shit!* One thing about my luck. It's consistent.

"But come, young sir, you do not seem pleased to see me."

"I think I'd be better off with the huetlacoatls."

Wrong answer. It made Foureagle frown and earned me a kidney punch from one of the Shadows. I sagged forward, retching.

"These ones with their costumes and silly antics have no idea of what they are doing," Foureagle said. "They've got it all wrong, dead wrong."

"They speak to the huetlacoatls well enough."

Foureagle snorted. "They speak as a dog speaks to its master. They sense emotion well enough but they understand only a little. The rest is deception. They deceive themselves and the huetlacoatls deceive and use them."

"Like you use the beasts in the menagerie?"

"The relationship between man and beast can be understood," he said, his eyes narrowed into slits, "but between man and these thinking, talking *creatures?* Where do we begin to know anything? How can we trust?"

"You understand them."

He shrugged. "I know when they are afraid. Even if their language is mostly a mystery, the prattling of the Speakers is easy to understand. The huetlacoatls are upset and they are driven to the point of hysteria. The thing you took from the body was very important to them." He smiled. "Important enough that the huetlacoatls brought the affair—forcefully—to the attention of the Emperor Himself. You were unwise to upset them so, young sir. If we cannot understand each other, we cannot trade, and the Emperor values the trade with the huetlacoatls very highly."

We were still in the intellectual fencing stage, which meant I would remain whole and functioning for a least another few minutes. What Foureagle said made sense. The huetlacoatls hadn't been really upset until they recovered the body with whatever-it-was missing. Then it took time for the word to reach the capital and for the Emperor to turn his Shadow's interest to this new case. All very logical, but I was damned if I could see how it helped me.

"Uncle, I swear to you I took nothing from the body."

"So Ninedeer maintained," the old man said, as if savoring a memory.

I shook off the sudden chill down my spine. "If something was taken, it must have been by someone else. The sailor who found the body, for instance. Or the city guards who investigated it."

A gauntleted fist slammed into my face. I had to cough and hack to clear the blood so I could breathe.

"These possibilities have been explored—thoroughly," Foureagle said. "So we come to you by a process of, ah, 'elimination.'"

"But I took—" This time the blow was from the front and knocked the breath out of me. Somewhere off to one side there was the sudden odor of burning charcoal as someone lit a brazier. I twisted and gasped and knew this was only the bare beginning of what they'd do to me before I died.

Unless . . .

The Speakers kept referring to the missing thing as "part of" the huetlacoatl. The huetlacoatls themselves might have continued that use, but the Speakers would have known enough to employ human usage when questioning a human.

Another blow to the face ended my speculation.

"Uncle," I gasped. "These things, how do they bear their young?"

"Eh?" This wasn't the way he expected the conversation to go. "Why, eggs, of course. Like crocodiles, or birds."

Shit! Another beautiful theory murdered by a gang of ugly facts.

"Although," Foureagle continued slowly, "not all of them lay the eggs in a nest. Some of them, like some snakes, hold the eggs in their bodies until the young hatch." He looked at me sharply. "Like the huetlacoatls."

"And the one who died was female." It wasn't a question. "Toltectecuhtli keeps talking about a great joining of humans, English, and even huetlacoatls. To make that work he's going to need something like the Speakers." The effort made me cough, which hurt my ribs even more. I wondered how many were broken.

"Except they would be huetlacoatls raised among humans rather than the other way around," the old man finished my thought. "Young sir, I believe you have it." He smiled, and I felt the grip on my arms loosen imperceptibly. Then he frowned. "But it is still just a theory, of course. And it does not tell us where the eggs are."

"I think I know," I said slowly. "Uncle, may I beg the boon of a handspan of days to find out?"

Foureagle rubbed his chin. "I will give you one day," he said.

Considering the obvious alternative, I took it.

One thing about being beaten up, it makes disguise easier — if you're disguising yourself as a cripple, that is. And I was. Some artificial scars and pockmarks helped the effect. But the bruises on my face and the swollen eye were real. So were the limping, halting gait and the painful, gasping breath. The ragged tunic was my servant's, but the sword underneath was mine.

The public parts of the temple were easily accessible. There was no service tonight, but a fair number of pilgrims wandered the halls, pausing at small shrines to pray and make offerings. No guards, of course. One would have to be truly mad *or very young and stupid* to profane or steal from a temple, even a temple of such an odd religion.

I hadn't really seen much of the place the last time. It turned out the inside was just as gaudy and probably just as disturbing as the outside. "Probably" because the place was lit by torches rather than gas lamps and much of it was lost in the gloom.

Now if I were a huetlacoatl egg, where would I be?

Someplace secure, of course. Out of the way, yet an important place. A sacred place. Then I remembered the use the Frogs traditionally made of their temples that the Reed folk did not. If this place followed the custom, there would be a crypt beneath the structure, a place for the burial of kings. *Or the birthplace of kings.*

The place had probably been a maze to begin with and the group's alterations hadn't improved that any. I drifted along the corridors, stopping at shrines to pay my respects and generally trying to look like I belonged.

Toltectecuhtli came striding down the corridor, resplendent in a headdress of quetzal plumes and beaten gold. He still wore the lizard-skin stomacher and the gold Quetzalcoatl gorget, but his elaborately embroidered kilt was new. From his belt hung a maquahatl, the flat wooden war club fitted with blades of keen obsidian along the edges. With his sloped head he looked like he had stepped out of a temple wall painting.

What the hell? I followed him. He went to the center of the ground floor, then down a stairway that was framed by the masterfully sculpted gaping jaws of gigantic huetlacoatls. It reminded me of stories of the underworld, the many Hells beneath the earth. An undistinguished soul on his way to oblivion, or one of the Lords of Death?

Down the stairs it grew dark, and the air became clammy. I heard moaning. Horrible moaning. I shuddered. Could the myths be true?

At the end of the narrow stair was a long corridor, with light showing from a side passage far down and off the right. I pressed myself against the wall and glided toward the light. The dank silence was broken only by an occasional moan.

Toltectecuhtli stood in the middle of a wide chamber lit with many lamps. The light flickered and shifted, making it hard to see things. Which was, perhaps, for the best.

The place was a ghastly parody of the Death Master's laying-out room. Stone tables dotted the room and forms covered with sheets lay on most of them. Toltectecuhtli was bending over one of the tables with his back to the door. He did something, and the thing on the table moaned like one who has been flayed but is not quite dead yet.

As Toltectecuhtli stood up I could see that the person on the table still had her skin, at least from the waist up. The priest strode away from the table to a door in the rear of the room. He unlocked it, passed through, and I heard the lock click as he relocked it from the inside.

I stayed where I was, listening hard. There was no sound through the damp, close air, not even from the tables. But there was a smell: the stink of strong tequila.

I moved carefully into the room and approached the table where Toltectecuhtli had uncovered the woman. She was young, with breasts that were full but had not yet begun to sag. She might have been pretty once, but suffering had drained all the beauty, and most of the humanity, from her.

"Fourflower?" I whispered. She turned drug-dimmed eyes to me. They were like the eyes of a dumb animal. No hope, no pleading.

Then I saw why. There was a gaping red wound from breastbone to groin. The belly skin was pink and healthy with no flush of infection, but the edges of the wound were separated by a hand-breadth and the belly was pushed out, as if bloated.

I looked closer and saw there was something in the wound, inside the woman.

It was grayish, rounded, and netted all over like a melon. I didn't have Foureagle's knowledge of human insides, but I knew that this thing didn't belong in a human belly. I shifted to get a better view and saw it was about twice the size of a large goose egg.

Eggs? Then all the fragments fell together. Like a shattered obsidian butterfly reassembling itself and flying away.

There are priest-surgeons, specialists, who can open a man up without killing him to treat a sickness of the body. They use the finest obsidian blades, take the greatest care not to cut into the bowels and carefully sew the flesh and skin together after dousing the area with the purest double-distilled tequila. Most of the time the patient even recovers.

Toltectecuhtli wanted a blending of huetlacoatl and human. What better way to blend the two essences than incubating huetlacoatl eggs within human bodies?

There was a crash behind me of something shattering on the stone. I whirled and saw Toltectecuhtli standing in the door I had come through. The remains of a jug at his feet and the stronger smell of tequila told me where he'd been. In the semi-darkness with the lamps hitting him from below he looked like a vengeful wall painting come to life. About a ten-foot-tall wall painting.

"Good evening," I said pleasantly, to distract him while I figured out whether I'd have to take him out or could just run.

If Toltectecuhtli's eyes were crossed, there was nothing wrong with his hearing. "You do not belong here, Tworabbit."

"I couldn't agree with you more," I said amiably. "So I'll just be going."

"Your part was ignorance! I told you to play your part in the great change."

"Ignorance is an expensive commodity," I said, moving sideways toward the main door. "Too expensive for a lowly person such as me."

He growled in inarticulate fury and leaped to the door, blocking my way out. In a single swirling motion he went for the bladed war club at his belt and launched a furious overhand swipe at my head.

I ducked and barely got my sword up to parry. The force of the blow drove my forearm down onto my forehead and twisted my sword in my grip. But the club went skittering off my sword and missed my body altogether. I tried a fast counterslash to his chest, but the old man twisted away easily and brought his maquahatl up in a disemboweling blow. I parried and gave ground and he came after me swinging left-and-right at my head.

That damn club was heavy, which made it hard to parry, and the obsidian blades set along the edge could open me up as efficiently as any steel sword. In spite of his age this priest was strong as an ox and fast as a teenager. I was neither and I was in a lot of trouble.

I tried to dodge around to his left side, but he spun on his toes before I could complete the move. He aimed another at my head. I raised my sword to parry and with a twist of the wrist he dropped the blow toward my legs. I scrambled back, but the tip raked me across the shins, leaving bright wellings of blood on both legs.

Frantically I dodged around a stone table. He struck at me over it and I flinched back, feeling the air stir as the maquahatl whistled past my face. The person on the table looked at me with dumb, pain-ridden eyes.

As Toltectecuhtli came around the table, I whipped my cloak off and threw it at his face, trying to blind him. While the cloak was still in the air I followed through with a lunging thrust. I missed but his reflexive return stroke didn't—quite. The club came down on the point of my right shoulder and tore an ugly gaping wound that left my whole arm numb.

He saw what he had done to me and started forward in triumph, his club coming up for an overhand blow.

I tossed the sword to my left hand and parried. This time his eyes widened and he stepped back. "Huitzilopochtli," he whispered hoarsely. "Lord Left-Handed Hummingbird."

I don't know what was going on in that god-ridden, madness-fogged brain, but obviously I had triggered something. I pressed the advantage ruthlessly, striking left and right in my turn before he could recover his composure.

He parried, but more clumsily. Madness aside, fighting a left-handed swordsman is difficult for a right-handed. You have to do some things backward and very few nobles ever train in the art because left-handedness is considered unlucky. Uncle Tlaloc's retainers are more practical about such things.

Then I remembered there was another difference between a maquahatl and a sword. I faked a downward slash at his belly, which brought his club up in a parry that made my blade slip off. Then instead of continuing with another slash, I brought the point up and lunged toward his belly with my hand low.

I felt a moment's resistance as the point pierced the lizard-skin stomacher, then a slow, easy slide as I sliced into his bowels. The blow forced him back against the edge of the one of the tables and his eyes widened. I leaned into the sword, putting my weight behind it, forcing the point deeper into his belly and ripping up until it grated on the breastbone. His eyes widened, his mouth moved, but only blood came out to run down the beaten gold gorget of the god Quetzalcoatl. I eased the pressure and he slumped to the floor, my sword still in him.

I leaned back against the wall, my chest heaving. The cuts on my legs were bleeding profusely, my shoulder was still numb with pain, but there was more blood running down my right arm and that side of the chest. My left wrist was throbbing as if I had sprained it. All in all, I looked like the victim of a particularly inept sacrificial priest. But I was alive, and right now that felt better than being crowned Emperor Himself.

"Well done, young sir," came an all-too-familiar voice from the doorway, "well done indeed."

Foureagle came stumping into the room, accompanied by five or six hard-looking men. "I trust you have recovered the missing items."

I gestured toward the still figures on the tables. "In there. One in each."

The old man bent over the nearest table and examined its burden. "Ah, yes. Ingenious and even, perhaps, theologically sound—from Toltectecuhtli's perspective, of course."

"What will you do with them?" Not that I really cared.

"Why, return them to the huetlacoatls, of course. Oh, you mean the people? We will save them, if we can." He gestured to the men behind him and they disappeared down the corridor.

"You look as if you could use some tending to yourself." He laid his hands, oddly gentle, on my shoulder, testing the wound. "Yes, we must get that attended to. But not here. Can you walk? Ah, excellent. I am afraid this place will shortly suffer an unfortunate accident. A fire, I believe." He looked around appraisingly, nodded, and stroked his chin. "Yes, I think a fire will do nicely."

He half-supported me as he guided me toward the door. "But I do hope you will come and visit me. After you have healed, of course. We have so much to discuss. Your future, for example, and perhaps some additional employment. Yes, I think we must discuss that, young sir."

I thought about how I would explain working for the Emperor's Shadow to

Uncle Tlaloc. Then I thought about Uncle Tlaloc's probable reaction. Then I thought about what Foureagle certainly would do to me if I refused. Turning of the cycle or not, my luck hadn't changed.

With that thought, I let them guide me down the corridor and out into the piss-warm rain of night.

patient zero

TANANARIVE DUE

Tananarive Due has been making a name for herself as a horror writer in the course of the last few years, but only this year has she begun to venture into science fiction as well, with sales to The Magazine of Fantasy & Science Fiction *and* Dark Matter. *In the chilling and deceptively quiet story that follows, she paints a heartrending portrait of a life spent in ever-increasing isolation in an ever-darkening world. . . .*

Tananarive Due's books include the horror novels The Between *and* My Soul to Keep, *which were both finalists for the Bram Stoker Award. Her most recent book is a sequel to* My Soul to Keep, *called* The Living Blood. *Upcoming is a memoir about Florida's civil rights movement,* Freedom in the Family, *written with her mother, Patricia Stephens Due. She lives in Longview, Washington, with her husband, SF writer Steven Barnes.*

September 19

The picture came! Veronica tapped on my glass and woke me up, and she held it up for me to see. It's autographed and everything! *For you,* Veronica mouthed at me, and she smiled a really big smile. The autograph says, TO JAY—I'LL THROW A TOUCHDOWN FOR YOU. I couldn't believe it. Everybody is laughing at me because of the way I yelled and ran in circles around my room until I fell on the floor and scraped my elbow. The janitor, Lou, turned on the intercom box outside my door and said, "Kid, you gone crazier than usual? What you care about that picture for?"

Don't they know Dan Marino is the greatest quarterback of all time? I taped the picture to the wall over my bed. On the rest of my wall I have maps of the United States, and the world, and the solar system. I can find Corsica on the map, and the Palau Islands, which most people have never heard of, and I know what order all the planets are in. But there's nothing else on my wall like Dan Marino. That's the best. The other best thing I have is the cassette tape from that time the President called me on the telephone when I was six. He said, "Hi, is Jay there? This is the President of the United States." He sounded just like on TV. My heart flipped, because it's so weird to hear the President say your name. I couldn't think of anything to say back. He asked me how I was feeling, and I said I was fine. That made him laugh, like he thought I was making a joke. Then his voice got real serious, and he said everyone was praying and thinking about me, and he hung up. When I listen to that tape now, I wish I had thought of something else to say. I used to think he might call me another time, but it only happened once, in the beginning. So I guess I'll never have a chance to talk to the President again.

After Veronica gave me my picture of Marino, I asked her if she could get somebody to fix my TV so I can see the football games. All my TV can play is videos. Veronica said there aren't any football games, and I started to get mad because I hate it when they lie. It's September, I said, and there's always football games in September. But Veronica told me the NFL people had a meeting and decided not to have football anymore, and maybe it would start again, but she wasn't sure, because nobody except me was thinking about football. At first, after she said that, it kind of ruined the autograph, because it seemed like Dan Marino must be lying, too. But Veronica said he was most likely talking about throwing a touchdown for me in the future, and I felt better then.

This notebook is from Ms. Manigat, my tutor, who is Haitian. She said I should start writing down my thoughts and everything that happens to me. I said I don't have any thoughts, but she said that was ridiculous. That is her favorite word, ridiculous.

Oh, I should say I'm ten today. If I were in a regular school, I would be in fifth grade like my brother was. I asked Ms. Manigat what grade I'm in, and she said I don't have a grade. I read like I'm in seventh grade and I do math like I'm in fourth grade, she says. She says I don't exactly fit anywhere, but I'm very smart. Ms. Manigat comes every day, except on weekends. She is my best friend, but I have to call her Ms. Manigat instead of using her first name, which is Emmeline, because she is so proper. She is very neat and wears skirts and dresses, and everything about her is very clean except her shoes, which are dirty. Her shoes are supposed to be white, but whenever I see her standing outside of the glass, when she hasn't put on her plastic suit yet, her shoes look brown and muddy.

Those are my thoughts.

September 20

I had a question today. Veronica never comes on Fridays, and the other nurse, Rene, isn't as nice as she is, so I waited for Ms. Manigat. She comes at one. I said, "You know how they give sick children their last wish when they're dying? Well, when Dr. Ben told me to think of the one thing I wanted for my birthday, I said I wanted an autograph from Dan Marino, so does that mean I'm dying and they're giving me my wish?" I said this really fast.

I thought Ms. Manigat would say I was being ridiculous. But she smiled. She put her hand on top of my head, and her hand felt stiff and heavy inside her big glove. "Listen, little old man," she said, which is what she calls me because she says I do so much worrying, "You're a lot of things, but you aren't dying. When everyone can be as healthy as you, it'll be a happy day."

The people here always seems to be waiting, and I don't know what for. I thought maybe they were waiting for me to die. But I believe Ms. Manigat. If she doesn't want to tell me something, she just says, "Leave it alone, Jay," which is her way of letting me know she would rather not say anything at all than ever tell a lie.

October 5

The lights in my room started going on and off again today, and it got so hot I had to leave my shirt off until I went to bed. Ms. Manigat couldn't do her lessons the way she wanted because of the lights not working right. She said it was the emergency generator. I asked her what the emergency was, and she said something that sounded funny: "Same old same old." That was all she said. I asked her if the emergency generator was the reason Dr. Ben took the television out of my room, and she said yes. She said everyone is conserving energy, and I have to do my part, too. But I miss my videos. There is nothing at all to do when I can't watch my videos. I hate it when I'm bored. Sometimes I'll even watch videos I've seen a hundred times, *really* a hundred times. I've seen *Big* with Tom Hanks more times than any other video. I love the part in the toy store with the really big piano keys on the floor. My mom taught me how to play Three Blind Mice on our piano at home, and it reminds me of that. I've never seen a toy store like the one in *Big*. I thought it was just a made-up place, but Ms. Manigat said it was a real toy store in New York.

I miss my videos. When I'm watching them, it's like I'm inside the movie, too. I hope Dr. Ben will bring my TV back soon.

October 22

I made Veronica cry yesterday. I didn't mean to. Dr. Ben said he knows it was an accident, but I feel very sorry, so I've been crying too. What happened is, I was talking to her, and she was taking some blood out of my arm with a needle like always. I was telling her about how me and my dad used to watch Marino play on television, and then all of a sudden she was crying really hard.

She dropped the needle on the floor and she was holding her wrist like she broke it. She started swearing. She said Goddammit, goddammit, goddammit, over and over, like that. I asked her what happened, and she pushed me away like she wanted to knock me over. Then she went to the door and punched the number code really fast and she pulled on the doorknob, but the door wouldn't open, and I heard something in her arm snap from yanking so hard. She had to do the code again. She was still crying. I've never seen her cry.

I didn't know what happened. I mashed my finger on the buzzer hard, but everybody ignored me. It reminded me of when I first came here, when I was always pushing the buzzer and crying, and nobody would ever come for a long time, and they were always in a bad mood when they came.

Anyway, I waited for Ms. Manigat, and when I told her about Veronica, she said she didn't know anything because she comes from the outside, but she promised to find out. Then she made me recite the Preamble to the Constitution, which I know by heart. Pretty soon, for a little while, I forgot about Veronica.

After my lessons, Ms. Manigat left and called me on my phone an hour later, like she promised. She always keeps her promises. My telephone is hooked up so people on the inside can call me, but I can't call anybody, inside or outside. It hardly ever rings now. But I almost didn't want to pick it up. I was afraid of what Ms. Manigat would say.

"Veronica poked herself," Ms. Manigat told me. "The needle stuck through her hot suit. She told Dr. Ben there was sudden movement."

I wondered who made the sudden movement, Veronica or me?

"Is she okay?" I asked. I thought maybe Ms. Manigat was mad at me, because she has told me many times that I should be careful. Maybe I wasn't being careful when Veronica was here.

"We'll see, Jay," Ms. Manigat said. From her voice, it sounded like the answer was *no*.

"Will she get sick?" I asked.

"Probably, yes, they think so," Ms. Manigat said.

I didn't want her to answer anymore questions. I like it when people tell me the truth, but it always makes me feel bad, too. I tried to say I was sorry, but I couldn't even open my mouth.

"It's not your fault, Jay," Ms. Manigat said.

I couldn't help it. I sobbed like I used to when I was still a little kid.

"Veronica knew something like this could happen," she said.

But that didn't make anything better, because I remembered how Veronica's face looked so scared inside her mask, and how she pushed me away. Veronica has been here since almost the beginning, before Ms. Manigat came, and she used to smile at me even when nobody else did. When she showed me my picture from Dan Marino, she looked almost as happy as me. I had never seen her whole face smiling like that. She looked so pretty and glad.

I was crying so much I couldn't even write down my thoughts like Ms. Manigat said to. Not until today.

November 4

A long time ago, when I first came here and the TV in my room played programs from outside, I saw the first-grade picture I had taken at school on TV. I always hated that picture because Mom put some greasy stuff in my hair that made me look like a total geek. And then I turned on the TV and saw that picture on the news! The man on TV said the names of everyone in our family, and even spelled them out on the screen. Then, he called me Patient Zero. He said I was the first person who got sick.

But that wasn't really what happened. My dad was sick before me. I've told them that already. He got it away on his job in Alaska. My dad traveled a lot because he drilled for oil, but he came home early that time. We weren't expecting him until Christmas, but he came when it was only September, close to my birthday. He said he'd been sent home because some people on his oil crew got sick. One of them had even died. But the doctor in Alaska had looked at my dad and said he was fine, and then his boss sent him home. Dad was really mad about that. He hated to lose money. Time away from a job was always losing money, he said. He was in a bad mood when he wasn't working.

And the worse thing was, my dad wasn't fine. After two days, his eyes got red and he started sniffling. Then I did, too. And then my mom and brother.

When the man on TV showed my picture and called me Patient Zero and said I was the first one to get sick, that was when I first learned how people tell lies, because that wasn't true. Somebody on my dad's oil rig caught it first, and then he gave it to my dad. And my dad gave it to me, my mom and my brother. But one thing he said was right. I was the only one who got well.

My Aunt Lori came here to live at the lab with me at first, but she wasn't here long, because her eyes had already turned red by then. She came to help take care of me and my brother before my mom died, but probably she shouldn't have done that. She lived all the way in California, and I bet she wouldn't have gotten sick if she hadn't come to Miami to be with us. But even my mom's doctor didn't know what was wrong then, so nobody could warn her about what would happen if she got close to us. Sometimes I dream I'm calling Aunt Lori on my phone, telling her please, please not to come. Aunt Lori and my mom were twins. They looked exactly alike.

After Aunt Lori died, I was the only one left in my whole family.

I got very upset when I saw that news report. I didn't like hearing someone talk about my family like that, people who didn't even know us. And I felt like maybe the man on TV was right, and maybe it was all my fault. I screamed and cried the whole day. After that, Dr. Ben made them fix my TV so I couldn't see the news anymore or any programs from outside, just cartoons and kid movies on video. The only good thing was, that was when the President called me. I think he was sorry when he heard what happened to my family.

When I ask Dr. Ben if they're still talking about me on the news, he just shrugs his shoulders. Sometimes Dr. Ben won't say yes or no if you ask him a question. It doesn't matter, though. I think the TV people probably stopped showing my picture a long time ago. I was just a little kid when my family got sick. I've been here four whole years!

Oh, I almost forgot. Veronica isn't back yet.

November 7

I have been staring at my Dan Marino picture all day, and I think the handwriting on the autograph looks like Dr. Ben's. But I'm afraid to ask anyone about that. Oh, yeah—and yesterday the power was off in my room for a whole day! Same old same old. That's what Ms. M. would say.

November 12

Ms. Manigat is teaching me a little bit about medicine. I told her I want to be a doctor when I grow up, and she said she thinks that's a wonderful idea because she believes people will always need doctors. She says I will be in a good position to help people, and I asked her if that's because I have been here so long, and she said yes.

The first thing she taught me is about diseases. She says in the old days, a long time ago, diseases like typhoid used to kill a lot of people because of unsanitary conditions and dirty drinking water, but people got smarter and doctors found drugs to cure it, so diseases didn't kill people as much anymore. Doctors are always trying to stay a step ahead of disease, Ms. Manigat says.

But sometimes they can't. Sometimes a new disease comes. Or, maybe it's not a new disease, but an old disease that has been hidden for a long time until something brings it out in the open. She said that's how nature balances the planet, because as soon as doctors find cures for one thing, there is always something new. Dr. Ben says my disease is new. There is a long name for it I can't remember how to spell, but most of the time people here call it Virus-J.

In a way, see, it's named after me. That's what Dr. Ben said. But I don't like that.

Ms. Manigat said after my dad came home, the virus got in my body and attacked me just like everyone else, so I got really, really sick for a lot of days. Then, I thought I was completely better. I stopped feeling bad at all. But the virus was already in my brother and my mom and dad, and even our doctor from before, Dr. Wolfe, and Ms. Manigat says it was very *aggressive*, which means doctors didn't know how to kill it.

Everybody wears yellow plastic suits and airtight masks when they're in my room because the virus is still in the air, and it's in my blood, and it's on my plates and cups whenever I finish eating. They call the suits hot suits because the virus is *hot* in my room. Not hot like fire, but dangerous.

Ms. Manigat says Virus-J is extra special in my body because even though I'm not sick anymore, except for when I feel like I have a temperature and I have to lie down sometimes, the virus won't go away. I can make other people sick even when I feel fine, so she said that makes me a carrier. Ms. Manigat said Dr. Ben doesn't know anybody else who's gotten well except for me.

Oh, except maybe there are some little girls in China. Veronica told me once there were some little girls in China the same age as me who didn't get sick either. But when I asked Dr. Ben, he said he didn't know if it was true. And Ms. Manigat told me it might have been true once, but those girls might not be alive anymore. I asked her if they died of Virus-J, and she said no, no, no. Three times. She told me to forget all about any little girls in China. Almost like she was mad.

I'm the only one like me she knows about for sure, she says. The only one left.

That's why I'm here, she says. But I already knew that part. When I was little, Dr. Ben told me about antibodies and stuff in my blood, and he said the reason him and Rene and Veronica and all the other doctors take so much blood from me all the time, until they make purple bruises on my arms and I feel dizzy, is so they can try to help other people get well, too. I have had almost ten surgeries since I have been here. I think they have even taken out parts of me, but I'm not really sure. I look the same on the outside, but I feel different on the inside. I had surgery on my belly a year ago, and sometimes when I'm climbing the play-rope hanging from the ceiling in my room, I feel like it hasn't healed right, like I'm still cut open. Ms. Manigat says that's only in my mind. But it really hurts! I don't hate anything like I hate operations. I wonder if that's what happened to the other little girls, if they kept getting cut up and cut up until they died. Anyway, it's been a year since I had any operations. I keep telling Dr. Ben they can have as much blood as they want, but I don't want anymore operations, please.

Dr. Ben said there's nobody in the world better than me to make people well, if only they can figure out how. Ms. Manigat says the same thing. That makes me feel a little better about Virus-J.

I was happy Ms. Manigat told me all about disease, because I don't want her to treat me like a baby the way everybody else does. That's what I always tell her. I like to know things.

I didn't even cry when she told me Veronica died. Maybe I got all my crying over with in the beginning, because I figured out a long time ago nobody gets better once they get sick. Nobody except for me.

November 14

Today, I asked Ms. Manigat how many people have Virus-J.

"Oh, Jay, I don't know," she said. I don't think she was in the mood to talk about disease.

"Just guess," I said.

Ms. Manigat thought for a long time. Then she opened her notebook and began drawing lines and boxes for me to see. Her picture looked like the tiny brown lines all over an oak-tree leaf. We had a tree called a live oak in our backyard, and my dad said it was more than a hundred years old. He said trees sometimes live longer than people do. And he was right, because I'm sure that tree is still standing in our yard even though my whole family is gone.

"This is how it goes, Jay," Ms. Manigat said, showing me with her pencil-tip how one line branched down to the next. "People are giving it to each other. They don't usually know they're sick for two weeks, and by then they've passed it to a lot of other people. By now, it's already been here four years, so the same thing that happened to your family is happening to a lot of families."

"How many families?" I asked again. I tried to think of the biggest number I could. "A million?"

Ms. Manigat shrugged just like Dr. Ben would. Maybe that meant yes.

I couldn't imagine a million families, so I asked Ms. Manigat if it happened to her family, too, if maybe she had a husband and kids and they got sick. But she said no, she was never married. I guess that's true, because Ms. Manigat doesn't look that old. She won't tell me her age, but she's in her twenties, I think. Ms. Manigat smiled at me, even though her eyes weren't happy.

"My parents were in Miami, and they got it right away," Ms. Manigat said. "Then my sister and nieces came to visit them from Haiti, and they got it, too. I was away working when it happened, and that's why I'm still here."

Ms. Manigat never told me that before.

My family lived in Miami Beach. My dad said our house was too small—I had to share a room with my brother—but my mother liked where we lived because our building was six blocks from the ocean. My mother said the ocean can heal anything. But that can't be true, can it?

My mother wouldn't like it where I am, because there is no ocean and no windows neither. I wondered if Ms. Manigat's parents knew someone who worked on an oil rig, too, but probably not. Probably they got it from my dad and me.

"Ms. Manigat," I said, "Maybe you should move inside like Dr. Ben and everybody else."

"Oh, Jay," Ms. Manigat said, like she was trying to sound cheerful. "Little old man, if I were that scared of anything, why would I be in here teaching you?"

She said she *asked* to be my teacher, which I didn't know. I said I thought her boss was making her do it, and she said she didn't have a boss. No one sent her. She wanted to come.

"Just to meet me?" I asked her.

"Yes, because I saw your face on television, and you looked to me like a one-of-a-kind," she said. She said she was a nurse before, and she used to work with Dr. Ben in his office in Atlanta. She said they worked at the CDC, which is a place that studies diseases. And he knew her, so that was why he let her come teach me.

"A boy like you needs his education. He needs to know how to face life outside," she said.

Ms. Manigat is funny like that. Sometimes she'll quit the regular lesson about presidents and the Ten Commandments and teach me something like how to sew and how to tell plants you eat from plants you don't, and stuff. Like, I remember when she brought a basket with real fruits and vegetables in it, fresh. She said she has a garden where she lives on the outside, close to here. She said one of the reasons she won't move inside is because she loves her garden so much, and she doesn't want to leave it.

The stuff she brought was not very interesting to look at. She showed me some cassava, which looked like a long, twisty tree branch to me, and she said it's good to eat, except it has poison in it that has to be boiled out of the root first and the leaves are poisonous too. She also brought something called akee, which she said she used to eat from trees in Haiti. It has another name in Haiti that's too hard for me to spell. It tasted fine to me, but she said akee can never be eaten before it's opened, or before it's ripe, because it makes your brain swell up and you can die. She also brought different kinds of mushrooms to show me which ones are good or bad, but they all looked alike to me. She promised to bring me other fruits and vegetables to see so I will know what's good for me and what isn't. There's a lot to learn about life outside, she said.

Well, I don't want Ms. Manigat to feel like I am a waste of her time, but I know for a fact I don't have to face life outside. Dr. Ben told me I might be a teenager before I can leave, or even older. He said I might even be a grown man.

But that's okay, I guess. I try not to think about what it would be like to leave. My room, which they moved me to when I had been here six months, is really, really big. They built it especially for me. It's four times as big as the hotel room my mom and dad got for us when we went to Universal Studios in Orlando when I was five. I remember that room because my brother, Kevin, kept asking my dad, "Doesn't this cost too much?" Every time my dad bought us a T-shirt or anything, Kevin brought up how much it cost. I told Kevin to stop it because I was afraid Dad would get mad and stop buying us stuff. Then, when we were in line for the King Kong ride, all by ourselves, Kevin told me, "Dad got fired from his job, stupid. Do you want to go on Welfare?" I waited for Dad and Mom to tell me he got fired, but they didn't. After Kevin said that, I didn't ask them to buy me anything else, and I was scared to stay in that huge, pretty hotel room because I thought we wouldn't have enough money to pay. But we did. And then Dad got a job on the oil rig, and we thought everything would be better.

My room here is as big as half the whole floor I bet. When I run from one side of my room to the other, from the glass in front to the wall in back, I'm out of breath. I like to do that. Sometimes I run until my ribs start squeezing and my stomach hurts like it's cut open and I have to sit down and rest. There's a basketball net in here, too, and the ball doesn't ever touch the ceiling except if I throw it too high on purpose. I also have comic books, and I draw pictures of me and my family and Ms. Manigat and Dr. Ben. Because I can't watch my videos, now I spend a lot of time writing in this notebook. A whole hour went by already. When I am writing down my thoughts, I forget about everything else.

I have decided for sure to be a doctor someday. I'm going to help make people better.

November 29

Thanksgiving was great! Ms. Manigat cooked real bread and brought me food she'd heated up. I could tell everything except the bread and cassava was from a can, like always, but it tasted much better than my regular food. I haven't had bread in a long time. Because of her mask, Ms. Manigat ate her dinner before she came, but she sat and watched me eat. Rene came in, too, and she surprised me when she gave me a hug. She never does that. Dr. Ben came in for a little while at the end, and he hugged me too, but he said he couldn't stay because he was busy. Dr. Ben doesn't come visit me much anymore. I could see he was growing a beard, and it was almost all white! I've seen Dr. Ben's hair when he's outside of the glass, when he isn't wearing his hot suit, and his hair is brown, not white. I asked him how come his beard was white, and he said that's what happens when your mind is overly tired.

I liked having everybody come to my room. Before, in the beginning, almost nobody came in, not even Ms. Manigat. She used to sit in a chair outside the glass and use the intercom for my lessons. It's better when they come in.

I remember how Thanksgiving used to be, with my family around the table in the dining room, and I told Ms. Manigat about that. Yes, she said, even though she didn't celebrate Thanksgiving in Haiti like Americans do, she remembers sitting at the table with her parents and her sister for Christmas dinner. She said she came to see me today, and Rene and Dr. Ben came too, because we are each other's family now, so we are not alone. I hadn't thought of it like that before.

December 1

No one will tell me, not even Ms. M., but I think maybe Dr. Ben is sick. I have not seen him in five whole days. It is quiet here. I wish it was Thanksgiving again.

January 23

I didn't know this before, but you have to be in the right mood to write your thoughts down. A lot happened in the days I missed.

The doctor with the French name is gone now, and I'm glad. He wasn't like Dr. Ben at all. I could hardly believe he was a real doctor, because he always had on the dirtiest clothes when I saw him take off his hot suit outside of the glass. And he was never nice to me—he wouldn't answer at all when I asked him questions, and he wouldn't look in my eyes except for a second. One time he slapped me on my ear, almost for nothing, and his glove hurt so much my ear turned red and was sore for a whole day. He didn't say he was sorry, but I didn't cry. I think he wanted me to.

Oh yeah, and he hooked me up to IV bags and took so much blood from me I couldn't even stand up. I was scared he would operate on me. Ms. Manigat didn't come in for almost a week, and when she finally came, I told her about the doctor taking too much blood. She got really mad. Then I found out the reason she didn't come all those days—he wouldn't let her! She said he tried to bar her from coming. *Bar* is the word she used, which sounds like a prison.

The new doctor and Ms. Manigat do not get along, even though they both speak French. I saw them outside of the glass, yelling back and forth and moving their hands, but I couldn't hear what they were saying. I was afraid he would send Ms. Manigat away for good. But yesterday she told me he's leaving! I told her I was happy, because I was afraid he would take Dr. Ben's place.

No, she told me, there isn't anyone taking Dr. Ben's place. She said the French doctor came here to study me in person because he was one of the doctors Dr. Ben had been sending my blood to ever since I first came. But he was already very sick when he got here, and he started feeling worse, so he had to go. Seeing me was his last wish, Ms. Manigat said, which didn't seem like it could be true because he didn't act like he wanted to be with me.

I asked her if he went back to France to his family, and Ms. Manigat said no, he probably didn't have a family, and even if he did, it's too hard to go to France. The ocean is in the way, she said.

Ms. Manigat seemed tired from all that talking. She said she'd decided to move inside, like Rene, to make sure they were taking care of me properly. She said she misses her garden. The whole place has been falling apart, she said. She said I do a good job of keeping my room clean—and I do, because I have my own mop and bucket and Lysol in my closet—but she told me the hallways are filthy. Which is true, because sometimes I can see water dripping down the wall outside of my glass, a lot of it, and it makes puddles all over the floor. You can tell the water is dirty because you can see different colors floating on top, the way my family's driveway used to look after my dad sprayed it with a hose. He said the oil from the car made the water look that way, but I don't know why it looks that way here. Ms. Manigat said the water smells bad, too.

"It's ridiculous. If they're going to keep you here, they'd damn well better take care of you," Mrs. Manigat said. She must have been really mad, because she never swears.

I told her about the time when Lou came and pressed on my intercom really late at night, when I was asleep and nobody else was around. He was talking really loud like people do in videos when they're drunk. Lou was glaring at me through the glass, banging on it. I had never seen him look so mean. I thought he would try to come into my room but then I remembered he couldn't because he didn't have a hot suit. But I'll never forget how he said, *They should put you to sleep like a dog at the pound.*

I try not to think about that night, because it gave me nightmares. It happened when I was pretty little, like eight. Sometimes I thought maybe I just dreamed it, because the next time Lou came he acted just like normal. He even smiled at me a little bit. Before he stopped coming here, Lou was nice to me every day after that.

Ms. Manigat did not sound surprised when I told her what Lou said about putting me to sleep. "Yes, Jay," she told me, "For a long time, there have been people outside who didn't think we should be taking care of you."

I never knew that before!

I remember a long time ago, when I was really little and I had pneumonia, my mom was scared to leave me alone at the hospital. "They won't know how to take care of Jay there," she said to my dad, even though she didn't know I heard her. I had to stay by myself all night, and because of what my mom said, I couldn't go to sleep. I was afraid everyone at the hospital would forget I was there. Or maybe something bad would happen to me.

It seems like the lights go off every other day now. And I know people must really miss Lou, because the dirty gray water is all over the floor outside my glass and there's no one to clean it up.

February 14

6-4-6-7-2-9-4-3   6-4-6-7-2-9-4-3   6-4-6-7-2-9-4-3

I remember the numbers already! I have been saying them over and over in my head so I won't forget, but I wanted to write them down in the exact right order to be extra sure. I want to know them without even looking.

Oh, I should start at the beginning. Yesterday, no one brought me any dinner, not even Ms. Manigat. She came with a huge bowl of oatmeal this morning, saying she was very sorry. She said she had to look a long time to find that food, and it wore her out. The oatmeal wasn't even hot, but I didn't say anything. I just ate. She watched me eating.

She didn't stay with me long, because she doesn't teach me lessons anymore. After the French doctor left, we talked about the Emancipation Proclamation and Martin Luther King, but she didn't bring that up today. She just kept sighing, and she said she had been in bed all day yesterday because she was so tired, and she was sorry she forgot to feed me. She said I couldn't count on Rene to bring me food because she didn't know where Rene was. It was hard for me to hear her talk through her hot suit today. Her mask was crooked, so the microphone wasn't in front of her mouth where it should be.

She saw my notebook and asked if she could look at it. I said sure. She looked at the pages from the beginning. She said she liked the part where I said she was my best friend. Her face-mask was fogging up, so I couldn't see her eyes and I couldn't tell if she was smiling. I am very sure she did not put her suit on right today.

When she put my notebook down, she told me to pay close attention to her and repeat the numbers she told me, which were 6-4-6-7-2-9-4-3.

I asked her what they were. She said it was the security code for my door. She said she wanted to give the code to me because my buzzer wasn't working, and I might need to leave my room if she overslept and nobody came to bring me food. She told me I could use the same code on the elevator, and the kitchen was on the third floor. There wouldn't be anybody there, she said, but I could look on the shelves, the top ones up high, to see if there was any food. If not, she said I should take the stairs down to the first floor and find the red EXIT sign to go outside. She said the elevator doesn't go to the first floor anymore.

I felt scared then, but she put her hand on top of my head again just like usual. She said she was sure there was plenty of food outside.

"But am I allowed?" I asked her. "What if people get sick?"

"You worry so much, little man," she said. "Only you matter now, my little one-of-a-kind."

But see I'm sure Ms. Manigat doesn't really want me to go outside. I've been thinking about that over and over. Ms. Manigat must be very tired to tell me to do something like that. Maybe she has a fever and that's why she told me how to get out of my room. My brother said silly things when he had a fever, and my father too. My father kept calling me *Oscar*, and I didn't know who Oscar was. My dad told us he had a brother who died when he was little, and maybe his name was Oscar. My mother didn't say anything at all when she got sick. She just died very fast. I wish I could find Ms. Manigat and give her something to drink. You get very thirsty when you have a fever, which I know for a fact. But I can't go to her because I don't know where she is. And besides, I don't know where Dr. Ben keeps the hot suits. What if I went to her and she wasn't wearing hers?

Maybe the oatmeal was the only thing left in the kitchen, and now I ate it all. I hope not! But I'm thinking maybe it is because I know Ms. Manigat would have brought me more food if she could have found it. She's always asking me if I have enough to eat. I'm already hungry again.

6-4-6-7-2-9-4-3
6-4-6-7-2-9-4-3

February 15

I am writing in the dark. The lights are off. I tried to open my lock but the numbers don't work because of the lights being off. I don't know where Ms. Manigat is. I'm trying not to cry.

What if the lights never come back on?

February 16

There's so much I want to say but I have a headache from being hungry. When the lights came back on I went out into the hall like Ms. M told me and I used the numbers to get the elevator to work and then I went to the kitchen like she said. I wanted to go real fast and find some peanut butter or some Oreos or even a can of beans I could open with the can opener Ms. M left me at Thanksgiving.

There's no food in the kitchen! There's empty cans and wrappers on the floor and even roaches but I looked on every single shelf and in every cabinet and I couldn't find anything to eat.

The sun was shining really REALLY bright from the window. I almost forgot how the sun looks. When I went to the window I saw a big, empty parking lot outside. At first I thought there were diamonds all over the ground because of the sparkles but it was just a lot of broken glass. I could only see one car and I thought it was Ms. M's. But Ms. M would never leave her car looking like that. For one thing it had two flat tires!

Anyway I don't think there's anybody here today. So I thought of a plan. I have to go now.

Ms. M, this is for you — or whoever comes looking for me. I know somebody will find this notebook if I leave it on my bed. I'm very sorry I had to leave in such a hurry.

I didn't want to go outside but isn't it okay if it's an emergency? I am really really hungry. I'll just find some food and bring it with me and I'll come right back. I'm leaving my door open so I won't get locked out. Ms. M, maybe I'll find your garden with cassavas and akee like you showed me and I'll know the good parts from the bad parts. If someone sees me and I get in trouble I'll just say I didn't have anything to eat.

Whoever is reading this don't worry. I'll tell everybody I see please please not to get too close to me. I know Dr. Ben was very worried I might make somebody sick.

A colder war

CHARLES STROSS

Here's another brilliant story by Charles Stross, whose story "Antibodies" appears elsewhere in this anthology. In this one, he gives us a scary look at the proposition that, even in wartime, new allies may sometimes cost you more than they're worth . . . more, in fact, than you have to spend. . . .

ANALYST

Roger Jourgensen tilts back in his chair, reading.

He's in his mid-thirties: fair hair razor-cropped, skin pallid from too much time spent under artificial lights. Spectacles, short-sleeved white shirt and tie, photographic ID badge on a chain around his neck. His office is air-conditioned and has no windows.

The file he is reading frightens him. Once, when Roger was a young boy, his father took him to an open day at Nellis AFB, out in the California desert. Sunlight glared brilliantly from the polished silver-plate flanks of the big bombers, sitting in their concrete-lined dispersal bays behind barriers and blinking radiation monitors. The brightly colored streamers flying from their pitot tubes lent them a strange, almost festive appearance. But they were sleeping nightmares: once they were awakened, nobody—except the flight crew—could come within a mile of the nuclear-powered bombers and live.

Looking at the gleaming, bulging pods slung under their wingtip pylons, Roger had a premature inkling of the fires that waited within, a frigid terror that echoed the siren wail of the air-raid warnings. He'd sucked nervously on his ice cream and gripped his father's hand tightly while the band ripped through a cheerful Sousa march, and only forgot his fear when a flock of Thunderchiefs sliced by overhead, rattling car windows for miles around.

He has the same feeling now, as an adult reading this intelligence assessment, that he had as a child watching the nuclear-powered bombers sleeping in their concrete beds.

In the file there's a blurry photograph of a concrete box, snapped from above by a high-flying U-2 during the autumn of '61. Three coffin-shaped lakes, bulking dark and gloomy beneath the arctic sun; a canal heading west, deep in the Soviet heartland, surrounded by warning trefoils and armed guards. Deep waters saturated with calcium salts, concrete coffer-dams lined with gold and lead. A sleeping giant pointed at NATO, more terrifying than any nuclear weapon.

Project Koschei.

RED SQUARE REDUX

Warning:
The following briefing film is classified SECRET GOLD JULY BOOJUM. If you do not have SECRET GOLD JULY BOOJUM clearance, leave the auditorium *now* and report to your unit security officer for debriefing. Failing to observe this notice is an imprisonable offense.

You have sixty seconds to comply.

Video clip:
Red Square in springtime. The sky overhead is clear and blue; there's a little wispy cirrus at high altitude. It forms a brilliant backdrop for flight after flight of four-engined bombers, thundering five at a time across the horizon to drop behind the Kremlin's high walls.

Voice-over:
Red Square, the May Day parade, 1962. This is the first time that the Soviet Union has publicly displayed weapons classified GOLD JULY BOOJUM. Here they are:

Video clip:
Later in the same day. A seemingly endless stream of armor and soldiers marches across the square, turning the air gray with diesel fumes. The trucks roll in line eight abreast, with soldiers sitting erect in the back. Behind them rumble a battalion of T-56s, their commanders standing at attention in their cupolas, saluting the stand. Jets race low and loud overhead, formations of MiG-17 fighters.

Behind the tanks sprawl a formation of four low-loaders: huge tractors towing low-slung trailers, their load beds strapped down under olive-drab tarpaulins. Whatever is under them is uneven, a bit like a loaf of bread the size of a small house. The trucks have an escort of jeep-like vehicles to either side. In the back of each, armed soldiers sit to attention.

There are big, five-pointed stars outlined in silver on each tarpaulin. Each star is surrounded by a stylized silver circle; unit insignia, perhaps, but not in the standard format for Red Army units. There's lettering around the circles, in a strangely stylized script.

Voice-over:
These are live servitors under transient control. The vehicles towing them bear the insignia of the Second Guards Engineering Brigade, a penal construction unit based in Bokhara and used for structural engineering assignments relating to nuclear installations in the Ukraine and Azerbaijan. This is the first time that any

Dresden Agreement party openly demonstrated ownership of this technology: in this instance, the conclusion we are intended to draw is that the Second Guards Engineering Brigade operates four units. Given existing figures for the Soviet OR-BAT we can then extrapolate a total task strength of two hundred and eighty-eight servitors, if this unit is typical.

Video clip:
Five huge Tu-95 Bear bombers thunder across the Moscow skies.

Voice-over:
This conclusion is questionable. For example, in 1964 a total of two hundred and forty Bear bomber passes were made over the reviewing stand in front of the Lenin Mausoleum. However, at that time technical reconnaissance assets verified that the Soviet air force had hard stand parking for only one hundred and sixty of these aircraft, and estimates of airframe production based on photographs of the extent of the Tupolev bureau's works indicate that total production to that date was between sixty and one hundred and eighty bombers.

Further analysis of photographic evidence from the 1964 parade suggests that a single group of twenty aircraft in four formations of five made repeated passes through the same airspace, the main arc of their circuit lying outside visual observation range of Moscow. This gave rise to the erroneous capacity report of 1964, in which the first strike delivery capability of the Soviet Union was overestimated by as much as three hundred percent.

We must therefore take anything that they show us in Red Square with a pinch of salt when preparing force estimates. Quite possibly these four servitors are all they've got. Then again, the actual battalion strength may be considerably higher.

Still photographic sequence:
From very high altitude — possibly in orbit — an eagle's eye view of a remote village in mountainous country. Small huts huddle together beneath a craggy outcrop; goats graze nearby.

In the second photograph, something has rolled through the village leaving a trail of devastation. The path is quite unlike the trail of damage left by an artillery bombardment: something roughly four meters wide has shaven the rocky plateau smooth, wearing it down as if with a terrible heat. A corner of a shack leans drunkenly, the other half sliced away cleanly. White bones gleam faintly in the track; no vultures descend to stab at the remains.

Voice-over:
These images were taken very recently, on successive orbital passes of a KH-11 satellite. They were timed precisely eighty-nine minutes apart. This village was the home of a principal Mujahedin leader. Note the similar footprint to the payloads on the load beds of the trucks seen at the 1962 parade.

These indicators were present, denoting the presence of servitor units in use by Soviet forces in Afghanistan: the four meter wide gauge of the assimilation track; the total molecular breakdown of organic matter in the track; the speed of destruction. The event took less than five thousand seconds to completion, no survivors were visible, and the causative agent had already been uplifted by the time of the second orbital pass. This, despite the residents of the community being armed with DShK heavy machine guns, rocket-propelled grenade-launchers and AK-47s. Lastly: there is no sign of the causative agent ever deviating from its course, but the entire area is depopulated. Except for excarnated residue there is no sign of human habitation.

In the presence of such unique indicators, we have no alternative but to conclude that the Soviet Union has violated the Dresden Agreement by deploying GOLD JULY BOOJUM in a combat mode in the Khyber pass. Without nuclear support, there are no grounds to believe that a NATO armored division would have fared any better than these Mujahedin . . .

PUZZLE PALACE

Roger isn't a soldier. He's not much of a patriot, either: he signed up with the CIA after college, in the aftermath of the Church Commission hearings in the early seventies. The Company was out of the assassination business, just a bureaucratic engine rolling out National Security assessments: that was fine by Roger. Only now, five years later, he's no longer able to roll along, casually disengaged, like a car in neutral bowling down a shallow incline toward his retirement, pension and a gold watch. He puts the file down on his desk and, with a shaking hand, pulls an illicit cigarette from the pack he keeps in his drawer. He lights it and leans back for a moment to draw breath, force relaxation. He stares at the smoke roiling in the air beneath the merciless light until his hand stops shaking.

Most people think spies are afraid of guns, or KGB guards, or barbed wire, but in point of fact the most dangerous thing they face is paper. Papers carry secrets. Papers can carry death warrants. Papers like this one, this folio with its blurry eighteen-year-old faked missile photographs and estimates of time/survivor curves and pervasive psychosis ratios, can give you nightmares, can drag you awake screaming in the early hours. It's one of a series of highly classified pieces of paper that he is summarizing for the eyes of the National Security Council and the President Elect—if his head of department and the Deputy Director CIA approve it—and here he is, having to calm his nerves with a cigarette before he turns the next page.

After a few minutes, Roger's hand is still. He leaves his cigarette in the eagle-headed ashtray and picks up the intelligence report again. It's a summary, itself the distillation of thousands of pages and hundreds of photographs. It's barely twenty pages long: as of 1963, its date of preparation, the CIA knew very little about Project Koschei. Just the bare skeleton, and rumors from a highly placed spy. And their own equivalent project, of course. Lacking the Soviet lead in that particular field, the USAF fielded the silver-plated white elephants of the NB-39 project: twelve atomic-powered bombers armed with XK-Pluto, ready to tackle Project Koschei should the Soviets show signs of unsealing the bunker. Three hundred megatons of H-bombs pointed at a single target, and nobody was certain that would be enough to do the job.

And then there was the hard-to-conceal fiasco in Antarctica. Egg on face: a subterranean nuclear test program in international territory! If nothing else, it had been enough to stop JFK running for a second term. The test program was a bad excuse: but it was far better than confessing what had really happened to the 501st Airborne Division on the cold plateau beyond Mount Erebus. The plateau that the public didn't know about, that didn't show up on the maps issued by the geological survey departments of those governments party to the Dresden Agreement of 1931 — an arrangement that even Hitler had kept. The plateau that had swallowed more U-2 spy planes than the Soviet Union, more surface expeditions than darkest Africa.

Shit. How the hell am I going to put this together for him?

Roger's spent the past five hours staring at this twenty-page report, trying to think of a way of summarizing its dryly quantifiable terror in words that will give the reader power over them, the power to think the unthinkable. But it's proving difficult. The new man in the White House is a straight-talker, who demands straight answers. He's pious enough not to believe in the supernatural, confident that just to listen to one of his speeches is an uplifting experience, if you can close your eyes and believe in morning in America. There is probably no way of explaining Project Koschei, or XK-Pluto, or MK-Nightmare, or the gates, without watering them down into just another weapons system — which they are not. Weapons may have deadly or hideous effects, but they acquire moral character from the actions of those who use them. Whereas these projects are indelibly stained by a patina of ancient evil . . .

He hopes that if the balloon ever does go up, if the sirens wail, he and Andrea and Jason will be left behind to face the nuclear fire. It'll be a merciful death compared with what he suspect lurks out there, in the unexplored vastness beyond the gates. The vastness that made Nixon cancel the manned space program, leaving just the standing joke of the shuttle, when he realized just how hideously dangerous the space race might become. The darkness that broke Jimmy Carter's faith and turned Lyndon B. Johnson into an alcoholic.

He stands up, nervously shifts from one foot to the other. Looks around at the walls of his cubicle. For a moment the cigarette smoldering on the edge of his ashtray catches his attention: wisps of blue-gray smoke coil like lazy dragons in the air above it, writhing in a strange cuneiform text. He blinks and they're gone, and the skin in the small of his back prickles as if someone had pissed on his grave.

"Shit." Finally, a spoken word in the silence. His hand is shaking as he stubs the cigarette out. *Mustn't let this get to me.* He glances at the wall. It's nineteen hundred hours; too late, too late. He should go home, Andy will be worrying herself sick.

In the end it's all too much. He slides the thin folder into the safe behind his chair, turns the locking handle and spins the dial, then signs himself out of the reading room and submits to the usual exit search.

During the thirty-mile drive home, he spits out of the window, trying to rid his mouth of the taste of Auschwitz ashes.

LATE NIGHT IN THE WHITE HOUSE

The Colonel is febrile, jittering about the room with gung-ho enthusiasm. "That was a mighty fine report you pulled together, Jourgensen!" He paces over to the niche between the office filing cabinet and the wall, turns on the spot, paces back to the far side of his desk. "You understand the fundamentals. I like that. A few more guys like you running the Company and we wouldn't have this fuck-up in Tehran." He grins, contagiously.

The Colonel is a firestorm of enthusiasm, burning out of control like a forties comic-book hero. He has Roger on the edge of his chair, almost sitting at attention. Roger has to bite his tongue to remind himself not to call the Colonel 'sir' — he's a civilian, not in the chain of command.

"That's why I've asked Deputy Director McMurdo to reassign you to this office, to work on my team as Company liaison. And I'm pleased to say that he's agreed."

Roger can't stop himself: "To work here, sir?" *Here* is in the basement of the Executive Office Building, an extension hanging off the White House. Whoever the Colonel is he's got *pull*, in positively magical quantities. "What will I be doing, sir? You said, your team —"

"Relax a bit. Drink your coffee." The Colonel paces back behind his desk, sits down. Roger sips cautiously at the brown sludge in the mug with the Marine Corps crest.

"The president told me to organize a team," the Colonel says, so casually that Roger nearly chokes on his coffee, "to handle contingencies. October surprises. Those asshole commies down in Nicaragua. 'We're eyeball to eyeball with an Evil Empire, Ollie, and we can't afford to blink' — those were his exact words. The Evil Empire uses dirty tricks. But nowadays we're better than they are: buncha hicks, like some third-world dictatorship — Upper Volta with shoggoths. My job is to pin them down and cut them up. Don't give them a chance to whack the shoe on the UN table, demand concessions. If they want to bluff I'll call 'em on it. If they want to go toe-to-toe I'll dance with 'em." He's up and pacing again. "The Company used to do that, and do it okay, back in the fifties and sixties. But too many bleeding hearts — it makes me sick. If you guys went back to wet ops today you'd have journalists following you every time you went to the john in case it was newsworthy.

"Well, we aren't going to do it that way this time. It's a small team and the buck stops here." The Colonel pauses, then glances at the ceiling. "Well, maybe up there. But you get the picture. I need someone who knows the Company, an insider who has clearance up the wazoo who can go in and get the dope before it goes through a fucking committee of ass-watching bureaucrats. I'm also getting someone from the Puzzle Palace, and some words to give me pull with Big Black." He glances at Roger sharply, and Roger nods: he's cleared for National Security Agency — Puzzle Palace — intelligence, and knows about Big Black, the National Reconnaissance Office, which is so secret that even its existence is still classified.

Roger is impressed by this Colonel, against his better judgment. Within the Byzantine world of the US intelligence services, he is talking about building his very own pocket battleship and sailing it under the Jolly Roger with letters of marque and reprise signed by the president. But Roger still has some questions to ask, to scope out the limits of what Colonel North is capable of. "What about Fever Dream, sir?"

The Colonel puts his coffee-cup down. "I own it," he says, bluntly. "And Nightmare. And Pluto. '*Any means necessary*,' he said, and I have an executive order with the ink still damp to prove it. Those projects aren't part of the national command structure anymore. Officially they've been stood down from active status and are being considered for inclusion in the next round of arms reduction talks. They're not part of the deterrent Orbat anymore; we're standardizing on just nuclear weapons. Unofficially, they're part of my group, and I will use them as necessary to contain and reduce the Evil Empire's war-making capabilities."

Roger's skin crawls with an echo of that childhood terror. "And the Dresden Agreement . . . ?"

"Don't worry. Nothing short of *them* breaking it would lead me to do so." The Colonel grins, toothily. "Which is where you come in . . ."

THE MOONLIT SHORES OF LAKE VOSTOK

The metal pier is dry and cold, the temperature hovering close to zero degrees Fahrenheit. It's oppressively dark in the cavern under the ice, and Roger shivers inside his multiple layers of insulation, shifts from foot to foot to keep warm. He has to swallow to keep his ears clear and he feels slightly dizzy from the pressure in the artificial bubble of air, pumped under the icy ceiling to allow humans to exist here, under the Ross Ice Shelf; they'll all spend more than a day sitting in depressurization chambers on the way back up to the surface.

There is no sound from the waters lapping just below the edge of the pier. The floodlights vanish into the surface and keep going—the water in the sub-surface Antarctic lake is incredibly clear—but are swallowed up rapidly, giving an impression of infinite, inky depths.

Manfred is here as the Colonel's representative, to observe the arrival of the probe, receive the consignment they're carrying, and report back that everything is running smoothly. The others try to ignore him, jittery at the presence of the man from DC. They're a gaggle of engineers and artificers, flown out via McMurdo base to handle the midget sub's operations. A nervous lieutenant supervises a squad of marines with complicated-looking weapons, half gun and half video camera, stationed at the corners of the raft. And there's the usual platform crew, deep-sea rig-maintenance types—but subdued and nervous looking. They're afloat in a bubble of pressurized air wedged against the underside of the Antarctic ice sheet: below them stretch the still, supercooled waters of Lake Vostok.

They're waiting for a rendezvous.

"Five hundred yards," reports one of the techs. "Rising on ten." His companion nods. They're waiting for the men in the midget sub drilling quietly through three miles of frigid water, intruders in a long-drowned tomb. "Have 'em back on board in no time." The sub has been away for nearly a day; it set out with enough battery juice for the journey, and enough air to keep the crew breathing for a long time if there's a system failure, but they've learned the hard way that fail-safe systems aren't. Not out here, at the edge of the human world.

"I was afraid the battery load on that cell you replaced would trip an undervoltage isolator, and we'd be here till Hell freezes over," the sub-driver jokes to his neighbor.

Roger shuffles some more. Looking round, he sees one of the marines cross himself. "Have you heard anything from Gorman or Suslowicz?" he asks quietly.

The lieutenant checks his clipboard. "Not since departure, sir," he says. "We don't have comms with the sub while it's submerged: too small for ELF, and we don't want to alert anybody who might be, uh, listening."

"Indeed."

The yellow hunchback shape of the midget submarine appears at the edge of the radiance shed by the floodlights. Surface waters undulate, oily, as the sub rises.

"Crew-transfer vehicle sighted," the driver mutters into his mike. He's suddenly very busy adjusting trim settings, blowing bottled air into ballast tanks, discussing ullage levels and blade count with his number two. The crane crew are busy too, running their long boom out over the lake.

The sub's hatch is visible now, bobbing along the top of the water: the lieutenant is suddenly active. "Jones! Civatti! Stake it out, left and center!" The crane is already swinging the huge lifting hook over the sub, waiting to bring it aboard. "I want eyeballs on the portholes before you crack this thing!" It's the tenth run—seventh manned—through the eye of the needle on the lake bed, the drowned structure so like an ancient temple, and Roger has a bad feeling about it. *We can't get away with this forever,* he reasons. *Sooner or later . . .*

The sub comes out of the water like a gigantic yellow bath toy, a cyborg whale designed by a god with a sense of humor. It takes tense minutes to winch it in and maneuver it safely onto the platform. Marines take up position, shining torches in through two of the portholes that bulge myopically from the smooth curve of the sub's nose. Up on top someone's talking into a handset plugged into the stubby conning tower; the hatch-locking wheel begins to turn.

"Gorman, sir." It's the lieutenant. In the light of the sodium floods everything looks sallow and washed-out; the soldier's face is the color of damp cardboard, slack with relief.

Roger waits while the submariner—Gorman—clambers unsteadily down from the top deck. He's a tall, emaciated-looking man, wearing a red thermal suit three sizes too big for him: salt-and-pepper stubble textures his jaw with sandpaper. Right now, he looks like a cholera victim; sallow skin, smell of acrid ketones as his body eats its own protein reserves, a more revolting miasma hovering over him. There's a slim aluminum briefcase chained to his left wrist, a bracelet of bruises darkening the skin above it. Roger steps forward.

"Sir?" Gorman straightens up for a moment: almost a shadow of military attention. He's unable to sustain it. "We made the pickup. Here's the QA sample; the rest is down below. You have the unlocking code?" he asks wearily.

Jourgensen nods. "One. Five. Eight. One. Two. Two. Nine."

Gorman slowly dials it into a combination lock on the briefcase, lets it fall open and unthreads the chain from his wrist. Floodlights glisten on polythene bags stuffed with white powder, five kilos of high-grade heroin from the hills of Afghanistan; there's another quarter of a ton packed in boxes in the crew compartment. The lieutenant inspects it, closes the case and passes it to Jourgensen.

"Delivery successful, sir." From the ruins on the high plateau of the Taklamakan desert to American territory in Antarctica, by way of a detour through gates linking alien worlds: gates that nobody knows how to create or destroy except the Predecessors—and they aren't talking.

"What's it like through there?" Roger demands, shoulders tense. "What did you *see?*"

Up on top, Suslowicz is sitting in the sub's hatch, half slumping against the crane's attachment post. There's obviously something very wrong with him. Gorman shakes his head and looks away: the wan light makes the razor-sharp creases on his face stand out, like the crackled and shattered surface of a Jovian moon. Crow's feet. Wrinkles. Signs of age. Hair the color of moonlight. "It took so long," he says, almost complaining. Sinks to his knees. "All that *time* we've been gone . . ." He leans against the side of the sub, a pale shadow, aged beyond his years. "The sun was so *bright.* And our radiation detectors . . . Must have been a solar flare or something." He doubles over and retches at the edge of the platform.

Roger looks at him for a long, thoughtful minute: Gorman is twenty-five and a fixer for Big Black, early history in the Green Berets. He was in rude good health two days ago, when he set off through the gate to make the pick-up. Roger glances at the lieutenant. "I'd better go and tell the Colonel," he says. A pause. "Get these two back to Recovery and see they're looked after. I don't expect we'll be sending anymore crews through Victor-Tango for a while."

He turns and walks toward the lift shaft, hands clasped behind his back to keep them from shaking. Behind him, alien moonlight glimmers across the floor of Lake Vostok, three miles and untold light years from home.

GENERAL LEMAY WOULD BE PROUD

Warning:
The following briefing film is classified SECRET INDIGO MARCH SNIPE. If you do not have SECRET INDIGO MARCH SNIPE clearance, leave the auditorium *now* and report to your unit security officer for debriefing. Failing to observe this notice is an imprisonable offense.

Video clip:
Shot of huge bomber, rounded gun turrets sprouting like mushrooms from the decaying log of its fuselage, weirdly bulbous engine pods slung too far out toward each wingtip, four turbine tubes clumped around each atomic kernel.

Voice-over:
"The Convair B-39 Peacemaker is the most formidable weapon in our Strategic Air Command's arsenal for peace. Powered by eight nuclear-heated Pratt & Whitney NP-4051 turbojets, it circles endlessly above the Arctic ice cap, waiting for the call. This is Item One, the flight training and test bird: twelve other birds await criticality on the ground, for once launched a B-39 can only be landed at the two airfields in Alaska that are equipped to handle them. This one's been airborne for nine months so far and shows no signs of age."

Cut to:
A shark the size of a Boeing 727 falls away from the open bomb bay of the monster. Stubby delta wings slice through the air, propelled by a rocket-bright glare.

Voice-over:
"A modified Navajo missile — test article for an XK-Pluto payload — dives away from a carrier plane. Unlike the real thing, this one carries no hydrogen bombs, no direct-cycle fission ramjet to bring retaliatory destruction to the enemy. Travelling at Mach 3 the XK-Pluto will overfly enemy territory, dropping megaton-range bombs until, its payload exhausted, it seeks out and circles a final enemy. Once over the target it will eject its reactor core and rain molten plutonium on the heads of the enemy. XK-Pluto is a total weapon: every aspect of its design, from the shockwave it creates as it hurtles along at treetop height to the structure of its atomic reactor, is designed to inflict damage."

Cut to:
Belsen postcards, Auschwitz movies: a holiday in hell.

Voice-over:
"*This* is why we need such a weapon. *This* is what it deters. The abominations first raised by the Third Reich's Organization Todt, now removed to the Ukraine and deployed in the service of New Soviet Man, as our enemy calls himself."

Cut to:
A sinister gray concrete slab, the upper surface of a Mayan step pyramid built with East German cement. Barbed wire, guns. A drained canal slashes north from the base of the pyramid toward the Baltic coastline, a relic of the installation process: this is where it came from. The slave barracks squat beside the pyramid like a horrible memorial to its black-uniformed builders.

Cut to:
The new resting-place: a big, concrete monolith surrounded by three concrete-lined lakes and a canal. It sits in the midst of a Ukraine landscape, flat as a pancake, that stretches forever in all directions.

Voice-over:
"This is Project Koschei. The Kremlin's key to the Gates of Hell . . ."

TECHNOLOGY TASTER

"We know they first came here during the Precambrian age." Professor Gould is busy with his viewgraphs, eyes down, trying not to pay too much attention to his audience. "We have samples of macrofauna, discovered by paleontologist Charles D. Walcott on his pioneering expeditions into the Canadian Rockies, near the eastern border of British Columbia —" a hand-drawing of something indescribably weird appears on the screen "—like this *opabina*, which died there six hundred and forty million years ago. Fossils of soft-bodied animals that old are rare; the Burgess shale deposits are the best record of the Precambrian fauna anyone has found to date."

A skinny woman with big hair and bigger shoulder-pads sniffs loudly; she has no truck with these antediluvian dates. Roger winces sympathy for the academic. He'd rather she wasn't here, but somehow she got wind of the famous paleontologist's visit—and she's the Colonel's administrative assistant. Telling her to leave would be a career-limiting move.

"The important item to note—" photograph of a mangled piece of rock, visual echoes of the *opabina* "—is the tooth marks. We find them also—their exact cognates—on the ring segments of the Z-series specimens returned by the Pabodie Antarctic expedition of 1926. The world of the Precambrian was laid out differently from our own; most of the landmasses that today are separate continents were joined into one huge structure. Indeed, these samples were originally separated by only two thousand miles or thereabouts. Suggesting that they brought their own parasites with them."

"What do tooth-marks tell us about them, that we need to know?" asks the Colonel.

The doctor looks up. His eyes gleam: "That something liked to eat them when they were fresh." There's a brief rattle of laughter. "Something with jaws that open and close like the iris in your camera. Something we thought was extinct."

Another viewgraph, this time with a blurry underwater photograph on it. The thing looks a bit like a bizarre fish—a turbo-charged, armored hagfish with side-skirts and spoilers, or maybe a squid with not enough tentacles. The upper head is a flattened disk, fronted by two weird, fern-like tentacles drooping over the sucker-mouth on its underside. "This snapshot was taken in Lake Vostok last year. It should be dead: there's nothing there for it to eat. This, ladies and gentlemen, is *Anomalocaris*, our toothy chewer." He pauses for a moment. "I'm very grateful to you for showing it to me," he adds, "even though it's going to make a lot of my colleagues very angry."

Is that a shy grin? The professor moves on rapidly, not giving Roger time to fathom his real reaction. "Now *this* is interesting in the extreme," Gould comments. Whatever it is, it looks like a cauliflower head, or maybe a brain: fractally branching stalks continuously diminishing in length and diameter, until they turn into an iridescent fuzzy manifold wrapped around a central stem. The base of the stem is rooted to a barrel-shaped structure that stands on four stubby tentacles.

"We had somehow managed to cram *Anomalocaris* into our taxonomy, but this is something that has no precedent. It bears a striking resemblance to an enlarged body segment of *Hallucigena*—" here he shows another viewgraph, something like a stiletto-heeled centipede wearing a war-bonnet of tentacles "—but a year ago we worked out that we had poor *hallucigena* upside down and it was actually just a spiny worm. And the high levels of iridium and diamond in the head here . . . this isn't a living creature, at least not within the animal kingdom I've been studying for the past thirty years. There's no cellular structure at all. I asked one of my colleagues for help and he was completely unable to isolate any DNA or RNA from it at all. It's more like a machine that displays biological levels of complexity."

"Can you put a date to it?" the Colonel asks.

"Yup." The professor grins. "It predates the wave of atmospheric atomic testing that began in 1945; that's about all. We think it's from some time in the first half of this century, or the latter half of the last. It's been dead for years, but there are older people still walking this earth. In contrast—" he flips to the picture of *Anomalocaris* "—this specimen we found in rocks that are roughly six hundred and ten million years old." He whips up another shot: similar structure, much clearer. "Note how similar it is to the dead but not decomposed one. They're obviously still alive somewhere."

He looks at the Colonel, suddenly bashful and tongue-tied: "Can I talk about the, uh, thing we were, like, earlier . . . ?"

"Sure. Go ahead. Everyone here is cleared for it." The Colonel's casual wave takes in the big-haired secretary, and Roger, and the two guys from Big Black who are taking notes, and the very serious woman from the Secret Service, and even the balding, worried-looking Admiral with the double chin and coke-bottle glasses.

"Oh. All right." Bashfulness falls away. "Well, we've done some preliminary dissections on the *Anomalocaris* tissues you supplied us with. And we've sent some samples for laboratory analysis—nothing anyone could deduce much from," he adds hastily. He straightens up. "What we discovered is quite simple: these samples didn't originate in Earth's ecosystem. Cladistic analysis of their intracellular characteristics and what we've been able to work out of their biochemistry indicates, not a point of divergence from our own ancestry, but the absence of any common ancestry at all. A *cabbage* has more in common with us than that creature. You can't tell by looking at the fossils, six hundred million years after it died, but live tissue samples are something else.

"Item: it's a multicellular organism, but each cell appears to have multiple structures like nuclei—a thing called a syncitium. No DNA, it uses RNA with a couple of base pairs that don't occur in terrestrial biology. We haven't been able to figure out what most of its organelles do, or what their terrestrial cognates would be, and it builds proteins using a couple of amino acids that we don't. That *nothing* does. Either it's descended from an ancestry that diverged from ours before the archaeobacteria, or—more probably—it is no relative at all." He isn't smiling anymore. "The gateways, Colonel?"

"Yeah, that's about the size of it. The critter you've got there was retrieved by one of our, uh, missions. On the other side of a gate."

Gould nods. "I don't suppose you could get me some more?" he asks hopefully.

"All missions are suspended pending an investigation into an accident we had earlier this year," the Colonel says, with a significant glance at Roger. Suslowicz died two weeks ago; Gorman is still disastrously sick, connective tissue rotting in his body, massive radiation exposure the probable cause. Normal service will not be resumed; the pipeline will remain empty until someone can figure out a way to make the deliveries without losing the crew. Roger inclines his head minutely.

"Oh well." The professor shrugs. "Let me know if you do. By the way, do you have anything approximating a fix on the other end of the gate?"

"No," the Colonel says, and this time Roger knows he's lying. Mission four, before the Colonel diverted their payload capacity to another purpose, planted a compact radio telescope in an empty courtyard in the city on the far side of the gate. XK-Masada, where the air's too thin to breathe without oxygen; where the sky is indigo, and the buildings cast razor-sharp shadows across a rocky plain baked to the consistency of pottery under a bloodred sun. Subsequent analysis of pulsar signals recorded by the station confirmed that it was nearly six hundred light years closer to the galactic core, inward along the same spiral arm. There are glyphs on the alien buildings that resemble symbols seen in grainy black-and-white Minox photos of the doors of the bunker in the Ukraine. Symbols behind which the subject of Project Koschei lies undead and sleeping: something evil, scraped from a nest in the drowned wreckage of a city on the Baltic floor. "Why do you want to know where they came from?"

"Well. We know so little about the context in which life evolves." For a moment the professor looks wistful. "We have — had — only one datum point: Earth, this world. Now we have a second, a fragment of a second. If we get a third, we can begin to ask deep questions not like, 'Is there life out there?' — because we know the answer to that one, now — but questions like 'What *sort* of life is out there?' and 'Is there a place for us?' "

Roger shudders: *Idiot*, he thinks. *If only you knew you wouldn't be so happy.* He restrains the urge to speak up — to do so would be another career-limiting move. More to the point, it might be a life-expectancy-limiting move for the professor, who certainly doesn't deserve any such drastic punishment for his cooperation. Besides, Harvard professors visiting the Executive Office Building in DC are harder to disappear than comm-symp teachers in some flyblown jungle village in Nicaragua. Somebody might notice. The Colonel would be annoyed.

Roger realizes that Professor Gould is staring at him. "Do you have a question for me?" the distinguished paleontologist asks.

"Uh — in a moment." Roger shakes himself. Remembering time-survivor curves, the captured Nazi medical atrocity records mapping the ability of a human brain to survive in close proximity to the Baltic Singularity. Mengele's insanity. The SS's final attempt to liquidate the survivors, the witnesses. Koschei, primed and pointed at the American heartland like a darkly evil gun. The 'World-Eating Mind' adrift in brilliant dreams of madness, estivating in the absence of its prey: dreaming of the minds of sapient beings, be they barrel-bodied wing-flying tentacular *things*, or their human inheritors. "Do you think they could have been intelligent, professor? Conscious, like us?"

"I'd say so." Gould's eyes glitter. "This one —" he points to a viewgraph — "isn't alive as we know it. And *this* one —" he's found a Predecessor, God help him, barrel-bodied and bat-winged " — had what looks like a lot of very complex ganglia, not a brain as we know it, but at least as massive as our own. And some specialized grasping adaptations that might be interpreted as facilitating tool use. Put the two together and you have a high level technological civilization. Gateways between planets orbiting different stars. Alien flora, fauna, or whatever. I'd say an interstellar civilization isn't out of the picture. One that has been extinct for deep geological time — ten times as long as the dinosaurs — but that has left relics that work." His voice is trembling with emotion. "We humans, we've barely scratched the surface! The longest-lasting of our relics? All our buildings will be dust in twenty thousand years, even the pyramids. Neil Armstrong's footprints in the Sea of Tranquility will crumble under micrometeoroid bombardment in a mere half million years or so. The emptied oil fields will refill over ten million years, methane percolating up through the mantle: continental drift will erase everything. But *these* people . . . ! They built to last. There's so much to learn from them. I wonder if we're worthy successors to their technological crown?"

"I'm sure we are, professor," the Colonel's secretary says brassily. "Isn't that right, Ollie?"

The Colonel nods, grinning. "You betcha, Fawn. You betcha!"

THE GREAT SATAN

Roger sits in the bar in the King David hotel, drinking from a tall glass of second-rate lemonade and sweating in spite of the air conditioning. He's dizzy and disoriented from jet-lag, the gut-cramps have only let him come down from his room in the past hour, and he has another two hours to go before he can try to place a call to Andrea. They had another blazing row before he flew out here; she doesn't understand why he keeps having to visit odd corners of the globe. She only knows that his son is growing up thinking a father is a voice that phones at odd times of day.

Roger is mildly depressed, despite the buzz of doing business at this level. He spends a lot of time worrying about what will happen if they're found out—what Andrea will do, or Jason for that matter, Jason whose father is a phone call away all the time—if Roger is led away in handcuffs beneath the glare of flash bulbs. If the Colonel sings, if the shy, bald Admiral is browbeaten into spilling the beans to Congress, who will look after them then?

Roger has no illusions about what kills black operations: there are too many people in the loop, too many elaborate front corporations and numbered bank accounts and shady Middle Eastern arms-dealers. Sooner or later someone will find a reason to talk, and Roger is in too deep. He isn't just the Company liaison officer anymore: he's become the Colonel's bag-man, his shadow, the guy with the diplomatic passport and the bulging briefcase full of heroin and end-user certificates.

At least the ship will sink from the top down, he thinks. There are people *very* high up who want the Colonel to succeed. When the shit hits the fan and is sprayed across the front page of the *Washington Post*, it will likely take down Cabinet members and Secretaries of State: the President himself will have to take the witness stand and deny everything. The republic will question itself.

A hand descends on his shoulder, sharply cutting off his reverie. "Howdy, Roger! Whatcha worrying about now?"

Jourgensen looks up wearily. "Stuff," he says gloomily. "Have a seat." The redneck from the embassy—Mike Hamilton, some kind of junior attaché for embassy protocol by cover—pulls out a chair and crashes down on it like a friendly car wreck. He's not really a redneck, Roger knows—rednecks don't come with doctorates in foreign relations from Yale—but he likes people to think he's a bumpkin when he wants to get something from them.

"He's early," Hamilton says, looking past Roger's ear, voice suddenly all business. "Play the agenda, I'm your dim but friendly good cop. Got the background? Deniables ready?"

Roger nods, then glances around and sees Mehmet (family name unknown) approaching from the other side of the room. Mehmet is impeccably manicured and tailored, wearing a suit from Jermyn Street that cost more than Roger earns in a month. He has a neatly trimmed beard and mustache and talks with a pronounced English accent. Mehmet is a Turkish name, not Persian: false, of course. To look at him you would think he was a westernized Turkish businessman—certainly not an Iranian revolutionary with heavy links to Hezbollah and (whisper this) Old Man Ruholla himself, the hermit of Qom. Never, ever, in a thousand years, the unofficial Iranian ambassador to the Little Satan in Tel Aviv.

Mehmet strides over. A brief exchange of pleasantries masks the essential formality of their meeting: he's early, a deliberate move to put them off-balance. He's outnumbered, too, and that's also a move to put them on the defensive, because the first rule of diplomacy is never to put yourself in a negotiating situation where the other side can assert any kind of moral authority, and sheer weight of numbers is a powerful psychological tool.

"Roger, my dear fellow." He smiles at Jourgensen. "And the charming doctor Hamilton, I see." The smile broadens. "I take it the good Colonel is desirous of news of his friends?"

Jourgensen nods. "That is indeed the case."

Mehmet stops smiling. For a moment he looks ten years older. "I visited them," he says shortly. "No, I was *taken* to see them. It is indeed grave, my friends. They are in the hands of very dangerous men, men who have nothing to lose and are filled with hatred."

Roger speaks: "There is a debt between us—"

Mehmet holds up a hand. "Peace, my friend. We will come to that. These are men of violence, men who have seen their homes destroyed and families subjected to indignities, and their hearts are full of anger. It will take a large display of repentance, a high blood-price, to buy their acquiescence. That is part of our law, you understand? The family of the bereaved may demand blood-price of the transgressor, and how else might the world be? They see it in these terms: that you must repent of your evils and assist them in waging holy war against those who would defy the will of Allah."

Roger sighs. "We do what we can," he says. "We're shipping them arms. We're fighting the Soviets every way we can without provoking the big one. What more do they want? The hostages—that's not playing well in DC. There's got to be some give and take. If Hezbollah don't release them soon they'll just convince everyone that they're not serious about negotiating. And that'll be an end to it. The Colonel *wants* to help you, but he's got to have something to show the man at the top, right?"

Mehmet nods. "You and I are men of the world and understand that this keeping of hostages is not rational, but they look to you for defense against the great

Satan that assails them, and their blood burns with anger that your nation, for all its fine words, takes no action. The great Satan rampages in Afghanistan, taking whole villages by night, and what is done? The United States turns its back. And they are not the only ones who feel betrayed. Our Ba'athist foes from Iraq . . . in Basra the unholy brotherhood of Takrit, and their servants the Mukhabarat, hold nightly sacrifice upon the altar of Yair-Suthot; the fountains of blood in Tehran testify to their effect. If the richest, most powerful nation on earth refuses to fight, these men of violence from the Bekaa think, how may we unstopper the ears of that nation? And they are not sophisticates like you or I."

He looks at Roger, who hunches his shoulders uneasily. "We *can't* move against the Soviets openly! They must understand that it would be the end of far more than their little war. If the Taliban want American help against the Russians, it cannot be delivered openly."

"It is not the Russians that we quarrel with," Mehmet says quietly, "but their choice of allies. They believe themselves to be infidel atheists, but by their deeds they shall be known; the icy spoor of Leng is upon them, their tools are those described in the Kitab al Azif. We have proof that they have violated the terms of the Dresden Agreement. The accursed and unhallowed stalk the frozen passes of the Himalayas by night, taking all whose path they cross. And will you stop your ears even as the Russians grow in misplaced confidence, sure that their dominance of these forces of evil is complete? The gates are opening everywhere, as was prophesied. Last week we flew an F-14C with a camera relay pod through one of them. The pilot and weapons operator are in Paradise now, but we have glanced into Hell, and have the film and radar plots to prove it."

The Iranian ambassador fixes the redneck from the embassy with an icy gaze. "Tell your ambassador that we have opened preliminary discussions with Mossad, with a view to purchasing the produce of a factory at Dimona, in the Negev desert. Past insults may be set aside, for the present danger imperils all of us. *They* are receptive to our arguments, even if you are not: His Holiness the Ayatollah has declared in private that any warrior who carries a nuclear device into the abode of the eater of souls will certainly achieve Paradise. There will be an end to the followers of the ancient abominations on this Earth, Doctor Hamilton, even if we have to push the nuclear bombs down their throats with our own hands!"

SWIMMING POOL

"Mister Jourgensen, at what point did you become aware that the Iranian government was threatening to violate UN Resolution 216 and the Non-Proliferation Protocol to the 1956 Geneva accords?"

Roger sweats under the hot lights: his heartbeat accelerates. "I'm not sure I understand the question, sir."

"I asked you a direct question. Which part don't you understand? I'm going to repeat myself slowly: When did you realize that the Iranian Government was threatening to violate resolution 216 and the 1956 Geneva Accords on nuclear proliferation?"

Roger shakes his head. It's like a bad dream, unseen insects buzzing furiously around him. "Sir, I had no direct dealings with the Iranian government. All I know is that I was asked to carry messages to and from a guy called Mehmet, who I was told knew something about our hostages in Beirut. My understanding is that the Colonel has been conducting secret negotiations with this gentleman or his backers for some time—a couple of years now. Mehmet made allusions to parties in the Iranian administration, but I have no way of knowing if he was telling the truth, and I never saw any diplomatic credentials."

There's an inquisition of dark-suited Congressmen opposite him, like a jury of teachers sitting in judgment on an errant pupil. The trouble is, these teachers can put him in front of a judge and send him to prison for many years, so that Jason really *will* grow up with a father who's only a voice on the telephone, a father who isn't around to take him to air shows or ball games or any of the other rituals of growing up. They're talking quietly to each other, deciding on another line of questioning: Roger shifts uneasily in his chair. This is a closed hearing, the television camera a gesture in the direction of the congressional archives: a pack of hungry Democrats have scented Republican blood in the water.

The Congressman in the middle looks toward Roger. "Stop right there. Where did you know about this guy Mehmet from? Who told you to go see him, and who told you what he was?"

Roger swallows. "I got a memo from Fawn, like always. Admiral Poindexter wanted a man on the spot to talk to this guy, a messenger, basically, who was already in the loop. Colonel North signed off on it and told me to charge the trip to his discretionary fund." That must have been the wrong thing to say, because two of the Congressmen are leaning together and whispering in each other's ears, and an aide obligingly sidles up to accept a note, then dashes away. "I was told that Mehmet was a mediator," Roger adds, "in trying to resolve the Beirut hostage thing."

"A mediator." The guy asking the questions looks at him in disbelief.

The man to his left—who looks as old as the moon, thin white hair, liver spots on his hooked nose, eyelids like sacks—chuckles appreciatively. "Yeah. Like Hitler was a diplomat. 'One more territorial demand'—" he glances round. "Nobody else remember that?" he asks plaintively.

"No sir," Roger says, very seriously.

The prime interrogator snorts. "What did Mehmet tell you Iran was going to do, exactly?"

Roger thinks for a moment. "He said they were going to buy something from a factory at Dimona. I understood this to be the Israeli Defense Ministry's nuclear weapons research institute, and the only logical item—in the context of our discussion—was a nuclear weapon. Or weapons. He said the Ayatollah had decreed that a suicide bomber who took out the temple of Yog-Sothoth in Basra would achieve paradise, and that they also had hard evidence that the Soviets have deployed certain illegal weapons systems in Afghanistan. This was in the context of discussing illegal weapons proliferation; he was very insistent about the Iraq thing."

"What exactly are these weapons systems?" the third inquisitor demands. He's a quiet, hawk-faced man sitting on the left of the panel.

"The shoggot'im, they're called: servitors. There are several kinds of advanced robotic systems made out of molecular components: they can change shape, restructure material at the atomic level—act like corrosive acid, or secrete diamonds. Some of them are like a tenuous mist—what Doctor Drexler at MIT calls a utility fog—while others are more like an oily globule. Apparently they may be able to manufacture more of themselves, but they're not really alive in any meaning of the term that we're familiar with. They're programmable, like robots, using a command language deduced from recovered records of the forerunners who left them here. The Molotov Raid of 1930 brought back a large consignment of them; all we have to go on are the scraps they missed, and reports by the Antarctic Survey. Professor Liebkunst's files in particular are most frustrating—"

"Stop. So you're saying the Russians have these, uh, Shoggoths, but we don't have any. And even those dumb Arab bastards in Baghdad are working on them. So you're saying we've got a . . . a Shoggoth gap? A chink in our strategic armor? And now the Iranians say the Russians are using them in Afghanistan?"

Roger speaks rapidly: "That is minimally correct, sir, although countervailing weapons have been developed to reduce the risk of a unilateral pre-emption escalating to an exchange of weakly godlike agencies." The Congressman in the middle nods encouragingly. "For the past three decades, the B-39 Peacemaker force has been tasked by SIOP with maintaining an XK-Pluto capability directed at ablating the ability of the Russians to activate Project Koschei, the dormant alien entity they captured from the Nazis at the end of the last war. We have twelve Pluto-class atomic-powered cruise missiles pointed at that thing, day and night, as many megatons as the entire Minuteman force. In principle, we will be able to blast it to pieces before it can be brought to full wakefulness and eat the minds of everyone within two hundred miles."

He warms to his subject. "Secondly, we believe the Soviet control of Shoggoth technology is rudimentary at best. They know how to tell them to roll over an Afghan hill-farmer village, but they can't manufacture more of them. Their utility as weapons is limited—though terrifying—but they're not much of a problem. A greater issue is the temple in Basra. This contains an operational gateway, and according to Mehmet the Iraqi political secret police, the Mukhabarat, are trying to figure out how to manipulate it; they're trying to summon something through it. He seemed to be mostly afraid that they—and the Russians—would lose control of whatever it was; presumably another weakly godlike creature like the K-Thulu entity at the core of Project Koschei."

The old guy speaks: "This foo-loo thing, boy—you can drop those stupid K prefixes around me—is it one of a kind?"

Roger shakes his head. "I don't know, sir. We know the gateways link to at least three other planets. There may be many that we don't know of. We don't know how to create them or close them; all we can do is send people through, or pile bricks in the opening." He nearly bites his tongue, because there *are* more than three worlds out there, and he's been to at least one of them: the bolt-hole on XK-Masada, built by the NRO from their secret budget. He's seen the mile-high dome Buckminster Fuller spent his last decade designing for them, the rings of Patriot air defense missiles. A squadron of black, diamond-shaped fighters from the Skunk Works, said to be invisible to radar, patrols the empty skies of XK-Masada. Hydroponic farms and empty barracks and apartment blocks await the Senators and Congressmen and their families and thousands of support personnel.

In event of war they'll be evacuated through the small gate that has been moved to the Executive Office Building basement, in a room beneath the swimming pool where Jack used to go skinny-dipping with Marilyn.

"Off the record, now." The old Congressman waves his hand in a chopping gesture: "I say *off*, boy." The cameraman switches off his machine and leaves. The old man leans forward, toward Roger. "What you're telling me is, we've been waging a secret war since, when? The end of the second world war? Earlier, the Pabodie Antarctic expedition in the twenties, whose survivors brought back the first of these alien relics? And now the Eye-ranians have gotten into the game and figure it's part of their fight with Saddam?"

"Sir." Roger barely trusts himself to do more than nod.

"Well." The Congressman eyes his neighbor sharply. "Let me put it to you that you have heard the phrase, 'The Great Filter.' What does it mean to you?"

"The Great—" Roger stops. *Professor Gould*, he thinks. "We had a professor of paleontology lecture us," he explains. "I think he mentioned it. Something about why there aren't any aliens in flying saucers buzzing us the whole time."

The Congressman snorts. His neighbor starts and sits up. "Thanks to Pabodie and his followers, Liebkunst and the like, we know there's a lot of life in the universe. The Great Filter, *boy*, is whatever force stops most of it developing intelligence and coming to visit. Something, somehow, kills intelligent species before they develop this kind of technology for themselves. How about meddling with relics of the Elder Ones? What do you think of that?"

Roger licks his lips nervously. "That sounds like a good possibility, sir," he says. His unease is building.

The Congressman's expression is intense: "these weapons your Colonel is dicking around with make all our nukes look like a toy bow and arrow, and all you can say is 'It's a good possibility, sir?' Seems to me like someone in the Oval Office has been asleep at the switch."

"Sir, executive order 2047, issued January 1980, directed the armed forces to standardize on nuclear weapons to fill the mass destruction role. All other items were to be developmentally suspended, with surplus stocks allocated to the supervision of Admiral Poindexter's Joint Munitions Expenditure Committee. Which Colonel North was detached to by the USMC high command, with the full cognizance of the White House—"

The door opens. The Congressman looks around angrily: "I thought I said we weren't to be disturbed!"

The aide standing there looks uncertain. "Sir, there's been an, uh, major security incident, and we need to evacuate—"

"Where? What happened?" the Congressman demands. But Roger, with a sinking feeling, realizes that the aide isn't watching the House Committee members: and the guy behind him is Secret Service.

"Basra. There's been an attack, sir." A furtive glance at Roger, as his brain freezes in denial: "If you'd all please come this way . . ."

BOMBING IN FIFTEEN MINUTES

Heads down, through a corridor where congressional staffers hurry about carrying papers, urgently calling one another. A cadre of dark-suited Secret Service agents closes in, hustling Roger along in the wake of the committee members. A wailing like tinnitus fills his ears. "What's happening?" he asks, but nobody answers.

Down into the basement. Another corridor, where two marine guards are waiting with drawn weapons. The Secret Service guys are exchanging terse reports by radio. The committee men are hustled away along a narrow service tunnel: Roger is stalled by the entrance. "What's going on?" he asks his minder.

"Just a moment, sir." More listening; these guys cock their heads to one side as they take instruction, birds of prey scanning the horizon for prey. "Delta four coming in. Over. You're clear to go along the tunnel now, sir. This way."

"What's *happening?*" Roger demands as he lets himself be hustled into the corridor, along to the end and around a sharp corner. Numb shock takes hold, but he keeps putting one foot in front of the other.

"We're now at Defcon One, sir. You're down on the special list as part of the house staff. Next door on the left, sir."

The queue in the dim-lit basement room is moving fast, white-gloved guards with clipboards checking off men and a few women in suits as one by one they step through a steel blast door and disappear from view. Roger looks around in bewilderment. He sees a familiar face. "Fawn! What's going on?"

The secretary looks puzzled. "I don't know. Roger? I thought you were testifying today."

"So did I." They're at the door. "What else?"

"Ronnie was making a big speech in Helsinki; the Colonel had me record it in his office. Something about not coexisting with the Evil Empire. He cracked some kinda joke about how we start bombing in fifteen minutes. Then this —"

They're at the door. It opens on a steel-walled airlock and the marine guard is taking their badges and hustling them inside. Two staff types and a middle-aged brigadier join them and the door thumps shut. The background noise vanishes, Roger's ears pop, then the inner door opens and another marine guard waves them through into the receiving hall.

"Where are we?" the big-haired secretary asks, staring around.

"Welcome to XK-Masada," Roger says. Then his childhood horrors catch up with him and he goes in search of a toilet to throw up in.

WE NEED YOU BACK

Roger spends the next week in a state of numbed shock. His apartment here is like a small hotel room — a hotel with security, air-conditioning, and windows that only open onto an interior atrium. He pays little attention to his surroundings. It's not as if he has a home to return to.

Roger stops shaving. Stops changing his socks. Stops looking in mirrors or combing his hair. He smokes a lot, orders cheap bourbon from the commissary, and drinks himself into an amnesiac stupor each night. He is, frankly, a mess. Self-destructive. Everything disintegrated under him at once: his job, the people he held in high regard, his family, his life. All the time he can't get one thing out of his head: the expression on Gorman's face as he stands there, in front of the submarine, rotting from the inside out with radiation sickness, dead and not yet knowing it. It's why he's stopped looking in mirrors.

On the fourth day he's slumped in a chair watching taped *I Love Lucy* re-runs on the boob tube when the door to his suite opens quietly. Someone comes in. He doesn't look around until the Colonel walks across the screen and unplugs the TV set at the wall, then sits down in the chair next to him. The Colonel has bags of dark skin under his eyes; his jacket is rumpled and his collar is unbuttoned.

"You've got to stop this, Roger," he says quietly. "You look like shit."

"Yeah, well. You too."

The Colonel passes him a slim manila folder. Without wanting to, Roger slides out the single sheet of paper within.

"So it *was* them."

"Yeah." A moment's silence. "For what it's worth, we haven't lost yet. We may yet pull your wife and son out alive. Or be able to go back home."

"Your family too, I suppose." Roger is touched by the Colonel's consideration, the pious hope that Andrea and Jason will be all right, even through his shell of misery. He realizes his glass is empty. Instead of refilling it he puts it down on the carpet beside his feet. "*Why?*"

The Colonel retrieves the sheet of paper from his numb fingers. "Probably someone spotted you in the King David and traced you back to us. The Mukharabat had agents everywhere, and if they were in league with the KGB . . ." He shrugs. "Things escalated rapidly. Then the president cracked that joke over a hot mike that was supposed to be switched off . . . Have you been checking in with the desk summaries this week?"

Roger looks at him blankly. "Should I?"

"Oh, things are still happening." The Colonel leans back and stretches his feet out. "From what we can tell of the situation on the other side, not everyone's dead yet. Ligachev's screaming blue murder over the hotline, accusing us of genocide: but he's still talking. Europe is a mess and nobody knows what's going on in the middle east—even the Blackbirds aren't making it back out again."

"The thing at Takrit."

"Yeah. It's bad news, Roger. We need you back."

"Bad news?"

"The worst." The Colonel jams his hands between his knees, stares at the floor like a bashful child. "Saddam Hussein al-Takriti spent years trying to get his hands on Elder technology. It looks like he finally succeeded in stabilizing the gate into Sothoth. Whole villages disappeared, Marsh Arabs, wiped out in the swamps of Eastern Iraq. Reports of yellow rain, people's skin melting right off their bones. The Iranians got itchy and finally went nuclear. Trouble is, they did so two hours before *that* speech. Some asshole in Plotsk launched half the Uralskoye SS-20 grid—they went to launch-on-warning eight months ago—burning south, praise Jesus. Scratch the middle east, period—everything from the Nile to the Khyber Pass is toast. We're still waiting for the callback on Moscow, but SAC has put the whole Peacemaker force on airborne alert. So far we've lost the eastern seaboard as far south as North Virginia and they've lost the Donbass basin and Vladivostok. Things are a mess; nobody can even agree whether we're fighting the commies or something else. But the box at Chernobyl—Project Koschei—the doors are open, Roger. We orbited a Keyhole-eleven over it and there are tracks, leading west. The Pluto strike didn't stop it—and nobody knows what the fuck is going on in WarPac country. Or France, or Germany, or Japan, or England."

The Colonel makes a grab for Roger's Wild Turkey, rubs the neck clean and swallows from the bottle. He looks at Roger with a wild expression on his face. "Koschei is loose, Roger. They fucking *woke* the thing. And now they can't control it. Can you believe that?"

"I can believe that."

"I want you back behind a desk tomorrow morning, Roger. We need to know what this Thulu creature is capable of. We need to know what to do to stop it. Forget Iraq; Iraq is a smoking hole in the map. But K-Thulu is heading toward the Atlantic coast. What are we going to do if it doesn't stop?"

MASADA

The city of XK-Masada sprouts like a vast mushroom, a mile-wide dome emerging from the top of a cold plateau on a dry planet in orbit round a dying star. The jagged black shapes of F-117s howl across the empty skies outside it at dusk and dawn, patrolling the threatening emptiness that stretches as far as the mind can imagine.

Shadows move in the streets of the city, hollowed-out human shells in uniform. They rustle around the feet of the towering concrete blocks like the dry leaves of autumn, obsessively focussed on the tasks that lend structure to their remaining days. Above them tower masts of steel, propping up the huge geodesic dome that arches across the sky: blocking out the hostile, alien constellations, protecting frail humanity from the dust storms that periodically scour the bones of the ancient world. The gravity here is a little lighter, the night sky whorled and marbled by diaphanous sheets of gas blasted off the dying star that lights their days. During the long winter nights, a flurry of carbon dioxide snow dusts the surface of the dome: but the air is bone-dry, the city slaking its thirst from subterranean aquifers.

This planet was once alive—near the equator there is still a scummy sea of algae that feeds oxygen into the atmosphere, and a range of volcanoes near the north pole indicates plate tectonics in motion—but it is visibly dying. There is a lot of history here, but no future.

Sometimes, in the early hours when he cannot sleep, Roger walks outside the city, along the edge of the dry plateau. Machines labor on behind him, keeping the city tenuously intact: he pays them little attention. There is talk of mounting an expedition to Earth one of these years, to salvage whatever is left before the searing winds of time erases it forever. Roger doesn't like to think about that. He tries to avoid thinking about Earth as much as possible, except when he cannot sleep. Then he walks along the clifftop, prodding at memories of Andrea and

Jason and his parents and sister and relatives and friends, each as painful as the socket of a missing tooth. He has a mouthful of emptiness, bitter and aching, out here on the edge of the plateau.

Sometimes Roger thinks he's the last human being alive. He works in an office, feverishly trying to sort out what went wrong; and bodies move around him, talking, eating in the canteen, sometimes talking *to* him and waiting, as if they expect dialogue. There are bodies here, men and some women chatting, civilian and some military—but no people. One of the bodies, an army surgeon, told him he's suffering from a common stress disorder, called survivor's guilt. This may be so, Roger admits, but it doesn't change anything. Soulless days follow sleepless nights into oblivion.

A narrow path runs along the side of the plateau, just downhill from the foundations of the city power plant, where huge apertures belch air warmed by the nuclear reactor's heat-exchangers. Roger follows the path, gravel and sandy rock crunching under his worn shoes, dust trickling over the side of the cliff like sand into the undug graves of his family. Foreign stars twinkle overhead, forming unrecognizable patterns that tell him he's far from home. The trail drops away from the top of the plateau, until the city is an unseen shadow looming above and behind his shoulder. To his right is a vertiginous panorama, the huge rift valley with its ancient city of the dead outstretched before him. Beyond it rise alien mountains, their peaks as high and airless as the dead volcanoes of Mars.

About half a mile away from the dome, the trail circles an outcrop of rock and takes a downhill switchback. Roger stops at the bend and looks out across the desert at his feet. He sits down, leans against the rough cliff-face and stretches his legs across the path, so that his feet dangle over nothingness. Far below him, the dead valley is furrowed with rectangular depressions; once, millions of years ago, they might have been fields, but nothing of that survives. They're just dead, like everyone else on this world. Like Roger.

In his shirt pocket, a crumpled, precious pack of cigarettes. He pulls a white cylinder out with shaking fingers, sniffs at it, then flicks his lighter under it. Scarcity has forced him to cut back: he coughs at the first lungful of stale smoke, a harsh, racking croak. The irony of being saved from lung cancer by a world war is not lost on him.

He blows smoke out, a tenuous trail streaming across the cliff. "Why me?" he asks quietly.

The emptiness takes its time answering. When it does, it speaks with the Colonel's voice. "You know why."

"I didn't want to do it," he hears himself saying. "I didn't want to leave them behind."

The void laughs at him. There are miles of empty air beneath his dangling feet. "You had no choice."

"Yes I did! I didn't have to come here." He pauses. "I didn't have to do anything," he says quietly, and inhales another lungful of death. "It was all automatic. Maybe it was inevitable."

"—Evitable," echoes the distant horizon. Something dark and angular skims across the stars, like an echo of extinct pterosaurs. Turbofans whirring in its belly, the F117 hunts on: patrolling to keep the ancient evil at bay, unaware that the battle is already lost. "Your family could still be alive, you know."

He looks up. "They could?" Andrea? Jason? "Alive?"

The void laughs again, unfriendly: "There is life eternal within the eater of souls. Nobody is ever forgotten or allowed to rest in peace. They populate the simulation spaces of its mind, exploring all the possible alternative endings to their lives. There *is* a fate worse than death, you know."

Roger looks at his cigarette disbelievingly: throws it far out into the night sky above the plain. He watches it fall until its ember is no longer visible. Then he gets up. For a long moment he stands poised on the edge of the cliff nerving himself, and thinking. Then he takes a step back, turns, and slowly makes his way back up the trail toward the redoubt on the plateau. If his analysis of the situation is wrong, at least he is still alive. And if he is right, dying would be no escape.

He wonders why hell is so cold at this time of year.

The Real World

STEVEN UTLEY

Steven Utley's fiction has appeared in The Magazine of Fantasy & Science Fiction, Universe, Galaxy, Amazing, Vertex, Stellar, Shayol, *and elsewhere. He was one of the best-known new writers of the seventies both for his solo work and for some strong work in collaboration with fellow Texan Howard Waldrop, but fell silent at the end of the decade and wasn't seen in print again for more than ten years. In the last decade he's made a strong comeback, though, becoming a frequent contributor to* Asimov's Science Fiction *magazine, as well as selling again to* The Magazine of Fantasy & Science Fiction, Sci Fiction, *and elsewhere. Utley is the coeditor, with George W. Proctor, of the anthology* Lone Star Universe, *the first—and probably the only—anthology of SF stories by Texans. His first collection,* Ghost Seas, *was published in 1997, and he is presently at work on a novel/collection based on his Silurian stories, such as the one that follows. His most recent books are collections of his poetry,* This Impatient Ape *and* Career Moves of the Gods. *He lives in Smyrna, Tennessee.*

Here, part of a long sequence of stories that Utley has been writing throughout the nineties, detailing the adventures and misadventures of time-traveling scientists exploring the distant Silurian Age, millions of years before the dinosaurs roamed the Earth, he offers us a parable of what's important and what's not—and wonders how you can be sure that you can tell the difference when you can't even be sure of the very ground under your feet.

Everything felt like a dream. The flight attendants seemed to whisper past in the aisle. The other passengers were but shadows and echoes. Through the window, he could see the wing floating above an infinite expanse of cloudtop as flat and featureless as the peneplained landscapes of the Paleozoic. I'm just tired, he thought, without conviction.

Ivan forced his attention back to the laptop. He had called up an did documentary in which he himself appeared. "Resume," he said, very softly, and the image on the screen unfroze, and a familiar, strange voice said, "Plant life may actually have invaded the land during the Ordovician Period." Is that really me? he thought. My face, my eyes, I look so unlived-in. "We know about two dozen genera of land plant in the Silurian," and the screen first showed a tangle of creeping green tendrils at his younger self's feet, "such as these, which are called psilophytes," then a glistening algal mat. "The big flat things you see all over the mudflats are Nematophycus. The point is—"

His earphone buzzed softly. "Pause," he murmured to the laptop, and the image on the screen froze once more. He said, "Hello?" and heard his brother say, "How's the flight?"

"Don. I hope you're not calling to rescind my invitation."

"Michelle'll pick you up at the airport as planned. I'm just calling to warn you and apologize in advance. I just got an invitation I can't refuse to a social event tomorrow evening."

"No need to apologize."

"Sure there is. This is a soirée of Hollywood swine."

"I can use the time to rest up for Monday."

"Well, actually, I'd sort of like to take you along. In case I need somebody intelligent to talk to. Unless, of course, you think you'd be uncomfortable."

Ivan examined the prospect for a moment, then said, "On Tuesday I'm going to read a paper on Paleozoic soils at the Page Museum. Young snotnoses keen to establish their reputations on the ruins of mine will be there. In light of that, I can't imagine how people who undoubtedly don't know mor from mull could possibly make me uncomfortable."

"Good. To the extent possible, I'll camouflage you in my clothing."

"What's the occasion for the party?"

"The occasion's the occasion."

"Let me rephrase the question. Who's hosting the party?"

"Somebody in the business who's throwing himself a birthday party. None of his friends will throw one for him, because he doesn't have any friends. If I hadn't come within an ace of an Oscar last month—which by the way is the limit of his long-term memory—it'd never have occurred to him to invite a writer. If I was a self-respecting writer and not a Hollywood whore, I'd duck it. But, hey, it'll be entertaining from a sociological point of view."

"As long as I get to ogle some starlets."

"Starlets'd eat you alive."

"That would be nice, too. Look, please don't think you have to entertain me the whole time I'm out there."

"Oh, this place'll afford you endless opportunities to entertain yourself."

"I look forward to it."

"See you soon."

"Goodbye."

"Resume," he murmured to the laptop. "The point is."

"The point is," his younger self said, "they can't have sprung up overnight, even in the geologic sense. The Silurian seas are receding as the land rises, and the plant invasion's not a coincidence. But there were also opportunities during the Ordovician for plants to come ashore in a big way. Only they *didn't*. Maybe there was lethal ozone at ground level for a long time after the atmosphere became oxygen-rich. If so, a lot of oxygen had to accumulate before the ozone layer rose to the higher levels safe enough for advanced life-forms. Our—"

"Stop," he said, and thought, What a lot of crap. Then he sighed deeply and told the laptop, "Cue the first Cutsinger press conference."

After a moment, Cutsinger's image appeared on the screen. He was standing at a podium, behind a brace of microphones. He said, "I am at pains to describe this phenomenon without resorting to the specialized jargon of my own field, which is physics. Metaphor, however, may be inadequate. I'll try to answer your questions afterward."

This is afterward, Ivan thought bitterly, and, yes, I have a question.

"The phenomenon," Cutsinger's image went on, "is, for want of a better term, a space-time anomaly—a hole, if you will, or a tunnel, or however you wish to think of it. It appears, and I use the word advisedly, appears to connect our present-day Earth with the Earth as it existed during the remote prehistoric past. We've inserted a number of robot probes, some with laboratory animals, into the anomaly and retrieved them intact, though some of the animals did not survive. Judging both from the biological samples obtained and from the period of rotation of this prehistoric Earth, what we're talking about is the Siluro-Devonian boundary in mid-Paleozoic time, roughly four hundred million years ago. Biological specimens collected include a genus of primitive plant called Cooksonia and an extinct arthropod called a—please forgive my pronunciation if I get this wrong—a trigonobartid. Both organisms are well-known to paleontologists, and DNA testing conclusively proves their affinities with all other known terrestrial life-forms. Thus, for all practical purposes, this is our own world as it existed during the Paleozoic Era. However, it cannot literally be our own world. We cannot travel directly backward into our own past."

Ivan looked up, startled, as a flight attendant leaned in and said something.

"I'm sorry, what?"

"We'll be landing soon. You'll have to put that away now."

"Of course."

She smiled and withdrew. He looked at the laptop. "The anomaly," Cutsinger was saying, "must therefore connect us with another Earth."

"Quit."

Michelle met him as he came off the ramp. For a second, he did not recognize her and could only stare at her when she called his name. He could not immediately connect this young woman with his memories of her as a long-limbed thirteen-year-old girl with braces on her teeth; then, he had never been quite able to decide whether she was going to grow up pretty or goofy-looking. It had been a matter of real concern to him: he had first seen her cradled tenderly in her mother's arms, eyes squeezed shut and oblivious of her beatific expression; baby Michelle was not asleep, though, but had seemed to be concentrating fiercely on the mother's warmth, heartbeat, and wordless murmured endearments. Tiny hands had clasped and unclasped rhythmically, kneading air, keeping time, and when Ivan had gently touched one perfect pink palm and her soft digits closed on, but could not encircle, his calloused fingertip, the contrast smote him in the heart.

He had no children of his own, and had never wanted any, but he knew immediately that he loved this child. He had murmured it to her, and to Don and Linda he said, "You folks do good work."

The discontinuous nature of these remembered Michelles, lying unconformably upon one another, heightened his sense of dislocation as he now beheld her. She was fresh out of high school, fair-skinned, unmade-up, with unplucked eyebrows and close-cropped brown hair. It cannot be her, he told himself. But then the corners of her mouth drew back, the firm, almost prim line of her lips fractured in a smile, and she delivered herself of pleasant, ringing laughter that had a most unexpected and wonderful effect on him: his head suddenly seemed inclined to float off his shoulders, and he found himself thinking that a man might want to bask for years in the radiance of that smile, the music of that laughter. Now he was convinced, and he let himself yield to the feeling of buoyant happiness. As a child she had had the comically intent expression of a squirrel monkey, but her father and her uncle had always been able to make her laugh, and when she had the effect was always marvelous. She closed with him and hugged him tightly, and his heart seemed to expand until it filled his chest.

As they headed into the hills north of Hollywood, she concentrated on her driving and he stole glances at her profile. He decided that the haircut suited her vastly better than the unfortunate coiffures she had been in the habit of inflicting upon herself. Well, he thought, you turned out pretty after all.

And he thought, I love you still, darling, and I always shall. Whether it's really you or not.

Seated at the metal table, screened from the sun by the eucalyptus tree and with his book lying open on his lap, he admired the blue and orange blooms and banana-shaped leaves of the bird of paradise flowers in his brother's backyard. He could look past them and the fence and right down the canyon on the hazy blur of the city. The morning had begun to heat up, and there was a faint ashy taste to the air. He noticed a small dark smudgy cloud where the farthest line of hills met the sky.

Michelle emerged from the house carrying two ice-flecked bottles of imported beer on a tray. She set it on the table and sat down across from him and said, "Daddy's still talking to the thing that would not die."

He nodded in the direction of the smudgy cloud. "I hope that's not what I think it is."

She looked. "Fires in the canyons. It's the season." She opened one of the beers and handed it to him. "What're you reading?"

Unnecessarily, he glanced at the spine. "*The Story of Philosophy*, by Will Durant."

She clearly did not know what to say in response.

"It's about the lives of the great philosophers," he went on after a moment, "and their thoughts on being and meaning and stuff."

She made a face. "It sounds excruciating."

"It is. I think the great philosophers were all wankers, except for Voltaire, who was funny. Nietzsche was probably the wankiest of the lot."

"Why're you reading it if you think it's so awful?"

"Let's just say I'm in full-tilt autodidact mode these days. Nowadays I carry the same three books with me everywhere I go. This one, a book about quantum mechanics, and the latest edition of the *People's Almanac*. The almanac's the only one I really enjoy."

"What's that, quantum mechanics?"

"Didn't they teach you anything in school? Advanced physics. Probably just a lot of philosophical wanking set to math. But it interests me. Somewhere between physics and philosophy is the intersection of the real world. Out of our subjective perception of an objective reality of energy and matter comes our interpretation of being and meaning."

"Whatever you say, Uncle Ivan."

"Are you going to this party tomorrow night?"

She shook her head emphatically. "I'm going to a concert with my boyfriend. Anyway, I don't much care for movie people. Oh, some of them are nice, but—I've never been comfortable around actors. I can never tell when they aren't acting. No, that's not it, it just makes me tired trying to figure out when they're acting and when they're not. The directors are mostly pretentious bores, and the producers just make Daddy crazy." She gazed down the canyon. "The fact is, I don't much like movies. But my boyfriend"—she gave him a quick, self-conscious glance—"my boyfriend loves 'em. And he *loves* dinosaurs. He says he judges a movie by whether he thinks it'd be better or worse with dinosaurs in it."

"Did he have anything to do with that recent version of *Little Women?*"

"No. He's not in the industry, thank God. I wouldn't go out with anybody who is. I wonder what genius thought of setting *Little Women* in prehistoric times. Anyway, you'd be surprised how many movies flunk his dinosaur test."

"Probably I wouldn't."

"He and Daddy like sitting around coming up with lunatic premises for movies. What they call high-concept. He cracks Daddy up. Daddy says he could be making movies every bit as bad as anybody else's if he just applied himself."

"Give me an example of high-concept."

"'Hitler! Stalin! And the woman who loved them both!'" They laughed together. Then she suddenly regarded him seriously. "I hope you're not going to let yourself be overawed by these people."

"People don't awe me." She looked doubtful, so he added, "They can't begin to compete with what awes me."

"What's that? What awes you?"

He leaned sideways in his chair, scooped some dirt out of a flowerbed. "This," he said, and as he went on talking he spread the dirt on his palm and sorted through it with his index finger. "When we were kids, teenagers, while your daddy sat up in his room figuring out how to write screenplays, I was outdoors collecting bugs and fossils. We neatly divided the world between us. He got the arts, I got the sciences. Even our tastes in reading—while he was reading, oh, Fitzgerald and Nabokov, I'd be reading John McPhee and Darwin's journal of the voyage of the *Beagle*. There was a little overlap. We both went through phases when we read mysteries and science fiction like mad. I'd read *The Big Sleep* or *The Time*

Machine and pass 'em onto Don, and then we'd discuss 'em. But we were usually interested in different parts of the same books. Don was interested in the characters, the story. Who killed so and so. I loved Raymond Chandler's, Ross Macdonald's descriptions of the southern California landscape. I was like a tourist. My feeling was that setting is as vital as plot and characterization. A good detective-story writer had to be a good travelogue writer, or else his characters and action were just hanging in space. Don argued that a good story could be set anywhere, scenery was just there to be glanced at. If the plot was good, it would work anywhere."

"Daddy says there are only three or four plots. At least he says that out here there are only three or four."

"Well, anyway, your dad and I have art and science all sewed up between us. Science to help us find out what the world is. Art to—I don't know, art's not my thing, but I think—"

"Daddy says you're trying to write a book."

"Trying is about as far as I've got so far. I have all the raw material, but . . ." But. "I'm not creative. Anyway, I think we have to have both science and art. Everything in the universe partakes in some way of every other thing."

"What about philosophy?"

"Maybe it's what links science and art."

"Even if it's a lot of wanking?"

"Even wanking has its place in the scheme of things. What about this boyfriend?"

"Interesting segue."

"Is this a serious thing? Serious like marriage?"

She shrugged, then shook her head. "I want to do something with my life before I get into that."

"What?"

"I wish I knew. I feel I have so much to live up to. Your side of the family's all overachievers. My father's a hot Hollywood screenwriter. My uncle, the scientist, has done just the most amazing things. My grandparents were big wheels in Texas politics. It's almost as bad as having movie-star parents. The pressure on me to achieve is awful."

"It was probably worse for the Huxleys."

"Mom's always felt outclassed. Her family'd always just muddled along. She felt utterly inadequate the whole time she and Dad were married."

"With a little help from him, she made a beautiful daughter."

She looked pleased by the compliment but also a little uncomfortable. "Thank you for saying that."

"It's true."

"You used to call me Squirrel Monkey."

Don came outside looking exasperated. "Ever reach a point in a conversation," he said, "where, you know, you can't go on pretending to take people seriously who don't know what they're talking about?"

"Are we talking rhetorically?"

Don laughed a soft, unhappy sort of laugh. He indicated the unopened bottle of beer. "Is that for me?"

"Just that one, Daddy."

"I need it." He said to Ivan, "Tell me the stupidest thing you've ever heard. I'm trying to put something into perspective here."

Ivan thought for a moment. "Well, there was the low point, or maybe it was the high point, of my blessedly short stint as a purveyor of scientific knowledge to college freshman. I had a student tell me in all earnestness that an organism that lives off dead organisms is a sacrilege."

Don laughed again, less unhappily than before. "Been on the phone with someone who makes deals and gives off movies as waste. He's got the hottest idea of his life. He's doing a full-blown remake of *The Three Musketeers* in Taiwan."

Ivan felt his eyebrows go up. He made them come back down.

Don nodded. "That was my reaction. I said to him, I gather you've taken a few liberties with the novel. And he said, Novel? By Alexandre Dumas, I said. You mean it? he said. Excuse me for a moment, and he gets on his AnswerMan and says, To legal, do we have exclusive rights to alleged novel by Doo-dah-duh. Dumas, I scream, *Dumas*, you dumbass!" He shook his head as though to clear it of an irritating buzz. "Well. I go on and tell him the novel's in the public domain, Dumas has been dead for a little while now. He drums his fingers on his desktop. He screws his face into a mask of thoughtfulness. He says, Well, it's always best to be sure, because if what you say is true, we'll have to see about getting it pulled out of circulation. I beg his pardon. He says, We don't want people confusing it with our book based on the movie."

Ivan said, "He's going to novelize a movie based on a novel?"

"Sure. The novel based on *Pride and Prejudice* was on the best-seller list?"

Michelle said, "Hooray for Hollywood," and Ivan raised his bottle in a toast.

Don raised his as well. "Here's to L.A., Los Angeles del Muerte!"

Then Michelle excused herself and went inside. Ivan said, "Every time I see her, she's bigger, smarter, prettier, and nicer."

"That's how it works if you only see her once every few years. Move out here, be her doting uncle all the time."

"Oh, I would love to. It would be good to see more of you, too. But—" To avoid his brother's expectant look, Ivan turned toward the canyon. "Call me a crank on the subject, but I'll never live on an active plate margin."

"Christ."

"Geologically speaking, these hills have all the structural integrity of head cheese. They piled up here after drifting in across a prehistoric sea from God knows where. One of these times, Don, the earth's going to hiccup, and all these nice houses and all you nice people in them are going to slide all the way down that canyon."

Don shrugged. "Mobility is what California's all about. Everything here is from someplace else. The water comes from Colorado. These flowers," and he extended his arm and delicately touched a leaf on one of the bird-of-paradise flowers as though he were stroking a cat under its jaw, "are South African. The jacaranda you see all over town are from Brazil, the eucalyptus trees are from Australia. The people and the architecture are from everywhere you can think of." He took a long pull on his bottle, draining it. "That's the reason California's such a weird goddamn place. Because nothing really belongs here."

"I think it's fascinating. I wouldn't live here for anything—not even for you and Michelle, I'm sorry. But it is certainly fascinating."

"Oh, absolutely, I agree, it is. In a big, ugly, tasteless, intellectually numbing kind of way."

"What do you do for intellectual stimulation?"

"I read your monographs."

"Really?"

"No, but I have copies of all of them."

Later, stretched across the bed with his eyes closed and the cool fresh sheet pulled up to his sternum, Ivan thought, Clever, talented Don. It had never occurred to him before that his brother considered his work at all. . . .

He did not think he had fallen asleep, yet he awoke with a start. He was hot and parched. He slipped into a robe and eased into the hallway. In the kitchen, he filled a glass with cold filtered water from the jug in the refrigerator and sat down with his back to the bar to look out through the glass doors, at the lights of the city. There was a glowing patch of sky, seemingly as distant as the half moon, where the dark smudgy cloud had been that afternoon.

When he returned to his room, he sat on the edge of the bed and took his well-thumbed *People's Almanac* from the nightstand. He opened it at random and read a page, then set it aside and picked up the laptop. "Where were we?"

The screen lightened. "That's a good question," Cutsinger was saying. He chuckled into the microphones. "I know, because my colleagues and I have asked it of each other thousands of times since the anomaly was discovered. Every time, the answer's been the same. Simply traveling through time into the past is impossible. Simply to do so violates the laws of physics, especially our old favorite, the second law of thermodynamics. Simply to enter the past is to alter the past, which is a literal and actual contradiction of logic. Yet the fact is, we have discovered this space-time anomaly which connects our immediate present with what from all evidence is the Earth as it existed during mid-Paleozoic times. The only way the laws of physics and logic can accommodate this awkward fact is if we quietly deep-six the adjective 'simply' and run things out to their extremely complicated conclusion. We must posit a universe that stops and starts, stops and starts, countless billions of times per microsecond, as it jumps from state to state. As it does so, it continually divides, copies itself. Each copy is in a different state—that is, they're inexact copies. A separate reality exists for every possible outcome of every possible quantum interaction. Inasmuch as the number of copies produced since the Big Bang must be practically infinite, the range of difference among the realities must be practically infinite as well. These realities exist in parallel with one another. Whatever we insert into the anomaly—probes, test animals, human beings—are not simply going to travel directly backward into our own past. Instead, they're going to travel somehow to another universe, to another Earth which resembles our Earth as it was in the Paleozoic. Yes? Question?"

From offscreen came a question, inaudible to Ivan, but on the screen Cutsinger nodded and answered, "Well, it's probably pointless to say whether this sort of travel occurs in any direction—backward, sideward, or diagonally."

From offscreen, someone else asked, "If there are all these multiple Earths, when you're ready to come back through this hole you're talking about, how can you be sure you'll find your way back to the right Earth?"

"To the very best of our knowledge, this hole as you call it has only two ends. One here and now, one there and then. Next question?"

You glib son of a bitch, Ivan thought.

After the robot probes had gone and apparently come back through the space-time anomaly, the next step was obvious to everyone: human beings must follow. It was decided that two people should go through together. At the outset, in the moment it had taken the phrase "time travel to the prehistoric world" to register in his mind, Ivan had made up his mind—yes, absolutely, I want to go! "Presented with the opportunity to traverse time and explore a prehistoric planet," he had written to Don, "who *wouldn't?*" In the weeks and months that followed, however, through all the discussion and planning sessions, he had never quite believed that he had a real chance to go. Partly it was a matter of funding: x amount of money in the kitty simply equaled y number of people who would get to go on any Paleozoic junket. Partly it was a matter of prestige: given, practically speaking, an entire new planet to explore—everything about it, everything about the cosmos it occupied, for that matter, being four hundred million years younger, any scientist could make a case for his or her particular field of inquiry. Ivan did not, of course, despise his work in the least or see any need to apologize for it; moreover, he did not take personally—too personally, anyway—one or another of the likelier candidates' feigned confusion over pedology, the study of the nature and development of children, and *pedology*, soil science. The first few times, he affected amusement at the joke fellow soil scientists told on themselves, which in its simplest form was that the insertion of a single soil scientist into Silurian time would result in that remote geological period's having more scientist than soil. It was the sort of extremely specialized joke specialists told. Like any specialized joke, its charm vanished the instant that an explanation became necessary. Real soil would have only just started, geologically speaking, to collect amid the Silurian barrens; pedogenesis would be spotty and sporadic; rock could weather away to fine particles, but only the decay of organic matter could make sterile grit into nurturing dirt, and while organisms abounded in the Silurian seas, they would have only just started, again, geologically speaking, to live and die—and decompose—on land.

"Oh. I see. Ha, ha."

The joke had escaped from the soil scientists at some point and begot tortuous variations in which twenty-first-century pedology overwhelmed and annihilated the reality of primordial soil: why (went one version), the weight of the terminology alone—soil air, soil complexes, associations and series, soil horizons, moisture budgets, aggregates and peds, mor and mull and all the rest of it—would be too much for such thin, poor, fragile stuff as one might expect to find sprinkled about in mid-Paleozoic times.

He had tried to look and sound amused, and to be a good sport overall, whenever he heard the joke in any of its mutated forms. After all, it was never intended really maliciously; it merely partook of a largely unconscious acceptance of a hierarchy of scientists. Physics and astronomy were glamour fields. Geology and paleontology were comparatively rough-hewn but nonetheless logical choices;

moreover, they were perennially popular with the public, a crucial concern when public money was involved. Pedology was none of the above. He liked to think that he did not have it in himself to be envious, and so, with unfailing good humor, he agreed that there certainly would be a lot of geology at hand in the Paleozoic, mountains, valleys, strata, and the like. And, as for paleozoology, the Paleozoic would be nothing if not a big aquarium stocked with weird wiggly things and maybe a few big showy monsters.

And as for the crazy night skies, my oh my!

And even Kemal Barrowclough, paleobotanist, could get up and describe some harsh interior landscape enlivened only by the gray-green of lichens, "the first true land plants, because, unlike the psilophytes and lycopods we find clinging to the low moist places, close to water, always looking over their shoulders, so to speak, to make sure they haven't strayed too far, lichens, by God, *have taken the big step,*" and there would scarcely be a dry eye among the listeners, except for Kemal's sister, Gulnar, herself a paleobotanist. Gulnar specialized in psilophytes.

Throughout the discussions, Ivan had felt that, in effect, DeRamus had but to point to his rocks and say, "*Old!*" or Gabbert to his sky and say, "*Big!*" and nothing, *nothing*, he could have said about microbiotic volume in the histic epipedon, or humic acid precipitation, or the varieties of Paleozoic mesofauna he expected to sift through a tullgren funnel, would have meant a damn thing. Rather than enter his saprotrophs in unequal and hopeless competition against thrust faults, sea scorpions, or prehistoric constellations, he would wait until all around the table had settled back, glowering but spent, then softly clear his throat and calmly explain all over again that the origin and evolution of soil ranked among the major events in the history of life on Earth, that soil was linked inextricably to that major event of mid-Paleozoic time, life's emergence onto land.

It had been by dint of this stolid persistence that he had, in the minds of enough of his peers, ultimately established himself as precisely the sort of knowledgeable, dedicated, persevering person who should be a member of the Paleozoic expedition — and had also established, by extension, all soil scientists everywhere, in every geologic age, as estimable fellows. When finally, Stoll had announced who would go, Ivan stunned to speechlessness, could only gape as each of his colleagues shook his hand; almost a minute passed before he found his voice. "Wonders never cease," he had said.

Almost the next thing he remembered was looking over the back of the man who had knelt before him to check the seals on his boots. Cutsinger had stood leaning back against the wall with his arms crossed and watched the technicians work. He smiled ruefully at Ivan and said, "Tell me how you *really* feel."

"Like the first astronaut to spacewalk must've, just before he went out and did it."

"That guy had an umbilical cord," said Dilks, who sat nearby, surrounded by his own satellite system of technicians. He did not go onto say the obvious: We don't.

"Just don't lose sight of the anomaly once you're through," Cutsinger said.

"Right now," Ivan said, "getting back through the anomaly doesn't concern me quite as much as going through the first time and finding myself sinking straight to the bottom of the sea."

"We sent a probe in to bird-dog for you. The hole's stabilized over solid ground. You'll arrive high and dry." Cutsinger nodded at Dilks. "Both of you, together."

Ivan flexed his gloved fingers and said, "It's just the suit," and thought, It isn't *only* just the suit, but part of it *is* the suit. The suit was bulky and heavy and had to be hermetic. He and Dilks had to carry their own air supplies and everything else they might conceivably need, lest they contaminate the pristine Paleozoic environment and induce a paradox. The physicists, Ivan and Dilks privately agreed, were covering their own asses.

Cutsinger asked Dilks, "Anything you're especially concerned about?"

Dilks grinned. "Not liking the scenery. Not seeing a single prehistoric monster."

Cutsinger smiled thinly. "Careful what you wish for."

"Time to seal up," said one of the technicians. Another raised a clear bubble helmet and carefully set it down over Ivan's head. The helmet sealed when twisted to the right.

"All set?" said the chief technician's voice in the helmetphone.

"All set," said Ivan.

Technicians stood by to lend steadying hands as the two suited men got to their feet and lumbered into an adjoining room for decontamination. They stood upon a metal platform. Their equipment had already been decontaminated and stowed.

Ivan gripped the railing that enclosed the platform; he did not trust his legs to hold him up. This is it, he told himself, and then, This is what? He found that he still could not entirely believe what he was about to do.

The wall opposite the door pivoted away. The metal platform began to move on rails toward a ripple in the air.

Everything turned to white light and pain.

They considered their reflections in the full-length mirror. Don and Ivan were two solidly built, deep-chested, middle-aged men, unmistakably products of the same parents. Michelle stood framed in the doorway. Her expression was dubious. "Daddy," she said, "they'll never accept him as one of their own. No offense, Uncle Ivan, but you don't have Hollywood hair and teeth. They'll be horrified by what you've done to your skin. Daddy's tanned and fit because he works out. You're brown and hard and leathery because you work."

Don said to Ivan, "Maybe they'll mistake you for a retired stuntman."

"Why retired?"

"What other kind is there anymore?"

"I feel strange in these clothes, but I have to admit that they feel good and look good. They look better that I do."

"This is up-to-the-moment thread."

"I look like a rough draft of you."

"Whatever you do," Michelle said, "don't say you're a scientist. 'Scientist' cuts no ice here."

Don flashed a grin along his shoulder at his brother and said, "Absolutely do not say you're a pedologist. They won't have any idea what a pedologist is, unless they think it's the same thing as a pedophile."

"Someone asks what you are," Michelle said, "they mean, What's your astro-logical sign?"

"I don't know my astrological sign."

She made a horrified face. "Get *out* of California!"

"Tell 'em anything," Don said, "It doesn't matter, they'll run with it, tell you they just knew all along you were a Taurus or whatever."

"Say you're a time-traveler," Michelle told him. "But don't be hurt if they're not even impressed by that. It's not like they've ever done anything real."

The afternoon was warm, golden, perfect, as they wound their way along Mul-holland Drive. Don had put the top down, though it meant wearing goggles to screen out airvertising. Ivan sat fingering the unfamiliar cloth of his borrowed clothing and admiring the fine houses. They turned in at a gate in a high stucco wall, passed a security guard's inspection, and drove on. Around a bend in the driveway, Ivan saw a monstrous house, an unworkable fusion of Spanish and Jap-anese architectural quirks framed by the rim of hills beyond. Don braked to stop in front of the house and simply abandoned the car — if he gave the keys to some-one, Ivan did not see it happen. Just at the door, Don turned to Ivan and said, "Let me take one more look at you."

Ivan held his arms away from his body, palms forward.

Don laughed. "You're the most confident-looking guy I've ever seen. You look like Samson about to go wreak havoc among the Philistines."

"What've I got to be nervous about?"

They went inside and immediately found themselves in a crowd of mostly gor-geous chattering people, all seemingly intent upon displaying themselves, all dressed with an artful casualness. As he followed Don through the room, Ivan admired their physical flawlessness. The women were breathtaking. They were shorter or taller than one another, paler or darker, blond or brunette, but nearly all fashioned along the same very particular lines — slim and boyish save for improbably full breasts. On two or three occasions, Don paused and turned to introduce Ivan to someone who smiled pleasantly, shook Ivan's hand, and looked through or around him.

Ivan was, therefore, taken aback when a lovely woman approached from his brother's blind side, touched Ivan fleetingly on the forearm, and said, "I'm so glad you came, it's so good to see you." She wore a short skirt, belted at the waist. Her back, flanks, and shoulders were bare. The tips of her breasts were barely covered by two narrow, translucent strips of fabric that crossed at the navel and fastened behind her neck.

"It's so good to see you, too," Ivan said. She said, "I have to go get after the help for a second, but don't you go away," and vanished.

Ivan caught up with Don and said, "Who was that?"

"Who was who?"

A simply pretty rather than gorgeous girl paused before Ivan with a food-laden tray and smiled invitingly; he helped himself to some unrecognizable but delicious foodstuff. Before he could help himself to seconds, she was gone. He consoled himself with a drink plucked from another passing tray.

The singer fronting the combo was Frank Sinatra, who snapped his fingers and smiled as he sang "My Way." According to a placard, the skinny, artfully scruffy young men accompanying him were The Sex Pistols. Although none of the real people in the room appeared to notice when the song ended, Frank Sinatra thanked them for their applause and told them they were beautiful. Ivan caught up with the girl with the food tray and had helped himself to a snack before he realized that she was a different girl and it was a different snack. She was pretty in her own right, however, and the snack was as mysterious and delicious as the first had been. The combo began playing again, somewhat picking up the tempo. As Frank Sinatra sang that he didn't know what he wanted, but he knew how to get it, Don turned, pointed vaguely, and said to Ivan, "I see somebody over there I have to go schmooze with. I'd introduce you, but he's a pig."

"So go schmooze. I can look after myself."

"You sure?"

"Positive."

"Okay. Ogle some starlets—I'll be back in a mo."

As though she had rotated into the space vacated by Don, a long tawny woman appeared before Ivan. Her waist was as big around as his thigh. Her high breasts exerted a firm, friendly pressure against his lapels. He thought she had the most kissable-looking mouth he had ever seen. She said, "I'm sure I know you."

Ivan smiled. "I was one of the original Sex Pistols."

"Really!" She glanced over her shoulder at the hologram, then peered at Ivan again. "Which one?"

Ivan nodded vaguely in the band's direction. "The dead one."

She pouted fetchingly. "Who are you, really?"

He decided to see what would happen if he disregarded Don and Michelle's advice. He said, "I'm a pedologist."

"Oh," she said, "you specialize in child actors? No, wait, that's a foot specialist, right?" She looked doubtfully at his hands, which were big and brown, hard and knobby. "Is your practice in Beverly Hills?"

"Gondwanaland."

"Ah," she said, and nodded, and looked thoughtful, and lost interest. Ivan let her rotate back the way she had come and then sidled into and through the next room. The house was a maze of rooms opening onto other rooms, seemingly unto infinity; inside of five minutes, he decided that he was hopelessly lost. Surrounded by small groups of people talking animatedly among themselves, he turned more or less in place, eavesdropping casually. He quickly gathered that most of the people around him believed in astrology, psychics, cosmetic surgery, and supply-side economics, and that some few among them were alarmed by the trend toward virtual actors. He overheard a tanned, broad-shouldered crewcut man say to a couple of paler and less substantial men, "What chance have I got? I'm losing parts to John Wayne, for chrissake! He's been dead for decades, and he's a bigger star than ever."

"Costs less than ever, too," said the wispier of the other two men, "and keeps his right-wing guff to himself."

The broad-shouldered man scowled. "I don't want what happened to stuntmen to happen to actors!"

"Oh, don't be alarmist," the wispy man said. "No one's going to get rid of actors. Oh, they might use fewer of them, but—besides, stuntmen're holding their own overseas, and—"

"Crazy goddamn Aussies and Filipinos!"

"—and," the wispy man said insistently, "the films do have a significant following in this country. For some viewers, it's not enough to see an actor who looks like he's risking his life. They want the extra kick that comes from knowing an actor really *is* risking his life."

The third man had a satisfied air and was shaped like a bowling pin; his white suit and scarlet ascot enhanced the resemblance. "Until that happens," he told the broad-shouldered man, "better get used to playing second fiddle to John Wayne. Right now, I got development people e-synthing old physical comedians from the nineteen-whenevers. Buster Keaton, Harold Lloyd, and Jackie Chan. People still bust a gut laughing at those guys."

"Never heard of 'em."

"You will. Because I'm putting 'em together in a film. Lots of smash-up, fall-down. Sure, we use computers to give 'em what they never had before—voices, color—personalities! But when people see Buster Keaton fall off a moving train, they know there's no fakery."

"Who the hell cares if some dead guy risks his life?"

The bowling-pin-shaped man jabbed a finger into the air. "Thrills are timeless!"

Glimpsing yet another pretty girl with a food tray, Ivan exited right, through a doorway. He somehow missed the girl, made a couple of turns at random, and was beginning to wonder amusedly if he had happened upon another space-time anomaly when he suddenly and unexpectedly found himself outdoors, on the tiled shore of a swimming pool as big, he decided, as the Tethys Sea—Galveston Bay, at least. There were small groups of people ranged at intervals around the pool and one person in the water, who swam to the edge, pulled herself up, and was revealed to be a sleekly muscular Amazon. As she toweled her hair, she let her incurious gaze alight fleetingly on Ivan, then move on; she was as indifferent to his existence as though he were another of the potted palms. She rose lithely, draped her towel over one exquisite shoulder, and walked past him into the house.

Ivan sipped his drink, thrust his free hand into his trousers pocket, and ambled toward the far end of the pool and an array of women there. At a table in their midst, like a castaway on an island circled by glistening succulent mermaids, a bald, fat, fortyish man sat talking animatedly to himself. A waiter stood at the ready behind a cart laden with liquor bottles. A large rectangular object, either a man or a refrigerator stuffed into a sports jacket, took up space nearby. Just as this large object startled Ivan by looking in his direction, the fat man suddenly laughed triumphantly, leaped to his feet, and clapped his hands. He pointed at bottles on the cart, and the waiter began to fuss with them. The fat man turned, looked straight at Ivan, evidently the only suitable person within arm's reach, and pulled him close. "Help me celebrate," he said, and to the large object, "Larry, get the man a chair." Larry pulled a chair back from the table, waited for Ivan to sit, then moved off a short distance. The fat man introduced himself as John Rubis and looked as though he expected Ivan to have heard of him. Ivan smiled pleasantly and tried to give the impression that he had.

"I am *real* happy!" Rubis pointed at his own ear, and Ivan realized that there was an AnswerMan plugged into it. "The word from the folks at Northemico is *go!*" He indicated the liquor cart. "What can I get you?"

"Brought my own. Congratulations." Ivan toasted him, and they drank. Rubis smacked his lips appreciatively. Ivan said, "You work for Northemico?"

"I *deal* with Northemico. Their entertainment division."

"I didn't even realize Northemico had an entertainment division."

"Hey, they got everything." He turned toward the waiter and said, "Fix me up another of these."

"Sorry, I'm just a pedologist from Podunk." Rubis looked perplexed. "Pedologist," Ivan said, enunciating as clearly as he could.

"Ah." Rubis listened to his AnswerMan again. "As in child specialist—or soil scientist? No, that can't be right. Sorry about that, Doctor. Sometimes my little mister know-it-all gets confused. At least it didn't think you said you're a pederast, ha ha. So what is it, set me straight here, what's your claim to celebrity?"

Ivan mentally shrugged and asked himself, Why the hell not? and to John Rubis he said, "I was one of the first people to travel through time."

Instead of responding to that, Rubis held up a forefinger, said, "Incoming," looked away, and hunched over the table, listening intently to his AnswerMan and occasionally muttering inaudibly. Ivan's attention wandered. Light reflecting from the pool's surface shimmered on the enclosing white walls. The water was as brilliantly blue-green as that ancient sea—and as he pictured that sea in his mind, he also pictured a woman like a tanned and buffed Aphrodite rising from the waters. And when he told her that he was a foot specialist, she heaved a sigh of exasperation and dived back into the sea.

Rubis turned back to him and said, "Sorry. You aren't kidding about the time-travel, are you?"

"Well, I was part of the first team of time-travelers—half of it. There were just two of us. Afterward, I made other visits and helped establish a community of scientists in Paleozoic time. The base camp's the size of a small town now."

Rubis stared at him for what felt like a long moment. Then a light seemed to come on behind the man's eyes, and he snapped his fingers and pointed. "Yeah. The hole through time. Back to, what, the Stone Age?"

"Um, actually, back to quite a bit before. Back to the Paleozoic Era, four hundred million and some odd years ago. The Siluro-Devonian boundary."

"Yeah, that's right! The Age of Trilobites. So, what, you're out here pitching the story of your life to producers?"

"No, I'm just visiting my brother. He's the screenwriter in the family." That information did not seem to impress Rubis particularly, so Ivan added, "He was just up for a Best Screenplay Oscar. Donald Kelly." Rubis brightened. "My own fifteen minutes of fame are long past, and they really didn't amount to all that much."

"Mm. Any face minutes?"

"I'm sorry?"

"You know, your face on the TV screen. Media interviews. Face minutes."

"Ah. I turn up in some old documentaries. Everybody made documentaries for a while, until all six people who were remotely interested were sick of them."

Rubis rolled his eyes. "Documentaries! Even I watched part of one. No offense, but it was like watching grass grow. The most exciting thing you found was a trilobite, and it's basically just some kind of big water bug, isn't it?"

"Yes, basically."

"There've been bigger bugs in movies already. Like in—like in *Them and I*. And *The Thief of Baghdad*. Seen it?"

"Yes, as a matter of fact. I thought the Indonesian settings were interesting."

"Our first idea was to actually shoot it in Baghdad. But not much of Baghdad's standing anymore. So—besides, Indonesia, Baghdad"—Rubis made a gesture expressive of some point that was not altogether clear to Ivan—"eh!"

"Once upon a time," Ivan said, "if you wanted to make a movie about Baghdad, you built sets on soundstages here in Hollywood, right?"

"Aah, nobody makes movies in Hollywood anymore. Too expensive. Lousy unions. But this is still the place to be, the place to make deals. Anyway, like I was saying, about time-travel—I've always thought it's a sensational thing. When you think about it, it really is just the biggest thing since the early days of space travel. I wish it could be used for something more interesting than studying bugs and slime a million years ago, but don't get me wrong. I think it's a real shame the time-travelers never caught on with the public like those first guys who went to the moon—Armstrong, Altman. Now those guys were celebrities."

"It's not like we could do a live broadcast from the Paleozoic. The view wouldn't have commended itself to most people anyway. The Silurian Period looks like a cross between a gravel pit and a stagnant pond. And we didn't plant a flag or say anything heroic. In fact—" Ivan hesitated for a moment, considering. "Still, it was all tremendously exciting. It was the most exciting thing in the world."

The wall opposite the door had pivoted away. The metal platform had begun to move on rails toward a ripple in the air. Everything had turned to white light and pain. Ivan, blinded, felt as though someone had taken careful aim with a two-by-four and struck him across his solar plexus. There was a terrifying, eternal moment when he could not suck in air. Then he drew a breath and started to exhale, and his stomach turned over. The convulsion put him on his hands and knees. Too excited to eat breakfast that morning, he had only drunk a cup of coffee. Now burning acid rose in his throat. He felt cramps in his calf muscles. His earphones throbbed with the sound of—what was it, crying, groaning . . . ?

Retching. His vision cleared, and he saw Dilks nearby, lying on his side, feebly moving his arms. For some reason, part of Dilks's visor was obscured. Ivan threw his weight in that direction and half rolled, half crawled to the man's side. Now he could see Dilks' face through the yellow-filmed visor. Dilks had lost his breakfast inside his helmet. Ivan spoke his name, but it was quickly established that, though Dilks' helmetphone worked, his microphone was fouled and useless. There was nothing to be done for it now: they could not simply remove Dilks' helmet and clean out the mess; they were under strictest orders not to contaminate the Paleozoic.

Nearby, the air around the anomaly rippled like a gossamer veil. Ivan looked around at the Paleozoic world. He and Dilks were on the shingle just above the high-tide line and just below a crumbling line of cliffs. The sun stood at zenith in the cloudless sky. The sea was blue-green, brilliant, beautiful.

Ivan bent over Dilks again and said, "You're in bad shape. We've got to get you back. Come on, I'll help you."

Dilks vehemently shoved him away. He looked gray-faced inside his helmet, but he grimaced and shook his head, and though he could not say what he meant, Ivan understood him. *We didn't come all this way only to go right back.* Dilks patted the front of Ivan's suit and then motioned in the direction of the water.

Ivan nodded. He said, "I'll be right back." He staggered to his feet, checked the instruments attached to the platform, activated the camera mounted on his helmet, and collected soil and air samples in the vicinity of the platform. Then, with what he hoped was a reassuring wave to Dilks, he lumbered toward the water. The shingle made for treacherous footing, and yet, as he looked out upon the expanse of water, he experienced a shivery rush of pleasure so particular that he knew he had felt it only once before, during boyhood, on the occasion of his first sight of the sea off Galveston Island. He had never been mystically inclined, even as a boy, but, then as now, he had responded to something tremendous and irresistible, the sea's summons, had rushed straight down to the water and dived in happily.

Nothing moved along the whole beach, nothing except the curling waves and the tangles of seaweed they had cast up. The beach curved away to left and right. It must curve away forever, Ivan thought. Hundreds, thousands of miles of perfectly unspoiled beach. He knelt on the dark wet sand and collected a sample of seawater. As he sealed the vial, he saw something emerge from the foam about two meters to his right. It was an arthropod about as big as his hand, flattened and segmented and carried along on jointed legs. The next wave licked after it, embraced it, appeared momentarily to draw it back toward the sea. The wave retreated, and the creature hesitated. Come on, Ivan thought, come on. Come on. He entertained no illusions that he had arrived on the spot just in time to greet the first Earth creature ever to come ashore. Surely, a thousand animals, a million, had already done so, and plants before them, and microorganisms before plants. Nevertheless, he had to admire the timing of this demonstration. He crouched, hands on knees, and waited. Foam rushed over the creature again. Come on, Ivan commanded it, make up your dim little mind. It's strange out here on land, not altogether hospitable, but you'll get used to it, or your children will, or your great-grandchildren a million times removed. Eventually, most of the species, most of the biomass, will be out here.

The arthropod advanced beyond the reach of the waves and began nudging through the seawrack. Eat hearty, Ivan thought, taking a cautious step toward the animal. He reflected on the persistence in vertebrates of revulsion toward arthropods. He felt kindly toward this arthropod, at least. Both of us, he thought, are pioneers.

As last he reluctantly tore himself away and returned to Dilks, who had sagged to the ground by the platform. Ivan propped the stricken man up and pointed toward the ripple. "We've got to cut this short," he said.

Dilks indicated disagreement, but more weakly than before.

"You're hurt," Ivan said, holding him up, "and we've got to go back." There was a crackle of static in Ivan's helmetphone, and he heard Dilks speak a single word.

". . . failed . . ."

"No! We didn't fail! We got here alive, and we're getting back alive. Nobody can take that away from us, Dilks. We're the first. And we'll come again."

They got clumsily onto the platform. Ivan made Dilks as comfortable as possible and then activated the platform. The air around the ripple began to roil and glow. Ivan gripped the railing and faced the glow. "Do your goddamn worst."

Rubis had offered Ivan a cigar, which he politely refused, and stuck one into his own mouth, and Larry had lurched forward to light it. Now, enveloped in smoke, Rubis said, "Trilobites just never did catch on with the public. Maybe if you'd found a really *big* trilobite. On the other hand, trilobites didn't make for very cuddly stuffed toys, either, and that's always an important consideration. The merchandising, I mean."

"Candy shaped like brachiopods and sea scorpions? How about breakfast cereal? Sugar-frosted Trilo*bites?*"

Perfectly serious, Rubis nodded. "Now, if you'd've set the dial in your time machine for the age of dinosaurs instead."

"There wasn't actually a time machine. Just the space-time anomaly, the hole. And it just happened to open up where it did."

"That's too bad. And ain't it the way it always happens with science? We spent a godzillion dollars sending people to the Moon and Mars, and the Moon's just a rock and Mars's just a damn desert."

"Well, I don't know anyone honestly expected—"

"Now, *dinosaurs*, dinosaurs've been hot sellers forever. Dino toys, VR—they had all that stuff when I was a kid, and it still outsells every damn thing in sight. And every two, three years, regular as laxatives, another big dino movie. But what've you got? You got nothing, I'm sorry to say." He began to count on his fingers the things which Ivan did not have. "You got no big concept. You got no merchandisable angle. You got no crossover potential. Crossover potential's very big these days. You know, like Tarzan meets Frankenstein. James Bond versus Mata Hari. But, most of all, you haven't got dinosaurs, though. Everybody knows if you're going to tell a story set in the prehistoric past, there have to be dinosaurs. Without dinosaurs, there's no drama."

"I guess not," Ivan said, and took a long sip of his drink, and looked at the shimmering blue-green water in the pool. The slowly stirring air seemed to carry a faint smell of burning. He said to Rubis, "Let me bounce an idea for a different kind of time-travel story off you. Tell me what you think."

"Sure. Shoot."

"Okay. You have to bear in mind that when we speak of traveling backward through time, into the past, what we're really talking about is traveling between just two of infinite multiple Earths. Some of these multiple Earths may be virtually identical, some may be subtly different, some are wildly different—as different as modern and prehistoric times. Anyway, what you actually do when you travel through time is go back and forth between Earths. Earth as it is, here and now, and another Earth, Earth as it was in the Paleozoic Era."

Rubis murmured, "Weird," and smiled.

"Now let's say someone from our present-day visits a prehistoric Earth and returns. After a while, after the initial excitement's died down, he starts to ponder the implications of travel back and forth between multiple Earths. He's come back to a present-day Earth that may or may not be his own present-day Earth. If it's virtually identical, well, if the only difference is, say, the outcome of some subatomic occurrence, then it doesn't matter. But maybe there's something subtly off on the macro level. It wouldn't be anything major. Napoleon, Hitler, and the Confederate States would all've gone down to defeat. Or maybe the time-traveler only suspects that something may be subtly off. His problem is, he's never quite sure, he can't decide whether something is off or he only thinks it is, so he's always looking for the telling detail. But there are so *many* details. If he never knew in the first place how many plays Shakespeare really wrote or who all those European kings were . . ."

Rubis nodded. "I get it. Not bad." He chewed his lower lip for a moment. "But I still think it needs dinosaurs."

Ivan chuckled softly, without mirth. "You should look up my niece's boyfriend." He turned on his seat, toward the burning hills.

They swept down Mulholland. Ivan said to Don, "Thanks for taking me. I can't remember when I've had so much fun." Don gave him a curious look. "No, really. I had a very good time, a wonderful time."

"Probably a better time than I did."

Ivan made a noncommittal sound. "I needed this experience as a kind of reality check."

Don laughed sharply. "Hollywood isn't the place to come for a reality check."

"Well, okay. Let's just say I had a very enlightening and entertaining poolside chat with our host."

"Johnny Rubis? Christ. He wasn't our host. Our host was a swine in human form named Lane. He was holding court indoors the whole time. I went in and did my dip and rise and got the hell out as fast as I could. Whatever Rubis may've told you he was doing by the pool, he was just showing off. See what a big deal I am. There were guys all over the place doing the same thing—women, too. Dropping names and making a show of pissant phone calls. See what big deals we are. Whatever Rubis may've told you, he's not that high in the food chain. A year ago he was probably packaging videos with titles like *Trailer Park Sluts*. He's an example of the most common form of life in Hollywood. The self-important butthead. I know, I've worked for plenty like him."

"Writing novels based on movies based on novels?"

Don shook his head. "Not me. Not lately, anyway?"

Ivan wondered if Don despised himself as much as he apparently despised everyone else in Hollywood. He hoped it was not so. More than anything, he hoped it was not so. "Don," he said, "I'm sorry I said that. I'm really terribly sorry."

Don shrugged. "No offense taken." He gave Ivan a quick grin. "Hey, big brother,

I've been insulted by professionals. It's one of the things writers in Hollywood get paid for."

They rode in silence for a time.

Then Don said, "Do you know what a monkey trap is?

"Pretty self-explanatory, isn't it?"

"Yes, but do you know how it works? You take a dry gourd and cut a small hole in it, just big enough for the monkey to get its hand through. You put a piece of food inside the gourd and attach the gourd to a tree or a post. The monkey puts his hand into the gourd, grabs the piece of food, and then can't pull his fist back through the hole. He could get away if he'd only let go of the food, but he just can't make himself let go. So, of course, he's trapped."

"Is the money really that good?"

"Christ, Ivan, the money's incredible. But it *isn't* just the money. What it is, is that every great once in a long goddamn while, against all the odds — remember, before all this happened, I worked in the next best habitat favorable to self-important buttheads, which is politics. While you were off exploring prehistoric times, I was writing like a sumbitch on fire and trying to get the hell out of Texas. I paid the rent, however, by working for the state legislature. Whenever a legislator wanted to lay down a barrage of memorial resolutions, I was the anonymous flunky who unlimbered the 'whereases' and the 'be it resolveds.' Every now and then, I wrote about forgotten black heroes of the Texas Revolution, forgotten women aviators of World War Two — something, anyway, that meant something. But, of course, in those resolutions, everything was equally important. Most of my assignments were about people's fiftieth wedding anniversaries, high-school football teams, rattlesnake roundups. Finally, I was assigned to write a resolution designating, I kid you not, Texas Bottled Water Day. Some people from the bottling industry were in town, lobbying for God remembers what, and someone in the lege thought it'd be real nice to present them with a resolution. Thus, Texas Bottled Water Day. When I saw the request, I looked my boss straight in the eye, and I told him, This is not work for a serious artist. He quite agreed. First chance he got, he fired me."

"Maybe you should've quit before it came to that."

"Well, I'd've quit anyway as soon as the writing took off." Don changed his grip on the steering wheel. "But while I was a legislative drudge, I lived for those few brief moments when the work really meant something."

His face, it seemed to Ivan, was suddenly transformed by some memory of happiness. Or perhaps it was just the car. The car cornered like a dream.

The Thing about Benny

M. SHAYNE BELL

M. Shayne Bell first came to public attention in 1986, when he won first place in that year's Writers of the Future contest. Since then he has published a number of well-liked stories in Asimov's *— including a Hugo Finalist, "Mrs. Lincoln's China," and a loosely connected series of stories about life in a future Africa — as well as appearing in* Amazing, The Magazine of Fantasy & Science Fiction, Realms of Fantasy, Pulphouse, Starlight 2, Vanishing Acts, *and elsewhere, published a well-received first novel,* Nicoji, *and edited an anthology of stories by Utah writers,* Washed by a Wave of Wind: Science Fiction from the Corridor. *Bell has an M.A. degree in English from Brigham Young University, and lives in Salt Lake City, Utah.*

In the quiet little story that follows, he shows us how a small hope can bloom even on the edge of disaster . . . if you know how to look for it, that is.

Abba, Fältskog Listing 47: "Dancing Queen," day 3.
En route from the airport.

Benny said, apropos of nothing, "The bridge is the most important part of a song, don't you think?"

"Oh, yeah," I said, me trying to drive in all that traffic and us late, as usual. "That's all I think about when I'm hearing music — those important bridges."

"No, really." Benny looked at me, earphones firmly covering his ears, eyes dark and kind of surprised. It was a weird look. Benny never has much to say, but when he does the company higher-ups told me I was supposed to take notice, try to figure out how he does what he does.

The light turned green. I drove us onto North Temple, downtown Salt Lake not so far off now. "Bridges in songs have something to do with extinct plants?" I asked.

"It's all in the music," he said, looking back at the street and sitting very, very still.

"Messages about plants are in the music?" I asked.

But he was gone, back in that trance he'd been in since LA. Besides, we were minutes from our first stop. He always gets so nervous just before we start work. "What if we find something?" he'd asked me once, and I'd said, "Isn't that the point?"

He started rubbing his sweaty hands up and down his pant legs. I could hear the tinny melody out of his earphones. It was "Dancing Queen" week. Benny'd set his player on endless repeat, and he listened to "Dancing Queen" over and over again on the plane, in the car, in the offices we went to, during meals, in bed with the earphones on his head. That's all he'd listen to for one week. Then he'd change to a different Abba song on Sunday. When he'd gone through every Abba song ever recorded, he'd start over.

"Check in," Benny said.

"What?"

"The Marriott."

I slammed brakes, did a U-turn, did like he'd asked. That was my job, even if we were late. Benny had to use the toilet, and he would not use toilets in the offices we visited.

I carried the bags up to our rooms—no bellhop needed, thank you. What's a personal assistant for if not to lug your luggage around? I called Utah Power and Light to tell them we were still coming. Then I waited for Benny in the lobby. My mind kept playing "Dancing Queen" over and over. "It's all in the music," Benny'd said, but I failed to understand how anybody, Benny included, could find directions in fifty-year-old Abba songs to the whereabouts of plants extinct in the wild.

Benny tapped me on the shoulder. "It's close enough that we can walk," he said. "Take these."

He handed me his briefcase and a stack of World Botanics pamphlets and motioned to the door. I always had to lead the way. Benny wouldn't walk with me. He walked behind me, four or five steps back, Abba blasting in his ears. It was no use trying to get him to do differently. I gave the car keys to the hotel car people so they could park the rental, and off we went.

Utah Power and Light was a first visit. We'd do a get-acquainted sweep of the cubicles and offices, then come back the next day for a detailed study. Oh sure, after Benny'd found the *Rhapis excelsa* in a technical writer's cubicle in the Transamerica Pyramid, everybody with a plant in a pot had hoped to be the one with the cancer cure. But most African violets are just African violets. They aren't going to cure anything. Still, the hopeful had driven college botany professors around the world nuts with their pots of begonias and canary ivy and sword ferns.

But they were out there. Plants extinct in the wild had been kept alive in the oddest places, including cubicles in office buildings. Benny'd found more than his share. Even I take "Extract of *Rhapis excelsa*" treatment one week each year like everybody else. Who wants a heart attack? Who doesn't feel better with his arteries unclogged? People used to go jogging just to feel that good.

The people at UP&L were thrilled to see us—hey, Benny was their chance at millions. A lady from HR led us around office after cubicle after break room. Benny walked along behind the lady and me. It was *Dieffenbachia maculata* after *Ficus benjamina* after *Cycus revoluta*. Even I could tell nobody was getting rich here. But up on the sixth floor, I turned around and Benny wasn't behind us. He was back staring at a *Nemanthus gregarius* on a bookshelf in a cubicle just inside the door.

I walked up to him. "It's just goldfish vine," I said.

The girl in the cubicle looked like she wanted to pick up her keyboard and kill me with it.

"Benny," I said, "we got a bunch more territory to cover. Let's move it."

He put his hands in his pockets and followed along behind me, but after about five minutes he was gone again. We found him back at the *Nemanthus gregarius*. I took a second look at the plant. It looked like nothing more than *Nemanthus gregarius* to me. Polly, the girl in the cubicle, was doing a little dance in her chair in time to the muffled "Dancing Queen" out of Benny's earphones. Mama mia, she felt like money, money, money.

I made arrangements with HR for us to come back the next day and start our detailed study. The company CEO came down to shake our hands when we left. Last we saw of Polly that day was her watering the *Nemanthus gregarius*.

Abba, Fältskog Listing 47: "Dancing Queen," day 3. Dinner.

The thing about Benny is, he never moves around in time to the music. I mean, he can sit there listening to "Dancing Queen" over and over again and stare straight ahead, hands folded in his lap. He never moves his shoulders. He never taps his toes. He never sways his hips. Watching him, you'd think "Dancing Queen" was some Bach cantata.

I ordered dinner for us in the hotel coffee shop. Benny always makes me order for him, but god forbid it's not a medium-rare hamburger and fries. We sat there eating in silence, the only sound between us the muffled dancing queen having the time of her life. I thought maybe I'd try a little conversation. "Hamburger OK?" I asked.

Benny nodded.

"Want a refill on the Coke?"

He picked up his glass and sucked up the last of the Coke, but shook his head no.

I took a bite of my burger, chewed it, looked at Benny. "You got any goals?" I asked him.

Benny looked at me then. He didn't say a word. He stopped chewing and just stared.

"I mean, what do you want to do with your life? You want a wife? Kids? A trip to the moon? We fly around together, city after city, studying all these plants, and I don't think I even know you."

He swallowed and wiped his mouth with his napkin. "I have goals," he said.

"Well, like what?"

"I haven't told anybody. I'll need some time to think about it before I answer you. I'm not sure I want to tell anybody, no offense."

Jeez, Benny, take a chance on me why don't you, I thought. We went back to eating our burgers. I knew the higher-ups would want me to follow the lead Benny had dropped when we were driving in from the airport, so I tried. "Tell me about bridges," I said. "Why are they important in songs?"

Benny wouldn't say another word. We finished eating, and I carried Benny's things up to his room for him. At the door he turned around and looked at me. "Bridges take you to a new place," he said. "But they also show you the way back to where you once were."

He closed the door.

I didn't turn on any music in my room. It was nice to have it a little quiet for a change. I wrote my reports and e-mailed them off, then went out for a drink. I nursed it along, wondering where we stood on the bridges.

Abba, Fältskog Listing 47: "Dancing Queen," day 4.
UP&L offices.

World Botanics sends Benny only to companies that meet its criteria. First, they have to have occupied the same building for fifty years or more. You'd be surprised how few companies in America have done that. But if a company has moved around a lot, chances are its plants have not gone with it. Second, it's nice if the company has had international ties, but even that isn't necessary. Lots of people somehow failed to tell customs about the cuttings or the little packets of seeds in their pockets after vacations abroad. If a company's employees had traveled around a lot, or if they had family ties with other countries, they sometimes ended up with the kind of plants we were looking for. UP&L has stayed put for a good long time, plus its employees include former Mormon missionaries who've poked around obscure corners of the planet. World Botanics hoped to find something in Utah.

The UP&L CEO and the HR staff and Polly were all waiting for us. You'd think Benny'd want to go straight up to the sixth floor to settle the *Nemanthus gregarius* question, but he didn't. Benny always starts on the first floor and works his way to the top, so we started on floor one.

The lobby was a new install, and I was glad Benny didn't waste even half an hour there. Not much hope of curing cancer with flame nettle or cantea palms. The cafeteria on the second floor had some interesting *Cleistocactus strausii*. Like all cactus, it's endangered but not yet extinct in the wild—there are still reports of *Cleistocactus strausii* growiing here and there in the tops of the Andes. As far as anybody can tell, it can't cure a thing.

We didn't make it to the sixth floor till after four o'clock, and you could tell that Polly was a nervous wreck.

But Benny walked right past her *Nemanthus gregarius*.

"Hey, Benny," I said in a low voice. "What about the goldfish vine?"

Benny turned around and stared at it. Polly moved back into her cubicle so she wouldn't block the view, but after a minute Benny put his hands in his pockets and walked off. Well, poor Polly, I thought.

But just before five, I turned around and Benny wasn't behind me. I found him at the *Nemanthus gregarius*. Jeez Benny, I thought, we need to know the name of the game here. Declare extract of *Nemanthus gregarius* the fountain of youth or tell Polly she has a nice plant but nothing special. I steered him out of the building and back to the Marriott.

Abba, Fältskog Listing 47: "Dancing Queen," day 4. Dinner.

I ordered Benny's burger and a steak for me. We sat there eating, the only sound between us a muffled "Dancing Queen." After last night, I was not attempting conversation.

I'd taken time before dinner to look up *Nemanthus gregarius* on the Net. It is not endangered. It grows like weeds in cubicles. It can't cure a thing.

I didn't know what Benny was doing.

He sucked up the last of his glass of Coke and put the glass down a little hard on the table. I looked up at him.

"I want to find a new plant and name it for Agnetha," he said.

"What?"

"My goal in life," he said. "If you tell anyone, I'll see that you're fired."

"You're looking for a new plant species in office buildings?"

"I'd actually like to find one for each of the four members of Abba, but Agnetha's first."

And I'd thought finding *one* completely new species was too much to ask.

"When Abba sang, the world was so lush," Benny said. "You can hear it in their music. It resonates with what's left of the natural world. It helps me save it."

It was my turn to be quiet. All I could think was, it works for Benny. He's had plenty of success, after all, and who hasn't heard of crazier things than the music of dead pop stars leading some guy to new plant species?

When I wrote up my daily reports that night, I left out Benny's goals. Some things the higher-ups don't need to know.

Abba, Fältskog Listing 47: "Dancing Queen," day 5.
UP&L offices.
We spent the day looking at more sorry specimens of *Cordyline terminalis, Columnea gloriosa,* and *Codiaeum variegatum* than I care to remember. By the end of the day, Benny started handing out the occasional watering tip, so I knew even he was giving up.

"*Nemanthus gregarius?*" I asked in the elevator on the way down.

Suddenly he punched 6. He walked straight to Polly's cubicle and stuck out his hand. "I owe you an apology," he said.

Polly just sat there. She was facing her own little Waterloo, and she did it bravely.

"I thought your *Nemanthus gregarius* might be a subspecies not before described, but it isn't. It's the common variety. A nice specimen, though."

We left quickly. At least he didn't give her any watering tips.

Abba, Fältskog Listing 47: "Dancing Queen," day 5.
Wandering the streets.
The thing about Benny is, if it doesn't work out and we've studied every plant on thirty floors of an office tower without finding even a *Calathea lancifolia,* he can't stand it. He wanders up and down the streets, poking into every little shop. He never buys anything—he isn't shopping. I think he's hoping to spot some rare plant in the odd tobacconist or magazine shop and to do it fast. I have a hard time keeping up with him then, and heaven forbid I should decide to buy something on sale for a Mother's Day gift.

We rushed through two used bookstores, an oriental rug store, four art galleries, three fast food joints. "Benny," I said. "Let's get something to eat."

"It's here," he said.

"What's where?"

"There's something here, and we just haven't found it."

The Dancing Queen was resonating, I supposed. Shops were closing all around us.

"You check the Indian jewelry store while I check Mr. Q's Big and Tall," he told me. "We meet outside in five."

I did like I was told. I smiled at the Navajo woman in traditional dress, but she did not smile back. She wanted to lock up. I made a quick sweep of the store and noted the various species of endangered cacti and left. Benny was not on the sidewalk. I went into Mr. Q's after him.

He was standing perfectly still in front of a rack of shirts on sale, hands in his pockets.

"These are too big for you," I said.

"Window display, southeast corner."

Well, I walked over there. It was a lovely little display of *Rhipsalis salicornioides*, *Phalaenopsis lueddemanniana*, and *Streptocarpus saxorum*. Nothing unusual.

Then I looked closer at the *Streptocarpus saxorum*. The flowers weren't the typical powder blue or lilac. They were a light yellow.

The proprietor walked up to me. "I'm sorry," he said. "But we're closing. Could you bring your final purchases to the register?"

"I'm just admiring your cape primrose," I said. "Where do they come from?"

"My mother grows them," he said. "She gave me these plants when I opened the store."

"Did she travel in Africa or Madagascar?"

"Her brother was in the foreign service. She used to follow him around to his postings. I don't remember where she went—I'd have to ask her."

"Do you mind if I touch one of the plants?" I asked.

He said sure. The leaves were the typical hairy, gray-green ovals; the flowers floated above the leaves on wire-thin stems. It was definitely *Streptocarpus*, but I'd never seen anything like it described.

"I think you should call your mother," I said, and I explained who Benny and I were.

The store closed, but Mr. Proprietor and his staff waited with us for the mother to arrive. The whole time Benny just stood by the sale rack, eyes closed, hands in his pockets. "You've done it again," I whispered to him.

He didn't answer me. Just as I turned to walk back over to the cape primrose, he opened his eyes. "*Streptocarpus agnethum*," he whispered.

And he smiled.

Abba, Fältskog Listing 32: "I Have a Dream," day 2.
Agnetha's grave.

The thing about Benny is, he's generous. He took me to Sweden with him, and we planted *Streptocarpus agnethum*, or "dancing queen," around Agnetha's gravestone. Turns out the flower wasn't a cure for anything, but it was a new species and Benny got to name it.

"Agnetha would have loved these flowers," I told Benny.

He just kept planting. We had a nice sound system on the ground beside us, playing her music—well, just one of her songs. It talks about believing in angels. I don't know if I believe in angels, but I can see the good in Benny's work. Nobody's bringing back the world we've lost, but little pieces of it have survived here and there. Benny was saving some of those pieces.

"These flowers are so pretty," I told him.

Of course he didn't say anything.

He didn't need to.

The Great Goodbye

ROBERT CHARLES WILSON

*Here's a sly and ingenious little glimpse of what the new millennium ahead
may have in store for humanity, one of a weekly series of such speculations
about the future commissioned by the science magazine* Nature . . .

*Robert Charles Wilson made his first sale in 1974, to Analog, but little
more was heard from him until the late eighties, when he began to publish
a string of ingenious and well-crafted novels and stories that have since
established him among the top ranks of the writers who came to prominence
in the last two decades of the twentieth century. His first novel,* A Hidden
Place, *appeared in 1986. He won the Philip K. Dick Award for his 1995
novel* Mysterium, *and the Aurora Award for his story "The Perseids." His
other books include the novels* Memory Wire, Gypsies, The Divide, The
Harvest, A Bridge of Years, Bios *and* Darwinia. *His most recent book is a
new novel,* The Chroncliths. *He lives in Toronto, Canada.*

The hardest part of the Great Goodbye, for me, was knowing I wouldn't see my
grandfather again. We had developed that rare thing, a friendship that crossed the
line of the post-evolutionary divide, and I loved him very much.

Humanity had become, by that autumn of 2350, two very distinct human
species—if I can use that antiquated term. Oh, the Stock Humans remain a 'species' in the classical evolutionary sense: New People, of course, have forgone all
that. Post-evolutionary, post-biological, budded or engineered, New People are
gloriously free from all the old human restraints. What unites us all is our common
source, the Divine Complexity that shaped primordial quark plasma into stars,
planets, planaria, people. Grandfather taught me that.

I had always known that we would, one day, be separated. But we first spoke
of it, tentatively and reluctantly, when Grandfather went with me to the Museum
of Devices in Brussels, a day trip. I was young and easily impressed by the full-
scale working model of a 'steam train' in the Machine Gallery—an amazingly
baroque contrivance of ancient metalwork and gas-pressure technology. Staring at
it, I thought (because Grandfather had taught me some of his 'religion'): Complexity made this. This is made of stardust, by stardust.

We walked from the Machine Gallery to the Gallery of the Planets, drawing more than a few stares from the Stock People (children, especially) around us. It was uncommon to see a New Person fully embodied and in public. The Great Goodbye had been going on for more than a century; New People were already scarce on Earth, and a New Person walking with a Stock Person was an even more unusual sight—risqué, even shocking. We bore the attention gamely. Grandfather held his head high and ignored the muttered insults.

The Gallery of the Planets recorded humanity's expansion into the Solar System, and I hope the irony was obvious to everyone who sniffed at our presence there: Stock People could not have colonized any of these forbidding places (consider Ganymede in its primeval state!) without the partnership of the New. In a way, Grandfather said, this was the most appropriate place we could have come. It was a monument to the long collaboration that was rapidly reaching its end.

The stars, at last, are within our grasp. The grasp, anyhow, of the New People. Was this, I asked Grandfather, why he and I had to be so different from one another?

"Some people," he said, "some families, just happen to prefer the old ways. Soon enough Earth will belong to the Stocks once again, though I'm not sure this is entirely a good thing." And he looked at me sadly. "We've learned a lot from each other. We could have learned more."

"I wish we could be together for centuries and centuries," I said.

I saw him for the last time (some years ago now) at the Shipworks, where the picturesque ruins of Detroit rise from the Michigan Waters, and the star-traveling Polises are assembled and wait like bright green baubles to lift, at last and forever, into the sky. Grandfather had arranged this final meeting—in the flesh, so to speak.

We had delayed it as long as possible. New People are patient: in a way, that's the point. Stock Humans have always dreamed of the stars, but the stars remain beyond their reach. A Stock Human lifetime is simply too short; one or two hundred years won't take you far enough. Relativistic constraints demand that travelers between the stars must be at home between the stars. Only New People have the continuity, the patience, the flexibility to endure and prosper in the Galaxy's immense voids.

I greeted Grandfather on the high embarkation platform where the wind was brisk and cool. He lifted me up in his arms and admired me with his bright blue eyes. We talked about trivial things, for the simple pleasure of talking. Then he said, "This isn't easy, this saying goodbye. It makes me think of mortality—that old enemy."

"It's all right," I said.

"Perhaps you could still change your mind?"

I shook my head, no. A New Person can transform himself into a Stock Person and vice versa, but the social taboos are strong, the obstacles (family dissension, legal entanglements) almost insurmountable, as Grandfather knew too well. And in any case that wasn't my choice. I was content as I was. Or so I chose to believe.

"Well, then," he said, empty, for once, of words. He looked away. The Polis would be rising soon, beginning its eons-long navigation of our near stellar neighbors. Discovering, no doubt, great wonders.

"Goodbye, boy," he said.

I said, "Goodbye, Grandfather."

Then he rose to his full height on his many translucent legs, winked one dish-sized glacial blue eye, and walked with a slow machinely dignity to the vessel that would carry him away. And I watched, desolate, alone on the platform with the wind in my hair, as his ship rose into the arc of the high clean noonday sky.

Tendeléo's Story

IAN MCDONALD

Here's a powerful, compassionate, and darkly lyrical story of a young girl's coming-of-age in a future Africa that is literally being eaten by an alien invader, and, after passing through that invader's alien guts, as it were, is being transformed into something rich and strange and totally unexpected. A sea change that extends as well to the lives of the people who find themselves in its way. . . .

British author Ian McDonald is an ambitious and daring writer with a wide range and an impressive amount of talent. His first story was published in 1982, and since then he has appeared with some frequency in Interzone, Asimov's Science Fiction, New Worlds, Zenith, Other Edens, Amazing, *and elsewhere. He was nominated for the* John W. Campbell Award *in 1985, and in 1989 he won the* Locus "Best First Novel" Award *for his novel* Desolation Road. *He won the* Philip K. Dick Award *in 1992 for his novel* King of Morning, Queen of Day. *His other books include the novels* Out on Blue Six *and* Hearts, Hands and Voices, Terminal Cafe, Sacrifice of Fools, *and the acclaimed* Evolution's Shore, *and two collections of his short fiction,* Empire Dreams *and* Speaking in Tongues. *His most recent book is a new novel,* Kirinya, *and a chapbook novella* Tendeléo's Story, *both sequels to* Evolution's Shore. *Born in Manchester, England, in 1960, McDonald has spent most of his life in Northern Ireland, and now lives and works in Belfast. He has a web site at http://www.lysator.liu.se/ ^unicorn/mcdonald/.*

I shall start my story with my name. I am Tendeléo. I was born here, in Gichichi. Does that surprise you? The village has changed so much that no one born then could recognize it now, but the name is still the same. That is why names are important. They remain.

I was born in 1995, shortly after the evening meal and before dusk. That is what Tendeléo means in my language, Kalenjin: early-evening-shortly-after-dinner. I am the oldest daughter of the pastor of St. John's Church. My younger sister was born in 1998, after my mother had two miscarriages, and my father asked the congregation to lay hands on her. We called her Little Egg. That is all there are of us, two. My father felt that a pastor should be an example to his people, and at that time the government was calling for smaller families.

My father had cure of five churches. He visited them on a red scrambler bike the bishop at Nakuru had given him. It was good motorbike, a Yamaha. Japanese. My father loved riding it. He practiced skids and jumps on the back roads because he thought a clergyman should not be seen stunt-riding. Of course, people did, but they never said to him. My father built St. John's. Before him, people sat on benches under trees. The church he made was sturdy and rendered in white concrete. The roof was red tin, trumpet vine climbed over it. In the season flowers would hang down outside the window. It was like being inside a garden. When I hear the story of Adam and Eve, that is how I think of Eden, a place among the flowers. Inside there were benches for the people, a lectern for the sermon and a high chair for when the bishop came to confirm children. Behind the altar rail was the holy table covered with a white cloth and an alcove in the wall for the cup and holy communion plate. We didn't have a font. We took people to the river and put them under. I and my mother sang in the choir. The services were long and, as I see them now, quite boring, but the music was wonderful. The women sang, the men played instruments. The best was played by a tall Luo, a teacher in the village school we called, rather blasphemously, Most High. It was a simple instrument: a piston ring from an old Peugeot engine which he hit with a heavy steel bolt. It made a great, ringing rhythm.

What was left over from the church went into the pastor's house. It had poured concrete floors and louvre windows, a separate kitchen and a good charcoal stove a parishioner who could weld had made from a diesel drum. We had electric light, two power sockets and a radio/cassette player, but no television. It was inviting the devil to dinner, my father told us. Kitchen, living room, our bedroom, my mother's bedroom, and my father's study. Five rooms. We were people of some distinction in Gichichi; for Kalenjin.

Gichichi was a thin, straggly sort of village; shops, school, post-office, matatu office, petrol station and mandazi shop up on the main road, with most of the houses set off the footpaths that followed the valley terraces. On one of them was our shamba, half a kilometer down the valley. The path to it went past the front door of the Ukerewe family. They had seven children who hated us. They threw dung or stones and called us see-what-we-thought-of-ourselves-Kalenjin and hated-of-God-Episcopalians. They were African Inland Church Kikuyu, and they had no respect for the discipline of the bishop.

If the church was my father's Eden, the shamba was my mother's. The air was cool in the valley and you could hear the river over the stones down below. We grew maize and gourds and some sugar-cane, which the local rummers bought from my father and he pretended not to know. Beans and chillis. Onions and potatoes. Two trees of finger bananas, though M'zee Kipchobe maintained that they sucked the life out of the soil. The maize grew right over my head, and I would run into the sugar-cane and pretend that two steps had taken me out of this world into another. There was always music there; the solar radio, or the women singing together when they helped each other turn the soil or hoe the weeds. I would sing with them, for I was considered good at harmonies. The shamba too had a place where the holy things were kept. Among the thick, winding tendrils of an old tree killed by strangling fig the women left little wooden figures gifts of money, Indian-trader jewelry and beer.

You are wondering, what about the Chaga? You've worked out from the dates that I was nine when the first package came down on Kilimanjaro. How could such tremendous events, a thing like another world taking over our own, have made so little impression on my life? It is easy, when it is no nearer to you than another world. We were not ignorant in Gichichi. We had seen the pictures from Kilimanjaro on the television, read the articles in the Nation about the thing that is like a coral reef and a rainforest that came out of the object from the sky. We had heard the discussions on the radio about how fast it was growing—fifty meters every day, it was ingrained on our minds—and what it might be and where it might come from. Every morning the vapor trails of the big UN jets scored our sky as they brought more men and machines to study it, but it was another world. It was not our world. Our world was church, home, shamba, school. Service on Sunday, Bible Study on Monday. Singing lessons, homework club. Sewing, weeding, stirring the ugali. Shooing the goats out of the maize. Playing with Little Egg and Grace and Ruth from next door in the compound: not too loud, Father's working. Once a week, the mobile bank. Once a fortnight, the mobile library. Mad little matatus dashing down, overtaking everything they could see, people hanging off every door and window. Big dirty country buses winding up the steep road like oxen. Gikombe, the town fool, if we could have afforded one, wrapped in dung-colored cloth sitting down in front of the country buses to stop them moving. Rains and hot seasons and cold fogs. People being born, people getting married, people running out on each other, or getting sick, or dying in accidents. Kilimanjaro, the Chaga? Another picture in a world where all pictures come from the same distance.

I was thirteen and just a woman when the Chaga came to my world and destroyed it. That night I was at Grace Muthiga's where she and I had a homework club. It was an excuse to listen to the radio. One of the great things about the United Nations taking over your country is the radio is very good. I would sing with it. They played the kind of music that wasn't approved of in our house.

We were listening to trip hop. Suddenly the record started to go all phasey, like the radio was tuning itself on and off the station. At first we thought the disc was slipping or something, then Grace got up to fiddle with the tuning button. That only made it worse. Grace's mother came in from the next room and said she couldn't get a picture on the battery television. It was full of wavy lines. Then we heard the first boom. It was far away and hollow and it rolled like thunder. Most nights up in the Highlands we get thunder. We know very well what it sounds like. This was something else. Boom! Again. Closer now. Voices outside, and lights. We took torches and went out to the voices. The road was full of people; men, women, children. There were torch beams weaving all over the place. Boom! Close now, loud enough to rattle the windows. All the people shone their torches straight up into the sky, like spears of light. Now the children were crying and I was afraid. Most High had the answer: "Sonic booms! There's something up there." As he said those words, we saw it. It was so slow.

That was the amazing thing about it. It was like a child drawing a chalk line across a board. It came in from the south east, across the hills east of Kiriani, straight as an arrow, a little to the south of us. The night was such as we often get in late May, clear after evening rains, and very full of stars. We all saw a glowing dot cut across the face of the stars. It seemed to float and dance, like illusions in the eye if you look into the sun. It left a line behind it like the trails of the big UN jets, only pure, glowing blue, drawn on the night. Double-boom now, so close and loud it hurt my ears. At that, one of the old women began wailing. The fear caught, and soon whole families were looking at the line of light in the sky with tears running down their faces, men as well as women. Many sat down and put their torches in their laps, not knowing what they should do. Some of the old people covered their heads with jackets, shawls, newspapers. Others saw what they were doing, and soon everyone was sitting on the ground with their heads covered. Not Most High. He stood looking up at the line of light as it cut his night in half. "Beautiful!" he said. "That I should see such things, with these own eyes!"

He stood watching until the object vanished in the dark of the mountains to the west. I saw its light reflected in his eyes. It took a long time to fade.

For a few moments after the thing went over, no one knew what to do. Everyone was scared, but they were relieved at the same time because, like the angel of death, it had passed over Gichichi. People were still crying, but tears of relief have a different sound. Someone got a radio from a house. Others fetched theirs, and soon we were all sitting in the middle of the road in the dark, grouped around our radios. An announcer interrupted the evening music show to bring a news flash. At twenty twenty eight a new biological package had struck in Central Province. At those words, a low keen went up from each group.

"Be quiet!" someone shouted, and there was quiet. Though the words would be terrible, they were better than the voices coming out of the dark.

The announcer said that the biological package had come down on the eastern slopes of the Nyandarua near to Tusha, a small Kikuyu village. Tusha was a name we knew. Some of us had relatives in Tusha. The country bus to Nyeri went through Tusha. From Gichichi to Tusha was twenty kilometers. There were cries. There were prayers. Most said nothing. But we all knew time had run out. In four years the Chaga had swallowed up Kilimanjaro, and Amboseli, and the border country of Namanga and was advancing up the A104 on Kajiado and Nairobi. We had ignored it and gone on with our lives, believing that when it finally came, we would know what to do. Now it had dropped out of the sky twenty kilometers north of us and said, Twenty kilometers, four hundred days: that's how long you've got to decide what you're going to do.

Then Jackson who ran the Peugeot Service Office stood up. He cocked his head to one side. He held up a finger. Everyone fell silent. He looked to the sky. "Listen!" I could hear nothing. He pointed to the south, and we all heard it: aircraft engines. Flashing lights lifted out of the dark tree-line on the far side of the valley. Behind it came others, then others, then ten, twenty, thirty, more. Helicopters swarmed over Gichichi like locusts. The sound of their engines filled the whole world. I wrapped my school shawl around my head and put my hands over my ears and yelled over the noise but it still felt like it would shatter my skull like a clay pot. Thirty-five helicopters: They flew so low their down-wash rattled our tin roofs and sent dust swirling up around our faces. Some of the teenagers cheered and waved their torches and white school shirts to the pilots. They cheered the helicopters on, right over the ridge. They cheered until the noise of their engines was lost among the night-insects. Where the Chaga goes, the United Nations comes close behind, like a dog after a bitch.

A few hours later the trucks came through. The grinding of engines as they toiled up the winding road woke all Gichichi. "It's three o'clock in the morning!" Mrs. Kuria shouted at the dusty white trucks with the blue symbol of UNECTA on the doors, but no one would sleep again. We lined the main road to watch them go through our village. I wonder what the drivers thought of all those faces and eyes suddenly appearing in their headlights as they rounded the bend. Some waved. The children waved back. They were still coming through as we went down to the shamba at dawn to milk the goats. They were a white snake coiling up and down the valley road as far as I could see. As they reached the top of the pass the low light from the east caught them and burned them to gold.

The trucks went up the road for two days. Then they stopped and the refugees started to come the other way, down the road. First the ones with the vehicles: matatus piled high with bedding and tools and animals, trucks with the family balanced in the back on top of all the things they had saved. A Toyota microbus, bursting with what looked like bolts of colored cloth but which were women, jammed in next to each other. Ancient cars, motorbikes and mopeds vanishing beneath sagging bales of possessions. It was a race of poverty; the rich ones with machines took the lead. After motors came animals; donkey carts and ox-wagons, pedal-rickshaws. Most came in the last wave, the ones on foot. They pushed handcarts laden with pots and bedding rolls and boxes lashed with twine, or dragged trolleys on ropes or shoved frightened-faced old women in wheelbarrows. They struggled their burdens down the steep valley road. Some broke free and bounced over the edge down across the terraces, strewing clothes and tools and cooking things over the fields. Last of all came hands and heads. These people carried their possessions on their heads and backs and children's shoulders.

My father opened the church to the refugees. There they could have rest, warm chai, some ugali, some beans. I helped stir the great pots of ugali over the open fire. The village doctor set up a treatment center. Most of the cases were for damaged feet and hands, and dehydrated children. Not everyone in Gichichi agreed with my father's charity. Some thought it would encourage the refugees to stay and take food from our mouths. The shopkeepers said he was ruining their trade by giving away what they should be selling. My father told them he was just trying to do what he thought Jesus would have done. They could not answer that, but I know he had another reason. He wanted to hear the refugee's stories. They would be his story, soon enough.

What about Tusha?

The package missed us by a couple of kilometers. It hit a place called Kombé;

two Kikuyu farms and some shit-caked cows. There was a big bang. Some of us from Tusha took a matatu to see what had happened to Kombé. They tell us there is nothing left. There they are, go, ask them.

This nothing, my brothers, what was it like? A hole?

No, it was something, but nothing we could recognize. The photographs? They only show the thing. They do not show how it happens. The houses, the fields, the fields and the track, they run like fat in a pan. We saw the soil itself melt and new things reach out of it like drowning men's fingers.

What kind of things?

We do not have the words to describe them. Things like you see in the television programs about the reefs on the coast, only the size of houses, and striped like zebras. Things like fists punching out of the ground, reaching up to the sky and opening like fingers. Things like fans, and springs, and balloons, and footballs.

So fast?

Oh yes. So fast that even as we watched, it took our matatu. It came up the tires and over the bumper and across the paintwork like a lizard up a wall and the whole thing came out in thousands of tiny yellow buds.

What did you do?

What do you think we did? We ran for our lives.

The people of Kombé?

When we brought back help from Tusha, we were stopped by helicopters. Soldiers, everywhere. Everyone must leave, this is a quarantine area. You have twenty four hours.

Twenty four hours!

Yes, they order you to pack up a life in twenty four hours. The Blue Berets brought in all these engineers who started building some great construction, all tracks and engines. The night was like day with welding torches. They plowed Kiyamba under with bulldozers to make a new airstrip. They were going to bring in jets there. And before they let us go they made everyone take medical tests. We lined up and went past these men in white coats and masks at tables.

Why?

I think they were testing to see if the Chaga-stuff had got into us.

What did they do, that you think that?

Pastor, some they would tap on the shoulder, just like this. Like Judas and the Lord, so gentle. Then a soldier would take them to the side.

What then?

I do not know, pastor. I have not seen them since. No one has.

These stories troubled my father greatly. They troubled the people he told them to, even Most High, who had been so thrilled by the coming of the alien to our land. They especially troubled the United Nations. Two days later a team came up from Nairobi in five army hummers. The first thing they did was tell my father and the doctor to close down their aid station. The official UNHCR refugee center was Muranga. No one could stay here in Gichichi, everyone must go.

In private they told my father that a man of his standing should not be sowing rumors and half truths in vulnerable communities. To make sure that we knew the real truth, UNECTA called a meeting in the church. Everyone packed onto the benches, even the Muslims. People stood all the way around the walls; others outside lifted out the louvres to listen in at the windows. My father sat with the doctor and our local chief at a table. With them was a government man, a white soldier and an Asian woman in civilian dress who looked scared. She was a scientist, a xenologist. She did most of the talking; the government man from Nairobi twirled his pencil between his fingers and tapped it on the table until he broke the point. The soldier, a French general with experience of humanitarian crises, sat motionless.

The xenologist told us that the Chaga was humanity's first contact with life from beyond the Earth. The nature of this contact was unclear; it did not follow any of the communication programs we had predicted. This contact was the physical transformation of our native landscape and vegetation. But what was in the package was not seeds and spores. The things that had consumed Kombé and were now consuming Tusha were more like tiny machines, breaking down the things of this world to pieces and rebuilding them in strange new forms. The Chaga responded to stimuli and adapted to counterattacks on itself. UNECTA had tried fire, poison, radioactive dusting, genetically modified diseases. Each had been quickly routed by the Chaga. However, it was not apparent if it was intelligent, or the tool of an as-yet unseen intelligence.

"And Gichichi?" Ismail the barber asked.

The French general spoke now.

"You will all be evacuated in plenty of time."

"But what if we do not want to be evacuated?" Most High asked. "What if we decide we want to stay here and take our chances with the Chaga?"

"You will all be evacuated," the general said again.

"This is our village, this is our country. Who are you to tell us what we must do in our own country?" Most High was indignant now. We all applauded, even my father up there with the UNECTA people. The Nairobi political looked vexed.

"UNECTA, UNHCR and the UN East Africa Protection Force operate with the informed consent of the Kenyan government. The Chaga has been deemed a threat to human life. We're doing this for your own good."

Most High drove on. "A threat? Who 'deems' it so? UNECTA? An organization that is eighty percent funded by the United States of America? I have heard different, that it doesn't harm people or animals. There are people living inside the Chaga; it's true, isn't it?"

The politician looked at the French general, who shrugged. The Asian scientist answered.

"Officially, we have no data."

Then my father stood up and cut her short.

"What about the people who are being taken away?"

"I don't know anything. . . ." the UNECTA scientist began but my father would not be stopped.

"What about the people from Kombé? What are these tests you are carrying out?"

The woman scientist looked flustered. The French general spoke.

"I'm a soldier, not a scientist. I've served in Kosovo and Iraq and East Timor.

I can only answer your questions as a soldier. On the fourteenth of June next year, it will come down that road. At about seven thirty in the evening, it will come through this church. By Tuesday night, there will be no sign that a place called Gichichi ever existed."

And that was the end of the meeting. As the UNECTA people left the church, the Christians of Gichichi crowded around my father. What should they believe? Was Jesus come again, or was it anti-Christ? These aliens, were they angels, or fallen creatures like ourselves? Did they know Jesus? What was God's plan in this? Question after question after question.

My father's voice was tired and thin and driven, like a leopard harried by beaters toward guns. Like that leopard, he turned on his hunters.

"I don't know!" he shouted. "You think I have answers to all these things? No. I have no answers. I have no authority to speak on these things. No one does. Why are you asking these silly silly questions? Do you think a country pastor has the answers that will stop the Chaga in its tracks and drive it back where it came from? No. I am making them up as I go along, like everyone else."

For a moment the whole congregation was silent. I remember feeling that I must die from embarrassment. My mother touched my father's arm. He had been shaking. He excused himself to his people. They stood back to let us out of the church. We stopped on the lintel, amazed. A rapture had indeed come. All the refugees were gone from the church compound. Their goods, their bundles, their carts and animals. Even their excrement had been swept away.

As we walked back to the house, I saw the woman scientist brush past Most High as she went to the UNECTA hummer. I heard her whisper, "About the people. It's true. But they're changed."

"How?" Most High asked but the door was closed. Two blue berets lifted mad Gikombe from in front of the hummer and it drove off slowly through the throng of people. I remembered that the UNECTA woman looked frightened.

That afternoon my father rode off on the red Yamaha and did not come back for almost a week.

I learned something about my father's faith that day. It was that it was strong in the small, local questions because it was weak in the great ones. It believed in singing and teaching the people and the disciplines of personal prayer and meditation, because you could see them in the lives of others. In the big beliefs, the ones you could not see, it fell.

That meeting was the wound through which Gichichi slowly bled to death. "This is our village, this is our country," Most High had declared, but before the end of the week the first family had tied their things onto the back of their pickup and joined the flow of refugees down the road to the south. After that a week did not pass that someone from our village would not close their doors a last time and leave Gichichi. The abandoned homes soon went to ruin. Water got in, roofs collapsed, then rude boys set fire to them. The dead houses were like empty skulls. Dogs fell into toilet pits and drowned. One day when we went down to the shamba there were no names and stones from the Ukerewe house. Within a month its windows were empty, smoke-stained sockets.

With no one to tend them, the shambas went to wild and weeds. Goats and cows grazed where they would, the terrace walls crumbled, the rains washed the soil down the valley in great red tears. Fields that had fed families for generations vanished in a night. No one cared for the women's tree anymore, to give the images their cups of beer. Hope stopped working in Gichichi. Always in the minds of the ones who remained was the day when we would look up the road and see the spines and fans and twisted spires of the Chaga standing along the ridge-line like warriors.

I remember the morning I was woken by the sound of voices from the Muthiga house. Men's voices, speaking softly so as not to waken anyone, for it was still dark, but they woke me. I put on my things and went out into the compound. Grace and Ruth were carrying cardboard boxes from the house, their father and a couple of other men from the village were loading them onto a Nissan pick-up. They had started early, and the pick-up was well laden. The children were gathering up the last few things.

"Ah, Tendeléo," Mr. Muthiga said, sadly. "We had hoped to get away before anyone was around."

"Can I talk to Grace?" I asked.

I did not talk to her. I shouted at her. I would be all alone when she went. I would be abandoned. She asked me a question. She said, "You say we must not go. Tell me, Tendeléo, why must you stay?"

I did not have an answer to that. I had always presumed that it was because a pastor must stay with his people, but the bishop had made several offers to my father to relocate us to a new parish in Eldoret.

Grace and her family left as it was getting light. Their red tail lights swung into the slow stream of refugees. I heard the horn hooting to warn stragglers and animals all the way down the valley. I tried to keep the house good and safe but two weeks later a gang of rude boys from another village broke in, took what they could and burned the rest. They were a new thing in what the radio called the "sub-terminum," gangs of raiders and looters stripping the corpses of the dead towns.

"Vultures, is what they are," my mother said.

Grace's question was a dark parting gift to me. The more I thought about it, the more I became convinced that I must see this thing that had forced such decisions on us. The television and newspaper pictures were not enough. I had to see it with my own eyes. I had to look at its face and ask it its reasons. Little Egg became my lieutenant. We slipped money from the collection plate, and we gathered up secret bundles of food. A schoolday was the best to go. We did not go straight up the road, where we would have been noticed. We caught a matatu to Kinangop in the Nyandarua valley where nobody knew us. There was still a lively traffic; the matatu was full of country people with goods to sell and chickens tied together by the feet stowed under the bench. We sat in the back and ate nuts from a paper cone folded from a page of the Bible. Everywhere were dirty white United Nations vehicles. One by one the people got out and were not replaced. By Ndunyu there was only me and Little Egg, jolting around in the back of the car.

The driver's mate turned around and said, "So, where for, girls?"

I said, "We want to look at the Chaga."

"Sure, won't the Chaga be coming to look at you soon enough?"

"Can you take us there?" I showed him Church shillings.

"It would take a lot more than that." He talked to the driver a moment. "We can drop you at Njeru. You can walk from there, it's under seven kilometers."

Njeru was what awaited Gichichi, when only the weak and poor and mad remained. I was glad to leave it. The road to the Chaga was easy to find, it was the direction no one else was going in. We set off up the red dirt road toward the mountains. We must have looked very strange, two girls walking through a ruined land with their lunches wrapped in kangas. If anyone had been there to watch.

The soldiers caught us within two kilometers of Njeru. I had heard the sound of their engine for some minutes, behind us. It was a big eight wheeled troop carrier of the South African army.

The officer was angry, but I think a little impressed. What did we think we were doing? There were vultures everywhere. Only last week an entire bus had been massacred, five kilometers from here. Not one escaped alive. Two girls alone, they would rob us and rape us, hang us up by our heels and cut our throats like pigs. All the time he was preaching, a soldier in the turret swept the countryside with a big heavy machine gun.

"So, what the hell are you doing here?"

I told him. He went to talk on the radio. When he came back, he said, "In the back."

The carrier was horribly hot and smelled of men and guns and diesel. When the door clanged shut on us I thought we were going to suffocate.

"Where are you taking us?" I asked, afraid.

"You came to see the Chaga," the commander said. We ate our lunch meekly and tried not to stare at the soldiers. They gave us water from their canteens and tried to make us laugh. The ride was short but uncomfortable. The door clanged open. The officer helped me out and I almost fell over with shock.

I stood in a hillside clearing. Around me were tree stumps, fresh cut, sticky with sap. From behind came the noise of chain saws. The clearing was full of military vehicles and tents. People hurried every way. Most of them were white. At the center of this activity was what I can only call a city on wheels. I had not yet been to Nairobi, but I knew it from photographs, a forest of beautiful towers rising out of a circle of townships. That was how the base seemed to me when I first saw it. Looking closer, I saw that the buildings were portable cabins stacked up on big tracked flat-beds, like the heavy log-carriers up in Eldoret. The tractors and towers were joined together with walkways and loops of cable. I saw people running along the high walkways. I would not have done that, not for a million shillings.

I tell you my first impressions, of a beautiful white city—and you may laugh because you know it was only a UNECTA mobile base—that they put together as fast and cheap as they could. But there is a truth here; seeing is magical. Looking kills. The longer I looked, the more the magic faded.

The air in the clearing smelled as badly of diesel smoke as it had in the troop carrier. Everywhere was engine-noise. A path had been slashed through the forest, as if the base had come down it. I looked at the tracks. The big cog wheels were turning. The base was moving, slowly and heavily, like the hands of a clock, creaking backward on its tracks in pace with the advance of the Chaga. Little Egg took my hand. I think my mouth must have been open in wonder for some time.

"Come on then," said the officer. He was smiling now. "You wanted to see the Chaga."

He gave us over to a tall American man with red hair and a red beard and blue eyes. His name was Byron and he spoke such bad Swahili that he did not understand when Little Egg said to me, "he looks like a vampire."

"I speak English," I told him and he looked relieved.

He took us through the tractors to the tower in the middle, the tallest. It was painted white, with the word UNECTA big in blue on the side, and beneath it, the name, Nyandarua Station. We got into a small metal cage. Byron closed the door and pressed a button. The cage went straight up the side of the building. I tell you this, that freight elevator was more frightening than any stories about murdering gangs of vultures. I gripped the handrail and closed my eyes. I could feel the whole base swaying below me.

"Open your eyes," Byron said. "You wouldn't want to come all this way and miss it."

As we rose over the tops of the trees the land opened before me. Nyandarua Station was moving down the eastern slopes of the Aberdare range: the Chaga was spread before me like a wedding kanga laid out on a bed.

It was as though someone had cut a series of circles of colored paper and let them fall on the side of the mountains. The Chaga followed the ridges and the valleys, but that was all it had to do with our geography. It was completely something else. The colors were so bright and silly I almost laughed: purples, oranges, lots of pink and deep red. Veins of bright yellow. Real things, living things were not these colors. This was a Hollywood trick, done with computers for a film. I guessed we were a kilometer from the edge. It was not a very big Chaga, not like the Kilimanjaro Chaga that had swallowed Moshi and Arusha and all the big Tanzanian towns at the foot of the mountain and was now halfway to Nairobi. Byron said this Chaga was about five kilometers across and beginning to show the classic form, a series of circles. I tried to make out the details. I thought details would make it real to me. I saw jumbles of reef-stuff the color of wiring. I saw a wall of dark crimson trees rise straight for a tremendous height. The trunks were as straight and smooth as spears. The leaves joined together like umbrellas. Beyond them, I saw things like icebergs tilted at an angle, things like open hands, praying to the sky, things like oil refineries made out of fungus, things like brains and fans and domes and footballs. Things like other things. Nothing that seemed a thing in itself. And all this was reaching toward me. But, I realized, it would never catch me. Not while I remained here, on this building that was retreating from it down the foothills of the Aberdares, fifty meters every day.

We were close to the top of the building. The cage swayed in the wind. I felt sick and scared and grabbed the rail and that was when it became real for me. I caught the scent of the Chaga on the wind. False things have no scent. The Chaga smelled of cinnamon and sweat and soil new turned up. It smelled of rotting fruit and diesel and concrete after rain. It smelled like my mother when she had The

Visit. It smelled like the milk that babies spit out of their mouths. It smelled like televisions and the stuff the Barber Under the Tree put on my father's hair and the women's holy place in the shamba. With each of these came a memory of Gichichi and my life and people. The scent stirred the things I had recently learned as a woman. The Chaga became real for me there, and I understood that it would eat my world.

While I was standing, putting all these things that were and would be into circles within circles inside my head, a white man in faded jeans and Timberland boots rushed out of a sliding door onto the elevator.

"Byron," he said, then noticed that there were two little Kenyan girls there with him. "Who're these?"

"I'm Tendeléo and this is my sister," I said. "We call her Little Egg. We've come to see the Chaga."

This answer seemed to please him.

"I'm called Shepard." He shook our hands. He also was American. "I'm a Peripatetic Executive Director. That means I rush around the world finding solutions to the Chaga."

"And have you?"

For a moment he was taken aback, and I felt bold and rude. Then he said, "come on, let's see."

"Shepard," Byron the vampire said. "It'll wait."

He took us in to the base. In one room were more white people than I had seen in the whole of my life. Each desk had a computer but the people — most of them were men dressed very badly in shorts, with beards — did not use them. They preferred to sit on each other's desks and talk very fast with much gesturing.

"Are African people not allowed in here?" I asked.

The man Shepard laughed. Everything I said that tour he treated as if it had come from the lips of a wise old m'zee. He took us down into the Projection Room where computers drew huge plans on circular tables: of the Chaga now, the Chaga in five years time and the Chaga when it met with its brother from the south and both of them swallowed Nairobi like two old men arguing over a stick of sugar cane.

"And after Nairobi is gone?" I asked. The maps showed the names of all the old towns and villages, under the Chaga. Of course. The names do not change. I reached out to touch the place that Gichichi would become.

"We can't project that far," he said. But I was thinking of an entire city, vanished beneath the bright colors of the Chaga like dirt trodden into carpet. All those lives and histories and stories. I realized that some names can be lost, the names of big things, like cities, and nations, and histories.

Next we went down several flights of steep steel stairs to the "lab levels." Here samples taken from the Chaga were stored inside sealed environments. A test tube might hold a bouquet of delicate fungi, a cylindrical jar a fistful of blue spongy fingers, a tank a square meter of Chaga, growing up the walls and across the ceiling. Some of the containers were so big people could walk around inside. They were dressed in bulky white suits that covered every part of them and were connected to the wall with pipes and tubes so that it was hard to tell where they ended and alien Chaga began. The weird striped and patterned leaves looked more natural than the UNECTA people in their white suits. The alien growing things were at least in their right world.

"Everything has to be isolated." Mr. Shepard said.

"Is that because even out here, it will start to attack and grow?" I asked.

"You got it."

"But I heard it doesn't attack people or animals," I said.

"Where did you hear that?" this man Shepard asked.

"My father told me," I said mildly.

We went on down to Terrestrial Cartography, which was video-pictures the size of a wall of the world seen looking down from satellites. It is a view that is familiar to everyone of our years, though there were people of my parents' generation who laughed when they heard that the world is a ball, with no string to hold it up. I looked for a long time — it is the one thing that does not pale for looking — before I saw that the face of the world was scarred, like a Giriama woman's. Beneath the clouds, South America and South Asia and mother Africa were spotted with dots of lighter color than the brown-green land. Some were large, some were specks, all were precise circles. One, on the eastern side of Africa, identified this disease of continents to me. Chagas. For the first time I understood that this was not a Kenyan thing, not even an African thing, but a whole world thing.

"They are all in the south," I said. "There is not one in the north."

"None of the biological packages have seeded in the northern hemisphere. This is what makes us believe that there are limits to the Chaga. That it won't cover our whole world, pole to pole. That it might confine itself only to the southern hemisphere."

"Why do you think that?"

"No reason at all."

"You just hope."

"Yeah. We hope."

"Mr. Shepard," I said. "Why should the Chaga take away our lands here in the south and leave you rich people in the north untouched? It does not seem fair."

"The universe is not fair, kid. Which you probably know better than me."

We went down then to Stellar Cartography, another dark room, with walls full of stars. They formed a belt around the middle of the room, in places so dense that individual stars blurred into masses of solid white.

"This is the Silver River," I said. I had seen this on Grace's family's television, which they had taken with them.

"Silver river. It is that. Good name."

"Where are we?" I asked.

Shepard went over to the wall near the door and touched a small star down near his waist. It had a red circle around it. Otherwise I do not think even he could have picked it out of all the other small white stars. I did not like it that our sun was so small and common. I asked, "And where are they from?"

The UNECTA man drew a line with his finger along the wall. He walked down one side of the room, halfway along the other, before he stopped. His finger stopped in a swirl of rainbow colors, like a flame.

"Rho Ophiuchi. It's just a name, it doesn't matter. What's important is that it's a long long way from us . . . so far it takes light—and that's as fast as anything can go—eight hundred years to get there, and it's not a planet, or even a star. It's what we call a nebula, a huge cloud of glowing gas."

"How can people live in a cloud?" I asked. "Are they angels?"

The man laughed at that.

"Not people," he said. "Not angels either. Machines. But not like you or I think of machines. Machines more like living things, and very very much smaller. Smaller even than the smallest cell in your body. Machines the size of chains of atoms, that can move other atoms around and so build copies of themselves, or copies of anything else they want. And we think those gas clouds are trillions upon trillions of those tiny, living machines."

"Not plants and animals," I said.

"Not plants and animals, no."

"I have not heard this theory before." It was huge and thrilling, but like the sun, it hurt if you looked at it too closely. I looked again at the swirl of color, colored like the Chaga scars on Earth's face, and back at the little dot by the door that was my light and heat. Compared to the rest of the room, they both looked very small. "Why should things like this, from so far away, want to come to my Kenya?"

"That's indeed the question."

That was all of the science that the UNECTA man was allowed to show us, so he took us down through the areas where people lived and ate and slept, where they watched television and films and drank alcohol and coffee, the places where they exercised, which they liked to do a lot, in immodest costumes. The corridors were full of them, immature and loosely put together, like leggy puppies.

"This place stinks of wazungu," Little Egg said, not thinking that maybe this m'zungu knew more Swahili than the other one. Mr. Shepard smiled.

"Mr. Shepard," I said. "You still haven't answered my question."

He looked puzzled a moment, then remembered.

"Solutions. Oh yes. Well, what do you think?"

Several questions came into my head but none as good, or important to me, as the one I did ask.

"I suppose the only question that matters, really, is can people live in the Chaga?"

Shepard pushed open a door and we were on a metal platform just above one of the big track sets.

"That, my friend, is the one question we aren't even allowed to consider," Shepard said as he escorted us onto a staircase.

The tour was over. We had seen the Chaga. We had seen our world and our future and our place among the stars; things too big for country church children, but which even they must consider, for unlike most of the wazungu here, they would have to find answers.

Down on the red dirt with the diesel stink and roar of chain-saws, we thanked Dr. Shepard. He seemed touched. He was clearly a person of power in this place. A word, and there was a UNECTA Landcruiser to take us home. We were so filled up with what we had seen that we did not think to tell the driver to let us off at the next village down so we could walk. Instead we went landcruising right up the main road, past Haran's shop and the Peugeot Service Station and all the Men Who Read Newspapers under the trees.

Then we faced my mother and father. It was bad. My father took me into his study. I stood. He sat. He took his Kalenjin Bible, that the Bishop gave him on his ordination so that he might always have God's word in his own tongue, and set it on the desk between himself and me. He told me that I had deceived my mother and him, that I had led Little Egg astray, that I had lied, that I had stolen, not God's money, for God had no need of money, but the money that people I saw every day, people I sang and prayed next to every Sunday, gave in their faith. He said all this in a very straightforward, very calm way, without ever raising his voice. I wanted to tell him all the things I said seen, offer them in trade, yes, I have cheated, I have lied, I have stolen from the Christians of Gichichi, but I have learned. I have seen. I have seen our sun lost among a million other suns. I have seen this world, that God is supposed to have made most special of all worlds, so small it cannot even be seen. I have seen men, that God is supposed to have loved so much that he died for their evils, try to understand living machines, each smaller than the smallest living thing, but together, so huge it takes light years to cross their community. I know how different things are from what we believe, I wanted to say, but I said nothing, for my father did an unbelievable thing. He stood up. Without sign or word or any display of strength, he hit me across the face. I fell to the ground, more from the unexpectedness than the hurt. Then he did another unbelievable thing. He sat down. He put his head in his hand. He began to cry. Now I was very scared, and I ran to my mother.

"He is a frightened man," she said. "Frightened men often strike out at the thing they fear."

"He has his church, he has his collar, he has his Bible, what can frighten him?"

"You," she said. This answer was as stunning as my father hitting me. My mother asked me if I remembered the time, after the argument outside the church, when my father had disappeared on the red Yamaha for a week. I said I did, yes.

"He went down south, to Nairobi, and beyond. He went to look at the thing he feared, and he saw that, with all his faith, he could not beat the Chaga."

My father stayed in his study a long time. Then he came to me and went down on his knees and asked me to forgive him. It was a Biblical principle, he said. Do not let the sun go down on your anger. But though Bible principles lived, my father died a little to me that day. This is life: a series of dyings and being born into new things and understandings.

Life by life, Gichichi died too. There were only twenty families left on the morning when the spines of the alien coral finally reached over the treetops up on the pass. Soon after dawn the UNECTA trucks arrived. They were dirty old Sudanese Army things, third hand Russian, badly painted and billowing black smoke. When we saw the black soldiers get out we were alarmed because we had heard bad things about Africans at the hands of other Africans. I did not trust their officer; he was too thin and had an odd hollow on the side of his shaved head, like a crater on the moon. We gathered in the open space in front of the church with our things piled around us. Ours came to twelve bundles wrapped up in kangas. I took the radio and a clatter of pots. My father's books were tied with string and balanced on the petrol tank of his red scrambler.

The moon-headed officer waved and the first truck backed up and let down its tail. A soldier jumped out, set up a folding beach-chair by the tail-gate and sat with a clip-board and a pencil. First went the Kurias, who had been strong in the church. They threw their children up into the truck, then passed up their bundles of belongings. The soldier in the beach-chair watched for a time, then shook his head.

"Too much, too much," he said in bad Swahili. "You must leave something."

Mr. Kuria frowned, measuring all the space in the back of the truck with his eyes. He lifted off a bundle of clothes.

"No no no," the soldier said, and stood up and tapped their television with his pencil. Another soldier came and took it out of Mr. Kuria's arms to a truck at the side of the road, the tithe truck.

"Now you get on," the soldier said, and made a check on his clip-board.

It was as bold as that. Wide-open crime under the blue sky. No one to see. No one to care. No one to say a word.

Our family's tax was the motorbike. My father's face had gone tight with anger and offense to God's laws, but he gave it up without a whisper. The officer wheeled it away to a group of soldiers squatting on their heels by a smudge-fire. They were very pleased with it, poking and teasing its engine with their long fingers. Every time since that I have heard a Yamaha engine I have looked to see if it is a red scrambler, and what thief is riding it.

"On, on," said the tithe-collector.

"My church," my father said and jumped off the truck. Immediately there were a dozen Kalashnikovs pointing at him. He raised his hands, then looked back at us.

"Tendeléo, you should see this."

The officer nodded. The guns were put down and I jumped to the ground. I walked with my father to the church. We proceeded up the aisle. The prayer books were on the bench seats, the woven kneelers set square in front of the pews. We went into the little vestry, where I had stolen the money from the collection. There were other dark secrets here. My father took a battered red petrol can from his robing cupboard and carried it to the communion table. He took the chalice, offered it to God, then filled it with petrol from the can. He turned to face the holy table.

"The blood of Christ keep you in eternal life," he said, raising the cup high. The he poured it out onto the white altar cloth. A gesture too fast for me to see; he struck fire. There was an explosion of yellow flame. I cried out. I thought my father had gone up in the gush of fire. He turned to me. Flames billowed behind him.

"Now do you understand?" he said.

I did. Sometimes it is better to destroy a thing you love than have it taken from you and made alien. Smoke was pouring from under the roof by the time we climbed back onto the truck. The Sudanese soldiers were only interested in that it was fire, and destruction excites soldiers. Ours was the church of an alien god.

Old Gikombe, too old and stupid to run away, did his "sitting in front of the trucks" trick. Every time the soldiers moved him, he scuttled back to his place. He did it once too often. The truck behind us had started to roll, and the driver did not see the dirty, rag-wrapped thing dart in under his wing. With a cry, Gikombe fell under the wheels and was crushed.

A wind from off the Chaga carried the smoke from the burning church over us as we went down the valley road. The communion at Gichichi was broken.

I think time changes everything into its opposite. Youth into age, innocence into experience, certainty into uncertainty. Life into death. Long before the end, time was changing Nairobi into the Chaga. Ten million people were crowded into the shanties that ringed the towers of downtown. Every hour of every day, more came. They came from north and south, from Rift Valley and Central Province, from Ilbisil and Naivasha, from Makindu and Gichichi.

Once Nairobi was a fine city. Now it was a refugee camp. Once it had great green parks. Now they were trampled dust between packing-case homes. The trees had all been hacked down for firewood. Villages grew up on road roundabouts, like castaways on coral islands, and in the football stadiums and sports grounds. Armed patrols daily cleared squatters from the two airport runways. The railway had been abandoned, cut south and north. Ten thousand people now lived in abandoned carriages and train sheds and between the tracks. The National Park was a dust bowl, ravaged for fuel and building material, its wildlife fled or slaughtered for food. Nairobi air was a smog of wood smoke, diesel and sewage. The slums spread for twenty kilometers on every side. It was an hour's walk to fetch water, and that was stinking and filthy. Like the Chaga, the shanties grew, hour by hour, family by family. String up a few plastic sheets here, shove together some cardboard boxes there, set up home where a matatu dies, pile some stolen bricks and sacking and tin. City and Chaga reached out to each other, and came to resemble each other.

I remember very little of those first days in Nairobi. It was too much, too fast—it numbed my sense of reality. The men who took our names, the squatting people watching us as we walked up the rows of white tents looking for our number, were things done to us that we went along with without thinking. Most of the time I had that high-pitched sound in my ear when you want to cry but cannot.

Here is an irony: we came from St. John's, we went to St. John's. It was a new camp, in the south close by the main airport. One eight three two. One number, one tent, one oil lamp, one plastic water bucket, one rice scoop. Every hundred tents there was a water pipe. Every hundred tents there was a shit pit. A river of sewage ran past our door. The stench would have stopped us sleeping, had the cold not done that first. The tent was thin and cheap and gave no protection from the night. We huddled together under blankets. No one wanted to be the first to cry, so no one did. Between the big aircraft and people crying and fighting, there was no quiet, ever. The first night, I heard shots. I had never heard them before but I knew exactly what they were.

In this St. John's we were no longer people of consequence. We were no longer anything. We were one eight three two. My father's collar earned no respect. The first day he went to the pipe for water he was beaten by young men, who stole his plastic water pail. The collar was a symbol of God's treachery. My father stopped wearing his collar; soon after, he stopped going out at all. He sat in the back room listening to the radio and looking at his books, which were still in their tied-up bundles. St. John's destroyed the rest of the things that had bound his life together. I think that if we had not been rescued, he would have gone under. In a place like St. John's, that means you die. When you went to the food truck you saw the ones on the way to death, sitting in front of their tents, holding their toes, rocking, looking at the soil.

We had been fifteen days in the camp—I kept a tally on the tent wall with a burned-out match—when we heard the vehicle pull up and the voice call out, "Jonathan Bi. Does anyone know Pastor Jonathan Bi?" I do not think my father could have looked anymore surprised if Jesus had called his name. Our savior was the Pastor Stephen Elezeke, who ran the Church Army Centre on Jogoo Road. He and my father had been in theological college together; they had been great footballing friends. My father was godfather to Pastor Elezeke's children; Pastor Elezeke, it seemed, was my godfather. He piled us all in the back of a white Nissan minibus with Praise Him on the Trumpet written on one side and Praise Him with the Psaltery and Harp, rather squashed up, on the other. He drove off hooting at the crowds of young men, who looked angrily at church men in a church van. He explained that he had found us through the net. The big churches were flagging certain clergy names. Bi was one of them.

So we came to Jogoo Road. Church Army had once been an old, pre-Independence teaching center with a modern, two-level accommodation block. These had overflowed long ago; now every open space was crowded with tents and wooden shanties. We had two rooms beside the metal working shop. They were comfortable but cramped, and when the metal workers started, noisy. There was no privacy.

The heart of Church Army was a little white chapel, shaped like a drum, with a thatched roof. The tents and lean-tos crowded close to the chapel but left a respectful distance. It was sacred. Many went there to pray. Many went to cry away from others, where it would not infect them like dirty water. I often saw my father go into the chapel. I thought about listening at the door to hear if he was praying or crying, but I did not. Whatever he looked for there, it did not seem to make him a whole man again.

My mother tried to make Jogoo Road Gichichi. Behind the accommodation block was a field of dry grass with an open drain running down the far side. Beyond the drain was a fence and a road, then the Jogoo Road market with its name painted on its rusting tin roof, then the shanties began again. But this field was untouched and open. My mother joined a group of women who wanted to turn the field into shambas. Pastor Elezeke agreed and they made mattocks in the workshops from bits of old car, broke up the soil and planted maize and cane. That summer we watched the crops grow as the shanties crowded in around the Jogoo Road market, and stifled it, and took it apart for roofs and walls. But they never touched the shambas. It was as if they were protected. The women hoed and sang to the radio and laughed and talked women-talk, and Little Egg and the Chole girls chased enormous sewer rats with sticks. One day I saw little cups of beer and dishes of maize and salt in a corner of the field and understood how it was protected.

My mother pretended it was Gichichi but I could see it was not. In Gichichi, the men did not stand by the fence wire and stare so nakedly. In Gichichi the helicopter gunships did not wheel overhead like vultures. In Gichichi the brightly painted matatus that roared up and down did not have heavy machine guns bolted to the roof and boys in sports fashion in the back looking at everything as if they owned it. They were a new thing in Nairobi, these gun-gangs; the Tacticals. Men, usually young, organized into gangs, with vehicles and guns, dressed in anything they could make a uniform. Some were as young as twelve. They gave themselves names like the Black Simbas and the Black Rhinos and the Ebonettes and the United Christian Front and the Black Taliban. They liked the word black. They thought it sounded threatening. These Tacticals had as many philosophies and beliefs as names, but they all owned territory, patrolled their streets and told their people they were the law. They enforced their law with kneecappings and burning car tires, they defended their streets with AK47s. We all knew that when the Chaga came, they would fight like hyenas over the corpse of Nairobi. The Soca Boys was our local army. They wore sports fashion and knee-length Manager's coats and had football team logos painted in the sides of their picknis, as the armed matatus were called. On their banners they had a black-and-white patterned ball on a green field. Despite their name, it was not a football. It was a buckyball, a carbon fullerene molecule, the half-living, half-machine building-brick of the Chaga. Their leader, a rat-faced boy in a Manchester United coat and shades that kept sliding down his nose, did not like Christians, so on Sundays he would send his picknis up and down Jogoo Road, roaring their engines and shooting into the air, but because they could.

The Church Army had its own plans for the coming time of changes. A few nights later, as I went to the choo, I overheard Pastor Elezeke and my father talking in the Pastor's study. I put my torch out and listened at the louvres.

"We need people like you, Jonathan," Elezeke was saying. "It is a work of God, I think. We have a chance to build a true Christian society."

"You cannot be certain."

"There are Tacticals . . ."

"They are filth. They are vultures."

"Hear me out, Jonathan. Some of them go into the Chaga. They bring things out—for all their quarantine, there are things the Americans want very much from the Chaga. It is different from what we are told is in there. Very very different. Plants that are like machines, that generate electricity, clean water, fabric, shelter, medicines. Knowledge. There are devices, the size of this thumb, that transmit information directly into the brain. And more; there are people living in there, not like primitives, not, forgive me, like refugees. It shapes itself to them, they have learned to make it work for them. There are whole towns—towns, I tell you—down there under Kilimanjaro. A great society is rising."

"It shapes itself to them," my father said. "And it shapes them to itself."

There was a pause.

"Yes. That is true. Different ways of being human."

"I cannot help you with this, my brother."

"Will you tell me why?"

"I will," my father said, so softly I had to press close to the window to hear. "Because I am afraid, Stephen. The Chaga has taken everything from me, but that is still not enough for it. It will only be satisfied when it has taken me, and changed me, and made me alien to myself."

"Your faith, Jonathan. What about your faith?"

"It took that first of all."

"Ah," Pastor Elezeke sighed. Then, after a time, "You understand you are always welcome here?"

"Yes, I do. Thank you, but I cannot help you."

That same night I went to the white chapel—my first and last time—to force issues with God. It was a very beautiful building, with a curving inner wall that made you walk halfway around the inside before you could enter. I suppose you could say it was spiritual, but the cross above the table angered me. It was straight and true and did not care for anyone or anything. I sat glaring at it some time before I found the courage to say, "You say you are the answer."

I am the answer, said the cross.

"My father is destroyed by fear. Fear of the Chaga, fear of the future, fear of death, fear of living. What is your answer?"

I am the answer.

"We are refugees, we live on wazungu's charity, my mother hoes corn, my sister roasts it at the roadside; tell me your answer."

I am the answer.

"An alien life has taken everything we ever owned. Even now, it wants more, and nothing can stop it. Tell me, what is your answer?"

I am the answer.

"You tell me you are the answer to every human need and question, but what does that mean? What is the answer to your answer?"

I am the answer, the silent, hanging cross said.

"That is no answer!" I screamed at the cross. "You do not even understand the questions, how can you be the answer? What power do you have? None. You can do nothing! They need me, not you. I am going to do what you can't."

I did not run from the chapel. You do not run from gods you no longer believe in. I walked, and took no notice of the people who stared at me.

The next morning, I went into Nairobi to get a job. To save money I went on foot. There were men everywhere, walking with friends, sitting by the road-side selling sheet metal charcoal burners or battery lamps, or making things from scrap metal and old tires, squatting together outside their huts with their hands draped over their knees. There must have been women, but they kept themselves hidden. I did not like the way the men worked me over with their eyes. They had shanty-town eyes, that see only what they can use in a thing. I must have appeared too poor to rob and too hungry to sexually harass, but I did not feel safe until the downtown towers rose around me and the vehicles on the streets were diesel-stained green and yellow buses and quick white UN cars.

I went first to the back door of one of the big tourist hotels.

"I can peel and clean and serve people," I said to an undercook in dirty whites. "I work hard and I am honest. My father is a pastor."

"You and ten million others," the cook said. "Get out of here."

Then I went to the CNN building. It was a big, bold idea. I slipped in behind a motorbike courier and went up to a good-looking Luo on the desk.

"I'm looking for work," I said. "Any work, I can do anything. I can make chai, I can photocopy, I can do basic accounts. I speak good English and a little French. I'm a fast learner."

"No work here today," the Luo on the desk said. "Or any other day. Learn that, fast."

I went to the Asian shops along Moi Avenue.

"Work?" the shopkeepers said. "We can't even sell enough to keep ourselves, let alone some up-country refugee."

I went to the wholesalers on Kimathi Street and the City Market and the stall traders and I got the same answer from each of them: no economy, no market, no work. I tried the street hawkers, selling liquidated stock from tarpaulins on the pavement, but their bad mouths and lewdness sickened me. I walked the five kilometers along Uhuru Highway to the UN East Africa Headquarters on Chiromo Road. The soldier on the gate would not even look at me. Cars and hummers he could see. His own people, he could not. After an hour I went away.

I took a wrong turn on the way back and ended up in a district I did not know, of dirty-looking two-story buildings that once held shops, now burned out or shuttered with heavy steel. Cables dipped across the street, loop upon loop upon loop, sagging and heavy. I could hear voices but see no one around. The voices came from an alley behind a row of shops. An entire district was crammed into this alley. Not even in St. John's camp have I seen so many people in one place. The alley was solid with bodies, jammed together, moving like one thing, like a rain cloud. The noise was incredible. At the end of the alley I glimpsed a big black foreign car, very shiny, and a man standing on the roof. He was surrounded by reaching hands, as if they were worshipping him.

"What's going on?" I shouted to whoever would hear. The crowd surged. I stood firm.

"Hiring," a shaved-headed boy as thin as famine shouted back. He saw I was puzzled. "Watekni. Day jobs in data processing. The UN treats us like shit in our own country, but we're good enough to do their tax returns."

"Good money?"

"Money." The crowd surged again, and made me part of it. A new car arrived behind me. The crowd turned like a flock of birds on the wing and pushed me toward the open doors. Big men with dark glasses got out and made a space around the watekni broker. He was a small Luhya in a long white jellaba and the uniform shades. He had a mean mouth. He fanned a fistful of paper slips. My hand went out by instinct and I found a slip in it. A single word was printed on it: Nimepata.

"Password of the day," my thin friend said. "Gets you into the system."

"Over there, over there," one of the big men said, pointing to an old bus at the end of the alley. I ran to the bus. I could feel a hundred people on my heels. There was another big man at the bus door.

"What're your languages?" the big man demanded.

"English and a bit of French," I told him.

"You waste my fucking time, kid," the man shouted. He tore the password slip from my hand, pushed me so hard, with two hands, I fell. I saw feet, crushing feet, and I rolled underneath the bus and out the other side. I did not stop running until I was out of the district of the watekni and into streets with people on them. I did not see if the famine-boy got a slip. I hope he did.

Singers wanted, said the sign by the flight of street stairs to an upper floor. So, my skills had no value in the information technology market. There were other markets. I climbed the stairs. They led to a room so dark I could not at first make out its dimensions. It smelled of beer, cigarettes and poppers. I sensed a number of men.

"Your sign says you want singers," I called into the dark.

"Come in then." The man's voice was low and dark, smoky, like an old hut. I ventured in. As my eyes grew used to the dark, I saw tables, chairs upturned on them, a bar, a raised stage area. I saw a number of dark figures at a table, and the glow of cigarettes.

"Let's have you."

"Where?"

"There."

I got up on the stage. A light stabbed out and blinded me.

"Take your top off."

I hesitated, then unbuttoned my blouse. I slipped it off, stood with my arms loosely folded over my breasts. I could not see the men, but I felt the shanty-eyes.

"You stand like a Christian child," smoky voice said. "Let's see the goods."

I unfolded my arms. I stood in the silver light for what seemed like hours.

"Don't you want to hear me sing?"

"Girl, you could sing like an angel, but if you don't have the architecture . . ."

I picked up my blouse and rebuttoned it. It was much more shaming putting it on than taking it off. I climbed down off the stage. The men began to talk and laugh. As I reached the door, the dark voice called me.

"Can you do a message?"

"What do you want?"

"Run this down the street for me right quick."

I saw fingers hold up a small glass vial. It glittered in the light from the open door.

"Down the street."

"To the American Embassy."

"I can find that."

"That's good. You give it to a man."

"What man?"

"You tell the guard on the gate. He'll know."

"How will he know me?"

"Say you're from Brother Dust."

"And how much will Brother Dust pay me?"

The men laughed.

"Enough."

"In my hand?"

"Only way to do business."

"We have a deal."

"Good girl. Hey."

"What?"

"Don't you want to know what it is?"

"Do you want to tell me?"

"They're fullerenes. They're from the Chaga. Do you understand that? They are alien spores. The Americans want them. They can use them to build things, from nothing up. Do you understand any of this?"

"A little."

"So be it. One last thing."

"What?"

"You don't carry it in your hand. You don't carry it anywhere on you. You get my meaning?"

"I think I do."

"There are changing rooms for the girls back of the stage. You can use one of them."

"Okay. Can I ask a question?"

"You can ask anything you like."

"These . . . fullerenes. These Chaga things . . . What if they; go off, inside?"

"You trust the stories that they never touch human flesh. Here. You may need this." An object flipped through the air toward me. I caught it . . . a tube of KY jelly. "A little lubrication."

I had one more question before I went backstage area.

"Can I ask, why me?"

"For a Christian child, you've a decent amount of dark," the voice said. "So, you've a name?"

"Tendeléo."

Ten minutes later I was walking across town, past all the UN checkpoints and security points, with a vial of Chaga fullerenes slid into my vagina. I walked up to the gate of the American Embassy. There were two guards with white helmets and white gaiters. I picked the big black one with the very good teeth.

"I'm from Brother Dust," I said.

"One moment please," the marine said. He made a call on his PDU. One minute later the gates swung open and a small white man with sticking-up hair came out.

"Come with me," he said, and took me to the guard unit toilets, where I extracted the consignment. In exchange he gave me a playing card with a portrait of a President of the United States on the back. The President was Nixon.

"You ever go back without one of these, you die," he told me. I gave the Nixon card to the man who called himself Brother Dust. He gave me a roll of shillings and told me to come back on Tuesday.

I gave two thirds of the roll to my mother.

"Where did you get this?" she asked, holding the notes in her hands like blessings.

"I have a job," I said, challenging her to ask. She never did ask. She bought clothes for Little Egg and fruit from the market. On the Tuesday, I went back to the upstairs club that smelled of beer and smoke and come and took another load inside me to the spikey-haired man at the Embassy.

So I became a runner. I became a link in a chain that ran from legendary cities under the clouds of Kilimanjaro across terminum, past the UN Interdiction Force, to an upstairs club in Nairobi, into my body, to the US Embassy. No, I do not have that right. I was a link in a chain that started eight hundred years ago, as light flies, in a gas cloud called Rho Ophiuchi, that ran from US Embassy to US Government, and on to a man whose face was on the back on one of my safe-conduct cards and from him into a future no one could guess.

"It scares them, that's why they want it," Brother Dust told me. "Americans are always drawn to things that terrify them. They think these fullerenes will give the edge to their industries, make the economy indestructible. Truth is, they'll destroy their industries, wreck their economy. With these, anyone can make anything they want. Their free market can't stand up to that."

I did not stay a runner long. Brother Dust liked my refusal to be impressed by what the world said should impress me. I became his personal assistant. I made appointments, kept records. I accompanied him when he called on brother Sheriffs. The Chaga was coming closer, the Tacticals were on the streets; old enemies were needed as allies now.

One such day, Brother Dust gave me a present wrapped in a piece of silk. I unwrapped it, inside was a gun. My first reaction was fear; that a sixteen year-old girl should have the gift of life or death in her hand. Would I, could I, ever use it on living flesh? Then a sense of power crept through me. For the first time in my life, I had authority.

"Don't love it too much," Brother Dust warned. "Guns don't make you safe. Nowhere in this world is safe, not for you, not for anyone."

It felt like a sin, like a burn on my body as I carried it next to my skin back to Jogoo Road. It was impossible to keep it in our rooms, but Simeon in the metal shop had been stashing my roll for some time now and he was happy to hide the gun behind the loose block. He wanted to handle it. I would not let him, though I think he did when I was not around. Every morning I took it out, some cash for lunch and bribes, and went to work.

With a gun and money in my pocket, Brother Dust's warning seemed old and full of fear. I was young and fast and clever. I could make the world as safe or as dangerous as I liked. Two days after my seventeenth birthday, the truth of what he said arrived at my door.

It was late, it was dark and I was coming off the matatu outside Church Army. It was a sign of how far things had gone with my mother and father that they no longer asked where I was until so late, or how the money kept coming. At once I could tell something was wrong; a sense you develop when you work on the street. People were milling around in the compound, needing to do something, not knowing what they could do. Elsewhere, women's voices were shouting. I found Simeon.

"What's happening, where is my mother?"

"The shambas. They have broken through into the shambas."

I pushed my way through the silly, mobbing Christians. The season was late, the corn over my head, the cane dark and whispering. I strayed off the shamba paths in moments. The moon ghosted behind clouds, the air-glow of the city surrounded me but cast no light. The voices steered me until I saw lights gleaming through the stalks: torches and yellow naphtha flares. The voices were loud now, close. There were now men, loud men. Loud men have always frightened me. Not caring for the crop, I charged through the maize, felling rich, ripe heads.

The women of Church Army stood at the edge of the crushed crop. Maize, potatoes, cane, beans had been trodden down, ripped out, torn up. Facing them was a mob of shanty-town people. The men had torches and cutting tools. The women's kangas bulged with stolen food. The children's baskets and sacks were stuffed with bean pods and maize cobs. They faced us shamelessly. Beyond the flattened wire fence, a larger crowd was waiting in front of the market; the hyenas, who if the mob won, would go with them, and if it lost, would sneak back to their homes. They outnumbered the women twenty to one. But I was bold. I had the authority of a gun.

"Get out of here," I shouted at them. "This is not your land."

"And neither is it yours," their leader said, a man thin as a skeleton, barefoot, dressed in cut-off jeans and a rag of a fertilizer company T-shirt. He held a tin-can oil-lamp in his left hand, in his right a machete. "It is all borrowed from the Chaga. It will take it away, and none of us will have it. We want what we can take, before it is lost to all of us."

"Go to the United Nations," I shouted.

The leader shook his head. The men stepped forward. The women murmured, gripped their mattocks and hoes firmly.

"The United Nations? Have you not heard? They are scaling down the relief effort. We are to be left to the mercy of the Chaga."

"This is our food. We grew it, we need it. Get off our land!"

"Who are you?" the leader laughed. The men hefted their pangas and stepped forward. The laughter lit the dark inside me that Brother Dust had recognized, that made me a warrior. Light-headed with rage and power, I pulled out my gun. I held it over my head. One, two, three shots cracked the night. The silence after was more shocking than the shots.

"So. The child has a gun," the hungry man said.

"The child can use it too. And you will be first to die."

"Perhaps." the leader said. "But you have three bullets. We have three hundred hands."

My mother pulled me to one side as the shanty men came through. Their pangas caught the yellow light as they cut their way through our maize and cane. After them came the women and the children, picking, sifting, gleaning. The three hundred hands stripped our fields like locusts. The gun pulled my arm down like an iron weight. I remember I cried with frustration and shame. There were too many of them. My power, my resolve, my weapon, were nothing. False bravery. Boasting. Show.

By morning the field was a trampled mess of stalks, stems and shredded leaves. Not a grain worth eating remained. By morning I was waiting on the Jogoo Road, my thumb held out for a matatu, my possessions in a sports bag on my back. A refugee again. The fight had been brief and muted.

"What is this thing?" My mother could not touch the gun. She pointed at it on the bed. My father could not even look. He sat hunched up in a deep, old armchair, staring at his knees. "Where did you get such a thing?"

The dark thing was still strong in me. It had failed against the mob, but it was more than enough for my parents.

"From a Sheriff," I said. "You know what a sheriff is? He is a big man. For him I stick Chaga-spores up my crack. I give them to Americans, Europeans, Chinese, anyone who will pay."

"Do not speak to us like that!"

"Why shouldn't I? What have you done, but sit here and wait for something to happen? I'll tell the only thing that is going to happen. The Chaga is going to come and destroy everything. At least I have taken some responsibility for this family, at least I have kept us out of the sewer! At least we have not had to steal other people's food!"

"Filth money! Dirt money, sin money!"

"You took that money readily enough."

"If we had known . . ."

"Did you ever ask?"

"You should have told us."

"You were afraid to know."

My mother could not answer that. She pointed at the gun again, as if it were the proof of all depravity.

"Have you ever used it?"

"No," I said, challenging her to call me a liar.

"Would you have used it, tonight?"

"Yes," I said. "I would, if I thought it would have worked."

"What has happened to you?" my mother said. "What have we done?"

"You have done nothing," I said. "That's what's wrong with you. You give up. You sit there, like him." My father had not yet said a word. "You sit there, and you do nothing. God will not help you. If God could, would he have sent the Chaga? God has made you beggars."

Now my father got up out of his deep chair.

"Leave this house," he said in a very quiet voice. I stared. "Take your things. Go on. Go now. You are no longer of this family. You will not come here again."

So I walked out with my things in my bag and my gun in my pants and my roll in my shoe and I felt the eyes in every room and lean-to and shack and I learned Christians can have shanty-eyes too. Brother Dust found me a room in the back of the club. I think he hoped it would give him a chance to have sex with me. It smelled and it was noisy at night and I often had to quit it to let the prostitutes do their business, but it was mine, and I believed I was free and happy. But his words were a curse on me. Like Evil Eye, I knew no peace. You do nothing, I had accused my parents but what had I done? What was my plan for when the Chaga came? As the months passed and the terminum was now at

Muranga, now at Ghania Falls, now at Thika, Brother Dust's curse accused me. I watched the Government pull out for Mombasa in a convoy of trucks and cars that took an hour and a half to go past the Haile Selassie Avenue cafe where I bought my runners morning coffee. I saw the gangs of picknis race through the avenues, loosing off tracer like firecrackers, until the big UN troop carriers drove them before them like beggars. I crouched in roadside ditches from terrible fire-fights over hijacked oil tankers. I went up to the observation deck of the Moi Telecom Tower and saw the smoke from battles out in the suburbs, and beyond, on the edge of the heat-haze, to south and north, beyond the mottled duns and dusts of the squatter towns, the patterned colors of the Chaga. I saw the newspapers announce that on July 18th, 2013, the walls of the Chaga would meet and Nairobi cease to exist. Where is safe? Brother Dust said in my spirit. What are you going to do?

A man dies, and it is easy to say when the dying ends. The breath goes out and does not come in again. The heart stills. The blood cools and congeals. The last thought fades from the brain. It is not so easy to say when a dying begins. Is it, for example, when the body goes into the terminal decline? When the first cell turns black and cancerous? When we pass our DNA to a new human generation, and become genetically redundant? When we are born? A civil servant once told me that when they make out your birth certificate, they also prepare your death certificate.

It was the same for the big death of Nairobi. The world saw the end of the end from spy satellites and camera-blimps. When the end for a city begins is less clear. Some say it was when the United Nations pulled out and left Nairobi open. Others, when the power plants at Embakasi went down and the fuel and telephone lines to the coast were cut. Some trace it to the first Hatching Tower appearing over the avenues of Westlands; some to the pictures on the television news of the hexagon pattern of Chaga-moss slowly obliterating a "Welcome to Nairobi" road sign. For me it was when I slept with Brother Dust in the back room of the upstairs club.

I told him I was a virgin.

"I always pegged you for a Christian child," he said, and though my virginity excited him, he did not try and take it from me forcefully or disrespectfully. I was fumbling and dry and did not know what to do and pretended to enjoy it more than I did. The truth was that I did not see what all the fuss was about. Why did I do it? It was the seal that I had become a fine young criminal, and tied my life to my city.

Though he was kind and gentle, we did not sleep together again.

They were bad times, those last months in Nairobi. Some times, I think, are so bad that we can only deal them with by remembering what is good, or bright. I will try and look at the end days straight and honestly. I was now eighteen, it was over a year since I left Jogoo Road and I had not seen my parents or Little Egg since. I was proud and angry and afraid. But a day had not passed that I had not thought about them and the duty I owed them. The Chaga was advancing on two fronts, marching up from the south and sweeping down from the north through the once-wealthy suburbs of Westlands and Garden Grove. The Kenyan Army was up there, firing mortars into the cliff of vegetation called the Great Wall, taking out the Hatching Towers with artillery. As futile as shelling the sea. In the south the United Nations was holding the international airport open at every cost. Between them, the Tacticals tore at each other like street dogs. Alliances formed and were broken in the same day. Neighbor turned on neighbor, brother killed brother. The boulevards of downtown Nairobi were littered with bullet casings and burned out picknis. There was not one pane of glass whole on all of Moi Avenue, nor one shop that was not looted. Between them were twelve million civilians, and the posses.

We too made and dissolved our alliances. We had an arrangement with Mombi, who had just bloodily ended an agreement with Haran, one of the big sheriffs, to make a secret deal with the Black Simbas, who intended to be a power in the new order after the Chaga. The silly, vain Soca Boys had been swept away in one night by the Simbas East Starehe Division. Custom matatus and football managers' coats were no match for Russian APCs and light-scatter combat-suits. Brother Dust's associations were precarious: the posses had wealth and influence but no power. Despite our AK47s and street cool uniforms—in the last days, everyone had a uniform—even the Soca Boys could have taken us out. We were criminals, not warriors.

Limuru, Tigani, Kiambu, in the north. Athi River, Matathia, Embakasi to the south. The Chaga advanced a house here, a school there, half a church, a quarter of a street. Fifty meters every day. Never slower, never faster. When the Supreme Commander East African Protection Force announced terminum at Ngara, I made my move. In my Dust Girl uniform of street-length, zebra-stripe PVC coat over short-shorts, I took a taxi to the Embassy of the United States of America. The driver detoured through Riverside.

"Glider come down on Limuru Road," the driver explained. The gliders scared me, hanging like great plastic bats from the hatching towers, waiting to drop, spread their wings and sail across the city sowing Chaga spores. To me they were dark death on wings. I have too many Old Testament images still in me. The army took out many on the towers, the helicopters the ones in the air, but some always made it down. Nairobi was being eaten away from within.

Riverside had been rich once. I saw a tank up-ended in a swimming pool, a tennis court strewn with swollen bodies in purple combats. Chaga camouflage. Beyond the trees I saw fans of lilac land-coral.

I told the driver to wait outside the Embassy. The grounds were jammed with trucks. Chains of soldiers and staff were loading them with crates and machinery. The black marine knew me by now.

"You're going?" I asked.

"Certainly are, ma'am," the marine said. I handed him my gun. He nodded me through. People pushed through the corridors under piles of paper and boxes marked Property of the United States Government. Everywhere I heard shredders. I found the right office. The spikey-haired man, whose name was Knutson, was piling cardboard boxes on his desk.

"We're not open for business."

"I'm not here to trade," I said. I told him what I was here for. He looked at me as if I had said that the world was made of wool, or the Chaga had reversed direction. So I cleared a space on his desk and laid out the photographs I had brought.

"Please tell me, because I don't understand this attraction," I said. "Is it that, when they are that young, you cannot tell the boys from the girls? Or is it the tightness?"

"Fuck you. You'll never get these public."

"They already are. If the Diplomatic Corps Personnel Section does not receive a password every week, the file will download."

If there had been a weapon to hand, I think Knutson would have killed me where I stood.

"I shouldn't have expected any more from a woman who sells her cunt to aliens."

"We are all prostitutes, Mr. Knutson. So?"

"Wait there. To get out you need to be chipped." In the few moments he was out of the room I studied the face of the President on the wall. I was familiar with Presidential features; is it something in the nature of the office, I wondered, that gives them all the same look? Knutson returned with a metal and plastic device like a large hypodermic. "Name, address, Social Security Number." I gave them to him. He tapped tiny keys on the side of the device, then he seized my wrist, pressed the nozzle against forearm. There was click, I felt a sharp pain but I did not cry out.

"Congratulations, you're an employee of US Military Intelligence. I hope that fucking hurt."

"Yes it did." Blood oozed down my wrist. "I need three more. These are the names."

Beside the grainy snaps of Knutson on the bed with the naked children, I laid out my family. Knutson thrust the chip gun at me.

"Here. Take it. Take the fucking thing. They'll never miss it, not in all this. It's easy to use, just dial it in there. And those."

I scooped up the photographs and slid them with the chip gun into my inside pocket. The freedom chip throbbed under my skin as I walked through the corridors full of people and paper into the light.

Back at the club I paid the driver in gold. It and cocaine were the only universally acceptable street currencies. I had been converting my roll to Kruger rands for some months now. The rate was not good. I jogged up the stairs to the club, and into slaughter.

Bullets had been poured into the dark room. The bar was shattered glass, stinking of alcohol. The tables were spilled and splintered. The chairs were overturned, smashed. Bodies lay among them, the club men, sprawled inelegantly. The carpet was sticky with blood. Flies buzzed over the dead. I saw the Dust Girls, my sisters, scattered across the floor, hair and bare skin and animal prints drenched with blood. I moved among them. I thought of zebras on the high plains, hunted down by lions, limbs and muscle and skin torn apart. The stench of blood is an awful thing. You never get it out of you. I saw Brother Dust on his back against the stage. Someone had emptied a clip of automatic fire into his face.

Our alliances were ended.

A noise; I turned. I drew my gun. I saw it in my hand, and the dead lying with their guns in their hands. I ran from the club. I ran down the stairs onto the street. I was a mad thing, screaming at the people in the street, my gun in hand, my coat flying out behind me. I ran as fast as I could. I ran for home, I ran for Jogoo Road. I ran for the people I had left there. Nothing could stop me. Nothing dared, with my gun in my hand. I would go home and I would take them away from this insanity. The last thing the United Nations will ever do for us is fly us out of here, I would tell them. We will fly somewhere we do not need guns or camps or charity, where we will again be what we were. In my coat and stupid boots, I ran, past the plastic city at the old country bus terminal, around the metal barricades on Landhies Road, across the waste ground past the Lusaka Road roundabout where two buses were burning. I ran out into Jogoo Road.

There were people right across the road. Many many people, with vehicles, white UN vehicles. And soldiers, a lot of soldiers. I could not see Church Army. I slammed into the back of the crowd, I threw people out of my way, hammered at them with the side of my gun.

"Get out of my way, I have to get to my family!"

Hands seized me, spun me around. A Kenyan Army soldier held me by the shoulders.

"You cannot get through."

"My family lives here. The Church Army Centre, I need to see them."

"No one goes through. There is no Church Army."

"What do you mean? What are you saying?"

"A glider came down."

I tore away from him, fought my way through the crowd until I came to the cordon of soldiers. A hundred meters down the road was a line of hummers and APCs. A hundred yards beyond them, the alien infection. The glider had crashed into the accommodation block. I could still make out the vile bat-shape among the crust of fungus and sponge spreading across the white plaster. Ribs of Chaga-coral had burst the tin roof of the teaching hall, the shacks were a stew of dissolving plastic and translucent bubbles that burst in a cloud of brown dust. Where the dust touched, fresh bubbles grew. The chapel had vanished under a web of red veins. Even Jogoo Road was blistered by yellow flowers and blue barrel-like objects. Fingers of the hexagonal Chaga moss were reaching toward the road block. As I watched, one of the thorn trees outside the center collapsed into the sewer and sent up a cloud of buzzing silver mites.

"Where are the people?" I asked a soldier.

"Decontamination," he said.

"My family was in there!" I screamed at him. He looked away. I shouted at the crowd. I shouted my father's name, my mother's name, Little Egg's, my own name. I pushed through the people, trying to look at the faces. Too many people, too many faces. The soldiers were looking at me. They were talking on radios, I was disturbing them. At any moment they might arrest me. More likely, they would take me to a quiet place and put a bullet in the back of my skull. Too many people, too many faces. I put the gun away, ducked down, slipped between the legs to the back of the crowd. Decontamination. A UN word, that. Headquarters

would have records of the contaminated. Chiromo Road. I would need transport.
I came out of the crowd and started to run again. I ran up Jogoo Road, past the
sports stadium, around the roundabout onto Landhies Road. There were still a
few civilian cars on the street. I ran up the middle of the road, pointing my gun
at every car that came toward me.

"Take me to Chiromo Road!" I shouted. The drivers would veer away, or hoot
and swear. Some even aimed at me. I sidestepped them, I was too fast for them.
"Chiromo Road, or I will kill you!" Tacticals laughed and yelled as they swept
past in their picknis. Not one stopped. Everyone had seen too many guns.

There was a Kenyan Army convoy on Pumwani Road, so I cut up through the
cardboard cities into Kariokor. As long as I kept the Nairobi River, a swamp of
refuse and sewage, to my left, I would eventually come out onto Ngara Road. The
shanty people fled from the striped demon with the big gun.

"Get out of my way!" I shouted. And then, all at once, the alley people diso-
beyed me. They stood stock still. They looked up.

I felt it before I saw it. Its shadow was cold on my skin. I stopped running. I
too looked up and it swooped down on me. That is what I thought, how I felt—this
thing had been sent from the heart of the Chaga to me alone. The glider was
bigger than I had imagined, and much much darker. It swept over me. I was
paralyzed with dread, then I remembered what I held in my hand. I lifted my gun
and fired at the dark bat-thing. I fired and fired and fired until all I heard was a
stiff click. I stood, shaking, as the glider vanished behind the plastic shanty roofs.
I stood, staring at my hand holding the gun. Then the tiniest yellow buds appeared
around the edge of the cylinder. The buds unfolded into crystals, and the crystals
spread across the black, oiled metal like scale. More buds came out of the muzzle and grew back down the barrel. Crystals swelled up and choked the cocked
hammer.

I dropped the gun like a snake. I tore at my hair, my clothes, I scrubbed at my
skin. My clothes were already beginning to change. My zebra-striped coat was
blistering. I pulled out the chip injector. It was a mess of yellow crystals and
flowers. I could not hope to save them now. I threw it away from me. The photographs of Knutson with the children fell to the earth. They bubbled up and
went to dust. I tore at my coat; it came apart in my fingers into tatters of plastic
and spores. I ran. The heel of one knee-boot gave way. I fell, rolled, recovered,
and stripped the foolish things off me. All around me, the people of Kariokor were
running, ripping at their skin and their clothes with their fingers. I ran with them,
crying with fear. I let them lead me. My finery came apart around me. I ran
naked, I did not care. I had nothing now. Everything had been taken from me,
everything but the chip in my arm. On every side the plastic and wood shanties
sent up shoots and stalks of Chaga.

We crashed up against the UN emergency cordon at Kariokor Market. Wicker
shields pushed us back; rungu clubs went up, came down. People fell, clutching
smashed skulls. I threw myself at the army line.

"Let me through!"

I thrust my arm between the riot shields.

"I'm chipped! I'm chipped!"

Rungus rose before my face.

"UN pass! I'm chipped!"

The rungus came down, and something whirled them away. A white man's voice shouted.

"Jesus fuck, she is! Get her out of there! Quick!"

The shield wall parted, hands seized me, pulled me through.

"Get something on her!"

A combat jacket fell on my shoulders. I was taken away very fast through the lines of soldiers to a white hummer with a red cross on the side. A white man with a red cross vest sat me on the back step and ran a scanner over my forearm. The wound was livid now, throbbing.

"Tendeléo Bi. US Embassy Intelligence Liaison. Okay Tendeléo Bi, I've no idea what you were doing in there, but it's decontam for you."

A second soldier—an officer, I guessed—had come back to the hummer.

"No time. Civs have to be out by twenty three hundred."

The medic puffed his cheeks.

"This is not procedure . . ."

"Procedure?" the officer said. "With a whole fucking city coming apart around us? But I guarantee you this, the Americans will go fucking ballistic if we fuck with one of their spooks. A surface scrub'll do . . ."

They took me over to a big boxy truck with a biohazard symbol on the side. It was parked well away from the other vehicles. I was shivering from shock. I made no complaint as they shaved all hair from my body. Someone gently took away the army jacket and showed me where to stand. Three men unrolled high-pressure hoses from the side of the truck and worked me from top to bottom. The water was cold, and hard enough to be painful. My skin burned. I twisted and turned to try to keep it away from my nipples and the tender parts of my body. On the third scrub, I realized what they were doing, and remembered.

"Take me to decontam!" I shouted. "I want to go to decontam! My family's there, don't you realize?" The men would not listen to me. I do not think they even knew it was a young woman's body they were hosing down. No one listened to me. I was dried with hot air guns, given some loose fatigues to wear, then put in the back of a diplomatic hummer that drove very fast through the streets to the airport. We did not go to the terminal building. There, I might have broken and run. We went through the wire gates, and straight to the open back of a big Russian transport plane. A line of people was going up the ramp into the cavern of its belly. Most of them were white, many had children, and all were laden with bags and goods. All were refugees, too . . . like me.

"My family is back there, I have to get them," I told the man with the security scanner at the foot of the ramp.

"We'll find them," he said as he checked off my Judas chip against the official database. "That's you. Good luck." I went up the metal ramp into the plane. A Russian woman in uniform found me a seat in the middle block, far from any window. Once I was belted in I sat trembling until I heard the ramp close and the engines start up. Then I knew I could do nothing, and the shaking stopped. I felt the plane bounce over the concrete and turn onto the runway. I hoped a terrible hope: that something would go wrong and the plane would crash and I would die. Because I needed to die. I had destroyed the thing I meant to save and saved the thing that was worthless.

Then the engines powered up and we made our run and though I could see only the backs of seats and the gray metal curve of the big cabin, I knew when we left the ground because I felt my bond with Kenya break and my home fall away beneath me as the plane took me into exile.

I pause now in my story now, for where it goes now is best told by another voice.

———

MY name is Sean. It's an Irish name. I'm not Irish. No bit of Irish in me, as you can probably see. My mum liked the name. Irish stuff was fashionable, thirty years ago. My telling probably won't do justice to Tendeléo's story; I apologize. My gift's numbers. Allegedly. I'm a reluctant accountant. I do what I do well, I just don't have a gut feel for it. That's why my company gave me all the odd jobs. One of them was this African-Caribbean-World restaurant just off Canal Street. It was called I-Nation—the menu changed every week, the ambience was great and the music was mighty. The first time I wore a suit there, Wynton the owner took the piss so much I never dressed up for them again. I'd sit at a table and poke at his VAT returns and find myself nodding to the drum and bass. Wynton would try out new grooves on me and I'd give them thumbs up or thumbs down. Then he'd fix me coffee with this liqueur he imported from Jamaica and that was the afternoon gone. It seemed a shame to invoice him.

One day Wynton said to me, "You should come to our evening sessions. Good music. Not this fucking bang bang bang. Not fucking deejays. Real music. Live music."

However, my mates liked fucking deejays and bang bang bang so I went to I-Nation on my own. There was a queue but the door staff nodded me right in. I got a seat at the bar and a Special Coffee, compliments of the house. The set had already begun, the floor was heaving. That band knew how to get a place moving. After the dance set ended, the lead guitarist gestured offstage. A girl got up behind the mic. I recognized her—she waitressed in the afternoons. She was a small, quiet girl, kind of unnoticeable, apart from her hair which stuck out in spikes like it was growing back after a Number Nought cut with the razor.

She got up behind that mic and smiled apologetically. Then she began to sing, and I wondered how I had never thought her unnoticeable. It was a slow, quiet song. I couldn't understand the language. I didn't need to, her voice said it all: loss and hurt and lost love. Bass and rhythm felt out the depth and damage in every syllable. She was five foot nothing and looked like she would break in half if you blew on her, but her voice had a stone edge that said, I've been where I'm singing about. Time stopped, she held a note then gently let it go. I-Nation was silent for a moment. Then it exploded. The girl bobbed shyly and went down through the cheering and whistling. Two minutes later she was back at work, clearing glasses. I could not take my eyes off her. You can fall in love in five minutes. It's not hard at all.

When she came to take my glass, all I could say was, "that was . . . great."

"Thank you."

And that was it. How I met Ten, said three shit words to her, and fell in love.

I never could pronounce her name. On the afternoons when the bar was quiet and we talked over my table she would shake her head at my mangling the vowel sounds.

"Eh-yo."

"Ay-oh?"

The soft spikes of hair would shake again. Then, she never could pronounce my name either. Shan, she would say.

"No, Shawn."

"Shone . . ."

So I called her Ten, which for me meant Il Primo, Top of the Heap, King of the Hill, A-Number-One. And she called me Shone. Like the sun. One afternoon when she was off shift, I asked Boss Wynton what kind of name Tendeléo was.

"I mean, I know it's African, I can tell by the accent, but it's a big continent."

"It is that. She not told you?"

"Not yet."

"She will when she's ready. And Mr. Accountant, you fucking respect her."

Two weeks later she came to my table and laid a series of forms before me like tarot cards. They were Social Security applications, Income Support, Housing Benefit.

"They say you're good with numbers."

"This isn't really my thing, but I'll take a look." I flipped through the forms. "You're working too many hours . . . they're trying to cut your benefits. It's the classic welfare trap. It doesn't pay you to work."

"I need to work," Ten said.

Last in line was a Home Office Asylum Seeker's form. She watched me pick it up and open it. She must have seen my eyes widen.

"Gichichi, in Kenya."

"Yes."

I read more.

"God. You got out of Nairobi."

"I got out of Nairobi, yes."

I hesitated before asking, "Was it bad?"

"Yes," she said. "I was very bad."

"I?" I said.

"What?"

"You said 'I.' I was very bad."

"I meant it, it was very bad."

The silence could have been uncomfortable, fatal even. The thing I had wanted to say for weeks rushed into the vacuum.

"Can I take you somewhere? Now? Today? When you finish? Would you like to eat?"

"I'd like that very much," she said.

Wynton sent her off early. I took her to a great restaurant in Chinatown where the waiters ask you before you go in how much you'd like to spend.

"I don't know what this is," she said as the first of the courses arrived.

"Eat it. You'll like it."

She toyed with her wontons and chopsticks.

"Is something wrong with it?"

"I will tell you about Nairobi now," she said. The food was expensive and lavish and exquisitely presented and we hardly touched it. Course after course went back to the kitchen barely picked over as Ten told me the story of her life, the church in Gichichi, the camps in Nairobi, the career as a posse girl, and of the Chaga that destroyed her family, her career, her hopes, her home, and almost her life. I had seen the coming of the Chaga on the television. Like most people, I had tuned it down to background muzak in my life; oh, wow, there's an alien life-form taking over the southern hemisphere. Well, it's bad for the safari holidays and carnival in Rio is fucked and you won't be getting the Brazilians in the next World Cup, but the Cooperage account's due next week and we're pitching for the Maine Road job and interest rates have gone up again. Aliens schmaliens. Another humanitarian crisis. I had followed the fall of Nairobi, the first of the really big cities to go, trying to make myself believe that this was not Hollywood, this was not Bruce Willis versus the CGI. This was twelve million people being swallowed by the dark. Unlike most of my friends and work mates. I had felt something move painfully inside me when I saw the walls of the Chaga close on the towers of downtown Nairobi. It was like a kick in my heart. For a moment I had gone behind the pictures that are all we are allowed to know of our world, to the true lives. And now the dark had spat one of these true lives up onto the streets of Manchester. We were on the last candle at the last table by the time Ten got around to telling me how she had been dumped out with the other Kenyans at Charles de Gaulle and shuffled for months through EU refugee quotas until she arrived, jet-lagged, culture-shocked and poor as shit, in the gray and damp of an English summer.

Afterward, I was quiet for some time. Nothing I could have said was adequate to what I had heard. Then I said, "would you like to come home with me for a drink, or a coffee, or something?"

"Yes," she said. Her voice was husky from much talking, and low, and unbearably attractive. "I would, very much."

I left the staff a big tip for above-and-beyondness.

Ten loved my house. The space astonished her. I left her curled up on my sofa savoring the space as I went to open wine.

"This is nice," she said. "Warm. Big. Nice. Yours."

"Yes," I said and leaned forward and kissed her. Then, before I could think about what I had done, I took her arm and kissed the round red blemish of her chip. Ten slept with me that night, but we did not make love. She lay, curled and chaste, in the hollow of my belly until morning. She cried out in her sleep often. Her skin smelled of Africa.

The bastards cut her housing benefit. Ten was distraught. Home was everything to her. Her life had been one long search for a place of her own; safe, secure, stable.

"You have two options," I said. "One, give up working here."

"Never," she said. "I work. I like to work." I saw Wynton smile, polishing the glasses behind the bar.

"Option two, then."

"What's that?"

"Move in with me."

It took her a week to decide. I understood her hesitation. It was a place, safe, secure, stable, but not her own. On the Saturday I got a phone call from her. Could I help her move? I went around to her flat in Salford. The rooms were tatty and cold, the furniture charity-shop fare, and the decor ugly. The place stank of dope. The television blared, unwatched; three different boomboxes competed with each other. While Ten fetched her stuff, her flatmates stared at me as if I were something come out of the Chaga. She had two bags—one of clothes, one of music and books. They went in the back of the car and she came home with me.

Life with Ten. She put her books on a shelf and her clothes in a drawer. She improvised harmonies to my music. She would light candles on any excuse. She spent hours in the bathroom and used toilet paper by the roll. She was meticulously tidy. She took great care of her little money. She would not borrow from me. She kept working at I-Nation, she sang every Friday. She still killed me every time she got up on that stage.

She said little, but it told. She was dark and intensely beautiful to me. She didn't smile much. When she did it was a knife through the heart of me. It was a sharp joy. Sex was a sharpness of a different kind—it always seemed difficult for her. She didn't lose herself in sex. I think she took a great pleasure from it, but it was controlled . . . it was owned, it was hers. She never let herself make any sound. She was a little afraid of the animal inside. She seemed much older than she was; on the times we went dancing, that same energy that lit her up in singing and sex burned out of her. It was then that she surprised me by being a bright, energetic, sociable eighteen-year-old. She loved me. I loved her so hard it felt like sickness. I would watch her unaware I was doing it . . . watch the way she moved her hands when she talked on the phone, how she curled her legs under her when she watched television, how she brushed her teeth in the morning. I would wake up in the night just to watch her sleep. I would check she was still breathing. I dreaded something insane, something out of nowhere, taking her away.

She stuck a satellite photograph of Africa on the fridge. She showed me how to trace the circles of the Chaga through the clouds. Every week she updated it. Week by week, the circles merging. That was how I measured our life together, by the circles, merging. Week by week, her home was taken away. Her parents and sister were down there, under those blue and white bars of cloud; week by week the circles were running them out of choices.

She never let herself forget she had failed them. She never let herself forget she was a refugee. That was what made her older, in ways, than me. That was what all her tidiness and orderliness around the house were about. She was only here for a little time. It could all be lifted at a moment's notice.

She liked to cook for me on Sundays, though the kitchen smelled of it for a week afterward. I never told her her cooking gave me the shits. She was chopping something she had got from the Caribbean stores and singing to herself. I was watching from the hall, as I loved to watch her without being watched. I saw her bring the knife down, heard a Kalenjin curse, saw her lift her hand to her mouth. I was in like a shot.

"Shit shit shit shit," she swore. It was a deep cut, and blood ran freely down her forefinger. I rushed her to the tap, stuck it under the cold, then went for the medical bag. I returned with gauze, plasters and a heal-the-world attitude.

"It's okay," she said, holding the finger up. "It's better."

The cut had vanished. No blood, no scab. All that remained was a slightly raised red weal. As I watched, even that faded.

"How?"

"I don't know," Ten said. "But it's better."

I didn't ask. I didn't want to ask. I didn't want there to be anything more difficult or complex in Ten's life. I wanted what she had from her past to be enough, to be all. I knew this was something alien; no one healed like that. I thought that if I let it go, it would never trouble us again. I had not calculated on the bomb.

Some fucking Nazis or other had been blast-bombing gay bars. London, Edinburgh, Dublin so far, always a Friday afternoon, work over, weekend starting. Manchester was on the alert. So were the bombers. Tuesday, lunch time, half a kilo of semtex with nails and razor blades packed around it went off under a table outside a Canal Street bar. No one died, but a woman at the next table lost both legs from the knees down and there were over fifty casualties. Ten had been going in for the afternoon shift. She was twenty meters away when the bomb went off. I got the call from the hospital same time as the news broke on the radio.

"Get the fuck over there," Willy the boss ordered. I didn't need ordering. Manchester Royal Infirmary casualty was bedlam. I saw the doctors going around in a slow rush and the people looking up at everyone who came in, very very afraid and the police taking statements and the trolleys in the aisles and I thought: It must have been something like this in Nairobi, at the end. The receptionist showed me to a room where I was to wait for a doctor. I met her in the corridor, a small, harassed-looking Chinese girl.

"Ah, Mr. Giddens. You're with Ms. Bi, that's right?"

"That's right, how is she?"

"Well, she was brought in with multiple lacerations, upper body, left side of face, left upper arm and shoulder . . ."

"Oh Jesus God. And now?"

"See for yourself."

Ten walked down the corridor. If she had not been wearing a hospital robe, I would have sworn she was unchanged from how I had left her that morning.

"Shone."

The weals were already fading from her face and hands. A terrible prescience came over me, so strong and cold I almost threw up.

"We want to keep her in for further tests, Mr. Giddens," the doctor said. "As you can imagine, we've never seen anything quite like this before."

"Shone, I'm fine, I want to go home."

"Just to be sure, Mr. Giddens."

When I brought Ten back a bag of stuff, the receptionist directed me to Intensive Care. I ran the six flights of stairs to ICU, burning with dread. Ten was in a sealed room full of white equipment. When she saw me, she ran from her bed to the window, pressed her hands against it.

"Shone!" Her words came through a speaker grille. "They won't let me out!"

Another doctor led to me a side room. There were two policemen there, and a man in a suit.

"What the hell is this?"

"Mr. Giddens. Ms. Bi, she is a Kenyan refugee?"

"You fucking know that."

"Easy, Mr. Giddens. We've been running some tests on Ms. Bi, and we've discovered the presence in her bloodstream of fullerene nanoprocessors."

"Nanowhat?"

"What are commonly know as Chaga spores."

Ten, Dust Girl, firing and firing and firing at the glider, the gun blossoming in her hand, the shanty town melting behind her as her clothes fell apart, her arm sticking through the shield wall as she shouted, I'm chipped, I'm chipped! The soldiers shaving her head, hosing her down. Those things she had carried inside her. All those runs for the Americans.

"Oh my God."

There was a window in the little room. Through it I saw Ten sitting on a plastic chair by the bed, hands on her thighs, head bowed.

"Mr. Giddens." The man in the suit flashed a little plastic wallet. "Robert McGlennon, Home Office Immigration. Your, ah . . ." He nodded at the window.

"Partner."

"Partner. Mr. Giddens, I have to tell you, we cannot be certain that Ms. Bi's continued presence is not a public health risk. Her refugee status is dependent on a number of conditions, one of which is that . . ."

"You're fucking deporting her . . ."

The two policemen stirred. I realized then that they were not there for Ten. There were there for me.

"It's a public health issue, Mr. Giddens. She should never have been allowed in in the first place. We have no idea of the possible environmental impact. You, of all people, should be aware what these things can do. Have done. Are still doing. I have to think of public safety."

"Public safety, fuck!"

"Mr. Giddens . . ."

I went to the window. I beat my fists on the wired glass.

"Ten! Ten! They're trying to deport you! They want to send you back!"

The policemen prised me away from the window. On the far side, Ten yelled silently.

"Look, I don't like having to do this," the man in the suit said.

"When?"

"Mr. Giddens."

"When? Tell me, how long has she got?"

"Usually there'd be a detention period, with limited rights of appeal. But as this is a public health issue . . ."

"You're going to do it right now."

"The order is effective immediately, Mr. Giddens. I'm sorry. These officers will go with you back to your home. If you could gather up the rest of her things . . ."

"At least let me say goodbye, Jesus, you owe me that!"

"I can't allow that, Mr. Giddens. There's a contamination risk."

"Contamination? I've only been fucking her for the past six months."

As the cops marched me out, the doctor came up for a word.

"Mr. Giddens, these nanoprocessors in her bloodstream . . ."

"That are fucking getting her thrown out of the country."

"The fullerenes . . ."

"She heals quick. I saw it."

"They do much more than that, Mr. Giddens. She'll probably never get sick again. And there's some evidence that they prevent telomere depletion in cell division."

"What does that mean?"

"It means, she ages very much more slowly than we do. Her life expectancy may be, I don't know, two, three hundred years."

I stared. The policemen stared.

"There's more. We observed unfamiliar structures in her brain; the best I can describe them is, the nanoprocessors seem to be re-engineering dead neurons into a complementary neural network."

"A spare brain?"

"An auxiliary brain."

"What would you do with that?"

"What wouldn't you do with that, Mr. Giddens." He wiped his hand across his mouth. "This bit is pure speculation, but . . ."

"But."

"But in some way, she's in control of it all. I think—this is just a theory—that through this auxiliary brain she's able to interact with the nanoprocessors. She might be able to make them do what she wants. Program them."

"Thank you for telling me that," I said bitterly. "That makes it all so much easier."

I took the policemen back to my house. I told them to make themselves tea. I took Ten's neatly arranged books and CDs off my shelves and her neatly folded clothes out of my drawers and her toilet things out of my bathroom and put them back in the two bags in which she had brought them. I gave the bags to the policemen, they took them away in their car. I never got to say goodbye. I never learned what flight she was on, where she flew from, when she left this country. A face behind glass. That was my last memory. The thing I feared—insane, out of nowhere—had taken her away.

After Ten went, I was sick for a long time. There was no sunshine, no rain, no wind. No days or time, just a constant, high-pitched, quiet whine in my head. People at work played out a slightly amplified normality for my benefit. Alone, they would ask, very gently, How do you feel?

"How do I feel?" I told them. "Like I've been shot with a single, high velocity round, and I'm dead, and I don't know it."

I asked for someone else to take over the I-Nation account. Wynton called me but I could not speak with him. He sent around a bottle of that good Jamaican import liqueur, and a note, "Come and see us, any time." Willy arranged me a career break and a therapist.

His name was Greg, he was a client-centered therapist, which meant I could talk for as long as I liked about whatever I liked and he had to listen. I talked very little, those first few sessions. Partly I felt stupid, partly I didn't want to talk, even to a stranger. But it worked, little by little, without my knowing. I think I only began to be aware of that the day I realized that Ten was gone, but not dead. Her last photo of Africa was still on the fridge and I looked at it and saw something new: down there, in there, somewhere, was Ten. The realization was vast and subtle at the same time. I think of it like a man who finds himself in darkness. He imagines he's in a room, no doors, no windows, and that he'll never find the way out. But then he hears noises, feels a touch on his face, smells a subtle smell, and he realizes that he is not in a room at all—he is outside: the touch on his face is the wind, the noises are night birds, the smell is from night-blooming flowers, and above him, somewhere, are stars.

Greg said nothing when I told him this—they never do, these client-centered boys, but after that session I went to the net and started the hunt for Tendeléo Bi. The Freedom of Information Act got me into the Immigration Service's databases. Ten had been flown out on a secure military transport to Mombasa. UNHCR in Mombasa had assigned her to Likoni Twelve, a new camp to the south of the city. She was transferred out on November Twelfth. It took two days searching to pick up a Tendeléo Bi logged into a place called Samburu North three months later. Medical records said she was suffering from exhaustion and dehydration, but responding to sugar and salt treatment. She was alive.

On the first Monday of winter, I went back to work. I had lost a whole season. On the first Friday, Willy gave me print-out from an on-line recruitment agency.

"I think you need a change of scene," he said. "These people are looking for a stock accountant."

These people were Medecins Sans Frontiers. Where they needed a stock accountant was their East African theater.

Eight months after the night the two policemen took away Ten's things, I stepped off the plane in Mombasa. I think hell must be like Mombasa in its final days as capital of the Republic of Kenya, infrastructure unravelling, economy disintegrating, the harbor a solid mass of boat people and a million more in the camps in Likoni and Shimba Hills, Islam and Christianity fighting a new Crusade for control of this chaos and the Chaga advancing from the west and now the south, after the new impact at Tanga. And in the middle of it all, Sean Giddens, accounting for stock. It was good, hard, solid work in MSF Sector Headquarters, buying drugs where, when, and how we could; haggling down truck drivers and Sibirsk jet-jockeys; negotiating service contracts as spare parts for the Landcruisers gradually ran out, every day juggling budgets always too small against needs too big. I loved it more than any work I've ever done. I was so busy I sometimes forgot why I was there. Then I would go in the safe bus back to the compound and see the smoke going up from the other side of the harbor, hear the gunfire echo off the old Arab houses, and the memory of her behind that green wired glass would gut me.

My boss was a big bastard Frenchman, Jean-Paul Gastineau. He had survived wars and disasters on every continent except Antarctica. He liked Cuban cigars and wine from the valley where he was born and opera, and made sure he had them, never mind distance or expense. He took absolutely no shit. I liked him immensely. I was a fucking thin-blooded number-pushing black rosbif, but he enjoyed my creative accounting. He was wasted in Mombasa. He was a true front-line medic. He was itching for action.

One lunchtime, as he was opening his red wine, I asked him how easy it would to find someone in the camps. He looked at me shrewdly, then asked, "Who is she?"

He poured two glasses, his invitation to me. I told him my history and her history over the bottle. It was very good.

"So, how do I find her?"

"You'll never get anything through channels," Jean-Paul said. "Easiest thing to do is go there yourself. You have leave due."

"No I don't."

"Yes you do. About three weeks of it. Ah. Yes." He poked about in his desk drawers. He threw me a black plastic object like a large cell-phone.

"What is it?"

"US ID chips have a GPS transponder. They like to know where their people are. Take it. If she is chipped, this will find her."

"Thanks."

He shrugged.

"I come from a nation of romantics. Also, you're the only one in this fucking place appreciates a good Beaune."

I flew up north on a Sibirsk charter. Through the window I could see the edge of the Chaga. It was too huge to be a feature of the landscape, or even a geographical entity. It was like a dark sea. It looked like what it was . . . another world, that had pushed up against our own. Like it, some ideas are too huge to fit into our everyday worlds. They push up through it, they take it over, and they change it beyond recognition. If what the doctor at Manchester Royal Infirmary had said about the things in Ten's blood were true, then this was not just a new world. This was a new humanity. This was every rule about how we make our livings, how we deal with each other, how we lead our lives, all over-turned.

The camps, also, are too big to take in. There is too much there for the world we've made for ourselves. They change everything you believe. Mombasa was no preparation. It was like the end of the world up there on the front line.

"So, you're looking for someone," Heino Rautavana said. He had worked with Jean-Paul through the fall of Nairobi; I could trust him, Jay-Pee said, but I think he thought I was a fool, or, all at best, a romantic. "No shortage of people here."

Jean-Paul had warned the records wouldn't be accurate. But you hope. I went to Samburu North, where my search in England had last recorded Ten. No trace of her. The UNHCR warden, a grim little American woman, took me up and down the rows of tents. I looked at the faces and my tracker sat silent on my hip. I saw those faces that night in the ceiling, and for many nights after.

"You expect to hit the prize first time?" Heino said as we bounced along the dirt track in an MSF Landcruiser to Don Dul.

I had better luck in Don Dul, if you can call it that. Ten had definitely been here two months ago. But she had left eight days later. I saw the log in, the log out, but there was no record of where she had gone.

"No shortage of camps either," Heino said. He was a dour bastard. He couldn't take me any further but he squared me an authorization to travel on Red Cross/Crescent convoys, who did a five hundred mile run through the camps along the northern terminum. In two weeks I saw more misery than I ever thought humanity could take. I saw the faces and the hands and the bundles of scavenged things and I thought, why hold them here? What are they saving them from? Is it so bad in the Chaga? What is so terrible about people living long lives, being immune from sickness, growing extra layers in their brains? What is so frightening about people being able to go into that alien place, and take control of it, and make it into what they want?

I couldn't see the Chaga, it lay just below the southern horizon, but I was constantly aware of its presence, like they say people who have plates in their skulls always feel a slight pressure. Sometimes, when the faces let me sleep, I would be woken instead by a strange smell, not strong, but distinct; musky and fruity and sweaty, sexy, warm. It was the smell of the Chaga, down there, blowing up from the south.

Tent to truck to camp to tent. My three weeks were running out and I had to arrange a lift back along the front line to Samburu and the flight to Mombasa. With three days left, I arrived in Eldoret, UNECTA's Lake Victoria regional center. It gave an impression of bustle, the shops and hotels and cafés were busy, but the white faces and American accents and dress sense said Eldoret was a company town. The Rift Valley Hotel looked like heaven after eighteen days on the front line. I spent an hour in the pool trying to beam myself into the sky. A sudden rain-storm drove everyone from the water but me. I floated there, luxuriating in the raindrops splashing around me. At sunset I went down to the camps. They lay to the south of the town, like a line of cannon-fodder against the Chaga. I checked the records, a matter of form. No Tendeléo Bi. I went in anyway. And it was another camp, and after a time, anyone can become insulated to suffering. You have to. You have to book into the big hotel and swim in the pool and eat a good dinner when you get back; in the camps you have to look at the faces just as faces and refuse to make any connection with the stories behind them. The hardest people I know work in the compassion business. So I went up and down the faces and somewhere halfway down some row I remembered this toy Jean-Paul had given me. I took it out. The display was flashing green. There was a single word: lock.

I almost dropped it.

I thought my heart had stopped. I felt shot between the eyes. I forgot to breathe. The world reeled sideways. My fucking stupid fingers couldn't get a precise reading. I ran down the row of tents, watching the figures. The digits told me how many meters I was to north and east. Wrong way. I doubled back, ducked right at the next opening and headed east. Both sets of figures were decreasing. I overshot, the cast reading went up. Back again. This row. This row. I peered through the twilight. At the far end was a group of people talking outside a tent lit by a yellow petrol lamp. I started to run, one eye on the tracker. I stumbled over guy-ropes, kicked cans, hurdled children, apologized to old women. The numbers clicked down, thirty five, thirty, twenty five meters . . . I could see this one figure in the group, back to me, dressed in purple combat gear. East zero, North twenty, eighteen . . . Short, female, Twelve, ten. Wore its hair in great soft spikes. Eight, six. I couldn't make it past four. I couldn't move. I couldn't speak. I was shaking.

Sensing me, the figure turned. The yellow light caught her.

"Ten," I said. I saw fifty emotions on that face. Then she ran at me and I dropped the scanner and I lifted her and held her to me and no words of mine, or anyone else's, I think, can say how I felt then.

––––––––––

NOW our lives and stories and places come together, and my tale moves to its conclusion.

I believe that people and their feelings write themselves on space and time. That is the only way I can explain how I knew, even before I turned and saw him there in that camp, that it was Sean, that he had searched for me, and found me. I tell you, that is something to know that another person has done for you. I saw him, and it was like the world had set laws about how it was to work for me, and then suddenly it said, no. I break them now, for you Tendeléo, because it pleases me. He was impossible, he changed everything I knew, he was there.

Too much joy weeps. Too much sorrow laughs.

He took me back to his hotel. The staff looked hard at me as he picked up his keycard from the lobby. They knew what I was. They did not dare say anything. The white men in the bar also turned to stare. They too knew the meaning of the colors I wore.

He took me to his room. We sat on the verandah with beer. There was a storm that night—there is a storm most nights, up in the high country—but it kept itself in the west among the Nandi Hills. Lightning crawled between the clouds, the distant thunder rattled our beer bottles on the iron table. I told Sean where I had been, what I had done, how I had lived. It was a story long in the telling. The sky had cleared, a new day was breaking by the time I finished it. We have always told each other stories, and each other's stories.

He kept his questions until the end. He had many, many of them.

"Yes, I suppose, it is like the old slave underground railroads," I answered one.

"I still don't understand why they try to stop people going in."

"Because we scare them. We can build a society in there that needs nothing from them. We challenge everything they believe. This is the first century we have gone into where we have no ideas, no philosophies, no beliefs. Buy stuff, look at stuff. That's it. We are supposed to build a thousand years on that? Well, now we do. I tell you, I've been reading, learning stuff, ideas, politics. Philosophy. It's all in there. There are information storage banks the size of skyscrapers, Sean. And not just our history. Other people, other races. You can go into them, you can become them, live their lives, see things through their senses. We are not the first. We are part of a long, long chain, and we are not the end of it. The world will belong to us; we will control physical reality as easily as computers control information."

"Hell, never mind the UN . . . you scare me, Ten!"

I always loved it when he called me Ten. Il Primo, Top of the Heap, King of the Hill, A-Number-One.

Then he said, "and your family?"

"Little Egg is in a place called Kilandui. It's full of weavers, she's a weaver. She makes beautiful brocades. I see her quite often."

"And your mother and father?"

"I'll find them."

But to most of his questions, there was only one answer: "Come, and I will show you." I left it to last. It rocked him as if he had been struck.

"You are serious."

"Why not? You took me to your home once. Let me take you to mine. But first, it's a year . . . And so so much . . ."

He picked me up.

"I like you in this combat stuff," he said.

We laughed a lot and remembered old things we had forgotten. We slowly shook off the rust and the dust, and it was good, and I remember the room maid opening the door and letting out a little shriek and going off giggling.

Sean once told me that one of his nation's greatest ages was built on those words, why not? For a thousand years Christianity had ruled England with the question: "Why?" Build a cathedral, invent a science, write a play, discover a new land, start a business: "why?" Then came the Elizabethans with the answer: "Why not?"

I knew the old Elizabethan was thinking, why not? There are only numbers to go back to, and benefit traps, and an old, gray city, and an old, gray dying world, a safe world with few promises. Here there's a world to be made. Here there's a future of a million years to be shaped. Here there are a thousand different ways of living together to be designed, and if they don't work, roll them up like clay and start again.

I did not hurry Sean for his answer. He knew as well as I that it was not a clean decision. It was lose a world, or lose each other. These are not choices you make in a day. So, I enjoyed the hotel. One day I was having a long bath. The hotel had a great bathroom and there was a lot of free stuff you could play with, so I abused it. I heard Sean pick up the phone. I could not make out what he was saying, but he was talking for some time. When I came out he was sitting on the edge of the bed with the telephone beside him. He sat very straight and formal.

"I called Jean-Paul," he said. "I gave him my resignation."

Two days later, we set out for the Chaga. We went by matatu. It was a school holiday, the Peugeot Services were busy with children on their way back to their families. They made a lot of noise and energy. They looked out the corners of their eyes at us and bent together to whisper. Sean noticed this.

"They're talking about you," Sean said.

"They know what I am, what I do."

One of the schoolgirls, in a black and white uniform, understood our English. She fixed Sean a look. "She is a warrior," she told him. "She is giving us our nation back."

We left most of the children in Kapsabet to change onto other matatus; ours drove on into the heart of the Nandi Hills. It was a high, green rolling country, in some ways like Sean's England. I asked the driver to stop just past a metal cross that marked some old road death.

"What now?" Sean said. He sat on the small pack I had told him was all he could take.

"Now, we wait. They won't be long."

Twenty cars went up the muddy red road, two trucks, a country bus and medical convoy went down. Then they came out of the darkness between the trees on the other side of the road like dreams out of sleep: Meji, Naomi and Hamid. They beckoned; behind them came men, women, children . . . entire families, from babes in arms to old men; twenty citizens, appearing one by one out of the dark, looking nervously up and down the straight red road, then crossing to the other side.

I fived with Meji, he looked Sean up and down.

"This is the one?"

"This is Sean."

"I had expected something, um . . ."

"Whiter?"

He laughed. He shook hands with Sean and introduced himself. Then Meji took a tube out of his pocket and covered Sean in spray. Sean jumped back, choking.

"Stay there, unless you want your clothes to fall off you when you get inside," I said.

Naomi translated this for the others. They found it very funny. When he had immunized Sean's clothes, Meji sprayed his bag.

"Now, we walk," I told Sean.

We spent the night in the Chief's house in the village of Senghalo. He was the last station on our railroad. I know from my Dust Girl days you need as good people on the outside as the inside. Folk came from all around to see the black Englishman. Although he found being looked at intimidating, Sean managed to tell his story. I translated. At the end the crowd outside the Chief's house burst into spontaneous applause and finger-clicks.

"Aye, Tendeléo, how can I compete?" Meji half-joked with me.

I slept fitfully that night, troubled by the sound of aircraft moving under the edge of the storm.

"Is it me?" Sean said.

"No, not you. Go back to sleep."

Sunlight through the bamboo wall woke us. While Sean washed outside in the bright, cold morning, watched by children curious to see if the black went all the way down, Chief and I tuned his shortwave to the UN frequencies.

There was a lot of chatter in Klingon. You Americans think we don't understand Star Trek?

"They've been tipped off," Chief said. We fetched the equipment from his souterrain. Sean watched Hamid, Naomi, Meri and I put on the communicators. He said nothing as the black-green knob of cha-plastic grew around the back of my head, into my ear, and sent a tendril to my lips. He picked up my staff.

"Can I?"

"It won't bite you."

He looked closely at the fist-sized ball of amber at its head, and the skeleton outline of a sphere embedded in it.

"It's a buckyball," I said. "The symbol of our power."

He passed it to me without comment. We unwrapped our guns, cleaned them, checked them and set off. We walked east that day along the ridges of the Nandi Hills, through ruined fields and abandoned villages. Helicopter engines were our constant companions. Sometimes we glimpsed them through the leaf cover, tiny in the sky like black mosquitoes. The old people and the mothers looked afraid. I did not want them to see how nervous they were making me. I called my colleagues apart.

"They're getting closer."

Hamid nodded. He was a quiet, thin twenty-two year old . . . Ethiopian skin, goatee, a political science graduate from the university of Nairobi.

"We choose a different path every time," he said. "They can't know this."

"Someone's selling us," Meji said.

"Wouldn't matter. We pick one at random."

"Unless they're covering them all."

In the afternoon we began to dip down toward the Rift Valley and terminum. As we wound our way down the old hunters' paths, muddy and slippery from recent rain, the helicopter came swooping in across the hillside. We scrambled for cover. It turned and made another pass, so low I could see the light glint from the pilot's heads-up visor.

"They're playing with us," Hamid said. "They can blow us right off this hill any time they want."

"How?" Naomi asked. She said only what was necessary, and when.

"I think I know," Sean said. He had been listening a little away. He slithered down to join us as the helicopter beat over the hillside again, flailing the leaves, showering us with dirt and twigs. "This." He tapped my forearm. "If I could find you, they can find you."

I pulled up my sleeve. The Judas chip seemed to throb under my skin, like poison.

"Hold my wrist," I said to Sean. "Whatever happens, don't let it slip."

Before he could say a word, I pulled my knife. These things must be done fast. If you once stop to think, you will never do it. Make sure you have it straight. You won't get another go. A stab down with the tip, a short pull, a twist, and the traitor thing was on the ground, greasy with my blood. It hurt. It hurt very much, but the blood had staunched, the wound was already closing.

"I'll just have to make sure not to lose you again," Sean said.

Very quietly, very silently, we formed up the team and one by one slipped down the hillside, out from under the eyes of the helicopter. For all I know, the stupid thing is up there still, keeping vigil over a dead chip. We slept under the sky that night, close together for warmth and on the third day we came to Tinderet and the edge of the Chaga.

TEN had been leading us a cracking pace, as if she were impatient to put Kenya behind us. Since mid-morning, we had been making our way up a long, slow hill. I'd done some hill-walking, I was fit for it, but the young ones and the women with babies found it tough going. When I called for a halt, I saw a moment of anger cross Ten's face. As soon as she could, we upped packs and moved on. I tried to catch up with her, but Ten moved steadily ahead of me until, just below the summit, she was almost running.

"Shone!" she shouted back. "Come with me!"

She ran up through the thinning trees to the summit. I followed, went bounding down a slight dip, and suddenly, the trees opened and I was on the edge.

The ground fell away at my feet into the Rift Valley, green on green on green, sweeping to the valley floor where the patterns of the abandoned fields could still be made out in the patchwork of yellows and buffs and earth tones. Perspective blurred the colors—I could see at least fifty miles—until, suddenly, breathtakingly, they changed. Browns and dry-land beiges blended into burgundies and rust reds, were shot through with veins of purple and white, then exploded into chaos, like a bed of flowers of every conceivable color, a jumble of shapes and colors like a mad coral reef, like a box of kiddie's plastic toys spilled out on a Chinese rug. It strained the eyes, it hurt the brain. I followed it back, trying to make sense of what I was seeing. A sheer wall, deep red, rose abruptly out of the chaotic landscape, straight up, almost as high as the escarpment I was standing on. It was not a solid wall, it looked to me to be made up of pillars or, I thought, tree trunks. They must have been of titanic size to be visible from this distance. They opened into an unbroken, flat crimson canopy. In the further distance, the flat roof became a jumble of dark greens, broken by what I can only describe as small mesas, like the Devil's Tower in Wyoming or the old volcanoes in Puy de Dome. But these glittered in the sun like glass. Beyond them, the landscape was striped like a tiger, yellow and dark brown, and formations like capsizing icebergs, pure white, lifted out of it. And beyond that, I lost the detail, but the colors went on and on, all the way to the horizon.

I don't know how long I stood, looking at the Chaga. I lost all sense of time. I became aware at some point that Ten was standing beside me. She did not try to move me on, or speak. She knew that the Chaga was one of these things that must just be experienced before it can be interpreted. One by one the others joined us. We stood in a row along the bluffs, looking at our new home.

Then we started down the path to the valley below.

Half an hour down the escarpment, Meji up front called a halt.

"What is it?" I asked Ten. She touched her fingers to her communicator, a half-eggshell of living plastic unfolded from the headset and pressed itself to her right eye.

"This is not good," she said. "Smoke, from Menengai."

"Menengai?"

"Where we're going. Meji is trying to raise them on the radio."

I looked over Ten's head to Meji, one hand held to his ear, looking around him. He looked worried.

"And?"

"Nothing."

"And what do we do?"

"We go on."

We descended through microclimates. The valley floor was fifteen degrees hotter than the cool, damp Nandi Hills. We toiled across brush and overgrown scrub, along abandoned roads, through deserted villages. The warriors held their weapons at the slope. Ten regularly scanned the sky with her all-seeing eye. Now even I could see the smoke, blowing toward us on a wind from the east, and smell it. It smelled like burned spices. I could make out Meji trying to call up Menengai. Radio silence.

In the early afternoon, we crossed terminum. You can see these things clearly from a distance. At ground level, they creep up on you. I was walking through tough valley grasses and thorn scrub when I noticed lines of blue moss between the roots. Oddly regular lines of moss, that bent and forked at exactly one hundred and twenty degrees, and joined up into hexagons. I froze. Twenty meters ahead of me, Ten stood in one world . . . I stood in another.

"Even if you do nothing, it will still come to you," she said. I looked down. The blue lines were inching toward my toes. "Come on." Ten reached out her hand. I took it, and she led me across. Within two minutes walk, the scrub and grass had given way entirely to Chaga vegetation. For the rest of the afternoon we moved through the destroying zone. Trees crashed around us, shrubs were devoured from the roots down, grasses fell apart and dissolved; fungus fingers and coral fans pushed up on either side, bubbles blew around my head. I walked through it untouched like a man in a furnace.

Meji called a halt under an arch of Chaga-growth like a vault in a medieval cathedral. He had a report on his earjack.

"Menengai has been attacked."

Everyone started talking asking question, jabbering. Meji held up his hand.

"They were Africans. Someone had provided them with Chaga-proof equipment, and weapons. They had badges on their uniforms: KLA."

"Kenyan Liberation Army," the quiet one, Naomi said.

"We have enemies," the clever one, Hamid said. "The Kenyan Government still claims jurisdiction over the Chaga. Every so often, they remind us who's in charge. They want to keep us on the run, stop us getting established. They're nothing but contras with western money and guns and advisers."

"And Menengai?" I asked. Meji shook his head.

"Most High is bringing the survivors to Ol Punyata."

I looked at Ten.

"Most High?"

She nodded.

We met up with Most High under the dark canopy of the Great Wall. It was an appropriately somber place for the meeting: the smooth soaring trunks of the trees; the canopy of leaves, held out like hands, a kilometer over our heads; the splashes of light that fell through the gaps to the forest floor; survivors and travelers, dwarfed by it all. Medieval peasants must have felt like this, awestruck in their own cathedrals.

It's an odd experience, meeting someone you've heard of in a story. You want to say, I've heard about you, you haven't heard about me, you're nothing like I imagined. You check them out to make sure they're playing true to their character. His story was simple and grim.

A village, waking, going about its normal business, people meeting and greeting, walking and talking, gossiping and idling, talking the news, taking coffee. Then, voices; strange voices, and shots, and people looking up wondering, What is going on here? and while they are caught wondering, strangers running at them, running through, strangers with guns, shooting at anything in front of them, not asking questions, not looking or listening, shooting and running on. Shooting, and burning. Bodies left where they lay, homes like blossoming flowers going up in gobs of flame. Through, back, and out. Gone. As fast, as off-hand as that. Ten minutes, and Menengai was a morgue. Most High told it as casually as it had been committed, but I saw his knuckles whiten as he gripped his staff.

To people like me, who come from a peaceful, ordered society, violence like that is unimaginable.

I've seen fights and they scared me, but I've never experienced the kind of violence Most High was describing, where people's pure intent is to kill other people. I could see the survivors—dirty, tired, scared, very quiet—but I couldn't see what had been done to them. So I couldn't really believe it. And though I'd hidden up there on the hill from the helicopter, I couldn't believe it would have opened up those big gatlings on me, and I couldn't believe now that the people who attacked Menengai, this Kenyan Liberation Army, whose only purpose was to kill Chaga-folk and destroy their lives, were out there somewhere, probably being resupplied by airdrop, reloading, and going in search of new targets. It seemed wrong in a place as silent and holy as this . . . like a snake in the garden.

Meji and Ten believed it. As soon as we could, they moved us on and out.

"Where now?" I asked Ten.

She looked uncertain.

"East. The Black Simbas have a number of settlements on Kirinyaga. They'll defend them."

"How far?"

"Three days?"

"That woman back there, Hope. She won't be able to go on very much longer." I had been speaking to her, she was heavily pregnant. Eight months, I reckoned. She had no English, and I had Aid-Agency Swahili, but she appreciated my company, and I found her big belly a confirmation that life was strong, life went on.

"I know," Ten said. She might wear the gear and carry the staff and have a gun at her hip, but she was facing decisions that told her, forcefully, You're still in your teens, little warrior.

We wound between the colossal buttressed roots of the roof-trees. The globes on the tops of the staffs gave off a soft yellow light—bioluminescence, Ten told me.

We followed the bobbing lights through the dark, dripping wall-forest. The land rose, slowly and steadily. I fell back to walk with Hope. We talked. It passed the time. The Great Wall gave way abruptly to an ecosystem of fungi. Red toadstools towered over my head, puff-balls dusted me with yellow spores, trumpetlike chanterelles dripped water from their cups, clusters of pin-head mushrooms glowed white like corpses. I saw monkeys, watching from the canopy.

We were high now, climbing up ridges like the fingers of a splayed out hand. Hope told me how her husband had been killed in the raid on Menengai. I did not know what to say. Then she asked me my story. I told it in my bad Swahili. The staffs led us higher.

"Ten."

We were taking an evening meal break. That was one thing about the Chaga, you could never go hungry. Reach out, and anything you touched would be edible. Ten had taught me that if you buried your shit, a good-tasting tuber would have grown in the morning. I hadn't had the courage yet to try it. For an alien invasion, the Chaga seemed remarkably considerate of human needs.

"I think Hope's a lot further on than we thought."

Ten shook her head.

"Ten, if she starts, will you stop?"

She hesitated a moment.

"Okay. We will stop."

She struggled for two days, down into a valley, through terribly tough terrain of great spheres of giraffe-patterned moss, then up, into higher country than any we had attempted before.

"Ten, where are we?" I asked. The Chaga had changed our geography, made all our maps obsolete. We navigated by compass, and major, geophysical landmarks.

"We've passed through the Nyandarua Valley, now we're going up the east side of the Aberdares."

The line of survivors became strung out. Naomi and I struggled at the rear with the old and the women with children, and Hope. We fought our way up that hillside, but Hope was flagging, failing.

"I think . . . I feel . . ." she said, hand on her belly.

"Call Ten on that thing," I ordered Naomi. She spoke into her mouthpiece.

"No reply."

"She what?"

"There is no reply."

I ran. Hands, knees, belly, whatever way I could, I made it up that ridge, as fast as I could. Over the summit the terrain changed, as suddenly as Chaga landscapes do, from the moss maze to a plantation of regularly spaced trees shaped like enormous ears of wheat.

Ten was a hundred meters downslope. She stood like a statue among the wheat-trees. Her staff was planted firmly on the ground. She did not acknowledge me when I called her name. I ran down through the trees to her.

"Ten, Hope can't go on. We have to stop."

"No!" Ten shouted. She did not look at me, she stared down through the rows of trees.

"Ten!" I seized her, spun her round. Her face was frantic, terrified, tearful, joyful, as if in this grove of alien plants was something familiar and absolutely agonizing. "Ten! You promised!"

"Shone! Shone! I know where I am! I know where this is! That is the pass, and that is where the road went, this is the valley, that is the river, and down there, is Gichichi!" She looked back up to the pass, called to the figures on the tree-line. "Most High! Gichichi! This is Gichichi! We are home!"

She took off. She held her staff in her hand like a hunter's spear, she leaped rocks and fallen trunks, she hurdled streams and run-offs; bounding down through the trees. I was after her like a shot but I couldn't hope to keep up. I found Ten standing in an open space where a falling wheat-tree had brought others down like dominoes. Her staff was thrust deep into the earth. I didn't interrupt. I didn't say a word. I knew I was witnessing something holy.

She went down on her knees. She closed her eyes. She pressed her hands to the soil. And I saw dark lines, like slow, black lightning, go out from her fingertips across the Chaga-cover. The lines arced and intersected, sparked out fresh paths.

The carpet of moss began to resemble a crackle-glazed Japanese bowl. But they all focused on Ten. She was the source of the pattern. And the Chaga-cover began to flow toward the lines of force. Shapes appeared under the moving moss, like ribs under skin. They formed grids and squares, slowly pushing up the Chaga-cover. I understood what I was seeing. The lines of buried walls and buildings were being exhumed. Molecule by molecule, centimeter by centimeter, Gichichi was being drawn out of the soil.

By the time the others had made it down from the ridge, the walls stood waist-high and service units were rising out of the earth, electricity generators, water pumps, heat-exchangers, nanofacturing cells. Refugees and warriors walked in amazement among the slowly rising porcelain walls.

Then Ten chose to recognize me.

She looked up. Her teeth were clenched, her hair was matted, sweat dripped from her chin and cheekbones. Her face was gaunt, she was burning her own body-mass, ramming it through that mind/Chaga interface in her brain to program nanoprocessors on a massive scale.

"We control it, Shone," she whispered. "We can make the world any shape we want it to be. We can make a home for ourselves."

Most High laid his hand on her shoulder.

"Enough, child. Enough. It can make itself now."

Ten nodded. She broke the spell. Ten rolled onto her side, gasping, shivering. "It's finished," she whispered. "Shone . . ."

She still could not say my name right. I went to her, I took her in my arms while around us Gichichi rose, unfolded roofs like petals, grew gardens and tiny, tangled lanes. No words. No need for words. She had done all her saying, but close at hand, I heard the delighted, apprehensive cry of a woman entering labor.

————

WE begin with a village, and we end with a village. Different villages, a different world, but the name remains the same. Did I not tell you that names are important? Ojok, Hope's child, is our first citizen. He is now two, but every day people come over the pass or up from the valley, to stay, to make their homes here. Gichichi is now two thousand souls strong. Five hundred houses straggle up and down the valley side, each with its own garden-shamba and nanofactory, where we can make whatever we require. Gichichi is famous for its nanoprocessor programmers. We earn much credit hiring them to the towns and villages that are growing up like mushrooms down in the valley of Nyeri and along the foothills of Mt. Kenya. A great city is growing there, I have heard, and a mighty culture developing; but that is for the far future. Here in Gichichi, we are wealthy in our own way; we have a community center, three bars, a mandazi shop, even a small theater. There is no church, yet. If Christians come, they may build one. If they do, I hope they call it St. John's. The vine-flowers will grow down over the roof again.

Life is not safe. The KLA have been joined by other contra groups, and we have heard through the net that the West is tightening its quarantine of the Chaga zones. There are attacks all along the northern edge. I do not imagine Gichichi is immune. We must scare their powerful ones very much, now. But the packages keep coming down, and the world keeps changing. And life is never safe. Brother Dust's lesson is the truest I ever learned, and I have been taught it better than many. But I trust in the future. Soon there will be a new name among the citizens of Gichichi, this fine, fertile town in the valleys of the Aberdares. Of course, Sean and I cannot agree what it should be. He wants to call her after the time of day she is born, I want something Irish.

"But you won't be able to pronounce it!" he says. We will think of something. That is the way we do things here. Whatever her name, she will have a story to tell, I am sure, but that is not for me to say. My story ends here, and our lives go on. I take up mine again, as you lift yours. We have a long road before us.

honorable mentions: 2000

Daniel Abraham, "Chimera 8," *Vanishing Acts*.
Linda Addison, "Twice, At Once, Separated," *Dark Matter*.
Brian W. Aldiss, "Cognitive Ability and the Light-Bulb," *Nature*, January 20.
———, "Steppenford," *F&SF*, February.
Poul Anderson, "Consequences," *Nature*, May 13.
Eleanor Arnason, "The Cloud Man," *Asimov's*, October/November.
———, "Origin Story," *Tales of the Unanticipated* 19.
Catherine Asaro, "A Roll of the Dice," *Analog*, July/August.
Fiona Avery, "Luring the Tiger Out of the Mountain," *Bookface*, August.
Kage Baker, "Black Smoker," *Asimov's*, January.
———, "Merry Christmas from Navarro Lodge, 1928," *Asimov's*, December.
———, "Two Old Men," *Asimov's*, March.
———, "The Young Master," *Asimov's*, July.
Dale Bailey, "Inheritance," *F&SF*, July.
Tony Ballantyne, "Single-Minded," *Interzone*, December.
William Barton, "Heart of Glass," *Asimov's*, January.
Barrington J. Bayley, "The Sky Tower," *Spectrum SF 2*.
Stephen Baxter, "Behold Now Behemoth," *Asimov's*, January.
———, "Cadre Siblings," *Interzone*, March.
———, "The Gravity Mine," *Asimov's*, April.
———, "Open Loops," *Skylife*.
———, "Reality Dust," PS Publishing.
———, "Saddle Point: The Children's Crusade," *Science Fiction Age*, March.
———, "Sheena 5," *Analog*, May.
———, "Silver Ghost," *Asimov's*, September.
Greg Bear, "Deep Ice and DNA Languages," *Nature*, January 13.
Chris Beckett, "Snapshots of Apirania," *Interzone*, October.
———, "The Welfare Man Retires," *Interzone*, August.
Susan Beetlestone, "Fly," *Interzone*, March.
M. Shayne Bell, "At Bud Light Old Faithful," *Interzone*, February.
———, "Balance Due," *Asimov's*, December.
———, "Homeless, with Aliens," *Science Fiction Age*, March.
Gregory Benford, "Taking Control," *Nature*, August 20.
Christopher L. Bennett, "Among the Wild Cybers of Cybele," *Analog*, December.
Judith Berman, "Dream of Rain," *Interzone*, May.
Michael Bishop, "Blue Kansas Sky," *Blue Kansas Sky*.
———, "How Beautiful with Banners," *Century 6*.
Russell Blackford, "The King with Three Daughters," *Black Heart, Ivory Bones*.

———, "Two Thousand Years," *Eidolon* 29/30.

James Blaylock, "The War of the World," *Sci Fiction*, May 24.

Ben Bova, "Death on Venus," *Analog*, March.

———, "High Jump," *Amazing*, Summer.

David Brin, "Stones of Significance," *Analog*, January.

Damian Broderick, "Infinite Monkey," *Eidolon* 29/30.

Keith Brooke, "Liberty Spin," *Interzone*, August.

———, ".zipped," *Spectrum SF 2*.

——— & Eric Brown, "Mind's Eye," *Spectrum SF 1*.

Eric Brown, "The Crimes of Domini Duvall," *Science Fiction Age*, May.

———, "Destiny on Tartarus," *Spectrum SF 2*.

———, "The Kings of Eternity," *Science Fiction Age*, January.

———, "The Miracle at Kallithea," *Spectrum SF 3*.

———, "The Ultimate Sacrifice," *Spectrum SF 4*.

Stephen Brown & Alison Tokloy, "A Serpent in Eden," *Eidolon* 29/30.

Chris Bunch, "Queen Bee," *Fantastic*, Spring.

Michael A Burstein, "Kaddish for the Last Survivor," *Analog*, November.

Eugene Byrne, "H.M.S. Habakkuk," *Interzone*, May.

Pat Cadigan & Chris Fowler, "Freeing the Angels," *Sci Fiction*, May 19.

James L. Cambias, "A Diagram of Rapture," *F&SF*, April.

Orson Scott Card, "The Elephants of Poznan," *GalaxyOnline*, January.

Michael Carroll, "The Terrible Lizards of Luna," *Asimov's*, June.

Amy Sterling Casil, "Letters from Arles," *Talesbones*, 14.

———, "Mad for the Mints," *F&SF*, July.

Robert R. Chase, "Cheetahs," *Analog*, July/August.

———, "From Mars and Venus," *Asimov's*, April.

Ted Chiang, "Catching Crumbs from the Table," *Nature*, June 1.

———, "Seventy-two Letters," *Vanishing Acts*.

David Ira Cleary, "In the Squeeze," *Science Fiction Age*, May.

Hal Clement, "Under," *Analog*, January.

Jim Cowan, "The True Story of Professor Trabuc," *Asimov's*, January.

Albert E. Cowdrey, "Mosh," *F&SF*, December.

F. Brett Cox, "The Light of the Ideal," *Century 5*.

Jack Dann, "Marilyn," *F&SF*, August.

Stephen Dedman, "A Sentiment Open to Doubt," *Ticonderoga On-Line*, May.

———, "Chosen," *Altair V*.

———, "The Devotee," *Eidolon* 29/30.

———, "Shades of Green," *Science Fiction Age*, May.

Jack Deighton, "The Gentlemen Go By," *Spectrum SF 2*.

A. M. Dellamonica, "Nevada," *Sci Fiction*, October 11.

Bradley Denton, "Bloody Bunnies," *F&SF*, April.

O'Neil De Noux, "Tyrannous and Strong," *Asimov's*, February.

Paul Di Filippo, "The Reluctant Book," *Science Fiction Age*, May.

———, "Singing Each to Each," *Interzone*, May.

———, "Stealing Happy Hours," *Interzone*, March.

———, "Stink Lines," *F&SF*, February.

Cory Doctorow, "At Lightspeed, Slowing," *Asimov's*, April.

——, "A Place So Foreign," *Science Fiction Age*, January.

——, "The Fundamental Unit of Memory," *On Spec*, Fall.

——, "The Rebranding of Billy Bailey," *Interzone*, August.

——, "Return to Pleasure Island," *Realms of Fantasy*, April.

—— & Michael Skeet, "I Love Paree," *Asimov's*, December.

Stefano Donati, "After the Rain," *Terra Incognita*, Summer.

——, "1900 Night," *Talesbones*, 14.

Terry Dowling, "The Saltimbanques," *Eidolon 29/30*.

L. Timmel Duchamp, "The Daddy's Little Helper," *Terra Incognita*, Summer.

——, "How Josiah Taylor Lost His Soul," *Asimov's*, February.

Tananarive Due, "Like Daughter," *Dark Matter*.

Andy Duncan, "Fenneman's Mouth," *Beluthahatchie & Other Stories*.

——, "Lincoln in Frogmore," *Beluthahatchie & Other Stories*.

——, "The Pottawatomie Giant," *Sci Fiction*, November 1.

J. R. Dunn, "Arcadia," *F&SF*, August.

——, "For the Sake of Another Man's Wife," *Century 5*.

Greg Egan, "Only Connect," *Nature*, February 10.

Harlan Ellison, "The Toad Prince or, Sex Queen of the Martian Pleasure-Domes," *Amazing #600*.

Dennis Fisher, "Waterdogs," *Aboriginal SF*, Summer.

Lawrence Fitzgerald, "Snowball's Chance," *The Age of Wonder*.

Michael F. Flynn, "Built Upon the Sands of Time," *Analog*, July/August.

——, "Maiden Flight," *Analog*, April.

Jeffrey Ford, "Exo-Skeleton Town," *Black Gate 1*.

——, "The Fantasy Writer's Assistant," *F&SF*, February.

——, "Malthusian's Zombie," *Sci Fiction*, May 31.

John M. Ford, "In the Days of the Comet," *Nature*, June 22.

Esther M. Friesner, "Big Hair," *Black Heart, Ivory Bones*.

——, "The Shunned Trailer," *Asimov's*, February.

Neil Gaiman, "The Facts in the Case of the Departure of Miss Finch," *Tales of the Unanticipated*, 20.

R. Garcia y Robertson, "Bird Herding," *F&SF*, May.

——, "The Iron Wood," *F&SF*, August.

——, "One-Eyed Jacks and Suicide Kings," *Asimov's*, August.

James Alan Gardner, "Ars Longa, Vita Brevis," *Nature*, November 9.

Carolyn Ives Gilman, "Dreamseed," *F&SF*, October/November.

Greer Gilman, "Jack Daw's Pack," *Century 5*.

Alexander Glass, "The Language of the Dead," *Interzone*, November.

——, "The Watcher's Curse," *Interzone*, December.

Jewelle Gomez, "Chicago 1927," *Dark Matter*.

Ed Gorman, "The Broker," *Fantastic*, Summer.

Peni R. Griffin, "The Troops," *Realms of Fantasy*, February.

Nicola Griffith, "Lessons in What Matters," *Realms of Fantasy*, June.

Jim Grimsley, "Peggy's Plan," *Asimov's*, October/November.

James Gunn, "Pow'r," *Analog*, January.

Joe Haldeman, "Brochure," *Nature*, May 25.

Peter F. Hamilton, "Watching Trees Grow," *PS Publishing*.

Elizabeth Hand, "Chip Crockett's Christmas Carol," *Sci Fiction*, December 6–27.

Charles Harness, "The Money Tree," *Analog*, June.

——, "Red Skies," *Analog*, February.

M. John Harrison, "The Neon Heart Murders," *F&SF*, April.

David J. Hoffman-Dachelet, "They're Not Coming Home," *Terra Incognita*, Summer.

Nalo Hopkinson, "Ganger (Ball Lightning)," *Dark Matter*.

——, "Greedy Choke Puppy," *Dark Matter*.

Charlee Jacob, "White Phantom," *Space & Time*, Spring.

Matthew Jarpe, "Vasquez Orbitial Salvage and Satellite Repair," *Asimov's*, July.

Kij Johnson, "The Horse Raiders," *Analog*, May.

Gwyneth Jones, "Total Internal Reflection," *Nature*, February 17.

Graham Joyce, "Partial Eclipse," *Sci Fiction*, Aug. 9.

——, "Xenos Beach," *The Third Alternative*, 23.

Michael Kandel, "Aliens," *Century* 6.

James Patrick Kelly, "Feel the Zaz," *Asimov's*, June.

Garry Kilworth, "Bonsai Tiger," *Spectrum SF 1*.

Ellen Klages, "Flying Over Water," *Lady Churchill's Rosebud Wristlet* 7.

Nancy Kress, "To Cuddle Amy," *Asimov's*, August.

——, "Wetlands Preserve," *Sci Fiction*, September 27. Douglas Lain,

Geoffrey A. Landis, "A History of the Human and Post-Human Species," *Science Fiction Age*, January.

David Langford, "Comp.basilisk.FAQ," *Asimov's*, September.

——, "Different Kinds of Darkness," *F&SF*, January.

Chris Lawson, "Matthew 24:36," *Eidolon* 29/30.

Mary Soon Lee, "Pause Time," *Spectrum SF 4*.

Rand B. Lee, "Tales from the Net: The Prince of Love," *F&SF*, January.

Sharon Lee & Steve Miller, "Changeling," *Absolute Magnitude*, Summer.

Tanith Lee, "The Eye in the Heart," *F&SF*, March.

——, "La Vampiresse," *Interzone*, April.

——, "Rapunzel," *Black Heart, Ivory Bones*.

——, "The Woman in Scarlet," *Realms of Fantasy*, April.

Ursula K. Le Guin, "The Flyers of Gy," *Sci Fiction*, 11/8.

——, "The Royals of Hegn," *Asimov's*, February.

Fred Lerner, "Rosetta Stone," *Artemis*, Spring.

Kelly Link, "The Glass Slipper," *Lady Churchill's Rosebud Wrislet*, 6.

—— & Gavin Grant, "Sea, Ship, Mountain, Sky," *Altair* 6&7.

Ian R. MacLeod, "Chitty Bang Bang," *Asimov's*, June.

——, "Two Sleepers," *Century* 6.

Ken Macleod, "The Oort Crowd," *Nature*, July 13.

Paul J. McAuley, "A Very British History," *Interzone*, July.

——, "Danger—Hard Hack Area," *Nature*, March 2.

——, "Interstitial," *Asimov's*, July.

——, "Making History," PS Publishing.

——, "The Rift," *Vanishing Acts*.

——, "Straight to Hell," *The Third Alternative*, 24.

Ian McDowell, "Sunflowers," *Vanishing Acts*.

Terry McGarry, "The Child Ephemeral," *Terra Incognita*, Winter.

Sean McMullen, "Colors of the Soul," *Interzone*, February.

Elisabeth Malartre, "Words, Words, Words," *Nature*, August 24.

Geoffrey Maloney, "The Elephant Sways As It Walks," *Eidolon 29/30*.

——, "The World According to Kipling," *Aurealis*, June/July.

George R. R. Martin, "Path of the Dragon," *Asimov's*, December.

David Marusek, "VTV," *Asimov's*, March.

Kain Massin, "Wrong Dreaming," *On Spec*, Fall.

A. R. Morlan, "Cine Rimettato," *Sci Fiction*, August 16.

——, "Fast Glaciers," *Vanishing Acts*.

Mike Moscow, "A Day's Work on the Moon," *Analog*, August.

Derryl Murphy, "Last Call," *On Spec*, Fall.

Linda Nagata, "Goddesses," *Sci Fiction*, July 26.

R. Neube, "Rules of the Game," *Tales of the Unanticipated*, 19.

——, "The Wurst King vs Aluminum Foil Boy," *Asimov's*, August.

Kim Newman, "Tomorrow Town," *Sci Fiction*, November 15.

Larry Niven, "Fly-By-Night," *Asimov's*, October/November.

——, "Loki," *Analog*, January.

——, "The Missing Mass," *Analog*, December.

——, "The Wisdom of Demons," *Analog*, July/August.

G. David Nordley, "The Forest Between the Worlds," *Asimov's*, February.

Jerry Oltion, "A Star is Born," *Analog*, February.

Kate Orman, "Cactus Land," *Realms of Fantasy*, August.

Susan Palwick, "Wood and Water," *F&SF*, February.

Severna Park, "The Golem," *Black Heart, Ivory Bones*.

Richard Parks, "The God of Children," *Asimov's*, December.

——, "Golden Bell, Seven, and the Marquis of Zeng," *Black Gate* 1.

Michaelene Pendelton, "The Great Economy of the Saurian Mode," *Asimov's*, July.

Therese Pieczynski, "Eden," *Asimov's*, January.

Brian Plante, "School of Thought," *The Age of Wonders*.

Frederik Pohl, "Brain Drain," *Nature*, November 23.

Tom Purdom, "The Noise of Their Joye," *Asimov's*, May.

——, "Romance in Extended Time," *Asimov's*, March.

——, "Sergeant Mother Glory," *Asimov's*, October/November.

Ken Rand, "Good Dog," *Aboriginal SF*, Summer.

Robert Reed, "Birdy Girl," *Sci Fiction*, September 20.

——, "Due," *F&SF*, February.

——, "Father to the Man," *Asimov's*, September.

——, "Frank," *Interzone*, April.

——, "Grandma's Jumpman," *Century* 6.

——, "The Gulf," *F&SF*, October/November.

——, "Hybrid," *F&SF*, July.

——, "The Prophet Ugly," *Asimov's*, April.

——, "Two Sams," *Asimov's*, May.

——, "When it Ends," *Asimov's*, August.

Jessica Reisman, "The Arcana of Maps," *The Third Alternative*, 23.

Mike Resnick, "The Elephants on Neptune," *Asimov's*, May.

——, "Redchapel," *Asimov's*, December.

Alastair Reynolds, "Hideaway," *Interzone*, July.

———, "Merlin's Gun," *Asimov's*, May.

Keith Roberts, "Virtual Reality," *Spectrum SF* 4.

Kim Stanley Robinson, "How Science Saved the World," *Nature*, January 6.

Bruce Holland Rogers, "Little BrotherTM," *Strange Horizons*, October 30.

Leone Ross, "Tasting Songs," *Dark Matter*.

Chuck Rothman, "Occurance at Arroyo de Buho Bridge," *Strange Horizons*, October 9.

Mark Rudolph, "Words of Love, Soft and Tender," *Strange Horizons*, December 4.

Kristine Kathryn Rusch, "Chimera," *Sci Fiction*, June 7.

———, "Millennium Babies," *Asimov's*, January.

———, "Results," *Asimov's*, March.

———, "The Retrieval Artist," *Analog*, June.

Richard Paul Russo, "Watching Lear Dream,"

James Sallis, "Upstream," *Amazing*, Summer.

William Sanders, "Creatures," *The Age of Wonders*.

James Sarafin, "Downriver," *Asimov's*, February.

Charles M. Saplak, "Something About a Sunday Night," *The Third Alternative*, 23.

Pamela Sargent, "Dream of Venus," *Star Colonies*.

———, "Too Many Memories," *Nature*, November 30.

Stanley Schmidt, "Generation Gap," *Artemis*, Spring.

Darrell Schweitzer, "The Fire Eggs," *Interzone*, March.

Cecily Scutt, "Indicator Species," *Eidolon* 29/30.

Rebecca M. Senese, "The Echo of Bones," *On Spec*, Spring.

Nisi Shawl, "At the Huts of Ajala," *Dark Matter*.

Robert Sheckley, "The New Horla," *F&SF*, July.

Charles Sheffield, "The Art of Fugue," *Asimov's*, June.

———, "Nuremberg Joys," *Asimov's*, March.

Lewis Shiner, "Primes," *F&SF*, October/November.

Robert Silverberg, "The Millennial Express," *Playboy*, January.

———, "Pluto Story," *Nature*, January 27.

Dan Simmons, "Madame Bovary, c'est moi," *Nature*, September 14.

Joan Slonczewski, "Tuberculosis Bacteria Join UN," *Nature*, June 29.

Dave Smeds, "The Cookie Jar," *The Age of Wonders*.

Bud Sparhawk, "The Debt," *Analog*, May.

William Browning Spencer, "The Foster Child," *F&SF*, June.

Dana Stabenow, "No Place Like Home," *Star Colonies*.

Brian Stableford, "Chanterbelle," *Black Heart, Ivory Bones*.

———, "The Ladykiller, as Observed from a Safe Distance," *Asimov's*, August.

———, "The Incubus of the Rose," *Weird Tales*, Summer.

———, "The Last Supper," *Science Fiction Age*, March.

———, "The Mandrake Garden," *F&SF*, July.

———, "Regression," *Asimov's*, April.

———, "Tenebrio," *Vanishing Acts*.

———, "Victims," *Science Fiction Age*, January.

Michael A. Stackpole, "The Lazarus Murder," *Amazing*, Summer.

Allen M. Steele, "Agape Among the Robots," *Analog*, May.

———, "The Boid Hunt," *Star Colonies*.

———, "Warning, Warning," *Fantastic*, Spring.

Charles Stross, "Bear Trap," *Spectrum SF 1*.

Tim Sullivan, "Hawk on a Flagpole," *Asimov's*, July.

Lucy Sussex, "The Gloaming," *Eidolon 29/30*.

Michael Swanwick, "The Madness of Gordon Van Gelder," *F&SF*, March.

———, "Moon Dogs," *Asimov's*, March.

Cecilia Tan, "In Silver A," *Absolute Magnitude*, Summer.

John Alfred Taylor, "Calamity of So Long Life," *Asimov's*, May.

———, "Tinkerbell Is Dying," *Asimov's*, September.

Mark W. Tiedemann, "Links," *Vanishing Acts*.

———, "The Song of the Neanderthal," *Nature*, March 9.

Lois Tilton, "The Enclave," *Asimov's*, September.

———, "The Goddess Danced," *Graven Images*.

——— & Noreen Doyle, "The Chapter of Coming Forth by Night," *Realms of Fantasy*, February.

Steven Utley, "Chain of Life," *Asimov's*, October/November.

———, "Cloud by Van Gogh," *F&SF*, December.

———, "The Despoblado," *Sci Fiction*, November 22.

Rajnar Vajra, "His Hands Passed Like Clouds," *Analog*, October.

Tamela Viglione, "Triage," *Strange Horizons*, September 9.

Vernor Vinge, "Win a Noble Prize!" *Nature*, October 12.

James Van Pelt, "The Comeback," *Analog*, April.

Howard Waldrop, "Our Mortal Span," *Black Heart, Ivory Bones*.

———, "Winter Quarters," *Sci Fiction*, August 2.

Ian Watson, "Tales from Weston Hollow," *Weird Tales*, Spring.

Don Webb, "The Prophecies at Newfane Asylum," *Interzone*, March.

Scott Westerfeld, "The Movements of Her Eyes," *F&SF*, April.